To Rachel,

SURVIVAL The Event [1]
Thomas A Dawson

16/07/24

This is a work of fiction. Names, characters and incidents are simply the product of the author's imagination. Any resemblance to persons, living or dead, is coincidental.

SURVIVAL The Event [1]

Published by HappyDaze Publications, in association with HappyDaze Pictures and HappyDaze Productions.

With

BADLANGUAGE?PRESS and ARTIDENTITY MEDIA

And,

Published by Lulu

Copyright © 2013 by Thomas A Dawson

All rights reserved by the author. No part of this publication may be reproduced, stored in a retrieval system or transmitted in any form or by any means electronic, mechanical, photocopying, recording or otherwise, without prior written permission of the author.

Cover design Copyright © 2013 by Al Davis

All rights reserved by the artist. No part of this image may be reproduced, stored in a retrieval system or transmitted in any form or by any means electronic, mechanical, photocopying or otherwise, without prior written permission of the artist.

ISBN: 978-1-291-89138-6

ACKNOWLEDGEMENTS

I would like to thank all those people who
supported me through the writing of this novel.

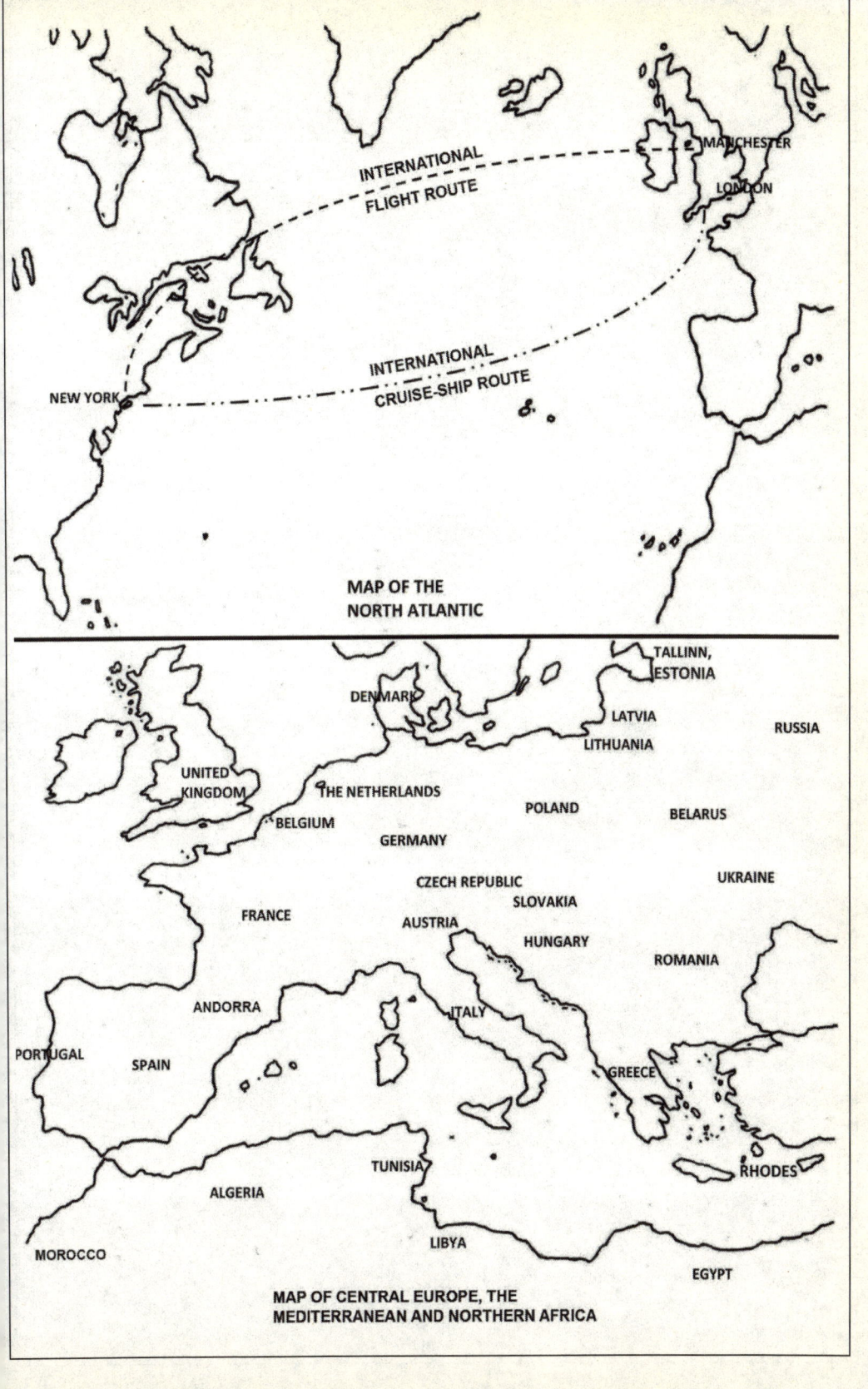

PROLOGUE

In Trafalgar Square, in central London, an innocuous unmarked white van pulled to the side of the road, beneath the shade of a line of planetrees alongside Canada House. It was 11:00am.

The van's brakes *squeaked* as it came to a halt; the driver's body sank into the worn, suede-rubbed seat. The chair was pock-marked and stuffing had fallen out and been replaced haphazardly at the edges. The driver's hand smoothed over the shiny plastic-coated steering-wheel, then he exited the vehicle, throwing the door closed behind him. He locked the vehicle, then passed the lock a second time with the flat of his thumb. A high-pitched *meep* sounded, then a tickling hair-raising static *fuzz* filled the air around the van. The hairs on the man's forearms tingled and stood on end, the pores became excited, the nerves undulated and prickled with energy.

The driver stole away Southeast towards the river.

Within seven minutes of the driver abandoning the van, two police officers were sent to check it.

Two more police officers were sent in pursuit of the driver, following his desertion of the van. The driver's movements were tracked to a service entrance into the London Underground near the Westminster Bridge, by London Transport Police; through the CCTV main-office and several satellite stations around the city. Facial recognition software was initiated to attempt to discover the driver's identity, however this proved useless. And pointless.

CCTV operators monitored both pairs of officers, as they moved to the van, and in their pursuit.

The first officer, the younger of the two, strode confidently in approach to the van, reaching his hand out to check the driver's-side door-handle. Observing personnel held their breath in various CCTV rooms, as superior's wailed at their screens in stubbornness for protocol. But he was stopped, when four more officers arrived on the scene to begin cordoning the area off from the public, and assessing the threat.

The first officer shrugged casually, then outstretched his hand again without hesitancy.

Less than three millimetres from the arched plastic shell above the handle, a tiny lightning bolt extended from the vehicle. The charge exploded up the officer's hand, and he was electrocuted and died one second later on the cool pavement-slab where he lay.

Immediately the second police officer screamed into her radio.

The other police officers reached the service entrance near Westminster Bridge and approached with extreme caution.

CHAPTER 1 - THE PLAGUE - The Scottish Highlands

The present. Kitchen – 11.03pm.
JOHN RAMSAY, 43 year old Englishman – awoke suddenly lying sprawled on his kitchen-floor. He had a rugged beard and untidy hair – a few days worth of no care and disinterest. Sticking to his shoulders he wore a filthy, speckled dried-blood stained white shirt, dirty trousers hung around his waist, and comfortable, but blood-splattered leather boots *creaked* quietly around his feet as he shifted on the floor. He blinked, trying to find the shapes of things in the dim light, sweeping away broken glass, debris and splintered pieces of wood, before preparing to stand. A thin layer of dust sat on everything. He exhaled, watching a tiny swirl of particles carry off the work-surface edge, dancing then vanishing. With muscles aching, he pulled himself onto his knee, pushing his elbow across the work-surface top to gain some purchase, pinching his toes tightly in his shoes to grip the floor firmly.

A noise, distant but blaring, sounded from the outside. A car horn *beep*.

John stared into the dimness, scanning the room, trying to pinpoint the origin of the noise, seeing the shapes of cupboards and the rim of the sink.

The kitchen was wrecked – smashed glasses, vases and cups; broken and bent pots and pans were scattered everywhere. He could see that more debris and dust had readily accumulated across each surface. A spider's-web had started to form in one of the alcoves, as dim pulses of light bled into the kitchen. The windows were boarded-up from the inside – a make-shift barricade of wooden planks, floorboards and non-machined logs; which, through some of the cracks in this barricade, car-headlights shone brightly in aurora-sunbursts, forming a series of tiny pin-lights. He wanted to be able to shut out all of the light and slink back into the darkness, but he knew he could not.

In the speeding car outside.
CIARA DEWLEY, 21 year old Scots young woman – steered the groaning vehicle down the bumpy, pot-hole minefield driveway to John's two-storey stone-built cottage, repeatedly beating her palm until it had become raw on the car-horn, in the hard centre of the steering-wheel column. She wore a loose Barbour jacket, her uncle's old one, over a dirty and dried-blood-stained grey vest, black jeans and blood-stained trainers. She shivered, hugging the Barbour close around her torso.

She wiped dirty, sweaty grime from her forehead, flicking a few strands of hair from her eyebrows and eyes.

She bit her lip, not-quite drawing blood, but steadying herself enough to lock her elbows and at her shoulders, gripping and clamping the wheel more tightly, keeping her right foot pressed to the accelerator, keeping her left foot hovering and wavering over the clutch.

Inside the house.
John saw through one of the cracks in the boarded-up window that it was Ciara's car approaching his house.

"Oh, Christ!" he murmured, then his head dropped. A bead of sweat coursed down his cheek and rested in his moustache. Another droplet rolled down his nose, tickling, and dropped to the worktop below. He cleared his throat.

One month earlier. Land Rover – 10.23am.
John drove, on a bi-monthly supply-run to the nearest town – Tobermory, eighty miles northwest of Glasgow on the Isle of Mull. It was a small, charming town on the Irish Sea -side of Scotland, protected by a long, large cove to the north. Tobermory had two tiny harbours, located in a small bay surrounded by heavy, grey rock and scrubland areas. The residents were pleasant and friendly, maintaining happy relations amongst one-another, observing a polite neighbourhood-watch scheme for the extended farms and small cottage-owners of the larger local area. Main Street – the A848 – passed along the front part of the beach and harbour, dotted with cars, several holiday-makers and locals. He wore a crisp white shirt under a woollen jumper and Barbour, denim jeans and comfortable boots.

He pulled the Land Rover to the side of the road and climbed out. His mobile rang and he answered.

A few cars idled down the main road. Two stopped side by side for the occupants and local residents – Dale McGurvey and Rick Stellon – to talk. Two fishermen – Everett MacIntyre and Fergus Mulroney – pulled in short-haul nets onto the larger pier of the two, wrapping the nets loosely around their forearms. Maisie MacFayden – a local white-witch and farmer's wife – trundled along the road, stopping to gossip with Annie McArthur – the owner of the Carnaburg Hotel. Dougal MacAllen – a local obese, balloon of a man – exited Tobermory Chocolate, a local patisserie and confectionery shop, carrying three large, luxury paper-bags with swinging string handles smiling from dimple to dimple, then climbed onto a mobility-scooter. Several old people combined into a posse and began their journey to the pavement along Main Street. A few children gathered along the beach-front, throwing stones into the water, and occasionally at sea-birds that perched or soared low near them.

John crossed to the public telephone-box near the large pier, and entered it. He spoke into the microphone of his mobile, pressed between his ear and shoulder. He leant on the phone-box's wall, haphazardly rolling and licking the Rizla paper of a cigarette.

As he spoke a smile lightly formed at the corner of his mouth. "...Yeah. --Um-hmm... –yes," John said, rubbing his beard, then listening for a long moment. "Right-yeah... --Okay mate.. Okay... See you soon... Yep... Yep... Yeah... Okay-great... I'll see you in two-weeks... Yeah, great... Bye mate... Bye..." he said, then: "Good... Good... I'll see you in two weeks then, mate..."

As John hung up a girl passed him on the other side of the road – it was Ciara. She turned when she saw him and stopped and waved, waiting for him to see her as he fidgeted a lighter from his jeans-pocket. John pocketed his mobile and looked at Ciara through the scratched, graffiti-tagged and greasy phone-box door-glass, seeing her waiting to talk to him. He waved. It had become obvious, though he would not fear to acknowledge it, that Ciara had a small crush on him. She mimed that she would see him later, through the door, before he had pushed it fully open, and turned.

She walked away, down the road, away from John.

He wandered casually from shop to shop and managed to finish his shopping encounter-free – he had often been cornered by locals, and occasionally some tourists, into small talk, enquiries about his books, or personal queries that sometimes went beyond personal. He endured fans, but not crazy fans.

He had shopped for two-weeks' worth of food, and had then carefully packed it into the back of his Land Rover. He broke a piece of dried mud from the wheel-arch, then gently pushed the boot closed. Since moving to Scotland, John had shopped for two-weeks' worth of food, every two weeks – this limited any unwanted encounters, however, for Ciara, made John an enigma – a tantalising mystery – that John did not discourage or support in equal measure.

He lit the cigarette, the roll-up he had saved in his well-worn Barbour jacket pocket from the phone-box. He poked it in the corner of his mouth, lighting it, scanning the road beyond. He pocketed the lighter and blinked several times, tugging on the loosely-rolled roll-up, as ashy smoke broke free from the end. He pulled on it, watching at each inhale how far the small cherry burned closer to his finger-knuckles. Exhaling hot smoke, and coughing slightly, John rolled the roll-up between his index, thumb and middle; then pulled on it again. Deciding the roll-up was done, he dropped it, then stomped on it, feeling each muscle along his foot and leg ache and lightning with nerves, feeling the balls of his feet press against the inside of his shoes, then finding himself walking away already.

He walked down the road and into the pub – The MacDonald Arms. Ciara's uncle – ARTHUR DEWLEY, 57 year old Scotsman, the landlord of the pub – stood, as he always did, behind the bar, always polishing a glass. He wore a grey wool jumper over a chequered-shirt, black jeans and snug tartan slippers.

"Mornin', John, how's it goin'?" he said, placing the cleaned glass on the shelf under the bar.

And Ciara, once again, greeted John warmly, perching beside her uncle on a tall bar-stool, holding a novel. "Morning..." A smile.

"Good morning, Arthur, Ciara... Everything is... --good at the moment, thank you," John replied, feeling a momentary twinge of discomfort, feeling himself rocking from one foot to the other. John saw Arthur notice his anxiety in the flicker of his eyes, prompting him into action.

"I'll get on it, now, then," Arthur asserted, then began to gather John's order. He pinched a medium-sized cardboard box from the floor between his fingers, flicked it lightly and caught it in his arms. He took a well-worn, finger-rubbed and creased scrap of paper from behind the bar – where it had been pinned under a bent nail in the wooden frame. John's eyes rolled across the room, as Ciara slid along the back edge of the bar, placing the novel down, almost sidling towards him, smiling warmly and looking across the poorly-lit bar at him.

"How're you?" she asked.

"I'm fine, thank you... And you?"

John felt himself backing away, whilst breathing in, and taking hold of the front edge of the bar. He found a smile, and it seemed to calm him considerably.

Ciara saw it.

"I'm great," she started, "I sent my application off!"

Their eyes met for a moment.

"That's good. That's great. I'm glad to hear that."

A little while later.
John and Ciara carried two large boxes of wine and spirits up the road to John's Land Rover, as the day moved into early evening. A light breeze and cloud-cover drifted in from the West. Until they reached the car, they walked in silence, before John broke it, *jingling* his keys at his side.

"When would you... When would you start university?" he asked, unable to come up with another thing to say.

"It would be late-September," Ciara said. "For Fresher's Week..."

"So, are you... --looking forward to it?"

"Absolutely. Even though the application is pretty late in..."

"It's great you applied. That's great. You'll really enjoy it."

She smiled. "Really? Did you go?"

"Yes... Years ago now. In London. It's where I met–..." he stopped. "It's where I had a fantastic time..."

"It's only in Glasgow. So... Not very far afield, I'm afraid."

"No... It'll be great. Where-ever you go. Really."

They packed the boxes in the car.

"It was really-nice seeing you," she said, "I'll see you later. Bye." She ever-so-slightly leaned in to kiss his cheek, then chose not to and walked away.

John caught himself watching her then turned back to his seat – the driver's door already open. John looked at the back seat, in the glow of the weak interior car-light and saw his life for the next two weeks. He could make it last longer and not need to come to town again for a month, but he would probably get through it all. He thought about Ciara's application – it was to study Art at the Glasgow School of Art. Charles Rennie MacIntosh met his wife there. They married in 1900. John always remembered that fact. Maybe something he heard Stephen Fry say on QI. Or maybe he had read it somewhere.

John looked again at the groceries and other packages and bags and products in the back-seat.

He glanced back at Ciara, as she walked down the road, back to the pub.

John climbed in the car and strapped the seatbelt across his body, *clicking* it in place, and put his right hand to the wheel, and left to the gear-stick.

He breathed in, filling his lungs.

A few minutes later.
John stopped at the Post Office, pulling the hand-brake to lock. He dismounted, crossing to the shop and entered. Every two weeks he received newly-published books from his editor, new articles from various sources, a small consignment of letters and several newspapers, magazines and flyers. He had not been to the Post Office in a month, as they had been closed due to sickness the last time he had come into town.

He carried out a large box filled with letters, parcels and smaller boxes.

The present.
John scrambled to his front-door, snatching an axe from an umbrella-stand, unlocking the door and throwing it open. He rushed outside. He immediately raced into the body of a blood-soaked man. He ducked back a step then charged at the man with the axe and cut him down, hacking at him again and again and again.

Ciara skidded to a stop in front of his house, kicking up gravel in a wide, spraying arc.

John winced as shards of gravel chipped and cut at his shirt and trousers, his body and legs, his face and hands. He gasped, letting out a sort of *yelp*, flicking his head from side to side, trying to see, as a stinging dust cloud engulfed him at the front of Ciara's car.

The man lay on the ground, coughing out dark mouthfuls of blood, steaming in the beam of the headlights.

Ciara stared at John, who stood up, pulling the axe from the man's broken-open chest. Their eyes met across the bonnet of Ciara's Land Rover, as a fine curtain of mist began to rise from the vents and edges of the bonnet-plate. Ciara was frightened and panting. Her left eye was almost completely bloodshot and flickered around John, seeing a halo around his head.

John's eyes bored into Ciara's. His felt blurry and distant; they hurt and trembled with his pulse.

A moment of silence drenched the scene.

John could only hear Ciara's muffled panting-breaths, and his own raging heartbeat.

Ciara could only hear her own panicked gasps for air, trying with all her strength to control her breathing and calm herself. Her knuckles were white with tension, still gripping the steering-wheel tightly.

The engine of her Land Rover *ticked* and *hissed*, then died altogether.

Another man charged at John from the darkness, chest-barging into him, and slamming him against the side of the car.

The man was frantic, violent and attacked John with a rage he had never seen in another person. He roared and screamed, coughing up thick, oily mouthfuls of blood. The man spat blood at John and gargled more out of its mouth. He charged at John again, swinging his arms in sweeping arcs.

John snatched the man's clothes and shoved him away, immediately advancing on him and punching him, as hard as he could. The man did nothing to block John's attack and so he fought harder. John kicked and punched the man to the ground. He grabbed the axe while the man lay on the floor stunned and wielded it swiftly, as Ciara watched perplexed. The man gargled and vomited blood as John brought the axe down on his chest, sending it rushing out of his mouth. Then John swung the axe down backwards, crushing the man's neck to pulp and sinew. Blood gushed from the wound soaking the axe-head and gravel around.

Dragging his body to stand, resting on the Land Rover's steaming bonnet, John looked at the two men's bodies. He could no longer see them as men, not in any normal sense – they were not human anymore; ghostly-pale and violently-deranged; beasts of pure rage and hunger – a hunger not to feed, but something else entirely. The men had transformed into something other than a true human – bloodshot eyes, bleeding from their mouths and nostrils, pale and clammy skin, driven by some internal engine to transmit their disease. They were infected by design and operation, disease-carrying predators, motivated to proliferate their affliction and infect any- and everyone left truly human.

John leapt to the driver's door still gripping the axe. It looked like it was itself bleeding profusely, dripping with blood and gore.

He helped Ciara out of her car.

John felt her arms encircle his shoulders, felt her weight as she landed on the gravel drive, felt her heart beating through her ribs and breasts; and saw her eyes look into his; and her breath on his face, ear and neck; and his arm was around her waist, touching her side and holding her from the ground, pressing his fingers flat against her back. And one second later, they stood, breathing, in the open maw of the Land Rover's doorway, embracing tightly in a tiny moment of complete silence as eddies of dust settled around them, dancing in the beams of the headlights.

The moment passed quickly.

John looked away and down the long distance of his uneven driveway, down to where his eyes could not see the boundary of his land anymore – into the darkness. He saw several of the infected sprinting headlong at them.

After a moment's thought, John blinked several times, realising immediately, angrily, that the infected had been attracted by the beeps of Ciara's horn.

He took Ciara's hand and glanced at the bonnet of the Land Rover, silently cursing the horn inside it.

John and Ciara rushed through the open front-door, throwing it to slam behind them, as the first of the infected reached the house and beat on the other side. A second and third quickly followed, drumming on the door with bloodying fists.

Two weeks ago. John's upstairs study – 4.40pm.
John typed on his computer, heavily drunk. He stubbed out a cigarette in an ashtray that resembled a porcupine back, filled to bursting with nicotine-brown and orange butts, when Ciara pulled up in her car outside his house.

John's eyes squinted in the light and he could see she had his two-week supply of food and drink in boxes in the back of her car – an older model Land Rover to John's, and grey, where John's was the traditional farmer's-green. He was surprised to see her, and walked slowly and carefully, but drunkenly, to the top of the stairs. He stumbled slightly on the staircase, hanging onto the balustrade to steady himself, feeling hot whiskey swill in his stomach and firework in his brain. He made it to the bottom step, nudging a photograph on the wall, pushing it a tiny amount off-alignment, where it stayed.

He reached the front-door and unlocked it. He stood a moment, then opened the door.

Moments later, Ciara walked into John's hall carrying the first of many boxes, leaving John puzzled and unable to account for the last few minutes. She smiled at him, breaking his trance, letting him realise she had been speaking.

"...So Uncle Arthur told me to come drop your stuff off, before going round to the Lanning Farm... We deliver her shopping every week, although Gary – her son – comes in the pub most-days... Lazy fucking bastard – he could bring it up to her himself any day..." she said, sliding another bag onto the work-surface.

"I've met him – Gary – a few times," John murmured.

"Lazy, lazy, stupid fucker, if you ask me..."

John smiled. "I agree... He always gives me a strange look," he said – a tense twinge bursting on his back, making him wince and stand taller. "The first time I met him he told me that he thought all of my books were shit. He had only read one of them, mind you.. And he was drunk. And being a prick."

John's dog Bobby – a German Shepherd (he had been told never to call them 'Alsatians', as they were originally from Germany and not France) – ran passed him in the hall and circled Ciara's feet. Ciara patted Bobby's neck and stroked his head softly, smoothing the fur around his ears, much to his liking. Bobby rubbed the side of his face against Ciara's leg.

"Would you like a drink? Tea, coffee... Beer, whiskey?"

"A beer would be great."

John picked up two bottles and turned to her, she said, "You've never been in my house before, have you?"

"I've been outside," she said, beaming a smile.

A little later. In John's living-room.
John and Ciara sat comfortably on sofas.

"I could only compare you to Nick Hornby."

"Well, thanks. If only I could get some of them made into films. That would be wonderful."

"You could. Definitely. *Highness and Lowness* and *Red Sky, Blue Wall* could easily be films!"

"You liked *Highness and Lowness*? The reviews said it wasn't 'girl-friendly,'" he admitted. "I hadn't written it to be particularly girl-friendly, anyway..."

"Fuck the reviews!" she said with a laugh.

"My editor sends me some. I ignore most of them. I think he does it to wind me up."

"I hope you read the good ones?" she laughed.

"Mostly... Not really any, to be totally truthful."

"You could be like the new J D Salinger."

"Because I live alone?"

"Because you're ever-so-slightly like the reclusive writer-guy that lives away on his own and barely sees any human existence at all. I mean, Tobermory people, but not cities or New York or Tokyo or anywhere else. But instead you're up-here, away in the Highlands. Like a recluse," she said and sipped from a bottle of beer. "Like a Stephen King character or something..."

"Well I hope the devil doesn't send anyone to kill me," he quipped. He half-smiled at the thought of the Salinger and King references and looked at Ciara, who sat on his sofa, shoes-off, laid back.

She noticed him noticing her and smiled to herself, blushing across her cheeks.

After a moment of lull, Ciara sat forward. "What kind of art do you like?"

"All sorts. Why do you ask?"

Ciara began to roll a cigarette, resting a small-skin Rizla paper on one of the creases in her woolly-jumper, pulling it up to reveal a few inches of her flat, smooth midriff. "I was... I was thinking of submitting something to one of the competitions or exhibitions this summer. I'd like you to give it a look and tell me what you think. Please."

"I would do that. You should enter... From what Arthur showed me – you are really, really talented," he said honestly.

"Thank you – you don't need to say anything... Just be honest..." Ciara licked the glue on the edge of a Rizla paper and wrapped the cigarette. She sipped the bottle of beer again. She crossed her legs and sat forward, closer to John.

"I am honest... You are really good. I think you'll do so well at uni," he said. "I'm no authority..."

"You're our local celebrity!" Ciara exclaimed, lighting the cigarette pinched between index and middle.

"No... No... I'm not... Not really... No."

"You are in town!" she beamed. "I don't know if you've ever noticed, but my uncle has all of your books.. His own copies and another set for the bookshelf in the pub... So do most of the people in town... You are quite well-liked, John... Even if you hadn't noticed."

"God! Why?.. Nobody needed to buy my books... I would have given–..."

Ciara interrupted, "Yes, but my uncle especially liked them, and wanted to buy them for himself... And the pub too, for that matter... That's how I read them... And I really, really like them too... I mean, not all of them the same amount, but most of them..."

Ciara's head rolled onto the back of the sofa, craning her neck to look around the room. John felt gravity increase on his brain, finally pulling it down, hinging his neck with no strain. They both daydreamed for a long moment, encapsulated in their own thoughts.

After a moment, "How come your living-room is on the upstairs?" Ciara asked.

"When we--... I... --bought the house... --it was one of the small rooms downstairs... Then, I only needed a bedroom, bathroom, study and living-room on the upstairs... --so I got a builder to knock-through some of the walls.. Downstairs became the kitchen, larder, a bathroom, a small workshop and the garage – then upstairs became what I wanted it to be... I get a really beautiful view from my study, when I write... Especially in winter when everywhere is... --snowy... And white..."

"You're so eloquent!" she giggled. "You'll have to show me it," Ciara flirted, "in the wintertime..."

The daylight outside had almost all but gone, leaving dark traces of trees, hills and the vague horizon.

"When it's brighter and snowier outside," she added.
John nodded.
A long moment of silence, then, "How come you moved up-here in the first place?"
A flicker of tension passed over John's eyes, then he said, "My... My... Well, I... I needed to get away from London... I needed to be as far away as I could be... So I put my house down-there on the market, got some builders to fix this place up quickly, then got all of my stuff together, said my goodbyes to friends..." he said, then cleared his throat. "This house was supposed to be a holiday home.. --when I first looked at it, then bought it..."
Ciara could see John was struggling.
"So you're always on holiday?" she said, lightly.
"Something like that..."

Later. In John's hall – 9:48pm.
Ciara kissed John's cheek, before walking out of his house.
"Are you sure you're okay to drive?" he asked.
"I only had one beer," she replied, smiling. "See you soon..."
John closed the front-door with a *click*, smiling uncontrollably. He leaned on the back of the door.

The present.
John was stood in exactly the same position and pose, but now Ciara was inside the hall again – and they were both filthy from their divergent encounters. John turned to Ciara angrily – It was clear to her he was drunk. He shouted, "Why?! Why did you come here?! Why did you come here?! What good was it coming here?... Why did you bring those things here?!" then he fell silent, and they stood for a long moment with the infected beating on the outward side of the front-door. Finally he said, "Go and wait in the kitchen, sit at the breakfast-table... Don't make a sound."
"Where're you going?" Ciara asked, panicked from the thought of being left alone in the dark.
"Upstairs," John answered. His head dropped. He started for the stairs, then continued, "We have a guest."
Ciara gasped with shock, but John did not hear it.

John took the first step up the staircase, slowly creeping upwards. Lights blinked on, paintings straightened automatically, glass pictures un-shattered and reformed on their hooks, a plant re-potted itself, blood-sprays and -splatters wiped clean from the walls and vanished as time unfurled and blossomed. John changed too, from slow deliberate steps to a casual hop. Time had changed around him – night had turned to day. Days had been peeled away.
John reached the top of his staircase and turned into his living-room. It was empty.
The fire-place had a healthy fire in it eating large piled logs with a Victorian fire-guard stood in front of it. Heat radiated from the licking flames. The fire *crackled* occasionally.
He walked in and slumped on the arm-chair. He put his feet up on a small pillow-topped stool.
Across from John, Bobby lay – looking as languid, placid and lazy as a cat. Bobby took up most of the sofa opposite John. The dog stirred, then rolled onto his front and stared at his master.
John smiled at Bobby. He reached over the side of the arm-chair's oversized arm and picked up a large ash-tray. He put the ash-tray on his stomach and lit a cigarette that sat abandoned in the ash-tray. As he puffed on the cigarette, he poured himself a large glass of wine. John blew out a huge cloud of smoke, then swallowed down a huge mouthful of wine.
He rested his head on the arm-chair, and closed his eyes.
His eyes eventually reopened and he looked out of the window.

Outside.
A wind was blowing and the tree-branches were swaying and the grass undulated in waves.

John stared, glassy-eyed, at the outside world.

Bobby stirred and whined.

The German Shepherd stretched, then stood up and wandered out of the room and downstairs. John watched Bobby go.

A few hours passed and the sky slowly darkened, then night closed in, and then day broke. Dawn set in, as a few more hours passed. Clouds rolled across the sky behind swaying treetops.

Across the stairs from the living-room was John's study, really an extension to his living-room, but with hundreds and hundreds of books covering every space on the walls – all ordered into sections for authors, subjects and fields. John slumped in front of his computer, asleep. A wet-ended, semi-smoked cigarette hung out of the side of his mouth – the blackened cherry-tip resting on a scorched circle the size of a 2p coin in the wood of the desk.

John stirred.

The wind blew outside, and John came awake with a start.

He looked at what he had written – read it painfully carefully, focusing and tracing the lines with his fingertips. He continued with it for some time, stopping again and again to re-read it.

He reached for the half-smoked cigarette in his mouth, and lit it.

Coils of smoke sprang from the cigarette cherry.

John picked up a nearby glass, sloshing in two inches of whiskey, then gulped it down in one. He smoked and carried on typing, letting the cigarette hang out of the side of his mouth, once again, at a droopy angle. It burned away.

John finished typing, mock-dramatically with the flair of an orchestra conductor or a jazz pianist, then stared at it.

His brow furrowed, and anger took over.

He relit and smoked, then tapped the ash from the end of the cigarette in the ashtray.

"...Shit!... What shit..." he said, standing, then sat back down, unsteadily, drunk. He poured another drink. He stared at the words closely. "I hate... all... of this..." he whispered.

He stared at the screen, his fist gripping so tightly his knuckles turned white. He looked from his fist to the screen, imagining smashing it, then the phone rang.

John reached out and grabbed the receiver, which sat next to the computer on a tower of piled books. He struggled, turning the phone in his hand to get it the correct way up, before he answered, pressing the receiver to his ear.

"Hello?"

On Princess Street, Edinburgh.

A man stood near a phone-box, making a call on his mobile phone – he was GRAHAM HARDING, 44 year old Scotsman, and John's friend and book-editor. He held the phone to his ear. He had short brown hair, going grey from the temples to the sides – side-parted and gelled. He was a handsome man and looked young for his age – younger than John did and was a year his senior. He was slim and gym-fit, healthy from a mostly-organic diet. He wore a dark grey suit over a spotless ice-blue shirt with comfortable tan shoes. "Hello?" he said with a smirk.

John rocked in his seat, sliding down the chair-back to put his feet up on the desk.

"Hello?" John repeated the greeting, slightly slurring his words.

"John?... Hello... Are you drunk?" Graham said, trying to sound surprised, but was not at all. He frowned.

John looked at a large digital clock on the wall. "Why would I be drunk, Graham?... It is only nine fifty-six...?" he said with a wry-ish smile. "Besides... I'm writing."

"Cool... Okay, mate," he started, getting to it, "I only rang because I'm runnin' a bit late, and I'll be late gettin' to yours... And... Well... Um, it is still good for me t'be stayin' at yours... --for five whole days?... You are still sure?"

"It's fine," John asserted. He was drunk, and was finding it more and more difficult to concentrate on being sober than he could take. He took a deep breath. Graham heard it too.

"Listen, bud, I'm gonna have to go, I've got breakfast on... See you soon... Later."
"Cool. Great. See you later on, dude."
John hung up the phone.

Graham stopped a moment, staring at his mobile for proof John had actually hung up on him. He felt concerned, but amused. He shrugged it off, and set off down the street, hailing a taxi.

John stared at the computer screen. His head rolled on his neck, as he analysed his words. He *huffed* at it, and rose to his feet. He stumbled out of the room, slowly regaining his senses. He slapped his own cheeks, feeling instant red-hot burns.

A little later.
John stood in the kitchen, cooking eggs and bacon together in a large frying-pan. Bread warmed in the toaster. He poured a large glass of whiskey. He switched the hob off and threw the frying-pan into the sink, rejecting it and the idea of food entirely. He gulped whiskey down. A drip rolled into his beard.
On his way out of the room, with the whiskey glass and bottle in hand, the toast ejected and left two sunburned slices behind in the toaster.

The next day.
John jumped-out-of-his-skin-awake with a nightmare. Sweating heavily and still wearing the clothes from yesterday, he felt dirty. He had collapsed on his arm-chair, again. He was confused and looked around the room dozily.
He caught his reflection in the window. He looked awful. He swept hair away from his forehead, itched his beard around his chin, then slapped himself across the cheek, again. A red mark manifested itself.
Bobby twitched, lying along the sofa opposite him, awakened by the noise.
John peeled himself from the seat. Sweat marks remained on the sofa-cushion where his head had been.
John stared at Bobby, as embarrassment and disgrace bubbled inside him. He rolled his neck and it *cracked* and *crackled* with synovial release. He shook and rubbed his head and face, waking up, pulling out from a sizzling hangover. "You'll..." he croaked, then cleared his throat. "You're going to need walking, aren't you?" he said as Bobby's head lifted and a smile broke across John's face.
John rose to his feet. He stumbled out of the room. "...But you'll want feeding first...!" he growled from the hall.
Bobby sprang to life and leapt to follow John downstairs.

Later that day. On the hills.
John walked, as Bobby ran around, playing with a short stick. John looked across the vast golden-green open space, breathing in the fresh cool air.
A handful of clouds fluttered across the horizon.
John and Bobby walked for several hours, following a wide, loose figure of eight.

Later that day. At John's house.
John sauntered down the long driveway to his property, with Bobby on the end of a very long lead. Graham had pulled up in front of John's house in a blue 2010 Mazda 3 rental-car.
"Alright you-old-bastard!" Graham shouted, climbing out of his car, after catching a glimpse in the rear-view.
"Awww-ight-mate!" John shouted back, meeting him with an embrace.
"Been a long while, dude."
"Yeah."
They parted, sizing each other up carefully.
"How's things?" Graham beamed, slapping John's shoulder.

"Good.. Having a lot more sober days recently," John stated. "Trying to, at least," he laughed.

"That's good news," Graham began. "Have you been writing, then?" he quickly added. "You said earlier…"

"A bit, yeah," he interrupted and beamed back a smile.

Graham reciprocated. The German Shepherd sniffed his leg. He squatted next to Bobby, rubbing his neck-fur, he said, "Hello you lazy old bastard… How's he been treating you, hey?.. Good, huh? Huh?" He retrieved some dried bacon dog-food from his overcoat-pocket and fed it to Bobby. Bobby wolfed it out of Graham's hand, leaving shiny marks of spittle behind on his palm.

"Last time you came, you fed him so much of that shit, Bobby shit green for a week… Calm it down this stay, will you? Please?"

Graham nodded, rising.

"I thought you were gonna be here in a few hours..?"

"The traffic was behind me," Graham smirked. "Plus, these roads… You can drive fairly fast… And I got on an earlier ferry…"

John unlocked the front-door and walked in, with Graham following a short distance behind.

"Tell me, why do you lock your door? Honestly, who's gonna steal this place, miles out-here, absolute middle-of-fucking-nowhere, Johnny-Bean…"

"I don't know… Deranged fans?"

Graham laughed, following John into the hall, before stopping. "Oh shit! My bag…" He trotted to the car. John paused in the doorway, watching his friend dither with the car-alarm, lock and boot-handle.

"Did you bring your granny-outfit? I love that one the best!" John joked. "Or the French-maid?"

John and Graham laughed, entering the house, closing and locking the front-door.

Later.
They sat and relaxed in John's living-room above the kitchen. They had drunk a lot of wine and whiskey, and chatted and smoked cigarettes and cigars. Their conversations meandered around the time of John's first book, their first encounter, the usual events that they always spoke of with fondness and nostalgia. And it served another purpose, to offer Graham the chance to capitalise on their reminiscences.

Later.
John and Graham lay back on the sofas.

"So, then… How is it livin' up-here in the sticks?"

"Imagine:… Peaceful… --and lovely and quiet… Just… --quiet," John said sombrely with a diminutive sigh.

Graham saw the tiny inflexion of melancholy and brusquely moved passed it. "I can imagine… Being locked away – away from everything – away from my friends and my family… Away from the bright lights of London," he stammered a laugh. "It's my hell. It's like fuckin' prison. Or being on the island in *Lost*…"

Graham caught John's eye – he was not happy with this conversation.

"That's where we disagree then. For me it's peaceful. No smoke monsters, either."

"Yeah, I guess," Graham said and sipped some whiskey.

"I am working on… --something… Thanks for not asking," John said changing the subject, necking the last swig of whiskey from a tumbler, then refilled it to half a centimetre shy of the rim. He poured Graham some more.

"Moving back to the land of the living? Leaving this paradise? Please tell me it's that!"

"…A book, is all."

"Good… Well… Good! I like hearing that! A lot, I might add," he said around a cigar clamped between his teeth.

John began to roll another cigarette.

"Have you been to see them?" Graham said soberly. "At all?... Since--..."
The air in the room thickened.
Focused on rolling the cigarette, John interrupted him, "I haven't left Tobermory."
"For how many years is it now?"
The room was a gas chamber.
"Does it matter, Gram?..."
"Will you ever leave?"
An ocean of heavy fog and choking mist filled the room.
"No... No..." John said. "No."
Minutes passed.
"I'm sorry. I'm sorry, I shouldn't have brought it up," Graham apologised.

He pulled a contract from his laptop bag and slapped it on the coffee-table between them. He relaxed back into the sofa, pulling on the fabric-thighs of his trousers to extricate the tightness around his crotch. He ran his fingers through his hair, finger-combing it back over his skull.

"I have a copy in my bag, in the car, of the sales for your last book... D'you want me to go get it?"

Graham's eyes traced over John. He relaxed. His shoulders drooped. His body sank.
"No, thanks... Tomorrow, maybe."
"It's good news, Johnny-boy.. Good-good news.. People are buying lots of copies..."
"Good for the publishers... Good for you.. Good for me."
"Speaking of the pubes... They've been asking me about a small tour...?"

John scanned Graham quickly – he had definitely noticed, like always, that Graham, although drunk, was still doing his job, still doing the business.

Later.
They laughed hysterically.

The present. In John's hall.
John crept up the staircase, holding the small-handle axe tightly. He reached the top of the stairs and stood by the door to the living-room. He hesitated even before reaching for the handle.

John knocked on the door gently and lightly, then an entity the other side charged at the door and banged against it violently. It beat and thrashed and punched the obstruction. There was something or someone behind the door – it banged on the other side of the door again and again and again making the door rattle with every tremor.

John gripped the axe and the door-handle, then, twisting the handle, body-slammed his whole weight against the door, knocking the stranger backwards. He barged into the room, then descended heavily upon the body of the intruder that lay across the coffee-table.

John leapt up, as the intruder bucked underneath him, then fell to kneel on the living-room floor, grappling and struggling and fighting with the figure. John was glad the lights were off, and that it was almost impossible to tell who he was fighting with face-to-face. He rolled the person over and hit down once with the back of the axe to stun him, then he said, "I'm sorry, mate."

John struck the figure again and again and again and again and again and again.

Two days ago. John's driveway – 11.08am.
Graham had packed to leave John's house, putting his last bag in the boot of his rental-car. He said, "I hope to come up and over to see you again, in a month or so..."
John laughed at this comment, he said, "That's unlikely."
Graham got in his car and said his goodbye and left.
John watched him go, then went inside with Bobby. He cooked breakfast, then fed Bobby, telling him he would take him for a walk a little later.

Later.
John walked with Bobby across the island's hilly scrubland. He checked his watch — it was ten past twelve. He whistled for Bobby to come to him.

Later.
Bobby *barked* at something over a hill-rise. John jogged slowly, avoiding sharp craggy rubble that dotted the landscape, to see what was drawing his dog's attention. He ascended the rise to get a better view to the main-road. He got to the peak of the small rise and saw a stationery car, with the driver still seated inside it. The driver struggled violently against their seatbelt, labouring hard to get out of a car, trying to fight their way out. The figure finally unhooked their arm from the belt, then turned, locating John — and Bobby's *barks* — from his side.

The figure sprinted straight at its target — John. The person no longer resembled the ordinary — blood seeped from their mouth and nose; all of their skin had turned pallid and lifeless, sweaty and pale; the sound from its lungs and throat had become animal and ravenous; its motions had become directed and instinctual.

John watched the person speeding toward him, seeing clearly something was horrifically wrong. He could see that it was a man, not a local, but similarly dressed to many locals; he wore a wool jumper over flannel shirt, brown jeans and wellington boots — he had significant trouble running in these. It looked like human rabies, or some other kind of disease, but with no froth at the mouth.

John glanced beyond the infected person, noticing the car he had run away from was skewed in the road, leaving skid marks behind its tyres, as if it was stopped with some urgency. It appeared the driver had been able to stop, before the disease had taken and they had changed into a monster, into one of the infected.

Its blood-red eyes were locked onto John, as Bobby continued to *bark*, bucking and bouncing on the spot, loyally standing by John's heel.

John started to retreat, asking rationally, projecting his voice down the hill, "Is this a joke?... Is it?... What—What's wrong with you?..."

He backed away a few more paces.

The infected did not stop, and plainly it did not appear to be a joke — could not possibly have been staged. It continued to race disturbingly towards him, swigs of blood splashing and leaking from its loose-hanging jaw.

Bobby barked aggressively at the infected — growling and snarling at it, but with no effect — no effect at all.

John backed away again, scooping up a small, sharp rock and gripping it in his palm.

The infected advanced incredibly fast and tackled John, weightily, knocking the wind out of him. Sprawling on the ground, the infected grabbed and snatched at John, then vomited a choking, thick, dark pint of blood on him. The blood mostly missed John, splashing his arm and coat, as he and the infected struggled and fought on the ground. He gripped the jaw of the infected, twisting it away from his face to prevent it from vomiting on him again.

John managed to locate the rock with his free hand. It had been knocked free in the first assault. He clutched it in his hand, turning it in his fingers to find the sharpest point. He killed the infected with five rapid blows to the side of its head. He immediately shoved the body from above him, stumbling to stand, then staggered backwards, staring at the body. Blood pooled, streaked and squirted from the head-wounds. The grass around its head quickly stained with rich, dark redness.

John turned away, vomiting his breakfast. He coughed, then vomited more.

Bobby circled around John and the body, *whining*, with his brow furrowed, looking up at John submissively. He *barked* twice at the corpse, then backed away, rounding to the direction home.

John rushed away from the body, to Bobby's side, and started to calm him, stroking his neck and shoulders. The infected gasped out its last, bloody, bubbling breath, then expired on the ground where it lay, shocking John and Bobby one final time.

John watched the man die. He put a knee on the grass and stroked Bobby, cradling his head.

Minutes passed as seconds then John, panicked and panting for air, suddenly rushed to the body and searched its pockets. He found a mobile-phone and tried 999. The message came back: "We are currently experiencing technical difficulties, please hang up and try again later," then the line cut off.

      John pocketed the mobile and started away, calling Bobby to his side.

Later. On the path home – 1:42pm.
John tried the mobile-phone again. This time it was completely dead, all trace of a signal was gone. He dropped it, looking across a shallow grassy valley to his house, in the middle-distance. He saw a person stalking around it. The person – another one infected with the disease – staggered and stumbled around the front of the house, *crunching* gravel under its feet. It lurched back and forth, scanning the windows and driveway. It looked like a crazy fan – a camera hung around his neck and he wore an old parka jacket, with a comic-book character adorned backpack looped over both arms. The infected turned and turned again on the spot.

      John stared, motionless, at the figure, about three hundred metres away from them, until Bobby *barked*. The noise immediately attracted the attention of the infected, when another appeared from the south of its position.

      The second infected sprang into a run. Its arms swung at its sides, as it charged along at a quick-walking pace, steadily increasing in acceleration. Blood poured out of its mouth, soaking its jumper-chest and –stomach. It was a local farmer, one of the ones John did not know the name of. Bobby *barked* again. The infected swung its eyes around and locked onto John and Bobby, quickening to a lumbering quick-jog. The infected near to the house also turned in their direction, and began its journey, taking unsteady steps one after the other, watching its own feet.

      John ran to his wood-shed and locked himself and Bobby inside it. He panted for air, gasping, feeling trapped and confined and claustrophobic, when the infected farmer made it to the wood-shed and started to smash its way in. Wood splintered, cracked and shattered as the farmer beat against the door and frame. John caught tiny glimpses of the blood-stained woollen sleeve of the man's jumper.

      John grabbed a small-handle axe from a nail-hook and moved to the door of the wood-shed.

      As the infected banged against the door, snarling and spitting blood from behind it, John unlocked the door quietly. He burst out, knocking the farmer to the grass, then he launched at him with the axe.

      The shed-door banged in the wind, as Bobby cowered and *barked* one solitary time, and John slashed and hacked and chopped the infected to pieces.

      He chanced a glance at his home and saw the other infected sprinting headlong at him.

The present. John's living-room.
John smashed the back of the axe down on the guest, when Ciara appeared behind him – she said, "John stop... Stop... Stop, John... Stop... Please..."

      John froze, then turned on her – he said, "We have got to get out of this house!"

One day ago. John's kitchen.
John had boarded-up the windows in the ground-floor rooms from the inside. He picked at a pile of wood and nailed another plank to the frame across the kitchen window. He wore gloves, avoiding splinters, feeling the sweat build up inside, making his fingers slippery and squirm around the hammer and barricade logs.

      He could make out signs of daylight through the windows, but had nailed the boards across the curtains and only small pin-pricks of light glimmered through.

      Something hit the back side of the window, cracking the glass.

      John froze. He held his breath. He stared at the window, standing stock-still, trying not making a sound, fighting to hold his breath, trying not to pass-out and knock something over, trying to be invisible, trying to sense any sign of the infected, and trying to hide from them by being a statue.

Later.
John watched at a tear in the curtain through a crack in the kitchen window, as a figure stalked around the perimeter of his property.

    Daylight beamed through the trees like spider's-webs beyond the infected as it circled and paced.

    John squinted in the light, ducking away into the dimness of his house.

Later.
John drank heavily, talking nonsensically to Bobby, sitting in the upstairs living-room with the lights out, watching the outside world at the window.

    He gulped down a large shot of whiskey, when he heard a noise coming from outside.

    He scrambled on all-fours to the window and pressed his face against the cool glass.

    He could not see anything.

Outside.
Graham sprinted down the driveway, hurtling towards John's house, legs whirling and arms flapping, screaming at the top of his lungs for "John!" and for John to "Open the door! Open the door! Open the door!" between enormous gasps for air. Graham's suit-jacket had been ripped, and dried blood had splattered the arms and his shirt underneath.

    Two infected jog-limped, launching down the driveway after him.

Inside.
John saw Graham.

    He rushed to the stairs but tripped and fell back, sliding down the carpet on four steps with a few dull *thuds*. He tumbled into the banister-rail catching his right knee. He groaned with pain, then steadied himself by snatching hold of the nearest balustrade. He leapt to the front-door, where dozens of spy-holes had been drilled and awaited him. He squinted to look through some of the holes, ducking and weaving to catch a glimpse of Graham. He threw the door open, but just as Graham got into the opening one of the infected collided with him and they hit the ground hard in a dusty cloud.

    John threw the door open and dove outside. He swung a golf-club in wheeling wide arcs, making the air *whistle*, then took out the other oncoming infected with a hard swipe. He turned to help Graham, who was being beaten and blood-puked-on by the first figure – spills and splashes of blood landed on Graham's writhing and twisting face, neck and body. He just-managed to push the infected woman off before John clubbed her several times on the arms, chest and head; before helping his friend to his feet and into the house. He slammed the door behind them and locked it a number of times.

    John turned to Graham, who lay back on the staircase, quite badly hurt. John ducked under his friend's right armpit and hoisted him to his feet, helping him up the stairs – one by one – and into the living-room, lowering him into an arm-chair.

    John sat opposite Graham, biting his lip to not to interrogate his friend with too many questions, trying to let his friend speak, trying to tend to a few of his more-visible wounds, cleaning them and applying bandages and surgical-tape.

    Graham sputtered and stammered with his words – his jaw and nose had been broken. Blood bubbled at one of his nostrils as he spoke, "I nearly got to Glasgow," he slurred, coughing lightly "...When, when, when cars started crashing and people started just, just, just going ape-shit and... And... And..." Graham's breathing shifted and slowed, becoming more and more difficult. He continued, "People were vomiting blood on other people... Puking... --on people that were okay... --or not one of them... --already..." he coughed, then finished, "Go to London... Live... Live... Living... People will flock there... You have to go... People will get there... --to safety... Go to your family."

    John could not believe his ears. He started to shake his head, tears filled his eyes.

    Graham coughed, then he shook his head.

    "No... No... Everything is gone... You don't understand," Graham stammered. "London... There will be more people... And some... More... And some... --hope..." He coughed up blood, then looked at John, he said, "Oh shit.." then Graham Harding died. For several seconds his heart did not beat.

John stared at his friend across the room, unblinkingly. He clenched his teeth.

John leant across the space and took Graham's wrist, holding it to check for a pulse, water streaming from his eyes.

There was no pulse. None at all.

The still and lifeless body of Graham twitched, making John jump and pin himself to the back of his chair.

Graham started to turn – the infection had caught him. Graham's skin started to redden, then softened, paling and losing all colour. His eyes snapped open – showing red, bruised and bloodshot pupils.

"Christ!" John screamed.

The infected pulled itself to its feet, then launched straight at John.

John managed to push and throw the infected Graham across the room and escape, slamming the door shut behind him. The infected banged and banged against the door, making the wood buck and tremble.

John fell to the floor against the wall opposite the living-room door, and stared at it, obsessively. His heart pounded inside his chest. Sweat beaded his forehead. Tears filled his eyes.

His body began to shudder.

Later. At night.
John remained opposite the living-room door, watching it intently. He got up, in a very-laboured way, feeling his muscles burn and quiver. He stumbled very-slowly downstairs. He moved sullenly into the kitchen and lit a candle on the breakfast-table. He slid a box of cereal in front of the candle to obscure the light from the windows, and the outside. It worked fairly well as a dampener, but he had no idea at all how many of the infected were outside.

John collected a bottle of whiskey from a knee-level cupboard and started to drink it. He sat at the breakfast table for a while, drinking quickly, gulping it down in great mouthfuls. He finished the bottle, tossing and smashing it against the wall. He got up to get another, then exploded – he smashed the pots and pans and plates from the top of his work-surface, breaking everything and knocking over the candle, which extinguished itself on the wet floor, where a smashed bottle of fruit-juice had puddled. John swung his arms wildly, beating the work-surface top with the flat bottoms of his hands, punching eye-level cupboard doors. He fell to the floor, where he passed out, dropping and sinking away into absolute blackness.

One of the cupboard-doors snapped off its hinge and fell to the floor next to John's body.

Later.
Ciara sped towards the house in her car, beeping her horn.

John awoke on his kitchen floor.

Moments later.
John peered through one of the cracks between the window-boards. He saw Ciara's car coming.

The present.
John had packed a large rucksack with clothes, food and alcohol. He snapped a family photo out of its frame – it showed John, his wife and son standing in front of the London Eye – he tucked it in his inside jacket-pocket.

Ciara walked into the kitchen, carrying another rucksack and asked, "Where are we goin' to go to?"

John replied, "London."

Later.
John stood by his front-door, when Ciara carried down a second small rucksack from the upstairs.

"What's the plan?" she whispered.

"You go out the back-door, while I go out the front... You'll have the car-keys," John replied in a growling whisper.

Ciara looked overwhelmed, but nodded. "Where's Bobby?" she asked.

John looked at her, pained and upset. He said, "When I killed one of those... --people... --outside the wood-shed... --another one puked blood all over him, and he died... --right there in my arms. After I killed the other one." John's eye-lid blinked a tear into surrender and disappeared. "I buried him yesterday."

"I'm sorry."

John nodded.

Ciara watched him for a moment, he swayed, agitated. "Go time?" she asked.

John nodded.

He watched her vanish into the darkness beside the stairs, leading to the back-door, before he started to bang on the front-door with his fists. After a long pause, he beat on the door again. He turned and shouted, "Go now!" into the darkness, and he threw the front-door open.

John immediately bolted up the stairs, as the first of three infected burst into the house and charged after him up the staircase. John twisted around on the middle stairs and cut the first infected down with a swipe of his axe, then turned and ran as fast as he could up the final eight stairs, as the body fell backwards. He darted across the hall-landing and into his bedroom. The other two infected shoved passed the falling body of the first and hotly pursued John to the top of the stairs, before beating on the bedroom door.

At the back of the house.
Ciara rushed around the outer-wall, carrying a golf-club and the small bag. She turned the final corner, and saw John's Land Rover. She breathed in – her eyes darting back and forth across the front of the house – and hesitantly crept toward the car. She looked around awkwardly, trying to minimise the sound her shoes made on the gravel drive, attempting to tip-toe with the lightest *crunch*es of gravel.

She looked to see if John was somewhere, somewhere close maybe, somewhere near the house, but there was nobody there. Ciara rushed the last three steps to the car, unlocked it, climbed in and threw the small bag onto the back-seat. The interior light dimmed as Ciara pulled the door closed enough to fool the censor into believing the door was shut. She shifted across the front of the car, dodging the gear-stick and sat in the passenger-seat, looking for John through the windscreen and driver's door-window. She pushed the keys in the ignition.

A window smashed – one of the window's in John's bedroom. The broken pieces of glass landed on the slanting-roof of the garage alongside the house. John clambered through the window, dragging the large rucksack behind him. He only-just managed to jump from the garage roof to the ground without hurting himself – but still landed with a groan. He scrambled to his feet and ran to the Land Rover, as Ciara pushed the driver's-side door open.

John leapt inside, starting the engine and wrenching the steering-wheel into a tight U-turn.

The car skidded off at speed.

John and Ciara disappeared in a cloud of dust, smoke and gravel.

One of the two remaining infected rushed out of the house. It slowed to a stop, staring up the driveway at the distant Land Rover's taillights shining and disappearing into the distance. It immediately started to run after them, pulling away with furious pursuing pace.

Later. On the A849 – 6:19am.
John slowed down and stopped the Land Rover. The sun had started to rise, and he noticed that both he and Ciara looked and more-than-likely felt exhausted.

The engine of the Land Rover *ticked* and *hissed*, then cut out.

"What are we going to do?" Ciara whispered.

"Graham thought people would flock to London. Any survivors who're left. I'm not sure where anyone would go."

"What about those things? Those people?"

"We can avoid them. Try to," John offered.

"I... I'll go with you, John. I don't have any better options right now. I don't have anything left behind."

"That makes two of us, then."

Ciara tried to smile, but could not, her cheek muscles would not allow it.

"We only have a few miles of petrol left. Then... We're going to have to find some way to cross to the mainland."

"I don't want to get out of the car again," Ciara said, resolute.

John looked at her, lifted his shoulders, trying not to shrug and said, "I don't know what the best plan is..."

"We are on an island, John."

"I know..." he admitted slowly. "We could be fairly safe here for quite some time... But we need to find other people... And that means we have to cross to the mainland.. After some time our food will run out..."

They agreed to walk from whatever point the car ran out of petrol, if they could not find any other transport. John put the car in gear and they pulled away and continued South and East as far as they could go.

Later. On the South-Eastern coast of The Isle of Mull.
John and Ciara trekked across the shore, slowing when they found a row boat, tied up with a wet rope.

"This'll do," John stated, pulling the large rucksack off his back and depositing it in the rowboat.

Ciara's brow furrowed. She shivered.

A little later.
John rowed hard, pulling away from his island home.

The row boat was quickly taken by the current and they moved without much need of their own energy. Ciara helped him to pull the oars into the boat. Occasionally John steered using the soggy, salt-crusted rudder, guiding the small boat along and across the dark North Sea.

Three days later. Four miles Southeast of Alexandria, eight miles from the centre of Glasgow – 3:20pm.
John walked along a shallow hillside, tugging and struggling with an eight foot long, two by two inch wooden stick in his hands. Attached to the other end a belt had been twisted and nailed in place; the belt was wrapped into a noose that was coiled around Ciara's neck. She had been lost to the plague: her infected figure struggled against the restraint, fighting with it, snapping her teeth, trying to reach for John, but the wood was too long for her to be able to reach him. Stains of dark ooze coated the nearer two feet of the pole, black like charred wood.

John stopped for a moment, glaring out over the hills surrounding him.

Green-golden grass, freckled with rocks and dark purple and brown heather bushes stretched in every direction.

Nothing stirred. No birds flew and he could hear no birdsong.

The infected, restrained behind him, gargled and hacked. It ejected a stream of gore out of its mouth, wetting the pole once again. Drips and dribbles fell from the wood at the feet of the infected.

Later. Six miles from the centre of Glasgow – 6:46pm.
John pegged the wooden-stick into the earth, fastening the infected Ciara to the ground.

He walked away a few metres, preparing to build a make-shift camp, as the sky grew darker and night loomed. He erected a small tent, pushing his large rucksack, and the small bag that Ciara had been carrying, into the tent. He zipped the tent closed from the outside and stood to survey the area. He picked up a camping-lantern, then walked away, ensuring Ciara was firmly anchored to the ground.

The infected chomped and spat congealed gobs of blood at his receding form.

Later. 9:50pm.
John watched the outskirts of North-eastern Glasgow from a hill nearby with binoculars. There were very few house-lights on in very few of the houses, but streetlight still illuminated the roads and buildings and businesses and some other homes.

He surveyed the way forward, staring along the roads lit up by gloomy orange neon. He could only make out one of the infected, wandering the middle of a side-street.

He moved on.

Dawn.
John climbed over a garden-wall, slowly and silently, making sure not to knock over any plant-pots. He crept down the side walkway of the house, opened the side-gate and wedged it fully ajar with a small terracotta plant-pot where a bunch of yellow tulips grew.

John walked down many empty streets, creeping cautiously between shadows and against walls, avoiding bright pools of light.

Later.
John found a small supermarket and walked inside through the automatic-door, listening for any sign of movement. He tiptoed into the open entrance space, holding his breath, listening for any sound. He gripped the small-handle axe, leading himself with it, until he found the shop abandoned.

He crossed to the tinned-goods aisle and saw three bodies on the ground. Each of them had expired the moment the virus reached them and had collapsed on the spot.

John pulled open a small rucksack, a new bag he had found behind the cigarette-counter. He had caught himself considering gathering some boxes of cigarettes, but decided the better for it. He looped the bag's straps across his lower left arm and picked up a can of tomatoes.

Further down the aisle, one of the three bodies blinked and resuscitated, *cracking* and craning its neck to peer along the linoleum floor to John.

As John selected some food from a large variety of tinned-goods, the infected silently got to its feet then charged at him, knocking him into the middle of one of the aisles.

Food tumbled around John, broke open and voided their contents, as he twisted to his feet and attacked the predator.

The fight escalated quickly, as the infected launched at John, vomiting blood in a horrendous gush from its throat. It grabbed at John's clothes and pulled at him roughly, trying to hug him close. John pushed its face away from his and squeezed its neck tightly. Simultaneously they both punched each other and fell back down the aisles. John stood quickly and the infected rose to its feet again clumsily.

Suddenly, seemingly from nowhere, the sharpened points of a pitchfork jabbed through the infected. Blood seeped from the four pointed ends, coursing down the abdomen of the infected. It tried to lift its arms, but could not.

John instantly fell, backing away, a wall of relief carrying him off his feet.

The infected squirmed on the pitchfork, streams of blood emptying out of the corners of its mouth. It hacked.

A moment later.
John met a small group of survivors in the back-room of the supermarket. PIOTR HOOGESTERN, 42 year old Dutchman; He was taller than John and more muscular, a strong skeletal frame underpinned his shape. His hair was cut short and dirty-blonde, covering his head. His face was sharp and furrowed with a thick jaw, big brow and high cheekbones. He wore a dirty black jacket, bloodied grey t-shirt, faded and torn dark-blue jeans and taupe hiking-boots. He was the one carrying the pitchfork; DONALD ETHERIDGE, 36 year old Scotsman; He had wide frame with a doughy round head. He wore

spectacles that magnified his eyes like the bottoms of a Coke bottles and had a thick ginger-brown beard, hiding most of his spotty and greasy skin. He had a sheepish, reluctant flicker to his eyes, weakly looking away from John, but then looking back when he wasn't being noticed. He was short and rotund, a small Ewok of a man. He wore a loosening tight t-shirt over muddied brown jeans and hiking-boots; BRIAN LOWRY, 41 year old Scotsman; He was average and slim, did not appear athletic or strong in any way. He stood shiftily at the back of the group, hidden amongst them. He seemed distant and evasive, never directly looking into John's eyes. He had receding grey hair, parted on both sides into a muddled peak, with a pair of short sideburns that curled down his cheeks. He wore a white shirt and grey suit under a tattered overcoat and smart shoes; PIPPA HEMMINGS, 38 year old Scotswoman; She was meek and frail, always keeping her arms together, embracing her own body to prevent shock from taking over. She had long grey-blonde hair, tied back in a long plait. Her face was slim and thin from worry, darkened rings encircled her eyes, the colour had gone from her lips. She wore the clothes she had been wearing for the last week: an aquamarine tracksuit over a white vest and Nike running trainers; JASON MACPHERSON, 20 year old Scotsman; He was tall and stout, muscular and fit, the type of person who would play rugby and football at the weekends and go to the gym most nights. He face was cut, lean and angular: he had a sharp nose planted between wide cheekbones and above a square jaw. He had short brown hair, recently cut by Pippa. He wore a body-hugging black long-sleeve t-shirt, khaki trousers and hiking-boots; and, ELLA LANNING, 23 year old Scotswoman; She was the first to smile, the first to place a comforting arm on John's. She was warm and calm, alert and seemed quite intuitive. She had auburn-copper hair, pulled back into a ponytail away from her face. Her eyes were quick and lively, watching John intently. She was slim and shapely, energetic with youthful enthusiasm. She wore a green tracksuit over a black vest and muddy hiking-boots.

John quickly learned the group had gathered together from the surrounding areas over the last few days.

"And, you've been hiding here since?" John asked.

"Yes, we were waiting for... --the army... Someone to help us, find us," Pippa replied quietly.

"We've been here, safe for two days now," Brian interjected. "They haven't showed up yet."

"I don't think hiding is the best plan," John responded. "I honestly think–..."

"I don't care what you think, where've you been?" Brian interrupted.

"I came from my house, North-West of here... About ninety miles... And, I don't think anyone is coming to rescue you. I haven't seen any rescue operation, or the army."

"Why? Why would no-one rescue us?" Ella asked, looking around the group.

"Why would no-one come?" Donald echoed.

"I've tried radios, mobile-phones, televisions – and there's nothing... Nothing left," John asserted.

"Don't you think we haven't?... Where's your suggestion, then, John?" Brian spat.

John looked from face to face – from Piotr to Brian, to Ella, to Jason, to Pippa, to Donald.

"London," he admitted.

Every face froze in a moment, only John moved – looking again around the group.

"Do you think it's safe there?" Donald asked in a tiny voice. He looked up at John from the floor, his back resting against a pile of magazines half his sitting-height. It looked like a makeshift arm-chair, or throne, built of glossy publications.

Piotr watched John, studied him.

"I don't know," John replied eventually. "But I think it's our best chance at finding any other survivors... I think people will be drawn to London... --for reason and for hope," he said gravely. "If any of you want to join me, you are most welcome... I can't make any promises... --but I think we can make it to London. There aren't that many of the infected. Just a lot of bodies. Millions of bodies. I think we can evade and hide and barricade ourselves away from the infected and make it all the way. It is far. It will be dangerous. We might not all make it, but we have to see what is left of the world, if there is anything left. And if there are more survivors, we have to help them. We have to gather in numbers in order to survive... That's the only plan I have."

Later.
John led the small group through the outskirts of Glasgow, taking the exact same route he took earlier that day. They passed the same house John passed earlier.

As they walked down the side walkway of the house, one of the infected launched through a side-window, and immediately blood-puked on Pippa, filling her mouth and nostrils, and painting her eyes.

Pippa's scream rent the air. She gargled and gasped, immediately falling to her knees. She tipped back, hacking, and landed on her back, clutching at her throat, spitting blood.

Piotr and John rushed down the passage and attacked the infected. They clubbed it and hammered at its head, arms and chest.

The rest of the group rushed through the gate and into the garden passed John and Piotr, as Pippa rose to her feet, the colour draining from her skin, infected. Her neck twitched and blood dribbled from her mouth. Her arms dragged her body up the wall as more blood rushed uncontrollably out of her mouth.

The infected leapt toward John.

He killed her with his axe.

Piotr stood by, breathing heavily, watching John through squinted eyes.

Later.
John stopped the group, as they walked up the hill he had descended earlier that day.

"How is it we're heading North-West?" Brian shouted, pushing passed Piotr to stand face-to-face with John. "I thought we were going South?"

"I need to tell you all something," John began, "I had a friend with me... --when I left my house... She... She got infected... When we realised, I made a neck-brace for her, so I could get her to London..."

"What the fuck?!" Brian screamed. "Why would you do that?!"

"John? Is this true?" Ella asked, shuddering at the thought.

"Yes."

"Why have you got her?" Ella asked, taking hold of Jason's arm.

"I needed to know how long they live like that," he explained.

Brian argued, roared, shouting, "You just killed Pippa! Why didn't we harness her and drag her with us?!"

"She turned before we could do anything."

"Bull-shit, fella, that's bull-shit!" Brian yelled, pacing in circles.

"If you and the others had dragged her away, while Piotr and I fought the other one, maybe, then–..."

Interrupting, "Fuck you!" he spat. Brian stepped toward John again, but Piotr stood between them, facing Brian. Piotr put out his hand and held it a few inches from Brian's chest. Brian took two paces backwards.

Jason put his arm around Ella. She whimpered.

"Where've you got her?" Jason asked calmly.

"I staked the harness to the ground about three hundred metres away."

"Do you think there's a cure in London?... If there is, then we should at least try," Jason resolved. "If not, you can use her to see... --how long they live... I guess."

Ella, although shaken, agreed with a nod.

Donald looked at the rest of the group and shrugged his shoulders apathetically.

Brian clenched his fists, pacing back and forth, gritting his teeth painfully.

Piotr watched Ella, who sat down on a tree-stump. Her eyes were red and watery, and her nose had flushed and was snotty.

"Is everyone agreed?" John asked. "I can fetch her?"

The group resolved to a silent agreement.

"I'll be back in a few minutes," he said and walked away to retrieve Ciara. He reached a small copse of trees and bushes, pushing through some brambles – following the path he took earlier. John passed a large tree, where Brian had rushed ahead to and had hidden and waited. He knocked John out with a broken tree branch.

Later.
The fog of darkness cleared. John woke up with Ella nursing him, patting his forehead with a wet cloth. He had been dragged back to camp. He sat up drowsily and looked around for Ciara.

"Brian went to get her," Donald said weakly. "To kill her."

"What direction did they go?" John asked, and Piotr pointed.

John rushed off into the woods, leaving the others to build a small camp in a dry ditch for the night.

A little while later.
John crept through the woods.

He stopped, hearing a noise, and closed in on it. He imagined the worst. He reached a clearing where he saw Brian trying to have sex with the Ciara over a fallen-tree. Her pale skin could easily be made out. She hissed and hacked, letting blood pour out of her mouth in intermittent flushes. The knotted belt around her neck was strained, pulling downwards, where Brian had wedged the stick. Brian's trousers sagged and bunched over his shoes, his underpants taut between his ankles, his shirt-flaps fluttered above his rear, the elastic around the bottom of his jumper rode up. Brian pumped the backside of the infected girl, as she growled, groaned and gasped. But that was not it.

John pushed between a thatch of twigs and found them. Brian, stood in front of the infected girl, wavered on his feet. His arms were raised and his hands had a slippery, uncomfortable grip around her neck. Ciara hacked and spat a stream of blood at Brian. He dodged it and looked away, feeling his sleeves wet with blood. His eyes were glassy wide, glinting in the poor, dim moonlight. John crept closer.

"I have to do this," Brian challenged the infected girl. "I have to do this!"

John raced towards them and hit Brian with all his strength, knocking him to the ground.

As they wrestled and fought, Ciara was knocked down a sheer-slope and rolled out of sight. John punched Brian several times in the face, then hit him hard in the throat with his knuckles. He watched Brian choke and flush red, still fighting away, his hands thrusting and shoving and pushing and slapping and punching. John moved back, watching the man fight his own body for his life. Red Vines of veins and muscles gripped his neck. John lifted himself to his feet and watched Brian for a long moment, watching the panic in his bulging eyes, the strain in his body, and the fear.

Then John kicked him down the slope with complete disdain.

Brian tumbled and rolled and flipped and spun and bounced, kicking up mud and wet leaves, agitating the air.

John's heart pounded. Sweat slicked his forehead. The hairs on his forearms twitched and stood on end.

He slowly moved to look down the slope, to look for Ciara. He scrambled down the harsh gradient, kicking up clods of mud and leaves, caking his boots, pulling sprouts, roots and small growths out of the earth, getting grime and dirt under his fingernails.

He crouched beside the body and saw that her neck had broken in the fall. He stared at the body, tears starting to form in his eyes. He cradled her head with his hands. Her hair was damp and greasy and felt alien in his fingers.

Brian twitched, gargling, trying to breathe, trying to survive, then he died.

John sniffed, smearing a tear into a muddy-streak across his cheek, then walked away.

Two days later.
They took shelter in a complex of small farm-buildings with breeze-block walls and flimsy corrugated-iron roofs, as a torrent of rain poured from the skies. Heavy dark-grey cloud cover rolled and massed in the sky. Thunder *rumbled*, followed by the flickers of lightning.

John stood by the doorway, staring up at roiling grey clouds. The rain soaked his face, but it was cooling and he did not mind. He looked across the surrounding fields: there were no infected anywhere. Rain coursed down the contours of his face, dripping and soaking through his beard.

He looked inside at the group, before he pulled the door shut and locked it with a solid bolt.

Donald and Jason had started to boil water in a saucepan and prepare their dinner. Piotr and Ella laid out their sleeping-bags and rucksacks. The rain *rattled* the roof in thousands of tiny tip-taps.

Three days later. M6 - Six miles West of Manchester, near Warrington – 2.12pm.
John arched his neck and looked at the sky, watching one small fluffy stratus cloud drift by. It was an almost completely cloud-free, clear blue sky.

John led the group, walking a few metres ahead of the others. John was followed by Piotr, Jason and Ella. Six others followed behind them: DAMIEN FLYNN, 33 year old Englishman. He had a Hollywood body; from personal fitness experts and yoga instructors and dieticians and health professionals and doctors and organic food-store workers. He had modelled in his early twenties and had maintained that physique. He had a California tan, but not to excess, and slight wrinkles and age-marks that he did not care to cover up. He was a handsome man, but not extremely so – this had stopped him from entering the mainstream, but had helped him carve a career with legs – he had spent very little time not-working in seventeen years. He had a thick mane of perfect black hair ruffled and swept back across the top of his head. His bright blue eyes sometimes betrayed him – through his confident exterior, the events of the last two weeks had taken a lot out of him. He wore a muddy and blood-splattered white shirt under a battered black suit, with comfortable but scuffed black boots. He carried a large backpack and a hammer in each hand; EVA LAMBERTON, 21 year old English young-woman. She had loose brown curls, cascading around the sides of her striking face and down her back over her shoulder-blades. Her eyes were an intense, serious hazel. A light speckling of freckles dotted across her cheeks and the bridge of her sharp, small nose. She was slight of build: a tiny waist, small breasts and rear; slim arms and legs made of thin coils of muscle. She had small, delicate hands, undecorated and plain. She wore a grey vest-top, faded and dirty jeans, and hiking-boots. She carried a large back-pack with a bow and quiver full of arrows attached to the sides; GRANT SANDS, 37 year old Englishman from Manchester. He was short and lean with a small, unassuming frame. He had short-cropped brown hair, thinning at the temples and a long, angular face. His teeth were uneven, his nose was long and bony, his chin jutting out to a point. He wore a brown wool jumper over a white shirt, black jeans and tan-suede brogues; MITCHELL YATES, 64 year old Canadian. His hair was cropped short, grey and thinning. He was average build, but with a healthy padding of fat that had enlarged and loosened with age. His wrinkled hands were tough and strong and hard-worked, the muscles in his arms and legs still strong and adept. He had been a jogger for many years and his heart was in perfect working order. He had a gentle nature and was careful with his gestures and mannerisms. He wore a grey suit with a white polo shirt underneath and brown leather brogues; KATYA VOLOVASKI, 28 year old Englishwoman of Polish descent. She had thick dark hair, pulled back into a ponytail, stretching her forehead overly smooth. She was an average height, with slim, curved shoulders and long bony arms. She had a sharp nose, arched brows and hotrod-red lipstick. She wore a black vest with black tracksuit-bottoms and duck-egg blue Nike Free running trainers; and JANE STAPLETON, 30 year old Englishwoman from Blackburn. She had streaky-brown hair, cut to her shoulders, framing a round face. She had a small button-nose, round cheeks and a sloped, wide forehead. She was small with long arms and legs and a short, round abdomen. She wore a blue v-neck t-shirt, three-quarter-length khaki trousers and small, black-and-white Gola Classics trainers.

The group walked carefully, and in a loose single-file line down the side of the main-road.

Damien overtook a few people to catch up to the front, where John walked in silence with Piotr.

"I was thinking," Damien started. "Do you think we should find a car? Or two?"

"Walking is the quietest way of getting around..."

"But also the slowest," added Damien.

"We should definitely think about it," John resolved.

"Maybe a van," Piotr stated.

"A security van..." John thought aloud. "That could work."

"Or a bus."

"An army truck would be great," Damien said, running his hand through his hair, then flattening spiky stubble around the point of his chin. "I just thought," he said with a hint of smugness.

Later that day.
Jason, Eva and Damien walked across the vast fourth floor of a concrete-block multi-storey car-park. They moved in a triangle formation, each holding different weapons – Eva had a bow with an arrow at the ready, Jason had a cricket-bat, and Damien carried a long-handle axe.

Their foot-falls gave off dull echoes within the space.

Outside.
John, Piotr and the rest of the group huddled in an underground pedestrian-walkway that passed under the road where the entrance to the car-park was built.

John guarded one exit of the passage, and Piotr and a few others guarded the other end. Katya, hugging her knees, sat against Mitchell, who stroked her shoulder warmly. Grant looked at the wall to the walkway. Blood stained the walls in several places, graffiti covered everywhere else.

John crept up one of the ramped-pathways gripping his small-handle axe and a golf-club in his hands. He thought he had heard something, and continued vigilantly up the ramp, very alert, eyes wide.

Inside the multi-storey car-park.
Eva's bow-string *twanged*, sending an arrow flying straight into the heart of an oncoming infected. Damien tripped another infected and leapt knee-first on its backbone, then broke its neck with a hit from the side of the axe-head.

Jason ducked inside a people-carrier, trying to hot-wire it speedily, his fingers twitchy and shaking with adrenaline. The engine started. Damien's and Eva's attentions turned toward it, when another three infected raced down the exit-ramp from several upper floors.

Eva put another arrow against her bow.

Damien rushed to the car and slid the back-door open. "Get this thing in gear, Jason, we need to be off! Go – Go – Go!"

"I'm trying... I'm trying," he replied, stabbing a screwdriver into the ignition.

Eva fired-off another arrow – it hit the first oncoming infected in the neck, piercing a hole straight through and embedded there. The car swung back, and Eva leapt in the open door. Jason sped forward and killed the second infected, shattering its ankles under the bumper and ribs on the bonnet, then slammed into the other arrow-impaled infected, knocking it over, when the third ran straight into the driver's-side window, cracking it badly with the flat of its forehead.

Jason yelped, spinning the wheel.

In the pedestrian-walkway.
John fought an infected, when three more attacked the rest of the group from the other end of the tunnel. It looked a lot like football-hooligans fighting after a match in the confined space of an underpass. Grant punched and kicked at one of the infected, while Mitchell flapped and shoved, forcing another away from him.

John clubbed the infected with the side of his elbow, gasping after being slightly winded. He winced, feeling himself black-out, but he pulled himself free, and focused instantly. He slapped his face, then cut down the infected with one blow to the head with his axe.

He stumbled into the tunnel, his feet dragging.

In the multi-storey car-park.
The people-carrier's brakes *squealed* and *shrieked* as Jason skidded to a stop.

Damien jumped out of the car and grabbed the third infected. He threw it to the floor with a yank of its collar. He chopped the top of its head off, across the temples, clean through.

Jason snatched a walkie-talkie from his belt and tried to contact the others, screaming, "John?! John?!" repeatedly, when Eva climbed out of the car. She rushed to the side of the car-park building and leaned over the cold metal balustrade at the edge.

"Eva! Eva – what're you doing?!" Jason shouted at her, panicked.

Damien looked across at Eva, concern burning lines in his face.

Eva looked down and saw the scene below.

Three-floors-below, John struggled with one of the infected, when the rest of the group breached the other end of the underground-walkway. They were surrounded. Numerous of the infected viciously attacked them. None of the group tried to break and flee, but tried as well as they could to remain together, fending off their attackers in a tight-knit ball.

A pack of five infected charged into the road, drawn to the noise two hundred metres away. Each was bleeding from its mouth, ravenous, and sprinting headlong at the group.

An arrow sailed through the air in a high, wide arc, and found its target: one of the infected was skewered by the arrow, puncturing through its open mouth and into its spine. It dropped to his knees and ploughed into the tarmac.

Eva let two more arrows go, killing two more of the infected, when Damien appeared at her side. He saw the chaos breaking-out on the ground below them. And saw Eva's effect, but he grimaced. "We need to get to the car," Damien shouted quickly.

Eva said, "Leave me here, I'll make my own way down."

Damien stared at her, then nodded and rushed back to the car. He and Jason sped off rapidly, as Eva loosed more arrows down on the pack of infected that were rushing towards the underground-walkway. She took down two with precise aim.

Halfway to the top of the pathway to the underground walkway.

John killed the infected that was attacking him with a blow from the small-handle axe. He ran up the ramp to ground-level, when Eva killed an infected that was advancing in front of him, before he even had time to react to its presence. He dodged the falling, slain arrow-impaled infected, scrambling along the rough tarmac-ground, and looked up to the car-park to the source of the arrows. He gave Eva a tiny salute, when the people-carrier *screeched* out of the exit and skidded to a stop, side-swiping and killing another infected.

Damien leapt out, immediately helping John to kill a slow-jogging oncoming infected.

Two days later. On the A542 – 3:48pm.

The group moved down a country road in a large Securicor-type security truck. Hedgerows lined the side of the road with fields beyond them. The truck was followed by the people-carrier, with Jason still at the wheel.

Jason put his hazard-lights on, signalling to stop; something Piotr had thought to implement, before they had started with the transportation. John had thought it a sensible precaution as well.

John pulled the truck to one side of the road, and Jason stopped the people-carrier.

Further down the road, about two hundred metres, a red Volvo V50 estate had rolled into the hedgerow. It had veered off the road, up the gentle bank and wedged itself across the top of the hedgerow, blocking over half of the road. John saw the Volvo and without making any comment to Piotr, who was in the passenger seat, climbed out of the truck's cabin.

John walked toward the people-carrier, as Jason opened the driver's door, leaning out.

"Is there a problem, Jason?" John asked.

Jason looked blankly at John, as Damien leaned across from passenger seat. At the same time, Piotr climbed out of the truck, checking through a pair of binoculars the way behind them; it was clear. He walked to the back of the van and climbed the welded-on ladder to the roof; he used the binoculars again, turning and turning to look in all directions, turning like a compass needle, but deliberately, stopping at points, then turning again.

Jason swallowed. "No... I just thought we could talk about how we're getting to London."

"I agree," Damien said, climbing out of the car and circling the engine-block. "I'd like to know... --what's going on?" he asked. "Why aren't we taking the motorway? Surely it'd be easier? What's goin' on?"

"Nothing," John replied with a quick shake of his head. "We're just taking the quiet routes..."

"I was looking at map, and I think we pass Birmingham," Piotr added.

"I was thinking the same," John said, nodding. "We can look for more survivors."

"Okay then, let's get moving," Damien said, turning to walk back around the car.

"Keep your eyes open for other survivors."

Five days later. On the M1 near Hemel Hempstead – 6:16pm.

The group had swelled further. John, Piotr and Damien led with Eva and Ella following closely behind them. Then Katya, Jane and GILLIAN NOLAN, 38 year old Englishwoman, and twenty-four others marched along in the back, with Grant and Mitchell at the immediate rear. They resembled the survivors of a plane crash or shipwreck, dirty and torn clothes, overgrown beards and unwashed hair, cobbled together back-packs and makeshift weapons. Gillian had streaky blonde hair, tied back in a pony-tail. She was a direct person with sharp features and quick eyes. She had a small frame, but was lean and tall, a little sinewy and thin. She wore a dirty white vest-top, muddy black jeans and hiking-boots.

They had abandoned the truck and people-carrier a few hours earlier.

They walked down the hard-shoulder of the motorway. Hundreds and hundreds of cars had crashed or stopped, skidded and skewed left and right. Some infected still stirred and vomited blood on the insides of the cars, but they were trapped and could not undo their seatbelts and could not escape their enclosure, and had started to weaken through bodily-motionlessness; withering and drying and shrivelling. The polyester seatbelt fabric had cut into the arms and necks of many of the infected, causing many to have bled-out and expired in their safety harnesses.

The group walked fairly slowly, in a scattered line-formation.

John looked down the motorway and saw a sign for (M25) London.

Gillian watched John from the middle of the group. She talked casually with two of the other survivors, not really paying attention to the conversation, trying to casually observe John without being noticed. "I'm going to so miss my holidays to Spain, to visit my cousin," she said absent-mindedly, looking away from John at the sun, burning hot and high in the sky.

"Spain sounds fucking amazing right-now," Jane said. "If it's free of those things!"

After a moment, Ella said, "I used to hate swearing... But now, I don't think it even comes close to describing our situation."

"The world is fucked."

"Yes," Ella said. "Fucked."

"I liked my holidays to Bognor Regis when I was a kid," Jane admitted.

"I never really went on any holidays..." Ella said slowly.

John asked a few of the survivors to stop, and started for the side of the motorway. Gillian thought he looked like he had heard something. Everyone slowed and huddled in between a line of cars. Gillian hushed the survivors, and most dropped to their knees, crouching by the nearest cars. Mitchell held a farmer's rifle at the back and left of the group, Damien held a long-handled axe at front and left, Grant held a small-handle axe at front and right, and Eva crouched at the very-back right side holding her bow with an arrow ready.

John climbed across the motorway's central reservation and crossed the northbound lanes. He reached the side of the motorway and ascended the grassy bank to the bridge-road that passed over the motorway. Pulling on the sharp top of the barrier he lifted himself onto the road, crouching and surveying the area quickly.

Piotr broke from the group and scrambled after John, hurrying between the cars.

John stopped at the peak of the overpass, pulling himself onto a car roof, when Piotr joined him at the side of the car, looking up and down the road himself.

"I remember visiting family near-here as a teenager," John said nostalgically. "I lived down the road from here with my foster-parents... In St Albans..."

John gritted his teeth, living for a millisecond in the memory.

"I can't see any of the infected," Piotr said, disregarding John's words.

Piotr looked across the roof of the car by John's feet. He passed John the binoculars. He looked down the road perpendicular to the motorway, around the junction; up and down as far as he could see; and at a cluster of buildings a short distance away: a large Regus office-building and a BP garage down the road, and a collection of large warehouse buildings northwest.

"I remember a supermarket further down this road," John said. "We need to get a group together to get some supplies, otherwise we'll run low on food. The store isn't too far."

"How do you know it's still there? Where you remember it?"

"I don't imagine many supermarkets move... Once they're where they are."

"O-kay... Alright."

John and Piotr crossed back to the group, who formed an alert huddle around them.

"There's a big supermarket down the road over the way," he started. "It's not far... And, there's a hotel nearby – people can find some empty rooms near the kitchen and hole-up there, ready for the food-run to return..."

John looked around the group at the thirty-three ashen expressions that faced him.

"I'm not going to make anyone come who doesn't want to," he started again. "I just... I want people to volunteer."

"I'll come," Eva said, sitting on the front row of the huddle.

"Me too," volunteered another – one John remembered was called Jim. His name was JAMES 'JIM' BARCLAY, 28 year old Englishman. He was short and stocky, with broad, thickset shoulders and muscular arms. He had a large, oval head with short-shorn wiry straw-hair, a heavy sloped forehead with blonde eyebrows separated by a wide, stout nose. His eyes were chocolate-brown and were creased at the edges into deep crows'-feet. He wore a grey hoodie, black t-shirt, black tracksuit-bottoms and black, cheap, market-stall knock-off Nikes.

"I'm fast – I used to run at school," volunteered another – called Gregory. He was GREGORY STIPE, 25 year old Englishman. He had a boyish face with youthful features, no signs of wrinkles or laughter lines. He was a tall beanpole with lanky legs, gangly arms and a lithe, stretched torso. His neck was long and his small head teetered on the stem. He had short dark hair with articulate, expressive eyebrows, a long, beaky nose and a thick-slab jaw. He wore a dirty grey t-shirt, black Adidas tracksuit-bottoms and scuffed white Nike Classics trainers.

"Me too," Piotr added lastly.

"That's enough – five is fine," John said, then picked up his bag and slung it over his shoulder.

A little while later.

John, Piotr, Eva, Gregory and Jim started away from the rest of the group, leaving them in the field behind the Holiday Inn, along the road from the Regus office-building. Light was beginning to dim and John checked his watch.

"We'll be back in four hours, before it gets too dark."

Damien nodded to John. "See you in four hours," he said, leading the rest of the group away, with Mitchell still at the back, still clutching the rifle.

"I don't want you to go," Jim's partner Gemma pleaded. Her name was GEMMA GREENE, 26 year old Englishwoman. She was short and skinny with an all-over carrot-tan and vibrant makeup highlighting non-features. She was overly made-up with a lot of hair product, and varnished and decorated nails. She had a sharp little face, half-disguised under an excess of creams, pastes, gloss and colour. She wore a matching black hoodie and bottoms, a baby-pink vest and pink Vans skater-trainers.

Jim crossed back to her, put a reassuring arm on her shoulder. "But we need to eat."

"I know that, but... I... I want you back, Jim, I want you to come back."

A little later.
The food-run party made their way slowly down the side of the A414, sticking to the far side of the strip of grass running beside the road, stopping now and then to check for any of the infected. Jim asked if they should try some of the houses around them, rather than to risk going any further to the supermarket, but Gregory said they could kill everyone in a shop and get a lot of food, rather than risk going into one house at a time for little reward. John said they should continue on to the supermarket without too much conversation.

Eva *twanged* her bow-string, as one of the infected turned into the road eighty metres ahead of them, near a Catholic church. The arrow hit the infected in the breast-plate and knocked it off its feet and sailing into a crashed car.

The small group crouched, freezing on the spot. A tiny bubble of relief burst, when no alarm sounded, and the infected dropped to the floor dead beside the car.

John said, "Be careful, Eva, we don't want to draw any more of those things with any car alarms... We have to be quiet."

She nodded in agreement.

They moved on.

A little later. Inside the supermarket.
There were bodies everywhere. Grisly blood stains polka-dotted the products, aisles and the dead.

Gregory crept down an aisle, when an infected grabbed his ankle. He fell face-first onto a seemingly-dead body, which suddenly awoke and coughed a clot of blood into his face. The infected that had grabbed Gregory's ankle rose painfully and looked around, thin channels of blood escaping its blackened lips.

At the back of the shop.
John and Eva crept toward the back-door that led to the service-entrance at the back of the shop – hoping to find a larger quantity of supplies. They walked slowly and quietly, keeping their absolute cool, eyes flicking everywhere, staying alert, hearing poised to catch a pin drop.

In the middle of the shop.
Jim walked to the alcohol section and grabbed a beer from a refrigerated cabinet. He opened it and drank quickly.

A *scratching*-noise alerted him to something behind him, and he snatched a vodka-bottle, aiming to use it as a club. Jim turned slowly on the spot and was instantly blood-puked on, spraying his hands and chest, but not infecting him. He immediately attacked the oncoming infected with the bottle, beating it to death, when Gregory appeared and vomited blood over Jim's face.

Jim gasped, falling back onto his rear, trying desperately to spit away the blood.

The infected Gregory seemed to regard Jim for a long moment, standing away from him, as if studying him, preying on him with bloodshot, feral eyes. Then he launched at Jim again and blood-puked a further time. Splashes of wine-dark ooze landed in Jim's mouth and eye.

Jim kicked and barged the infected to the floor and they struggled and fought, their shoes *squeaking* on the linoleum flooring.

In the back of the shop.
Eva and John slowly advanced down the plain, bland, air-cooled corridor to the back rooms, when one of the infected appeared ahead of them, blocking their way.

At first the infected did not see either of them, then Eva fired an arrow into its body, causing it to turn. It locked onto them and accelerated forward. Eva fired another, hitting its torso again, making it lurch and stumble sideways, slowing its advance on them. But it did not stop; its weight and instinct propelled it onward.

John rushed forward, when another infected pitched out of the shadows and shoulder-barged into him, shoving him into the oncoming infected. With a blow to the throat from his axe, he killed the double arrow-spiked infected, then turned to the second, when an arrow hit its head, imbedding itself there, an inch above the left ear. The infected dropped to its knees, its eyes rolling back. Its mouth dropped open, bouncing loosely on its chest, then it face-planted into the floor.

Eva pointed down the dim corridor at a refrigerated-section, whispering, "Let's go..."

They entered the first of four back-rooms.

In the middle of the shop.
Jim shoved the infected Gregory away from him, as he washed the blood out of his mouth with overflowing mouthfuls of vodka and splashing it over his face. He coughed, spitting and spitting, gargling more vodka then spitting it out. The infected charged at him once again, and Jim fell back, smashing the bottle of vodka; the bottle-neck broke into a perfect glass-shard-weapon.

Jim grabbed the neck of the bottle-shard and leapt to his feet, stabbing Gregory viciously in the neck and chest. A fountain of blood sprayed out, soaking Jim's screaming face and upper body.

He fell back to the floor and let out a pained scream, knowing his own fate, clutching his temples. Then he attacked Gregory again, violently, beating his head with his bare fists.

He screamed, wailing and yelling.

He held up the glass-shard, considering using it on himself, tears filling his eyes.

A little while later.
John and Eva walked out of the back of the shop – weighed-down by a few rucksacks each full of food. They walked out onto the 'floor' of the supermarket, and passed a few aisles, when an infected Jim stalked into the end of the aisle, saw them both and rushed toward them.

John reacted quickly, dropping the rucksacks and hammering the infected across the head, snapping its neck and killing it in a short, simple motion.

John and Eva shared a brief look, then started across the shop.

They reached the exit, putting down the rucksacks.

"We've got to find Gregory," Eva said. "We can't just leave."

"Yeah," John agreed. "Okay."

Eva walked along the rows of tellers – some were dead and slumped in their chairs, some had disappeared from their stations, presumably to escape, or to infect. She turned an aisle at the mid-way point, and instantly saw Gregory's body. His neck was ripped apart with the bottle-weapon discarded beside it. Blood pooled and soaked the aisle, spreading dark and venomous, oily and thick across the linoleum.

In the car-park.
Eva and John hurried along a line of parked cars, meeting Piotr at a trolley-shelter.

"What happened – where is Gregory and Jim?" Piotr asked.

"Not with us."

Piotr looked at both of their disturbed faces, then at the shop beyond them.

"We've got to push on," John said, passing Piotr two of the rucksacks.

Later. Behind the Holiday Inn, on the A414 – 9:57pm.
John, Piotr and Eva clambered down from a hedgerow onto the field near the hotel, when Jim's partner Gemma saw that Jim was not with them. She walked out into the open of the rear car-park of the hotel. She started to cry and scream and shout at John, Piotr and Eva.

Gillian and Ella rushed outside and pulled her into the dark of the hotel, trying to comfort her.

Piotr stared at Gemma with no expression, then looked away, craning his neck to look around the car-park for any sign of the infected – anything that had been attracted to the screams. It was getting quite dark, but all of the streetlights were still operating, illuminating the roads around them, the motorway and the car-park.

The returning three walked inside.

Grant shut and locked the door behind them, clutching a golf-club.

Other survivors tried to read John's expression.

Damien greeted Eva and helped her with the bags.

A few of the others helped John with his bags.

A little while later. In the hotel's kitchen – 10.51pm.

Most of the survivors had settled in the windowless kitchen – on piled pillows and sheets and clothes and duvets in cleared corners and spaces where shelving units had been removed. Several candles had been lit and placed around the room and on the central island. One of the ovens was set to full and opened, letting out gradual heat. Bowls of pasta and sauce had been passed around, and most people ate it while it steamed – there had been infrequent hot food during the last few nights – it was not always easiest or safest staying in hotels or houses.

John looked at the group; a mixed bag of the haunted and the positive. He sat near the corridor that led to the exit and had been taking regular trips to the exit-door to check the road nearby. He thought about the people they had lost, then buried the thought.

A few people kept watch around the perimeter, in rooms adjacent to the kitchen – Grant and Jane sat near the back-door in a small side-lobby, where the window had been covered with a blanket and generous amount of Duct tape. Grant occasionally checked under the corner of the blanket.

Damien and Piotr stood at the stove, putting the last of the pasta into Tupperware boxes.

"I had lessons – cookery lessons – for a TV show I was on in New York... I co-starred with this hot young girlie-chef-actress over-there," Damien whispered. "I fucked her loads. She was hot..."

Piotr smiled.

"I guess I learned a little bit."

"About cookery?" Piotr asked.

"Yeah, no, yeah," Damien laughed, but kept it low.

Eva sat a few metres away from the stove with Gillian, who was talking to Ella about the prospect of finding any safe-havens and the obtuse value of hope. Ella and a few others sat around her listening.

"Do you think it'll be safe in London? I don't," Gillian said. "I can't imagine how many of those infected people are out-there... Maybe no-one died and everyone is infected. Maybe everywhere is totally overrun. How can we be expected to just be silent and follow..."

"I hope we find somewhere safe... Truly safe," Ella mumbled.

"If we all make it there in one piece," Gillian exclaimed. "We've lost so many people."

"John came from Scotland, didn't he? Why would he risk everything?"

"He's got some other motive," Gillian whispered. "He must."

"What?"

"Why?"

"What could it be?"

"What if he doesn't care about any of us?" Gillian posed.

"Why would he?"

"Why would he help us?"

Eva sat in complete silence. She glanced at Damien, then back at Gillian, as she continued to stir. She looked back to Damien, as he moved away from the stove. Piotr watched him go, then caught Eva studying them.

Damien crossed out of the kitchen and walked to John, who had stood by the exit, watching the road. It was still and quiet and empty, for now. He whispered, "We haven't seen any sign of the army or many other people, for that matter... Not since this-all happened.. Hardly any people at all... It seems quite hopeless... Don't you think?"

John replied, "It definitely does... --but I don't want to turn into one of those things, and if we can keep it together until we can make some kind of order out of this, find some answers, find out how and why this happened... -- then it'll be an okay start... It'll be a step in the right direction..."

Damien looked at John, trying to read him, trying to tell whether John believed his own spiel.

"Then that's what you have to do," Damien said.

"We."

"Excuse me?"

"That's what we have to do," John asserted. "I can't do this alone."

"I have my own mission right-now, John."

Two days later.
John and the group – now thirty-eight people strong – walked through a small woods in a large north London park. They stopped at the tree-line, checking the open grass-area.

John was at the lead, checking the way forward. He snuck through some bushes and used his binoculars.

Piotr pushed through the group to be at John's side. He reported, "There are plenty... --in the park... --but they might not see us."

John nodded. "Okay. We're moving on."

A while later.
The last member of the group – Damien – carefully ran across the open grass of the park. He dashed into the farther tree-line and made it out of the sight of several roaming infected, as they lurched along in a loose pack.

They continued on through the small wood at the other side of the park, trampling dried leaves underfoot.

Gillian caught up with John.

"Hello," she said with a half-smile.

"Hi," John said, trudging on.

"I wanted a word."

"Okay." John slowed. Piotr looked back at him. "Go on for a bit in the lead, I'll catch up in a bit." Piotr nodded and led the group away through the wood. John and Gillian were passed by the last few members of the group, Eva and Ella.

"What can I help you with?" John said sharply.

"I want to know... Is there any other reason, any other agenda, we are here – in London!?"

"No. There isn't," he said, his voice wavering with a little uncertainly.

Gillian detected this. "I've noticed you've become quite withdrawn the last few days... Since Gregory and Jim."

John shuddered.

"And I think you're keeping secrets," she claimed.

"I... I..."

"What is it with you?"

"I don't have to explain myself to you," John snapped. He pointed at her angrily. "I don't have to explain anything to you!"

"You do if you expect these people to keep following you?"

"I've noticed what you've been doing, Gillian... Do you really want to be the leader? I don't..."

"It's about having the right leader."

"Oh yeah?"

"Yes! You can't expect these people to follow a leader they can't trust!"

John shook his head and walked away. Gillian watched him go, before following a second later.

A little while later.
John led the group down a back-street. His eyes were glassy and his fists were clenched. He was bitterly angry and his teeth *clicked* and *grated* as he ground them. He ducked down a side alleyway, with the group loosely following behind him. He reached the dead-end of the alleyway where a wall blocked their path.

They climbed over the wall one by one, and found that it was the boundary-wall of a vast graveyard. Once John had made-sure the last person was over the wall, he determinedly strode away into the graveyard, looking straight-forward, not seeming to take anything in, not seeming to notice he was outrunning the group, not seeming to notice if there were any infected nearby. His heart beat against his ribcage, pounding and jerking and thumping and thudding. Sweat poured down his forehead and he felt his anger balloon inside himself. Tears filled his eyes and he could barely see as they streaked down his face.

The group quickly began to catch up with their leader and watched him concernedly, but followed him all the same, some jogging to keep up with him, others hurrying in the rear.

Gillian ran ahead and caught up and asked him, "What are we doing here, John?"

John did not answer.

Gillian slowed to a walk, watching John accelerate away from her. A few people passed by, slowing when they caught sight of John, as he raced away from them all. They all slowed and formed a wall of watchers.

Moments later, John found what he was looking for – a pair of graves, one for Miranda Ramsay and one for Carl Ramsay, who "died tragically and suddenly" six years ago.

John felt his legs buckle under his weight and he fell to his knees and started to cry.

"I'm sorry," John whispered through gasps and cries.

The group watched John, and nervously waited for someone to say something, someone to break the uncomfortable moment. But nobody stopped John. The group bunched twenty metres from their leader, watching, waiting; scared, confused, perplexed.

Damien looked at Piotr. He shrugged. Damien shook his head.

Gillian looked around the group, trying to read everyone's reactions. She smiled inwardly.

Eva watched John sympathetically and bit her bottom lip.

John cried uncontrollably. Through his tears, he said, "What do I do?!... What am I supposed to do?!" His hands knotted into balls, gripping tightly, fingernails digging into the soft meat. Tears fell from his eyes, as the clouds shifted overhead, pointing rays of sunlight across the graveyard.

As if shocked by lightning, John pulled himself together, wiped away his tears, snorted, and cleared his throat. He stood, suddenly looking stable and determined. He gritted his teeth.

"I'm okay now. I know what to do. I know what we have to do."

Three infected appeared ahead of them and charged towards the group.

John grabbed his axe, before anyone else had time to react.

Somewhere near.
Someone was watching the group.

CHAPTER 2 - SANCTUARY - Chelsea, London

Seven months ago. East London.
Down the length of a dark, densely weed-strangled side-alley stood an old, derelict warehouse. It had a dark interior, overgrown black and ashen plants gripped it around its foundation, smashed and broken windows tarnished the riverside-face, graffiti and stains covered the lower-walls. River-water lapped gently against the crumbling brick sidings to the bank. Across the river, several men loaded boxes into a small fishing boat. Dirty-yellow streetlights illuminated the road beyond the warehouse, neon-orange across the river.

ADAM HILTON, 36 year old Englishman; waited to meet a new acquaintance. Under cropped, gingery strawberry-blonde hair, his face was soft and jovial. He had bright green eyes that shone out beneath thin lids. He had a slim-build but had acquired a potbelly over the last few years – devoting more time to work and eating poorly than caring for himself. He was slightly lanky with long, sinewy arms and legs. He wore a long, black overcoat over a dark-brown suit, white shirt and brown shoes. He stood a few metres from the door, propped open with a breeze-block. He gritted his teeth, preventing himself from looking at his wristwatch once more. His mobile-phone would have created too much light, but it was more difficult to read the watch's face in the dim.

A man entered the space – CHRISTOPHER DALLOW, 53 year old Englishman. He looked old for his age, wrinkled and jowly. He had deep-set eyes, glimmering under heavy hoods and thick, dark but greying eyebrows. His skin was pale, dry and broken, and a sprinkling of dandruff showed on his shoulders. He wore a black suit a few sizes too large, black tie, grey shirt and scuffed black shoes. He carried an umbrella and a small black-leather satchel. Adam had only located and spoken to Dallow three times before this meeting and it had taken him a long time to arrange another. Dallow crossed the warehouse staying in all of the most poorly-lit places, a shadow man, and stood near the decaying back wall. Adam thought it was an eerie and hostile place, and imagined rats pouring out of every hole, crack and pipe. The thought disgusted him. He shivered, but tried not to show it.

"I have some things for you," Dallow said quickly, not looking at Adam, retrieving a small black-felt satchel from a shoulder-holster, hidden from view under his armpit. Dallow gave Adam the satchel – it contained a tiny vial of "Substance OX3311-H", a photocopied collection of file-folders and records, a hydraulic-syringe-gun, and some copied DVD-discs. Adam examined the syringe-gun, smoothing his hand over it – he had never seen one before. He twisted the vial between his fingers, reading the tiny printed label.

Dallow looked straight into Adam's eyes. "Take the Substance and trust me... Or don't... It's your choice," he said glumly, then shrugged his shoulders.

Adam watched, as Dallow's eyes darted around the building, a deep undercurrent of paranoia showing under the surface. He could see from the man's scattered and unpredictable movements – especially his head, cocking from side to side, jittering up and down – that something was disturbing him. He had seen movements like this in Gulf War veterans, mental health hospitals, secure units and several prisons. Dallow said nothing, twitching on the spot.

"If I do take it?" Adam asked slowly.

Dallow stared at him again, wide-eyed. "Then, at least, at least, you will be safe... --and safe," he started quickly, head twitching. "You will be safe, you will be safe, you will be – but... Only if you're smart, young man, only if you last long enough anyway... At least you might have a chance... Only if you value your life, of course..."

Adam did not take his eyes from Dallow, watching him pace and shift from side to side, like a child caught in a lie in front of its parents, or head teacher, or needing to go to the toilet excruciatingly badly.

"'Last long enough'? How will I–?"

Dallow interrupted, "Mr Hilton, you have very little time to get your affairs in order."

"What do you mean by that? Is that a threat?"

"...It might be. It might be..."

"What does that mean?"

"They are dangerous, and they will do anything they want to... Anything they want... The manifesto tells it all..."

Before Adam could cough the word 'what', Dallow moved toward a door he had not previously noticed, hidden in the shadows at the back of the room, concealed by grime and dirt and what looked like large, strangling ivy plant. Dallow disappeared through the doorway and was gone. Adam stood in the room another four minutes, as instructed, before leaving the way he came in.

The present.
Adam awoke in his bedroom, in the morning – the alarm clock read 10:05am – his right-leg encased in a plaster-cast. He moaned and rocked himself up from the shoulders, trying to kick some life back into his sleeping free-leg. The skin under the plaster-cast itched and tingled with heat. His hair was long and straggly, uncut for some time.

He struggled to get up and get dressed. He wore a pair of track-suit bottoms, hacked at the knee on one side so he could pull them on over his cast. He tugged on a t-shirt, then pulled a hoodie over the top. Before moving from his bed, he reached for the folded-concertina of a wheelchair and snapped it open to unfold, locking it into a wide canvas seat. Using his bedside table, Adam hoisted his body, hopping on his left leg, and dropped into the seat.

He had wheeled around his small flat, in the hospital-supplied wheelchair, for what seemed like many, many months, but in reality was only a number of weeks. He wheeled into the living-room and picked up a laptop, turning the power on.

The flat was small but comfortable – almost every wall was lined with books, archive boxes, articles, newspaper clippings, small pieces of art and other small trinkets, covering a dull brownish-yellow paint. Certain pathways had been cleared for the wheelchair to pass through – stacks of books and boxes were pushed aside to make wider streams.

Two hours later.
Adam sat reading the newspaper in his kitchen. He turned the page and folded the paper down.

A loud *boom* filled the air and all of the panes of glass in the windows rippled and shook.

Adam folded the newspaper down, away from his face, crumpling it to twist across his stomach. He looked at the window, wheeled himself closer and peered outside. He could not see anything. He glanced down at the ground and saw a car rolling slowly down the road and out of sight.

A little later.
Adam used his cordless-phone to call his sister, glancing at the clock and seeing it was 12:56am. Her mobiles' voicemail message sprang into action, giving him the automated response – he complained to the machine about her being late, he hated it when people were late, that she should hurry, and bring food, nice food. He hung up and felt dejected momentarily, before his mind drifted somewhere else.

Adam put music on – *The Beach Boys Greatest Hits* – with a remote-control to his iPod docked in a stereo-system and started to make himself breakfast.

Over a short period of time, noises from outside his building got louder and louder, making Adam increase the volume on the stereo button-push by button-push. He loved listening to music whilst cooking. He briefly glanced out of the window, but took no notice of what was outside and fried his bacon further, to crisp, darken, spit and steam. He pulled doughy white bread from a bag, squeezing it lightly as he dropped it into the toaster.

On the pavement below.
One of the infected chased a man down the street. The man screamed and wailed, waving his arms in the air, sprinting for his life. The infected ravenously bolted after the man, its feet pounding the street, arms swinging loosely behind it.

A little while later.

Adam sunk his teeth into a three-layered bacon and egg sandwich. He finally turned the music down to call his sister again. He tried her mobile using his cordless, but the network was down. He moaned and tossed the handset on the kitchen table.

He thought about concerts and political marches and football matches ending and the many disasters that caused the networks to be jammed with calls. He struggled to find his mobile-phone. He dug around under a pile of magazines on the kitchen table – but found the signal was dead in that as well. He shook the phone, pointing it at the exterior-wall of the building, trying to find any trace of signal.

Adam put the phone down.

He wheeled along the table and flipped open his laptop. He slid his finger across the touch-pad and found Chrome. He double-tapped the pad and the window opened. The screen loaded. It read: Connection unavailable at this time, please try again later.

Suddenly, a heavy-banging came from his front-door – intense, urgent banging – it made Adam jump in his seat.

He wheeled the chair back into the hallway to get a full view of the front-door, as the banging continued.

"Who is it?" Adam shouted out, all of a sudden feeling extremely frail and useless. And helpless.

"Let me in, mate, it's Craig," called a voice, trying to be heard, but not too loudly.

Behind the door stood CRAIG CHARLTON, 44 year old Englishman. He was swaddled in a padding of fat – enclosed around tight, toughened muscle. He was a small bear of a man; strong but doughy on top. His head was shaved to grade one, leaving a rug of thinning spiky sandy-blonde hair. He had many tattoos on each arm – from wrist to shoulder, with various symbols, characters and images from around the world adorning each arm-sleeve. He wore a white t-shirt under a grey hoodie, faded denim jeans and blood-stained black shoe-boots. "One of them is coming, Adam! One of them is coming! Come on, open the fucking door! Let me in! Please!" he screamed. "Please! Come on, man!"

Adam struggled to move at-speed in his wheelchair, then rejected it, and started hobbling and hopping and limping to the door on his good foot. His exposed toe caught on a stack of boxes and he tripped and fell to the carpet flat.

"I'm coming!" he shouted at the door. "I'm nearly there!"

He dragged himself down the hallway, struggling to get himself back onto his good leg, pulling books and small cardboard boxes from their perches, as Craig's banging continued uninterrupted. "Please, mate, please!" Craig cried, pressed against the door.

Adam made it, reaching up to the lock, straining the muscle along his arm, fingers outstretched.

Some time ago. Soho. At night.

Adam walked along the road humming the tune to *Good Vibrations*, thinking about his imminent meeting with Dallow – at a pub called The Quiet Man. He called Dallow on his mobile. "I'm running-late," he said pressing the phone to his ear.

A sound of *static*. Then another *fuzzy* tone.

"Fine. I am as well... I'll see you seven minutes later than planned."

"I took it – the Substance..." Adam offered, registering fear in Dallow's voice.

"Great... Good for you!" Dallow replied, short. Adam heard Dallow's words as a flippant–comment that cut deeply. It was something he did not want to hear, something he had heard on another case which had led to a dud story, something that made him truly believe Dallow was talking conspiratorial bull-shit. Adam hoped this was not the same situation played out again, but with heavier paranoia, shadows and bigger piles of shit. Adam gritted his teeth, unwilling to say another word, but he knew Dallow was still on the other end and had not yet hung up.

"Don't go inside the meeting-place. Meet me outside. Meet me on the opposite street-corner," Dallow said in hushed tones, then hung up.

Moments later.
Adam turned the corner of a street. He could hear the noise of people sat outside the pub, around the corner. He started to slow, looking at the side-door, then continued passed it when he saw Dallow. He was walking towards him down the opposite street about one hundred metres away, lit by infrequent street-lights and shop-window displays. Adam looked at the side-door to the pub again. He felt so sceptical now, seeing him face to face.

Dallow saw him too, and acknowledged him with a sweaty nod, then he was shot powerfully in the heart. The bullet hit him below the collarbone and exploded through him. He was dragged backwards a few paces, but righted himself and stood up hunchbacked. His arms tucked up to his body, shaky and straining.

Dallow stumbled into the road ahead of him, taking five slow, painful steps – the lifeless paces of a dead man – stepped off the curb and onto the tarmac shakily. He coughed-up a mouthful of blood, his lids drooping down over his eyes.

Adam watched with wide eyes, frozen to the ground where he stood, mouth dropped open.

An unmarked van with black-tinted windows accelerated along the street and mowed Dallow down, ploughing into him, then shredding him under the ridged, uneven chassis, bouncing and breaking and rolling him under the speeding vehicle.

Adam was close enough to be sprayed with Dallow's blood, which he found immediately repellent and wiped his face with his sleeve. But shock did not take over: Adam had seen other people killed in front of him; in Afghanistan, Iraq, Somalia, Russia, Ireland and Greece. He took stock of the situation and it felt like slow-motion for a moment.

Adam's eye caught Dallow's satchel. It had been knocked out of his hand when he was shot. It lay on its own in the wet shadows across the road. Adam paused, not wanting to turn to look up at the building behind him for the shooter. He became breathless, or felt his natural instinct to hold his breath, as adrenaline flooded his system. He glanced behind him and saw an empty open window in a high-rise a few roads away. A sheet of plastic unfolded across the open window frame, flapping in the wind. He thought that might be a decoy, but did not care. He pushed his feet to move forward.

Several of the patrons from the pub quickly reacted to the murder, standing or staring or turning away, with even more people exiting the pub to see what was going on. A gathered noise started to build as the alert amongst the assembly began to call for the police. A small crowd formed around Dallow's mangled body.

The van had sped away immediately and nobody seated outside the pub could recall the license plate to tell to the police. A murmur of voices swept across the crowd. As the people flocked loosely around the body, Adam crossed the road, moving between a few of them, blending in. He snatched the satchel off the ground and ducked into the shadows.

Seconds later he ran.

As Adam dashed away he began to glance a few men taking notice of him, who seemed to be spying on him. And he bolted.

He ran and ran and ran, hugging the satchel, panting for breath, feeling the lactic build-up in his muscles, feeling the burn, sweating all over, hugging that satchel.

The present.
Adam threw his front-door open. Craig immediately pushed inside, slamming the door behind him, taking hold of Adam by his shirt to stop him from being knocked over. He gently sat Adam on a small stack of boxes and pressed himself against the door. Craig twisted three shiny-new locks shut and attached the security-chain with a *jingle*.

The door shook when somebody behind it banged and pounded against it. Craig pushed against the door, as Adam sat forward and pushed a knee-high dead-bolt into place.

The beating on the other side of the door continued.

"What's wrong with your flat?" Adam asked abruptly.

"...The key snapped in the lock..." Craig, breathing extremely heavily, responded between *huffs*.

"What the fuck is going on?" Adam screamed. "Why is there blood on you?"

"Haven't you been outside today?" Craig replied, finally levelling his breathing with a few more *huffs* of air.

Their eyes both moved to Adam's leg-cast at the same time. Craig half-smirked. Adam's eyebrows instantly raised. "D'you wanna do me a favour?" he asked.

A little while later.
Craig carefully cut the plaster-cast off Adam's leg – scissoring and ripping at the layers of plaster and gauze. It took a long time and broke two pairs of scissors. Craig was patient, while Adam enthusiastically ripped chunks of the plaster-infused gauze from the cast, dropping the shreds on the dust-white carpet.

"This is fuckin' tough stuff," Craig said.
"Yeah... But my leg's under-there and it wants out!"
"We're getting there."
"Excellent."

A little while later.
Adam and Craig looked out of two of the windows in Adam's study.

"...People were dropping like flies... Dead. Others just seemed to get sick, and then they were chasing people around, and then they'd catch them and blood would pour out all over them... It was fucking disgusting," Craig said with a sad laugh.

Adam noted that Craig looked slightly haunted. "What were you out for?"
"I only went for a pack of cigarettes and a sandwich for lunch," Craig laughed. "Fucking day!"
"Can I have a cigarette?"
"Yeah."
Craig took the packet of Marlboro reds and pulled two out. He passed Adam his and the lighter and placed the second in his mouth. Adam lit his cigarette and pulled on it, then released a cloud of white smoke.

"I haven't smoked in years!" he admitted.
Adam passed the lighter back and Craig lit his own. "Why would you ever quit?" he said around the cigarette.

They smoked for a moment and Adam noticed Craig's attention had waned and he looked bored. He finished his cigarette first and flicked it into space. It spun through the air then landed with a bounce on the pavement before being swept away by the wind and into a gutter.

"Why don't we watch the telly? Nothing's happening out here right-now."
"My television's broken."
Craig was shocked by the statement. Adam pointed and the shock doubled when he saw the smashed television-set under the tiny, thin hall-table. The screen was split by a large crack running through the middle from top to bottom.

"I don't know how you live without a TV!"
"It was broken... --only recently, and I haven't been able to buy a new one, because... Well," Adam said and looked at the ripped white mountain on the floor that had been his plaster-cast for months.

"Mobile check?"
"Alright," Craig agreed with a nod.
They each dug out their mobiles, then Adam checked his landline-cordless and the laptop again for the internet. Nothing worked. No signals. No connections.

"What the fuck is going on?! And where is my fucking sister?!"
"It's like I told you... The world's fucked..."
"The loss of the internet reminds me when the Syrian government pulled the plug on theirs... No-one could communicate outside of the country unless their mobiles could dial out."
"Well someone's done the same thing here, right-now," Craig said coldly.
"Whoopee!"

Some time ago.
Adam walked down a London back-street, when a black van pulled up behind him.

"Okay, Scary-Mary, thank you for the fifteen-thousandth reminder," Adam moaned into his mobile-phone, holding it an inch from his ear.

His sister Mary spoke.

"Yes. Yes. Yes. Okay," he answered. "Love you to. Speak soon."

The van curb-crawled, just out of Adam's sight, a few metres behind him. One second after he hung up the call, a black cotton bag was pulled over his head and he was dragged into the van and the door was slid-slammed shut.

The van sped off down the street with a *squeal* of its tyres.

A little later.
Adam woke up in an interrogation room. It was a concrete-box twenty-by-twenty feet with a microphone/speaker system positioned on the wall, a metal stool that was bolted to the floor, a large mirror-window that Adam instantly knew had to be two-way, and the sleek black panel, without a handle, that was the entry- and exit-door. There was a tiny intercom-box next to the door but Adam could not make it out clearly.

He felt the headache-daze immediately, like the worst, longest head-rush, but managed to stand up unsteadily.

A loud *crackle* of static came from the speaker and made Adam jump. Then a voice started to speak, "Please sit down, Mr Hilton." It was a robotic voice, heavily filtered and modified. There would be no way to identify the speaker.

Adam took the stool in his hands. It felt cold. And he sat down. He hugged his arms and shivered. He could see the mist of his own breath, drifting away into his own reflection.

"Your name is Adam Hilton. You are thirty-six point five-two years old. You were born in St Albans City Hospital. Your parents are Kenneth and Marjorie Hilton – we have their address and current location in Buckingham. Your sister is Mary Hilton – we have her address and current location in Harrow. We know where you work, how much you are paid, where you live, your local shop, your regular pub... Where all of your favourite places are, who your nearest and dearest are, all of your friends, where they live, where their children go to school... We know your life inside out."

Adam stood a moment, digesting the words, looking at himself in the mirror. He looked awful.

"What do you want?" he said finally.

A noise of static came from the speaker, followed by no sound.

Adam tried to ask more questions, but when he got no answer he sat, staring at his reflection, perplexed and cold.

After four hours, Adam's captors asked for him to gather everything Dallow gave him together. Adam asked how he will reach them. The voice said, "Instructions will follow." Then another static-*crackle* sounded.

The room started to fill with thick white clouds of gas, building into cumulonimbus walls of white, pouring from unseen vents at the lower edges of each side wall.

Just before the lights blinked off, Adam passed out.

The next day.
Adam woke up lying on his bed in his bedroom, fully clothed in yesterday's wardrobe. His eyes detected only blurry shapes at first, gradually adjusting to the sunlight streaming in through his window. His head ached in pulsing beats and waves of pain like multiple holes being drilled into his skull. He found bruises on his wrists from hand-cuffs. He looked around his bedroom, dazed. He rubbed his temples. His mouth was dry and gammy and his tongue felt ashy. A powdery white residue covered his clothes, hair and skin. He patted a tiny white nebula from his sleeve.

Feeling momentarily stable, he rose and entered his hallway. He found it in disarray. Boxes and files had been searched and the contents were strewn about the flat. Huge paper waves had collected across the carpet. He knew those people had not found either satchel he had received from

Dallow. They had not found them, because they were not in the flat. They were somewhere nobody would anticipate. They were safe.

Adam began to tidy the papers back into their respective boxes and files.

It was going to be a very long, very late night.

The present.

Adam and Craig continued to watch the street below the apartment building. It was deserted, except for the body of the man from earlier in the day that Craig pointed out. Adam had not seen him until that moment. He studied the corpse from the window. He had been soaked with the blood-emission of one of the infected, and had expired on the ground, in a wide and messy bloody puddle.

"It looks like hell on earth," Adam said woefully. "And I can only see one body."

"It looks like modern art to me," Craig quipped. "This whole thing shrieks of one of those mass things... Loads of people," he said. "Like freezing or singing or dancing or other bull-shit... They did one in the Grand Central Terminal in New York, everyone froze at the exact same time... Flash-mobs... That's it," he said with a satisfied smirk.

Adam sighed and shook his head. He could not understand it. "Except it's real."

"Good... I hated flash-mobs... And.... At least we won't have to queue for anything anymore," Craig amused.

"That's in bad-taste."

"Oh yeh? What's 'taste' anymore, dude?"

"God knows."

"I hope that's just an expression for you?" Craig asked tentatively. "The 'God' bit...?"

"'God knows'? No... No, yeah – just an expression... I don't believe in anything," Adam replied. "Atheist all the way to the end. Then nothing..."

"No offence to religious people, but thank fuck for that! If this is an end-of-the-world scenario, then I don't want to be holed-up with a religious-nut!"

"Fuck no. That would be awful," Adam agreed with a laugh.

They saw a thick tower of smoke rise from behind a building several hundred metres away.

"I hope the virus isn't everywhere... Hopefully the rest of the world is safe," Craig said. "Can I eat something?" Then without hesitation, he walked straight into the kitchen and started making something to eat: Kellogg's Special K cereal with lots of milk and lots of sugar. Piling and *crunching* the cereal-bites into his mouth, Craig spilled milk on his t-shirt and the floor without noticing.

"Tasty shit," Craig said around a mouth full of cereal. "For women's breakfast food."

Adam felt spurned into speaking, "My sister. Mary. She bought it. Because of my cast. I couldn't go shopping."

"S'alright, pal... Huh, you're actually taller than I remembered."

"You look fatter... Who says 'dude' anymore?"

Craig chuckled.

Adam stared out the window, when he saw a woman and boy running and hiding, trying to evade the infected that was lurching after them.

"Fuck! Craig! Look down there!"

Craig plopped the cereal-bowl down on the coffee-table wetly and rushed to Adam's side. "What?" he yelled, spitted shards of cereal out of his mouth.

They opened another window in the living-room, wide enough for both of them to hang out of.

"Hey!" Adam shouted into the road. "Hey! Up here!"

The woman, hidden with the boy in a recess where two buildings met, saw Adam and waved. She smiled dumbly.

"Come into the building, we'll buzz you in... But wait in the lobby!"

"Why wait in the lobby?" Craig whispered.

"Remember that fucker the other side of the front-door?!"

"Oh yeh."

They had tuned out the banging on the door. The infected still beat against it, and now they heard it again, all too close, and much louder than before. The door shook and quivered with each punch.

Craig jogged to the front-door and stood by the buzzer.

Adam watched as the women dashed along the building, dragging the boy by his hand. The infected saw them again and quickened its pace, arms outstretched.

"Now, Craig!" Adam shouted.

Craig pressed the buzzer hard, letting the woman and boy inside.

Moments later.
Adam stood sheepishly at one side of the flat.

"Okay," Craig said gripping Adam's shoulders and repositioning him a foot to the left. "Good. Stay here."

"Am I the bait?"

"Yeh, dude. You are," he replied casually and handed him two sauce-pans. "When I say go, you start making loads of noise. Yeah? Have you got that massively intricate plan?"

Adam twitched.

"Ready? Adam?" Craig barked.

"Yes. Yes. Mmm-hmm. Yes."

Adam waited, stood at the other side of the flat, shaking nervously. Sweat dripped down his forehead.

"Okay. Now!"

He started banging and beating and clattering and hammering the sauce-pans together.

Craig flung the door open, letting the infected inside. He instantly caught it by its belt and smashed the claw of a claw-hammer into its head, lifting it off its feet. He then slammed it to the ground, in one seamless move. Adam watched, startled and slightly awestruck. It appeared that Craig was a lot more resourceful or possibly violent than Adam had previously believed him to be. Adam's mind fluttered back to all of the encounters he had ever had with Craig – none of them led him to believe Craig was the warrior he appeared to be today. Adam was impressed.

He quickly stopped banging the pans and moved to join Craig in the hallway. "Nice one," Adam blurted.

"Drag the body into the corridor, you don't want it in here," Craig ordered, then jogged down the corridor to the stairwell at the end. "Catch you in a minute!" he yelled, then cautiously opened the door and looked into the stairwell, then he disappeared from Adam's sight.

Adam stared down the corridor at the door as it swung closed with a *click*.

The body of the infected twitched. Adam grimaced, then reached to pick it up by its ankles. He laboured with extreme difficulty, dragging the body into the corridor. As he dropped the legs, two doors opened around him and two people came out of their respective flats.

"Hello?"

"Hello? Do you know what's happening?"

They were two other near-neighbours along the corridor – ANGELA GARCIA, 52 year old Spanish woman – and MARISA FLENKMAN, 54 year old English woman of Israeli descent. Angela had a round face with a round nose at the centre, between large, round cheeks. She had a natural smile that made her eyes upturn at the sides with several crows-feet. She had long hazel hair with a rolled fringe. She wore a red hoodie over a white t-shirt, denim jeans and pink Lacoste trainers. Marisa had greying, black hair swept into a loose ponytail. She had a sharp jaw and laughter-lines either side of a stubby nose. She had interested, calm, dark eyes under sharp brows. She had a small frame and was athletic and slim. She wore a black and cream polka-dotted shirt over a white vest, black jeans and small, black-leather shoes.

"I don't know what is going on," Adam admitted looking from Angela to Marisa and back again.

"They seem to attack everything that moves, except each other... I've been watching them for the last two hours, at my window," Marisa stated. "I think this is the end of the world."

Adam's expression was blank.

"Are we safe?" Angela asked. "Do you know anything, Adam?"

"I don't know... For now, we're safe... For sure," he said, trying to sound positive.

"I hope to have your confidence," Marisa said.

"You are welcome to sanctuary in my flat... --if you're alone...?"

As Angela and Marisa decided the boy, the woman and Craig burst out of the stairwell and came sprinting down the corridor.

"Run! Run! Get in the flat!" Craig bellowed.

"Quick, quick, make up your minds," Adam said hurriedly to the ladies. They all rushed into Adam's flat, followed incredibly-quickly by the boy, the woman and Craig.

The door slammed shut with a *bang*.

Some time ago. At *The Sentinel* news-paper.

Adam stood in front of his boss's desk. He felt like he was being judged. His boss was PAUL TRIKE, 50 year old Englishman; He was going white at the temples of a curly knotted mane of grey-brown hair. He had round shoulders and was slightly overweight, his shirt was tight around his chubby body. He had a warm face, dimpled on both sides, thoughtful brown eyes behind thin-rimmed spectacles and a broad nose. He wore a light grey suit, white shirt with no tie, and beaten and cracked brown shoes. He eyed Adam over a cardboard folder with an article paper-clipped to it. He looked at Adam sharply, his brow furrowing.

"This is nonsense, Adam. Speculative nonsense. The stuff of pure fabrication, paranoid delusion and weak writing. Topped off with conspiracy theory... I can't print this nonsense, Adam."

"I have the evidence."

"DVDs with footage from the seventies and eighties are not evidence. Neither are any of these allegations and loose conspiracies that this man – Dallow – provided you with. For God's sake, Adam. Even if he did die, get assassinated, or whatever."

Adam was taken aback by Paul's directness. He was normally more free-thinking, willing to believe. "But... But... But there's something to these claims," Adam argued.

"No. There is not."

"There is..."

"We could go on like this all day."

"What about Dallow being shot? What about the van? What about his fucking death in front of me?! That cannot mean nothing, and it cannot mean you'd do nothing!"

"Calm yourself. And lower your voice."

"What about my kidnapping, for fuck's sake?!" Adam blurted through gritted teeth.

"If there are these people who are doing these things, building these grand schemes, conspiracies... --whatever... Then obviously they don't want anyone to know about it, they cover everything up.. What you have is speculation without the closest thing to proof, so I can't print it... And you'll have to drop it... Or..." Paul stated slowly.

"If you'd let me show you the tapes!" Adam begged.

"I'm sorry. My hands are tied. I can't see anything you have to offer."

"How can you be so obtuse?"

Paul was momentarily taken aback. He paused, took a breath to regain his composure, then cleared his throat. "This isn't *The Shawshank Redemption*, Adam... I'm not the warden."

"But–..."

"There are no more 'buts', Adam. This is the third time you've brought to my desk some elaborate conspiracy that just hasn't panned-out, has it?... I don't mean to sound harsh, Adam, but I did think you had an okay future. Not bright, but okay... But I don't see that now. You're like a walking cliché... Chasing UFOs and Atlantis and whatever this is, is not good journalism..."

A little later.

Adam left the building holding a full box of office-stuff, desk-stuff and the general-stuff that he could carry. He stopped on the pavement, turned to look back at the grey monolith-of-a-building he had just vacated permanently. His lids sank over his eyes and he thought about his first interview. His hands balled into fists and his fingernails dug into his palms. His eyes snapped open and he stared at the building. All that occupied it now, all of the work carried out in its bowels, all of the pomp and prestige. All of it that he now hated with every atom in his body.

He sighed.

He had loved his job there, at *The Sentinel*. He had worked for many years to be at that desk, where now the contents were packed into one archive box gripped in his hands. Another box to be placed somewhere in his flat, possibly under his bed where there was still a small area free to use.

He wielded the box in front of him and walked to a local MacDonald's restaurant. He sat down after ordering a coffee and sipped it slowly. The box taunted him from the other side of the booth.

Later that day. In Adam's study – 10:12pm.
Adam placed one of Dallow's DVDs into his player and pressed the Play-button. He sat back, stirring a fresh cup of coffee – Nescafé Alta Rica Coffee, grown in the mountains of Costa Rica – when the video began.

The videos had a title-card and stated they came from "Field Operations", all with their own case designates, from central Africa, northern Russia and southern South America.

The videos showed commandos in helicopters, landing under the cover of night, then storming various villages and complexes: blowing holes in buildings, entering in formation and firing machine-guns on unseen targets. The videos were heavily edited and choppy. They included black-panels, blurry-smears and pixelated-blotches covering the names of soldiers and officers, actual locations, any signposts, all advertising and the unknown 'enemies' themselves. The videos were poor reproductions of degraded copies of vintage originals. The footage was mostly shot in colour. Some tiny edited highlights showed the visuals from old-tech helmet-mounted pen-cameras, which was particularly bad and grainy black and white footage. Some scenes appeared to be shot on Super-8 while most were deteriorated VHS and Betamax video.

Adam sipped the strong, rich coffee, swashing it around his mouth before swallowing. He lit a cigarette and tugged on it. He scribbled some notes on a folded, paper notepad.

On two of the videos, visible dates that Adam glimpsed referred to operations undertaken in March 1986 and December 1979. Adam stared at the screen. It was the twentieth time maybe that he had watched the videos.

The last section of the video featured commandos, all blurred-out, sitting in the back of a sleek, military-green Boeing Chinook HC1 tandem-rotor helicopter. It appeared as though they were preparing to land for a new operation. The commandos were all young men, however very seasoned and experienced. A word was spoken, ever-so quietly in the background and Adam tapped the Rewind-button for two seconds. He turned the volume up, then played the clip again. He repeated the Rewind, then adjusted the Bass and Treble settings on his television. He replayed the clip.

Voice: "En... don..."

He replayed the clip again. And again. And again, each time adjusting the settings, until the recording was much clearer. He pressed play.

Voice: "...Enchiridion..."

Adam let the video play on. He noted the word.

On the video, the Chinook helicopters were shown flying low above and over a jungle-canopy, branches whipping and swaying. Then came footage of a missile being fired from the deck of a British warship stationed somewhere in the Mediterranean. The last glimpse of footage was of a doctor beginning a speech in a lecture-theatre, subtitled in overlaid German and French, when a loud banging-*knock* came from Adam's flat door.

He switched the DVD player off, ejected the disc, snapped it into its case then slid the pack into a long, thin crack in the plaster between his kitchen and living-room.

"One sec," he shouted in the vague direction of the door.

He replaced a thin sliver of plaster behind the DVD case, concealing it completely.

Adam walked casually into the hall and to the front-door, when it burst open, splintering the lock from the wooden frame. Two men wearing balaclavas entered and Adam was immediately knocked to the floor with one club from a mace, then sprayed with a tiny bottle, liquid glinting in the daylight.

He instantly fell unconscious.

Inky blackness danced and swirled around him. He felt like he was flying through the air. Or falling upwards. He felt wind rushing between each hair on his head, each follicle excitedly fidgeting. He felt the sensation of riding a rollercoaster, being buffeted left and right, feeling zero-gravity, feeling his stomach pitch and fall, feeling his cheeks balloon then deflate, feeling the blood rush around his body, feeling lightheaded.

He awoke tied to a chair with an abrupt start, like he had just been slapped. His cheek burned. The chair was one of the cheap Ikea wooden-chairs from his kitchen table, which he was tied to with expert knots and climbing rope from the bottom of his bedroom wardrobe. One of the two men interrogated him, as the other ransacked the flat, bagging almost all of Dallow's items from the kitchen table and his bedroom. The interrogator took out a surgical-knife; a scalpel with a slightly curved end, almost like a craft-knife. He gestured toward Adam's kneecaps. Adam groggily panicked, dribbling on his shirt, and gave everything up, telling them exactly where to look for everything they were looking for.

The interrogator smiled from beneath his Balaclava. He said, "You don't get away that easy," and shook his head to the second man, who was standing behind Adam, out of his sight.

The second man finished packing Dallow's evidence into one of Adam's holiday suitcases, and passed the interrogator a large, iron crowbar.

The interrogator circled Adam, then pushed the chair-back; it fell backwards and Adam hit the floor hard.

Adam plead, "Please... Please don't kill me... Please..."

The interrogator raised the crowbar, then hammered down on Adam's leg. He hit the same leg five times – breaking it in three places.

Adam screamed and screamed and screamed, then passed-out.

The present.

Adam stood in his living-room with the woman from the street. They were leaning on an open window-frame that looked out over the street below; not quite a balcony, a box or a bay, but bigger and deeper than a normal window. Craig talked with Angela and Marisa across the room on the sofa. Adam and the woman smoked cigarettes out of the window.

"So... Where were you, when all this happened, then?" Adam asked smarmily.

The woman half-smiled. She said, "I was near Earl's Court... Visiting my friend..."

"Until just-earlier I had a plaster-cast on my leg. Craig," he said and gestured across the room, "he helped me cut it off... It was due to be cut off today anyway... All healed ish."

The woman stared at her hands, seeing some stain that was not there. "I can't believe what's happening," she whispered.

"It's a total fucking nightmare," Adam blurted with a light laugh.

The boy from the street sat on the other sofa from Craig. He shook a little bit, tiny body tremors, head tics; without anyone noticing.

"It's completely absurd, really. I bet there were people who'd seen the Romero Living Dead films that wished and dreamed that a day like today would happen. Would've jizzed their pants," Adam joked. "And I bet most of those-people shit themselves!"

The boy had been taken by the infection. He leapt to his feet and sprinted directly at the woman. As the boy hit her, launching from the ground and diving face-first at her head, blood dribbling off his lips, they became top-heavy and flipped and tumbled over the window-edge and plummeted three floors to the ground below with a *crunching* and *bursting* sound.

Adam hung over the window-ledge and stared down open-mouthed on the scene below. He exhaled heavily.

He saw one of the infected run down the street. It stopped over the bodies of the boy and woman. It vomited blood on the now severely disabled woman's face, as she gargled on the tarmac, blowing glossy wine-red bubbles. Then she died from the impact wounds.

Craig and Angela joined Adam at the window. Angela put her arm on Adam's shoulder, as Craig leant on the window-frame to look down on the street.

"Holy fuck!" Craig roared.

Marisa stood against the back wall of the living-room. Her eyes fluttered open and closed, as her bones shook inside her body and her teeth shattered nervously. "Oh my God! Oh my God! Oh my God!" she muttered.

The infected craned its neck to stare up at the window. It blinked its bloodshot eyes twice, then started off down the street.

The boy had died on impact with the road.

Angela turned and saw Marisa shaking. She went to her and stroked her arm, hugged her, then held her hands, sitting on the arm-rest of the two-seater sofa. Craig turned and sat down on a tall stack of books.

"Geez," Craig murmured, breathing out a heavy, tired breath.

Adam turned to the others. He said desperately, "What the fucking hell're we supposed do now?!"

The clock on the wall behind Adam read 5:19pm.

Earlier that day. On the Southbank of the Thames, near Battersea Park – 11:49am.

Craig swung a thin, white-plastic bag across his fingers letting the book inside rock to and fro, bumping into each corner with each swing. He whistled an unidentifiable tune to himself: it sounded vaguely African, tribal.

With his free hand, he patted the hand-rail that ran along the riverside. He thought about the antique book store. The smell of the ancient volumes piling the walls and spreading out from looming bookcases like crumbling columns of paper and leather. The book store had provided him with exactly the manuscript he had been searching for, for many years. He felt pleased with himself and had adopted a slight smirk since the owner had told him about the delivery of the book. It was a copy of the original, incredibly rare; very difficult and time consuming to uncover any version.

He felt his shoe unloosen, heard the laces *creak* against leather.

He stopped to tie the laces on his left-foot shoe, drawing them tight, pulling his shoes close around his foot. He was wearing black thick-leather ankle-boots, more shoes than proper boots – they were durable and long-lasting, good for hill-walking and commuting alike.

He continued on.

Moments after passing the Peace Pagoda, he noticed a young man huddled on the ground, gripping his stomach and moaning in pain. Craig froze. He watched the young man intently. He baby-crawled a few feet along the ground, then began to cough, gutturally, from his core. The young man spat and coughed, still holding his stomach and making no attempt to cover his mouth, unable due to the pain.

Like a flashbulb in Craig's mind, his eyes started to spring around the Park. He saw three other groups of people: a woman pushing a pram, three Chinese students and two construction workers in high-visibility vests. The woman pushing the pram collapsed to her knees and fell face-first onto the ground. The three Chinese students had all been engaged by the virus proper and were beginning to transform into the infected. One of the two construction workers had turned already and grabbed at his colleague, attacking violently, trying to vomit blood on him, and succeeded, filling his mouth with oily mess.

Craig looked at the young man, paralysed with the virus, groaning and crying in front of him, gravel and grit embedded under his fingernails and in his clammy palms, the look of absolute shock and paralysing fear etched into his face. His eyes bugged, boring into Craig's.

He stepped up to the young man and kicked him solidly in the torso, rolling him onto his back. In three short movements, Craig stamped on the young man's face. First the nose broke and collapsed in. With the second stamp the cheek bone and eye-socket cracked and spread. And with the third stamp the bridge of the nose fractured and the forehead split down the middle. Blood gushed around the sole of the shoe.

Craig leapt away and started running down the riverside path, screwing the book into a tube in his hand and shoving it into the pocket of his hoodie.

He dashed along the path that curved at the end and exited onto the Albert Bridge Road. He charged passed three corpses lying near the spiked, black-painted wrought-iron fence where the exit was, and barrelled out onto the road. He launched down the bridge, passed the old, wooden tollbooth, passed a sign that read: *All troops must break step when marching over this bridge*.

He ran down the Albert Bridge, a white, soft pink, powder blue and minty green-painted part cable-stayed, part suspension bridge that crossed the churning grey-brown waters of the Thames.

An Air France narrow-body jet airliner bound for Paris-Orly airport swooped low. It was two hundred metres from the ground and falling fast.

A storm of wind blasted the bridge.

One of the infected on the Chelsea side of the bridge was taken off the ground and thrown into a parked 1999 Volvo V70 estate car, smashing the farthest-back window and snapping its neck.

As Craig reached the middle of the bridge he stopped and ducked alongside the barrier. It was painted soft pink and had portholes cut into it at regular intervals with decorative iron wreaths set into them. He locked onto the plane.

The jet airliner wheeled through the sky, coming down fast. The tail-cone broke free and spun into the air, hitting and taking a large chunk out of the Battersea Bridge. Its starboard wing-tip clipped the water, spitting up a fountain-wall, and it took the airliner into a spin, cartwheeling it across the Thames. The back-section of the plane, its tail and upper rudder ripped apart and Craig saw over a dozen people topple out and fall into the River. The airliner lifted and pitched then crashed cockpit-first into two of the tall Chelsea Wharf blocks of luxury flats, before swinging wildly again, losing an engine, and crashing into a huge abandoned factory, detonating underneath the structure and taking down its immense twin chimney-stacks.

The shockwave sent a ripple of dust and smoke from the epicentre, spilling down streets, along the surface of the river and into the clouds.

A huge nimbus of smoke and dust and debris and smog quickly filled the air, rolling up into the sky, licked at the centre by intense, climbing fingers and tongues of flame.

Craig's eyes widened and he let out a tiny cry. He picked himself up and darted across the bridge.

Seconds later. On the crossroads of Chelsea Embankment and Oakley Street – 12:15pm.
Craig dashed into the low bushes and hid behind a tree, overlooking the crossroads. He waited for a long moment, surveying the mess of crashed cars and bloody carnage around him. Bodies lay on the pavements, rested against cars and buildings, or slumped behind the steering-wheels of the wrecks. Blood puddles pooled around all of the corpses, and there were more out in the open, along the pavement, in the road, sprayed across a zebra-crossing.

Smoke billowed from the factory and blocks of flats, drifting overhead and trailing to the ground.

One of the infected idled in front of the Mercedes-Benz dealership across from the crossroads, gargling and swilling blood in its mouth, letting it pour down its chin and soak the chest of its t-shirt. It stopped, seeming to sniff the air, but it was not. It arched its neck and looked away down the road, then stumbled along the embankment road running parallel to the river, eventually vanishing behind a row of trees.

Several of the infected idled across the bridge, following Craig at a distance. They were far enough away to ignore for the moment, he decided.

Craig's eyes did not leave a closer infected that was walking along the road, stumbling to cross the cross-roads. He breathed a sigh of relief as it disappeared from view. He darted across the road, dodging around some roadside metal railings. He rushed down Oakley Street, circling behind the first of many large brick planters; eight foot by twenty foot flower-beds with large bushes, small trees and shrubs growing in them. It was the perfect cover for moving down the street.

A little later. In the Tesco's Express on King's Road — 13:45pm.
Craig ducked behind the cigarette counter, pushing a Biro deep into the throat of one of the infected, pressing its chin away from it, locking its mouth shut and stopping the spittle-flow of blood-vomit from spraying out. Instead thick, warm blood oozed between its teeth, dripping from the dry edges of its mouth and jaw, collecting in the hollow at the top of the sternum, before running down its chest, neck and shoulders. The Biro punched deep into the neck between twines of tense muscle.

He withdrew the pen and pushed the motionless body away, kicking it further from him, then heaving his body to sit up against the soft racks of plastic-bags. Blood drained from the mouth of the infected still, its body slumped along the rough hessian carpet tiles.

An infected stumbled to the front of the counter and moved deeper into the shop. It groaned and made deep choking sounds.

Craig took a breath then stealthily reached for a bottle of whiskey, taking it from the shelf and unscrewed the cap. He poured half on his hand that was lined with rivulets of blood, then took a long draught. It burned as it went down. He returned the bottle to the shelf, wiping his hand with a rag, then got to his feet, crouching behind the counter-top. He scurried to the end of the counter and swung the entrance-hatch up in silence, locking it in place with a hook. He crept through the channel to the edge of the space, peering around the corner to look across the shop. He could not see any of the infected, but heard several moans and indistinguishable noises.

A trolley-attendant raced through the shop, but was tackled by two of the infected. Her screaming face was quickly covered with heavy vomits of blood, filling her mouth and drowning her. After several moments, the infected deserted the woman, rapidly being taken by the virus.

Craig used the attack as a chance to manoeuvre into a vacant aisle, pressing his book deeper into his hoodie pocket. He walked towards a body and picked up the record-bag that lay beside it. He looped the strap over his shoulder and head, and moved further into the shop, further from the tills and further from the exit. He made sure his footsteps were quiet, but still moved hurriedly.

He turned into the small neon-lit space in front of the small bakery with a dozen shelves and a deli-counter at the back of the shop. One of the bakers had collapsed then had vomited blood over the inside of one of the bread-cabinets, discolouring the glass-front with streaks of bloody mess.

One of the infected stumbled down the canned-fruit and soup aisle and made a line for Craig. It sniffed the air, blowing small bubbles of blood out of its nostrils.

Craig saw it coming.

The infected lurched, blood pooling at the corners of its mouth, gaining speed.

Craig retreated a pace, letting the infected get closer, then he booted its legs, swiping them out from under it. He stepped around its flailing limbs, then stomped on the back of its head, cracking its skull like a plastic-globe against the beige hard, polished-concrete floor.

He moved into the aisle and packed the record-bag with tinned goods.

A noise, maybe a scream, alerted Craig to another aisle, but he ignored it, and packed more food into his bag. This was not the time to be rescuing anyone. Now was the time to be moving. Getting home. Getting away.

He started for the exit, when the trolley-attendant, infected and ravenous. blocked his path. Craig shifted on his feet, retrieving a can of pineapple-rings from the record-bag. He palmed the can, then struck the attendant, hard, over the left eye-socket.

The attendant hit the ground, dark ooze and brain leaking from a crescent fracture along the temple.

Craig stepped over the body, as its fingers twitched and curled into a gnarled fist, and continued reaching for its prey, before it expired. Blood bubbles formed like froth between its thin lips.

Outside, on King's Road.
Craig ducked by the shop door, crouching in the tiny square of shade behind a National Lottery sign.

A local bus had crashed through a shop-window front several shops down, breaking both panels of glass either sides of the entrance-doorway. The crash had allowed several of the infected inside the shop the freedom to escape, and others free-reign to enter easily. The rear of the bus hung out of the shop like the huge head-end of a sperm whale. One of the infected stood in the centre of the bus, one that had not yet climbed out. It lurched back and forth, almost deciding what it should do. It teetered on the brink of a decision. From Craig's position he could see that its attention was drawn to several pigeons that had landed on the bonnet of a silver 2002 Honda Civic that had side-swiped the bus. The pigeons *cooed* and gave out tiny rattling-whistles. The infected turned in the other direction, ignoring the pigeons, staring through the back window of the bus.

Another of the infected roamed into the road about fifty metres behind the bus. A dozen more joined it, shuffling across the tarmac. They exited shops and businesses through broken glass-doors and shop-front windows.

Craig swallowed spit that had started to clag in his mouth. He was surrounded.

Something caught his eye. A glint of light.

He beamed across the road at the entrance-door to above-business flats. It inched open. A face appeared in the crack that formed, a middle-aged Asian man. He looked terrified. The man peaked around the blackened metal door-frame, pushed from behind by an unseen force. He saw the pack of the infected spanning the road, and retreated quickly backwards into the hallway, with much difficulty. The door swung on its hinge, not fully opening and not fully closing.

Craig looked at a corpse that sat near the Tesco's entrance. It was an old man that had collapsed on the ground, causing the door-sensor to keep the doors permanently open. He reached for it, dragged it near to him, then removed the man's shoe. He untied the laces then held both ends, wrapping his hand in three coils. It was now the perfect tool to strangle somebody. Or one of the infected.

The man appeared again at the doorway across the road. He was tense and trying with all his might to claw his way back inside. He was being pushed from behind by several men. He was immediately followed out onto the pavement by five other men. They pushed and shoved at each other, forcing their journey forward, down the other side of the road.

Craig watched them. Like a spectator.

The infected standing in the rear of the bus dove through the window and fell onto the roof of the Honda below it. The noise of contact with the roof awoke the driver of the car; one of the many latent infected. It awoke from its stupor filled with violent compulsion. The driver beat and thrashed inside the car hitting the steering-wheel and horn several times. Its seatbelt trapped it inside the car, locking it in place.

The group of men froze, each turning to the road behind them.

The infected at the front of the pack saw the men. It led the charge. The four infected immediately behind the first sprinted headlong at the group of men, berserk and raging, whilst the others jog-shuffled behind them, following as quickly as their bodies would let them.

"Oh Christ," Craig whimpered, backing away into the darker shade of the Tesco store. He shook his head. He did not want to be a spectator anymore. But he was safe.

The first infected struck the group, knocking three of the men flat. The remaining three men took off down the road running, with half of the pack hotly pursuing them. One of the infected grappled with one of the men, striking him and letting off wave after wave of violent, gut-wrenching bursts of blood that poured from its open-hanging mouth. The other two men were quickly dispatched by the faster-moving of the pack who had reached them swiftly. The second wave of the pack sauntered up the road; these infected had mostly been older people, the extremely skinny and the overweight who had succumbed to the virus and were unable to support greater speed.

Craig unknotted his fists from the shoelace and tucked it into his jean-pocket. He was safe. For now. He still needed a proper weapon. He thought about the shop. His mind raced across each aisle, scanning every item for its value as a weapon: nothing, nothing, nothing. Then his brain froze on a tiny section devoted to kitchenware, containing a small assortment of knives. He blinked, then scrambled into a crouch position. His eyes never left the infected ambling along the street in plain view, moving in the direction the three men took. He could see that their numbers had begun to swell.

He crossed directly to the small kitchenware section and crouched by it, huddling to be invisible. He selected two soft-grip utility knives with six-inch blades. He used a pair of scissors to cut the knives from the plastic sleeve and put the scissors in his bag.

Craig held a knife in each hand, then moved to the exit.

A little later. On Elm Park Gardens - 15:03pm.
Craig charged into his flat-building, closely followed by two of the infected, who were matching his pace. He raced into the stairwell and skidded to a stop. He stood his ground, watching the infected charging along the hallway almost side by side, as the door slowly swung closed on the automatic-arm at the top-hinge. The first of the infected lurched into the stairwell and Craig stabbed it through the bottom of its mouth, stabbing up through the soft-tissue of the mouth repeatedly, through the lashing tongue and the hard roof, into the nasal cavity and lodging it in the base of the brain. He twisted the knife.

The infected gasped and coughed, letting out spits of blood. It growled and exhaled.

Craig yanked the knife free and the infected crumpled to the floor.

The second of the infected bowled into Craig, knocking the knives free and throwing him onto the lower staircase. He groaned with pain but immediately reached for the scissors in his bag, when the infected ripped the bag's strap. Cans fell to the ground, *clattering* and tumbling down the oak floor-boarded stairs. Craig and the infected fought, struggling, grappling, jolting. They wriggled on the stairs, twisting and kicking, when Craig's fingers found good purchase on the finger-loops of the scissors.

Craig drove the twin blades into the temple of the infected, whipping his head to look away, as blood sprayed the wooden steps around him, like opening a shaken barrel of Coke.

He felt momentarily relieved.

He was panting for air, but lucid. His heart pounded.

He glanced through the open door into the hallway. The body of the first infected had stopped it from closing. And then he saw a third sprinting towards him.

"For fuck's sake!" he screamed, pulling his body to stand. Then he started up the staircase.

The infected piled into the stairwell, smacking the door back on its hinges, as Craig reached the second floor. He had only two more floors to climb, so he pushed on, feeling the lactic burn in his leg muscles, feeling his arms ache and tense, feeling his ankles erupting with searing pain. His brain screamed at him.

He burst into the hallway of the fourth floor and jogged down the corridor, slowing, panting for air, the last candle-flame of energy he had left burning low, but he forced himself on. He could hear the echo of shoes pounding up the stairs, not breaking pace for a second, and a vague growling moan rising on the air.

Craig pulled his key free from his pocket and pushed it into the lock, when the infected appeared at the end of the hall, menacing him, still charging, still going, still gunning for him.

He twisted the key, as the infected charged headlong at him.

The present.
Craig glanced at Adam, looking at his profile; at his long, thick nose, at the two tufts of golden hair that formed his eyebrows and at the pile of gingery-blonde hair on his head. As he stood, the top book in the stack slid from its perch, sliding away beneath him. Craig caught then replaced the book, then started toward the door.

"Where're you going?" Adam asked with a start.

"I've got some things in my flat that I wanna get," Craig replied, exiting the room.

Adam followed. "Do you think that's safe?"

Moments later. At Craig's flat door.
Craig took a step back from the door, before kicking it with all of his strength. The door buckled, and wood splintered and sprang from the frame. It burst open and wedged itself against a rough patch of dusty grey carpet.

Adam watched from his door, wide-eyed and gawping.

"Lock your door, Adam, wait for my knock – I won't be long," Craig said, then disappeared inside his flat.

His flat was considerably different from Adam's. His was empty, sparse, void; where he felt Adam's was crowded, overfilled and cramped. The walls were the same colour, but Craig could see more of his. There were no books, photographs or paintings anywhere. There was very little furniture; a bed and small chest of drawers in the bedroom, a seat and a television-set perched on a plastic milk-crate in the living-room and a tall wooden stool in the kitchen. The only appliance he had apart from a fridge-freezer, oven and microwave was a solitary toaster next to the sink.

Craig entered the bedroom and sat for a moment on the plain-white duvet, looking at the plain-white pillow resting on plain-white sheets. He had lived in this flat for eight years. He found himself nodding. Coming to some agreement with himself. His jaw locked tightly, then he unlocked it. He bounced himself free of the bed with a small shove, then stepped up to the open-fronted wardrobe recess, where no clothes hung or sat. He picked up a small metal mallet and placed his hand on the blank wall-space next to the recess. He counted two palm-widths across the wall, then planted the mallet in the plaster. It broke through easily, letting plaster chunks fall free.

Craig pounded the wall four more times, uncovering a square sided metal-box that had been previously invisible. He prised the metal cube from the hole in the wall. He slid the box free, letting small chunks of plaster and powder fall from its ends. He whirled about in the room and dropped the box on the bed. He opened the small chest of drawers next to the bed and retrieved a hard-wearing backpack from the bottom shelf.

He opened the box.

Moments later. At Adam's front door.
Craig knocked twice.

"Craig?"

Craig thought about saying something smart, then decided against it. "Yeh."

The door unlocked and Craig entered, carrying the backpack over one shoulder.

Marisa and Angela sat in the living-room, while Adam followed Craig into the kitchen.

"What did you get?"

"A few personal things," he replied offhandedly. "I think we need to think about the long-term."

"How so?"

"Look... You seem... You're a smart guy, Adam... Outside, everything is fucked. Everything."

Adam was momentarily taken aback. He felt his heart beat and he swallowed to steady himself.

"The world has had it," Craig continued. "We need to get to the nearest Police Station – it's about a kilometre from here... I think we can make it there."

"Why do we need to go there? Won't there be infected inside?"

"We need to set up an emergency signal..."

"An emergency signal? For what purpose?"

"To tell people where to go..."

"That isn't our responsibility, Craig, seriously," Adam stammered.

"This situation were in," Craig said, "is only going to get worse. More of those things will make it onto the streets and anyone else left alive will be infected."

"How do you know that? How can you guess that?"

"What's going on?" Marisa asked; she had entered without either of the men seeing her.

Adam and Craig looked at each other, then sheepishly away.

"I think we need to make plans to move," Craig asserted, looking into Marisa's small dark eyes. "To move on."

"Really?" she said.

"Yeh."

"I don't think it's a great idea," Adam added.

A little later. In the living-room.
Craig, sat on the floor, watched the clock. Adam sat in his wheelchair, beside the broken television, tapping his fingers together rhythmically. Marisa and Angela sat on the sofa; Marisa rubbed her hands together and Angela sat with her hands under her armpits. The room was silent.

    Adam sat up in the wheelchair, rocking the handles back against the wall.

    "I'll make some dinner," he said, and walked slowly out of the room, wincing twice as tremors of pain ran up his leg.

    Craig rose and joined him in the kitchen.

The next day. In Adam's bedroom – 08:11am.
Craig lay on the floor, covered in his own coat with a rolled-up towel for a pillow. Adam lay on his bed, staring at the patterns of light from the window that made the wall above the doorway glow.

    Adam took a deep breath, then became quickly alert to the fact that Craig was not asleep; his breathing was calm and measured.

    "You sound awake," Adam offered quietly.

    "I am," Craig replied, sitting up, "I don't know how you slept so well…"

    "My dreams were pretty shit, to be honest. If that's any consolation?"

    Craig half-smiled, then stood, letting out a tiny groan and touched his lower back tenderly. He used both of his hands to massage the back of his neck, tilting it and hearing small, sharp *cracks*.

    "What are we gonna do?"

    "If no-one else wants to set up the signal, then I'll go alone… But it's something that needs to be done."

A little later. In the living-room – 10:22am.
Craig picked up his backpack and slung it over his shoulder. Adam wavered by the window, looking down on the road below. Marisa and Angela sat on the sofa together.

    "If I'm not back by this evening, assume I'm dead," Craig said flatly.

    "Then what do we do?" Marisa asked.

    "Try an' fend for yourselves."

CHAPTER 3 - THE VOYAGER - New York City, USA

Upper East Side, Manhattan – 04:51am.
NICHOLAS 'BRODIE' BRODESON, 29 year old Englishman, stepped out of the polished steel and mirrored elevator. He was dressed smartly, but comfortably – wearing a black cotton suit, white shirt and snug shoes. He was fairly short and quite slim, the average build of a scientist and geek: He was not athletic in any way. He had walnut-coloured hair, in short curls, cut only a few days ago. His expression was always serious and grave, but his grey eyes were kind and gentle.

He walked out of his apartment block, dragging a large wheeled-suitcase behind him. He felt worn out and shattered, but somewhere underneath happy. He ruffled his hair, feeling the breeze running down the canyon-street. The air was cool and clean and felt refreshing.

He breathed deeply, waiting for the cab he had had ordered.

The taxi-cab appeared shortly and Brodie climbed in, pushing his suitcase onto the backseat next to him.

Brodie watched as Manhattan passed him by – The Guggenheim, then the Met, the zoo, and the whole of Central Park beyond. He would miss it. And he did actually believe that. He would miss the streets and the people, the noise and the tourists, the sights, smells, foods and ambience. He would not miss work. He promised himself that. He would not miss Wanda. He would not miss his apartment; he had always had aspirations for something bigger, something better, something newer, something cooler. He had slowly had to realise that even though he had lived in New York City, he no longer did.

He sank back into the faux-leather beige seat, breathing in the cab's last few occupants. He opened the window and watched the buildings flash and streak and blur and pass by.

The cab slowed as they reached his uncle's hotel.

JFK Airport, Departure Gate 23 – 05:42am.
Brodie sat with his uncle – ERIC BRODESON, 58 year old Englishman – waiting for their plane. Eric was a chubby, stocky and greying duplicate of his nephew. His face was fleshy and portly, dark plum rings under his eyes, deep dimples in his cheeks and lips the colour of shale. He wore a grey suit, blue shirt with no tie and smart brown shoes. His hair was slightly longer than Brodie's, and slightly more receded, but it waved and rippled in similar dark curls. Eric ran his fingers through his hair.

"It's great that we could both meet up on our way back-home," Eric offered. He smiled and nodded at Brodie.

"Yeah," Brodie replied warily.

"It is good. And I haven't seen you in a few years. We've got the whole ride back to catch up."

Brodie nodded.

"The last time I saw you, I think, was the time when we met up at Southbank... That was quite a nice afternoon with your dad... Was it good seeing my kids? Your cousins?"

"Yeah. It was good."

Eric cleared his throat. "I was so sorry to hear about your reason for leaving..."

"Thanks."

"Funerals aren't the best reasons for family to meet, are they?"

Brodie shook his head.

"How is your work?" Eric asked kindly.

"I quit shortly after I found out that dad had died."

"I'm sorry... I'm sorry to hear that."

Brodie ruffled his hair, curling parts of his side-burn behind his ear.

"What about that girl you were seeing? Wendy?"

"Wanda."

"What about Wanda?"

"Well..."

"Go on..."

"We split-up a week ago..."

Eric felt and knew he was making Brodie feel uncomfortable, so he stopped asking questions and stared at the tourists and business-men and –women and the airport staff and security, the shop, café and the people that handed out flyers. He watched a queue forming at one of the coffee-kiosks and sighed; he wanted a coffee, did not want to wait.

Brodie excused himself and went to the toilet. "Just going to cool off," he said, walking away.

In the toilet, Brodie found an empty cubicle and locked himself inside it.

He stood back from the door, rolling his sleeve above the elbow, peeling back a small, quarter-sized plaster on his forearm, revealing the red dot of a needle's puncture-hole. It resembled any normal, benign example of blood-taking at a doctor's surgery. He re-covered the hole, then unrolled his sleeve, buttoning the sleeve at the wrist.

He exited the cubicle and glanced at the departure information on a screen above the sinks, as he splashed water on his face, rubbing it across his forehead and the nape of his neck.

One week earlier. The rooftop garden of 230 Fifth Avenue.
Brodie sat at the side of the rooftop garden on a backless wooden bench next to the row of dwarf conifers that lined the roof-edge. He had just sat down, after admiring the spectacular New York skyline. He had stared at the Empire State Building and watched as the evening lights were flicked on, illuminating the towering spire with lilacs and purples. He always loved seeing the skyline from the roofs of buildings, any roof, anywhere in the city. He was wearing a pair of Tom Ford sunglasses: He had seen Brad Pitt wearing them in photos from Cannes and at premieres, and thought he could pull the look off, and could easily afford them.

A black and white-suited waiter crossed to Brodie's table, and placed a bottle of Taittinger champagne in a silver bucket full of ice, standing on a two-foot stem with round base, beside it. The waiter poured a glass and he stood back as Brodie took a sip.

Brodie nodded and the waiter wandered away. He took a place near the door to the rooftop garden and remained aware of each table he was servicing with a stony look.

A woman exited the doorway and stepped out into the evening sunlight. She was WANDA BRIDGES, 28 year old North Carolinian American. She was a tall, slim, vivacious young lady with a winning, yet manipulative smile and intelligent, fierce eyes. She wore a white intricately patterned sundress, with a lace top and feathery skirt from the Dutch designer Egon Jakobsen, whom she worked for, and Christian Louboutin white-satin, peep-toe high heels. She strode across the rooftop to Brodie, who rose when he saw her. The sunset glinted and beamed from the large, dark sunglasses she was wearing, also by Jakobsen, as she stared at Brodie from behind them.

Brodie smiled at Wanda. "Hi," he said and kissed her cheek, then the other.

"Hi," she said in a bored and solemn tone.

Brodie's brow creased momentarily, before she sat in front of him, and he sat down on the bench.

"How was your day?"

"Nicholas... I'm going to just cut to the chase," she said, and eyed the waiter.

He returned to the table and stood by.

Wanda looked over the top-rim of her Jakobsen's and glared at the waiter. "I would like a drink," she said. Her eyes flicked to the bottle of Taittinger, which had beads of condensation forming on the glass. The waiter nodded sharply, snapping his ankles together like a Nazi's ankle-*click*, coming to attention, and poured her a frothing, bubbling glass of champagne.

The waiter nodded again, then retreated back to the door.

"I don't think our relationship is going anywhere," she said matter-of-factly. She sipped from the glass.

Brodie was stopped, his lips parted to form a question, then they closed.

"I don't think we are anywhere-near as compatible as you think," she told him, then took another sip of the fizzing champagne.

"We've been together now for–..."

She interrupted him, "That doesn't matter now. I am..." she trailed off. "I imagine I'll see you around," she said with a slight smirk, then took a swig from the glass, then another. "You enjoy your work... You're finding some success..." she said and finished the champagne. She placed the glass down and stood. "I'll see ya..."

Brodie watched her stride purposefully back across the rooftop garden and entered the penthouse bar.

Later that day.
Brodie stretched his body out on the luxury suede sofa in the living-room in his apartment. He was reading *West of right here* by John Ramsay. He was halfway through the book and took a break, folding over the page-corner. He sat up from the tremendously lush, huge and comfortable sofa and rubbed his face.

His mobile phone rang.
"Hello," he said answering it with the tap of the screen.
"Hello, Nicholas, it's Ed Epstein from HR..."
Then Brodie knew he was about to be fired.

The present. At the departure Gate.
Brodie and Eric had joined the queue to board their plane. It was already about sixty people long, with dozens more people joining the line, snaking back and forth along the rows of seats.

Brodie eventually handed the tickets to an air-steward and they boarded without any disruptions.

"Enjoy your flight," one of the stewardesses said, pointing and ushering them into the plane with her arm.

Brodie took his seat by the window.
Eric sat beside him and immediately *clicked* his belt closed.
"I'm not a fan of flying," Eric said.
"Me neither."
"Must be a Brodeson family thing."
"Hmm, yeah."

A little later. On the Boeing 747-400.
The stewards and stewardesses performed the safety-procedure.

"You will find the emergency exits here, here, and here," said the pre-recorded message as the stewards and stewardesses mimed the routine.

Brodie looked out of the oval-window as the JFK terminal sank away into the distance. He was tired and could not disguise a yawn that erupted from within him.

"Take a nap," Eric suggested, patting Brodie's knee.
"Yeah... I think I will."
"It's not like the plane's gonna crash!"
"I think I'll just stare out the window for the time being," Brodie said, pushing his face near to the Perspex interior-window. The sky was pale greyish-white, brightening by the minute.

A little later.
Eric glanced at Brodie and he was finally falling asleep; his lids fluttered and his eyes rolled underneath. He told his nephew, "Crash out... I'm going to watch one of the films. I think there's a Bruce Willis one on..."

The Captain started his announcement, as Brodie fell asleep. The bassy drawl of the Captain deepened and softened, until it was a droning, muffled echo.

A hollow, reverberating pitch sounded, as Brodie fell asleep. He had folded one of the airline-pillows in half and braced it between his head and the wall of the aircraft.

Eric put on the cheap, wiry headphones that the airline had provided and switched the channel using the arm-rest. *RED* starring Bruce Willis began to play, the credits rolled. Eric tried to make himself as comfortable as he could, but struggled.

A while later.
Brodie snapped awake at the panicked-scream of the Captain over the speaker-system.
"Hello?! Hello?!... Is there anyone still alive back there? Is there anyone alive back there?!" the Captain shrieked, and repeated himself over and over.
Brodie felt startled, like he had been dragged backwards out of a dream. He checked his wristwatch – it was 7:16am. He turned to his uncle and immediately saw that he was dead. Blood rivulets had run from his nose and out of the corners of his mouth. Brodie checked his uncle's pulse. His heart had stopped, or he could find no remnant of a beat. Eric had lost his colour, was drained of it, and had been taken by the virus. Brodie let out a whimper, pressing himself against the side of the plane, wanting to create a distance between himself and the corpse of his uncle.
The Captain repeated his call. "Is there anyone alive back there?!"
Brodie cried out again.
He looked around, panicked, sweat rushing out of every pore, his head pounding, his heart racing, his eyes flicking around at what he could see of the cabin.
Brodie unbuckled his seatbelt shakily and, as he stood, he saw the rest of the cabin. Everyone appeared to be dead; all of the passengers looked like Eric, with blood around their noses and mouths. The smell of death circulated in the air, blown and remixed by the air-conditioning.
Something attracted Brodie's attention: A man. He cried uncontrollably, dementedly repeating: "Oh God! Oh God! Oh God!" over and over again. The man was obviously distressed, clutching at his own shoulders and rocking on his hips, twisting and turning in his seat, his knees knocking into the seat in front.
Brodie awkwardly climbed over his uncle without touching him. He stepped into the aisle and then slowly crossed to the man, squeezing passed a line of three bodies.
"Hey," Brodie said with a whisper.
"Oh God! Oh God! Oh God!" the man repeated, hysterical and huffing air in and out of his lungs.
"Hey!" Brodie said with a hint of anger in his voice and grabbed the man's arm. "What the hell happened?" he fumed. "What's going on?"
"Oh God! Oh God! Oh God!" he repeated. The man did not even look up at Brodie, his eyes fixed on the tray-table folded up on the seat-back.
"What the fuck is–..." Brodie stopped.
A stewardess slowly paced forward, taking short, nervous steps down the gangway towards him. She said, "Everyone just... died... They starting coughing... Everyone started coughing... --then they died!" She began to whimper, lifting her fragile hands to her face.
Brodie stared at her for a moment, stepping back down the aisle, seeing behind the stewardess's hands a thick coating of blood had soaked the lower-half of the her face, dripping from the tip of her chin. She pitched over and fell face-first onto the aisle-floor, as an infected passenger stepped into the shear valley between the seats, at the other end of the cabin. The infected charged toward Brodie, grabbing and reaching for him even at quite a distance, blood gushing from its mouth. It met Brodie and tried to snatch him, when a large bubble of blood popped out its jaw. It tried to spit and spray the blood on Brodie, aiming it at his face, snarling and prowling closer.
Brodie managed to shove the infected away from him and gave it a nervous kick.
"Please... Is there anyone alive back there?!" the Captain screamed out again, as Brodie evaded the infected. But it noticed the man, still rocking in his seat, and it rushed to him, pouncing and puking blood on him, until he was left choking and gasping as blood rushed into his mouth, lungs and stomach.
Brodie took the opportunity to run for the cockpit, scrambling backwards down the aisle, when he saw the stewardess straighten up, clambering to her knees and elbows, pulling herself onto her unsteady feet, gripping the seat-backs with talon-like fingers.

Brodie rushed down the plane, but stopped urgently, seeing three more of the infected ahead of him, blocking his way. He was frantic. He looked for any weapon, but found only plastic cutlery. He took a plastic-knife and snapped it lengthways, turning it into a sharp-point with a handle. It resembled a prison shiv he had seen in *Oz* on television.

One of the infected started towards him.

He climbed away, over dead-bodies in their seats, trampling hands and thighs, crotches and knees.

The infected followed him.

Brodie's eyes followed it.

The infected leapt up and scrambled over the seats, scrambling towards Brodie, when it stopped, then gasped violently, spitting a sprinkler-rain of blood. The infected gargled and roared, as its kicks and arm-swings lessened and lessened – something held it in place, not allowing it move any more, clamping it where it was.

Brodie fell shoulder-first into the aisle, landing with a bump. He got back to his feet quickly. He rose, picking up the shiv. His eyes darted around the cabin.

Something near Brodie moved, making him leap with a shock.

A large Texan had grabbed the infected from the under-side and had stabbed it in the neck with a sleek, black Meisterstück Montblanc Diamond fountain-pen. The man threw the infected into the seat-row in front of him, standing. He wore a prototypical cowboy-hat, a dark brown Stetson, over short, greying hair which merged into a dusty-blonde beard and moustache. He had on a grey-brown three-piece suit over a cream shirt and black tie with dark-grey cowboy-boots.

Brodie stood in the gangway, staring at the infected, as blood continued to drain from its slack jaw, then beamed at the emerging Texan.

"If you stay perfect-still... --they cain't see ya..." he said, tipping his blood-dotted hat.

Brodie could not speak. The Texan moved into the gangway.

"How long were you out for?" he asked calmly.

"Out?... Excuse me?..."

"Sleepin'... You were out afore we'd even taken off, kid," the Texan said with a wry smile. "I noticed you snorin' when I boarded the plane... I was ever-so-slightly the reason we departed a few minutes late..."

Brodie nodded, then looked along the fuselage to the next cabin, in the direction of the nose of the plane and the cockpit. He said, "What are we gonna do about the Captain? There are more of those people up that end..."

The Texan climbed over a body next to Brodie: They did not stand, they crouched behind the seats for cover. The Texan introduced himself – his name was ALLEN LAWRENCE BRIGHT, 58 year old American. Brodie introduced himself.

"Pleased to meet you, kid," Bright whispered with a half-smile.

"I'm just happy not to be the only person left alive on this fucking plane," Brodie blurted. "Well, except for that fucking loudmouth Captain..."

Bright laughed.

"So, we're going to the cockpit?" Bright asked, his brow furrowing seriously.

Brodie nodded. "I guess so. There's not many other places to hide..."

"Huh, yeah," Bright agreed. "But we find the Sky-Marshall first... After we get to a steward's-station and find the flight-manifest."

"How do you know to do that?"

"I watched *Lost*."

They scampered along the aisle until they reached the steward's-station and crept in, pulling the thin, blue curtain closed across the aisle.

Bright found the manifest easily. He stated, "I've been on so many business trips, you pick up on where the important stuff gets tucked away..." He routed through the flight-manifest and found the likely Sky Marshall. He crossed the station to the other aisle, stepping lightly over the body of a stewardess. A puddle of blood pooled around her head.

Brodie watched him, holding his breath, stepping over the body.

Bright pointed at one of the bodies, a thickly-set man in his thirties with a moustache and sunglasses. "That's our man," Bright whispered. "I'll make a move to him. You stay here."

Brodie clasped the door-frame into the steward's-station, crouching, bouncing on his tensed thighs, watching Bright tip-toe down the aisle four rows. He stopped, holding the fountain-pen in one hand and reached under the Marshall's coat with the other.

A moment passed, and Bright had recovered a gun – a Sig Sauer P229 service pistol – a telescopic-baton, two spare clips and a box of bullets. He tucked the gun in his pocket and threw the baton to Brodie, who caught it with both hands.

Bright returned to the steward's-station and crouched next to Brodie, checking the gun. It was loaded already, and with the two extra magazines it meant there were thirty-six bullets.

"Right, now, son, let's get movin'," Bright said, slapping Brodie's shoulder softly to comfort him.

"Okay. Lead the way..."

They crept up the gangway. Bright said, "Get down, kid..." and they ducked, as one of the infected prowled down the opposite aisle, moving in the direction of the back of the plane, blood dripping from its mouth. It groaned, swinging its head from side to side, sniffing the air like a wolf. Snotty splatters of blood popped out of each nostril with each breath.

The high-pitched whine of the plane whistled through the cabin and both Brodie and Bright had to stop a moment as a pain stung their ears. Brodie pinched his nose and blew, un-popping his ears from a hollow underwater murmur.

A young woman, sat the other side of the cabin, holding herself in her seat, whispered, "Is there someone there?"

The young woman started to rise, looking across the central column of seats toward Brodie and Bright. She had thought the infected had completely passed, but her statement was loud enough for it to hear. The infected turned back, having walked straight passed the young woman, and locked its eyes on her. It shifted on its legs, blood dripping from the edges of its mouth, stalking its prey with its bloodshot-red eyes.

"That girl!" Brodie whispered.

"Oh geez!" Bright said, then stood. "Hey! Hey ugly! Over here!" he shouted, attracting the attention of the infected immediately.

The infected whipped its head around, seemingly now completely un-phased by the woman, hovering above her in her chair. She froze, halfway between standing and crouching. It faced Bright head-on: its new target, where its prior one had just vanished from its senses. The infected bounded forward, then clambered onto the seats in the central column.

The woman stared, wide-eyed at the infected only a few meters away from her, struggling to hold her breath. She bit her lip and was silent, keeping her full attention on the monster, her eyes bugged out. Her shoulder-length blonde hair fell in front of her eyes, but she did not move to curl it behind her ear as was her habit, and it tickled.

Brodie and Bright watched as the infected climbed; its full awareness locked onto Bright. It lumbered over the seats, falling awkwardly at points. Its mouth snapped and blood splashed and fell out of it.

"Don't worry, kid," Bright said reassuringly.

Brodie whimpered.

Three years ago. Five miles north of Carupano, off the Northern coast of Venezuela.

Brodie stumbled down the side-deck of the 32-passenger, 84m blue-water research vessel *Solaris*. He hugged the handrail as the ship lifted and fell over a wave at anchor. He felt his stomach buck and sink. He grabbed the handrail to stabilise himself and stopped from vomiting into the sea.

A young woman walked out of the radio room and hopped skilfully and lightly down the ladder, and stood at Brodie's side. She stroked his back. Her name was PORTIA BAPTISTE, 26 year old Spanish-American. She had a light tan, scorching Spanish eyes that glowed green, lips that were lean but shapely, high cheekbones, a sharp, small nose, and perfectly-plucked eyebrows. She was extraordinarily attractive, distinguished by a tiny scar that ran one inch down her forehead to her left eyebrow, and a beauty-spot mole. She wore a dark-blue overalls with a visible white vest underneath and comfortable hiking-boots that gripped well to the deck.

"How are you, buddy?"

"Feeling better."

"You're looking a bit better. A bit more colour," she flirted.

"Oh, yeah?"

"Yesterday, after the dive, you looked quite peaky."

"I've felt worse."

"You couldn't've possibly looked any worse," she said with a bright smile.

Brodie's shoulders raised and he felt shy for a moment.

"I think you'd better take a look at what we found yesterday..." she said, and snatched his hand in hers.

"Why?" he asked excitedly. "Was there something there?"

"Come see," she teased.

They walked through the outer-door and Portia pulled it closed behind them. She led him down the corridor, around the bend and into a laboratory. Brodie's eyes widened when he saw the writing on the main computer monitor that faced the door. It blinked on and off the screen. It read: *Sample Found – Formula Identified – APPROVED*.

"It's great news, huh?"

Brodie kissed Portia's cheek.

"It's great news!"

"We still need to do further tests, but as a preliminary find... I think we may have found the Missing Piece."

"The 'Missing Piece'?" Brodie snorted.

"That's what Caldwell, Hall and Kidd have been calling it."

"...I've never heard them call it that before."

"Maybe, you aren't in the secret circle? Huh?"

The present.
The infected scrambled down the cabin, over the chairs and their dead occupants, breaking and snapping trays, bumping and scratching seat-backs, nudging and butting the overhead-lockers, trying to get its best, clumsy purchase on the climb. On one of the seat-backs, it ripped a fingernail clean from its right index finger: The infected was indifferent to the pain, ravenously scrambling forward, all focus on the Texan, blood spots flicking and leaping from its snapping mouth.

When the infected was two rows from them, Brodie pointed the gun, aiming. He was a moment from pulling the trigger when he looked at Bright, who stared at the oncoming infected, eyes glued to it.

"Everybody stay calm," Bright suggested, glancing at Brodie. "Don't use that gun, kid."

"O-Okay," he said and retracted his arm. He agreed it was best not to fire the gun, for fear of missing and puncturing the fuselage, nodding a couple of times. He wedged the gun in his belt and opened an overhead-locker behind them. Brodie closed the overhead-locker dejectedly, moving away from the infected as it struggled forward, growling. He opened another overhead-locker and snatched a small, hard carry-on-case.

The infected lurched, throwing an arm out at Brodie, when he smacked it hard with the carry-on-case. Bright, still holding the bloody Montblanc fountain-pen, launched at the infected. He grabbed it tightly around the shoulders, snatching a fistful of collar, and stabbed into its neck with the 14 karat gold nib. The pen punctured the soft neck-skin, reaching veins and arteries. Blood *hissed* as it sprayed from the gashes. More thick, oozing blood pooled around Bright's fist: dark red erupted and flooded out from the creatures neck, soaking an empty seat.

Bright pushed the infected down, wedging the corpse in the leg space between the rows.

Brodie started, hesitantly, across a row, keeping a close watch on each of the passengers. He looked closely at each of their faces; white and sallow, blood drying on their lips, in crusting rings around their nostrils and browning drips on shirts, t-shirts and blouses.

"Oh, shit!" Brodie whispered. "Stay calm. Stay calm. Stay calm."

Brodie reached the woman and she introduced herself – her name was KARA SCHOFIELD, 25 year old Englishwoman. She wore a smart grey business suit over a white shirt. Her clothes were creased, as Kara had fallen asleep after the plane took off. Brodie helped her away from her seat.

Brodie introduced Bright, who stared at them, then held his index finger in front of his mouth, signalling for silence.

Bright crept up the opposite-side aisle. An infected appeared in the aisle ahead of him, and Bright leapt at it, disappearing from Brodie's and Kara's sight.

After a moment, a loud *crunch* sound rent the air, then more noises of scrambling and fighting, and the noise of vomiting and coughing, then they heard more noise of fighting. Brodie craned his body and neck to see, but the back few rows of seats obscured the fight from view. He ventured up the aisle, retrieving the gun from his belt.

Kara stopped Brodie, putting her hand around his wrist. They stood, frozen to the floor, and could do nothing more than watch the space that Bright occupied last. "Don't use the gun. We have to be as quiet as we can," she whispered into his ear. He felt her breath tickle his side-burns and the hair behind his ear.

A second later, the man who had been crying "Oh God!" came crashing down the aisle, having been infected. He groaned as he closed-in on Brodie and Kara, coming along to the rear.

Kara, moving too quickly and too resourcefully, and too accurately and too professionally, and too calm all-of-a-sudden, grabbed the gun from Brodie's hand and fired at the infected.

Brodie stared at the infected man. Kara had shot him in the heart. Dark ribbons of blood spilled out of the hole. The infected coughed up blood, gasped and wheezed, took two more paces forward, then collapsed onto his knees and fell face-first into the aisle-floor. Blood wet the emergency strip-lights that ran along either side of the aisles.

Sunlight beamed into the plane from the right side, as a cloud skittered away from it.

Dust motes floated and twinkled in the light.

Brodie turned to Kara. "What do you do?!" he snapped suspiciously. He looked at her inquisitively, and Kara noted the look. She did not respond and remained blank-faced. She blinked, emotionlessly.

Bright snapped the neck of the infected he had been fighting near the front steward's-station, and climbed to his feet. Kara instantly pointed the gun on Bright, but Brodie stood in between them. "Whoa!" he shouted, putting his hand on the top of the gun and lowering it. He looked at Bright. "You okay?"

"All in one piece," the Texan replied with a half-smile and wink.

"Good. Let's get to the cockpit."

"Yeah, I'd say so! That shot probably woke a lot of these fuckers up! Let's move!"

At the door to the cockpit.
Kara crouched in the left aisle, Bright in the right and Brodie squatted between them in the front row of Business Class. Bright crept forward and knocked on the door to the cockpit, then picked up the intercom-receiver and passed it to Brodie, who had crawled up behind him. Brodie pressed the receiver to his ear.

"Hello, Captain?" he started. "Are you there?"

"Who is that?"

"My name is Nicholas Brodeson," he replied. "I'm one of three other survivors back-here..."

"There's no-one out-there!... No other planes!..." the Captain exclaimed shakily. "I can't reach anyone! No air-traffic-control, no open channels – no-one is replying!"

The three of them shared a look.

"Can you let us in?... Please."

"There's no air-traffic-control... Nowhere... There's nobody left alive! Everyone is dead! The world has gone!"

Bright took hold of the receiver. "We ain't turned inta one o' those things, pal! You gotta let us in! We're sittin' ducks out-here!... Unless you let us in..."

The Captain mumbled hysterically, then raised his voice, responding. "I came out and I saw everyone, after the co-pilot died in his seat... I put the plane on auto-pilot!... And, and... Everyone was dead!... How do I know you're safe?!... How do I know you aren't infected?"

Bright passed the receiver back to Brodie.

"How do I know you aren't one of those things? I saw one kill another passenger..." the Captain yelled.

"You're just going to have to trust us," Brodie replied sincerely. "We haven't been infected!"

The Captain heard and believed the honesty in Brodie's voice.

The door lock *clicked* open.

They entered cautiously.

A little while later.
Bright and Brodie moved the co-pilot's body into the cabin while Kara kept watch, holding the gun, pointing it across the Business Class compartment, swinging wide arcs across the seat-tops.

The Captain sat in the pilot's-chair, head held in his hands. His name was ROBIN LEACH, 45 year old Canadian. He wore the Captain's uniform for the airline, a hint of purple in the blue-black uniform. He had a large beak of a nose, jutting out of a face that was long and thin but pinched and angular. He was tall and stringy, lanky with bandy arms and legs.

Leach reached out and took a loose grip on the steering-wheel. His eyes were watering.

Kara glanced into the cockpit and saw Leach wipe a tear from his eye with his shirt-sleeve.

"Are you okay?" she asked bluntly.

"Are you?"

"I was only being–..."

"Are any of us okay right-now? I don't think so... That man you're laying to rest... His name was James Callaway. We went through training together. I've known him for fourteen years!... He's not okay... No, I'm not okay, Miss Schofield."

An hour later. In the cockpit.
Bright, Brodie, Kara and Leach sat in the cockpit; Bright and the Captain had taken the pilot's and co-pilot's seats, Brodie and Kara sat on the floor behind them.

"...I don't think there's any other option," Brodie said. "Other than to go on to Manchester. As planned."

"It's our destination. For now," Leach said. He had calmed a lot in the last hour, and was more level and alert.

"If we can land," Kara said.

"If there's room on the runway," Leach agreed.

"Well, let's jus' try an' stay focused on the positive, yeah?"

"So... We head for Manchester, then... We see where we can land," Leach stated. "That about all of it?"

"Yes."

"Okay, then."

An hour later.
None of them spoke. They sat, confined to the cockpit, lost in their own thoughts. Brodie stared at his feet. He tried not to think about anything, trying to keep his attention completely fixed on the stitching in his shoes, counting each stitch dozens of times over and over.

Leach broke the silence by trying to communicate with air-traffic-control again, but to no avail. He turned to Bright and Brodie, he said, "We'll be landing in the late-afternoon... There's no telling what we've got waiting for us when we land! I'm gonna circle to see if we can see anything before I take us down fully..."

"Then I suggest we take care of all of those things back-there, that are up on their legs – before we land," Kara stated, standing up and stretching her legs.

Brodie noticed Bright's reaction to Kara's suggestion: he became more alert, raising an eyebrow, agreeing with her with a tiny nod.

"Is that a wise plan?" Brodie asked hesitantly.

"We don't wanna hafta deal with them when we land, kid..."

"Wouldn't it be safer? No windows getting blown-out and us-all getting sucked out into the sky?!"

"I am an excellent shot, Nicholas," Kara said.

"What is it with you? What job do you do, again?"

"Security... I was in security."

"Well, okay. You-two can handle them better than I can... I'm gonna go to the toilet and cry!"

An hour later.
Brodie stared through one of the windows in the Business Class section, as Bright and Kara corralled and attacked several of the infected in the mid-section of the plane.

Outside he saw England below through thinning cloud.

The flight lifted then fell, dropping in altitude. Silvery feathers of wind sliced over the wing.

Brodie saw two plane crashes: One plane looked like it had nose-dived shortly after takeoff, gauging a deep furrow through a field, then it had flipped and skidded on its roof for another fifty metres. Fire had raged over the wreckage and one of the engines had exploded, ripping a wing clean from the body. The other crash was in a village; The plane's belly had hit the ground, tearing all three of its landing-gear wheels from their places. The plane had then careened through the village, tearing through houses, a Post Office, a pub and a Chinese takeaway. A huge gulley of destruction lay behind the plane, a three hundred metre long trail of dirt and rubble. Several fires continued to burn, coughing towers of black smoke into the air.

He looked away and swallowed deeply.

Below them on the M6 motorway, thousands of cars filled the roadway, motionless: They were locked in place, like the twisted, rainbow-reflection from the scales on a tropical snake's back. A dozen infected, smaller than ants, dashed along the motorway.

An hour later.
Brodie stood in the toilet facing the mirror. His eyes were glazed, and he stared at himself with detached interest. He splashed water on his face, rubbing his temples, kneading the skin down to the skull. He could feel sweat seeping from his forehead. He snatched a wad of paper-towels and patted his face.

He heard occasional gunshots – with every shot he flinched.

Kara and Bright were now in the tail section of the plane, and finishing their task.

He splashed more water on his face then buried it in a pile of bundled paper-towels.

A while later. In the cockpit.
Leach prepared to land, automatically transforming into an astute, able Captain. Kara sat in the co-pilot's seat and Bright and Brodie took fold-down steward's chairs at the back of the small space. They had all strapped themselves in tightly.

Bright looked at Brodie. "This's where the fun starts, kid!"

Brodie replied sarcastically, "Great!"

CHAPTER 4 - BREAKDOWN - Manchester

FRANCOIS 'FRANK' LEBECK, 31 year old Frenchman – left his office on his lunch-break. He was tall and slim, wearing a sleek-fitted, grey three-piece suit that was tailored to his figure. He had short dark hair, almost black, with thick, dark eyebrows and -lashes. He had a muscular face with high cheekbones and an angular jaw. His eyes glittered under his broad brow. He had straight, sharp teeth behind full, plump lips. He wore a cornflower-blue shirt under the suit-jacket and waistcoat, with an indigo-blue tie and matching indigo handkerchief, and smart black shoes.

    He let the exit-door go, swinging closed behind him, as he breathed in the fresh midday air. He stood outside the building for a moment, deciding with himself whether to sneak a cigarette before his lunch-meeting or not.

    He decided against it, tucked the tip of his tie behind his belt-buckle, then strode off down the pavement.

    His shoes *clacked* on the pavement as he marched away.

    He slid a pellet of chewing-gum into the corner of his mouth.

A little while later. In St John's Gardens – 11:58am.
Frank sat on a bench, crossed his legs, straightened his tie, tugged his trouser-leg down, then the other, and *squeaked* his finger slowly across his teeth. He checked his breath with a cupped hand, then ate another pellet of chewing-gum, flattened his hair with a casual stroke, and smoothed down his eyebrows with fingertips. He was waiting for someone and did not want to look impatient, did not want to be seen to be glancing at his watch.

    His eyes criss-crossed the space, from families to couples to singles to dogs racing around.

    ERIN FONTEIN, 28 year old Frenchwoman – walked toward Frank, greeting him with a tender, prolonged kiss on the cheek. She was tall, taller than Frank, especially so in tasteful, gracefully-stemmed, cleanly-detailed high-heels. She had the easy air of a supermodel: she had porcelain skin, was tall and slim and statuesque, and had beautiful, alluring features. She was elegant and graceful. She had short, boyish, reddish chestnut-coloured hair that she parted on the left, curling part of the fringe around her ear. She wore a tight-fitting grey business-suit, buttoned above her navel, showing off a low-cut white blouse underneath. She had Jimmy Choo shoes, a Cartier wristwatch, three platinum and gold rings, and diamond ear-rings.

    As they kissed for a second time, on the lips, several people in the park collapsed.

    A man fell, mid-step, onto his knee, then coughed violently; a fountain-spray of blood erupted from his mouth. He fell into a bush on the outside of the park, out of Frank and Erin's sight.

    Another man sat on a bench near the centre of the park, fifty metres from Frank and Erin, pitched forward and fell onto the ground face-first. The rough pavement grated across his face, peeling back several strips of his cheek and nose. He came to a stop, eyes wide open, bleeding from the wounds. The majority of the people coughed-up blood then died, while a few others stared wide-eyed with shock at the scene unfolding around them.

    Frank pulled away from Erin and smiled at her sweetly, but immediately noticed out of the corner of his eye that the people around him were now lying face-down on the ground. "What the hell," he started, "is going on?"

    "I don't know..."

    "Um..."

    "Is this a prank?" Erin asked. "What is this?"

    Frank turned in every direction. He saw bodies everywhere. Only three people, two at one gate, and the other further up the path, were seemingly aware of what was happening. They stood, as Frank and Erin did, surveying the park and their immediate surroundings.

    A heart-pounding panic started to grow inside Frank.

    "What is this?" she asked again. "What's going on, Frank? Is this a joke?"

    "I don't know," Frank replied, and took Erin's hand. "I don't know," he repeated quietly. They scurried to check on one of the people lying near them, as a dozen cars crashed loudly nearby on

Lower Byrom Street. One car rammed into the wrought-iron fence surrounding the park and wedged itself between the uprights. Smoke began to rise from the engine.

Erin was frightened. Her eyes darted across the park; to people lying on the ground dead, to a couple of people trying to resuscitate others, to people scrambling to their feet bleeding from their mouths, to people running away.

Frank let go of her hand, ran to check on three more people and found them all dead. His eyes met Erin's and he shook his head after each body.

On the road that encircled the park, a few more cars crashed into one-another. A fire had started inside one of the cars; flames licked the air as the inside of the car became an inferno. Toxic black smoke poured from cracks around doors, windows and air-intakes. The driver screamed, beating the windows and steering-wheel. Their arms flailed and whipped out, until they were fully engulfed in flames, black sooty patches forming on the windows.

Frank stared at the car. The occupant inside continued to beat at the windows around it from the driver's seat. They had not taken off their seatbelt. For a tiny moment, Frank was mesmerised by the flames, entranced by the figure inside; its arms flapping and striking out. Then all movement inside the car stopped, apart from the roaring flames.

"Frank, what's happening?!" Erin asked, panicked.

He snapped out of it. "I'm not sure. But we have to go."

"Where?"

"I don't know... Come with me... Come on, follow me..."

Frank took Erin's hand, and they dashed out into the centre of the road, onto St John Street.

The street was gridlocked with crashed cars. Every driver and passenger in all of the cars was dead, or being taken by the virus: becoming stricken and defeated, losing their colour. Those that had turned, fought with and thrashed against their restraints, roaring like caged beasts.

They moved along the pavement, passing cars that were skewed across the walkway. They ducked along the road, cutting down the wall-side, trying to be invisible.

A scream rent the air, then Frank pulled Erin into the recessed doorway to an office building. They huddled for a moment.

Four of the infected stalked into the park, a short distance behind Frank and Erin. Each one wore bloodied and tattered suits; office-workers on their lunch-breaks.

"What the fuck is this?!" Frank whispered to himself. He watched the infected scatter towards the remaining people, who in turn darted in every direction. Two people caused the death of another when they dodged one of the infected, only to let it vomit blood over the third person. The man gagged, spitting blood, then fell out of sight behind a grey 2002 Ford Focus.

Frank tried his mobile. There was no signal. He tried again. "I can't get any fucking reception!"

"What should we do?"

Frank glanced down the street. It was clear for now. "We should go to my office," Frank started. "It's the nearest place I know. It's two streets away from here. We might be safe there, until we can find out what is going on..."

Erin whimpered. She let go of Frank's hand.

"Okay?!"

"Okay," Erin replied, brimming with fear.

They crept down the road, when an infected stalked into the junction twenty metres ahead of them. They froze, huddling behind a crashed white 2013 Volvo V40. Blood soaked the chin of the infected, its shirt and chest, splatters covered its arms; rips and scratches had torn its suit. The infected lurched forward, teetering on its knees and ankles.

"What the fuck has happened to that man?!" Frank whispered.

Erin did not reply, she peered over the bonnet and watched the infected alert to something, then sprinted out of sight. Frank watched through the car's cracked side-window, and saw the infected disappear. He took Erin's hand and they continued along the road, ducking for cover and rushing between spaces where there were no cars.

A man crept into the street ahead of them. Frank recognised him and waved.

"Justin!" Frank whispered loudly.

The man was JUSTIN O'DWYER, 30 year old Englishman – he worked on the same floor as Frank in their building – Finley & Associates. Justin was of average height but over-average weight; he was a short man with a wide waistline. His face was oblong with bulging with plump cheeks and chin, his eyes were tiny dots behind large rectangular-spectacles, his lips were thickset and shiny. He wore a baggy pair of jeans, a Slipknot t-shirt and black Nike trainers.

Justin saw Frank and Erin, and crossed to them, huddling behind a crashed silver 2008 Citroen C4 Picasso people-carrier. "Do you-two know what's going on?" Justin asked.

"I have no idea, it's fucking insane," Frank started. "This--... This is Erin, my fiancée... This is Justin."

"Justin," he repeated, shaking Erin's hand. "I was walking away from Sainsbury's... When all this shit started."

"We were in the park," Erin offered, "down there."

Justin looked up and down the road. He noticed Frank looking away.

"Where were you going?"

"Back to the office."

"Seriously? Why? W--"

"Do you know anywhere else?" Erin interrupted.

"No," Justin admitted.

"My car is miles away at a Park and Ride," Frank said. "We need to find somewhere safe."

Justin agreed to go back to the office with a nod, the jolt wobbling his neck and jaw.

They shuffled off down the side of the road.

A few minutes later – Outside Finley & Associates building.
They reached Frank and Justin's office-building and headed towards the reception. An infected abruptly ran out of a street nearby and clothes-lined Justin. It leapt on him, dragging him away from the doorway and pinning him to the ground. It puked blood on him, thrashing at his flailing arms, beating down on him. One of its punches broke Justin's ribs and another cracked his cheekbone. Justin screamed and wailed, then gargled and spat as a torrent of bloody ooze poured into his mouth from the creature's.

Frank and Erin dashed to the reception and leapt inside. They watched through the glass-plate front-door, backing away up the entry stairs, as the infected retreated from Justin's body. They did not know whether to help or not, not knowing how to help and were terrified by the attack. They paced backwards from the doorway, half-step by half-step.

The infected stood up fully straightening its back then lurched around the entrance-way to the office, then ran away, leaving Justin blood-soaked and seemingly-dead body on the pavement.

Once the infected had gone, Frank tip-toed down the entry stairs and crossed to the window. "I'm going to check on Justin," he said quietly.

"Okay," Erin stated shakily. She watched as her fiancé stepped off the bottom stair and his foot met the carpet, reaching for the door-handle.

Frank glanced over his shoulder, then felt himself crouching.

Erin joined him moments later, hooking her hand around his elbow.

They pressed their hands to the window, staring at the body. They watched as the virus took Justin, and he rose, infected. His skin quickly paled, his eyes grew bloodshot and any semblance of a personality was completely lost. The infected snorted and blood dripped from its nose freely. Its jaws snapped. It scanned the window, unable to detect the frozen figures behind the pane of Frank and Erin. Their eyes bugged out of their heads, mouths unmoving; their faces were masks of terror.

The infected Justin turned and wandered away from the office-building without looking at either of them. It craned its neck, then shuffled off down the street, attracted by a distant sound.

They backed away further up the entry stairs and entered the stairwell. They stopped and waited. Frank leant against the wall, and Erin sat on the second stair.

"What should we do? What the fuck do we do?!"

"I don't know," Frank groaned through gritted teeth, thinking.

"Should we hide? Should we run?"

Frank did not reply. He pressed his hands together and ever-so slightly rubbed his palms. He looked at Erin; her eyes glistened with tears.

"Is this the end of the world?" she asked.

"I don't know."

"How long will we have to stay here? Do you think it is just Manchester?" she asked.

"I don't know..."

"What are we going to do for food?" she asked.

"We have to think," he blurted.

Erin looked at him. She shuddered.

"We should go up to the office, see what is happening on the news."

"The news?"

"Anything... The television... Someone must know what is going on," he said, drifting off. "If not, then we have to find some car-keys and try to get away."

Erin whimpered.

"We should also have a better view of the city..."

Erin nodded slowly.

A little while later.
Frank walked in the lead with Erin following closely behind, as they entered Frank's office, opening and peering around the door slowly.

A noise came from a back-room.

Frank grabbed an office-chair and held it up in front of him, unstably; the wheels spun. Erin stood behind him.

A bloody-man stepped out from an office doorway.

Erin held her breath.

Frank gasped and stepped back from the doorway, the chair wavering in his grip. He quickly noticed something about the man: he was not moving towards them, was not infected. He was KEVIN DUNLEVY, 46 year old Englishman – a work-colleague of Frank's. Kevin was as tall as Frank, but carried a lot more weight. He had light-brown hair that was greying evenly all over, baggy, tired-looking eyes, a deep, permanent frown, and a rigid turned-down mouth. He always looked bitter, exhausted and angry; today was like any other. He wore black suit-trousers, a grey shirt with sleeves rolled up and no tie, and beaten-up brown shoes.

Frank lowered the chair and pushed it under a desk weakly.

"Hello, Frank," Kevin said eventually.

Frank cleared his throat. "Hi, Kevin... Great day we're having, no?"

Kevin nodded slowly. "Yeah..."

"What happened in here?" Frank asked, finally noticing the signs of attack and carnage around the office. Cubicles had been smashed; computers, desks and chairs were strewn everywhere. Blood soaked and speckled a lot of the surfaces. Frank noticed Kevin was holding a belt. It was knotted around one hand and curled at the other end. Blood dripped from the belt, buckle and Kevin's hand, forming a small blotch on the carpet-tiles below.

"I killed five of those people... They just--... They just kept coming at me. One after the other..."

"We saw... Outside... It was chaos. We haven't got an idea as to what is happening!"

"Check your mobiles... Or the phones, the land-lines... Or the television, any channel... None of it works!"

Frank checked his phone again. It was dead.

"It's weird... The power still works... I don't know how if everyone is dead..." Kevin snorted.

Frank looked at the walls and ceiling, and saw that the lights were still on. He wiggled the mouse on a desk and the computer monitor blinked on. He typed his username and password into the window and hit enter.

"It's useless trying, Frank... There is no internet."

"What?! What?! How can this be?!" he asked, checking for himself anyway. Kevin was right.

"It just stopped working."

"That can't be! That can't, can't be!"

"We have to move... We have to leave... Get the fuck outta here."

"And go where?" Frank demanded.

"Out of the fucking city, man!" Kevin shouted.

"Where?! Go where, after we leave the city?"

"Away from all those fucking things!" Kevin argued, pointing out of the window at fifty or more infected that shuffled along the street below them.

Erin stared at the small herd of the infected. She gasped.

"We can't just leave. We'll be out in the open. We'll be killed!"

"My car is in the basement-car park. We get that, we leave!" Kevin said with the slightest hint of a smirk.

"Yes," Erin agreed.

"What?"

A little later. In the basement-car park.
Frank sat in the passenger seat as Erin got in the back of Kevin's Nissan SUV.

Kevin slammed the driver's door closed and made himself comfortable.

"What are you waiting for?" Frank snapped.

"What's your rush?"

Kevin started the engine then pulled across the car park. He pressed the security-gate sensor and the gate shook, then retracted from the exit with a metallic *rattle*. He accelerated up the ramp and took off into the street.

A little later. On Plymouth Grove, the A5184.
The Nissan slalomed between dozens of parked and crashed cars. At one point, Kevin deliberately let the back-end of the car swing out, ploughing one of the infected into a low-built wall that lined part of the road. The infected hit the wall above the hips, snapping its spinal cord, twisting it and doubling it over, and dumping it on the grass beyond in a heap.

There were hundreds of bodies lining the pavements at irregular intervals, blood-stained and motionless.

A halo of rainbow colours shone through trees, as Kevin swung the Nissan passed a car that was wedged into the fence around Swinton Green Park.

Kevin accelerated down the road, heading South-east.

"Where will we go?" Erin asked, bracing herself against the backseat. "There is nobody else left alive..."

"Anywhere... Anywhere away from here... South seems like a good punt!" Kevin responded.

Frank watched as they slowed behind the back of a bus.

Five infected were trapped inside the bus, wandering the central aisle. Three of them saw the Nissan and pounced against the window, beating it with their palms, fists and shoulders. One of the windows cracked and one of the infected burst forth, landing in a small mass on the road. Both of its elbows were scraped clean of skin and wept blood.

Kevin kicked the accelerator and the Nissan leapt forward, as the infected clambered to its feet. The car collided with the infected, shattering its ribs and breaking both its arms.

The car sped away, rolling over a body that lay in the centre of the roadway. Its legs snapped with disturbing *cracks*, and the car shot off down the road.

They passed Plymouth Grove Primary School and a large red-brick church, before speeding away down a three-hundred metre stretch of clear road.

A little later. On Wellington Road North, the A6, three miles north of Stockton.
The Nissan slowed, passing Conor's Bar and Longue.

Frank stared at the pub as they passed it, saw through the window the flicker of one of the infected charging at a woman. He screwed his eyes shut and gritted his teeth.

Erin placed her hand on Frank's shoulder and he put his on hers.

A little later. On Wellington Road North, the A6, north of the M60 motorway, one mile north of Stockton.

Kevin slowed, as the road appeared to be blocked. Two cars had collided with a moving-van, causing the contents of the van to spill out into the road: a wardrobe, a seven-foot long sofa, three bedside-tables and a chest of drawers lay broken and in pieces across the tarmac. One of the cars had rammed the van and had compacted under the side, crushing the engine-block and foot-wells. The second car had struck the back of the first and spun into the side of the van, pushing it into the road.

Frank looked through the windscreen and saw a huge, old factory-building that had been converted into a Safestore Self Storage facility. Opposite was a large church spire made of blackened sandy-coloured bricks. Beyond the Safestore facility there was a three-storey brick building, the sign on the front read Enterprise Rent-A-Car.

"What do we do?"

Four infected stumbled into the road behind the Nissan.

"There are some of those people back-here," Erin stated boldly, staring out of the back window.

"Fuck!" Frank yelled turning to see.

"We need to get out of the car and get inside... We need to find shelter."

Three more infected idled into the road a distance behind the others.

A little later. Inside the Safestore facility.

Kevin ambled along the corridor on the third-floor of the Safestore facility, with Frank and Erin creeping along behind him. Kevin held a kitchen-knife that he had liberated from the kitchenette at Finley and Associates; Frank and Erin carried batons that they had taken from the bodies of two security guards near the entrance.

They found the exterior wall and the passageway-access to the roof.

"Come on, we'll be okay," Kevin said and started up the staircase."I doubt there'll be anyone up there..."

Halfway up the stairs they heard glass smashing somewhere close. They ran to one of the windows and saw, across the road in the Enterprise building, something was happening. They watched, stunned, as shards of glass fell from the frame of a smashed-open window. They saw a young man run straight out of the broken-window, screaming and unable to stop himself. The man then plummeted fifty-feet to the tarmac-ground of the car park below. A second later, an infected that had been in pursuit followed him out of the window and fell to the ground, *crunching* on impact beside the young man.

Blood puddled around both bodies.

Frank and Erin stared at the man and the infected.

Kevin glanced back to the staircase when another window broke, but then nothing happened. They watched, captivated by the void, then one of the infected hurtled out of the second broken window. Then another joined it, flipping and tossing through the air before the impact.

The window stood empty: A painting framed with wood, presenting a perfect, deep, spotless grey.

Nothing happened for a long time, all of their eyes fixed on the window, then a stern-looking man stepped into the window-frame. He was TETSUO KATSUSHIKA, 48 year old Japanese man. He had a military-style moustache and haircut, regularly trimmed and neatly cropped. He had a regular, but strong build with sharp, square shoulders. He wore an expensive but bloodied and torn black three-piece suit, dirtied and bloody white shirt, a cherry-red tie and comfortable black shoes.

Tetsuo did not seem to see Frank, Erin or Kevin, looking down at the bodies below, and stepped out of sight without looking up at them.

"Should we go to him? Get his attention?"

"No. Fuck him. He seems to be doing fine," Kevin groaned.

"I don't know, Frank," Erin said softly. "Maybe we're safer as just us."

"You think we're safer here?!"

"Yes," Kevin said abruptly. "We are... We can look out for each other. Keep an eye on each other's backs. Work together. We can't risk our lives for that bloke across the road."

"What if there are more people around?" Frank asked. "He's the only other person we've seen... Someone who has survived these past few hours..."

Kevin grimaced.

Erin stroked Frank's arm.

"I'll keep watch out this window, then if you go hunting for food and weapons... See if any of the TVs are working in the guard-station downstairs – see if the news is on... Most of the building seems to be on lock-down... We'll be safe, so long as no-one opens any of the outside doors," Kevin said finally.

Kevin slouched by the window on the staircase, gripping the kitchen-knife. He looked outside and at the building opposite them. His eyes flickered to the window where they had last seen Tetsuo. It remained a grey canvas of emptiness.

Frank and Erin searched the guard-station cautiously, creeping around corners and being careful not to make any noise.

Later. At the guard-station.
Frank checked ten channels on a small LCD-screen television.

"Is there anything on?" Erin asked in a whisper, as she returned from a tiny kitchenette.

"There is no news..." Frank said, deflated.

On one of the ten news-channels, the television studio and news-desk were both empty, but the broadcast was still being made. As Frank changed the channel to another news station, the screen flickered. There was some movement in the television-studio. But neither Frank or Erin noticed it.

"At least the power is still on, that must be a good sign... Don't you think, Frank?" Erin asked.

Frank looked at the light above them and said, "It won't last! I bet it won't last..."

Erin tried to read Frank's expression, but was unable. She looked through the guard-station's door at the corridor beyond. "We should maybe go and sit with Kevin..?"

Later. In the evening.
Only a sprinkling of the lights in Manchester were switched on, except those in office-blocks that remained on all day and a few houses dotted around. This gave the city and the streets an eerie darkness, lit now mostly by street-light, apart from inside the acerbic, clinical office-towers, facilities and residential blocks.

A horde of sixty of the infected trudged around the surrounding streets.

Inside the Safestore facility.
Frank, Erin and Kevin switched off almost all of the lights in the building. They sat by the window on the staircase to the roof, and watched the street and car-park below them, and the Enterprise offices opposite.

They sat in the light of one fluorescent strip-beam.

Outside.
Several of the infected wandered down the road, clambering over the broken belongings that spread from the van's broken back roller-shutter.

One of the infected paused in the road, looking up at the Safestore building. It gazed at the glow from the fluorescent light, then turned away from it, shambling across the tarmac around the van and cars.

A few metres away a pair of the infected stared up at the window, catching tiny fragments of shadow that flickered along the upper-sill and frame. They stood motionless in the road, eyes affixed to the window.

Inside.
Erin kissed Frank's cheek and walked into one of the empty containers and lay on a pile of coats on the floor, away from Frank and Kevin. She lay still, resting, thinking. She started to cry, trying to do so as quietly as she could manage.

    Kevin and Frank could hear every one of her suppressed sobs.

    Suddenly, Kevin had an idea and got to his feet.

    "What are you doing?" Frank asked.

    "There must be bags, handbags, lost items and things downstairs... And loads of things in these containers that we can use," he said excitedly. "Have you ever watched Auction Hunters? With Ton and Allen?"

    Frank and Kevin started searching the building. They found a couple of Swiss Army knives, two torches, one can of mace, four lighters and three cans of hair-spray. Kevin went into the guard-station. Frank stared at him.

    Moments later, Kevin came out of the room. He said, "I'm not sitting around and waiting, Frank... I'm gonna get out of here! We were stupid to stop and look for other people, or to hide and stop for the night... And... And, the army obviously isn't coming!... I've got to get to my family, Frank... I have to go! I need to know if they're dead!"

    "We should find food first, not risk all of our lives... But... --we should wait for daylight... Wait for the morning."

    A beam of light shone from the building opposite, blinking on and off.

    Kevin and Frank turned to look through the window.

    The light swung from the open window where they had made camp, across the side wall of the building. Traces and flares shone into the downstairs floors, through grease and smog-smudged windows, momentarily illuminating Frank and Kevin. They dashed for the stairs.

    Erin rolled over and stared at the light shining at her. She sat up, shielding her eyes.

Moments later.
They all stood watching the Enterprise building across the road, as Tetsuo flashed a focused Maglite torch at them.

    Tetsuo stared straight at them, framed in one of the broken windows.

    Frank grabbed one of the torches and flashed it on and off, aiming it at the mysterious stranger across the street.

    "We should go to the roof and shout to him... We can't risk smashing a window..."

    Erin agreed with a nod.

    Frank waved at Tetsuo, who nodded in return. Frank pointed upwards and Tetsuo nodded again.

    Kevin looked at the entrance-door to the third-floor. It was obvious to Frank and Erin that even with his momentary bravado he was scared of leaving the space, and even to climb the stairs upwards. He started to weep. "I... I can't kill any more people, Frank. I can't do it."

    "They are not 'people' anymore."

A little while later.
Kevin sat on the staircase. He watched Frank and Erin stepping towards the rooftop-exit. "There will definitely be more of those people on the way to the roof, judging on how many people I saw that were turned into them... I'll stay behind – leave me behind." Kevin was juddering, behaving erratically, unpredictable and paranoid. He hugged himself, as Frank pushed the door open.

    Frank and Erin entered the stairwell.

One of the infected, prowling around on the ground-floor, growled. It vomited blood on the concrete floor and its shoes, hearing the door *bang* behind Frank and Erin. It sprinted up the stairs, taking two steps at a time, hacking and snapping its jaw.

"Oh my God!" Erin screamed.

They raced up the stairs as fast as they could, pushing themselves.

Kevin covered his ears, panicking and sobbing. "Oh fuck! Oh fuck! Oh fuck!" he whimpered.

The infected charged up the stairs after them, speeding up as it went. It bounded up several stairs at a time tirelessly, and closed the gap quickly, getting nearer and nearer and nearer to Frank and Erin.

Moments later.
Frank and Erin stopped running and stared down the stairwell, as loud noises echoed around them, crashing- and beating-sounds could be heard, then silence.

They watched, unblinkingly, down the staircases.

Frank grabbed Erin's hand and they raced to the roof.

On the roof.
Frank broke a fire-axe free from its safety-case, as Erin rushed to the roof-edge and started shouting "Hello?!" repeatedly.

Frank stood in front of the roof-door, readying the axe, when Kevin stepped out, a lot more bloody than before, but unhurt. He half-smiled at Frank.

"I couldn't let you kids go off on your own..." Kevin admitted.

Frank relaxed a little. He said, "Thank you Kevin..." breathing a sigh of relief.

The word "Silence!" cut Erin off and she stopped shouting.

Tetsuo stood in another broken-window, one floor down, looking up and across the car-park at them.

"What should we do?" Erin called out to Tetsuo quietly.

"Meet us downstairs in twenty minutes," he said soberly, then he disappeared.

They watched the window for a long moment in silence.

"He said 'us', so that must mean there are more people with him," Frank suggested.

Kevin remained suspicious of Tetsuo, watching the window where he had just been standing. "I don't like it."

"It might be safer at night for us to cross the street, than in daylight – we might get seen more easily in daylight..." Erin said slowly.

Kevin grumbled, but agreed. He said, "In principle."

Frank looked up at the stars and took a deep breath.

Later.
They moved down the staircase floor-by-floor, closing and locking all of the doors behind them. When they reached the ground-floor, they could see three of the infected stalking across the road.

"We'll have to kill those people in order to cross the road, or we'll definitely become one of them!"

"Shit... I don't want to kill..." Frank began.

"Well, you'll have to!" Kevin interrupted.

"No," Frank stated firmly. "I won't. I won't do it."

"I don't think I can either, Kevin," Erin added.

"You wanted to get to those other people. So... We have to get across the road..."

"Then we run fast," Erin suggested.

"I'm not getting turned into one of those... Just because you-two won't defend yourselves!"

"It's not about that!"

"Yeah? What is it?"

"What if they're still awake inside? What if they can't stop themselves? What if they can't stop what they're doing?" Frank argued.

"Look, we have to leave this place..." Kevin asserted. "At some point or another... Your friend over-there says now is the time to go... It's your choice... But, I'm going with or without you-two."

Moments later.
They ran outside, throwing the side-door open.

From across the street, Tetsuo and some other survivors emerged to fend off any oncoming infected and help Frank, Erin and Kevin cross, but all of the noise attracted more infected to their location. A dozen or more shuffled and filed in from surrounding roads and streets.

They rushed for the fire-exit of the building opposite, where one of Tetsuo's companions waited, hand on the handle. Kevin punted one of the infected out of his way, as Erin sped past him. He punched then elbowed another infected, hitting it out of his path and raced for the door. Tetsuo and two others backed away to the door.

As Frank was about to get to the fire-exit door, he was grabbed from behind by one of the infected and tackled to the ground aggressively. He kicked it away and darted for the fire-exit door, when it slammed shut in front of him.

Silence fell over the scene, as if a giant had upturned an enormous glass bowl above his head, containing the road around him in a bubble. Frank stared wide-eyed and open-mouthed at the closed fire-exit door, then he started to hear again; the muffled-sounds of Erin screaming from behind the door, one of the infected vomiting blood on one of Tetsuo's companions, his own breath and his raging heartbeat. He stared at his arms, his hands pounding against the back of the door, drumming on it.

He was momentarily frozen to the ground, unable to move, unable to turn around.

He jolted into movement as if the ground had been electrified, and he ran and hid behind the Nissan SUV. One of the infected rushed at Frank, but before it reached him a bullet tore a hole through its head. It toppled forward. Blood splattered the ground between Frank's shoes.

The infected juddered and twitched on the tarmac in front of him, blood pooling around its head.

Frank stared at it, shock taking over his system, eyes stretched wide.

Silenced-machinegun-fire erupted all around as two soldiers wearing woodland-camouflage uniforms jogged down the street in parallel, moving toward Frank. His mouth feel open. They were Sergeant DANNY NEWTON, 39 year old Englishman – and Private EVAN HASTINGS, 38 year old Englishman. Newton had an average build and square-shoulders; he was muscular and footballer-fit, and carried himself with an imposing yet charming manner. His hair was shaved to grade one and was still full and dark. He had a serious face with kind eyes and a thin, muscular bone-structure. He wore a bloodied woodland-camouflage, battle-dress uniform which was torn in several places – along one arm and two pockets had been ripped clean off. His boots carried dried mud with dried blood caked around the heel and toe. Hastings was taller than Newton and lean; he was also muscular, but his muscles were stretched and taught around a broader and bigger skeleton. His sandy-brown hair was shaved to grade one, and was receding and thinning in spots. He had a gentle, long face with dark eyes under a heavy brow. His cheeks, jaw and nose jutted out of his lean face. He also wore a bloodied woodland-camouflage, battle-dress uniform which was also torn in several places – across the shoulder and along one leg. His boots were piled with dried mud around the edges.

The soldiers were followed by an Armoured-Personnel-Carrier (APC), which drove down the road knocking a few cars out of the way, before it stopped.

Relief flooded over Frank and he rushed to the fire-exit. He beat heavily on the door, shouting, " Open this door, open this door! The army are here!"

He stopped banging on the door, staring at it, bewildered, turning to the soldiers.
Sergeant Newton jogged towards him.
Then the doors burst open and Erin leapt forward and grabbed hold of Frank.
They hugged for a long moment, tightly wrapping their arms around each other.
Newton looked from Frank and Erin to Tetsuo to Kevin to three other survivors. He said, "Let's get inside quick and have a chat.."

CHAPTER 5 - CASUALTIES - North Yorkshire

B6409 – Blackwell, 3 miles East of Buxton near the Peak District National Park– 12:01pm.
The brakes of a British Army Bedford MK 4x4 personnel-truck *squealed* loudly, as it skidded to a halt in the middle of the road. The tyres came to a stop leaving a dirty skid-mark of burned rubber behind it, kicking arcs of gravel across the road. The truck stopped eighty metres from a crossroads with woods on one side, and some fields and cottages on the other.

In the cab, Sergeant DANNY NEWTON, 39 year old Englishman – looked at the driver, gripping the dashboard and roof-handle for stability. He said, "What in the fuck is goin'-on over there, Haste?"

He squinted through the mud-speckled windscreen. Newton had an average build and square-shoulders; he was muscular and footballer-fit, and carried himself with an imposing yet charming manner. His hair was shaved to grade one and was still full and dark. He had a serious face with kind eyes and a thin, muscular bone-structure. He wore a moderately battered woodland-camouflage, battle-dress uniform. It was dirty and scuffed, worn out from the weekend. His boots were slightly muddy and scratched from heel and toe, top to bottom.

The driver of the truck was Private EVAN HASTINGS, 38 year old Englishman, and Newton's life-long wing-man, loyal friend and comrade. Hastings was taller than Newton and lean; he was also muscular, but his muscles were stretched and taught around a broader and bigger skeleton. His sandy-brown hair was shaved to grade one, and was receding and thinning in spots. He had a gentle, long face with dark eyes under a heavy brow. His cheeks, jaw and nose jutted out of his lean face. He also wore a dirtied and well-worn woodland-camouflage, battle-dress uniform. His boots were slightly scuffed and matte, but were generally free of dried mud. Hastings stared ahead, transfixed by the same thing that had captured Newton's focus. Their eyes widened.

On the crossroads ahead of them, a woman was being chased-down by one of the infected, and was knocked to the ground. The infected then vomited blood over the woman, shaking ferociously, roaring and beating her as it ejected vile, oozing red from its mouth. The infected whipped its head up and looked around, then stormed off in the direction of some distant screaming that rent the air fleetingly. The infected had not noticed the truck at all.

Newton climbed down from the truck's cab and fired at the infected with a pistol.

The bullet ripped through the parietal bone, clipped off the back quarter of the its head, spraying out blood and brain into the air like a stringy, blotchy mist. The infected tripped and fell nose-first into the ground, face-butting a clod of earth and parting the grass with the prow of its head.

Newton breathed a sigh of relief.

Hastings looked out of the open passenger door at his Sergeant. "What the fuck?!"

Newton shrugged.

Thirty seconds ago.
In the back of the truck there were more soldiers – Privates: BURT FOOST, 32 year old Welshman; Gorden, Jayson, "Munster", Callow, ILHAN NAHAR, 33 year old Hindu Englishman; Wade and "Conan". Foost was small and wiry, skinny but as fit as a sprinter; he had brown hair shaved to grade one, light stubble wrapped around a thin, pointy and kind face. Nahar was taller and lanky, with a solemn and sometimes overly-serious face; he had thick dark hair, shaved to grade one, thick eyebrows over dark, sunken brown eyes, a long statuesque nose and a wide, full mouth ringed by dark heavy stubble.

They lurched together, as the truck came to a stop.
"Why've we fuckin' stopped?" Gorden snapped, shoving away from Munster.
"How should we know, brainiac?"
"Yeah... I don't know, why don't you text your mum?"
"...Maybe a cow's dead in the road..."
"Maybe it's Callow's mum dead in the road!"
"Oi! Fuck you!"
"Maybe it's a UFO..."
"Shut-the-fuck-up!"

"Poke your head out... Take a look."

"Fuck you. You look!"

The second they heard Newton's pistol-shot, they immediately launched into action. They armed themselves with automatic-rifles from three large Army-trunks that were bolted to the floor in the back of the truck with them.

Callow, Munster and Wade leapt out and rushed to be the back-up for their Sergeant.

As they joined Newton, and before they could even ask what was going on, Wade collapsed to his knees. Both of his knees *cracked* arthritically as they hit the tarmac, and he let out a groan.

Another of the infected saw them from one of the cottages, across the field from the road, and charged at them, arms hanging behind it, mouth hanging open. The infected had once been a farm-hand, a young man, and wore blood-soaked jeans, a t-shirt with jumper pulled over it and boots. It moved quickly, eyes fixed on Newton.

Through the trees across the cross-roads, Munster saw another infected wriggling from a car.

Munster opened-fire on the infected, ripping it to shreds and bloody-mess. Bullets *tinged* into the car, popping holes and tearing the metal to scraps.

Newton paced cautiously towards the woman's body in the road, only a few metres ahead of him.

The infected farm-hand reached Wade, who was crouched on the ground gripping his stomach, wincing in pain. The infected knee-butted Wade into the side of the truck. He yelped and the infected lurched up, then puked blood over his face. Dark, glossy ooze erupted from the mouth of the infected, raining down on Wade, filling his mouth, dribbling up his nose, pooling in his eye-sockets.

The infected whipped its body around, still crouching, and turned on Munster and Callow who had momentarily frozen, when another of the infected appeared down the road behind them. It had clambered out of a car that was at rest in a ditch fifty metres down from the crossing. The infected whirled its arms as it launched into a sprint, charging face-first at the soldiers.

Wade coughed up blood, gasping, crawling on all-fours. He peered at Callow, and his terror evaporated.

Callow threw himself at the on-coming infected farm-hand, barrelling it away into the hedgerow.

"Sarge!" Munster screamed.

The infected, crouching over Wade, stepped towards him. Then Newton rushed it from the side and punted it onto the grass. It twisted on the ground, poised to attack, then it sprang forward.

Munster and Newton killed the infected, firing shot after shot into its torso.

Its body, straightened by the bullets, tumbled forward and landed on the muddy edge of the road.

Callow gripped the slimy, bloody neck of the infected, rolling through thorny bushes. He took firm hold and crushed. The infected kicked and elbowed him, but its strength lessened and lessened and it went limp. He pushed the body aside and found Newton and Munster's outstretched hands waiting for his. They hoisted him upright.

Gunfire erupted out of the side of the truck, ripping through the side-canvas. Three bullets hit Callow and killed him where he stood. The bullets dashed through his head and he died instantly, collapsing on the spot, falling back into the crater of broken branches in the hedge. The expression of relief now permanently frozen to his face.

Another distant infected charged down the road from the collection of cottages, drawn by the sound of gunfire. It sprinted headlong down the road. Newton aimed quickly and shot the infected, as the woman in the crossroads rose from the ground and started towards them, gargling blood and dragging a twisted leg behind. It hobbled up the road, arms outstretched, lurching forward, blood oozing from its hung-open mouth. Its eyes seared and raged, searching for them. Newton turned, and shot the infected woman through the eye. She stumbled, then tripped and landed flat in the crossroads' centre.

Foost, Nahar and Conan jumped out of the back of the truck and rushed around the side, joining Newton and Munster: An infected Gorden scrambled to pursue them. It leapt on Foost, who struggled it off his back and kicked it backwards, then Conan machine-gunned it at close-range, firing at its abdomen, blasting huge chunks of flesh free. The infected gargled and spat blood, then faded; its jaw loosened and dropped open, then its eyes sunk closed.

"Fuckin' hell, that was a bit close, Conan!" Foost said in a slow, exasperated breath.

Conan turned to Foost, expressionless. "Sorry," he shrugged.

Newton, Munster and Nahar stood motionless, as Conan helped Foost to his feet.

The door to the truck *clunked* loudly, then swung open. Hastings half-climbed out of the cabin, hanging on the door, and shot another infected that was running up the road towards them, a stomach-full of blood emptying down its collar and chest.

Everything went silent.

Each man in turn turned to look at one-another. They arranged themselves in a back-to-back formation and swung their weapons in every feasible direction around them. They were all frightened, but alert and ready, steady and calm. Hastings peered over the roof, picking up some binoculars from the dashboard. He pressed them to his eyes, firing his eyesight in every direction.

Newton looked at each of his remaining soldiers. Their faces were ashen.

The wind rustled through the trees.

Nahar noticed the truck's right indicator light was still blinking, shining bright-yellow in his eyes. He looked away.

Conan gripped his machinegun, his knuckles whitening.

Munster bit his bottom lip, chewing lightly on it, his eyes flashing around the location. He crouched, getting better purchase on his weapon.

Conan was the first to speak – he said, "Does anyone know what the fuck is going on?!"

Newton looked around cautiously, then finally examined one of the corpses – he said, "It looks like some kind of infection... A virus or a poison... A chemical attack... Maybe."

"At least it's clear for now."

"Keep your eyes wide open."

"Jayson started reacting to it... --from the air... Then he choked to death... Then he came up spitting blood like a fucking fountain... We struggled to put him down," Munster said slowly. "The three of us."

Newton gritted his teeth – he said, "Clear out the back and get back in... We'll continue on to the base – we're close..."

"Sir," Foost was first to say, acknowledging the order.

Later.

The truck stopped on the outskirts of the base – the Bufford Mann Army Barracks, a small training base for operations, exercises and field-tests in Yorkshire. It had a ten-foot tall chain-link fence around its complete perimeter, except at the entrance, where two guard-posts sat either side of a large gate and a set of automatic parking-barriers.

Behind the fence there was a fifteen-foot grass-covered mound constructed all of the way around the base so that the public could not look inside, with a small break at the entrance. The base comprised of dozens of buildings used for training, education, housing, equipment, vehicles and instruction.

Newton and Hastings watched from the cab.

Both of the guard-posts appeared empty from their position, but it would be unclear until closer inspection was carried out. Newton gritted his teeth and leaned forward, staring beyond the gate along the small driveway to the Barracks.

"The world has gone to shit, mate. It's a fucking disaster," Newton said. "What do we do?"

"What d'we do?... Get some beers, some ice to keep 'em cool, and fuck-off to Spain?" Hastings replied with a short laugh. His brow furrowed and he swallowed.

Newton smiled, then nodded.

"I'll consider it," he said, then lost his smile.

"Do that..."

A while later.
Newton, Foost, Nahar and Munster crept stealthily alongside the buildings around the Barracks, guns at the ready, in single-file. They passed a dormitory, then stopped, watching one of the infected, dressed in a bloodied Private's uniform, cross the road ahead of them.

All around them corpses of soldiers littered the entire grounds.

The sun beamed in the sky.

Foost wiped sweat from his forehead with the sleeve of his uniform.

In the back of the truck. Inside the entrance of the Bufford Mann Army Barracks.
Conan sat pointing his gun outward, ready to fire, and also making quick moves to check through the gunfire-ripped-hole in the canvas-side. Hastings sat in the cab, controlling his breathing, when he saw an infected stalking around the base. It meandered towards the truck, eyes not particularly locked onto anything. It lolloped from side to side, peering into the distance.

Hastings ducked in his seat, breathing more heavily. He shut his eyes and whispered, "Everything's going to be fine."

The infected stumbled to one side, then started off in a new direction. It wandered away from the truck and up the side of the grass-covered mound.

In the barracks.
Nahar and Munster climbed a staircase cautiously, machineguns aimed at the top of the stairs. They took careful, quiet paces up the wooden staircase. A floorboard *creaked*. Both men froze. A bead of sweat rolled down Nahar's cheek. He shook it off, continuing up, giving a little nod to Munster, arching his eyebrow to relate signs of calm.

Newton and Foost walked down a corridor, and each entered an office.

As Foost entered, three infected rushed towards him headfirst. He screamed.

Newton joined him in the doorway, and they started firing on the infected. Taking short, quick bursts at each one.

The infected were knocked back by the bullets and taken down. Blood stained the back wall, as dislodged paperwork skittered and coasted through the air, eventually settling on the floor in disarray.

"That was fairly close."

"And fairly loud... We have to find suppressors or silencers for all of our guns!"

Later.
The back of the truck was half-filled with supplies, equipment, guns and ammunition. It had been done at some speed, and boxes and bags were piled together, stacked haphazardly and in crooked piles.

Conan and Munster sat in the back of the truck on boxes of ammunition, in silence. Their machineguns, now with silencers, were aimed out of the back at the road.

In the cab.
Hastings drove the truck carefully, pulling left out of the Barracks and heading down the road.

He glanced at the side-mirror and watched the vehicle that was following him for a few seconds. It was an Armoured-Personnel-Carrier (APC) – called a Saxon – it was a 4x4, 10.6 tonne battle-taxi capable of carrying ten passengers with two crew. It had a small turret armed with two machineguns.

Hastings focused back on the road.

In the APC.
Nahar drove, seated in the cab at the front of the vehicle, following the truck twenty metres ahead of them. His palms were clammy against the stiff plastic-coated steering-wheel.

Newton and Foost sat in the back. They were not strapped in, and crouched on the edges of two opposite seats. They held a map between them, bouncing with every bump or dip in the road.

"We should try to find other survivors," Newton said. He studied the map and saw Leeds, Bradford and Manchester. "One of these," he said and pointed.

"I suppose, Sarge, but–..."

"There's no question about it," Newton stated. "We have to help as many people as we can."

"Sarge... If it was like that, out on a flippin' crossroads in the middle o' nowhere, then... Can you imagine what a city will be like?"

Newton thought for a long moment, sliding back into the seat.

"All I'm sayin' is – we need to check it out before we decide anything."

"We treat all hostiles with force," Newton started. "And that way we can cut through to survivors."

"Yes, Sarge," Foost agreed.

Later – On Mudhurst Lane, 1 mile South of Disley, 10 miles Southeast of Manchester.
The truck and the APC stopped on a hillside road. They ate supermarket sandwiches, huddled beside the truck. Foost and Conan took first watch. Foost sat on the roof of the truck, sweeping binoculars South and East. Conan sat on the roof of the APC, covering the North and West.

"I agree with Foost, cities will be totally fucked, Sarge," Munster said frankly. Foost heard him from the roof.

"What if you were in a city right-now?" Hastings countered.

"I–... I–..."

"You'd want help."

"Exactly. People will be stranded."

"Yeah. Trapped goodness-knows-where..."

"They'll be frightened."

"Most will've probably been killed. Or turned."

"We use extreme force."

Newton said, "In the end, we still have to act like soldiers... I can't fucking do anything else..."

Nahar saw a dot in the sky and pressed binoculars to his eyes. "I see a plane!..." he screamed, elated.

Newton stepped onto the back of the truck, hanging onto part of the frame that was built as metal ribbing covering the rear-end, and was sheathed in resilient plastic-coated canvas. A few drops of rain fell from the sky. A drop landed under Newton's eye as he swung to look at the point in the sky where Nahar's finger aimed.

Newton said immediately to Hastings, "Haste – Go to the airport and see if you can rescue the people on that plane... Even if it's just the pilot. He may come in handy... We'll push on into Manchester to see if there are any people there. We'll meet back here... It may take a couple of days to get in and get out, so... Make sure you get back here, and make sure you wait for us if we aren't back... We can't stand around debating about this. It's going on. And we have to act as fast as we can. It's," he said and checked his watched. "Nearly six... We've still got a few hours of daylight left."

Hastings nodded, and the group separated into two.

Later. On Wellington Road South, the A6, south of Stockport.
The APC pulled down the road. Newton looked out of the windows at the buildings around them: mostly residential.

Nahar was sat at the computer monitor behind the driver's seat, looking through the onboard cameras, switching from view to view automatically. Nahar paused the computer on one of the cameras, a high-specification, long-range camera with infra-red and night-vision capabilities. He zoomed in down the road and saw some lights in two of buildings half a kilometre ahead of them.

"Sarge, I've got some flashing lights ahead half a click..."

Newton stood by Foost in the driver's seat and looked through the windscreen. "Let's go, then."

Twenty minutes later.
Foost and Newton leapt out of the APC and ran alongside it. They saw a man and rushed towards him – it was Frank Lebeck.

They paused, aimed and shot the infected that were racing down the street towards Frank, using their silenced-machineguns. The bodies of the infected were thrown to the ground, or bounced off walls or cars.

Frank picked himself up then ran away from them.

Foost shot an infected through the head two metres from Frank, who scrambled to some fire-exit doors, then started banging on them. Foost could not make out what he was shouting.

"Be careful," Newton shouted to Foost. He could see Foost was alarmed by Frank's actions. "Be careful," he repeated. Foost nodded in agreement to his Sergeant.

Newton knelt to take careful aim and shot two more infected, aiming for the bridges of their noses, when the fire-exit doors burst open with a *boom* and Erin Fontein ran out of the building and into Frank's arms.

Foost shot the last infected through the cheek-bone, sending blood-red sunburst onto the side of the wall behind it.

Kevin Dunlevy and Tetsuo Katsushika stood in the fire-exit doorway with some other survivors.

Newton walked towards them, he said, "Let's get inside quick and have a chat..."

They started to walk inside. "I'll wait in the APC with Nahar, Sarge... Keep a radio-link open," Foost said.

Newton agreed with a nod and walked inside.

Foost turned away. He marched a few metres to the front-door and climbed into the APC.

The fire-exit doors slammed shut behind them.

A little later.
Nahar and Foost listened to a walkie-talkie, hearing Newton talk to Frank, Erin, Kevin, Tetsuo and three others in the office-building.

Foost said, "At least we're gonna hear the Sarge tell these people what he thinks is goin' on..."

Newton began, "From what we can ascertain, a viral or chemical attack has taken place... We don't know the extent of its reach... All communications are down... To be honest... Things look pretty-bad at the moment. Things are incredibly dangerous and lethal. But we have to stick together and help as many others as we can. Then get to safety." He looked around the group, continuing, "Bradford and Leeds were completely overrun and impenetrable. We had to drive straight by... We saw a plane in the sky over Manchester, so half our squad went to the airport to rescue any survivors... While we came into the city... I don't think we can make it any further – to the centre... We saw your lights, and came here... I take it this is all of you?... Okay..."

"How many soldiers have you got?" one of the survivors said. His name was LAWRENCE GAIT, 44 year old Welshman. He was hunched, with a back almost crooked, shoulders slouched over the edges of his frame. His face looked up from under a mop of long, straight black hair. He had a weasely face, a long witch's nose, arched brows and sunken dark eyes that had purple rings around tops and bottoms.

The other people that had been sheltering with Tetsuo were BEN STANTON, 32 year old Englishman, and DAWN HALL, 25 year old Englishwoman. Ben had preppy good-looks that went with his slick-shined blonde hair and grey fitted-suit. He was one of the young executive types that showed CEOs, officials, delegates and ministers the car they were renting and how its specification matched their desire. He was sharp, educated and played a lot of sports in his free time. Dawn had long gingery-blonde hair, curled at the ends so that it would bob up and down when she walked. She was slim and attractive and wore a neat black business-suit. She was pretty and had a girl-next-door disposition about her, smart and impulsive but friendly and bubbly. She was Ben's assistant.

"Six," Newton answered. "Six soldiers left from my squad." He exhaled and looked around the group. Their faces were even more ashen and perplexed than his squad had been when he had last checked them.

"Don't mind me saying, but... What the fuck're we gonna do with only six soldiers?!" Kevin shouted.

Tetsuo spoke up – he said, "Seven. I was a soldier in Japan."

"Great. That's fantastic! A samurai," Kevin sneered.

"Hey, be nice," Frank said pointedly to Kevin.

"He's old! What use will he be?"

"Hey!" Erin said angrily.

"We have to work together. And put a lid on any animosity for the time being... When this is all done, you two can fight it out in an arena for all I care... Right-now, my only cares are for the survivors out-there, and keeping you safe. And getting back to the rest of my squad."

"Thank you," Erin said and touched Newton's shoulder.

Newton half-smiled.

"We should be fucking grateful!" Frank snapped. He beamed at Kevin, who looked away sulkily. "This man... These men did not have to come to rescue us!"

"Look. Just let me know... Is this all of you?"

"Yes," Tetsuo answered.

"Well, we've got to get out of here."

Two days later.
The truck and the APC were parked next to each other, on the empty hillside road. Munster sat on the roof of the truck, keeping watch, turning a rifle in his hands. The remainder of the survivors – Kevin, Tetsuo, Lawrence, Ben, Dawn and nine others – sat between the vehicles in a makeshift camp with two tents and a small camping cooker, with several suitcases, bags of food and linen dotted around them.

Nicholas 'Brodie' Brodeson sat with Foost in the back of the truck. "This is all fucked," Brodie said with a sigh.

"It's no picnic."

Foost bit into a sandwich.

"I hated picnics."

Foost smiled, chewing the bread. "I haven't been to any since I was a kid," he said around the mouthful.

"My girlfriend and I had a couple, back in New York. In Central Park... Ex-girlfriend..."

"Huh... There's none of that anymore," Foost said finally swallowing the remnants of the bite.

"No. I guess not."

"At least she might be dead now... Was it a bad break-up?"

"Ish..." Brodie conceded. "It does give me a nice feeling inside thinking that..."

"What?"

"That she might be dead... Or a mindless zombie."

Foost took another huge bite. "When this is all over, I'll have a picnic with you."

"Great. Cheers. Great. Thanks."

"No worries."

Newton climbed out of the APC and crossed directly to Hastings, who smoked a cigarette with Kara Schofield at the back of the truck, overlooking the road that swung away down the hill.

"Can I have a word?" Newton asked.

Hastings nodded.

They walked away from the group, a few metres into the field.

"You okay?" Hastings asked.

"I can't believe we rescued so few," Newton said.

"The airport was overrun."

"So was the city. We barely made it in and out. Thank god a few people saw the truck and came out of hiding."

"There were so many of the infected... Man, what're we gonna do?"

"The pilot was gone seconds after we got there. Couldn't get to him..."

Kara followed the sounds of their voices and paced to meet them.

"Danny, this is Kara," Hastings said, before Kara had even reached them.

"Pleased to meet you," Newton said, taking her hand and shaking it.

"Likewise," she stated.

"Can we help you with something?" Newton asked.

"I'd like to know what the plan is."

"There isn't a plan."

Hastings watched Kara for a reaction, but she let nothing out. "We should move south," she said slowly.

"Why do you think that? We need to find as many survivors as we can. And help them."

"As long as we do that, we'll lose more people than gain," she said matter-of-factly.

Hastings nodded slowly.

Newton said nothing, when Brodie walked towards them, with Bright following two paces behind him. The Texan reset his hat on his head, curling a few stray strands of grey-blonde hair from sticking to his head with sweat. Brodie stood awkwardly, trying to convince the others of his confidence, but failed.

"South should be the choice."

Hastings looked at Newton in agreement, but said nothing.

"If we go to Birmingham Hospital, or the university, I might be able to... I–... I might–... --be able to synthesise an anti-virus – if that's even possible," Brodie said awkwardly. "I looked at a couple of the corpses while we were in the airport... After I lost all sense that they were alive..."

"What d'you mean by that?"

"Well... After Allen shot one – shot one in the chest.. It was still capable of movement. Limited movement though. They did react to their wounds, but something drove them on for a short period of time. Until the injury killed them."

"Those bastards kept on going," Bright added. "And going, and going..."

"Meaning?" Hastings asked.

"That means there's hyper-coagulation happening in their blood... Their system is still running with potentially life-threatening wounds, for extended periods of time... They're able to bypass some vital systems or their extremities... And they still move! They are definitely still human, so shooting their heart is lethal, but shooting their arm, where a normal person would stop and react to the pain, they ignore it and keep coming."

"I shot several, an' they kept comin'," Bright said.

Both Newton and Hastings stared at Brodie, as did Kara.

"I–... I worked in a lab... Working in bio-chem... Um... A biological and chemical, um, laboratory... I think, if I can get to a hospital or a university or to some laboratory, I can check out the virus up-close... I'm not promising anything. I am not promising any cure..."

"Then we'll try for Birmingham," Newton asserted.

"And if we can't get there?" Kara questioned.

"We try somewhere else."

"Um," Brodie stammered. "There is one more thing..."

"What is it?" Newton asked.

"If we... If I don't find a way... Then our safest bet is to shoot them in the head... Or heart."

"Noted."

Four days later. The outskirts of Birmingham.
The APC and the truck were parked on a stubby wooded and grassy hill, north of Birmingham. The vehicles were positioned a short distance from the centre of the field, pointed toward the exit gate. The afternoon sun shone down on them, baking the APC and truck, exsiccating the short grass.

In the back of the APC, Brodie sat with Newton. "It's very difficult talking about the chemistry of a super-virus," Brodie stated. Sweat dotted both of their foreheads; a drip fell from Brodie's sideburn.

"Then I hope you'll be able to work some magic if we find a lab."

Kara listened to them, when Bright walked to the back. He leaned into the space and said, "Your boys're on their way back..." Bright nodded to his right, over his shoulder.

Newton climbed to the exit and left Brodie with Kara, who, after a short moment, climbed out of the APC to follow Newton. She had a determined expression on her face. Brodie sat alone.

"Fantastic!" he murmured to himself. "Everyone's left me on my own!..."

He let out a deep breath.

A cooling breeze met Newton as he stepped out into the air. He started for the shade of the woods that lined the field, where others were gathered. He felt Kara following him.

Hastings and Conan jogged up the hill to the group that were waiting to meet them – Newton, Kara, Bright and Tetsuo. Hastings measured their blank faces as he trudged through a patch of drying mud to stand in report in front of them. His eyes moved to Newton.

"Birmingham is completely overrun..! There's no way of going into the centre," he said with a deep frown.

Newton wanted to vent his anger by punching the truck-door, but he looked across at it, thirty metres away. "Fuck!" he blurted. He pressed his hand to a tree and wiped sweat from his face. He glanced to check for any of the others' reactions, but there were none – everyone felt exactly the same. "That's not good news," he admitted.

"Then we make camp somewhere," Bright suggested. "For a night or two. Recoup. Gather more food..."

"Where? Where? Where will be safe?" Conan asked twitchily.

Kara immediately responded with confidence, "A church."

Newton's eyebrows raised in surprise.

"Then tomorrow we cut through the bottom of Birmingham," Kara added, "so we can see if there is anyone around..."

Newton nodded.

Later.
The APC and the truck drove across a roughly-hewn field and pulled up by the grounds of a medieval church, which had a large graveyard surrounding it, and a hedgerow and fence around its perimeter.

Everybody got out of the vehicles in silence and assembled between them.

Munster and Nahar kept watch across the back-fields, checking the direction they had just come from, and Hastings and Foost kept watch across the graveyard, kneeling with their rifles raised and eyes to telescopic-sights.

In between the guarding-soldiers were: Newton, Bright and Brodie at the front, Kevin, Frank, Erin and Tetsuo behind them, Kara, Conan, Lawrence, Ben and Dawn a little further back, NANCY CRAFT, 56 year old Thai woman; JAMES KHALIQ, 28 year old English Muslim; WILSON ITUS, 39 year old Englishman of Nigerian descent; ALAN CREDDLE, 52 year old Englishman; and eight others forming the back. Nancy was small and wore comfortable clothes – a pair of jeans, tracksuit-top and trainers. James was average and lean, and wore a grey shirt with jeans and trainers. Wilson was tall and well-built, and wore a black hoodie, white t-shirt, grey jeans and white trainers. Alan was average but stood with a crooked back, hunched over, and wore an eight-year-old grey suit, charity shop shirt and tie, bright red socks and scuffed shoes.

Nancy stood with James and Wilson, while Alan stood with the others.

Newton gave out the orders, "Munster, Conan – you-two are sweeping the graveyard and getting to the front-door. Check if it's open, if it's locked, there must be a side-door, use that... Hastings, Foost – you-two are backing-them-up... After that, Tetsuo, Kara – you're up... Then we all move... Nahar – you're keeping watch, get up on the truck roof..."

Nahar nodded and clambered up the side of the truck as Munster and Conan moved to the fence and hedgerow, poised to climb over.

Newton watched as Hastings and Foost got in place behind the others.

Munster and Conan leapt over the fence then pushed through the hedgerow, and moved into the graveyard, pointing their rifles in every direction. They reached the side of the church and made their way to the two oversized, oak front-doors.

As Conan crouched by the door and Munster watched his back, Hastings and Foost made it to the side of the church building. They started along the rough stone wall, moving to the front-doors and their comrades.

Conan reached for the handle and breathed in, as Munster held his gun ready. The handle turned and the door swung open, revealing a small, darkened foyer, which seemed empty. Munster poked his head inside when one of the infected rushed out and head-butted him, knocking him backwards. It blood-puked on both Conan and Munster, infecting them with directed splashes.

Munster fell back on his behind and rolled to a stop, hacking and coughing violently. "No! God no!" he screamed around gargles and groans.

Conan pitched over and started convulsing instantly – bloody splatter gushed from his mouth and nostrils as if a balloon filled with gore had burst inside him.

Hearing the commotion, Hasting and Foost sprinted around the side of the church, as another infected exited from the front-door. It barged-passed Conan, stepping on his hand with a heavy *crunch*, and launched down the wall at Hastings.

Foost opened fire on the infected. The bullets *whistled* passed its head, not finding their target.

It reached him tremendously quickly, throwing a punch outward, snapping the silencer from the barrel of the gun. The gun was knocked aside and the infected punched Foost in the chest and abdomen, as Hastings brought his silenced-machinegun up. The infected slapped out at Hastings. The first infected circled back to both of them. It frenziedly beat out at them, leaking blood over their uniforms. In the frantic attack, Foost swung his rifle around letting off a few rounds, explosive and loud, trying to blow the head off the shoulders of the infected. The sound of gunfire alerted every-single one of the nearby infected to their presence.

"Oh, shit," Foost muttered from the ground. "Oh shit!" He stabbed the infected in the eye with a short-blade knife, digging it in and twisting it.

Hastings punched the other infected aside and shot it through the skull with a silenced-pistol. The infected was thrown to the ground, landing with a *crunch* on the corner of a broken gravestone. He caught Foost's arm above the wrist and yanked him to his feet.

"Fuck me, that was frightening!"

"You've felt worse," Hastings joked.

Seconds earlier. At the APC.
Newton heard the gunfire and reacted immediately, he said, "Oh fuck! Move up, move up!.. But, slowly!"

Tetsuo and Kara instantly leapt over the fence and dashed towards the church, moving in to pincer the side-door, as Newton leaned in close to Brodie. He said, "You move when I move, kid..."

Nahar, who was watching over the fields and had climbed to the roof of the APC, shouted to Newton, "We have multiple in-coming on the horizon, Sarge.. I count eight hostiles... And more coming now!"

"Everyone over the wall! Now!" Newton shouted to the others. He turned to look up at Nahar. "Open fire on the hostiles," he screamed. "Then lock yourself in the APC over-night – and keep a radio link open!"

"Yes, Sergeant!" Nahar replied. He climbed across the APC's roof and lay flat. He rested a 7.62mm L96 sniper's rifle on a tripod and aimed at the first target.

Nahar opened fire.

An infected, dressed in jogging-clothes, dashed down the muddy slope kicking up clumps of grassy-turf. The bullet blasted through the jaw and neck and skull, taking it down.

Another infected, dressed in everyday-wear, hobbled across and down the hill. The bullet took the top of the its head off, everything from the eyebrows up became a bloody mist.

Another infected, dressed in ripped golfing-attire, hop-jogged through the mud. The bullet passed through the chest, above the left nipple, blowing out the heart and lungs.

Nahar watched as even more infected charged over the rise. He counted eleven more. He sat up on the APC and took aim with his silenced-machinegun, as they drew closer and closer.

At the church.
The church came to life as thirteen infected raced outside into the graveyard. Hastings grabbed Foost and they narrowly escaped being blood-puked on and infected, as one the creatures charged towards them. Tetsuo and Kara stopped, aimed and fired, as Hastings and Foost retreated to their position.

Tetsuo pulled Foost behind a grave, as he busily unscrewed the broken silencer from the end of his barrel. His hands shook involuntarily. Tetsuo passed him a replacement, which he struggled to screw onto the rifle-barrel.

Kara shot three infected in their eyes, dropping them.

An infected leapt onto Foost, but he fought back, as Conan rose, blood gushing from his nostrils, and Kara killed him with a shot to the temple. Conan dropped to his knees and fell flat.

The infected gang rushed at Hastings, Foost, Tetsuo and Kara, when Nahar pressed the truck-horn once, then climbed into the APC through the roof-hatch, locking it behind him.

Newton saw Nahar give a final wave before dropping into the APC then yanking the hatch shut, when eight infected appeared, thundering through the hedgerow in the field beyond, about a hundred and fifty metres away, and raced in the direction of the receding figures dashing toward the church.

Newton, Brodie and Bright jumped the fence and dashed across the graveyard, following Frank, Erin, Kevin and the others, who had slowed and shuffled in a wide shambolic mob across the grounds. Ben stood to one side of the group. "Come on! Come on!" he yelled. "We've gotta move faster than this!"

An infected lumbered along the side of the APC and fixed to climb the ladder at the back. It took several long moments to turn and lift its face; its eyes locked and dried in one central position. At first it stumbled to gain purchase on the ladder, barely detecting it. Its hands were wet with fresh, bright blood and were slippery to grip the rungs. It heaved on its body, both of its scrawny biceps tensing like diseased, purpling rope under the top layer of pale, almost-opaque skin. It lifted a foot onto the lowest rung.

Newton chanced a look back at the APC and saw the infected scrambling onto the roof.

Alan sneered from the middle of the group.

"Quick! Quick!" Wilson called from the back.

Brodie was not coping, he felt his heart race and sweat soak him, as Kevin wilted and began to freak out a few metres away.

Kevin whined, a high-pitched desperate sound. He held his hands over his ears, pressing hard, then crouched behind a large headstone when bullets began to *whistle* around his position.

Bright grabbed Brodie's collar and hoisted him out of harm's way, saving him from a wave of bloody puke, and shot the accountable infected. The infected was thrown away with the force of the bullet, a gust of wind exhaled from its mouth. Brodie gasped, looking at the huddle of survivors, loosely following behind them, scattered and shell-shocked, wavering on a dozen spots.

"Come on, you guys!" Bright yelled forcefully. He started forward, leading the group, dragging Brodie at his side. Nancy, James, Dawn, Lawrence and the others were panicking, grouping together around some grave-stones between Newton, Brodie and Bright who dashed to join them, and Hastings, Foost, Kara and Tetsuo who had formed a front line of defence. Ben and Wilson tried to usher them on from within the huddle.

Alan crept through the group, looking for the best possible way ahead.

Munster rose to his feet unstable, infected. The other infected spread out across the graveyard. Each one seemed focused on finding one of the survivors. They stalked around, hissing, moaning, sniffing, hacking and growling.

"Come on, everyone! Get up and move! Now!" Newton shouted, trying to get some control back on the situation. He knew he had to do something, get these people safe, but they were spread out too thinly. He waved, motioning for them to move forward, between taking strategic shots at the infected.

Hastings, Foost, Tetsuo and Kara helped the others from the church. They killed three of the infected that were honing in on them.

Two of the infected that had been inside the church shuffled toward Bright and Brodie, as they backed away to the side-door. Bright raised his pistol and pulled the trigger, but the magazine was empty.

"What do we do now?" Brodie murmured.

"Stay with me," Bright assured him, stepping in front of his companion.

Kara reloaded her rifle and aimed it at the two infected closing in on Bright and Brodie. She shot with precision. Her one and only bullet planted itself in the nearest ear, exploding the far side of its head, and taking off the skull-plate of the farther infected. Blood sprayed the church wall in blossoms and blooms of dark wine-red.

Across the back-field, the eight infected that had been drawn to the sound increased by several more. They did not seem capable of climbing the fence at first and seemed impeded. Then one of the infected got inventive and adventurous and clambered over. It was quickly followed by the others.

Several more infected appeared over the crest of the hill.

Newton, Bright and Wilson shot at the infected as they climbed over the fence, when an extremely fast-moving creature appeared from within the church and broke through the line and divided the group. The infected barged into the middle of the group. It blood-puked on Nancy, splashing her and filling her mouth with vile, oozing blood. She spat out as much of the blood as she could and coughed violently, hacking and vomiting. She curled into a ball on the ground, gripping her stomach, convulsing.

One of the survivors broke and ran for it, but was tackled by another infected and then blood-puked on. The man sputtered and coughed, wincing and groaning, feeling pain knifing down his body. He wailed, crawling away on all-fours to the exit into the car-park.

Hastings shot the infected, then stepped over and aimed at the survivor. He rolled over, sensing Hastings' presence and held his arms up, pleading around deep, heavy coughs. "Please…"

Hastings shot the man.

Tetsuo grappled with another infected. Kara dashed to him and helped him to kill it, stabbing it through the eye with an army-issue knife.

One of the field-infected hurdled over the fence, leaping it in a single, athletic bound.

"Everyone! Get inside the church!" Newton commanded.

Foost killed the final infected near the entrance-door and ran to the opening. Then he and Hastings dashed inside.

The remaining people followed them into the church: James, Tetsuo and Wilson, Frank and Erin, Newton, Lawrence, Dawn, Ben and Wilson, Alan and four others.

Then the door slammed shut.

Hastings lifted a heavy table and with the help of Foost, pushed it against the front-door, wedging it closed.

A momentarily lull of silence fell over the large, impressive stone echo-space.

Newton looked around the room, at the remaining people. He sighed, then a thought popped into his head. "Where's Brodie?"

"Where's Allen and Kara, too?" Frank added with a concerned shrug.

Hastings sprinted to the side-door and threw it open. Newton dashed a few paces behind him, skidding to a stop and lifting his silenced-machinegun behind his friend's shoulder. Sunlight beamed into the small side-entranceway.

Brodie, Bright and Kara rushed inside and helped Hastings to force the door shut, as three of the infected struck the back side of the door.

In the graveyard.
Kevin sat behind a grave, crying, watching one of the other survivors being infected.

The infected crawled and scampered, bounded and scrambled, as gushes of blood poured from its open, slack mouth. The infected blood-puked on itself, grappling with a headstone to stand. It lurched across the graveyard and out of sight.

Kevin hugged his knees, sobbing and whimpering.

Inside the church.

The group huddled in the central aisle of the church. They looked around the interior from where they stood.

"We've got to check every body. Put a bullet in everyone. In the head," Newton ordered them.

The infected outside the church *banged* on the front- and side-doors violently, a ceaseless random drum-beat.

Bright said, "Looks like we're stuck here for the time bein'…"

CHAPTER 6 - HOLE - London

REGINALD 'REG' HERON, 40 year old Englishman of Nigerian descent – gazed around an art-gallery, studying several pieces of art closely and others from an aloof distance, when he received a phone-call. The Apple iPhone vibrated and *buzzed* in his inside suit-jacket pocket. He was tall and statuesque with a dark-bronze colour to his skin. He had a serious but shy manner and spoke softly and quietly. Reg was neatly attired; he wore a tan mohair overcoat over a black suit, white shirt, ice-blue tie and smart black shoes.

Static then *beeps* and *boops* sounded, then: "Please state your full name," a computerised-voice asked flatly.

"Reginald Achilles Vernon Heron."

"Please state your identification number."

"Eight-two-two-six-six-seven."

"Which station were you responsible for the design?" the voice asked.

"Four."

"Please state your current location."

"The Michael Bleich Gallery. London."

The phone went dead.

Reg put it away, replacing it in the inside suit-jacket pocket of his overcoat. He looked at his blue Storm Desert Laser wristwatch and walked out of the art-gallery. He slipped the phone out of his pocket and dropped it in the aluminium trash-bin near the exit without being noticed.

A few other patrons sauntered around the gallery.

As Reg left the gallery a tramp entered, overlooking him. The tramp was a small, hairy man with an extremely dirty Parka coat on, with the matted fur-lined hood up, pulled over his greasy, tanned face. The tramp was expressionless, eyes emotionless. The tramp stalked through the gallery hastily, moving through the six continuous, connected rooms with distinct purpose. His eyes snapped from patron to patron, scanning them robotically.

When the tramp saw a man that looked remarkably like Reg – another tall, smartly-dressed black man wearing a tan mohair overcoat over a grey Armani suit – he pulled out a four-inch knife and executed the look-alike viciously. The tramp stabbed the lookalike under the chin, stabbing through the tongue and up through the palate, then beat at the man's throat, punching deep slices and slashes through the soft meat of the neck.

The man collapsed to the ground and blood sprayed the gallery's polished wooden floor. The man's Salvatore Ferragamo *Raveena* penny loafer's kicked and skittered in a broken, wide and bloody spirograph on the shiny deck.

A number of other patrons dashed away from the murder, emitting screams and gasps.

Moments later.
Reg walked into the London Underground, completely oblivious to the scene at the gallery two streets behind him.

A siren sounded.

Seconds later a police car *screamed* passed the entrance, lights spinning and siren *wailing*.

Reg stomped down the escalator, passing a few tourists laden with shopping-bags.

Minutes later.
Reg found a vacant seat on an Underground train headed East and sat down. Opposite Reg sat GLENN MEAKINS, 54 year old Englishman. He was a large, bear-like man with a husky build, and heavyset face. He had a friendly, gentle manner; smile and laughter lines criss-crossed his face. Bushy eyebrows overcast beady but alert eyes, broad cheeks and a heavy jaw. He was bulky with thick arms and tree-trunk legs. He wore a rugby-jersey, faded denim jeans and steel-toe-cap boots. Paint, oil and grease stained his jeans and boots, his work clothes, but the jersey was immaculate, ironed and creased in straight lines.

Glenn massaged the back of his neck, feeling a twinge easing between his rough bear-paws. "Christ," he murmured to himself, squeezing and pushing against a knot. He glanced along the train carriage, at thirty or more passengers, wincing as he pressed harder on the knot.

Earlier that day. Wembley.
Glenn stood in the kitchen of his home; a 1930s two-storey house with a bay window upstairs and down on the front. A cordless phone was clamped between his ear and shoulder. He spread Flora thickly onto two thin slices of toast, before placing thick slabs of cheese across the first piece.

"Alright... Alright, then... I'll be at the site later," he said, "after I've been to see my mum in her old people's home..."

He listened for a long moment, hearing the foreman speaking between noises from a building site.

"Alright, Gaz, catch you up in a bit."

Minutes later.
Glenn said goodbye to his wife, kissed her cheek, then walked out of the house, taking a bag of builder's-tools with him. He stepped onto the pavement and avoided a trick-slab that had a pool of dirty water resting under and around it.

He wandered down the road, lightly swinging the bag.
The sun warmed the skin on his forehead and his lower arms.

The present.
The Underground train jolted, pushing forward then juddering back a few inches, then started moving. Glenn used both hands to massage his neck under each ear, pinching and pulling at the skin and muscle. He looked along the train at two men in business-suits.

The two men, two yuppies – RUSSELL CARTWRIGHT, 29 year old Englishman – and WAYNE BIGNALL, 28 year old Englishman – talked loudly. Russell had an average-build, sloped shoulders and a slight potbelly. He had a sneering, careless face with deep, assuming eyes. He wore a pin-stripe dark blue suit, baby-blue shirt and black shoes. Wayne was shorter than Russell, but larger and more burdened with weight. He had curly blonde hair, slicked back across his head with excessive, perfumed hair-gel. Wayne wore a dark-green suit with a charcoal-grey shirt and brown suede shoes.

"I can't believe you didn't fuckin' make it to The Precinct," Russell spat, poking Wayne in the shoulder. "You fuck!"

"I was so drunk, you have no idea!"

"Ha! You fuckin' lightweight!"

"I couldn't help it, for fuck's sake, I was out drinking earlier with Clifton and Reyes!"

"Clifton is a fuckin' sissy! And Reyes is a smelly shit!"

"Hey!" Wayne said uneasily.

"Hey, what?! I don't like those fuckin' dopes..."

Another man – ABDUL KASHIM, 29 year old Englishman of Indian descent – gritted his teeth, listening to the conversation. Abdul was distracted from his thoughts by the yuppies' noise. He looked at them with thinly-veiled contempt, then looked away shyly. Abdul was a slight man with a skinny frame and long, bandy arms and legs. He had warm, caring eyes under heavy, thick eyebrows and thick-glass spectacles. He was dressed neatly in a light-grey suit, black shirt, black tie and black shoes. He clutched a suitcase-satchel close to his body.

"Where did you go, in the end?" Russell asked in an accusatory tone.

"We didn't get far..."

Abdul pinched the bridge of his nose, holding his breath for five seconds.

Earlier that day. Chichester.
Abdul awoke in his single bed to the sound of his alarm's *beeps*. He pushed the alarm-button and the small bedroom fell silent. It was sparsely decorated with only three family photos on the wall near his wardrobe.

He got out of bed, showered, shaved, brushed his teeth, got dressed then combed his hair.

He picked up the suitcase-satchel that he had packed last night and left his empty but homely flat.

On his way out the door, Abdul telephoned his brother's secretary to assure her that he would be at the appointment later.

He listened patiently as the secretary reiterated the appointment details and Abdul was grateful for the confirmation. "Thank you," he said, then hung up with a gentle push of the disconnect button.

Abdul walked to the end of his road and got in a taxi that waited for him there.

Later.
Abdul sat on a main-line train, staring out of the window. He looked at his watch, it was eleven o'clock. He stared out of the window, his leg shaking nervously.

The West Sussex countryside *whizzed* by on the other side of the glass.

The present.
The Underground train jolted again and the lights flickered on and off. Glenn looked at some of the other passengers, and noticed Abdul – his leg was shaking nervously. Glenn drifted from Abdul, his eyes wandering and drifting along the carriage.

DUNCAN BERRY, 30 year old Englishman – looked around the carriage, drunk. He was a good-looking man with sharp, small features and a full head of thick, dark hair. He had high cheekbones, a straight nose, perfect teeth and sculpted eyebrows. He was tall, muscular and athletic. He wore a fitted black suit, white shirt, no tie, black belt and black shoes. Duncan's head rolled on his neck, swinging a little too freely and obviously not to be recognised by the other passengers as being intoxicated. The lights blinked on and off again. He rubbed his face and kneaded his temples with his palms. He felt warm inside; the alcohol sloshed in his stomach, giving rise to a tiny burp, which he tried to suppress without any luck.

People up and down the carriage started coughing – reacting to something – then a few coughed up blood. Other passengers took notice – standing or moving away from them. Only two passengers checked for responses, then pulses – Glenn was one of them. More people started getting agitated and coughed more and more. Some people choked to death, unable to breathe from coughing up too much thick, red oozing blood. Many people died quietly in their seats.

Glenn reached out to help some of the people, but hesitated, as they coughed and expired in front of him.

Abdul stared at the person opposite him. They looked like they had fallen asleep, except for the masses of blood draining out of their mouth and nostrils.

Reg looked on blankly at the people around him. He checked his watch.

Duncan stared at the dying and the dead, completely apathetic, when the train suddenly *screeched* to a halt. The lights blinked on and off several times. Everyone jerked forward. A dozen hands shot out to grab anything nearby that would stabilise the person attached. An eerie silence flooded the tunnel.

Further down the train from Duncan – MELANIE CANNON, 17 year old English girl – started to freak out, looking around at the horrific scene playing-out in front of her. She was petite with square-shoulders and a small frame. She had a pretty, cute nose between dazzling green eyes, under long-coils of streaky-brown hair. She wore a carmine-pink vest, three-quarter length denim jeans and white Nike trainers. She pulled her legs close to her body and whimpered and sobbed.

Duncan glanced at Melanie, then looked away.

Glenn finally checked the pulses of a few people near him. He found no trace of a heartbeat in any of the bodies.

Russell and Wayne stood up, with Abdul frozen to his seat near them, when one of the infected came to life and attacked Wayne, vomiting blood on him and beating him with clenched fists. Wayne, stunned and disoriented, was flooded and painted with blood.

Abdul watched, perplexed with fear, but then got to his feet slowly.

Russell punched the infected in the face and shoved him back down the carriage, as HEIDI PETERSON, 21 year old Swedish young-woman – climbed onto the seat and pressed her back against the window of the train. She nervously fell silent and wished to be invisible. She was beautiful with platinum-blonde hair long over her shoulders, piercing, intense blue eyes and full, poppy-red lips. She was tall, slim and model-fit. She had kind, sensitive eyes and a calm, dimpled smile. She wore a fitted black business-suit with a pencil skirt, a crimson-red blouse and crimson-red Garrison Handley shoes.

Glenn and Reg moved down the carriage, watching the fight further down the train.

The infected managed to punch Russell and winded him, as Abdul shoved it away from them.

Glenn grabbed a hammer out of his bag and ran down the train to help Russell and Abdul, but as he neared, the infected gargled and blood-puked on the ground in front of him. A little splatter wet the steel toecap of his right boot. Glenn, Russell and Abdul semi-circled around the infected, backing it into a corner.

In a millisecond-lull, the infected vomited blood on itself, then went to charge at Russell. It stretched out its arms, hands clenched to fists, then its mouth dropped open. It took a leap forward.

Russell grabbed the hammer out of Glenn's hand and killed the infected with five quick blows to the head. He paced back, pushing between Glenn and Abdul. "Jesus!" he groaned.

"What on earth is going on?" Glenn muttered.

Abdul crouched and picked up Wayne's arm at his wrist. "This man has no pulse," he reported, looking from Russell to Glenn and back again. "Your friend?"

"What d'you mean 'no-pulse', you fuckin' asshole?!" Russell screamed, barrelling forward. Glenn put out his arm and it blocked Russell's path to Abdul.

Abdul stared back at Russell blankly. He blinked twice, brow furrowed.

"Huh?!" Russell shouted. "Huh?!" but it was obvious he could not pass Glenn's arm, nor did he really want to.

Abdul once again blinked, unable to gauge how far Russell's posturing would go.

Melanie stood up, panting for breath, and looked at the hammered-in head of the infected. Her eyes widened. "Oh my god!" she whimpered. "You killed him! You killed that man!"

Russell beamed a menacing look at the young woman.

Earlier that day. In The Aquarium night-club – 1:41am.
Melanie was with four other girls – Sky, Amber, Lydia and Erica – dancing in the midst of a vast cloud of fake-smoke, bathed in flashing lights, on an oblong dance-floor in a packed night-club. Beads of sweat fell from the ceiling onto and around the dance-floor, as a cloud of moisture rose and fell above the swell of dancers.

The dance-floor was a crowded parade of drunken-dancers.

Melanie sipped a cocktail, when Amber hugged her tightly, causing Melanie to spill her drink down Amber's back.

"Shit!" Amber groaned. "Thanks a bunch!"

Melanie laughed uncontrollably.

A young man in a dark suit stood at the bar a few metres behind the dance-floor. His eyes did not leave Melanie, as she pranced and hopped on the spot, flapping her arms in the air.

Amber dipped her fingers in her own drink and flicked the droplets at Melanie.

Later.
Melanie and the other girls exited the night-club. Their shoes *clip-clopped* on the pavement outside.

Other revellers spread out, moving down the road in a slow march.

A dozen night-club patrons stood, idling, at a queue by a taxi rank

A little later.
The girls stumbled drunkenly along a quiet suburban street arm-in-arm singing, holding each other up.

Melanie and Sky laughed hysterically.

Later.
They walked through a quiet, empty park. Lydia teetered on her high-heels then fell over onto the grass and the others laughed. All of the girls moved to help their fallen friend, grabbing her arms by the wrists and hoisting her back onto her heels.

    Melanie giggled, holding her stomach.

Later.
They arrived on the doorstep of Lydia's house.

    None of the girls were wearing their shoes. They carried their heels by their ankle-straps, swinging with each step, with the heels occasionally *clicking* together between elbow and handbag.

    Lydia struggled to push the key in the lock, but managed on the third attempt.

    Amber looked huffily around the road.

    Melanie and Sky laughed, as Lydia pushed the front-door wide open.

Later.
Lydia's hippie-mum, with a full-head of thick uneven dreadlocks and wearing a flower-embroidered dressing-gown, made the girls breakfast in the small, bright and colourful kitchen. She cooked eggs, bacon and mushrooms whilst bread toasted; a spliff clamped in between her fingers the whole duration. She made a large percolator to the brim with hot coffee, as the girls took turns to shower.

    Melanie chewed the corner of a piece of toast, dipping it into a broken egg-yolk.

Later.
Melanie washed in the shower. She thought about her bed, as she ran her fingers through her shoulder-length hair, squeezing shampoo into the water. It would not be long before she got home, only a few hours – three tube changes and she'd be nearly there. Within three hours she would be lying down on her soft mattress, wrapping her duvet tightly around her body. She felt tired, but alcohol, Red Bull and the final traces of speedy ecstasy were still keeping her slightly buzzed. She blinked tightly as steaming-hot water washed down her head.

    She rubbed her temples, letting the water soak her face and the crown of her head.

Later.
Melanie exited the kitchen, kissing each of her friends and Lydia's mother, then walked to the front-door where Lydia waited for her. She was happy to be wearing fresh clothes. She kissed Lydia on the cheek and gave her a small hug.

    "Take care, babe," Lydia said.

    "You too, Lyd," Melanie replied and walked away down to the road, waving back to her friend.

    Lydia stood on the threshold, waving at Melanie's diminishing form.

Later.
Melanie walked into a music shop implanted in the side of a London Underground station. She perused a few DVDs, then lost interest and moved to the tiny section of books. She picked up a copy of *Jubilee Junction* by John Ramsay, read the back cover, then slotted it back in place between several other books.

    She sauntered to the exit and left the shop, turning to the barriers. She swiped her Oyster card and the barriers opened with a *clunk*. She walked through and started for the escalator down to the platforms.

    Melanie stepped onto the escalator and relaxed. It led down to the tunnels of the London Underground, for trains to the West and East.

Later.
Melanie got on an Underground train that arrived seven minutes later, headed East.

She filed between several people and found a seat. She crossed her legs and arms and rested her head against the window-glass.

The doors *hissed* then rolled closed.

The train jerked to a start and picked up speed, heading into the tunnels.

Melanie's head vibrated against the glass, as the train juddered along the tracks.

The present.
Melanie turned to look at Reg and Heidi, as SONNY HALLETT, 29 year old English hair-dresser of Italian descent – stood up. He was short and stocky, heavily tanned and oily-haired. He had a streetwise swagger and his hips swung as he stepped into the middle of the train. He wore a camel-brown leather jacket over a tight black t-shirt, dark-denim jeans and tan-leather Hush Puppies that were stitched like moccasins.

Sonny had a slight smirk on his face. He glared around the carriage.

Melanie could not stop herself from shaking. She gripped her own arms, trying to force herself still.

Reg backed away towards one of the exit-doors. He peered back at the next carriage, then stepped nearer to the door, shielding himself from sight behind Glenn and Melanie's huddled forms.

The lights flickered off, then came back on again after a moment.

Earlier that day. Chelsea.
Sonny talked on his mobile-phone as he strode down the road.

"Yes, sweetie, yes... Of course... After you pick up the kids, I'll bring us back a takeaway..." he said cheerily. "Love you, hun, bye."

He hung up the phone and switched the setting to Silent.

He swung across the clear road and walked into a restaurant – *Carlo's Ristorante*.

Sonny crossed to a table and kissed a beautiful woman, then sat down in front of her. "Hey, gorgeous... How are you?"

Later.
Sonny exited The *Palmerston Hotel,* stepping down the entrance-steps and hopping two feet to the pavement. He turned with a whirl, then started off down the road. He carried his camel-brown leather jacket, balled up in his hand. He put on a pair of fake Ray Ban sunglasses, pulling his phone out of his pocket. Without even turning it off silent he called back a Missed Call that showed up on his screen.

"Hey, gorgeous... I saw you rang, I haven't checked the message yet – you about in half an hour, hah?"

The present.
The lights flickered throughout the length of the train, off and on through each carriage in turn.

Melanie stared at everyone, losing control, freaking out. She pled, "What's going on? Is it an attack? What's happening?"

Duncan, sitting behind her, replied slowly, "It's the plague."

"What?!" she said exasperatedly.

Reg turned to Duncan, and they exchanged a look. Duncan shrugged.

Heidi could not take her eyes from the dead body of the infected at Russell's feet, or Wayne's body. She looked at Glenn, Russell and Abdul – she said, "What happened to that man?"

"He was spewin'-up blood, and... He wanted to get it on us..." Russell began, when an infected Wayne got to his feet.

"He's moving! He's standing up!..." Abdul yelled, backing away.

The infected Wayne teetered on its ankles.

Abdul stepped in front of Heidi.

Russell and Glenn stood in the middle of the carriage, watching the infected take its first tentative step forward.

Heidi shivered, backing away.

The infected charged at them, stomping down the central aisle, gargling blood and coughing out great gushes.

Heidi stared from the back of the carriage, as Glenn stepped forward and fought the infected Wayne. It barked and scratched at him, trying to gain purchase to launch its blood-fuelled attack. Glenn battered at it with the hammer, clipping one of its arms above the elbow. Blood streamed from the wound and the infected stopped moving forward.

Russell punched the infected in face, breaking its nose with a *crack*, taking it a few paces backwards. Glenn kicked out at its thigh and it fell to kneel in the aisle.

Heidi's eyes widened.

Earlier that day.
Heidi sipped a cup of steaming coffee. Her sister – ERIKA PETERSON, 25 year old Swedish youngwoman – sat opposite her in a small, neat coffee-shop down a shaded side-street. She was beautiful like her sister with even longer platinum-blonde hair down her back, piercing, intense blue eyes and full, poppy-red lips. She was tall and statuesque, slim and model-fit. She had serious, analytical eyes and a cold, downturned mouth. She wore a fitted white business-suit with loose, baggy trousers, a black silk blouse and grey Egon Jakobsen shoes detailed with blue droplets around the ankle.

"We have this conversation every time we meet, Heidi!" Erika said, infuriated.

"What?–... --that I don't like England very much, hate my new job and want to fucking quit – today! I want to move back to Sweden," Heidi said sulkily.

"You can't want to be a serious journalist and live in Sweden. That's a fact. You can't have your cake and eat it too, sis," Erika said warmly, when her mobile phone *buzzed* and vibrated on the tabletop, bumbling across the tabletop like a legless scarab. "I'm sorry. I have to take this."

Heidi nodded and smiled.

Erika listened to the phone, then hung up.

Heidi sat wordlessly.

"Excuse me, Heidi... Powerful people are way-too-demanding! I'm going to have to go. Right-now!"

"Oh-Okay..."

Erica stood up to leave.

A little later.
Heidi walked to the Underground entrance. She kissed Erika goodbye.

Heidi entered the station swiping her Oyster card on the top of the barrier, before it sprang open.

She walked through and started toward the downward escalator.

Erika watched her sister disappear from sight, then took off at pace down the road. A limousine with black-tinted windows waited for her at the end of the road. She climbed inside and the limousine sped away.

The present.
The infected Wayne fought with Glenn and Abdul, as Russell tried to pull it off them, hugging it from behind and avoiding the spraying blood rushing out of its mouth.

Duncan walked down the carriage pointing a black 9mm Smith and Wesson model 59 pistol at the head of the infected.

Russell saw the gun and leapt out of the way.

Duncan blew its brains out.

In a moment of respite, a thick, close silence fell over the carriage, as the gunshot sound echoed then died away, leaving a cold vacuum space. The infected fell down in the gangway, blood gushing from the head-wound. Rivulets of blood collected and streamed along the shallow gullies of the rubber flooring, lead to one side by the slight pitch of the carriage.

Everyone's circled around to Duncan, as another infected came awake near the fallen body.

He held a hand aloft and the pistol behind his body. "I'll explain to you-all why I have a gun in a while... But for now, everybody still alive get behind me," Duncan said, stepping forward. He raised the gun and aimed it tightly on the temple of the infected, just above the twitching and blood-encrusted eyebrow.

As the second infected stepped down the carriage, blood-puking on itself, instead of shooting it Duncan turned the pistol in his hand then beat it to death with the side of the gun.

Sonny grabbed Duncan from behind, pining his arms to his sides, interrupting the beating. He screamed, "Why don't you just shoot it – you asshole?"

Duncan shrugged Sonny off him easily and looked at the infected. He stamped on its head, cracking its skull open. "I don't want to attract any more of them... It was stupid to've shot that last one! We have to get to a train station, get to the surface," he answered angrily.

"Why the fuck should we do what you say?"

Duncan said directly, "We have to get somewhere safe, chances are some more people in this carriage, or the next, or the next – will've turned into these things... I don't want to be here, or there, when they wake up... Besides, I'm the one with a gun! So, actually, do what you want, but that's what I'm doing..."

"How do you know that will happen?" Heidi asked shakily. "That more of these people will wake up?"

Glenn cut her off. "That's not important right-now... Right... Okay, we get up to the surface... Where do we start, then?" he stated, then looked in Duncan's direction, his thick eyebrows peaked in the centre of his face.

Duncan looked across the carriage to the door that Reg was still hovering beside.

A little later.
Reg, Glenn and Duncan with Melanie, Sonny and Abdul in the middle, and Russell and Heidi following, made their way quietly through the next carriage. They were armed with tools from Glenn's bag – hammers, screwdrivers, knives and the heavier bits of gear.

Duncan led them, moving quickly between collapsed bodies and puddles of blood.

A little later.
The group trekked along the tunnel, lit by two torches – one held by Duncan at the front, the other held by Glenn at the back. Shuffling silhouettes and shadows danced around the arched blackened-concrete tunnel-walls.

"What do you think is going on?" Heidi asked Reg in a whisper.

"Keep quiet, we don't want any of those things hearing us," he whispered, then he quickened his pace, walking away ahead of her.

Sonny sped up and caught up to Abdul. He slapped his thighs, then he said, "Hey, man... Why?–... Why do you think this is happening to me?"

"It's happening to everyone, friend... There's nothing special about any of us."

Russell rubbed his temples, flattening sweaty hair across the sides of his head. They moved onward in silence for a few more paces, before Russell cleared his throat. "I can't believe my mate's gone," he said wearily, pushing between Sonny and Abdul. "I can't believe my mate's gone... What did he do to anyone?... He didn't do nothin'..."

Duncan increased his pace to be a few metres ahead of the group, when Melanie caught up with him.

"I think I can see light further down the tunnel," she said.

Duncan could not.

A little later.
The group reached the next station, along the dark, extended burrow. The next signs they saw were *Pickering Station*.

They gathered at the side of the platform. It was littered with bodies, some in piles, others in disorganised, crippled shapes. Blood splatters, pools and puddles bloomed across the platform; some sprays had hit the walls, like a dozen soaked paintbrushes had been fired at the walls, creating horrific patches of blood-stains; others had seeped over the edge of the concrete-siding, forming perfect dark, oily-red lagoons of blood, rounded and lustrous resting on top of a thick grey layer of dust, skin, hair, dirt and grime under the tracks.

Reg pulled a body off the platform onto the tracks, hastily stepped on it, and climbed up first. Glenn helped him, pushing his lower back to get him over the concrete-siding.

Sonny pushed to the front of the line, the second person to step on the body with a *squelch*, then used Glenn's shoulder to vault onto the platform. He kicked away and dashed a few paces forward. He did not look back at the others.

The lights in the station flickered erratically.

Reg crossed the platform slowly, inspecting several of the bodies, checking at the jugular and radial pulses. None that he scrutinised showed any signs of a heartbeat.

Sonny swaggered to the exit, passing Reg, who knelt by a body to check for another pulse at the wrist.

"Hey! Hey! Help us!" Heidi shouted, panicking, from the edge of the platform.

Reg glanced at her emotionlessly, then turned back to the corpse he was examining.

"Come on, guys!" Glenn yelled.

Sonny turned to face them and started wandering casually, idly back towards them.

An infected commuter ran onto the platform and skidded on seeing Sonny. It kicked off a body and started charging straight at him, blood falling out of its slack mouth.

As the infected passed one of the exits, machinegun-fire ripped it to shreds and it fell apart against the arched, tiled wall. The noise of the gunfire echoed loudly around the station, bouncing through every open void, as the body of the infected slumped and slid to the ground and came to rest.

A man appeared. He was wearing a uniform. The POLICE OFFICER, 28 year old Englishman – stepped out onto the platform, holding an ArmaLite AR-15 semi automatic rifle, smoking lightly at the tip of the barrel. He was bulky, imposing and restless: over six foot six, wide-shouldered and well-built. He had stern features but a bland face. His hair was cropped short all over, but full and dark. He was dressed in his normal uniform with Police riot-gear on top; he had a helmet, bullet- and stab-proof vest, elbow and chin protectors, a lower-back guard and knee-pads. He had a second AR-15 hung on a strap around his shoulder and two Sig Sauer P239s in holsters on his hips. He saw the group and stalked down the platform toward them. His head bucked as he counted each member.

Sonny crouched on the side of the platform over ten metres away. He had wet himself.

"I saw you on the security cameras," the Police Officer said, and crossed to them, hauling Glenn onto the platform in one easy tug. Reg moved to join him and stood by Glenn's side.

Glenn and Reg helped Melanie onto the platform, as Duncan, Russell and Abdul helped the others from the tracks, pushing them up, then passing them their weapons.

"Thank you," Melanie whispered to Glenn and hugged him lightly.

Reg started down the platform, creeping away from the group. Melanie watched him go, then looked to Glenn.

"Let him check it out, if he wants," Glenn said with a dismissive wave of his paw to Reg, as the Police Officer and Sonny reached for Heidi's arms and started to haul her up.

A second infected commuter rushed out of one of the passageways. It hobbled towards Sonny and the Police Officer, whose backs were turned to it. It blood-puked on both Sonny and Heidi, who was still being lifted to the platform.

Glenn knocked the infected out of the way with a powerful shoulder-barge. He snatched out at the air, grabbing for Heidi, as she fell off the platform in a slow, frosty blur. Her face was splattered with dots of thick ooze.

"No!" Melanie shrieked.

Glenn dove onto the track and cradled Heidi, who sputtered and cried and coughed up blood then died in his arms.

Duncan helped push Russell up onto the platform from the dirty track edge, as the Police Officer shot the infected, blasting it backwards so that it fell off the platform. Glenn saw the body of the infected fall roughly onto the tracks. He swept Heidi's fringe from her eyes. The infected sat up, sliding to the floor below the track. Its arm hooked the track and it hauled itself onto its feet.

The Police Officer moved to the edge of the platform and took a single shot with one of the Sigs and nailed the infected in the eye.

Reg glanced back from further down the platform twenty metres away, then looked away.

Duncan clambered onto the platform without assistance and crossed to Melanie. He took her by her arms, closing his fingers loosely above her elbows, and led her to a seat on the platform. He eased her down onto the moulded-plastic seat.

"Wait here," he said softly.

Another infected charged out onto the platform. It had once been a Spanish tourist, dressed in a baggy vest, cargo-shorts and blood-stained white Nike trainers. It barrelled towards the scattered group, centring on Russell. He stood firm, gripping a screwdriver in his hand.

The Police Officer grabbed at the infected tourist as it leapt at Russell. It tripped and he punched it. He managed to barge it a few metres away from the others. It landed with a skid, falling onto one knee, its arms flapping in the air like lame wings. Then it jumped to its feet, immediately moving forward. Blood dripped from its open mouth as it scowled and moaned and hacked.

Three more infected appeared fifty metres down the platform from Reg. He froze upon seeing them. They lurched forward arduously, but were gaining in pace with every step.

Sonny collapsed to his knees on the platform, coughing-up blood, gagging. His fingers scratched at his neck as he coughed and trembled and shook from his core. His hands slapped the platform, then scraped back. He screamed and groaned and spat blood.

The Police Officer was momentarily rooted to the spot. His eyes, wide enough to make them pop, beamed down the platform at the three oncoming infected; his entire focus was drawn to them.

The infected tourist sprinted across the platform and leapt on top of Russell. It slapped and struck at him, beating his flailing arms to either side. It forced his hands down, then drew its face up to his. It blood-puked on him, gushing out of its mouth and filling Russell's.

Sonny, on his knees, coughed violently, then straightened. A trickle of blood rolled out of his mouth, then he instantly launched up at the back-side of the Police Officer. Duncan shot Sonny in the eye, blasting a mist of brains into the air. He moved quickly to the platform edge, then hauled Abdul off his feet and onto his level.

Abdul hugged Duncan tightly. "I thought everyone had forgotten about me!" he exclaimed.

The Police Officer threw the infected tourist to the ground and shot it several times in the torso and head, then ran to Glenn's side. He pointed the Sig down the station and shot one of the oncoming infected through the throat. It gasped, snapped at them, then fell to the floor. Reg backed away a few paces.

Russell retched, crawling on his knees, slowly turning. His skin dimpled and paled.

Glenn placed Heidi's body on the ground beside the tracks.

The infected down the platform were joined by four more, who sauntered into the space from an adjoining platform. They alerted to the group and locked onto their movement.

Abdul backed away quickly.

Reg watched the infected mass, his eyes filling with tears, inching backwards, then turning and running.

Melanie stared wide-eyed across the station. She pulled her knees up to her chest, hugging them tightly.

Duncan glanced at Melanie. "You!" he shouted at Glenn, "get over here!"

Glenn's gaze slowly lifted to Duncan, his brow creased.

"Wake up! Move, move, move!"

Glenn dashed to the platform edge and met Duncan.

"You! Get over here and help me," Duncan screamed, pointing at Abdul.

Abdul rushed to the edge and helped Duncan lift Glenn up.

Reg stopped at the side of the Police Officer and they stood together at one end of the group, slowly backing away. "Know how to use this?" he asked, passing Reg one of the Sig Sauers.

"Yes."

Melanie sat against the wall behind them, still hugging her knees, shivering.

Glenn, Abdul and Duncan stood behind Reg and the Police Officer, watching the infected shift toward them.

"We have to get to the surface," Duncan asserted.

"No way," the Police Officer called back.

"What, then? Let those things get us?" Glenn asked.

"We get to the security point and lock in until these things have gone," the Police Officer stated.

Russell's body quivered.

"We have to move now," Duncan said, "or we'll run out of bullets."

The crowd of infected closed the distance to about twenty metres from the group. The divide was decreasing by the second.

The Police Officer lifted his machinegun and took aim.

"I wouldn't fire on them," Duncan said. "They're slow. We can outrun them."

The Police Officer shot a look at Duncan, before he and Reg joined the three men. Duncan took Melanie by the arm above her elbow and moved her along the platform quickly.

The group followed them.

They moved to the very end of the platform where a set of stairs led upward.

The Police Officer caught up with Duncan as they entered a long tunnel filled with bodies. They tip-toed between arms, heads, bodies and legs, moving stealthily and silently. Duncan released his hold of Melanie's arm, but she caught hold of his hand in hers and they moved single-file holding hands. He felt her arm quiver with every step.

Duncan stopped the group at the end of the tunnel, still holding Melanie's hand, and peaked into the next space. It was a small atrium room with a tunnel leading to another pair of platforms and a short bank of two escalators, completely tiled in cream and a cool duck-egg blue.

The Police Officer stopped behind Melanie, and Abdul and Glenn stopped behind him. They hugged the arched wall, not wanting to betray their presence to anyone else. Reg slowed and stopped at the back of the group.

"I don't think it's a good plan to get to the surface," the Police Officer stated in whispers.

"Why's that?" Duncan quipped.

"I saw the world outside on the monitors," he began. "And as far as I could see, everyone was dead. Or like those bloody things! We have to be extremely careful."

"We need to get to the surface, then find shelter... --and more weapons."

"What do you think is going on?!"

"I have an idea... But right now we need to get out of this hole."

"You know? I need answers right-now! You cannot expect me to follow you on a promise!"

"We don't even know how long the power will last... If everyone is dead, there will be nobody alive in the power-stations... So, no more power... Do you want to be down here in the absolute darkness?" Glenn announced.

The Police Officer said nothing.

"So, we're moving to the surface?" Duncan questioned.

"Okay."

"Do you know how to get out of here?"

"Yes... Fine... Follow me."

The Police Officer started around the corner. Melanie hugged Duncan's arm as they moved off. Abdul wrung the handle of a hammer as he stepped after the others.

Glenn moved labouredly around the corner.

Reg reluctantly followed after a moment, glaring down the tunnel behind them.

A little later.
Duncan led the group quickly along another arched tunnel, followed by Abdul and Reg, Melanie and the Police Officer, as Glenn slowed his pace, wheezing a little from their speed.

Duncan stopped, he said, "We need to move quickly. You cannot be walking that slowly!..."

Glenn huffed and puffed. "I'm coming. Don't leave me behind..."
Melanie took Glenn's arm and they walked together. "They won't."
"I might," Duncan cracked.

Earlier that day. West Hampstead.
Duncan walked up to the front-door of his home, unlocked the door and walked inside. He poured himself a large glass of whiskey. He glanced in the mirror above the fireplace. He looked exhausted. He felt exhausted.

"Lena?" he called out, but heard no answer. He repeated the call, but again heard nothing.

He walked up the stairs wearily, pausing every few steps to sip his drink.

Duncan entered his study and found his files were in total disarray. All of his paperwork and documents and files and folders had been ransacked. Someone had strewn papers across the room, ripped some pages and had stuffed many more in a waste-basket.

He stumbled out of the room, still calling for Lena, feeling twitchy and nervous.

He walked into his bedroom and found LENA BERRY, 29 year old Dutch woman – hanging from a noose. She had successfully hung herself. She looked at peace, her delicate small eyes lightly closed, giving her an angelic, somnolent appearance.

Later.
Duncan tumbled out of his house, carrying a litre bottle of Jack Daniels, leaving the front-door wide open.

He walked away down the street. The leather soles of his shoes *slapped* the pavement angrily. He stomped and kicked at the ground, pushing himself onward.

His free hand balled into a fist and his nails dug into his palm.

He swigged the whiskey.

The present.
The group moved along a tiled tunnel-walkway cautiously led by the Police Officer. There were more bodies littering the floor, like a gas chamber, reclined and laid down with the appearance of sleep.

Melanie muttered, "Everyone is dead..."

Glenn put a comforting arm around her shoulder. Abdul looked at his watch, then at the ground. Duncan noticed Reg was stone-faced and unemotional, a robot tip-toeing around the dead.

"It's not far," the Police Officer said with a wave of his hand. The lights blinked on and off.

Glenn watched Duncan and the Police Officer and saw that they were serious and driven, their expressions both stoic and unemotional and aware.

They reached a pair of lifts that were not in use and stopped by them for a moment's break.

"I know which way to go," the Police Officer announced. "Only a little way more."

Glenn caught his breath and Abdul comforted him.

The Police Officer set off and the group followed him to a small staircase that led to a huge, echo-chamber atrium with four corridors leading off it to the north and south, and a long, tall bank of four escalators the other side – two up and two down. None of the escalators were working.

"I guess we go up, if that's still the plan?" the Police Officer asked.

"Up we go!" Duncan retorted.

They started to climb, treading between bodies at various angles stretched out and broken over the motionless staircase steps. Bodies cluttered the escalators, up and down. It looked like a bomb had exploded, throwing people down the tunnels and depositing them at staggered points.

"Everyone stop!" the Police Officer whispered, and everyone froze in reply.

Duncan looked over Melanie's shoulder, up the shaft.

The noises of infected could be heard echoing down the space: a crescendo of groans and growls and footfalls.

The Police Officer pointed his machine-gun in front of him, aiming at the top of the staircases. The barrel and sight swung across the narrow space, flicking back and forth. Before the Police Officer could say more, a scream rent the air. One of the infected could be heard vomiting somewhere, but no-one could tell which direction it had come from. Duncan, at the back of the group, stared into the atrium, straining to decipher which corridor the scream might have emitted from.

An infected suddenly rushed out of one of the four corridors in the hall behind them and charged at Abdul, who was second from the back of the group. He tried to scramble away, clambering and climbing and dragging himself up the steps, over bodies and bloody mess.

The Police Officer killed the infected with one shot. But this signalled for more infected to emerge.

It was a race up the escalators, climbing over dozens of bodies, as the infected piled out of the corridors and chased them up the incline. Duncan and the Police Officer started shooting, when more infected appeared ahead of them, at the top of the escalators, rushing down at them.

The lights began to flicker.

Melanie started crying. "Oh God!" she repeated, as Glenn helped her to climb the stairs, when the lights went off completely.

The Police Officer shot a few rounds down the escalators, hitting one of the infected, but in the brief flicker of light, he could see more joining the pack, and joining the hunt.

Duncan could only hear the sounds of the groups' panicked breathing, scrambling and climbing. And the infected growling and advancing.

CHAPTER 7 - COLLAPSE - Cambridge

A greying and exhaust-stained orange and white Citi 2 stagecoach bus lurched to a halt at a bus-stop in a suburban neighbourhood. At the wheel was DONALD 'DON' CLEMENT, 44 year old Englishman. He was a stern-looking type with emotionless but clever eyes and a thick beard hiding a not unattractive face. He was six foot tall, fairly muscular and carried his weight with a light manner. He wore a black beanie, with a flap rolled up over his forehead, finger-less grey woollen-gloves, an army-green jacket, a grey t-shirt under a black round-neck jumper, black jeans and comfortable black hiking-boots.

Don was slow to reach for and pull the door-handle. Three people instantly pushed in and crowded onto the bus, staggering and shuffling into the cramped space. The bus was already nearly at capacity, and the extra people filled it. It *grumbled* and sagged onto the axles under the weight.

Don glanced at the passengers on-board over his shoulder: All of them seemed sickly-ill, pale and sweaty. He looked at himself in the rear-view mirror. He felt tired and a little rough, but was well and his cheeks were a little ruddy and a healthy red. It felt warm inside the bus, clammy and sticky; the air felt heavy and close.

The doors snapped shut and the bus pulled away quickly, juddering into action.

Don slammed on the brakes on the next turn on the road and pulled over onto the pavement and grass, digging out clods and furrows in the earth. Cars had crashed across the road, criss-crossing the intersection. Don stared at the wreck of cars, then looked more deeply – looking into them. A few people were dead in their cars, with more bodies on the sides of the road, collapsed or fallen. Blood pooled around the faces of some of the bodies scattered here and there. He glanced at the passengers in the bus. They huddled in a sickly crowd. A few people coughed. He could not see many of the back rows as standing passengers blocked his view.

All of a sudden something inside Don snapped. He felt a fierce and determined inner strength grow within himself. But he felt traces of shock and worry floating just-under the surface. His eye twitched, his brow creased. It was obvious he was thinking deeply. He shook his head, coming to. He gritted his teeth.

Don stared out the windscreen, glaring around and into each of the rear-view mirrors, jumping from place to place. He saw a middle-aged woman in a patchwork woollen jumper trying to resuscitate an old man. She was pushing on his chest, doing compressions, then blowing air into his lungs.

The sounds and tones of coughing increased rapidly from the inside, then that of bodies falling to the bus floor. Don turned suddenly and beamed down the bus again. Nearly all of people had died. Blood dripped from their noses and mouths. The standing passengers had fallen like bowling pins or chopped trees, meanwhile the sitting passengers were slumped against each other, the window-panes or the seat-backs. One of the bodies shook, then hocked and coughed up a mouthful of blood. The expelled blood trickled off an old man's chin and rolled down his neck and pooled in the ridge at the top of the breastbone. The remaining live passengers – three men and two women sat stunned, wide-eyed and silent.

A man banged on the door of the bus, causing it to shudder and quake.

Don stared at the man for a moment. Then blinked.

An old Polish man, sitting back from Don, shouted, "No! No room!" – he coughed – "Go to hospital!"

Don stared at the man outside the bus, then he pounded his foot on the accelerator and moved away down the grass. The wheels kicked and ripped at the grass and mud, then found traction and accelerated away.

The man chased the bus, still banging on the side, trying to be let aboard, screaming, "Please! Please! Please!"

A vicious-looking infected tackled him to the ground and blood-puked on him. It gargled and roared as blood splattered the man, spilling into his mouth and eyes. He coughed, gasping, then the infected retreated; its attention caught by the departing bus.

The infected sprinted down the road.

Inside the bus.
As it sped away, Don looked for the woman who had been trying to resuscitate the old man, but she had disappeared.

The bus careened down the pavement, bouncing half on and half off the curb.

The old man on the side of the road sat up infected. Its mouth hung open and it looked around with bloodshot and rage-filled eyes. A gob of blood rolled out of its mouth.

Minutes later.
Don pulled to a stop at the turning outside Addenbrooks hospital, or as near as he could get to it: the roadway all around the hospital was gridlocked by crashed, wrecked and carcass-entangled cars for four hundred metres, including the whole way to the hospital ambulance bay and Accident-and-Emergency entrance.

Three ambulances were trapped near the A-and-E entrance. Another one was wedged in place, trying to exit the hospital's grounds. Seven infected prowled between the cars, wandering aimlessly, searching.

Don looked down the bus. Everyone was dead and three infected stood up into the aisle. The other survivors had all been infected: Don had been so focused on driving, and the engine had been so loud, he had not paid attention to those inside his bus. Blood splattered the walls and windows, blotting out a lot of the light. The old Polish man had been infected and sat forward, sliding his backside to the edge of the seat. The infected was able to find its feet standing in the stationery bus, inching closer to Don.

Don got out and shut the door behind him before any of the other infected had noticed him.

The infected old Polish man slapped the door behind Don.

He strode away, when one of the infected blundered into the inside-window of the bus. More infected had begun moving inside the bus and were clamouring to exit, thrashing at their enclosure. A few shoved against the weak door-panels, some beat against the glass-box-walls surrounding them. One of the figures inside blood-puked over a blank spot on one of the windows, smearing it in thick, bloody vomit.

Don jogged away from the bus and away from the hospital.

He slowed, glancing in a car-window. The person inside was dead, slumped over, chin resting on chest, arms flopped on crotch, motionless, when suddenly an infected banged against the inside of the window of the car directly behind him. Don did not flinch. He turned slowly and quickly assessed his surroundings. There was no immediate danger.

He started jogging again, when one of the infected smashed out of his bus sending glass shards twinkling into the air and skittering across the road.

At first the infected inside the bus did not know what to do with their freedom. Then one of them ventured through the hole. It fell face-first to the ground and impaled itself with several pieces of glass. It was not fazed by its injuries at all. It clambered to its feet and stepped off down the road, *crunching* glass under its shoes, slowly picking up speed. One of its arms was broken in three places: the humerus was snapped below the shoulder leaving the socket in the scapula, and both the radius and ulna were twisted and split into four stems of bone. The forearm hung like a rubbery, useless piece of skin, flapping at its side. Greasy, thick blood oozed from the arm wounds, and around the pieces of glass wedged in its body and face.

Another infected appeared from a nearby road shuffling along the tarmac. It locked on to Don.

Don saw both of the infected coming, and ran to a motorcyclist who had collided with the back of a parked car and broken his neck. Don saw a spare helmet strapped to the back of the red 100cc Suzuki, and scooped it up. He gripped the face-mask through the visor window, swung it through the air and smashed the first infected across the cheek incredibly hard, snapping its neck, as the other infected leapt towards him, blood-puking across the back of his coat.

Don threw his coat off, and parried the attack with a twirl. He tripped the infected and booted-out its other leg, slamming it to the ground, then mashed its face into the tarmac with repeated hits with the top of the helmet. He stopped when there was little head left, and jogged away, ducking and weaving, dodging and observing, keeping hold of his make-do weapon.

A few columns of black smoke had started to rise into the sky at different points on the horizon.

Later. In *Branding's* – a small hardware shop.
Don collected a series of weapons from different shelves and locations in the shop: two claw-hammers, eight knives, two pairs of scissors and a twin-matching set of small-handle axes. He placed the axes into make-shift holsters that he had fixed onto a thick leather belt. He slid the knives into various sheaths: two on each leg, two on each side of the belt, two above his hips and two under his armpits. He scooped up the hammers and started around the shop.

The shop was quiet and empty, except for two dead attendants. One lay slumped behind the counter, the other was in the back-room, dead after the first bite of a sandwich. Deep chops had been taken out of both of their faces, a steak of bone and meat mashed away by the swipes of an axe. Don had made sure both of the bodies would not rise again.

Don collected nails, screws, bearings and matches, stuffing and placing them in a durable rucksack that he had lifted from the back-room. He found several Maglite torches of various sizes and took one of each, sliding batteries off a spindle and directly into the bag, falling in to sit with the scissors and the rest. He found lighter-fluid, a small hacksaw, a nail gun with a large box of nails, various sizes of screwdrivers and some steel-toe-cap boots – he took them all. He tugged the boots onto his feet and strapped two knee-guards around each lower-leg, one around the shin, one on the knee, with Duct tape. He found a sturdy, thick leather jacket in the back-room and pulled it on, throwing the rucksack over his shoulders, double strapping it across his back, then Duct taping the straps together across the chest.

Don left the shop and immediately had to dodge an oncoming infected that rallied towards him.

He threw the hammers upwards and caught its neck. It was knocked backwards and howled, tripping back a few paces. It instantaneously lurched straight into movement. Its right foot took a hesitant step towards Don, then it pitched forward, dragged into leaning its upper body and head in an advancing move. The infected chomped its teeth as it took another step.

Don stepped at it, kicking its knee aside with the heavy toe-capped boot. The infected twisted and fell to the ground. He pounded its skull twice with the hammer, spilling blood over the hammer's head. He wiped the hammer with a rag then discarded it with a wet *slap*.

Later.
Don climbed a large brick wall and walked carefully but steadily along the top of it. He reached a first-floor flat terrace with apartments built around three sides of the square, and jumped down to it. He landed well and rolled to his feet, then rushed to one of the front-doors, pulling his keys out.

An infected stalked out of the stairwell across the terrace, lurching towards Don.

He unlocked the door and raced inside, shutting and locking the door behind him.

Don hurried to his bedroom and threw his modest television set straight on the floor, smashing it, to get to a trunk underneath. He tore through the contents of the trunk, turning-over all sorts of army paraphernalia to get to a walkie-talkie. He spoke into it immediately, he said, "Sadie? Sadie? Sadie pick up!... Carl?... Carl?! Sadie?!... Are you okay? Are you there?!"

There was no answer.

Don pulled a heavy-duty back-pack out of the trunk and whipped open the top, flicking the draw-strings aside. He looked into the trunk at the contents.

Later.
Don charged down a suburban road, passed a few skewed cars, when two infected were alerted to him and rushed out into the road. They hurtled through bushes, passed the cars and down the pavement. Two infected turned into three as another ran into the road, then more appeared distantly down the road, slow and shambling. The faster moving infected bolted after Don's speedy footfalls.

Don saw the enemy with enough time and darted toward the nearest house to him. He raced to the front-door and kicked it hard. Wooden strips shattered from the lock and the door sprang open. He turned, as the first infected appeared at the end of the path, its legs beating toward the house. It fixed on Don and charged through the gateway.

He stood firm for a moment and stared at it, menacingly.

Don tossed one of the axes – tomahawk-style – at the infected. It hit and dug into its collarbone, knocking it down, but it did not kill it. Blood seeped around the wound. The infected gargled and heaved, scrambling to get to its feet.

Don ran inside, leaping up the staircase, as the second infected barged passed the first and followed hastily after him. Its breathing was hard and rasping and laboured and frantic.

As Don ran up the stairs he ripped a phone-cable from the skirting-board, and looped it into a primitive-noose. He tossed it over the balustrade and caught the third infected around the neck. He yanked on the cable and quickly hoisted the infected off its feet, dislocating then wrenching its neck to *snap*, when the second infected thundered along the hallway towards him and knocked him over. They landed on the floor, sprawling and *squeaking* across polished floorboards.

Don managed to grab a hold of one of the hammers and beat it to death on the hall-landing.

He stood up, breathing heavily, when a fourth infected appeared from behind him – the occupant of the house – and dove at him. They smashed through the balustrade and banisters, and fell across the void, landing on the middle of the stairs below.

Don groaned as fireworks of pain exploded inside him. He passed out. Blackness and emptiness filled his mind.

A little later.
Don awoke abruptly, finding the fourth infected impaled on the stair-banisters. Blood dripped down each of the banister-shafts, coursing down the staircase and wall below.

He picked himself up slowly, groaning and touching his ribs – he had broken two – when he heard static *crackling* from the walkie-talkie clipped to his belt. He grabbed the walkie-talkie and shouted impassionedly into it, "Sadie?! Sadie?! Can you hear me?!... Carl? Sadie?... Sadie?!"

But there was nothing – no noise.

Don regained his composure wiping at a glassy-eye, sitting on the middle stairs, looking around the hallway. A twinge of paranoia shot through him; that his shouting had alerted more of the infected. He watched and waited for a long moment, staring through the open front-doorway.

He saw nothing.

He picked himself up and eased himself down the stairs. He saw the infected that had been hit by the axe in the collarbone. It had been kicked either by the infected on the banisters, or by him, when they fell over the landing. He turned the motionless body over and pulled the axe free.

Thirty seconds later, Don jogged down the street, holding his side where his broken ribs ached and throbbed. He groaned, but kept his pace.

Later.
Don jogged up to a three-storey block of flats – twenty in total, built in two small towers of ten apartments. It was a grey double-lump of concrete from the sixties, rain-stained, pollution-coated and very dated.

He stared along the ground level car-park, up at the first-floor pedestrian entrance level.

He saw an infected stalking around near the entrances to the apartments.

Don ducked into a dumpster-bin bay and crawled between two large dumpsters. He kicked a wet and partially-rotted wooden-panel from the back-wall, exposing a disused, blocked-off entrance to the flats' gardens. He clambered through the opening into a heavily-overgrown garden.

He waded through eight-foot-high grass, brambles and weeds until he reached a fence, which he pushed and it hinged away from him, forming an acute-angled lean-to with the shed behind it. Don climbed through the gap into the next similarly heavily-overgrown garden.

As Don waded through the shoulder-height grass, a female infected saw him from a flat-window, one floor up. It launched through the window and hurtled to the ground in a cloud of broken glass.

Don fell back, as the infected lunged toward him. He spun the axe in his hand and clobbered it, with the flat, blunt side. The infected went down with one hit, face-first into a furrow of grass. A tiny fountain of blood sprayed, then drained down, wetting the long brown hair.

After a moment, Don lifted up its head. He thought the hair colour seemed familiar, and he thought he knew who it could be, then he saw who it was. It was his ex-wife, SADIE CLEMENT, 39 year old Englishwoman. He could not hold back his tears or his composure and he broke down awfully. Tears streamed out of his eyes, soaking his cheeks and beard.

A little later.
Don scaled the back-wall, climbing up to the tiny balcony of Sadie's flat. He gritted his teeth, climbing in through the broken-window. He searched the flat and found his son – CARL CLEMENT, 7 year old English body – dead. He was sat cross-legged on the floor in front of the television. He had been playing a computer game in his bedroom. He was wearing a school uniform – a neat little purple blazer, grey shirt, blue tie, grey shorts, white socks and small, black shoes. He was pale and had no colour at all in his cheeks. His face had fallen forward, his eyes were closed. A rivulet of blood had run out of his nose.

Don fought to hold backs his tears, but eventually he could not. He broke down again; holding his dead son in his arms, cradling him.

He screamed and wailed and cursed and swore and cried and sobbed and blubbered.

Carl's limp body juddered with every cry. Don hugged his son, then snapped the boy's neck.

Later.
Don sat in his ex-wife's front-room staring at a television set. The television was not switched on. The black LCD-screen showed a hazy, mirrored version of Don.

The curtains rippled and swayed with a gentle breeze.

He toyed with a whiskey bottle, rolling it between his palms. He took a one-shot swig, then placed the bottle softly on the carpet. He ate half a cheese and ham roll.

Then he drank more whiskey.

Later.
Don smashed the television. He stared at the detail-less wall opposite him. Pain and anger seared inside him, building to make him shudder wildly.

The television bucked, then ripped free of the wall. He kicked the screen, punting it backwards.

He sat down with a bump. He took his head in his hands, pressing his hands together, tensing his arms. Then he released the grip, spitting froth. Tears streamed from his eyes.

Night.
Don slumped in the same position – backside planted on the floor, legs bent, holding his head in his hands.

He sobbed uncontrollably, taking infrequent gulps of whiskey.

He finished the bottle, then tossed the empty vessel through the broken window. It disappeared silently into the night, nestling in a thatch of long grass.

Dark clouds coasted across the sky, revealing a full moon and thousands of brilliantine stars.

Later.
Don downed the bottle of whiskey. He squinted into the bottle and saw tiny dregs slipping around the base, then launched it at the wall, shattering it into a hundred pieces.

He blinked quickly as shards of glass rained down on him and the sofa behind him.

His fists clenched tightly and his body shuddered.

He let out a rough, grating primal roar from deep within. His neck craned and the sound blasted out; a torrent of rawness accelerating out of his mouth, escaping into the night.

Later.
Don cried uncontrollably, blubbing into his hands, as daylight flickered into existence outside. White light shone from the horizon, building and lightening the sky.

A light mist settled over the houses a few hundred metres away.

Day.
Don sat next to the television, with one arm loosely swung around it for stability. He drank a bottle of vodka, gulping it down, spilling more over the sides of his beard.

A little later.
Don clumsily, drunkenly stumbled out the front-door, leaving it wide open.

An infected, walking near to the staircase that led up to the pedestrian entrance-level, immediately alerted to Don and charged up the stairs. It sprinted headlong at him.

Don drunkenly fought it, punching and slapping at it, then killed it with an immense blow to the neck.

The infected crumpled on the concrete. It tried to vomit blood, but it bucked and let out an alien groan. It pitched over and died.

He kicked in Sadie's neighbour's front-door and burst into the hallway. He knocked ornaments, a couple of old newspapers and some post off the shelf near the door as he meandered inside.

Moments later, Don fought with another infected inside the flat. He stabbed it with a carving-fork into its left temple, putting it down.

Moments later, Don stumbled outside, drinking another bottle of whiskey. He had the tiniest twinkle in his eye, and the slightest of smiles on his lips.

Later.
Don carried his large back-pack, walking down a street, slightly aimless. He rambled down the centre of the road, swinging widely around ten stationery cars, making it into a slalom.

An idea came to him like an electric shock and he turned and jogged away in the opposite direction.

Later.
Don crouched in a ditch opposite a police-station.

He surveyed the area in front of him, then darted up the incline.

Don huddled by a white 2002 Daihatsu Terios 4x4, in the middle of the road with cars askew around it, stuffing the ripped-shirtsleeve of a corpse through the cap into its petrol-tank. He lit the end. He kicked the car hard and yanked on the door-handle, setting off the car's alarm.

The alarm *wailed*.

He ducked and rushed into the undergrowth on the side of the road. The alarm attracted six infected, that charged toward the car from all directions. A moment after the infected reached it, the car exploded in a ball of fire and metal, smoke folding in itself. It killed three of the infected in the initial blast and severely maimed the others. A large blade of metal shrapnel had cut one of the legs from an infected; it stumbled and tripped, tumbling into the ditch where Don had been moments before.

Seconds later, Don ran toward the police-station, followed-quickly by a late-coming infected. He noticed it and shoulder-barged it into a wall, then stabbed it straight in the heart with a large army knife. He twisted the knife, executing the infected.

He dashed into the police-station reception and dove over the counter-top. He paused for a moment, catching his breath, then looked around. He saw a police-man had died in the security-access-doorway, wedging the door open.

Don scrambled through the doorway. He stopped momentarily on the other side to slide the army knife into the back of the man's skull, then he scrambled away.

A little later.
Don kicked in the door to the communications-room, and immediately saw a yellow blinking light. He put on a headset, plugging the ear-piece in his ear, and hit the button.

"Hello? Is there anyone there?"

"Hello – yes!..."

"Where are you?" Don demanded.

"London... My name is Marc Sheridan – Transport Police on the Underground," the voice answered. "Who am I speaking to?"

"Don."

"Where're you?" Marc asked slowly.

"Cambridge. Police headquarters."

"It's pretty fucked what's going on, huh?..."

"It is – yeah."

"It's wild!... How's it been for you?" Marc asked.

"I've had some scrapes."

Marc let out a laugh. "That's an understatement, pal."

"What's the situation like in London?"

"It's been better... There's a lot of those people on the streets... But it's fairly easily to avoid most of them, though..."

"I've taken-out one, here and there... But I've generally tried to keep away from them at all costs. Don't let them get near you. I've seen them get too close to a few people today... And yesterday."

"I've seen that too."

Don cleared his throat. "So, what's your strategy, then?"

"I have no idea," Marc stated, "I guess... Get as many survivors to safety...?"

"That's a start."

"What do you suggest?"

"We move to the biggest police station in London... It's nearly central and it'd be easy to get people to it... Make it safe and find more survivors, from there on out..."

"Where's the biggest–? Pickering?"

Don interrupted, "Yes. There's a police academy bolted onto the back, there's a tower-block for good views and a hotel next door to cope with the survivors..." He cleared his throat, waiting for Marc's response.

"You've really thought that through... I have some good news – I'm here – in Pickering. In the Comms-room in the station... There are a few of us, so far."

"Seriously?"

"It's where I lived before I graduated, that's why I thought to come here... We have a permanent Police placement in the Tube station... I stayed in the area and they put me to work in the local Underground station. Now I live locally... How did you know that about this place?"

"I've known a few police."

"But, you're not one?"

"No."

"Then what...?"

"I served a little time in the Army... Now I drive buses."

"Buses?" Marc stammered.

"Public buses," Don said. "Well, not now anymore... Look... The focus has got to be to help those that can't help themselves... And we have to move as fast as possible."

"I couldn't agree more."

Don rubbed his chin around his beard, pondering.

"You should come here.. --to London," Marc said, then paused. He took a breath, then he continued, "We should set up a signal for people to find us... You should come here."

After a long pause, Don said, "Okay."

Later.
Don rushed down a road, then stopped and scouted around.

He stopped by a large white wall: the side of a late Victorian house, with a large, windowless wall on its side.

Two minutes later, Don ran away from the wall. He had spray-canned: "Go to London – Pickering Police Station. Be careful."

A few infected shambled into the street one hundred metres away, but Don was long gone. They groaned and stumbled, gradually making their laboured way down the slight hill the road was on.

Later – 4:44pm.
Don rode a black 1000cc Yamaha YZF motorbike down a main-road, weaving between stationary-cars. As Don passed one of the cars, an infected awakened inside it and started puking blood over itself. It banged its arms around the inside of the car and hit the horn a few times.

Don immediately slowed, and saw that the road was blocked ahead of him, impeding his journey. He looked around, trying to locate a way to go forward, when five infected appeared in the road near the roadblock.

"Great."

Don spun the motorbike around in what little space he had, and lit and tossed a Molotov-cocktail at the pack of infected, then sped away.

The cocktail spun through the air, smashing into a thousand tiny shards and exploded into a raging inferno. Splashes of the liquid landed on two of the infected and they combusted in the flames, their clothes igniting quickly.

Flames licked the infected, but they did not stop their pursuit.

Don cursed and kicked the motorbike into motion. He bolted away, speeding in the direction he had come from.

He pulled into a main-road, as the five infected, including two that were alight with fire, were joined by three others. Don jerked the motorbike around heavily and darted into a side-road. He sped on, turned and drove up the tight, inclining path that led to an over-ground train station.

The infected continued to follow at a sprinters' pace, knocking into each other to gain footing and charge after Don with one sole purpose – to infect him.

Don spun the motorbike into the station, then ploughed through the closed ticket-barrier. The motorbike barely made it through the gap, the handle-bars cracking each barrier-panel and bending them back on themselves. He sped through the station, passed dozens of bodies, skidding to a stop in a wide curve, leaving an arced rubber burn behind the wheel. He looked up another inclining path that led to the platforms and revved the engine. He pulled out a silenced-Sig Sauer P239 pistol, as the first of the eight infected charged into the station. But there were now eleven chasing toward him.

Don killed the front-row of four with single shots to the head, then hurried up to the platform, skidding around a few bodies and rolling straight over others.

On the platform there were dead people scattered around like fleshy matchsticks thrown liberally from the sky. Blood pooled around several of the bodies.

Three of the bodies suddenly started to move, sitting up or turning to look from their seats, somehow now awakened.

Don paused for a moment, picturing the scene as a hundred and fifty people suddenly collapsed where they stood and were preserved there what seemed like timelessly.

He grappled with his bag and found another bottle. He lit and threw the second Molotov-cocktail into the platform ramp's mouth, filling the outlet with flames.

He was quick to notice that some of the infected had gone up the other ramps and had reached the other platforms either side of him. They continued to pursue Don, leaping onto the tracks to cross to where Don sat on the motorbike.

Don shot another infected, and wounded a further three with bullets to their abdomens. He launched down the platform on the motorbike.

The infected followed, growing in numbers.

Don slowed the motorbike further down the tracks and stopped. He took a 7.62mm L96 sniper's rifle with a silencer screwed to the end of it from around his shoulders. He aimed carefully, taking a breath in before each shot. He killed all of the infected, one by one: each with single headshots that made their blood fountain in a dozen different and surprising ways.

He breathed deeply for a moment, then replaced the rifle, then cleared his throat, then rubbed his face, then drove on.

Later.
Don ditched the motorbike on the train-tracks. He removed a back-pack that he had slung over the fuel-tank and swung it onto his back. He clipped the arm-straps together across his chest, securing the pack firmly.

Ahead of him, sixty metres down the tracks, a train had collided with a van that had veered off the road. The van was a mangled ashtray of nonsense under the immense carnage of the train-wreck. Nine carriages and the engine were bent over, twisted and cracked and distorted and pounded into dented, crumpled shapes. Five of the train's cars were crushed under three of the others, mashed and pressed under the intense collision. Metal was frayed and splayed and splintered and torn apart up and down every carriage.

One of the carriages lay across the Southbound tracks, buckled in the middle. Don looked and saw that all of the windows were smashed and the empty holes just begged for the infected to start flooding out. But none did.

Don closed his eyes for a long moment, silently praying for the souls of the dead.

He scrambled up the grass-bank that sided the tracks and climbed the chain-link fence that acted as a barrier for the land. He dropped over the other side and landed with ease.

Later.
Evening was settling in, the light was beginning to fade. A gusty wind was picking up, and trees swayed and leaves danced on the breeze.

Don climbed a wooden fence between two alleyways. He jumped and landed, when an infected charged towards him. He elbowed it, as it tried to puke blood on him, then he struggled to fight with it. The infected pounced on him and he struck it twice in the eye with the butt of his pistol.

They both fell back and struck a pair of metal rubbish-bins, knocking them over. The sound alerted more infected to their presence. Don stamped on the neck of the infected and twisted, *crunching* it underfoot, as multiple shadows were cast over the end of the alleyway.

Don saw a door and kicked it in with one hard punt. It splintered into two halves. He barged through the broken-pieces of door and found himself in the basement of an old block of flats, in the bottom of a stairwell. He launched in and raced up the stairs, reaching the second floor, before three ravenous infected cannoned into the stairwell on the ground-floor and sprinted upwards in pursuit.

Don stumbled into the wall, panting and pressing his hand to his ribs. He threw the third-floor door open and ran into the corridor, followed quickly by the first infected, who reached the door before it swung closed.

Don shot it with the silenced-pistol and it fell back into the doorway, blocking the door from closing, as the next two infected charged in and down the corridor after him, stamping on the body with total disregard.

Don kicked in the nearest flat-door, and darted inside, slamming the door shut behind him and locking it with a chain-lock. The two infected in the hallway started attacking the door, breaking through the gap formed by the chain and forcing their arms inside. Don fired the pistol into the door in several places, injuring one of the infected. Suddenly, blood-puke sprayed over Don, narrowly missing his face. He turned and punched his pistol under the chin, then blew the brains out of the flat's occupant – an infected elderly woman – whose mouth dripped with oily dark ooze.

Don knee-butted the elderly infected away and ran deeper into the flat. He found the rest of the flat to be empty, but seemingly void of escape. He looked around, as the chain-lock sustained a heavy-beating. Don pointed the gun at the front-door and fired until there were no bullets left.

In the corridor, both infected expired quietly in a heap on the floor, spilling out a lake of blood on the carpet.

Don stood for a moment, his head spinning, then took out a map. He studied it, while he found an envelope with the flat's address on it.

He located himself on the map, then Pickering Police Station. He had circled it on the map. He was about six streets away. He felt close.

He walked to a tiny window above the kitchen sink and looked outside.

A little later.
Don hung out of the window, grabbing hold of a telephone-cable – one that stretched across the road below. He went hand-over-hand along the cable, dangling above the ground about twenty feet below, pushing the back-pack with rifle fastened to it ahead of him.

A few infected stared up at him, idling along the road, following him with their bloodshot eyes.

The cable quivered as he reached along the line. He pushed the bag, then inched after it. It was slow going.

A little while later.
Don climbed from the other end of the cable, replaced the back-pack and fastened it, then scaled the building-front opposite the flat, and clambered onto the roof.

He sat on the roof for a second, staring up at the darkening sky; grey clouds growing.

He picked himself up and brushed the thighs of his jeans. He continued along the roof, feeling the ridge running along the centre of his boots. He teetered slightly, but regained his footing and moved slowly away.

A little while later.
Don walked and climbed over several rooftops, hanging onto chimneys and television aerials as he went along. Some of the bricks were still warm to the touch from the day's sunlight.

He stopped and stared across at Pickering Police Station a few roads over. He saw the walled courtyard-car-park at the back of the Police Station, the tower standing out of the middle of the police-station building complex, the Academy at the back, beyond the dormitories and parade-ground and near the administrative office-buildings. He only saw parts of the parade-ground that were not obscured by other buildings or trees. He noticed an open-air garage near the Police Station, along the back-road where the access to the car-park was gained. He thought the garage would be a perfect place to get into the back-road, hopefully safely out of the sight of any local infected, and into the Police Station.

He reached the end of the rooftops where a road cut off the path.

The road was empty, for now.

Don clambered down the side of the house, hanging onto a drainpipe for stability. He slowed as he reached the roof of a ground floor extension and gently pressed his weight onto it, lightly releasing the drainpipe. He walked along the wall-edge of the roof and found a pergola to use as a climbing-frame to get to the ground.

He landed on the patio below safely, then crossed to a side-gate in the fenced garden.

He peeped though the iron bars of the side-gate, darting for a look into the road. It was still empty.

A little later – 8:15pm.
Don lowered himself onto a wall, then clambered down into the gated-courtyard of the garage behind the Police Station. He moved to the far-wall, climbed on a car bonnet. It *creaked* and bowed under his

weight. He stepped up onto the car roof. He hopped gingerly onto the surrounding-wall of the garage, putting a tentative foot atop the bricks.

A voice called out from the rooftop of the Police Station main-building, in the shadow of the tower. The voice said, "Hold-tight there for a second."

Don looked up and saw a sniper kneeling on the roof-edge of the Police Station between two bright security lights. He shaded his eyes with his hand to see the figure properly. At first he was just a silhouette, then the man waved to someone Don could not see and the lights dimmed considerably.

He could finally make out the man.

The man had a sniper-rifle pointed directly at Don.

Then the man waved at him.

The sniper was HARRY CHAPMAN, 34 year old English Police Officer. He was average and lean, moderately handsome and relatively clean-cut. He had short-back-and-sides dusty grey-blonde hair and light, golden stubble. He had gentle but very average features, nothing outstanding. He was dressed in a normal uniform with Police riot-gear on top: he had a helmet, bullet- and stab-proof vest, elbow and chin protectors, a lower-back guard and knee-pads. He carried a vintage Parker Hale M-85 sniper-rifle that he had liberated from the Police armoury.

"One sec," Harry said, then he disappeared for a long moment, then something exploded distantly the other side of the building. To Don it sounded like a firework had gone off in a galvanised, corrugated metal-bin. And that is exactly what had happened: Harry had dashed to the opposite roof-edge, threw a lit firework in the dustbin, then Duct taped it closed, then launched it from the roof.

Harry ran back to the roof-edge nearest to Don. He shouted, "You've got ten seconds... Marc, Craig?!..."

Another person behind the car-park wall shouted, "Ready!... Go! Get over the wall!"

Don leapt over and landed in the back-road, as an infected charged from the main-road end. It sprinted headlong down the alleyway, arms trailing behind it.

Don pointed the silenced-pistol and killed the infected with a shot to the eye, calm as a Hindu cow, then rushed across the back-road.

Don bolted toward the security-backdoor that led into the Police Station compound. He banged on it twice with the flat of his palm.

The door popped open and Don rushed inside.

The door slammed shut behind him. Locks turned.

CHAPTER 8 - MERCY - Milton Keynes

GILLIAN NOLAN, 38 year old Englishwoman – sat in her red 2011 BMW 640i cabriole outside the law firm, Grays and Shrim Associates. She had streaky blonde hair, smoothed carefully and tied back in a neat pony-tail. She was a direct person with sharp features and quick eyes. She had a small frame, but was lean and tall, a little sinewy and muscular: she enjoyed the gym and went as often as she could. She wore a smart, white Egon Jakobsen shirt-top under a black Armani business-suit and black Jimmy Choo shoes. She breathed deeply with her eyes shut, rhythmically rubbing her palms together to psych herself up. She looked at her car's clock - it read: 11.53am.

She got out of her car picking up her black Armani satchel, breathed out heavily, then strode up to the reception front-door.

Gillian waited patiently to be buzzed-in. She looked through the glass-panel door, checking to confirm the vacant expression on the receptionist's face. Several seconds later the receptionist waved at her.

Gillian glared.

The receptionist pressed the button under her desk.

Buzz – buzz and the door unlocked and rested an inch open.

Gillian exhaled, then pushed the handle, swinging the door inward.

She strode into the entrance-atrium, noting the *clip-clop* of her shoes on the faux-marble floor, passing a cleaner – RYAN RAINEY, 19 year old Englishman – walking to the reception-desk. Ryan had shoulder-length golden-blonde hair, greasy and tangled. He had a gentle face and demeanour, was soft-spoken, but carried himself with confidence and assertion. Light golden, coarse stubble spread like wiry-moss from the ball of his chin across his face. He was six foot tall and slim, wearing an oversized t-shirt with a cartoon rabbit on it, flared Smog denim jeans and black-and-white plaid-canvas Jack Purcell Converse low trainers. His trainers *squeaked* as he turned with the mop.

Ryan mopped the corner of the reception lazily, slapping the cloth-strands on the tiled floor, kicking the bucket to keep it rolling alongside him.

Minutes later.

A featureless, grey secretary led Gillian upstairs to the first-floor. Gillian was shown into a large office with a large, hand-worn and cracked-aged oval conference-table with six antique chairs arranged around it.

"Guy will be in to see you shortly," the secretary said, then left.

Gillian waited for a long while, then the secretary brought her a cup of coffee, and left again.

The secretary walked down the corridor away from the office to a small kitchenette. As she reached the kitchenette, a rumble of coughs escaped her throat. She began to cough uncontrollably, swatting at her mouth with limp, flapping hands. Her coughs grew violent, as GUY WATKINS, 44 year old Englishman – strutted passed her, confident, stiff and haughty.

He patted his hair down and brushed it across his forehead.

Guy coughed lightly as he entered the office, covering his mouth with the folder he was carrying.

He stood, noticing the demeanour of his visitor. He slapped the folder on the table and cleared his throat, trying to be noticed, trying to be heard then seen.

Gillian stood on the other side of the room, staring out of the window-wall. She did not turn to acknowledge Guy as he sat down, stifling to cover his irrepressible coughs.

"I'm not going to let you speak, Guy!... I have had just about enough of you!... For all of the foul, awful and pathetic excuses you've given me these past few days, weeks, months!... For all of the sly comments to the clients about me and my manner around them!..." she berated Guy, maintaining her stance, looking away from him, when his coughs fell silent. "You amaze me! You totally amaze me right-now, Guy! I'm really surprised you've sat there, quietly, for once, and taken what's coming to you! You are ridiculous, and I would take this statement right-now as concrete... You are fired, you useless, fucking idiot!" she said calmly.

She finally turned to acknowledge Guy. He had been infected, losing all of his colour and hiccup-spitting blood on himself. Penny sized blots of blood stained his stomach and chest.

She stared at him, for a long time, it seemed. Then his eyes seemed to flicker, trying to seek any movement.

Gillian flinched and took a tiny half-pace backwards.

The infected immediately leapt onto the table, crawling towards Gillian, focusing completely on her. Its fingernails scratched into the shiny tabletop as it swept forward, coughing up mouthfuls of blood, dragging itself through the wet patches.

The infected landed in front of Gillian and hit at her body and arms, punching and striking her with its fists and the sides of its arms. Then she heard what sounded like thunder. The window behind Gillian exploded into thousands of shattered pieces. Gillian and the infected smashed through the window, dropping through space, falling outward and crashing down onto the roof of a grey 2012 Audi A6 below.

The Audi's front side-windows cracked on impact, spider-webbing the glass.

Gillian whimpered and groaned, then blacked-out.

One minute ago. Inside the reception.
Ryan mopped idly, when the receptionist started coughing, each bark getting heavier and heavier. He stopped mopping and rested the mop in its bucket. The mop *clacked* against the side of the bucket as it slipped to a stable lean.

He stepped lightly across the floor to the reception desk. His Converse trainers *squeaked* again as he crossed the clean ceramic floor-tiles. "Um... Are you okay? Miss? Miss, are you okay?"

The receptionist held up a hand like a wrinkled talon, motioning to Ryan that she was fine, a smug smile creased at the corner of her mouth. She suddenly coughed up blood, spitting out several mouthfuls onto the keyboard and monitor on the desk in front of her. She gasped, staring shocked at the blood, then looked embarrassedly at Ryan, then coughed again. Then she choked to death in front of Ryan, gushes of blood forcing their way out of her mouth. Blood pooled on the keyboard and dripped off of the desk, wetting the receptionist's feet and heels.

Ryan stared at the receptionist wide-eyed and open-mouthed, not knowing what to do, when a window smashed upstairs.

He turned just in time to see two people falling out of the ground-floor window, then slamming painfully onto the roof of the Audi in the car park. Ryan knew that it was Guy Watkins' Audi. A tiny smile fluttered across his face, before a shock of reality surged through his body.

"Jesus!" he blurted uncontrollably, wincing empathically at the people's pain.

Ryan instantly saw the woman – Gillian – groan and black-out, as the other person slid off the roof, then got to his feet. He realised it was Guy immediately from the grey-blue faux-Armani suit, but a barely recognisable version of him. He could see there was something terrifically wrong with Guy. All of the colour had gone from his face, his eyes had become raged-filled and bloodshot, his mouth stained red from the torrents of blood issuing from it. It swallowed back the flow and glared at its surroundings. The infected coughed up sickening black-red ooze, stumbling back from the Audi, staring at the road ahead of it.

It caught sight of a man running along the opposite side of the road; its eyes tracking the man with an animalistic and ferocious manner. It had not registered that one of its arms was terribly-broken and hung at its side: muscle and sinew kept the limb attached like the ripped sleeve of a shirt.

The infected moved back to look at Gillian, to analyse her. It stared at her intently, like a wolf before it strikes. It growled from deep within its body. The infected reared back, like a cobra or a vampire, its mouth hanging open and slack.

Ryan snatched the mop and darted outside. He rushed towards the car and jump-kicked the infected away from Gillian, sending it sprawling out of the parking-space. It viciously scrambled to its feet and stood, blood raining from its snapping mouth. It fixed on Ryan, as he tried to pull Gillian from the roof onto the bonnet of the car. He stopped and snatched the mop again.

Ryan jabbed the infected away hard with his mop. It stumbled back into the road, as a car sped by and ran it down, killing it. The infected struck the ground with a *crunch* and rolled to a stop. Its neck had been broken on impact with the tarmac and had twisted the head to face the wrong direction.

Ryan stared at the body in shock, watched the car skid into the crossroads at the end of the road and stop.

He turned to Gillian, gently trying to shake her into being roused, at the same time stopping her from sliding off the bonnet to the pavement.

Another infected appeared further down the road, puked blood on itself, then bolted straight toward them.

Ryan saw it coming.

He dragged Gillian off the car, her heels *clicking* on the stone, and heaved her across to the reception-door. Struggling to hold her up, Ryan stretched to use his security-swipe-card to gain entry, as the infected charging at them closed in on their position, getting nearer and nearer and nearer and nearer.

He got the door open, but the infected reached them extremely quickly. They smashed through the glass-doors, sending shards of glass everywhere, landing sprawled across the floor, when TYRONE ROBINSON, 29 year old Englishman of West Indian descent, and the driver of the car – arrived to help them. He was tall and well-built with thick, bulging shoulders, chest and arms. He was strong, fit and dynamic. He had a warm, smiley face with chocolate-brown eyes, thick eyebrows and a broad, flat nose. He had short afro-hair, cut shorter on the sides. He wore a beige hoodie over a black shirt, baggy denim jeans and black Nike trainers.

Tyrone rushed from the car, parked near Guy's body, and grabbed the infected from behind by the collar.

Ryan hit the attacking infected with the mop-handle, as blood sprayed and bubbled from its mouth.

"What the fuck should I do?" Tyrone yelled, bear-hugging the infected.

"Kill the fucker!" Ryan shouted.

"Seriously?!"

"Seriously!"

"Just kill him?"

"Yeah!"

"I don't know..."

"Do it!"

"Really? Really-really?"

"Really-really!" Ryan yelled.

Tyrone grappled with the infected, twisting with it, getting a grip around its shoulder, then snapped its neck. He was slow to place the body on the ground, lowering it gently to the tiles.

"What the fuck is goin' on?!" he screamed. "Why the fuck did I just do that?!"

"I have no idea what's going on, dude," Ryan said, still holding the mop like a club. He stared at the body of the infected. It twitched and he stabbed at its temple with the mop-tip. "Fuck! Fuck!"

"I think he's dead."

"It's not a 'he', look at him..."

Tyrone studied the body for a second.

"It's the plague, or something..."

Tyrone glanced at Gillian, then back to Ryan. "Is she okay?" he asked, gesturing at her.

"I hope so," he replied, checking her pulse. "She still looks normal."

Ryan and Tyrone moved Gillian to a row of black Cretan-leather Barcelona chairs and lay her down gently. Her body sank into the soft cushions.

"What about the radio in my car?" Tyrone suggested.

"Okay, cool."

They stealthily dashed to the car, moving straight to the radio. Tyrone switched it on, then scrolled through the channels.

Every station produced static.

Tyrone and Ryan abruptly and disconcertingly noticed the scene around them – there was chaos in every direction – dozens of the infected prowled around or struggled in crashed cars; a few survivors wandered, confused and aimless and shell-shocked. Smoke rose from several of the collisions on the roads. Screaming could be heard distantly, then it faded away.

A black and yellow police EC135 helicopter zoomed overhead, swinging wildly through the air. It banked then dropped away behind one of the office-buildings two streets away.

One of the infected sixty metres down the road noticed a survivor climbing out of her car, looking wide-eyed at the carnage around her. The infected charged at the young woman, knocking her to the ground with a chest-barge. It retched and gargled, then puked-blood into her upturned face, then immediately raced away in another direction.

The noise of an explosion filled the air, then disappeared just as swiftly.

Moments later, the young woman rose from the ground, infected. It puked-blood on its own feet, then jogged away, attracted to the sound of the explosion. The infected gradually increased in speed to a run, then dashed behind a white van and out of sight.

Tyrone and Ryan rushed back to the reception, to Gillian, who was stirring and awakening.

"Hey. Hi. Hi…" Ryan said comfortingly.

"Hi. Who are you? How did I?–…" Gillian stammered.

"We brought you inside. We fought off that thing – whatever it was that Guy turned into!... We helped you… We've just checked the radios in the car. Nothing seems to be working."

"What's going on?" she asked drowsily. "You're the cleaner…"

"Fuckin' the end of the fuckin' world!"

"There are dozens of those things out there… Those people…" Tyrone stated. "Maybe everyone – maybe millions, then…"

"What should we do?" Ryan asked.

Gillian sat up and thought for a moment.

"Are there any TVs we can check?" Tyrone asked her.

"I don't know," Gillian started, "I don't work in this building. I was here for a meeting."

"With Guy?" Ryan said disdainfully.

Gillian walked to the front-door. She looked outside at three infected sprinting after another survivor. "Yes."

"I hated that fucking guy."

"Well, if it's any comfort to you, I was firing him… Right before we took a fall…"

"It's a little comfort," Ryan quipped.

"What do we do?" Tyrone asked, looking through the broken glass of the front-door passed Gillian.

Ryan sat down on the chairs and rested his head on his interlocked hands.

"We hide… We have to hide… For now, that's our only option," Gillian said decisively.

Ten days later. In the morning.
Gillian sat at a window on the first floor of the law firm. She held a pair of binoculars to her eyes.

Outside the streets were empty or seemed empty. They were never empty for too long. It looked like a war had happened, leaving no survivors and hundreds of corpses. Puddles of rain had collected on the pavements and in the roads. Beads of water on the leaves in the trees sparkled in the fleeting sunlight.

A solitary infected idled from a nearby street into the cross-roads a hundred metres away.

Gillian watched the infected.

It shuffled across the tarmac, stopping momentarily to look around, then continued on without stopping. She breathed a sigh of relief. The infected was alone.

She glanced at the wall opposite her. She, Ryan and Tyrone had barricaded themselves in the upstairs of the law firm. She sat in one of the board-rooms; it had been cleared and the table had been used to wedge the doors closed at the bottom of the stairwell, along with several of the desks from adjacent offices. They had made makeshift nests of clothes and sleeping-bags in separate offices: designated bedrooms for the time being. Food-rubbish had been bagged and thrown into the stairwell, their attempt to throw the infected off their scent. Gillian had noticed that sound – any kind – attracted the infected, and from that moment on, they had spoken in hushed whispers.

Tyrone entered and crouched next to her.

"I'm getting sick of keeping-watch, Gillian," he whispered. "We're running low on the food Ryan and I got three days ago. We'll need to get more food in the next day or so. It's does seem to be fairly clear at the moment..."

"What do you suggest doing, then?"

"I don't know... It's been two days since I've seen one of the infected..."

"I just saw one. Up the road," she stated. But she begrudgingly added, "It was alone... But God-knows whether there are anymore on the way... There might be a large group around any corner."

Gillian could see in his face that Tyrone was getting desperate; his eyes wandered and he was restless. He wrung his hands together, his biceps tensing.

"We should make a run for it."

"What?!"

Ryan walked along the main corridor that ran from one side of the law firm to the other. He thought about how many times he had walked up and down the corridor in the last week; two hundred times maybe. He shuddered, noticing Tyrone and Gillian huddled together at the window in the board-room. He moved inside.

"There must be a safe-zone or something, somewhere... The Army... Other survivors... I don't know... London will be overrun with those things, so we should go North... I think we should go North..."

Gillian looked at Tyrone for a long moment, watching his eyes pop and shiver, before finally agreeing with a slow, but deliberate nod. She noticed Ryan standing in the doorway. He looked haunted and ghostly.

"We were thinking of going North," she stated confidently. "What d'you think?"

"I don't want to go outside again, ever."

Tyrone did not say anything for a long time, then he stood up and started gathering his things.

"We can take my car. We've got to get out of here. My car will be good..."

"As soon as we're out of the city we can find a car – if one of those things hears us getting the engine started, then we're dead... It's not a good idea."

Tyrone removed his car-keys from his pocket, nodded, then dropped them on the floor. "Fine."

"We need to be sensible about this," Gillian began. "We need to make a list of all the items we'll need... Down to things like... --needles and thread, bandages, wire-cutters, torches, batteries – essentials... And weapons!"

Two hours later. Lower Fourth Street – 12:11pm.
Gillian jogged behind a long line of bushes that ran around the perimeter of large red-sided building with a ground-floor car-park built under the nearer half of it. Between the red-sided building and another stepped, glass-fronted office-block was a four-hundred space car-park, almost entirely filled with cars. Along one side of the car-park was lush green pubic park that had a winding path running through the middle of it. Along the other side of the car-park was Midsummer Boulevard – the main avenue that ran through Milton Keynes city centre.

Gillian stopped for a second to hide behind a car, before stopping fully near a parked silver 2006 Vauxhall Zafira people-carrier. She hid in the shade under the building beside the car. She looked down the line of cars and saw Tyrone dodging around the electric-barrier at the car-park entrance.

Ryan sat huddled in the bushes fifty metres behind Tyrone, watching him pause at the start of the bushes.

Tyrone had stopped. He was staring at something.

Ryan could not see Gillian, could not see what Tyrone saw, and rooted himself to the spot.

Gillian saw exactly what Tyrone saw. Three infected lurched off the Boulevard and started down the street, edging towards the car-park, slowly moving in their direction.

Tyrone motioned for Gillian to stay put. He discarded his rucksack, tucking it in the bushes out of sight. He gripped a bloodied baseball-bat that he had found in the boot of a car a few days ago on a food-run. He watched the closest infected. It prowled along the street, gargling and spitting blood. He glanced at Ryan – he had unsheathed a hunting-knife – one they had found in the back of a Chinese takeaway a little while after he had found the baseball-bat.

Ryan crawled backwards, out of Tyrone's sight, and hid in the bushes. Leaves curled around his face.

Gillian's eyes hovered over Tyrone, before turning to the closest infected. It lurched forward, limping towards the car-park. Gillian took a meat-cleaver in one hand and a large kitchen-knife in the other. She glanced to look at Tyrone again, as he moved into the road – immediately being seen by the closest of the infected.

The infected regarded him, then coughed, hacked, snapped its jaws and groaned.

The other two infected sought out Tyrone – one stepped quickly, gathering pace, turning into a steady but laboured jog; the other burst into immediate acceleration. The fast-moving infected was halfway to Tyrone before he took off and sprinted into the car-park.

The three infected, at varying speeds, set off after him.

Tyrone bolted down the first lane of the car-park, then dashed into the park, turning to a stop in the centre of the pathway.

The fastest moving infected clumsily clipped the side of a car and bounced away, skidding onto the pathway into the park. It did not stop for a single moment. The collision had only impeded it for a second and it launched back into a sprint.

Tyrone lifted the bat, readying a swing, when he saw five more infected hurtling into the car-park on the Boulevard side. Each of them dove down a different line of cars.

As the first infected charged forward, Tyrone advanced and swung out. The last three inches of the bat caught the infected across the chin, shattering it, and sending its body swirling onto the grass. Tyrone beat the back of its head until brains were dashed out onto the grass, dyeing it a putrid oily-red.

In an instant, Tyrone was bounding across the grass again, leaping down the winding path. He vaulted over a hedgerow and ran at the entrance-doors to the stepped, glass office-block. He burst inside and ran to the reception desk, where he hid, wheezing for air.

He glanced passed the wooden-edge of the reception desk.

The infected had all changed course.

Three hours later. Wetherspoons 'Moon Under The Water' pub – 3:25pm.
Gillian huddled beside one of the seating-booths, gripping the cleaver and knife in each hand. She was panting for breath and exhausted from the chaotic retreat from the small pack of infected.

Ryan sat beside her, holding the hunting-knife tightly between both of his hands. Both hands were soaked with blood and the sleeves to the elbow. Next to Ryan sat a doubled up bin-liner, knotted at the top: Gillian and he had searched the kitchen in the pub and had packed it into the bag.

Tyrone crept out of the Chiquito restaurant next door and waved to Gillian. He was carrying two rucksacks loaded with food.

"Get ready to go, Ryan," Gillian whispered.

Gillian crept to the entrance and pushed the door open. The door *pinged* on its hinges as it swung open and held in place. She looked up and down the Boulevard and saw no infected at all. They inched outside.

Three hours later. The cross-roads of Silbury Boulevard and Grafton Gate – 6:28pm.
Gillian huddled under the stone-flagged pedestrian walkway, staring vaguely up the ramp that led down to the underpass. She hid between two rucksacks, turning her head left and right, and keeping watch from the south walkway.

Tyrone skipped down a set of stone-block steps beside the underpass and peered quickly, maybe three times, into the walkway. He saw Gillian move between the two bin-bags and relaxed for a moment. He strode down the last few steps of the ramp and crouched next to his companion.

"I'm so relieved you're okay," she said.

"Me too," he replied, squeezing her shoulder lightly. "You too... I almost didn't see you.. The bags are a good cover."

Ryan appeared at the other end of the walkway and jogged to them.

"The way ahead looks clear for now."

"Good."

"We have to find somewhere to hide before it gets too dark," Gillian stated, standing. She gathered up the bags.

"We could try the Travelodge..? It's right over there," Ryan said, then pointed North.

"It would be enclosed."

"Is that a good thing, or a bad thing?" Tyrone questioned.

Two hours later. Travelodge – ground floor, room 12 – 8:39pm.

Gillian gently peeled back strips of black masking tape from a reel, tore the strip, then passed it to Tyrone. He carefully placed the strip across a sheet of thick, black felt that Ryan held in place across the left side of the window. The room was dark, except for the dim glow of a torch, placed three inches from the wall: The reflected light made from the torch's aurora on the wall produced silhouettes and heavy shadows.

"All done," Tyrone stated, as Ryan pressed the last strip of tape across the corner of the window.

Tyrone unfolded a large flat-packed cardboard box and pushed it into the window-frame, wedging it in place as an extra layer to shut out the light and sound.

"Cool," Ryan said, then flicked the bedside lamp on.

The room filled with a warm glow.

Tyrone sat at the head of the bed next to Gillian and Ryan sat on an arm-chair placed by the television.

One hour later.

Tyrone passed Gillian a bowl of noodles that he had cooked in the room's microwave. He had wrapped the two-cup kettle with two towels to dampen the noise. He stirred one cup of black coffee, wiping the spoon on the kettle-wrapped towel.

"I'll take the first shift... This should do," he said, gesturing with the coffee, as steam mushroomed from the surface.

"I'll take second," Gillian said. "I sleep better in short bursts."

"Remembering your old lawyer days?"

After a long pause, "Yeah," she admitted.

Tyrone placed the coffee next to the arm-chair, as Ryan ate his noodles. "How long should the shifts be?" he asked around cheekfuls of noodles and hard, dried pieces of vegetables.

"Every two hours or so."

"I can't believe we didn't leave sooner," Tyrone said with a deep breath.

"We've not made it out yet," Gillian countered.

"Yeah, but, we've got this far. We're nearly out of the city centre. It's time to be a little positive. For now."

Eight hours later.

Ryan sat beside the window. He had turned the bedside-lamp off an hour ago and peeled back the lower-corner of the cardboard and felt. Through a two and a half inch triangle of glass, Ryan could make out several infected stumbling down the Grafton Gate road. He swallowed, then pressed the cardboard back into place.

He gripped the handle of his sheathed hunting-knife tightly, twisting it in his grip.

Ryan looked at his wristwatch; a cheap replica he had bought in the market months ago, and was pleasantly surprised it still worked. He stood and moved to wake Gillian and Tyrone.

One hour later.
Tyrone watched through the peeled-back corner of the window swathe. There were fourteen infected in total, shiftily wandering around the road.

"What could be keeping them here?" Gillian asked.
"I don't know," Tyrone answered, "They can't know we're here..."
"We haven't made any noise," Ryan agreed.
"I know... But there's got to be some reason."

One hour later.
Tyrone stood by the locked door to the room, his hand hovering over the handle.

Gillian stood two paces behind Tyrone, carrying one of the back-packs.
Ryan crouched at the window, watching the road. "Do you think this'll work?"
"What other option is there?"

One day later.
Gillian, Tyrone and Ryan left Milton Keynes, slow and cautious.

They climbed down a short slope and crossed a band of mowed grass, then climbed a fence and hopped into a field of long rushes and lanky grass. They trudged across the field and the long grass wet the ankles of their trousers.

Ryan glanced back over his shoulder, then turned away.

Four days later. M40 near Redditch, South of Birmingham.
Gillian and Tyrone reached the southern outskirts of Birmingham. They walked side by side down the main-road. They moved between several cars, trying to keep to the side of the road.

An infected stumbled out of a side-street and saw them. It charged down the road, blood dripping from its mouth, when another infected appeared from an open car driver's-door and chest-barged into Tyrone, knocking him into the barrier at the edge of the road. Both Tyrone and the infected rolled over the barrier and fell down into a pedestrian under-pass.

The first infected raced off the road and darted into the under-pass, ignoring Gillian.

Gillian was momentarily paralysed with fear, staring at the edge of the under-pass, waiting to see Tyrone reappear. Her hands knotted into fists, tightly clenching, nails digging into her palms. She quivered on the spot, not knowing whether to hide, or run, or help.

She listened to her breathing. It was ragged and breathy and hollow and heavy.

The first infected reappeared, slicks of blood shining on its chin, and stalked around the edge of the under-pass. It moved to charge at Gillian.

She ran.

She tried the doors of a few crashed-cars, all of those immediately nearest to her, when one opened. She climbed inside. Gillian screamed instantly, feeling around that she had sat down on the lap of a corpse. She hesitated with a shudder, then slammed the door shut with a jerk. The infected arrived at the pale blue Hyundai Accent and pounded on the window. Its third hit cracked the glass, then it smashed through, punching a fist-sized hole. It violently grabbed and snatched at her, ramming its hands through the broken opening in the window. It started to shudder, as blood rushed up its throat and cascaded onto its own arms and through broken window.

An arrow hit the infected in the shoulder, impaling it above the right pectoral muscle, knocking it back a few steps, snapping and tearing its arm off at the elbow. Then another arrow hit the side of its head. Its head snapped back and another arrow whipped through the air. The infected groaned and then it dropped to its knees, dead. It slumped backwards and cracked its head on the tarmac, three arrows protruding from its body and head.

Gillian panted for breath in the Hyundai, glancing around, panicked, struggling to see which direction her salvation was coming from. She saw movement in the distance through the misty, greasy windscreen. It looked like a person, but it could have been one of the infected. She strained to see, wiping the glass with her sleeve. The view did not improve.

Two hundred metres down the road, a Securicor-truck gently nudged between two cars, in order to get down the road. Metal scraped and sparked as the truck forced its way through.

Gillian slowly reached for the door-handle, when Eva Lamberton appeared next to the car, eyes darting around. Gillian saw her through the broken hole in the window, still dripping with blood, before Eva moved to retrieve her arrows from the body and head of the infected. Eva looked back at Gillian and she smiled. "It's okay..." she said with a nod.

Jason Macpherson arrived next to Eva carrying a claw-hammer. He moved to the car and peered inside.

"She looks alive," he said quietly to Eva.

Eva gripped her bow, the quiver of arrows hanging across her back, replacing the spent arrows. "She is."

Gillian opened the car door. She looked at Eva and Jason, their eyes met.

"Watch out for another one... And the man that was with me... He's probably been infected," she said with a sob. "I don't know what happened..."

The truck pulled up and stopped.

John Ramsay and Damien Flynn opened the doors of the truck's cabin. John looked around at the road, before climbing down to meet Gillian. Damien stood on the seat-edge and peered into the distance down the road.

"Hello. I'm John... Where have you come from?" he asked, stepping close to Gillian with his hand outstretched.

Damien climbed onto the roof of the cabin. He looked up and down the road with a pair of binoculars, and away, at a small courtyard of shops where the under-pass led to.

"I was at work... In Milton Keynes... We hid... --for ages! For days!"

"Well, you're with us now... We'll try and keep you safe."

The back of the truck opened and Piotr Hoogestern climbed out.

"We found another survivor," Damien said to Piotr from the roof.

"Oh."

"A woman... Talking to John."

"Mmm."

Damien hung over the roof and looked into the back of the truck, where other survivors sat, huddled together. Ella, Grant and Mitchell sat near the doorway with weapons readied, Katya, Jane and twelve others sat deeper in the back. "We found another survivor... There's nothing to worry about... At least we aren't stopping for another toilet break!" he joked.

Grant and Mitchell grimaced.

Jason jogged across to the edge of the under-pass, then looked back, worriedly.

Two infected appeared – one of them was Tyrone. They raced up the grass-bank at the side of the under-pass and charged at the group. Jason stepped in to tackle the first infected, when four others erupted from the under-pass.

"Jason! Get back in the truck!" John shouted.

As Jason turned to catch John's eye, he was battered into the side of a car by one of the faster infected. He was blood-puked on, then disappeared from view, falling to the ground. Several infected puked blood on Jason as they passed him, then turned to rush the truck.

John reacted quickly, running to intercept an infected, as Eva let off two arrows into Tyrone. Both arrows met the oncoming body of the infected Tyrone, as he continued to advance on them. The arrows embedded in his chest blossomed with oily red-black, streaking down his bloodied t-shirt.

John beat one of the infected to death with a hammer, then glanced at Eva. She fought with the infected Tyrone, dodging his punches, when Damien joined her, swinging a cricket-bat, and they killed him with a dozen heavy hits.

"Get back in the truck!" John shouted, as more infected appeared, shambling and wandering and jogging and sprinting from surrounding houses, and the courtyard of shops.

Eighty metres down the road, three infected collapsed and toppled to the ground at the side of a small Post Office. Several pigeons took off from the Post Office's roof and ascended into the air, spreading out across the sky.

Four days later.
The group trekked away from the truck. John, Piotr, Damien and Eva led them; Ella, Grant, Mitchell and Katya marched closely behind; Jane, Gillian, Gregory, Jim and Gemma, a man called Leo and twenty-six others followed.

They walked in a loose-group down the side of the M1 motorway. They were six miles from Hemel Hempstead.

Gillian caught up with John and walked with him at the front of the group.

"Hi," John said warmly.

"Hello."

"Can I help you with something?"

"What do you expect to find in London, John?"

"I don't know. Something. Some structure left... More people, maybe some of the army will be left," he said hopefully.

Gillian did not look as hopeful. "I think you're going to be surprised."

"Why do you say that?"

"All of the cities... London will be no different. We're almost there and there are already more of those things."

"That may be so. But I've made it all the way here from Scotland. I'm not gonna stop yet."

"You have made it so far, that is true... But you are just a writer."

"I was a writer... I haven't done much writing in the last few weeks."

"But everyone seems to treat you as the leader...?"

"I'm not the leader."

"You are the default leader, John. And you're leading all of these people to a crowded, massively-populated city... Again, what do you expect to find?"

"Somewhere we can settle... Somewhere we can build a base. And find other people. Gather together."

"Building a settlement?"

"Well, yeah. Maybe a temporary place..."

"When I was hiding in that office, I felt trapped. I felt imprisoned. I felt like going outside was the worst option in the world..."

"So, now you see we can move about, without being attacked every minute?"

"That may be so, for now, John. But I don't think you're thinking long-term..."

"I don't think there is a long-term yet."

"How can you say that?"

"What we have is right-now... You need to think about that."

Two days later. The cemetery.
John led the group – thirty-eight other survivors – through the cemetery in a large, loose group. John was ahead of everyone – he cried uncontrollably. Through his tears, he said, "What do I do?!... What am I supposed to do?!" His hands knotted into balls, gripping tightly, fingernails digging into the soft meat. Tears fell from his eyes, as the clouds shifted overhead, pointing rays of sunlight across the graveyard.

As if shocked by lightning, John pulled himself together, wiped away his tears, snorted, and cleared his throat. He stood, suddenly looking stable and determined. He gritted his teeth.

"I'm okay now. I know what to do. I know what we have to do."

Three infected appeared ahead of them, and charged towards the group.

John grabbed his axe, before anyone else had time to react.

Damien and Piotr were the only others to stop watching John and leap into movement. They reacted immediately, rushing towards the first infected, when a car sped into the graveyard, driving down the road to the crematorium.

The car skidded, then ran into the second infected. It sent the body rolling through the air like a ragdoll, stopping at a gravestone, shattering its backbone on it, and killing it instantly.

Relief flooded over John for a millisecond.

Damien and Piotr momentarily hesitated at seeing the car, but quickly-turned, as the first infected tackled them both to the ground.

John ran at the third infected, looking and feeling wild and ferocious, when the driver of the car and the passenger leapt out: they were Sergeant Newton and Private Hastings.

Gillian and the rest of the group watched in stunned-silence.

Newton, armed with a silenced-pistol, shot the infected, splattering its brains into the air. It tripped and tumbled to a stop at John's feet, spilling blood onto the grass under the toes of his shoes.

Damien and Piotr beat the other infected to death, away from the sight of the group behind a gravestone. They stopped, when they noticed the men were dressed in soldiers' uniforms. They breathed a sigh of relief in unison.

Later.
Newton and Hastings stood with John's group, who had huddled and collected in front of them.

"We saw you walking along the motorway yesterday," Newton said. "We did try to intercept you-all earlier, but we ran into a little trouble... We've made a base in a police-station... It has a training academy and a hotel next door to it, so there's plenty of room for all of you... It's in the east-end of London... I think we should get you there as soon as possible."

"So, are you the army?" Gillian asked, sitting with her back straight.

"We are... Not officially speaking."

"What does that mean?" Grant asked.

"Well. There's nothing left..."

A rumble of fear and panic swam through the group.

"We were in the army... There are some of us left. And we've been trying to help and gather other survivors... With your help we could–..."

"With our help?!" Gillian interrupted. "What help can we offer the army?!"

"Well," Newton stuttered. "You've made it this far."

"So?!"

"So, you all worked together..."

"So?!"

"We have to stick together! And help others... If we can... Everybody has a skill, or set of skills, that will be useful."

John said nothing throughout this exchange. He listened as questions and answers rattled back and forth. Nobody seemed convinced, nobody's fears were allayed, nobody felt safe. Gillian eyed John from the other side of the huddle.

Private Foost and Tetsuo Katsushika emerged from the road to the crematorium. They approached and joined the group, circling around the side to stand next to Newton.

Hastings stood and crossed to them, taking them into an aside.

"How's the transport?" Hastings asked.

"We've found a bus, with some petrol in the tank... Bright and Kara are with it, coming to the entrance of the graveyard," Foost replied, when static came through on his walkie-talkie. "Excuse me a sec."

Piotr and Damien watched Foost walk away, pressing the walkie-talkie to his ear.

Tetsuo sat down on a headstone behind Hastings and Newton.

"Are there any – or do you know of any other safe-havens?" Gillian asked sternly.

"No others... None yet... None that we know of..."

Other members of the group asked more questions, without getting any solid answers from Newton. Gillian noticed this and watched him closely.

John sat, listening but not participating.

Damien glanced at Gillian and stepped aside of the group with Piotr.

"That woman is going to cause a lot of trouble."

"I thought the same thing," Piotr replied with a nod.

"John's gonna need to keep a cap on her."

"If he cares anymore," Piotr said and nodded at John, who rubbed his whiskery-beard and then massaged his temples. "He seems to have run out of energy."

"Or will-power."

"What about any other place outside of London?!" Gillian shouted at Newton.

Later.

The bus pulled up at the entrance to the cemetery. A few of the windows were missing or broken, and blood stained a lot of the existing-windows. Handprints and splatters dotted the sides of the bus.

Bright drove while Kara sat in one of the open-windows, holding a silenced-army rifle, a few rows behind him.

Hastings and Newton covered the sides of the bus with their silenced-machineguns, as Foost climbed aboard. He sat by another smashed-window, pointing his rifle outward, near the back of the bus.

Thirty-eight people boarded the bus, led by Gillian and Mitchell, in single-file.

John found a seat behind Kara and ducked out of sight, resting his head against the wall.

Tetsuo followed the last of the group, covering the graveyard.

Newton was last to board. He looked back at Tetsuo, who stopped on the pavement.

"I will rejoin you in Pickering in a few days," he said.

Newton stared into Tetsuo's eyes. He blinked emotionlessly at the soldier, then gave a tiny nod.

"Make sure you do," Newton instructed. He returned the nod.

Tetsuo half-smiled, waited for the bus to pull away, then walked back into the graveyard.

A little later.

Gillian stared out of one of the windows in the bus, gazing at ghostly, stark and empty streets, one after the other. There were crashed and abandoned and burned-out cars on every street; and even more bodies, peppering every road and pavement.

A few slow, roaming infected wandered the streets.

Gillian's eyes started to water. She gritted her teeth.

CHAPTER 9 - CONTROL - London

Eighteen months ago. South-East Spain.
Duncan Berry, 29 year old Englishman, exited from the only door in a small, non-descript concrete building that was set into the incline of a vast wooded hill. Red-brown dirt surrounded the building and the dust had settled over it, giving it a Martian hue. The building was hidden and heavily shaded by a forest of cork oak trees that masked it completely from the air.

Duncan was a good-looking man, with sharp, small features and a full head of thick, dark hair, trimmed a little short on the sides. He had high cheekbones, a straight nose, perfect teeth and sculpted eyebrows. He was tall, muscular and athletic. He wore a fitted black suit, white shirt, no tie, black belt with a silver buckle and smart black shoes.

A tiny plaque beside the plain entrance-door read: "Estacion Cinco".

He answered his mobile-phone, listening for a few seconds as muffled words emitted from the speaker.

"The site is ready and functioning," he said laconically. "All of the environmental conditions are working at optimum levels. All backups and assessments have been completed. All residential quarters have now been finished to the required standards... Yes, sir," he said, then hung up.

Duncan glanced at his watch.

A black 2009 Land Rover LR3 Discovery with blacked-out windows pulled up and Duncan got in the back-seat.

The car sped away, kicking up a cloud of swirling dusty-red sand.

The concrete building disappeared in the rear-window, collecting another fine layer of dust.

The Land Rover slowed before a guard-station, where four heavily-armed guards sat.

Duncan glanced through the tinted window at the guards, one of whom jumped out of his seat and moved to open the double-gate and raise a twin set of barriers. The guard saluted the driver, as the car took off down the dusty road.

The guard watched the car dissolve from sight in a long scud of dust and exhaust, then vanished behind a screen of trees and shrubs as it passed around the crest of a hill. He adjusted his silenced-machinegun, then pulled out his baton and joined the other guards in the station.

A little later. At night.
Duncan walked through an incredibly grand hotel. His shoes *clipped* on the marble and echoed as he crossed the vast foyer. There were no other people in the hotel, except two waiters who stood either side of the patio-doors, dressed in penguin-suits.

The waiters pushed the doors to the patio open as Duncan approached.

"Evenin' guys," he said, patting one of the waiter's shoulders.

He stepped from the cool, crisp air-conditioned foyer out into the warm, salty night.

Duncan walked toward the pool-side bar, taking a wide, sweeping arc around a giant oval swimming-pool. Decorative palms had been planted in rows, eight metres apart, lining the paths that criss-crossed the hotel complex. A light, warm breeze stirred through the trees.

At the pool-side bar, MALCOLM REID, 48 year old Scotsman and Duncan's work-partner – sat on his own. He was a husky man with hunched shoulders and a big frame underneath. His arms and legs were thick with muscle, but his body was doughy and tired. He had a rough face, deep with wrinkles, crows-feet and glabellar frown-lines. He had a strong nose in the centre of a strong, broad face with a sharp mouth hiding uneven, large teeth. He wore a dark-grey suit with an open-collared pink shirt and smart, black shoes.

Reid was drinking heavily. Empty beer bottles, pressed together like bowling-pins, formed a glass temple beyond his elbow, where he played with another bottle in his paw. His other hand, balled into a gnarled and scarred fist, pressed into his face under the cheek bone, stretching the skin under his eye, pulling it grotesquely open to reveal the crimson-red slit of veins under the dusty, quite bloodshot ball.

"Good evening," Duncan said, smiling at the sight of several empty bottles of McCutcheon whiskey behind the beer bottles. "I see your night is going well?"

Reid shot Duncan a look, as he took a seat.

"It's great!" Reid exclaimed. "But this beer is weak and shite!"

"I was just out at the Station..."

"Oh yeah, how was that?" Reid spat.

Duncan did not answer. He saw that Reid was too drunk to talk properly to him, so he would endure his mood and rising anger. Reid threw back two fingers of whiskey. His face had turned red, and was purpling. His teeth clenched then snapped open.

"Was it cosy? Was it spacious? Was it hunky-dory?"

"It was ready."

"Ready?!"

Duncan put his hand up, motioning for Reid to quieten.

"There's no-one else staying here, Duncan! Besides you and me! I can be as loud as I like!"

Duncan waved over one of the waiters.

"Another bottle of McCutcheon. A glass with ice."

The waiter nodded and vanished.

Reid's head lolled on his shoulder. It looked like he was minutes away from passing out.

Moments later the waiter appeared with two glasses, with three cubes of ice in each.

Duncan finished one glass in one gulp, then held the second in his hand, rolling the liquid around the tumbler.

Reid watched him. He watched the waiter place the bottle of whiskey on the bar next to Duncan. Saw Duncan sip his second drink, then poured more in. He saw Duncan had kept the bottle near to him, away from Reid's reach.

"I have a question for you, partner..."

Duncan sipped the hot, sharp, delicious whiskey. "Go on."

"How can you not say a word about what we're a part of – to your fiancée?!... To Lena, huh?... How can you be so complicit?!" he screamed, then shoved Duncan drunkenly in the shoulder. Duncan's stool slid back a few inches. Reid stood up, adding, "One day, she'll be out-here, and then the next day, after it's happened, she'll be somewhere completely new... How would you like that, Duncan? How would you--...?!"

Later.
Duncan stood in his hotel-suite's bathroom, splashing water on his face. His jacket lay on the bed, a leather shoulder-holster hung on the corner of the door. It carried a black 9mm Smith and Wesson model 59 pistol, held in place by a buttoned-down strap.

Duncan stared at himself in the mirror as beads of water rolled and gathered, streaming down his clean-shaven face. He rubbed his temples, then splashed more cold water at his face.

The next morning.
Duncan awoke lying on his bed, still wearing his suit, as someone banged on the door.

He answered it – it was Reid.

"Morning, princess..."

"I'll meet you downstairs in a little while, let me get... --re-dressed..."

Reid nodded and let the door swing closed.

A little later.
Duncan crossed to join Reid at the breakfast-table, on a beautiful balcony over-looking the sea. The balcony was lush and green, decorated with bright, colourful and vibrant flowers.

"I want to apologise for last night, for raising my voice," Reid said, then continued, "but we own the hotel, so who fucking cares, right, big man?... And, there's nobody else staying here besides us..."

"You said that last night," Duncan replied, studying Reid. His tone was particularly disrespectful and flippant.

Standing to leave, he said: "Be careful." Then added, "Enjoy your breakfast, I'll meet you in the reception... I can't stand all the fucking light and colour and green out-here... It's driving me fucking crazy! See you–..."

As Reid walked across the sand-coloured tiled patio and into the building, he pulled a black 9mm Smith and Wesson model 59 pistol from the holster under his armpit, and blew his brains out. The bullet lifted him slightly off his feet, then he went tumbling to the ground. Every joint in his body yielded as his hulking frame was propelled across the tiles. His head clipped the floor and blood leaked out of the wounds at the front and back.

Duncan heard the shot and sprinted inside. He came to a stop, skidding across the tiles a few feet from Reid's body.

A deep, rich pool of wine-red reflected the ornate chandelier above Duncan's head.

One year ago. Saratoga, upstate New York.
Duncan was finishing a game of golf with a colleague – ROB ALCOTT, 31 year old Harvard graduate and an American. Rob was athletic and sporting; a former rower, a boxer and a polo player. He had Masters degrees on three continents, spoke eight languages – Mandarin, Cantonese, Spanish, Russian, German, Arabic, Japanese and English, had a fighter-pilot's license, a deep-sea scuba diving license and had competed in some of the world's toughest endurance trials, races and expeditions. He was tall, broad-shouldered and superheroic in proportions. He had a Hollywood-handsome face with a straight nose, defined cheek-bones, a strong jaw and perfect lips. His hair was warm, thick cocoa-coloured, cropped and gelled by a New York stylist, parted on the side in a forties fashion. He wore grey suit trousers and an Aegean-blue shirt with the sleeves rolled up and grey, spiked golf-shoes.

Duncan wore a pair of black trousers, a canary-yellow shirt with the sleeves rolled up and black, spiked golf-shoes.

"You never told me how you got into the game?"

"Another time... Let me concentrate on this shot," Duncan replied, tapping the ball towards the hole. It rolled short. "That was appalling... I don't seem to get the time to practice these-days... How's your work coming along?"

"Fine, fine."

"And, Rachel and the kids?"

"They're great. Really great."

Duncan could sense something in Rob, bubbling under the surface. His eyes twitched as he went to retrieve another club. "How about we talk?"

"About?" Rob replied.

"About our little situation we have here. The act with our loved ones. The losses we've had to take."

"What, with talk of the uprising? They're just rumours..."

"Everything."

"Are you talking about Reid?"

"Reid, Lena, Rachel... Even Everest."

"Everest was a traitor."

"Was he, though?"

"I'm not sure I follow you–..."

"Haven't you ever wanted to talk to your own wife about all-of-this?" Duncan interrupted sternly.

"Of course, but–..."

"We have lives! You have children! For God's sake–..."

"You cannot talk about this here, Duncan!"

"I've blocked all transmissions and surveillance. We can talk. For a few minutes," Duncan said. He held up a standard six-sided dice: it was a telecommunications blocker. He smiled.

"We could... But we're not going to."

Duncan stared into Rob's eyes, the look of concern on his face plain to see. Rob glanced over Duncan's shoulder, and he turned to look. "Careful..."

An attendant drove a golf-trolley along a wide asphalt path and pulled in near to them. "Excuse me, sirs, but… --Mr Burton has arrived. And is waiting for you in the Dryden Suite, Mr Berry," he reported.

"Excuse me, Rob… Got to go," Duncan said calmly, and left with the attendant.

Rob watched them go. He replaced a putter in his bag next to the rest of the set. He slid a cover over the head of the club, then crossed to the tee and picked up his ball.

The trolley Duncan sat in rounded a small hill and disappeared from sight. As it went, Duncan held a hand in the air, waving to Rob.

A little later.
Duncan opened the door to the Dryden Suite and found MR BURTON, 58 year old Englishman and Duncan's boss — standing waiting for him. He was statuesque, straight-backed and square-jawed. He had a long, ridged brow, over intelligent, bright eyes and wide cheek-bones. He stood as a Spartan general, impressive and formidable. He wore a black three-piece suit over a pristine white shirt with a patterned red-and-gold tie. He had a vintage, gold 1970s Omega De Ville wristwatch, platinum cuff-links and a gold 1950s Patek Philippe & Co pocket-watch. He held a tumbler with ice and three inches of Suntory – Blend Hibiki, a seventeen year old Japanese whisky. He rolled the golden liquid in the glass, then sipped. His other arm sat across his lower back, as if he was permanently standing to attention.

"Good afternoon, Mr Berry," he said without looking at Duncan. He crossed to an unmarked antique, vintage red-leather Chesterfield. The couch was an eight-foot long beast of quilted leather upholstery and deep brass buttons. He sat in the middle, looking up at Duncan, who lingered by the entrance. His head tilted, as if deliberately displaying his confusion to Duncan as to why he had not yet moved. The attendant, clutching both door-handles, swung them closed behind him with a *whoosh* of air that rippled the back of Duncan's shirt.

"Good afternoon," he replied and walked around a second Chesterfield that mirrored the other. He sat facing Burton.

"How was your game with Mr Alcott?"

Duncan looked to one of the large, arched windows, crossed with tiny squares of lead. "It was good. I could play a lot better."

"We were monitoring your communications, until it mysteriously cut-out," Burton said flatly.

The hair on the back of Duncan's neck twitched. "I needed to speak to Mr Alcott. Alone."

"Was that really necessary?"

"Agendas," he said slowly.

Burton sat forward on the Chesterfield, his big hands clutching his thighs. "What about them?"

"Whether anyone can be trusted, when there are a lot of different agendas on the go…"

"That's bold. You're bold," Burton laughed, took another sip of his whiskey, then straightened. "I've read your most-recent psych-report, Duncan."

Duncan's right eye blinked.

"You understand my coming here…? Interrupting your game."

"I pieced it together," Duncan mocked.

"I know you would like to tell your fiancée about your job… Lena?"

"Yes."

"But you know you cannot?"

"Yes."

"Then you see my problem when your report tells me you aren't centred?"

"I see I may be a problem."

"But you may not have to be."

"No?"

"Neither you… Nor Lena… -- need be a casualty… You need some time-off. A holiday."

"And then I won't be a problem anymore?"

"If you behave, Duncan, if you behave… And that's up to you."

Burton stared at Duncan.

The room felt immediately quiet. Duncan looked from the floor into his boss's eyes.

Six months ago. London.

A coffee-cup sailed through the air and shattered, spilling black coffee onto the wall of Duncan's kitchen. He ducked and narrowly missed a plate. LENA BERRY, 29 year old Dutch young woman – stood at the other side of the room. She was slight, delicate and petite; Duncan towered over her. She had long, ice-blonde hair, fashionably styled. She had a beautiful face, stunning, deep blue-eyes, a small nose and sharp, pursed lips. She wore a tight cherry-red cardigan over a white silk blouse, a black pleated skirt and tiny black pumps. Duncan wore a simple grey suit and white shirt. "For fuck's sake, Duncan!" she screamed, tossing another plate. "I can't trust you! I can't talk to you! I can't be in the same room with you!"

Lena threw another plate, sending it across the room like a discuss at Duncan. It *zipped* by above his head and smashed against the wall. Duncan planted both hands on the table. He pled, "I would tell you, but it may cost us our lives...! Honestly... I work for people that do not take this type-of-thing lightly."

"What? What do you mean by that?"

"I can't explain."

"Explain! You have to!"

"Lena–..." he started.

"No!" she screamed, interrupting him. "Give me an answer!"

Duncan said nothing.

"I'm begging you!" she moaned.

Duncan finally nodded.

He led Lena up the stairs to their bedroom, and switched the stereo on, twisting the volume to its highest. He took her by the hand and they entered the en suite bathroom. He turned the shower on and climbed in, under the water. Lena took a hesitant step into the shower, then climbed in next to her husband. The door swung closed behind her.

Duncan hugged Lena close, and whispered to her as the water rushed around them and steam rose.

One minute later.

Duncan got out of the shower, peeling his soaked suit jacket off. He strode into the bedroom and reduced the volume of the stereo, dropping the jacket on the floor in a wet heap. He pulled a towel free from an exposed shelf and rubbed his face and hair with it.

Lena remained in the shower.

She sank to the floor and cried, hugging her knees.

Duncan glanced into the bathroom, then gritted his teeth, and looked away ashamedly.

The present. West Hampstead.

Duncan walked up to the front-door of his home, unlocked the door and walked inside. He poured himself a large glass of whiskey. He glanced in the mirror above the fireplace. He looked exhausted. He felt exhausted.

"Lena?" he called out, but heard no answer. He repeated the call, but again heard nothing.

He walked up the stairs wearily, pausing every few steps to sip his drink.

Duncan entered his study and found his files were in total disarray. All of his paperwork and documents and files and folders had been ransacked. Someone had strewn papers across the room, ripped some pages and had stuffed many more in a waste-basket.

He stumbled out of the room, still calling for Lena, feeling twitchy and nervous.

He walked into his bedroom and found her – hanging from a noose. She had successfully hung herself. She looked at peace, her delicate small eyes lightly closed, giving her an angelic appearance.

He pulled a knife from his inside jacket-pocket and righted the chair that lay beside her. He stood on the chair and sawed through the rope with the knife. Before it frayed and broke, he caught her body.

He cradled his wife, laying her down gently on the bed. Tears filled his eyes.

He screamed.

Duncan kicked and punched and smashed his way through his bedroom, hallway, landing and downstairs.

Later.

Duncan tumbled out of his house, carrying a litre bottle of Jack Daniels, leaving the front-door wide open.

He walked away down the street. The leather soles of his shoes *slapped* the pavement angrily. He stomped and kicked at the ground, pushing himself onward.

His free hand balled into a fist and his nails dug into his palm.

He swigged the whiskey.

His head dragged his body along the pavement, as he veered into the road, gulping down hot bolts of whiskey.

Later. The London Underground.

In absolute darkness, Duncan climbed up the left side of the bank of four escalators. He shot several infected that were surrounding the group from the top of the steps and at the bottom in the atrium.

Duncan and the Police Officer both fired their guns, as more infected appeared ahead of them, at the top of the escalators, groaning and roaring, rushing down at them.

The main lights flickered on then off. Then flashed alight.

Glenn dragged Melanie to her feet as she huddled next to a body, trying to hide from view.

Reg forced himself onwards and upwards, climbing the right side of the bank, furthest from Duncan. He took two shots with the pistol that the Police Officer had given him. Both bullets met their targets: two infected that were toppling down the escalators towards him.

The main lights flickered on then off again.

Melanie cried out, "Oh my god!" for the tenth time.

The Police Officer shot a few rounds down the escalators, hitting one of the infected, but in the glimmer of light at the end of the barrel, he could see more joining the hunt.

Duncan could only hear the sounds of the groups' panicked breathing, scrambling and climbing. And the infected growling and retching and advancing.

The Police Officer shot a single round down the escalators, illuminating the space in a flash of light. An infected charged at him through the darkness, hopping and jumping and leaping and tripping and stumbling over corpses as it bounded down the escalator swinging its arms.

Duncan and the Police Officer fired a few more times. One of the bullets from the Police Officer's machinegun bounced off the metal-plating between the escalators, ricocheting into Abdul's ear.

Melanie felt up the steps, feeling along the ridged edges. She climbed to the next step, then screamed when she put her hand in the mouth of a corpse. She felt her fingers run along the bottom set of the person's teeth. She gasped as Glenn reached her and put a comforting arm on her shoulder, gently guiding her up the stairs.

"It's going to be okay. It's going to be okay," Glenn reassured her.

The lights flickered, then came back on. A few fluorescent strip-lights blinked on and off – three did not come back on again. An emergency light glowed from the atrium behind them.

They regrouped in a huddle at the middle point on the steps.

Duncan and the Police Officer shot the remaining infected one by one, building piles of them at the foot and head of the escalator bank.

Abdul's body lay on the steps, blood seeping from the head-wound. He blinked three times, then died.

There was a momentary lull where no more infected appeared. Everyone still panted for breath. They looked down at where they had come from, and up to the top of the escalators. Duncan saw Abdul's body and moved to block Melanie's view to it. Glenn also saw the body and helped to hide it from Melanie with his bulky frame.

The Police Officer climbed ahead and checked that it was clear.

"Whoa... That was terrifying," Glenn whispered to Duncan.

Duncan looked around at the group, then at the pistol in his hand, then started to climb upwards again. He followed Glenn and Melanie up the last few steps and reached flat ground.

Reg followed after them, appearing from his hidden position behind two piled-up bodies.

"For a second there I thought you hadn't made it," Duncan quipped at Reg.

Reg looked sourly at Duncan as he clambered away up the escalator. "Sorry to disappoint."

A little later.
The group reached the exit of the Pickering Underground Station.

They huddled together, keeping-watch, making sure there were no infected roaming the street in front of the station. They stood at the edge of the wide entranceway, hiding behind two signs that had early closure notices written on them, beside a small newspaper stand built into a recess in the entrance-wall. The Police Officer dragged a body into the entrance and rocked it onto its side. He crouched behind it, scanning the street. There were three cars that had collided with each other, and another that had careened off the street and through the front window of a Starbucks coffee-shop. Three dozen or more bodies lay on the pavement and in the street around them.

The Police Officer took out his mobile-phone and saw there was no reception. He held it up, pointing it skyward. No signal bars appeared. He shook his head and replaced the phone in its case on his belt. He glanced at the four people beside him and sighed. He pursed his lips, thinking. He looked into Melanie's eyes and saw her near-paralysing fear. He looked at Duncan and saw his apathy. He saw Glenn's solidarity and Reg's cowardice.

The Police Officer said, "By the way... My name's Marc... Marc Sheridan."

"Glenn... Meakins," Glenn offered, shaking Marc's hand.

"Melanie," she whispered. "Melanie Cannon."

"Reg."

"Duncan."

Marc looked at Duncan, who lit a cigarette casually. "Where to now?" he said sternly.

"We have to find food, or shelter," Glenn proposed before Duncan could answer.

"I need to get to my wife," Reg stammered. "I need to go..."

"You don't have a wife, Reg... I've seen your file. And you aren't even wearing a wedding-ring, genius!" Duncan snapped mockingly.

"Do you-two fellas know each other?" Glenn enquired, brow furrowed.

"Look, stop that, we have to stick together! Whatever association you-two have, you can settle it when we're safe! We should get to the nearest police-station... It'll be safe in a police-station. And there'll be weapons."

"We should get food first," Duncan said, brooding.

"Head to a super-market, then...?" Glenn suggested.

They slowly crept out of the Underground station in single-file, when an infected saw them from further down the street. It lurched in their direction and started striding toward them, gradually gathering speed to a difficult jog-run.

The infected rushed around a car, but Marc intercepted it, catching it by the shirt-collar. He snapped its neck, bear-hugging it from behind. He turned to the group, ordering them, "Stay low and stay quiet..."

They ducked and weaved along the side of the road, when Glenn spotted a small supermarket.

A little later.
They were all safely inside the Arford's supermarket. Duncan secured his pistol against his back by his belt. Marc strapped the machineguns around his shoulders. They stood by the cigarette counter, huddled away from the aisles.

Marc saw a plastic tub filled with umbrellas of various colour, size and pattern. He picked up and passed an umbrella to each member of the party. "Use these if any of those people come at you," Marc said. "We have to be quiet from now on. Those things come at any sound... Right-now, we have to make sure this place is empty... Duncan, you move down this first aisle to the back, then we sweep across the shop... Glenn, you cover us in case we flush any up this way... Reg, look after Melanie, and watch the door. We don't need any more of them coming inside."

Marc moved across to the first aisle and stood ready with the umbrella, holding it by the handle in his right and three-quarters of the way down with his left. He felt it would work as a spear and it seemed to feel sturdy enough to punch through any eye, through the nasal cavity, or the roof of the mouth. Duncan stepped into the first aisle, and Glenn moved to stand behind Marc.

Duncan could see that there were four bodies in the aisle: two lay flat, while another had crumpled where they had been standing and was propped up against the shelves, and the other had fallen into a chiller with fresh pasta, pizzas and sauces in it. Duncan gripped the umbrella like a spear too, holding it in front of him like a warrior. He moved passed the first body, looking at the person: it was a young black woman, maybe in her early twenties, with the most serene expression on her face Duncan had seen, underneath splatters and drips of clotted and dried blood. He passed the second body, the one that was leaning against the shelves, almost fooling Duncan into believing they had sat down and were asleep: it was an overweight, middle-aged Greek man with a thick moustache and a balding head. Blood stained the man's shirt. A layer of blood, thick like paint, tarred his chin and neck. He passed the third body, lying face-down on the polished concrete floor: it was a middle-aged Greek lady with heavy eye-makeup and slicked, thinning dyed-black hair tied in a bun at the back. Blood pooled around her face in an abstract, broken lake. He glanced back at Glenn, who stood watching him from the open end of the aisle. He nodded at Duncan, giving a half-smile, then pursed his lips. Duncan moved on passed the fourth body, the one that lay in the chiller with one foot hanging out. A two-inch heeled shoe had fallen from the foot. The body belonged to a woman in her late twenties. She wore a business-suit jacket and an over-knee-length pencil-skirt. She had blood filling one nostril and stains around her mouth and on her hands.

He reached the end of the aisle and slowed to peer around the shelving unit at the end. He saw that there were two more bodies lying near to the small delicatessen-counter with two chillers across the front of it. There were no others. He waved down to Glenn and gave him a thumbs up.

Glenn patted Marc's arm and he slid along the shelving unit to the start of the second aisle.

A little later.
Marc and Duncan crossed back to the group at the front of the shop. Marc had found the manager's keys in a body at the back of the shop, he played with them, flicking the loop of six keys around his finger.

"Hi," Marc started. "It's all clear... I found the keys so we can lock ourselves in. I've already locked the back door. I'd suggest we should each go and find a sturdy bag, gather food essentials and any useful weapons. Meet back here by the counter away from the windows in ten minutes."

They each went for separate things: Duncan moved quickly to the alcohol aisle, Glenn walked to the chillers with sandwiches in them, Melanie went to the tiny clothes section to exchange her blood-stained ones for new, Marc crossed to the tinned and canned foods aisle, and Reg followed Duncan sneakily.

Reg stopped at the end of the aisle, watching Duncan as he took a bottle of whiskey, unscrewed the cap and poured it messily into his mouth. He menaced at the seemingly oblivious Duncan, when he gulped down a mouthful and righted the bottle. Duncan turned slowly to face Reg.

"I thought you'd try something," he said.

"What d'you want from me?" Reg growled.

"I don't want anything."

Reg eased into the aisle.

Duncan lit a cigarette and pulled on it. He blew smoke across the space between himself and Reg.

"...Except to see you dead..."

"Why? Why me? I don't even know you!"

"That's beside the point right now, Reginald," Duncan said, then took another long drink from the bottle.

"You won't kill me with these people around," Reg stated flicking his head in the direction of the others.

Duncan placed the bottle on the nearest shelf and took the pistol from behind his back and pointed it, straight-armed, at Reg's face. Reg did not flinch.

"Why shouldn't I put a bullet in your head, Reg?"

Reg did not answer.

Duncan closed the gap between them, pressing the barrel into the soft wrinkles of Reg's brow.

"Give me one good reason."

Reg did not answer.

"I'll give you to the count of three..."

Reg blinked, staring into Duncan's eyes.

"One... Two... Three."

"I have information," Reg blurted weakly.

"Hey! Duncan! Put that down," Marc shouted, marching angrily towards them. He slapped the pistol down. "You two need to stop this bull-shit! Now! Right now!"

Marc stared at both men.

"Now go and find bags and fill them with food... We have no idea what the situation is like in the rest of the country... Or the world, for that matter... Quit this shit right now! We have to do the best for all of us, otherwise we'll all be dead," Marc shouted, then turned and walked away.

Reg dropped his head, then sank into an aisle, slinking away from Duncan.

Duncan picked up a fresh bottle of whiskey and started along the aisle, walking towards a body with a backpack on. He pulled the backpack free without a care for the body. He unzipped the bag then emptied the contents on the floor. He jammed the whiskey bottle inside and slung the backpack over his shoulder.

Across the shop.
Melanie tucked in her new, slightly oversized t-shirt into a pair of fitted jeans. She pulled a tight, black v-neck jumper over her shoulder and tugged it down over her midriff, pressing down the folds of the t-shirt. She found a long-strapped satchel at the end of the tiny clothing section, hung it across her shoulder, and opened it. She entered various aisles, selecting salt and sugar, spices, some canned vegetables and frozen chicken breasts and legs.

She joined Glenn in the fresh food section. He was eating cream-cakes, sat on the floor with his legs spread, leaning back against the base of a chiller-cabinet. She selected a roast chicken and salad sandwich and sat opposite him.

"It's nice not to have to pay, for once," Glenn remarked.

"Yeah," Melanie whispered.

"Everything is so expensive at the moment... Ha!... My doctor kept telling me to stop eating so many cakes and sweets... I love having sweet teeth. Not just one sweet tooth. I have a whole set. And sweets are great."

"My dentist told me that when I was younger..."

Glenn smiled. "Good advice..." he chuckled.

Marc walked towards them and crouched, placing down his bag; a large camping backpack he had removed from the body of a hippie-looking traveller. He had collected tinned and canned goods, bottled water and medicine. He placed several packs of sandwiches and bottles of fruit juice into the top of the bag, filling it, then tied the straps securing the contents inside.

"We should meet the others at the counter," he suggested.

Glenn nodded and clambered to his feet, gripping shelves to pull his weight up onto his ankles.

Melanie stood and walked with Glenn, following Marc, to the counter.

Reg walked towards them from the left and joined them.

Duncan arrived a moment later. He checked his watch – it was 3:46pm.

"How far do we have to go?" Glenn asked softly.

"It's about a mile. Give or take routes we may not be able to cross."

"That's not too far," Glenn said and nodded. He squeezed Melanie's shoulder and she tried to smile.

"Is everyone armed?" Marc asked.

The group took out their weapons: Reg had a carving knife and one of Glenn's hammers; Duncan had a pair of scissors and a cricket-bat; Melanie gripped a carving knife; Glenn had an iron mallet with copper faces and a chisel-ended hammer; Reg held Marc's police-baton and a kitchen knife; and Marc held a meat cleaver and carving-fork.

"We'll be much-safer in the police station than out in the open, or holed-up somewhere like this."

Duncan said nothing. He necked more whiskey, then washed down two pain-killers.

"I'll lead the way, everyone else stay close behind. Reg, check the door. Glenn, Melanie – you two move over behind him and be ready to follow me."

Marc held Duncan back.

"I know you know what's going on... And I want to know, too... As soon as we're safe – you're gonna tell me everything..."

"Is that so?"

"Yeah. That's so," he said. "Reg, how's it looking out-there?"

"It's clear for now."

Marc walked to the front, to take the lead, and unlocked the door. He pulled the door open and crept into the daylight.

Reg took Duncan into an aside, pressing a hand on Duncan's chest. He said, "I'm going to be watching you..."

"I hope that's fun for you," Duncan smarted.

CHAPTER 10 - WITH A LITTLE HELP (AND THE GEEK KILLERS) - Plymouth

Sainsbury's supermarket, Crabtree, Plymouth.
JAMES 'JERRY' HARDBOLD, 21 year old Englishman – stood in the milk aisle. He had shoulder-length straggly-blonde hair under a brightly patterned beanie, overgrown sideburns and a Jesus-beard. He was average and lean, always slouching with low slung shoulders and an exhausted appearance. He wore a faded and paint-blotched t-shirt, worn-in stonewash jeans, and scuffed, dirty blue Adidas Classics. He loafed at the wall of milk, staring through glazed eyes and hooded lids. He blinked and his eyes darted from type to type and size to size. He yawned, shielding his mouth with the back of his hand.

He flicked hair from his eyes, then they wandered across the various varieties of milk in a stoned-daze. Then the shopper three paces away coughed-up blood over the plastic milk bottles in front of him.

Dark red spread across pristine white.

People started coughing and puking blood, doubling-over and ashamedly covering their faces. Others collapsed and died around Jerry in the aisle, dropping baskets with *clings* of metal on concrete. Some contents fell from a lop-sided basket – a six-inch pack of tinned tuna rolled free and passed Jerry's trainers.

He watched it roll by, following it down the aisle.

Then he noticed all of the other people.

Jerry looked around slowly, apathetic and disinterested, moving from body to body. A deep, sinking feeling tickled its way down his spine. Across the aisle and from what he could see of the cash registers, everyone was dead. He gently placed his basket on the floor where he stood, and walked away casually. His head swam and buzzed with thoughts like fireworks.

He crossed to the small book section and stopped. His eyes dashed across the shelves, reading every word, every name, every title.

Someone walked up to him, but he ignored them, when they asked, "Is this a terrorist attack? Or a chemical attack? Or a virus? Or a disease? What's.. What d'you think is going on?"

Jerry answered without looking at the person, "I don't know what's happening..."

He picked up a survival guide, then another, then walked out of the shop without paying, pushing the books in a shopping bag. The alarm came on like an air-raid siren.

Jerry marched into the car-park and headed towards the Premier Inn across the road, clutching the books under his arm, wrapped in tight orange plastic bag.

Across the car-park dozens of cars had collided or careened off the roads and grounds, through bushes, up turfed inclines and into street-lights.

Jerry glanced up at the sky as a tiny single-engine Cessna *buzzed* through the clouds, then darted toward land, rotor-first.

Three infected charged down a woman and beat at her. She fell to the ground and the infected spilled oozing blood-vomit onto her face.

Jerry reached the road and darted across, leaping between a blue 2003 Fiat Punto and a grey 2006 Hyundai Getz. He bolted for the side of the Premier Inn and raced across the rear car-park and through the foliage of the wood that surrounded the complex of buildings. The leaves of the oak-trees fluttered then settled.

Ten minutes ago. Follerton Manor.
An exclusive function was being held on the rear lawns of a large, converted country-house, enclosed in a huge stone wall. There were three marquees of different sizes across the main back-lawn, and a private dining area on a smaller secluded lawn near the gardener's tool shed. Dozens of waiters and waitresses served a hundred or more guests, seated in the marquees and standing around the fringes and lawns in small groups.

One of the waitresses – FIONA CARTER-BLYTHE, 20 year old English young woman – tried to waste time. She was a stunning, easy-on-the-eye young lady with long, sleek brown hair, an angelic face and bright, dazzling blue eyes. She was slim and petite, giving her a dainty look, but her demeanour and mannerisms were fiery and intense. She wore a white shirt with a thin black tie, a buttoned black waistcoat, a black pencil skirt and comfortable black flats. A traditional outfit for female waiting staff at occasions such as this.

The largest marquee faced the back of the mansion and the facing-wall had been removed so that the guests could look from the house across the lush, meticulous garden to the marquee and vice versa.

Fiona walked into the largest marquee through the open side and passed a dance-floor that had been built at the centre of a grand deck, pincered by tables on three sides. Twenty tables were spread around the marquee with eight guests sat around each.

Lunch had just been served and the dance-floor was empty, bar waiters criss-crossing to tables around its perimeter.

A band played softly from a small stage built at the head of the dance-floor.

Fiona crossed to the bar that lined most of the side wall of the marquee and stood near one of the six bar-men, who were waiting on guests, cleaning glasses and getting prepared for the next course. At both ends of the bar there were doorways leading to corridors built out from the marquee that acted as covered conduits to another marquee adjoining the largest one. This second marquee was where all of the food-courses were being prepared and served from.

"I'm going to have a ciggie-break out the back," she said, touching the bar-man's bicep, then walked through a slit-opening in the middle of the marquee wall behind the bar. The opening led to a roofless square-shaped clearing where barrels, boxes and food trolleys were being stored. This area was formed by the main marquee, the corridors at either end of the bar, and the second, catering marquee behind; an un-secret hiding place.

After smoking half of the cigarette, the Head Waiter appeared from another slit-opening, from the catering marquee. "Fiona! You are to ask me, and me alone, for your breaks! I will permit you them when I wish!" he said in a high-pitched squeal. He was French and was the exact character that almost seemed like a stereotype for a Head Waiter.

Fiona dropped her head and smirked. She knew how to play apologetic and was well practised, and hid her amusement with a submissive tip of her head.

He eventually said, with an infuriated drawl, "You have been especially-requested by Mr Dryden, to serve the head-table on the side-lawn... Maintenant!"

The Head Waiter puffed out his chest and pointed at the slit-opening he had pushed through one second earlier.

One minute later.
Fiona served the head-table from a trolley that a butler had brought outside to the side-lawn. He had pushed the trolley from the kitchens in the manor house two paces behind Fiona as she had walked to the table.

Mr DOUGLAS DRYDEN, 56 year old Englishman – sat at the head of the table. He had a stern face, with deep wrinkle-lines on his forehead and cheeks, a heavy brow, deep-set blue eyes and a blunt nose. He wore a black three-piece suit, a spotless white shirt, a black tie and perfectly-shined black shoes. He had an emerald green handkerchief folded in his jacket breast-pocket – the only colour he wore. He had no rings or jewellery, and no wristwatch.

The table was set forty metres away from the catering marquee and seated nine – all of whom looked elegant, officious, like powerful bureaucrats or former prime-ministers and presidents. This was the most exclusive-table at the exclusive affair.

Fiona served the nine, keeping her expression as blank as she could manage.

Dryden eyed her for a brief moment.

The other eight sat in silence, watching Dryden.

Two minutes later.
Fiona walked away from the head-table back to the manor house spitting chewing-gum into a flowerbed, when the all of the people at the exclusive-table started to cough and choke and expire –

all except Dryden, who disregarded the multiple pleading and shocked faces, then deaths, in front of him. He continued to eat his meal, uninterrupted.

He looked malevolently at the corpses.

He skewered a crayfish tail on his fork and dipped it in a mayonnaise and white truffle-infused olive oil sauce and delivered it swiftly to his mouth. He sliced four chopped heads of purple asparagus and stabbed his fork through them. He ate some of the buttery cabbage and used his napkin to catch a stray drip of butter from a crease in his chin. He stabbed at another crayfish tail.

Dryden's executive-secretary – MYLES FOREMANN, 41 year old Englishman – walked to the table from the shade of the gardener's shed, where he had been lingering. He was tall, stiff and lean, but with wide, swimmer's-shoulders making him look angular and top-heavy. He had short, grey-blonde hair, parted at the side. He had a thin-lipped mouth, bony cheeks and a sharp, pointy nose. His eyes were concrete-grey and beady, behind thin, coal-grey horn-rimmed glasses that possessed no style or fashion and made him look more a peculiar android than a man. He was dressed in a uniform grey-suit, white shirt, cornflower-blue tie and black work-shoes. He stood at his master's side, ever the lapdog, smiling evilly at the table's other guests. His emotionless eyes sparkled in the midday sun. He did not speak before Dryden spoke.

Dryden ate another of the crayfish tails and placed his fork neatly on the plate.

"What of the helicopter, Myles?"

"It's ready to take off on the west-lawn, Sir," Foremann announced.

Dryden nodded, smiled wickedly, then finished his food and glass of Romanée Conti, Côte de Nuits, 1970.

He placed the wine-glass on the table and savoured the vintage. His fingers knocked his knife and fork to close and angled them at ten twenty-five.

Dryden pursed his lips and dabbed the napkin across them, then he stood, discarding the napkin onto his plate without a care. Foremann's hands hovered over the back of Dryden's chair, impotent to touch it.

Dryden pushed his own chair back and stood.

Foremann walked a pace behind his master, as they crossed to the wood-shed, passing it, then ventured through an arched-doorway in the garden's wall. They marched along under a tall, arched arbour that was entwined and strangled by white Akito roses. They exited the arbour and crossed to another walled-garden, where a black five-seat Eurocopter Colibri awaited them.

The pilot started the engine and the blades wavered, then started to spin.

One minute ago. Inside the manor-house.
Fiona walked into the kitchen through a side-access into the pantry. One of the chefs lay on the floor choking to death, holding his own throat as he hacked violently. He rocked from side to side, straining every muscle. The veins and tendons in his neck pinched and tensed like strips of rope under a thin layer of paling skin.

Fiona gasped, and held her hands in front of her body, hesitating. She whimpered.

"What--... What should I do?"

The chef scrambled onto all fours, groaning, then coughed up blood, collapsing face-first onto white and black chessboard-tiles. The body twitched and wriggled on the floor.

Fiona stared at the chef for a long time, not knowing what to do, not knowing which way to turn. Her hands cupped around her mouth and chin, the moisture from her breath making them hot and clammy. She hovered on the spot, quavering, not knowing whether to check for a pulse or run for help. She tip-toed a step forward and back again.

"Oh my God!" she murmured.

Fiona rushed through the pantry door and outside. She jumped down a small, garden staircase of three steps, bounding down the broken-chalk path to find help in the marquee.

She skidded to a stop when she saw into the marquee.

She found a similar scene to the kitchen, only multiplied: every single person at every table was dead. Blood streaked down their faces from nostrils and lips. People had collapsed in huddles near standing-bars built around the marquees' six corner poles, but not around the centre-pole near the dance-floor; that was empty. There were many of the dead not present. And Fiona noticed their absence, glancing around for any signs of life. A scream rent the air making her jump on the spot. She looked for the source, but could not see anything through the marquee. She quickly started to notice blood stains near several of the exits. It looked like some people had been chased to the exits and outside.

Fiona gazed at the sight of disaster in front of her, wide-eyed with shock, horrified and temporarily frozen with fear. Her feet felt rooted to the spot. She stood in the open-side of the marquee, on the edge of the wooden flooring. Her shoes rested on the coconut matting that had been placed along the edge of the marquee, and had been trimmed and laid-out to guide guests to the broken chalk paths built around the existing garden. The matting felt spongy underfoot.

One of the guests stirred. Then several more started to shift and move.

The first infected stood up from a table. Two bodies were face-down in their meals, still sat in their chairs around the table. The infected vomited blood over itself, staining its chest dark red, hanging its mouth open and slack. It rocked on its ankles, finding its balance. The infected was four metres from Fiona, with a table that sat eight between it and her.

Fiona stared at the infected, unable to take her eyes from it, when she started to back away.

A dozen of the seemingly dead arose infected, from various spots around the marquee.

Fiona paced back until her foot found the *crunch* of the broken chalk path that the matted-paths to the marquees' openings had been positioned to meet. She felt the gravel *crunch* again under her flat as she twisted her ankle in small arcs, feeling the uneven surface through the slim, rubber soles of his shoe.

Only one of the infected had noticed Fiona, and it moved achingly slowly in her direction, eyes locked onto her.

Her other shoe met the gravel and it appeared that the infected had lost interest in her. Its head swung away from Fiona, alerted to the other infected shuffling and clambering to their feet. Cracks of light beamed momentarily from one of the exits at the far side of the marquee.

Something flashed by at the other end of the marquee and Fiona saw one of the infected chasing a guest beyond the marquee. It barrelled into the woman, who could not run in a knee-length silk dress, and pounced on her.

Like the starting shot of a race, Fiona whipped around, dashed up the path and darted passed the pantry door.

Blood gushed out of the mouth of the infected, soaking the woman, as she swung and flapped her arms at her attacker. It beat at her, still gargling and spitting blood. The woman tried to crawl away, but a second infected stopped her with an accidental kick to the face. The infected hanging onto her back hacked and coughed blood over her face. It stomped on her back as it got to its feet, then lurched off across the lawn.

At the side of the manor-house.
Fiona bounded along the path, passed the kitchen's windows; inside was a blood-soaked mess. An infected lurched into the path ahead of her and she skidded to a stop. She ran back to the pantry door and rushed inside, pulling the door closed behind her.

She found the toilets on the ground-floor and threw herself into the room. She leapt into one of the cubicles, palming the door shut, and locked herself in.

She tried her mobile-phone, but there was no signal. "Shit!" she moaned, gripping the useless plastic and electronic block in her hand.

She heard the familiar sound of a helicopter. It was loud and close to the building. Air *howled* at the windows. The sound grew, then subsided, fading gradually to nothing.

Eighteen minutes ago.
In a green 1998 Vauxhall Corsa with spotty paint and rust around the wheel-arches, BAHRUL 'BAZ' GOHIL, 20 year old Englishman of Bangladeshi descent – drove carefully and observantly amongst dozens of other cars. He was a small, heavy, dark-tanned young man with friendly, dark eyes, a cheerful smile and scruffy black hair. He was husky, stocky and doughy, but was a rugby-player in his

spare time which made his chubby exterior betray a small bull within him. He wore a faded *Superman* t-shirt, battered and torn denim jeans and Converse All-Stars with *The Flash* emblazoned on the fabric. He was travelling along the A38 motorway going West, tapping the steering-wheel with both hands. His mobile-phone buzzed from his jeans' pocket and a tinny, hollow sample of music started to play – Aphex Twin's *Come To Daddy*.

He checked the caller-ID before he answered it – it was Fiona. He pressed the green button.
"He–..."

"When am I going to be picked-up?" she asked impatiently, interrupting his greeting.

"I'm on my way... I'll be there in about twenty minutes – give or take," he replied. "The traffic looks to be getting a bit lighter." He scanned optimistically down the busy motorway.

"Just hurry up – gotta go," she said, and hung up.

Baz tossed his mobile onto the passenger seat.

"You can be a right bossy bitch, sometimes," he murmured to his phone. Then he switched the radio on.

He continued along the motorway, listening to what he considered to be awful music, for ten minutes and four songs. He tapped the steering-wheel with his thumbs as he saw a road-sign that showed a turning for Plymouth, Plympton and Kingsbridge.

"That song is tipped to be Number 1," the radio DJ announced. Then Baz heard him cough. Not something he normally heard on the radio. "Excuse me," he said. "Frog in my throa–..."

Baz stared at the radio. He moved into the slow-lane, pulling in behind a 40-tonne Mercedes haulage lorry, as traffic slowed down to a crawl, then stopped altogether. He took a deep breath and exhaled slowly, puffing his cheeks.

He drummed the steering-wheel again – waiting patiently for the traffic to start moving, when he saw something in his rear-view mirror. He turned in his seat to get a better view, twisting like a snake in the confines of the seatbelt. The driver in the car behind, a woman in her late forties, seemed to be having a fit, shaking violently and pounding out at every angle. Then the woman coughed-up blood over herself and over the inside of the windscreen of her car.

Baz's eyes widened, brows raised. He spun in his seat. Then he looked around the car, through every window, suddenly seeing other drivers in other cars. His mouth fell open. Each of the drivers appeared to be having a fit: each person struck out at their car interiors. Then he saw blood seeping out of their mouths.

He noticed the radio was silent. He tried the volume, but there was nothing.

Baz's attention was drawn back to the other drivers around his car. People raged in their seats, striking out in every direction with clenched fists; others seemed to be falling asleep; some had managed to unbuckle their seatbelts, but were trapped in their own cars as the virus swept over them.

Jerking forward, the lorry in front of the Corsa started moving away. Baz eyes widened further, staring across the bonnet of his car into the open space now manifested. The lorry accelerated and pushed a route through the stationary-cars, knocking them either side and pinning one flat against its front, until it hit the median, then ploughed on further, grating along the barrier, sparking a couple of times. It continued away, until it rolled over the back-wing of sports car and toppled into the median with a loud *bang* and *crunching* sounds.

A long void was left in front of the Corsa.

Baz looked at that the man in the car next to him. He had died, with blood dripping freely out of his nose and mouth. It looked like he had laid back against the head-rest and fallen asleep.

"Fuck this!" Baz screamed and pulled off the motorway onto the hard-shoulder.

He crawled down the side of the motorway, keeping his speed slow, peering and moving in his seat to glance into a lot of the cars.

Everyone appeared dead. Or infected and trapped, for now.

High-above the motorway.
Baz's green Corsa drove slowly up the hard-shoulder, beside the gridlocked motorway. Cars of all colours, stationary in a giant canal, glinted in the midday sun. The occupants of many of the cars beat at and vomited blood over the windows, growling, screaming, howling and roaring.

Higher-above the motorway.
Baz's car was the size of a finger-nail – and the only car moving along that stretch of the motorway, going both ways. On the other side of the motorway a 49-seater holiday coach had careened off the side of the road and ploughed into several trees before crashing.

Even-higher-above the motorway.
Baz's car was a tiny speck – driving down what looked like a river of cars that tailed off, becoming more erratic the less cars there had been on the road. The green Corsa was a tiny ember, zipping alongside the motorway, when it began to slow down. A little cloud crossed over the sun.

In the Corsa.
Baz slowed down. He saw a figure standing on the roof of one of the blocked-in cars, waving their arms in the air.
    He stopped beside two cars that were half-on and half-off the hard-shoulder. He unclipped his seatbelt, pushed the door open and stepped out. He looked across three car-roofs distance between himself and the figure.
    The figure stood on top of the car was LAYLA EDWARDS, 26 year old English young woman. She was pretty, ruddy and had a farmer's daughter, countryside-nature about her. She had curly, streaky-blonde hair tied back in a woolly bun, that glowed above a charming, smiley face. She had high, round cheeks, squinty but bright green eyes and a warm, mellow toothy-smile. Layla wore a dark blue vest, faded blue jeans and black Nike trainers. She looked startled and frightened and flapped her arms, dropping them at her sides when she saw Baz approach.
    "Hi," Baz shouted.
    "Hi. Can you help me?"
    Baz nodded quickly. "Yes. Yes... Yes."
    Layla climbed down from the car and took something from the car in her arms. It was her niece, VIVIENNE EDWARDS, 7 year old English girl. She looked like a miniature version of her aunt, with bright, fluffy blonde hair, loose and hanging down her back. She had small features, but the same high, round cheeks and constant mellow smile. Vivienne wore a white vest under a lime floral dress and buckled, shiny red shoes.
    "Can you make it through?" Baz called out.
    Layla beamed at him.
    "Shut your eyes," Layla told her niece.
    Vivienne screwed her eyes shut tightly and Layla dashed between the cars towards Baz.

A little later.
Baz continued to drive carefully and slowly, when Layla asked, "What's your plan?"
    "I've got to get to my friends!" Baz replied. "That's the only plan I have... Other than go home, make a cup of tea and sit down for a few minutes. Let this all sink in..."
    Layla frowned.
    They reached an exit from the motorway and Baz pulled off the road up the inclining off-ramp.
    An infected hurtled out of nowhere and raced at the car.
    Baz accelerated along the bridge and slalomed between five crashed cars and into an open stretch.
    The infected sprinted down the road after them, shoes beating the tarmac.

Later.
Baz, with Layla and Vivienne in the car, slowed to a stop on a winding country-road, stopping behind a stationary-car that blocked the way forward.

"Do I ram it? Then push it 'til we can get through?"

"I guess. It's a better idea than getting out and pushing," Layla said with a nod.

Baz slowly-bumped into the back of the car. The motion instantly awoke a dormant infected in the driver's seat, who scrambled around and tore at the seats. It puked blood and growled, roared and punched at the dashboard. It thrashed against the seatbelt, carving long gashes into its skin.

Baz and Layla watched, terrified.

"What do you think is happening?" Layla asked slowly. "Please don't speak too loudly."

She glanced into the backseat, where Vivienne sat with her pink iPod listening to Disney songs.

Baz also checked Vivienne in the rear-view mirror before answering.

"Honestly? I have no fucking idea," he whispered. "I only-just passed my GCSE science double-awards... But... I dunno. A virus. Some biological bull-shit... The government, aliens, conspiracy theories, the living dead, or I don't know what..."

Baz kicked down on the accelerator and butted the other car into the entrance of a field, then sped away down the road, kicking up gravel in his wake.

"It's frightening," Layla stated.

"Mmm-hmm."

Later.
Baz's car slowed outside the front of Follerton Manor, coming to a stop with a gentle *crunch* of gravel.

He glanced at the clock on his dashboard – it read: 13:02.

"Right, let me have a moment to think of a plan..."

"You're not thinking of going inside?!" Layla blurted.

"I have to – Fiona's my friend... And I can't leave her in there."

"You can't seriously want to risk all of us for her? We're safe out here for now."

"She is alive in there. She's way too stubborn to've been turned... I've gotta try."

Inside the manor-house.
Fiona remained hidden in the locked-cubicle in the toilet. She stifled her cries, pinching her nose and trying desperately to breathe through her mouth. She sat on the toilet with the lid closed, hugging her knees. She forced herself not to look at the cubicle's lock.

A *banging* noise echoed into the toilet from somewhere within the building.

In the Corsa.
Baz was about to slap his palm on the car-horn, when Layla stopped him.

"What if there are any more of those people outside?... Ones that aren't trapped in their cars? Or, were having their brunch on the lawn?"

"Okay," he agreed. "No horn."

Baz noticed his mobile-phone in the alcove below his radio; Layla must have moved it when she and Vivienne got in the car. It still was not working.

"Do you have your mobile?"

Layla took out her phone, but did not give it to Baz. "It's dead," she moaned.

Baz looked at the screen and saw there was no signal.

"How am I going to find Fiona?"

Layla did not have an answer.

A man appeared near the garages at the side of the manor house. He looked around frantically. He was HARLAN MADISON, 31 year old Australian. He had short curly brown hair, like a Greek statue, with a large brow and nose, and thick jaw. He had hooded grey eyes, alert and discerning, and wide, full lips. He wore a white shirt unbuttoned at the collar with speckles of blood on the chest, black trousers and shiny black shoes. He was one of the several barmen from the marquee. He had lost his tie and waistcoat.

Harlan saw Baz, and Baz saw him.

They stared at each other for a moment. Baz moved to open his car door and stood behind it, when Harlan held up a hand, signalling for Baz to stay where he was.

Baz nodded.

Harlan's eyes beamed back at Baz. He held up his hand again; thumb pinching down the little finger, with his three other fingers raised.

Baz nodded again. Harlan replied with a smirk. And Baz took the driver's seat, easing the door shut behind him. He and Layla watched, as Harlan ran into the courtyard in front of the garages and disappeared from sight.

"Who's that?"

"His name is Harlan. He's an Aussie... He works with Fiona at these parties... I've met him a couple of times."

"Where'd you think he's going?"

"Hopefully to get Fiona... If not, I haven't a clue."

"Let's both hope that, then."

Baz nodded. "Yeah."

Five minutes later.
Baz fidgeted, tapping his hands on the steering-wheel again, when Layla put a comforting hand on top of his, stopping them from moving. She removed her hand and placed it back in her lap. "We have to be patient," she insisted.

"I'm going to go inside," he said abruptly and reached for the door-handle.

"No, don't," Layla plead, putting a hand on his shoulder.

"I have to, Harlan might now be dead... Or zombified. Or whatever that is..."

"Don't. Baz, don't..."

"It's been longer than he said..."

As Baz opened the door, Harlan and Fiona raced outside hand-in-hand, followed quickly by one of the infected. The infected had been a guest, wearing a smart dark-green suit, stained and caked in thick patches of blood. It charged after them.

"Oh shit! Oh shit! Oh shit!" Baz screamed, panic taking hold. He hesitated, watching them running toward him, quavering on the spot.

Harlan let go of Fiona's hand, letting her run alone to the car. "Go! Go! Go! I'll be right behind you!" he shouted.

Fiona glanced back, as she raced away.

Layla threw the door open and immediately clambered into the back-seat with Vivienne, who had started to cry uncontrollably. "Hi, hey, no... Don't cry... Don't cry," she said, rubbing Vivienne's arm warmly.

Harlan dashed to a nearby parked, canary-yellow Jeep Wrangler Sport and pulled the door open, as the infected hurtled toward him. Its arms swung behind it slack, its face pointed and poised to attack.

Baz panicked and let out a squeaky sob, seeing the infected getting closer and closer to Harlan. He opened his door again, then pulled it shut. He gulped loudly, then finally got out of his Corsa, leaving one foot resting in the foot-well.

Fiona reached Baz's car and clamped her hands on the door and roof, staring back at Harlan. She hesitated on the spot, letting go of the car and returning a few paces towards Harlan.

"Hey you, you shithead!" Baz shouted, waving his arms, slashing them through the air.

Fiona turned to look at Baz, her mouth hanging open.

"Hey you, fuck-face! Come over here!"

The infected skidded along the path instantly changing course to advance on Baz. This afforded Harlan the seconds he needed to grab a golf-club, tug the novelty Captain America plush-cover free from its head, and turn. He beat the infected across the throat, exactly as it was about to dash passed him. He pounded it, creating blossoms of dark crimson, clubbing the temple to pulp.

"Harlan!" Baz shouted. Harlan glared at him, then softened. He nodded. "Move!"

Baz and Harlan shared a further look, when Fiona, from the passenger-seat, shouted, "Come on! Come on, Harlan!"

Fiona left the door open and climbed into the back-seat with Layla and Vivienne.

Harlan jogged to them.

Later.
Baz drove carefully down a suburban road, manoeuvring cautiously around several crashed cars.

"Be careful, slow down a bit!" Harlan barked from the passenger-seat.

"Look," Baz started impatiently. "I can fucking drive!" he snapped. "I'm only going twelve miles an hour! So–..."

"Easy on the swearing," Fiona interjected quietly.

Baz shot Fiona a look of barely concealed contempt, then watched the road.

"Watch the road!" Harlan yelled.

Baz gritted his teeth, swerving around a stationary rust and cream 1981 Volvo 240 estate.

"Hey! Hey! There's Jerry!" Baz hit the brakes lightly. They *screeched* and *squealed* as the car slowed down and turned into an adjoining road.

Jerry gently ambled down the side of a hill-road, holding a brick in one hand and an orange Sainsbury's plastic-bag in the other: The brick was covered and shedding blood, dripping between his soaked fingers.

Baz pulled across to the curb and crawled along, matching Jerry's pace, winding the window down.

"Dude! Get in! Where've you been?"

Jerry slowly turned to the car. He nodded a hello. "Shopping," he said, and held up the bag.

"When did you get back from holiday?"

"A few hours ago."

"Cool."

"How was it? Did you have a cool time?"

"Yeah, it was good."

"Do you wanna get in?" Fiona asked across Baz.

"Huh? Yeah, I guess."

"There's no room," Harlan moaned.

"I'll just walk, it's not far..."

"Mind out for the zombies," Baz said with a smirk. "Well. No. Seriously..."

"Mmm... Yeah. I saw some... Hmm..."

"So, when did you get back to town?"

"This morning, as planned... Look, I'll just meet you at the house..."

Later.
Baz's car slowed to a stop outside their three-storey Victorian townhouse. Vivienne sat huddled on Layla's lap in the backseat with Fiona. They all looked relieved to have arrived at their destination.

Harlan jumped out, keeping-watch along the road, as Baz helped the others to climb out.

Jerry sauntered down the road and hopped up to the front-door, still holding the brick, and unlocked the door, looping the bag over his wrist. Baz noticed that Jerry looked dazed and smiled. The lock turned and Jerry shoved the door open. He walked inside.

The others rushed in behind him. Fiona closed the door quietly, locking it twice; with a chain and a deadbolt.

Several infected stalked along the tarmac, from pavement to pavement.

Fifty metres up the road, one of the infected lay on the ground. Its head had been smashed in with a brick, several small geysers of blood flushed from its wounds.

Moments later. Inside the house.

They assembled them in the living-room; a knocked-through space conjoining the old front-room and the dining-room into a long, wide lounge. Harlan poured himself a large vodka, looking at Fiona, who poured herself, Layla and Vivienne a small glass of Bailey's each. Jerry rolled a large, thick spliff, as Baz paced the room, wringing his hands together, biting his lip.

The television set displayed nothing but a statement that there was no signal. A laptop on the dining-table at the back end of the room showed at internet page with the web browser showing that there was no signal. Another window on the laptop showed all digital radio reception had reduced to zero. Baz stopped in the centre of the room. "TV is gone. The radio is completely dead. Mobiles are gone. The internet is fucking gone! And everyone is dead or infected with that zombie-virus...!" Baz squawked, arms flapping.

"Hey!" Fiona said. "Language..."

Baz froze, consternation showing in his expression. "First things first..."

"Look," Harland started. "We have to do something. Go somewhere... I have some family in London, maybe this thing hasn't spread."

"If we go somewhere, the Army might stop us. What if Plymouth is quarantined! They might even fucking shoot us," Baz groaned. "There's no way of knowing if anywhere else is any safer!"

"We have to think about this... And stay quiet. And calm," Fiona asserted. She motioned for Baz to sit, and he did, flopping into an armchair. He huffed, then looked at the 42" Sony flat-screen television.

"If there's no TV, then there's no-one there to report the news, or to hear it..." he said despondently.

Jerry glanced at Baz.

"We have to at least try to do something. I don't think we'll be safe in this house for long," Layla said.

"What about a boat?"

"We're three miles from any boat in this house," Fiona replied. "And to get there would be through three miles of those people."

"We wouldn't stand a chance," Baz moaned. "Unless we were tooled-up..." he said, drifting off into his own thoughts. His thick, bushy eyebrows twitched.

"Then we go to London. There must be some safe-place with scientists and doctors and nerds and people with loads of fucking guns!" Harlan announced. "We should be safe there."

"If we do go to London, there has to be some-kind of army or MI5 or something..." Fiona agreed. She nodded, smiled, looked at Layla, then at Vivienne. She bit her lip.

Baz swallowed hard.

Jerry lit the spliff and walked to the back-window overlooking the compact garden. He slid the pane up and sat on the sill. "So we're going to London then?"

Fiona looked over at Jerry and her eyebrows raised. "I guess."

"I suppose I might be able to use my bat'leth and my two d'k tagh daggers..." Baz thought aloud.

"What's one of those?" Harlan asked.

"They're Klingon weapons from *Star Trek*..."

"Do you have any more?" Harlan asked, interest peaked. He edged forward on his chair.

"Well," Baz said calmly, "I have a replica of the Hattori Hanzo katana sword from *Kill Bill*, a replica of Ice from *Game of Thrones*, and a replica of the sword from *Serenity* with the jagged-y blade... Oh, and the two fighting-daggers that Legolas used, from *The Lord Of The Rings* films... And a Sting – Frodo's short-sword from *The Lord Of The Rings*..."

"Boy! You're a grade-A nerd, Baz!" Harlan chided, shaking his head. "What the fuck–!"

"Will any of them actually work?" Layla asked.

"Oh, yeah! They're all sharp! I sharpen them! And oil them... And polish them!... We replaced some of the blades!... Most of the blades, yeah..."

"You nerd!" Harlan groaned.

A little later. In Baz's bedroom.

Baz, Fiona, Harlan and Layla stood in the room; a poster-plastered, ornament, figure and toy filled box-room. Baz pulled a large, long trunk from underneath his bed, where a *Spider-man* duvet hung over the edge.

Layla eyed the replica of Sting that balanced on two nails on the wall above Baz's PC. The sword was a long, silver leaf-shaped blade with an overlapping twin tusk-shaped hilt and a florally decorated wooden handle. Layla thought about reaching out and taking it off the nails, then resisted.

Harlan looked around the room scornfully. "Dude, you have the bedroom of a twelve year old!"

Baz shot Harlan a look. "I don't really care, right-now... Dude... Ahem, at least I've got some weapons that might be useful."

Harlan snorted derisively.

"So, let's show you them all.."

Fiona watched Baz as he unlatched the trunk and pulled the lid open. Inside a Klingon bat'leth sat on the top of a pile of collectables and comic books. The bat'leth was draped in a red satin cloth. Baz pulled back the cloth, clutching the centre handle, of three, and showed off the curved, four-bladed weapon to the others. He placed the bat'leth gently on his duvet and took out the d'k tagh daggers, which were also wrapped in satin. He placed the daggers next to the bat'leth and straightened them. He pushed the trunk under the bed.

Above Baz's bed there was the katana, an 80cm long samurai sword with a long, black and pearl cross-laid grip for use with two hands. It sat on a short shelf where it was mounted on wooden pins. Eight inches above that shelf there was another, with the Serenity sword; a 40cm weapon with ridged and slightly curved blade and a wooden handle split into five segments by silver rings. Baz took both swords down and placed them next to the bat'leth and daggers.

Layla took Sting down and laid it with the others.

From the top of Baz's wardrobe, he took down two boxes, one long and thin, the other short and wide. He opened the first box and took out Ice; a 140cm long longsword with a large hilt, two-handed grip and large metal pommel. Inside the second box were Legolas' daggers; two 57cm fighting-knives with long, gently-curving delicate blades and hardwood handles.

Baz took a step back and reviewed the weapons.

Fiona's brow furrowed as she looked at each item.

Harlan slightly grimaced, looking from the weapons, to Baz, and back again.

Layla stared at the assorted swords, knives and bat'leth.

"How do know they'll even cut anything?" Harlan exclaimed.

"Some of my other friends and I go out to the woods and stage mini-battles..."

"That's pretty fucking gay, dude."

"Hey!" Baz shouted. "That's–..."

"Get to the point," Fiona interjected, cutting Baz off. "How do you know they'll even work?"

"Well, some of them... Like I said... We've changed a few of the blades... The ones that needed new blades, that is... So they're now made of stronger metals... And–..."

"And, what?" Harlan demanded.

"And, well... Um... We bought a pig once and... Um... We hung it up in the woods by a few ropes... Errr... And we took turns to chop it to bits... All of the swords and daggers work really well."

"That's gross!" Layla whimpered.

"That's fucking weird, guy!"

"Shut up, Harlan, you dick," Baz said defensively, momentarily dominating the room, then he shied back. Harlan was shocked into silence, and shied back as well. Fiona felt a tiny murmur of being impressed with Baz, but it was fleeting. "The pig was dead when we got it... It wasn't alive."

"So you know they'll be worthwhile?" Layla offered.

"Oh yeah... Mmm-hmm."

"And your friends must be fuckin' weirdos!"

"Bugger off."

"Err... Guys..." Jerry said from the doorway. All eyes turned on him. "The party's just got bigger."

"What does that mean?"

Downstairs.
Harlan was first to reach the bottom of the stairs and pushed his way inside. Fiona, Baz and Layla followed quickly after him. Jerry sauntered down the stairs, pulling a lighter free from his pocket.

Harlan stopped the moment he entered the room and the others had to file around him.

Two young men stood in front of them. They were BERNARD 'BERNIE' WALLACE, 21 year old Englishman of Afro-Caribbean descent – and SUTHEP KHAN, 20 year old Englishman of Indian descent. Bernie had a baby-face with round, dimpled cheeks and a long, round nose. His eyes were soft and dark chocolate colour, wide and alert. He was a short man with sloped shoulders and a slight stoop giving the impression his arms were longer than they were, even though they were often slung in his jacket pockets. He wore a black beanie that was flecked with blood, a blue and canary-yellow letterman jacket over a white t-shirt, baggy black jogging-bottoms and blue-and-grey *Batman* Converse ankle-high trainers. Bernie carried Storm Shadow's katana sword from *GI Joe*, a knife from *Rambo First Blood* with a 9" blade sheathed on his right hip, and a Roman Gladius sword sheathed on the left. Suthep had an unlined, oblong face with a large, ridged nose and thick, straight eyebrows. His eyes were beady and hooded, making the whole display of his face seem deadpan and robotic. He was tall and stringy with gangly arms and legs, although he appeared to be very articulate and nimble. He wore a black hoodie over a blue Captain America t-shirt, brown corduroy trousers and red-white-and-blue high-ankle *Captain America* Nike Dunk trainers. Suthep carried a Medieval club with twenty-one two-inch spikes arranged along and around its end, and a Medieval kite shield that had a large spiked, domed boss in the centre of the front. Their weapons and clothes were stained with drips, splashes and polka-dots of blood.

"What the hell? How did you two get here?!" Baz screamed with glee, and dashed towards the pair.

The three young men hugged, as Fiona, Harlan and Layla watched, and Jerry smoked.

"Who are these people?" Layla asked, directing her question at Fiona.

"Baz's friends... The ones he killed the pig with, presumably."

"It was already dead," Suthep added, peaking out over Baz's round shoulder.

"They're funny!" Vivienne exclaimed.

"What happened?" Baz enquired. "How did you get here?"

"We got out of our house, decided to come here..." Bernie revealed. "We thought if you were still alive, then you'd probably have a plan."

"That was your plan? Come here, and hope Baz has a plan?" Harlan accused.

"Yep."

"Well, yeah," Bernie admitted. "Baz likes horror films."

"I do. I do..."

"So? So what?!" Harlan shouted.

"Keep your voices down," Fiona asserted, wandering into the kitchen.

"Why do you have a shield?" Vivienne asked, staring at Suthep.

Suthep shrugged. "It came in handy."

A little later.
The group sat in the living-room. Fiona and Jerry had cooked chicken, vegetables and noodles in a spicy Thai sauce. They ate for a long time without speaking; the only sound was the *clinking* of cutlery on the bowls, and the chewing of food.

"What about our parents!" Harlan said, finally breaking the silence. "I can't ring my mum or dad... Who knows what Oz will be like... If I can't get through, do you think that means it's bad for Australia too, guys?"

"My parents flew to Bangladesh three-weeks ago... They're still there."

"I assume my parents would've been in Dorset by now," Layla said quietly.

Vivienne sat up. "My mum died three years ago."

Layla looked at her niece with soft, sad eyes. She looked at the others. "Vivienne has lived with me since then..."

"What about your parents, Fi?" Baz asked.

"They were on their sailboat in the Caribbean. As far as I'm aware," she replied nonchalantly.

"Jerry?"

"Um... Well... My dad would be in Plymouth somewhere. And my mum would be in Bristol, with my brothers."

"Aren't you worried about them?" Harlan asked boldly.

"Yeah. Of course. I guess."

"You-Brits are well-, well-emotionless about family!"

"I think everyone is feeling the same way. Where-ever any of them are... They're in exactly the same situation as we are... Quite fucking, fucked!" Jerry said. "Everyone we care about."

"My parents are with Bernie's in Florida... They went on a cruise," Suthep admitted slowly. "Around the Bahamas and West Indies..."

"Then they were going to Orlando," Bernie added. "To go to Disney World. To meet Mickey Mouse."

Jerry wandered to one of the front windows and pulled the curtain an inch across. He saw several infected roaming the street beyond Baz's Corsa. "It looks fairly bleak outside."

"Tell us something we don't know!" Harlan blurted.

Two days later. Four miles North of Yeovil.
The group crept along a thick, bramble-strangled hedgerow in a shallow sloping field, ducking under the low branches of trees and walking in single-file. The field was muddy and furrowed, between dried crusty mud thin gullies of water splashed around their boots and shoes.

Harlan led the group with the daggers and replica of Ice. Baz followed behind Harlan holding the katana in front him and the bat'leth lashed down his back. Jerry followed Baz holding the sword with the jagged blade in front of him. Fiona, Layla and Vivienne followed; Vivienne had her ear-phones in her ears again, clutching Layla's hand; Fiona carried the short-sword in one hand, and a claw-hammer in the other, with the two *Star Trek* daggers crossed at the back of her belt. She was careful and kept watched behind them, beaming down the path they had taken, where Suthep and Bernie prowled at the back. They all had backpacks strapped onto their backs; filled with food and supplies, and rolled sleeping-bags tied on top. Blood, wet and dry, stuck to all of their weapons and clothes.

They stopped when they found a small shed and took some shelter.

Baz stood at the window as Jerry and Fiona made sandwiches, sawing thick slabs of bread and spreading them with margarine and jam. Suthep crossed to join Baz.

"What if there are other survivors?" Layla asked, breaking the silence.

"What if there are?" Harlan replied sharply.

"We could try to find some," Layla suggested. "There must be other people out-there..."

"Yeah, it is possible," Bernie agreed. "We can't be the only people left."

"We could die trying," Baz said. "But... --We might help some people too. We should try to find a doctor or a nurse... Someone who's a sharp-shooter or an assassin..."

"Yeah, like there are dozens of hit-men running around the country!" Harlan snapped.

"The army would be nice, in the least."

"A nurse or doctor would be useful... Someone who can forage for food, too."

"I have these books," Jerry said slowly, rolling a spliff. "So we don't really need Ray Mears."

"They'll only go so far," Baz said. "We need to find practical people... If we find a safe place in London, we'll need traps and early-warning systems..."

"And CCTV access," Suthep added. "So we can watch all of the plague victims."

"That's thinking a bit far ahead," Layla said gloomily.

Fiona said nothing. She rubbed the edge of the sword with a whetstone.

Two days later. Five miles West of Andover.
They had taken shelter in a farmer's barn. They had lit six candles and placed them in a two-metre wide circle on the floor, where they had cleared away the hay and straw. Fiona stood at a large window on the mezzanine watching the fields on the northern and western sides of the barn. They had locked the barn doors and barricaded them with dozens of hay-bales. They had found loose nails and hung sheets of torn sacks around any parts of the walls where there were cracks in the planked-walls.

It was daylight outside and Fiona had been on watch since the sun had come up. She stared across the fields, as sunlight shone through the tree-line two hundred metres away. She had not seen any infected at all. She was pleased, but remained alert. Vivienne had brought her a cup of coffee a few minutes ago which was now drinkable. She sipped it, sitting on a hay-bale that she had placed in front of the window. There was a pitchfork sitting on the bale next to her, and the sword next to it.

She looked down into the barn. Vivienne, Baz and Layla sat to one side – they were talking, but she could not hear their whispers. Suthep and Bernie played a game of travel-chess on a miniaturised, magnetic board. She saw Harlan walk over to Jerry, who sat near the candle circle on his own reading a copy of Ray Mears' *Outdoor Survival Handbook*.

"We need to get some food from a shop nearby," he said. "I've okayed it with Fiona."

"That's great news," Jerry said sarcastically, putting his book down.

"Well, she's your friend..."

"You didn't need to get an okay from her about me."

"I felt I should ask."

"Then ask me, next time."

Baz played with Vivienne, as Layla climbed the ladder and joined Fiona.

"I was just reminiscing about nice things with Baz and Vivienne..."

"Oh yeah?" Fiona said with a smile. "Like what?"

"Fresh, clean clothes and showers, baths and soap... Actual other people... Teachers, parents, friends... I wish I could have a steaming bath right-now."

"Me too."

Vivienne lay back on her sleeping-bag. She stared at the cross-beams above her, then looked at Baz.

"Why did we leave the car?" she asked softly.

"We ran out of petrol... And, besides, having a car would've probably attracted more of those people..."

"What's wrong with everybody?"

"I have no idea," Baz said joylessly.

Suthep and Bernie were close enough to hear Vivienne's question. They both frowned at Baz, who smiled weakly back at them.

Two hours later.
Harlan stood on a thick branch in a tall oak tree, looking down a broad, sweeping hill at a village in the middle-distance. The ground stretched out across dozens of fields, and nestled amongst them was the village of Shipton Bellinger. He used binoculars to get a closer view.

"It looks pretty empty," Harlan shouted down the trunk.

Jerry stood at the base of the tree, clutching the handle of the razor-sharp katana sword. He swiped it through the air, cutting and slashing, twisting the handle in swirling arcs.

"The village looks empty, no-one's around... It's like a ghost town... Stop playing around, you stupid stoner!"

Jerry looked up at Harlan and lowered the sword.

Harlan could see that there was at least a pub. He started down the tree, using the branches like wonky-rungs on a twisted, uneven ladder. "There's a few places we can try down-there," he said.

"If there's a shop or a pub, then we should be okay," Jerry said with a sigh.

They started down the vast slope toward the village.

"What's your deal?"

"What?"

"You just seem like a carefree stoner... But–..."

"But what?" Jerry interrupted.

"I just can't read you."

"And?"

"That bothers me, dude."

Jerry slowed and Harlan glanced over his shoulder at him.

"I don't know what's going on right-now. And so I'm being quiet. And I'm waiting to see what happens next."

"As long as it is 'quiet' and not you spiralling into some unnerving murderous rampage, then that's fine..."

"Thanks for your support," Jerry stated.

One of the infected burst through a hedgerow a hundred metres from them, charging in their direction.

"How the fuck did that thing see us? Or hear us?" Harlan exclaimed.

They stood, watching the infected bounding across the field, kicking grass and earth behind it.

"I know this sword works, Harlan... I'm gonna take it out."

"Good luck with that," Harlan spat. "I'm gonna run for it."

The infected closed the gap to fifty metres.

Jerry lifted the katana and held it in front of himself, poised to strike. Harlan started away, pulling his daggers free. He paced backwards, then stopped, placing Jerry between himself and the infected. "This is ridiculous," Harlan moaned.

The infected lurched forward, blood dripping from its mouth, then it launched to attack. Jerry swung the katana and cut through the throat of the infected, slicing entirely through. The head rolled away and the body dropped to the ground. Blood gushed from the jugular and carotid artery, pooling around the body.

"Jesus! That was disgusting..."

"Yep."

"Now can you see why I'm disturbed by you?"

"No... What was the alternative?"

"I don't know, dude... But, still, that was pretty gnarly."

"Yeah. Yeah, it was..."

A little later.
Harlan led Jerry down the main-road through the village to the pub – The Boot Inn.

As they reached the door, Harlan placed the long-sword against the doorframe and placed his pack by the front door. He took out his hammer, still holding one of the daggers, and readied himself. He put his hand lightly on the doorknob, not quite gripping it, pinching it with his fingertips around the handle of the hammer.

"Get ready," he whispered.

Jerry, still holding the katana, entered first.

It was quite dark inside, and it felt hot and stifling. None of the lights were on and the curtains were half drawn. Several people had died and a raw, rotting stench rose and fell. A few bodies lay collapsed on the floor near the seating section, while others had dropped from bar-stools. Thick veils of smoke drifted up and down throughout the entire space. The smell hit both of them immediately. Jerry coughed and spat on the carpet.

"Shhhh!"

Jerry shot Harlan a look.

They made their way across the lounge, staying low, and entered the kitchen. Dark, smoky vapours and mist hung above their heads, sweeping in and out, back and forth through the building. A few of the windows had been smashed, including one at the back of the lounge, allowing air-flow in from the back-garden. Dirt and grime, blood spots and puddles showed all over the bar, tables, floor and walls. The ceiling was a deep, dark, rich murky brown-black and getting darker by the minute.

Harlan pointed the daggers in front of him, into every corner, around every surface.

Jerry slowly peered inside the kitchen, inching his face between the door and frame. He could see four large refrigerators at the back of the room and a freezer-room tacked onto the kitchen next to one of the fresh-food pantries. There was a central island of ovens and hobs, *buzzing* and gathering dust.

The room was awkward to see into and presented some difficulty to access: a wide part of the kitchen could not be seen from the door. Along the corridor in front of the kitchen Jerry saw another door. It was slightly ajar and there were stairs beyond it that led upstairs.

It was stiflingly hot in the kitchen; a wall of heat burned out of the fractionally-open door. Jerry turned away and let the door shut silently.

An infected emerged from the shadows at the back-exit, from the other end of the short corridor to the back-garden. It lurched down the path, groaning and hacking, then came to an abrupt stop.

Both of the young men froze, as the infected scanned the corridor, looking through them for a second. Blood poured from its mouth, as it open and closed, *clicking* shut each time against its teeth. A chip of tooth pinged from its mouth and landed in the deep, grey shag-carpet.

Harlan pushed the kitchen door open and it wedged itself in place on a doorstop. He edged into the kitchen, feeling the heat tingle up and down his sweaty arms and back. The cookers were still aflame, burning the contents of several pans and cooking pots that rested atop of them. Thick black columns of smoke coursed up from several places, blending into the sooty thunder-cloud that hovered a few inches from the ceiling; it drifted in waves and curtain-like veils, a gentle siphoning course dragging it to a blackened and soot-choked extractor vent.

Jerry ran at the infected and stabbed it through the neck above the tight, hard larynx. The force of the thrust pushed the infected backward, dragging Jerry with it.

A second infected entered the kitchen from the area near the cookers behind Harlan, and blood-puked over him. Harlan was instantly drenched in putrid, thick blood. He dropped the hammer, slicking blood mess back in his hair. He turned and slashed the infected across the cheek, slitting the flesh open and rewarding the attacker with a Chelsea-smile. He stabbed at it, as it recoiled, puncturing its chest cavity and abdomen. He dropped the dagger and punted the infected with his boot. The infected slammed back against an oven and fell. Harlan booted its face, sending teeth skittering across the floor. He jabbed the second blade through the forehead and frontal bone, pushing it deep into the brain. A line of blood streaked from the wound, then a solitary jet spurted across Harlan's fingers. The infected hacked and wheezed, sinking to the floor.

Jerry thrashed at the other infected, when a third appeared from the door leading upstairs. It tripped and stumbled down the bottom two steps, shunting the door open with the toe of its shoe and the flat of its forehead. Two of the infected were the middle-aged couple who owned the pub, and the other was dressed in filthy chef's whites. Jerry rolled on top of the first infected and it punched him square in the eye. They fell into the shadowy end of the corridor.

Harlan was momentarily cornered, away from any exit, when the third infected stumbled into the kitchen and bolted toward him.

Three minutes later. Outside The Boot Inn.
Harlan stumbled out of the pub shaking with adrenaline. He wiped the slick of blood off his arms and shoulders. He mopped his hair with a bar-towel. He steadied himself on one of the signs that listed meal deals and he coughed. He spat on the ground, then studied it. There was no blood. He sighed heavily and turned back to face the pub, stumbling backwards. He could not see or hear Jerry at all, did not see him as he sprinted out of the pub. Several shadows dodged about inside; Harlan only caught glimpses through the curtains.

Suddenly a silver 2007 Mazda 5 people-carrier roared down the main-road, hurtling toward Harlan. The roar of the engine grew louder with every passing second.

He saw the car and waved his arms frantically at the driver.

The car hopped on a bump in the road, skidded a few metres, then deliberately swung-out and hit Harlan, knocking him into a parked-car and onto the tarmac.

He winced and screamed, clutching his ribcage. Pain seared throughout his body. His fingers twitched uncontrollably, his breathing like an excited dog, electricity firing through his brain.

The car disappeared down the road.

Harlan passed-out where he lay. Absolute blackness veiled him.

Later. Night.
Harlan woke up with a groan and a yelp.

He looked around slowly, the muscles in his neck bunching and flaring with pain. He tried to orient himself to his surroundings, arching his back to look up at The Boot Inn behind him. He was alert, but suddenly terrified. He felt excruciating pain in every cell in his body. He crawled and dragged and pulled and climbed to his feet. One of his ankles was badly twisted, and his left arm was dead: he couldn't feel any sensation, but he could open and close his hand. He stared at his arm for a long moment, opening and balling his fist. Four of his ribs were broken, he was sure of that. He cringed with the pain, eyes instantly filling with water, leaning against a car, when he saw an infected slowly closing in on him.

The infected was about forty metres from him, lurching down the road, gathering speed. Its blood-red eyes beamed at him. A thin gush of blood escaped its mouth and splashed on the road between its feet.

Harlan looked around for his daggers, his sword, and saw them on the ground a few feet from him. He began a slow and painful journey to retrieve them.

As the infected moved nearer and nearer, Harlan hobbled closer and closer to the sword. Finally he got to it, and, in enormous pain, reached down and picked it up. He bellowed and groaned, pressing his side firmly with the flat of his hand.

The infected puked a tiny amount of blood down itself again, a lonely trickle escaping from within, shrinking the gap between it and Harlan.

Harlan swung the sword like a golf-club, and chopped the infected across its face, slicing the tip of the jaw and the tip of its nose clean off. The infected rocked backwards and fell, *cracking* its head on the pavement. It sat up and rocked back and forth, grappling with sitting up fully, scraping its elbows across the tarmac.

Harlan stared, as blood spewed from the hole in its face, spilling out and spreading across the pavement. He swung the sword with one hand and chopped off the top three-inches of the skull. The infected huffed and burbled, airy bubbles of blood popping on its lips, then it lay back on the ground. Blood oozed around the body, draining away between the thick iron-bars of a gutter.

He stared at the infected, the sword-tip *clanging* on the tarmac, as a brief satisfying relief settled over him.

Later.
Harlan stumbled and scrambled up the hill, groaning with pain. He passed the tree he climbed twelve hours earlier.

He had fashioned a crutch out of a tree-branch and carried the sword in his weaker-hand, dragging it along beside him. "Keep going. Keep going. Keep going. Keep going. Keep going," he told himself.

Later.
Harlan reached the field beyond the barn. Early morning light was beginning to show the edges of things, and his figure was one of them.

He waved at Layla, who sat in the window on the mezzanine. She stared at Harlan, then pointed a torch at him. The beam illuminated him: all of the blood stains and bruises. Layla waved back.

Harlan limped closer and knocked on the door, patting it lightly with the side of the sword-hilt.

"It's Harlan! Let him in," Layla called out.

Fiona unlocked and opened the door. She looked for Jerry, when all she could see was Harlan. "Jerry? Where's Jerry?" she asked sharply.

"He's not back?... Then, I don't think he made it."

Fiona froze, pushing passed Harlan to look at the fields and woods around them.

Harlan slid through the doorway, easing by Fiona and into the barn.

She closed and locked the door, stopping a second behind it, closing her eyes for a moment.

"Where's the food?" Vivienne asked from the candle circle.

"I was hit by a car. I couldn't carry it."

"I'm not surprised – looking the way you do... I would've run you over too."

"You looked pretty battered, dude," Bernie stated.

"I could barely carry this!" Harlan said holding up the sword.

"Where are the daggers? They were worth something!" Baz yelled.

"Look at me! Do you think I care about that?! What the fuck!"

"Shut up, and think of a way out of this situation," Fiona barked. "We can't afford to lose anyone else!"

"Shouldn't we look for him?" Suthep asked.

Layla helped Harlan to a makeshift-bed made from bales of hay. Harlan lay down. Baz offered him and he drank from a bottle of vodka from his back-pack.

"So, how did Jerry get got?" Baz asked with a pained expression.

"Huh?... We were in the kitchen of a pub trying to get us all some food..."

"And?"

"And we were overrun by those fucking things, man," Harlan said, then necked more vodka.

"Did you see him get infected?"

"No."

"That might not mean he was infected!" Baz exclaimed. "He might not be a zombie."

"That's true," Bernie agreed.

"If he hadn't been, then where is he? He would've come back by now, wouldn't he?... It's not like he got hit by a fucking car! Is it?"

"I don't know... Get some rest. Have a sleep... Chill out."

Fiona paced the barn, thinking. Layla sat with Vivienne watching Fiona. She stopped pacing when she noticed they were watching her and sat with them. Layla stroked her niece's hair then started to braid it. Vivienne remained still while her hair was looped and twisted then tied with two tiny red bows.

Fiona looked at all of them. She did not know what to do.

Baz climbed the ladder to the mezzanine and took his place at the window. Fiona followed him with her eyes and saw him settle on the bale. He picked up the pitchfork and turned it between his palms. He gritted his teeth.

Suthep and Bernie followed Baz to the window and sat with their friend.

Fiona's head dropped and she cupped it in her hands.

Bernie crouched, then slid to the floor near the window. Suthep stood on the other side. Baz looked from one to the other. "This is pretty messed up."

"You're telling me!" Bernie agreed, a dimple forming on his right cheek.

"There's no saying Jerry got got."

"Yeah..."

"So, he might come back and find us."

"I hope he's not been infected. I hope he isn't a zombie."

"The amount he smoked, it'd be difficult to tell the difference," Bernie joked.

Baz half-smiled. "I'm gonna fucking miss him. I hope he's okay."

"I know what you mean..." Suthep said. "I don't think I've spent this amount of time with anyone, except online, in the last ten years... Like, all together in one space... It's kinda like a never-ending camping trip..."

"You-two hang out a lot!" Baz said.

"Yeah," Bernie agreed, "but it's not all-day everyday for a week straight..."

"It's like being in a shit version of Big Brother, but the whole country... And no cameras. And just us."

"No audience..."

"Yeah..."

Suthep sat down next to Baz and he shuffled along the bale to make more room. He sighed. "I hope the cast of *Community* and *How I Met Your Mother* are okay... And the whole cast from *Game of Thrones,* too... Emilia Clarke..."

"That's an odd thing to say..." Baz said slowly.

"Nah, we were talking about it the other day, and thinking of which celebrities we hoped were still alive..."

"Like a game."

"Oh, right," Baz nodded. "I hope Olivia Wilde's alive..."

"I hope Comic Book Girl 19 is alive too... And Lizzy Caplan. And Zooey Deschanel."

"And Kirsten Dunst, Britt Robertson, Blake Lively, Amber Heard, Felicity Jones... And Rashida Jones, too!"

"And Nina Dobrev and the cast of *Vampire Diaries*!... And Mila Kunis, too..."

"And the cast of *The Big Bang Theory*..."

"Kate from *Lost*..."

"Yeah, you can't forget Kate from *Lost*..."

"And the cast of *Temple*, too... Except Damien Flynn..."

"That guy's a turd!"

"Yeah!"

"Yeah! I hate that guy..."

They sat a moment in silence, lost in their own thoughts.

"So," Suthep started, "if you think of any more to go on our list, let us know..."

"You-two have a list?" Baz asked. "Like, a real list? On paper, written in pen?"

"Yeah, man... We thought about remembering everyone, but the list got too long..."

Baz stifled a laugh.

Suthep pulled a scrap of note-paper free from his pocket, unfolded it several times and looked at it. "I forgot to say: Emma Watson, Willa Holland... Oh, and, Oprah..."

"Oprah?"

"Yeah."

"Add George R R Martin... And William Shatner and Patrick Stewart, too..."

Later. Morning.

The group was on the move again. They trekked through a small forest, sparsely peppered with trees.

Baz helped Harlan walk with the crutch under his other arm.

Fiona walked ahead of the group, reading a compass, hanging the pitchfork over her shoulder. She had made holsters for her daggers and a sheath for the short-sword out of rope and Duct tape.

Layla and Vivienne walked behind Fiona and a few paces ahead of Harlan and Baz. Suthep and Bernie were once again bringing up the rear.

"Can we...? Can we stop for a break, please?" Harlan muttered.

"We can't," Fiona stated. "We're too out-in-the-open."

"Please..."

"No. We keep going."

Harlan groaned and rested more of his weight on Baz's shoulder. Baz's feet sunk into the mud a little deeper.

"How're we out-in-the-open? We're in a wood!"

"We have to keep going," Fiona stated, and they kept walking.

Two days later. Three miles West of Reading.

Fiona marched at the head the group along the M4 motorway. She led them down the slight bank at the side of the road and stopped, huddling by the crash-barrier.

Baz still supported Harlan as he sat down next to the barrier and leaned against it.

Layla and Vivienne squatted next to Harlan.

Suthep crouched at the back, watching the other side of the motorway.

Bernie perched a few paces from Fiona, staring at the motorway behind her.

"We have got to keep moving down the motorway," Fiona said. "It's the quickest way forward."

The clouds parted and sunlight shone down on them, warming their skin.

"Can't we just stop here for a moment?" Harlan said breathlessly. "I really need to rest..."

"No. We have to keep on the move," Fiona insisted.

"We could take a five minute break, Fiona," Layla said.

"I'm not sure that's wise..." Suthep stated.

"Harlan needs a break."

"Fine. You-all, wait here. I'll go and check out the way forward," Fiona told them. She silently climbed over the barrier and crept around the back of an orange 2002 Ford Ka, holding the pitchfork at the middle of the pole. She approached a green 2005 Peugeot 307 and edged around the back wing. Her eyes widened and her jaw clenched shut. She immediately rushed back, bounding over the barrier, with an infected following quickly behind her.

As the infected and Fiona got closer to the group, she stopped, turned, and planted her feet on the ground, swinging the pitchfork in the air.

The infected ran chest-first into the fork.

Fiona's feet skidded back two and a half feet, as momentum carried her backwards. The grip on her shoes resisted and the infected came to a stop. It gargled, beaming at Fiona. She shoved the infected onto the ground, and stamped on the fork, ramming it deeper into its torso. The infected coughed up blood, wetting its cheeks and nose. It reached out limply, swinging its arms in Fiona's direction, trying desperately to touch her.

She pulled the fork out and swung it through the air, then brought it down in the face of the infected.

Layla covered Vivienne's eyes, as Baz helped Harlan down the grass-verge they were standing on and onto the tarmac of the onramp.

Another infected barrelled across the road and Bernie stabbed it through its open mouth with the Roman Gladius sword, punching out the back.

"What was it like over-there?" Baz asked.

"Quite dangerous," Fiona answered.

CHAPTER 11 - SALVATION - Oxford

The Bridge nightclub.
A girl danced across the dance-floor – NICOLA WEBB, 18 year old half-English, half-Lithuanian young woman. She had piercing blue eyes, winged with long black lashes and circled in dark eye-makeup, behind thick black-rimmed glasses. Folds of dark, rich hazel-brown hair cascaded onto her shoulders, parted on her left and swept over the top of her head. She was skinny and petite, with a tiny waist and skinny limbs. She wore tight-fitting, elasticy plain-black trousers, a loose-fitting t-shirt, with a *Guns and Roses* album cover printed on it with deliberate fade and distress, and black-and-white Converse High Tops that sat snugly around her feet, laced tightly. She was drunk and having a lot of fun, waving her arms in the air in time to the music.

She not hear at all but, could feel *squeaks* the rubber soles of her shoes made against the linoleum-chequered-squares that covered the dance-floor.

Nicola screamed and sang along to the vague lyrics, almost hidden beneath pulsing and pounding beats.

The dance-floor was filled with young people: chavs, emos, hip hop types, smartly dressed preppy-types, hippies, suits, business-men after a long week's work, some rockers, a few goths, some grungy-rockers, and dozens of alternatives.

Nicola swung her vision upwards and leant against a standing-bar that acted as the perimeter-fence around the dance-floor in broken stretches, leaving openings for access to the bars, toilets and exits.

Nicola picked up a drink, any drink, and took a sip. The cool liquid sank down her throat, leaving a bead to roll down her smooth, pale neck. She half-dropped, half-let go of the glass one inch from where she thought the table-top was. The glass clattered and wobbled between her sweat-filmed fingers, but righted itself and settled.

A miserable-looking couple who were sat on a small, round three-person table on the other side of the bar, grimaced and stared bitterly at her. They had been interrupted mid-argument by Nicola's drunken thievery. They glared at her. Nicola pulled an expression of faux-guilt.

"Sorry!" she exclaimed with a drunken, sweet smile. She threw a small handful of change, that she noticed she had been clutching in her sweaty palm for some time, at the couple. The coins bounced and clipped off their drinks and the empties that sat around theirs on the table-top, and fell to the floor by their feet.

Nicola shrugged and turned away from the couple.

Lights blinked on and off at random.

Fake-smoke drifted through the air, billowing and clouding.

Nicola danced drunkenly, moving away from the bar and into the centre of the dance-floor. Her arms flapped a little and her feet felt sticky and immovable in random bursts. She flirted with four of the young men in polo-shirts circling her, who were dancing lamely and awkwardly to the beat.

"Excuse me," she slurred.

She had aimed the comment at two of the young men, but neither of them noticed. Nicola did not notice their obliviousness and wandered off, shoving between them.

Nicola stumbled and nudged and parted and pushed through a crowd of people to get to the bar. She said nothing to any of the people, did not apologise once, including to two people whose drinks she knocked out of their hands and spilled and broke.

At the bar.
Nicola's friends, a young couple, were kissing: LLOYD SMITH, 19 year old mixed-race Englishman, of English and West Indian descent; and EILEEN DAUBAN, 18 year old English young woman, originally from Bristol. Lloyd had a large, rugby-playing and swimmer's body; tall and lean with wide shoulders and long limbs. He had short-cropped afro-hair with thick, straight eye-brows. He had a gentle, caring face with warm, milk chocolate-brown eyes and a full, toothy smile. He wore a tight white t-shirt that hugged his pecks, shoulders, biceps and triceps, and his visible, gym-worked six-pack; plain-black jeans from River Island and black-and-white Nike Blazers. Eileen was petite like Nicola, with a small, slim

frame. She had sleek blonde hair with a hair-salon sheen, curled at the ends and parted on one side and secured behind her ear and with a two Kirby-grips. She had clear, smooth skin with only one dimple on her left cheek, a shy, humble smile and alert, curious green eyes. She had a golden tan, highlighted with very little makeup: some hot pink lipstick, metallic-green eye-shade and a little blush on her cheeks. She wore a satin black shirt, unbuttoned down to her push-up bra, Smog denim jeans and two-inch black heels from Next.

Nicola interrupted their kiss, having a laugh, having fun, flirting with a dark-suited young man down the bar who smiled cheekily at her. They could barely make out their collective noises, over-lapping and interrupting one-another, muffled and incomprehensible.

Nicola laughed and turned away from the man down the bar, laughing embarrassedly.

Nicola, Eileen and Lloyd necked a shot each of Wray & Nephews white rum that Lloyd had managed to order.

Lloyd passed the barman a ten pound note and winked at him.

Later.
The three of them exited the club, as other clubbers left. Eileen hung onto Lloyd's arm, as Nicola wandered away smoking a cigarette.

"Hey," Lloyd called after Nicola. "Wait for us!"

"Okay!" she shouted in reply.

Eileen giggled.

"Where to now?" Nicola said with a tiny pirouette on her High Tops.

"Home!" Eileen murmured.

"Home?!" Nicola shouted dejectedly. "Boo!" she moaned.

A little later.
The three of them piled into a 2005 Vauxhall Vectra taxi, laughing hysterically.

"Thank you for stopping," Lloyd said gratefully, through the open passenger-side window. "It's taken fucking ages to get a cab... --at this time of night."

"Where-to, guys?" the taxi driver asked with a smile, a gold tooth inset on the top-left.

"10 Fielding Lane... Out near the motorway..."

"Then back to Jericho..." Lloyd added half-carrying Eileen, who slumbered and murmured softly to herself, eyes screwed shut. He pulled the door open and Lloyd lifted Eileen into the cab, letting Nicola follow, then jumped in himself.

"Alright," the taxi driver said jovially and alert, and put the car in gear. "It'll be eight-eighty... Then I'll let you off with four-sixty on the return journey."

"Fuckin' hell," Nicola exclaimed, falling into the back seat with a bounce that made her body jiggle.

Lloyd helped Eileen to buckle her seatbelt, then took a seat for himself.

A little later.
Lloyd helped Nicola from the backseat of the taxi outside her house. He held onto one of her arms, with his other hooked under her armpit.

Nicola burst into laughter.

"What's funny?" Lloyd asked.

"What?" she said with a laugh.

"You laughed? Out loud?"

"I thought you did," Nicola said flirtily.

Seconds later.
Lloyd helped Nicola unlock her front door. She put her weight on Lloyd, hugging him around his muscular middle. She whistled a tune badly.

Eileen hung out of the back window of the taxi, watching Lloyd and Nicola with a half-asleep, quite drunk leering-smile and a lot of stifled giggles.

"Thank you," Nicola whispered and kissed Lloyd's cheek wetly.

Minutes later.
Eileen still hung out the back window of the taxi, watching Nicola's house, empty and silent, through the open front-door. She saw several interior lights flick on and beam outside onto the small driveway, illuminating them and the taxi, but little else.

"Bye!" she shouted loudly, as Lloyd jogged to the taxi, pushing the front door shut, and hopped back inside, then the taxi pulled away.

Nicola waved from her bedroom window, a slim silhouette framed in the window-frame by the light from her desk-lamps.

Seconds later.
Nicola fell onto her bed fully clothed.
The lights from her desk shone brightly.
Nicola tugged the duvet to cover her head.

Morning.
Nicola's eyes snapped open. She had a very sore head, and sat up slowly on her elbows, lifting it behind her hands. Hair tangled between her fingers, stuck to her forehead and shaded her eyes. She smoothed the dark curls away from her face.

She *croaked* out a tiny noise.
The clock on her wall ticked loudly. It was 11:56am.
She slipped off her elbows and buried her face in the pillow, damping it with a few dots of sweat, before arching her back to flip the pillow to the cool side. She screwed her eyes shut and sank her face into the cool cotton.

Later – 1:06pm.
Nicola wandered downstairs in a bath-robe. She ruffled her hair with one hand, putting on her thick-black-rimmed glasses.

"Mum?... Mum?... Muuuum?... Mother?!" she shouted.
There was no reply.
"Mum?... I'm going to go for a swim," she called out, but again got no reply. "For fuck's sake, where the fuck are you?" she murmured.

She walked through the hall, the kitchen and went outside. Beyond the kitchen, inset into a modest patio, was a modest swimming-pool. Sunlight glinted off the surface of the water.

Later.
Nicola lazed on a half-air-filled lilo in the water, listening to a loud but compact stereo with an iPod plugged into it. She wore a small, two-piece sunflower-yellow bikini that sat snugly around her body. She kicked with one foot and the lilo wobbled then drifted in a rippling circle. She had replaced her glasses with the same type, but with dark, smoky lenses instead of her regular clear-lenses.

Nicola adjusted the sunglasses an inch down the bridge of her small, fine nose.
"Muuuum? Can you bring me a Coke?... A Diet Coke?... Pleeeease!"
There was no response.
"Mum?... Mum?... Mum?... Mum?... Muuuum?... Muuuuum?! Muuuuuum?!" she shouted.
Nicola stared at the doorway into the kitchen. Both half-doors were pulled slightly in, but she could see fully into the kitchen. She slapped the water, and eventually swam to the edge of the pool and got out. She scooped a beach-towel from a nearby patio-chair and wrapped it around her waist, tightly. She picked up a small hand-towel and patted beads of water from her chest and ribs and midriff.

As Nicola walked into the house, she shouted upstairs, through the hall, "Muuuum?!" but received no reply.

She stood in the kitchen doorway, idling, when she moved forward and crossed the room. And then discovered her mother's body on the floor. It had been hidden from view from the swimming pool and doorway by the island-unit in the centre of the room.

It looked like Nicola's mother had collapsed where she stood and hit the tiled-floor hard. Blood had dried in channels running from a wound on the woman's temple. She was completely still.

Nicola screamed.

Later.
Nicola cried her eyes out curled-up on the floor of the kitchen. She hugged her legs, pulling the hand-towel tightly around her upper body.

She shivered and whimpered as tears poured from her eyes.

A breeze from the outside carried some dust motes on the air.

Outside.
The stereo by the swimming-pool still played loudly. A happy, upbeat pop song came on. Nicola rose, and stormed over to the stereo and bashed the off-button with her finger. She kicked the stereo and the iPod skittered out of the dock.

She straightened and exhaled, momentarily relieved by the silence, then wiped away her tears. The towel loosened and she started to tighten it around her waist.

A noise came from the hedgerow near the pool, then one of the infected tore through. It clambered over the short fence, and fell to the patio floor.

It scrambled to pick itself up then rushed at Nicola.

She immediately backed away, dropping the towel, and launched into the house, slamming the patio-doors behind her and locking them. She stared through the glass panels at the infected as it bounded forward. It punched the glass and the wooden frame, roaring and groaning, rasping and choking up blood.

The infected paced back then bolted and launched itself at the doorway again. It smashed through the glass panels in the doors with its flailing and punching arms. It growled and gargled, hitting at the door with its body, its shoulders beating back and forth against the doors.

Nicola retreated from the attacker quickly, searching for a weapon. The infected smashed further into the kitchen. Its arms were outstretched through the broken panels, scratching at the air in between them.

Dozens of shards of glass spun through the air as the door was buffeted in its frame.

The infected rammed its face into the glass panel and puked blood through the hole onto the kitchen-floor, gasping and screaming and looking erratically for Nicola with its enraged, bloodshot eyes. It butted its face into the glass panel again; the glass ripped at its cheek- and jaw-flesh. Its mouth snapped and its teeth *clicked* together.

Nicola broke from the attacker and ran out of the kitchen and up the staircase to her bedroom, leaving the infected struggling in the broken-glass and door-frame. Its arms had temporarily immobilised it in the door-frame, pining it where it stood. It shrugged and tugged at its own arm, pushing then pulling to free itself.

Nicola ran into her bedroom and slammed the door behind her. She wedged a chair against the door-handle. She dressed quickly, looking in all directions for a weapon. She pulled on a vest over her bikini top and a pair of shorts over her bottoms. She stamped her feet into white and pink Gola trainers.

The infected twisted its hips and smashed through the kitchen doors. Chunks of glass stuck in its arms. It strode into the room. It looked around, only regarding the body of Nicola's mother for a second.

It stumbled through the kitchen into the hallway.

Nicola found her school hockey-stick and gripped it tightly. "This fucker is dead!" she murmured to herself.

A car-horn sounded from the outside.

Nicola reacted instantly.

The infected turned and ushered itself back out of the kitchen, onto the patio, *cracking* glass underfoot.

Outside the front of the house.
A car pulled up on the gravel, *crunching* it under the tyres. It was Lloyd and Eileen in a silver 2002 Ford Fiesta. Lloyd put the handbrake on and tapped the top arch of the steering-wheel, looking through the windscreen at Nicola's house. The sun shone across the polished glass, glinting in Lloyd's eyes, when thin clouds coasted by.

Eileen pressed the car's horn again. "What's taking her?"

Nicola pulled her bedroom-window open and leant through the opening.

They saw her immediately.

Eileen wound-down the passenger-side window and hung out to look at her friend.

"Stay in the car!" Nicola shrieked, before Eileen had a chance to speak. Their smiles vanished from their faces. Both Lloyd and Eileen could hear the panic in Nicola's voice and see the terror in her eyes and felt it exactly the same. They shared a frightened and concerned look between them.

"What's goin' on?"

Seconds ago. Downstairs.
The infected heard the car's horn again and jerked its body around on the spot. It raced out across the patio and dashed around the side of the house. As it passed the edge of the patio its shoulder caught the bottom of a hanging-basket and the contents were tipped and flung out. The basket swung on its chain, as the infected vaulted away.

Outside.
The infected pushed between the house and a large, farm-style gate and ran onto the gravel at the front of the house. The gate sprang backwards and *clicked* shut. It immediately saw Eileen's open window and bolted for the car.

Eileen saw it coming and rushed to wind the window up.

The infected reached the car and punched at the windows. It puked blood on the glass. It punched and slapped at the windows, smearing its greasy, oily mess in vile streaks.

Nicola saw the infected from her window and bolted downstairs after it, hockey-stick still firmly in her grip. She leapt three stairs at a time, swinging the stick in front of her.

Once she was downstairs, she moved through the house cautiously and made it to the side-door. She unlocked it and eased the door open. Sunlight beamed into the hallway. She crept across the gravel. She neared the farm-style gate that blocked the driveway along the side of the house.

The infected turned and charged at her.

Nicola made her arms a pendulum, swinging the hockey-stick up, then brought it down, battering the infected across its throat. The infected fell, gasping, hissing and spitting blood. It wriggled and writhed on the floor, hacking and wheezing for air.

Nicola beat it. She hit its neck and face, until Lloyd lifted her off the ground and pulled her away.

A little later.
Lloyd, Eileen and Nicola sat in Lloyd's car. Nicola sat in the back, crying uncontrollably.

"We should check the radio," Lloyd announced and turned it on.

Static noises sounded from the speakers.

Lloyd scanned to another channel – nothing again. He tried many, many channels, with no results.

"What the fuck is going on, Nic?" Eileen asked.

Nicola shook her head. "I don't know." She sniffed.

"What happened inside?"

"My mum..." she started, then cried out and whimpered. "She's dead. Inside. She's gone."

"Oh my God! I'm so sorry!" Eileen said and hugged Nicola tightly.

Lloyd stared at the house, then looked across at the body of the infected. It lay near the gate, crumpled and crippled, crushed and bent over double. Blood seeped out of it, soaking the gravel and dyeing it a dark, oily red.

"What the fuck are we going to do?"

"God knows! I'm... I'm just so glad you're both here... And alive."

"I'm glad I'm alive, too," Lloyd admitted.

"Me, too."

A little later.
Lloyd drove his car down a country-road. The trees and bushes separated for a wide, clearing and he slowed, and pulled up on a motorway-bridge. They all climbed out of the car and walked to the metal-barrier.

Up and down the motorway cars had collided and were tightly packed together.

In a lot of the cars people were dead. In several others they saw infected tussling with their seatbelt restraints.

"What the fuck is going on?! What has happened to all of those people?"

They stared at the motorway, looking both ways. In each direction there was carnage.

"What are those people? What's wrong with them?"

"They look infected. Or rabid... Or it's some plague," Nicola said slowly, trailing off. Her eyes filled with water. She wiped and rubbed them dry. "We have to go back to my house and bury my mum. I can't stand the thought of her just lying there in the kitchen."

"We should keep moving," Lloyd said, only seconds later realising his statement. "I'm sorry... I..."

"We need to have a plan," Nicola asserted. "And step one is to bury my mum. The rest comes after that."

Later. At night.
Nicola and Eileen sat in Lloyd's car, parked outside her house. They huddled together in the back seat, holding hands, fingers threaded together and pinching hard.

The headlights illuminated the front of the house like a gloomy ghost-house. Only two interior lights were on; in the living-room and kitchen, and in the hallway.

Eileen shivered.

Inside.
Lloyd pulled Nicola's mother's body into the dining room and put a jacket over her head.

He stared at the covered-form of the body, unable to move. He sighed.

He picked up a spade he had found in the shed and walked through the kitchen to the patio. He moved through a side-gate into the garden, shining a torch ahead of him, and started digging.

Later.
Lloyd walked out of the front-door and waved for the girls to come inside. They got out of the car, and Eileen turned the headlights off.

"It's clear inside," Lloyd said.

"Are you sure?" Eileen said, her voice quivering.

"I've moved the... --your... --your mum. And cleaned the kitchen floor... I've propped the kitchen doors closed, but we need to fix them."

Moments later.
Nicola and Eileen walked into the kitchen, and saw the makeshift job Lloyd had made of the smashed patio-doors.

Lloyd started collecting planks of wood from the wood-bin at the side of the house. He returned to the kitchen with a hammer and nails. "I'll start on the door."

Two minutes ago.
An infected sprinted through a field towards Lloyd's car's headlights, illuminating the side of Nicola's house, when they switched off, leaving only a few of the interior house-lights inside to guide its path.

    The infected bolted through the field, the grass whipping its legs and feet.

    It groaned, hacked and panted.

Inside.
Lloyd re-entered the kitchen for a third time, putting down a stack of wooden-planks.

    Eileen prepared vegetables and chicken to cook in a curry.

    "After we've got this secured and had dinner," Lloyd started, "what do you think we should do?"

    Nicola trawled through every television channel in an endless cycle, without finding any signs of life at all. She languidly turned her head to Lloyd, who stood, awaiting a response. "I'm working on it," she said, and turned back to the television.

    Lloyd placed the first plank against the broken door, nailing it in place, when the infected from the field charged across the patio and ploughed straight into the door, breaking it open once again, and throwing Lloyd onto the tiled-floor, and knocking him unconscious.

    Nicola immediately leapt to her feet, grabbing her hockey-stick. She charged at the infected, while Eileen backed away, frightened and whimpering.

    "Fuck you!" Nicola screamed as she beat and thrashed at the infected.

    The infected and Nicola came together, the hockey-stick between them. They twisted then cannoned into a large kitchen-cabinet, smashing dishes and glasses, when Lloyd woke up with a shiver. He instantly grabbed the hammer and jumped to help Nicola.

    Nicola shoved the infected further into the cabinet, knocking free several more dishes and cups, which tumbled and smashed on the floor. She flicked the end of the stick, clipping its shoulder, then threw herself forward, catching the infected under the chin. The tip of its tongue was almost bitten off by its own chomping jaws, and it hung down its chin by a rubbery, jelly-tether of meat.

    Lloyd pounded the infected heavily with the flat-end of the hammer, knocking it sideways, giving Nicola the time she needed to crush its throat between the shaft of her hockey-stick and the wall. The infected collapsed to the ground, crumpling under her. She turned the hockey-stick and stabbed it down into the face of the infected. The curved, hard wooden-end of the stick crushed the eye-socket and broke the bridge of its nose. She beat it again and again and again. But this time she stopped herself. She turned to Lloyd, "Thank you for your help."

A little later.
Lloyd, Nicola and Eileen nailed small-tables, chairs, planks of wood and any dark-coloured fabric over all of the downstairs windows, blanking out the light from within.

    "I can't believe what's happening," Eileen whispered.

    "Me neither, babe," Lloyd said and kissed the top of her head.

    Nicola picked up a small side-table and swung it to cover the window above the kitchen sink.

Four days later. In the morning.
Nicola made herself a cup of tea. She sipped it, walking to the television, and continued her search through all of the television channels. She pulled her legs up onto the arm-chair and held the cup with one hand, warming her palm, and the remote pointed-out in the other hand like a pistol.

    There was no news. There were no announcements. There was no media at all. There appeared to be nobody in front of any of the cameras that were showing live feeds. Her eyes were sore and glazed and ringed with crimson and purple.

    Nicola found herself staring at the carpet, before she even noticed. She picked up the remote that had fallen from her hand onto her lap and continued trawling the channels.

    She rubbed her eyes under her glasses, pinching the bridge of her nose, then thumbing her temples.

Upstairs.
Eileen and Lloyd slept soundly in Nicola's mother's bedroom. Lloyd was big-spoon, his arms wrapped tightly around Eileen's body.

The windows were closed and the curtains were pulled. The lights were extinguished. Daylight glowed from the outside.

There was no sound at all, apart from the light breaths of Eileen and Lloyd.

A little later.
Nicola used a telescope to look at a house further down her road from her bedroom window. She could not see very much, could not see into the house, except through one side-window. There were no signs of movement in the house at all.

She sipped a half-drunk cup of tea, when Eileen walked into the room, a dressing-gown folded around her.

"Hey... What's up?"

"I'm looking at the Webber house down the road."

"Have you slept at all?"

"I've been watching the house."

"Oh... Oh?"

"I was thinking about searching it for more food and any more weapons."

"We haven't seen any of those people in three days..."

"I want to go there."

"If you went alone... No... No, Lloyd and I would have to go with you..."

Nicola disagreed with a few shakes of her head. "No. No. No."

"If you go alone, we wouldn't know whether you were coming back... And if Lloyd goes with you, I won't know if either of you will come back... So, we would all have to go.... If you got hurt, we wouldn't know, Nic..."

"Then we're going to need to be very, very careful."

"Well, okay, then."

Later.
Nicola channel-surfed on the television, deeply lost in thought about her plan, as Lloyd and Eileen made dinner. Nicola twisted coils of her hair between her fingers, then licked her lips.

"I noticed your books, Nic," Lloyd said, glancing at her on the sofa.

She slowly moved to look at him. "Yeah," she replied noncommittally, turning back to the television screen. She sighed.

"You've got a good selection..."

"Yeh."

"Were they yours?"

"Some. A lot of them... Most were my mum's old books that she made me read..."

"I saw John Ramsay's new book upstairs," Eileen offered. "It must've only come out a week ago..."

Nicola looked at the bookshelf. Her eyes started to water. "Mmm."

A little later.
They ate, standing around the kitchen table-island-unit.

Nicola finished first and washed her plate. She turned to the others. "I've thought of a plan... Eileen needs to drive my mum's car across the field, to the hill at the top... Turn and watch us down the hill... If you see anything, beep the horn... Lloyd and I will run to the Webber's house and get inside, then get out quickly."

"That sounds risky."

"We need to get more food."

"We could move on, Nicola," Lloyd suggested.

"And go where?"

"I don't know. The coast? London? I don't know."

"Then, until we decide somewhere better to go, or a decent plan of what we should do, then we do this!"

A little later.
They went to bed in almost complete darkness. They walked into the hall with torches pointed at the floor. As they reached the stairs, they switched the torches off and groped their way to the bedrooms.

"Goodnight, Nic," Eileen whispered, then disappeared into the bedroom, following Lloyd.

Nicola went to the telescope and stared through the eye-piece at the Webber's house, down the road. She gritted her teeth, then bit her bottom lip. She replaced her glasses, then sat on her bed. Her small hands gripped the duvet, tightening into balls.

Morning.
Eileen stood by the front-door, gingerly holding the handle, when Lloyd hopped down the stairs.

"There's nobody around the Webber's house that I can see... Let's go now."

"Okay," Nicola said, determined.

A little later.
Eileen drove away from the house in Nicola's mother's green 1999 Land Rover Discovery. The engine *hummed* and *chugged* as she turned the wheel, and pushed against a farmer's-gate, moving into the field.

The five-bar wooden gate flexed and bent, then the metal latch popped and it swung open into the field.

Outside the house.
Nicola and Lloyd scurried through the front-door and raced up the hedgerow-line towards the Webber's house. They saw the Land Rover ease through the open gate and drive away up the slope, to the top of the field. The Land Rover swung out before Eileen turned the wheel.

Nicola and Lloyd ran down the road, moving hastily to the Webber's house.

Eileen parked the Land Rover facing down the field. She looked all around the car periodically, watching the back hedgerow behind her in the rear-view mirror. "This is not a good idea. This is not a good idea. This is not a good idea," she murmured to herself.

Outside the Webber's house.
Lloyd and Nicola reached the property and huddled by the side-door along the driveway.

"You okay?" Lloyd asked, catching his breath.

"Fine. Stay focused."

Lloyd nodded. He noticed that while he was slightly out of breath, Nicola was not at all; her breathing remained even, steady and slow.

"We have to get into the house through the back door... There's a key the Webber's kept hidden in a terracotta-pot near their rockery round-back."

An infected inside the house peered at them through a single-glazed pane of glass. Its bloodshot eyes flicked from Nicola to Lloyd and back again. It stepped onto the wide sill on the inside then leapt through the window. It hurtled to the ground, landing with a bump and a hundred tiny *clinks* of glass.

The infected hit the block-paving between Lloyd and Nicola. It struggled on its arms, trying to lift itself to stand. They beat it with the hockey-stick and cricket-bat until it was motionless. Nicola was about to swipe at the infected again, when Lloyd put a hand on her arm. "I think it's dead."

Nicola gritted her teeth. "There's no harm in making sure."

"There is, if you're gonna run out of energy... If we come across any more of those things you won't be so tired..."

"Don't worry. I'll be fine."

At the field.
One of the infected emerged from the hedgerow behind the Land Rover. Eileen saw it in the rear-view mirror and turned in the seat to look at it, trying not to betray her position. The infected shook and shuddered, vomited blood on itself then ran headlong at the car.

Eileen panicked momentarily, then put the car in reverse and moved slowly backwards towards the oncoming-infected. "Fuck you," she hissed.

The car sprang back and the infected charged into the boot. Eileen hit the brakes and stopped over the body. The infected quaked then clambered to its arms and legs, crawling out from the underside of the car. It hocked then vomited blood on the long grass, flattening it with splayed hands.

Inside the Webber's house.
Lloyd and Nicola slowly entered the utility room, then crept into the kitchen, leaving the key in the lock behind them.

"It doesn't look like there's anyone else in here," Lloyd whispered.

"We need to check the house, either way... That was Mr Webber outside... That means his wife could be here too. We need to know."

They separated and searched the house. They found no other sign of life.
They collected food and packed it in bags.

In the field.
Eileen pressed the accelerator and shifted the Land Rover across the field. She stopped at the far-top-side, overlooking several more oncoming infected. She stared at them as they swept towards the car.

An infected ran out of the woods twenty metres away, bounding rapidly, and smashed its fist through the side-window.

Eileen screamed and pounded the horn.

Outside the Webber's house.
Lloyd and Nicola rushed out of the house upon hearing the horn. They immediately saw three infected attacking the Land Rover, as four more closed in on it.

"Oh my god!" Nicola shrieked. "Eileen!"

"Oh, fuck no!" Lloyd shouted. "What the fuck?! What can we do?!"

In the field.
Eileen kicked her foot down, and ran one of the infected over, slamming the bonnet and bumper into the torso. The infected hanging onto the side of the Land Rover, with its arm punctured through the side-window, puked blood through the opening. Its arm clawed and swung around the space, trying to catch hold of Eileen's sleeve or arm, as the legs of the infected kicked and leapt, trying with all its might to cling on.

She pulled and tugged on the steering-wheel, leaning away from the attacker's reach.

She whimpered and yanked the steering-wheel.

The infected kicked and its arm pulled free from the window, shredded into a banana-peel to the wrist. It rolled to a stop, striking a particularly dry and dusty ploughed furrow.

Near the hedgerow.
Nicola grabbed Lloyd by the arm.

"We've got to help her!"

"No!" he groaned. "No way! We have to get back to the house!" he shouted. "She's in a car! She can get back to us! What can we do? We can't help her!"

Nicola watched as the Land Rover careened around the field, speeding away from the small pack of infected. The car jumped over a small ridge on the field and was lost from sight in the woods to the West.

"Keep watching to see her circle back to meet us..."

"There's no time... We've got to run for it, Nic!"
They started away.

On the road.
An infected tore through the hedgerow and appeared close behind Lloyd and Nicola. It snatched Lloyd and dragged him to the ground, knocking Nicola down with weighty blow. As Lloyd tried to crawl away, the infected puked blood over him. He screamed and roared, as the infected punched and beat his back and sides. Blood seeped over the side of Lloyd's head. The infected leapt onto him and clung onto his back. It spat and vomited more blood over him, still pummelling his body. He squawked and his mouth filled with blood. He screamed again, spitting blood.

Nicola ferociously attacked the infected, and killed it with three quick strikes. She turned to Lloyd.

Lloyd coughed and retched, his body curling on the ground, spitting up droplets of blood. "How did that happen?" he asked holding his breath. His body bucked. He spat on the road; a gob of blood landed on the tarmac.

"I'm sorry, Lloyd," Nicola whispered, lifting the hockey-stick.

"No," he coughed. "Wait. Please!" The colour started to drain from Lloyd's face. He coughed violently. "Please. Don't..." His raised hand, begging Nicola not to strike him. His arm went limp and fell to the road, scraping the skin.

Nicola beat Lloyd across the back of his head, knocking him flat. She hit violently and brutally until he was dead and his skull was cracked open. Her eyes watered.

She sprinted away down the road.

Later. Inside Nicola's house.
Nicola sat on the chair in front of the television crying her eyes out. She sobbed uncontrollably, when she heard a light tapping noise which stopped her tears. She sniffed.

She calmly stood and walked into the hall, closing the kitchen-door behind her, cutting out the light.

Nicola reached the front-door slowly, when she heard Eileen's voice.

"Nic, it's me... Let me in... Please..."

Nicola opened the door and Eileen pushed in quickly.

Nicola quietly shut and locked the front-door behind her friend.

They hugged tightly.

"Where's Lloyd?"

Later. In the kitchen. At night.
Nicola and Eileen sat in the breakfast-area, away from the television.

"I don't want to go outside ever again," Eileen murmured.

"I know what you mean... I'm sorry," Nicola blurted. "It's all my fault!"

Morning.
Nicola and Eileen woke up in Nicola's mother's bed. They lay on either side of the bed, back to back.

"Morning."

"Morning, Nic."

Nicola stared at the ceiling, counting the swirls of plaster like fish-scales. She screwed her eyes shut and pressed the pillow to the sides of her head.

A little later.
Nicola read a survivalist book and Eileen read a trashy romance novel.

Nicola placed a finger in between two pages. "We won't last long here, 'Leen.. --if we stay here."

Eileen looked at Nicola worriedly, holding her place in her book.

"I think we might be able to move onto to somewhere else. I think I might have a plan..."

Eileen put the book in her lap. "The thought of going outside is still horrible to me... I can't imagine..."

One day later. Three miles West of Reading, near the M4 motorway.

Nicola led Eileen down the side of the A34, travelling South away from Oxford. They had reached the point where the A-road met the motorway, the M4. The M4 split into two roads, the main motorway and the off-ramp. The off-ramp swung away from the motorway and curved back to join the A34. The motorway and off-ramp made two shaded bridges over the A34.

They both carried packs on their backs, and were tired and dirty.

Nicola hesitated.

"Did you see something up there?" Eileen asked nervously.

Nicola pulled a pair of binoculars out of her pack and scanned both the motorway and the off-ramp.

"Let's get up there quickly," Nicola said, grabbing a bread-knife and a claw-hammer. She rushed down the road and up the grass-slope that sided the A34 to the level of the off-ramp. She continued up until she found the motorway above them.

At the side of the motorway, Nicola saw two infected fighting with a small group of people. Fiona and Baz stood to one side, tackling one of the infected, while Suthep and Bernie fought off the other. Layla hovered on the spot in front of Harlan and Vivienne, who huddled by an orange 2002 Ford Ka, gripping one of the *Lord of the Rings* fighting-daggers ahead of her. Two bodies of other infected lay on the ground at their feet.

Baz was hit in the face by one of the infected, knocking him back a few paces. Fiona swiped at it with a pair of heavy fabric scissors. The blades slashed the infected across its throat. Baz scooped up his katana sword and lopped the top of the skull off the infected. The bowl of brain spun through the air and dropped from sight. Fiona shoved the infected away and the body crumpled.

Suthep swung the medieval club into the second infected. It dug into the flesh and meat of the face of the infected. Suthep twisted and pulled, when Bernie jabbed his own katana sword into its eye-socket.

Another infected appeared beyond Fiona, and raced to attack her, when Nicola rushed up and stabbed it in the back and side repeatedly with the bread-knife. The serrated-blade gouged chunks of meat away.

The infected peeled away from Fiona, gasping and trying to look over its shoulder.

Nicola tugged the back of the its collar and punted it into a green 2005 Peugeot 307. The infected slammed against the wing, denting it, and landed on the tarmac.

Bernie patted Suthep on his side and nodded at Nicola, who stood a short distance from the rest of them.

Harlan hung-back with Vivienne, crouching in front of her with his arms weakly held out in a protective stance, but he looked frightened and completely incapable of protecting her. Layla teetered on the spot, a metre in front of them.

Fiona helped Nicola fight another infected away, when Eileen appeared at the side of the motorway. She gasped.

Baz stabbed the seventh infected in the stomach with the curved, sharpened blade of the bat'leth. He twisted the weapon, then dashed it up, cutting the throat of the infected wide open. The infected fell back into Fiona and Nicola's arms. They tossed the body aside. Blood gushed from its wounds, pouring onto the road.

"May I?" Nicola said, holding her hand open to Baz.

He passed her the bat'leth and she stabbed the infected in the temple.

Eileen's face had dropped. She stared at the infected with a sickly expression. Nicola looked at her. Her glance was followed by Fiona, Baz and Layla.

"Hi," Eileen said cheerlessly, raising an arm.

Bernie and Suthep raised their arms to greet Eileen.

Fiona impaled the other infected with her garden-fork through its open mouth.

"Hi," Layla replied, taking Eileen's outstretched hand in hers.

"Hi," she repeated.

"So, where did you-two come from?" Harlan asked, leering at both of the girls from the side of the car.

A while later.
Nicola and Eileen sat with the others beside a white 2003 Ford Transit van that had rolled onto its side. Baz stood at the back end of the van, watching the motorway with a pair of binoculars. Suthep stood at the other end of the group, watching their backs, scanning the other end of the motorway with Nicola's pair of binoculars.

Layla and Vivienne smiled at Nicola and Eileen. Fiona hovered between a crouch and standing, her feet twitching on the ground next to Harlan's thigh, caked in dried blood. Bernie perched nearby, silently wiping the blade of his katana sword. He finished, sheathed the sword, then picked up Suthep's club to wipe clean.

"I'm Nicola. This is Eileen." Nicola said, looking from Layla to Fiona.

Fiona turned, her brow wrinkled. Her eyes met Nicola's. "Fiona... This is Vivienne, Layla, Harlan, Suthep, Baz and Bernie... We came from Plymouth. We came East... How about you? How about you-two?"

"Oxford. We were in Oxford. Just outside, actually."

"What was it like there?" Harlan asked. "A real shit storm?"

"I don't know... We don't know what the centre was like, because we were a little way out... But it wasn't good."

"What did you do for the last week, then?" Harlan said in an accusatory tone.

"Harlan," Layla said passively. "Let them explain in their own time..."

"No... It's okay... We hid," Eileen answered bashfully.

"Hid?" Fiona asked. Her eyebrow arched questioningly.

"We didn't leave my house until yesterday."

"That was probably the sensible plan," Layla admitted. "After all, we met. And now we're together. If you'd left earlier... Or stayed put...."

Fiona looked at the group, then back along the motorway. She beamed at Baz, who lowered his binoculars, sensing her glare. He glanced at her, then presented the mimic of a contented and calm expression.

Nicola scanned the road as well continually, restless, almost fidgeting, squatting on the road next to the strangers.

"We need to find a car or a van, something so I don't have to walk so much," Harlan moaned.

"We had a car for a little while... Earlier today... But it attracted too many of those things," Eileen stated.

Harlan looked crushed. Baz turned back to the road. "It looks clear for now," he stated.

"Well, we have to do something... And walking is going really slowly," Bernie added.

"We were going to London... At least some people will still be alive, in a place that big... -- you would have thought," Fiona offered. "The odds would suggest we might be right."

"There will also be a lot've those things there too!" Nicola said dryly. She looked up at the sky. There were no clouds. There were no birds. She swallowed and looked at Fiona.

"I hate those fucking things," Harlan added. "I fucking, fucking hate them."

"We were going to London, too, incidentally... We have to try and get there, otherwise we might as well sit here and rot... There will be soldiers there, there must be, and there will be some sort of safe-haven... There has to be..." Nicola said firmly. She swallowed again. Tried to push down the feeling that she was beginning to sound oblivious to all of the clear and obvious and present dangers, or being ridiculously optimistic in a totally hopeless situation. She did not know which. She blushed.

Baz sighed.

Bernie and Suthep shared a look.

Fiona noticed everything.

Four days later – 5:18pm.

The make-shift group arrived at the outskirts of Wimbledon and had gained three more people – KIT WALSH, 17 year old –English young man; MEREDITH MATTHEWS, 30 year old Englishwoman; and NIGEL FLETCHER, 41 year old Irishman. Kit had streaky blonde hair, highlighted by the sun, parted at the side and slicked down with hair-gel. He was a healthy young man with no fat on him at all; his body was angular and muscular, but immature and little. He had sharp features, a small nose, keen eyes and a thin mouth. He was still wearing a tattered school uniform. Meredith was very ordinary and plain; her hair was swept back and neatly tied in a ponytail. She wore very-little make-up and had quite a forgettable appearance. She was an average build with a modest frame and weak, sloped shoulders. She still wore her work clothes: a tracksuit with a polo shirt underneath. Nigel was short and dark, with bushy dark hair grown over his collar. He had dark brows with dark beads for eyes underneath, a long, crooked nose and a mouth full of large, pearly teeth. He had wide shoulders and a bent back, making his arms look extra long and his legs extra short. He was dressed in a tattered and bloodied brown suit, with a grey shirt, no tie, and comfortable brown brogues.

They had blockaded themselves in a small supermarket earlier that day and took time to rest and eat.

Baz sat by the nailed-shut entrance-door, looking through a letterbox-flap that he had cut from the cardboard covering, allowing access to the actual letterbox that was temporarily wedged open with an empty can of Coke, Duct taped in place. He watched the road in front of the shop through the limited viewpoint.

Bernie and Suthep sat near to Baz; Suthep played on a classic Gameboy with the volume turned low, and Bernie sharpened his katana sword. They sat in silence. Suthep had white iPod earphones pressed into his ears: classic Nintendo music seeped around the seal. Bernie placed the sword, whetstone and cloth aside, then pulled the piece of note-paper out. He took a pen from the inside-pocket of his body-warmer and wrote two more names on the list: Ian McKellen and Ai Wei Wei. He showed the paper to Suthep who scan-read the names, then smiled, then nodded at his friend, then went back to the Gameboy.

Harlan lay on a pile of blankets on a crooked staircase near the front-door that led to the first-floor. He was still in a lot of pain from the car accident, and he groaned and sweated and slept in a feverish state. He whispered and mumbled in his sleep, flushing in colour. He had sated his hunger with a plate of fish fingers and chips earlier. The plate lay discarded a few steps below him, knife and fork askew, half of the food uneaten.

Layla and Vivienne huddled in one of the aisles with Kit, Meredith and Eileen. They ate a chicken and vegetable stir-fry, with canned pineapple chunks and cream-powder for dessert. They spoke about their previous employment.

"I worked in a call-centre before all this... I feel... I feel totally useless in this situation. Absolutely and totally without any useful skills or training or attributes," Layla said. "Or any geeky weapons, like Baz and the other boys have... They seemed to be at least somewhat prepared for something like this..."

"In their wildest dreams..." Kit said around a smile.

"All I did was school-work.." Eileen offered. "A lot of work."

"Me, too," Kit said with a half-smile. Eileen could see through his attempt at flirtation and looked blankly back at him.

"That sounds nice, though," Layla said and half-smiled. "I didn't mind my time at school."

"I actually didn't mind mine, either," Kit stated slowly. "But I have no skills to bring to the table, either..."

"I don't think many people will be that resourceful... Or, would know how to deal with any or all-of-this... Nobody is qualified to deal with this... I wouldn't have survived at all without Nicola. And I bet the same goes for you-lot and Baz, Bernie and Suthep... And Nicola..."

"I used to work in the school Kit went to. I taught him PE in year 9," Meredith added. "I don't think I have any skills, really... Except working in a school..."

"Where was the school?"

"In Wimbledon," Meredith replied. "I lived about a mile and bit from here... Near the Park and the Pavilion... The school is just around the corner."

In the back of the shop.
Nicola, Fiona and Nigel huddled around a map of the area that Nigel and Meredith had added to with hand-drawn notes in Biro and crayon.

"Seeing as your mate watching the door has been counting more and more infected each day, you still want to leave here?!" Nigel accused. "Your little kill-squad of geeks won't be able to protect us all, if we leave here!"

Nicola started to nod.

"Do you agree?" Fiona asked Nicola.

"Look, Fi, I... I don't know... There are more of those things."

"There are..."

"So," Nigel plead, "you can see where we're coming from?"

"We have to keep moving, at least to see if there's anything actually happening in the world. Any other people alive... We found you... We found you, Nigel... And the others... We have to get further into London... --to the centre... --and see if there are any other people left... Plus, we'll run out of food soon, even being in this shop... What are we going to do then?!" Fiona stated firmly.

Nicola looked down at the map, looking away from Fiona's eyes.

Nigel shrugged.

Fiona exited, leaving Nigel to persuade Nicola. "We can't keep moving. And we aren't likely to run out of fucking food, in a fucking supermarket!"

"Watch your mouth, Nigel... And... She's right. Picking at this food will last a while. But it's all short-term. Nothing substantial. Nothing that will allow us to continue, will it?"

"You cannot be serious!"

"What?"

"You're talking about a future..."

"We're trying to talk about the future."

In the front of the shop.
Baz stood up with the look of shock on his face; his eyes popped and his mouth hung open gormlessly. He started pulling the nails from the door-frame, trying to get the entrance-door open, when Kit arose behind him.

"What're you doing?!" Kit shouted.

"What are you doing?" Bernie parroted.

"The army is outside!"

"What?" Suthep asked.

"The army is outside! There're soldiers out-there!"

Kit rushed to help Baz pull the door open, when an infected darted passed the door. Suthep and Bernie armed themselves with katana and club.

Pffft - Pffft

They pulled the door open wider and hurriedly stepped into the doorway. The infected had been shot dead. It tumbled and skipped and tripped and landed a few metres away, sliding along the ground and hitting a lamppost with a *crack* of its shoulder.

After a long moment, Baz and Kit hesitated in the doorway. They moved a little way out. Bernie and Suthep followed, remaining hesitant and swathed in shadow.

Baz and Kit stepped further outside, into bright sunlight, with their arms raised to shade their eyes. They found a black-painted APC stopped in the middle of the road. The APC's engine was running with a quiet *jigger-jigger* and a little smoke coughed out of the exhaust.

Smiles stretched across Baz's and Kit's faces. Baz turned to his friends. Bernie and Suthep remained stony.

Two soldiers, dressed in black army fatigues, riot helmets, gas-masks and dark sunglasses, sat on the roof armed with silenced-machineguns.

They instantly saw Kit and Baz, Bernie and Suthep, and aimed their weapons at them, frozen for a few seconds.

One of the soldiers pressed his finger to his ear and both soldiers lowered their guns and stared at the four young men from the roof of the APC, without a word.

The first black-fatigued soldier climbed down, covered by the other.

Then the second soldier clambered and slid down, with the first providing cover.

The first soldier walked toward Baz and Kit, who were still frozen to the spot, unable to move, arms wavering in the air.

They stared at the oncoming soldier, when Fiona appeared between the four of them in the doorway to the shop, looking unsettled.

The soldier looked at Baz and Kit, Suthep and Bernie, then at Fiona.

"How many of you are there?... We need to get you in the APC, and evacuated away from here."

Fiona looked relieved and surprised and happy and shocked and comforted and afraid.

She looked back inside the supermarket at Nicola, who entered from the back-room.

They smiled at each other, but they both saw deep pools of fear in each other's eyes.

CHAPTER 12 - THE RETURN - Bristol

DERMOTT KEANE, 44 year old half-English, half-Irishman; sat in his double prison-cell. He had thick shoulders and arms, a barrel chest and strong bulging legs. His dusty-brown hair was cropped short and slightly parted on one side. His eyes were cool, icy blue under heavy brows. He had a stern, angry expression permanently etched into his face: although he was cool and measured; a human glacier. He had tattoos covering both arms, from wrist to shoulder, and more on his neck, knuckles and calves. He wore prison-issue denim jeans with the legs rolled up at the ankle, a white t-shirt under a powder-blue shirt with the sleeves rolled up above the elbow, and black, cheap generic trainers.

Football posters and a few Page 3 topless models adorned the wall opposite two bunk-beds.

Dermott perched on the edge of the lower-bunk. His eyes fluttered back and forth to the door. The bed springs *squeaked* and *creaked* underneath the thin, plastic-coated mattress.

He wrung his tattooed-hands together, feeling like he looked impatient, when SEAN TULLY, 44 year old Englishman; was brought back to the cell chaperoned by two prison-guards. He was thinner than Dermott, but only slightly; with similar broad shoulders and muscular arms. He was taller than Dermott by a few inches and often they were mistaken for older and younger brothers. His hair was shaved to grade one, leaving a thick matt of spiky darker-brown hair, fuller and less receded than Dermott's. He had tattoos on his lower-arms, a Union Jack over his heart and a large block of text that ran down his right leg. He also wore the prison-issue clothing.

Sean stepped inside and sat down next to Dermott.

"They paroled me, mate," he said slowly, bitterly and sorely.

Neither of them appeared happy about the news. The guards backed away from the doorway.

Dermott gritted his teeth, "Well-done, mate... I'll see yer, then..."

Sean gave a tiny nod and pursed his lips. "I'll see you..."

Two weeks later – 11:02pm.
Sean stood at the bar of the White Horse pub. He was wearing a grey shirt, black jeans and a pair of reddish-brown Caterpillar Vinson boots, and did not look or feel comfortable. He rolled his sleeves to above his elbow and rubbed at the rough-fur that thinly-rugged his arm.

He finished the dregs at the bottom of a pint of beer, when the landlord rang the bell, indicating that it was the time for last orders. Sean glanced at the clock on the wall, hung behind the bar. He pushed the pint-glass across the top of the bar.

"Bye, mate," he said with a nod to the landlord and patted one of the regulars on the back. "Bye."

He exited.

A cool breeze ran fingers through his hair. He sucked in the air, then lit a cigarette.

As soon as Sean had left the White Horse, a tramp emerged from the shadows of an alleyway that ran down the side the pub, connecting the road in front with the road behind. This tramp will be the same man who will try to assassinate Reg Heron in the Michael Bleich Gallery in London in the future, but will be unsuccessful. The tramp wore layers of festering and ripped clothing under a worn, ripped and grease-blotched parka jacket with furred-hood, pulled up over a black beanie. His skin was filthy and smeared, oily and muddy; his face covered by a grotty, matted beard.

Sean sensed the tramp following him and heard the pursuers pace increase to match his own.

Moments later.
Sean crossed a silent street then walked down a poorly-lit side-road, with the tramp following him. The tramp increased his speed again and extricated a kitchen-knife from a hidden sheath in the parka's lining. Before reaching Sean, he turned and snatched the tramp's lower arm, gripping so hard the knife could not be used. His other hand enveloped the tramp's hand with his own, trapping the knife in his grip. His eyes widened, then he shoved forward and grappled with Sean.

Sean and the tramp fought, knocking the knife to the ground. They punched each other viciously, over and over, when another man ran across the street – another tramp – whose face was disguised and indistinguishable in the darkness of the side-road.

The second tramp stunned Sean with a handheld taser-device, hitting him hard in the fleshy abdomen-side between his ribs and pelvis. The electricity *buzzed* and *fizzled* and *ticked* on impact.

Sean dropped to his hands and knees groaning, when the first tramp kicked and punched at him, forcing the wind out of his lungs. The second tramp kicked Sean into a wooden-planked fence, sending him falling onto his side.

The first tramp retrieved his knife, scraping it across the pavement as he scooped it up, when the second tramp stunned Sean again, knocking him flat onto his body, sprawled-out on the ground.

As the first tramp returned with the knife, car headlights shone into the street and both tramps ran.

The car stopped and a man got out.

The man dialled 999 on his mobile, as he walked hesitantly toward the prone figure of Sean. "Ambulance, please."

Two months later.
Sean sat in the White Horse drinking a pint. There were a few old men sitting around the pub at different tables. He sat alone at the bar, when the landlord appeared, continuing their conversation, "So, when did you last see Dermott, then, Sean?"

Sean finished his pint, "Last week, Tuesday... I'm going for a piss... Do me another one, would ya, pal?" he said, rising to his feet. "I've got a job interview at two..." he laughed.

"Right-o. Good one..."

He winked at the landlord and walked to the double-doors that led to the toilets.

As the doors closed behind Sean and he entered the toilet, the landlord started to cough whilst pouring Sean's next pint. He managed to finish the pint unsteadily, then coughed more violently. He gripped the bar-top, then fell to his knees. He coughed uncontrollably, choking to get any air inside his lungs. He fell onto all-fours and barked. The colour drained from his face and his eyes became bloodshot.

The landlord rose up, puking blood on the bar and into Sean's pint. Blood sank into the glass in dark red mushrooms and snakes, coiling passed fizz and bubbles that floated up the glass in miniature columns.

The landlord stood, panting, gargling and hacking, hold down a torrent of blood inside itself. For a second the infected looked dozy, and it dropped to one knee, putting its hand out for stability. It seemed to collapse in slow-motion; its legs angular and awkward.

Two minutes later.
Sean walked out of the toilet drying his hands on the back of his jeans. He instantly saw that two of the three old men at the tables had died, with blood leaking out of their mouths and noses. They lay, bent-over across the tables, as if they had all suddenly fallen asleep in unison, or been stunned with a stun-gun.

The third old man had become infected. It blood-puked on itself, teetering on its ankles, then collapsed, expiring on the floor in a pool of blood.

Sean stared at the infected on the floor.

A jet of blood sprang from the mouth of the infected and it splashed the barstool's legs nearest it.

Sean casually crossed to the bar and picked up his pint. Before drinking it, he saw the blood; a red ooze had collected at the base of the pint-glass, dark and thick. He peered over the bar, when the landlord got to his feet and puked blood over the bar again, splattering thick gore over cardboard and rubberised bar-mats, around empty bottles and glasses; washing them over the edges. Immediately the landlord started to clamber over the bar towards Sean, who backed away quickly.

Sean was utterly nonchalant, not making a single sound, not modifying his expression, demeanour or speed whatsoever. He merely glanced from body to body, continuing to back away from the infected landlord.

He set his focus on the landlord as it fell over the top of the bar clumsily and flopped to the floor.

Sean looked for a weapon, and saw one. He stepped slowly to the wooden pool-cue-stand. He selected a cue and took it down, when the infected finally charged at him. Sean speared the infected under the ribs. They struggled and the infected tried to puke blood on him again. Sean dodged aside then shoved it back against the front of the bar, then lifted it over the top. It flipped over the bar and landed on the cue-end, impaling itself deeper.

The infected growled and moaned, striking out in all directions.

He picked up a large glass-block ashtray and launched it at the spirits, upside down in their optics, behind the bar. Glass shattered and alcohol spilled and pooled. He lit a match and tossed it onto the landlord's raging form.

Sean walked to the door slowly and exited the pub.

The infected landlord tried to get up as fire swelled around him, but it could not, the pool-cue had caught across both sides of the bar, pining it in place.

Flames erupted around the room.

Outside.
Sunlight flared in his eyes and then Sean saw what the outside looked like: people had died on the sides of the road, a few cars had crashed, and other people were now infected and prowling the streets.

Sean stepped out into the road, when one of the infected charged at him. He charged straight at it. He punched it to the ground and stamped on its head and neck.

He looked around and saw that he was safe, then turned and walked away when no more threats presented themselves.

Six minutes later. On Gloucester Road, the A38.
Sean rushed to a black 2004 Volkswagen Golf and found the driver dead. He immediately saw through the driver's side-window that the body still had the seatbelt drawn across its torso. He reached in, panting for breath. Something was chasing him and it was getting nearer and nearer and nearer. He managed to undo the seatbelt and dragged the dead driver out by their arm. He turned to briefly look up the road as eleven infected charged down the slight-hill road toward him. He climbed in the Golf, slamming the door shut in the nick of time, as the gang of the infected reached the car.

He turned the ignition and sped away.

Sean drove down a few back-roads, Weston Crescent onto Wellington Hill onto Church Road onto Maple Road, veering wildly around crashed- and stopped-cars. He was not able to drive faster than about fourteen miles an hour. He stopped at a road-block, where several cars had collided with each other and blocked the way forward.

Beyond the road-block there was another car: A silver 2003 Land Rover Freelander with both of its front-doors hanging open.

He leapt out of the Golf and dashed toward the road-block. He vaulted the first car, then jumped onto the roof of a second. He tore between three other cars, as a few of the passengers and drivers awoke infected.

Growls and moans and coughs emanated from within the road-block.

Sean ran to the Land Rover, as a slow-moving infected stalked out of the open front-door of a nearby house.

A little later.
Sean wiped blood and grime from his sleeve as he pulled the passenger door shut, and started the engine of the Land Rover. He swung the car around a white Pitter self-drive van that had swerved off the road and had nested in a large privet hedge. He turned off Maple and onto Radnor Road.

A little later.
Sean drove through a mechanical barrier, half-shearing and bending-back the metal beam and quarter-breaking it off its hinge. The Land Rover shot through the car-park in front of the prison – HMP Bristol – tyres *squealing*.

Sean broke hard, turning the wheel tightly. He drove at the left corner of the main office and processing building at the front of the complex and skidded through a large chain-link fence, crushing an infected against the wall in the sweep of the back wheels. The Land Rover darted down a thin passage, breaking a bicycle shelter to pieces. The car sped along the wall, fizzing and sparking against the fence on one side and the shelter on the other. The engine *roared* and then smashed through the original, large Victorian entrance-doors with a *boom*. The huge oak doors buckled and sprang back, splitting around reinforcing-beams, then fractured altogether in a cloud of dust and large, sharp splinters of wood.

The Land Rover skidded to a halt, sliding sideways into another large chain-link fence. The fence shivered and waved, bending backwards on itself.

Sean leapt out of the car, holding a large hammer in one hand and a bat in the other. He charged to the bent-over fence and climbed over the folded metal with *clangs* and *chinks*. He jumped to the ground the other side and found himself in a small compound, where a few dead visitors and prison-officers lay face-down. Blood-stains soaked the ground around their heads and tarnished the walls and doors near the exit in vicious, violent dark splatters.

Sean stared at the bodies for a short moment, then rushed to the back entrance-door of the prison's reception. He crept in silently and carefully, looking around in fast sweeps, then shook his head with irreverence and straightened up. He leapt over the counter-top in one bound and looked around again quickly, before continuing on at a faster pace.

He hesitated a moment, looking at the door at the back of the office and the door-handle. He found it was unlocked. Immediately as Sean opened the door, an infected charged at the other side of it, knocking him back a few paces and allowing it to enter the reception.

Sean did not feel any intimidation at all and a wave of determination and anger filled him. He saw the bat on the ground and went for it with lightning-speed. He lashed out even-faster, as the infected advanced on him.

Sean beat the infected until it did not move.

He moved to the door and pulled it open. He stomped through the doorway and into the corridor beyond. Eerie silence once again settled over the reception.

Later.
Sean frantically unlocked the gate in an iron-bar wall that divided two halves of a corridor. He panted for breath, briefly glancing over his shoulder.

He saw five infected walking slowly towards him in a loose line.

The infected made *gaaah* sounds and groaned, focusing entirely on Sean; all bloodshot eyes locked onto him.

He finally got the door open and jumped through, when a faster moving infected sprinted through the slower ones, knocking them aside. The infected stomped down the corridor, roaring and raging, blood dripping from its slack mouth, accelerating towards the gate.

Sean shoved the door backwards and broke the nose of the infected across the bridge, as it charged head-first into the bars. He bone *crunched* under the impact and the infected was knocked sprawling to the corridor floor. He pulled the gate straight and locked it, pocketing the keys. He looked back as the broken-nose infected clambered to its feet, stumbled to the gate and puked blood between the bars, spilling dark ooze onto the linoleum flooring. Trails of blood sprayed and ran out over the shattered fragments of nose cartilage and skin, squirting up into its eyes and running down its cheeks and into its eyes and into its mouth.

The other five infected reached the gate finally and eyed Sean through the gaps. Their arms stretched through the bars, clawing at thin air.

"Fuck you, you ugly fucks!" he spat.

Sean turned to jog away down the corridor, but chest-butted with an infected that blocked his path. They were both knocked over.

"Ouch!" Sean groaned. "Teach me to be arrogant, huh?"

The infected sat up.

Sean climbed to his feet and watched the infected. It tried to try to stand. Its arms flopped at its sides, trying to find purchase on the floor. Sean crossed to it, snatched its head in his arm, and snapped its neck in one quick motion.

A little later.

Sean arrived at a T-junction where one corridor met another. He speedily looked right, when an infected charged full-pelt at him from the left side.

Sean immediately batted the attacker to the ground and hit it repeatedly, when another emerged from an open cell behind him. The second infected sped towards him, but this time Sean stabbed the hammer forward at it, hitting its neck and crushing it.

The infected hit the ground gasping and coughing up blood.

"Try and sneak up on me, you fucker!" he shouted with a wry smile, then stamped on both of the temples of the infected with the heel of his boot with loud, echoing *cracks*.

He picked himself up, snatched the bat from the floor, and continued on.

A little later.

A much more bloodied and soaked Sean jogged down a metal-walkway toward one specific cell. He was in a large gallery of cells, criss-crossed by walkways and staircases and netted with fine mesh. It looked like every prison, in every country around the world. Beige walls, splattered with blood, lined the walkway.

He knocked on the cell-door, and waited.

After a moment, he spoke, "Dermott?... It's Sean... Are you in there?"

A second passed, then Dermott replied from behind the door, "Sean? What the fuckin'-hell are you doin' here?!"

"I'm here to rescue you, princess!" he answered with a laugh.

A noise, dull but noticeable, sounded from across the gallery.

Sean unbolted the cell door and reunited with Dermott. They hugged a moment.

Dermott was also quite bloody; he had had to kill his new cell-mate. The body was laid on the top bunk. Its neck was broken, its body and face peppered with stab wounds.

Sean took a quick look inside the cell, "I couldn't've let you rot in this cell, mate... After a day or two you'd've been bumming that bloke's body!" he said with a wink.

They both laughed.

"Fuck you, buddy... But, thanks for coming."

Sean continued, "I brought you your own pieces..."

He handed a knife in a sheath and a long-handled hammer to Dermott

"I can't believe you fought your way in here to rescue me... You asshole."

Sean looked through the gallery to the ground-floor, two floors below. He said, "Come on.. We gotta go."

Seconds later.

Sean and Dermott charged down the walkway and crossed to a staircase, when an alarm sounded continuously in a high-pitched *whir* and all of the prison-cell doors automatically unlocked and popped open a few inches.

Fifty infected started to creep out of the cells.

Sean and Dermott looked at each other, half-smiling at their new predicament. They turned, catching sight of every member of the surrounding pack, who advanced along the walkways toward them.

"This seems like fun," Dermott quipped.

"It's all good fun."

Several infected moved along the walkway, either side of Dermott and Sean.
"Like the old days…"
"Just like the old days…"

Across the gallery.
Somebody watched Sean and Dermott, eyeing them from the doorway to their cell.

Later.
Dermott helped Sean – who was injured on his right-side – out of the prison. They jogged across the road to a parked black 2008 Nissan Murano and pulled the driver out from the front seat.
The engine *roared* on ignition and they sped away.
"So, where to?"
"Fuck knows, mate. My plan was to get you out. That's where I sign off. It's your deal now…"

Five days later – 11:01am. Half a mile North of Andover.
Dermott and Sean walked casually through a field, keeping close to the hedgerow that lined the Eastern side. The hedgerow provided them with some shade from the morning sun.
"If this plague has infected the whole-world, we could go anywhere… Like… Anywhere," Dermott said positively.
"We could start by seeing if France is safe or not… And move on down and around to the Mediterranean."
Dermott smiled, "Yeah… Spain… The Costa Del Sol…"
They both smiled at the thought.
"Could be a good laugh."
"Yeah…"
"We could live like kings…"
"I just want a sun-tan. I hate being so white!"
"Yeah, a permanent tan…"
"We could go to Goa, or Australia… I mean… Sail anywhere… We could find Richard Branson's island…"
"Necker Island?"
"Yeah…"
"And hope the serving-staff are all still fine…"
"Ha – Yeah!"
"Excuse me?" a voice called from the other side of the hedgerow.
Dermott and Sean froze. Dermott lifted the long-handle hammer across his chest; Sean took a hunting-knife from its sheath and raised the claw-hammer. "Who's that, then?" Dermott called out.
"I'm Jerry…" the man said, snapping dried twigs under his shoes as he moved along parallel to them. Jerry Hardbold stepped through a gap in the hedgerow, dragging a backpack behind him. "Hi," he said, holding a hand up, a smile creasing across half of his face, where the other side showed a darkening, purpling black-eye.
"Hello."
"Alright, buddy."
"That's a nasty bruise…"
"I was fighting with one of those people… You have seen them, haven't you?"
"Oh yeah. We've seen them…"
"I was with a group… Some of my friends… Yesterday… I can't find them."
"You'll be alright with us."

Later – 10:11pm.
Sean, Jerry and Dermott took refuge in a supermarket. They ate snack food and sandwiches, huddled in the clothing section of the shop. They had pushed aside racks and piled t-shirts and jumpers to create a small living-room space with beds.

Jerry rolled a cigarette and lit it. "D'you reckon we're safe in here?" he asked.

"Yeah, man," Sean said and got up. "I'm gonna find something more to eat..."

Dermott followed, he said, "I'm sure we can find a microwave and a plug-socket somewhere... And some macaroni and cheese, or something in a can or tin..."

"You're still thinking like you're in prison! We have loads of things to eat here!"

"Prison?" Jerry repeated.

"Chill out, buddy... We were framed."

"Both of you were in–..."

"Yeah."

Jerry's eyes widened. Dermott saw it, and smiled. "Don't worry... If we can't find your friends, then you are actually okay with us... We can be useful."

"Speak for yourself," Sean added with a smirk, wandering down an aisle.

A little later.
Sean and Dermott sat in front of a microwave, watching as a macaroni and cheese microwave-meal spun on the glass plate inside. As soon as it was finished, the *ping* awoke an infected who had laid dormant in the next aisle. It came out of its slumber with a rasping *moan*.

The infected sat up and puked blood on itself.

The noise unsettled Dermott and he stood up, looking around. "Did you hear that?" he asked, turning again on the spot.

"No. Nothing."

"Jerry?"

"I thought so..."

"Fuck it," Dermott said, exhaling, then sat. He stabbed at the pasta in the plastic container, craning it to his open mouth.

"Check the TVs, again, see if there's anything on. Might be someone broadcasting something, somewhere."

"Maybe."

"It didn't seem like it," Jerry announced. "We tried loads of TVs..."

"It has been almost a week."

"We could find a DVD to watch..."

Dermott pushed the microwave meal aside and sat up.

"I might get some salt an' pepper," Sean said and started to rise. He immediately saw the oncoming infected stumbling towards him with its arms outstretched and blood dripping from its lips. He was caught off-guard and tripped backwards on the microwave. He fell to the ground, crushing several packets of dried-pasta and vegetables.

Dermott reacted quickly, snatching the long-handle hammer from the floor. He struck the infected hard. He leapt at it and they struggled on the floor. Sean regained his composure and joined Dermott. They fought the infected, finally stamping on its head and breaking it open.

"That was stupid."

"You're telling me?" Dermott said exhaling slowly.

"We need to check every single body there is."

"We need to stab them through the eye!" Jerry added.

"That's not a bad idea!"

Later.
They sat on the floor near the microwave, drinking from cases of beer. All of them picked at their microwave macaroni dishes, laughing, listening to music quietly on a tiny, pink girls' stereo.

"I kinda missed music," Dermott admitted.

"I just missed someone decent to talk to."

"You sound so gay."

"Thanks, Derm, love you too, bro."

"I missed the freedom to put music on, whatever I wanted to listen to..."

"You had the internet."

"I couldn't be fucked with that. It always seemed like a chore."

"You're a chore," Sean said with a laugh and slapped Dermott's face lightly.

"Sod off."

Jerry watched the two men quietly.

"Just eat your food, con," Sean said around a smile.

"So," Dermott started, "tell us about you, Jerry..."

"What? Like what?"

"Anything about you."

"I think I met the girl of my dreams a week ago," he replied blankly, staring at the centre of their circle. "And, right-now, I don't think there's the slightest thing I can do about it... Or find my friends, for that matter."

"Where'd you meet her?"

Jerry cleared his throat. "I went to Amsterdam for a couple of days. The day I got home all-of-this started..."

"The virus?"

"Yeah... The day I got home. Got off the plane. Got the bus back to the house."

"At least you met us!"

"Mmm..."

"You might get to see her again..." Dermott said quietly. "It's a possibility..."

"Slim..." Jerry murmured.

"If she's still alive... And has her wits about her," Sean added. "She could be..."

"I guess... If she's alive... Sticking with you-two might mean I get to see her again, I guess..."

"Yeah. Be positive," Dermott sang and slapped Jerry's shoulder.

A little later.

Sean and Dermott twisted-off the fluorescent light-beams above the clothing section, where they had laid out three air-mattresses as beds on top of the piles of clothes. Jerry lay asleep on his own bed.

Dermott and Sean placed a large camping lantern in the centre between their beds and sat. They were still drinking, but had moved on to whiskey. "You are one stupid, crazy fuckin' idiot," Dermott slurred.

"Thanks."

"I mean it."

"Like I said, the first thing I thought was... --that I couldn't leave you in there. If you were even alive."

"Barely."

"You did seem to be warming to your bunk-mate!"

"Oh yeah!"

"Were you gonna braid his hair?"

"Yeah. And do his makeup, too!"

They laughed.

"What're we gonna do?" Sean said solemnly.

Jerry slumbered.

A little later.

Sean and Dermott had passed-out on their beds, with the lantern still on and glowing warmly.

Jerry hugged his backpack, sleeping soundly.

Dermott snored.

Sean momentarily woke up. He kicked the lantern and it went out. He fell asleep.

The next day.
Dermott and Sean collected the final amount of goods and survivalist-provisions that they could fit into large backpacks; backpacks that dwarfed Jerry's and those that regular campers or travellers would use.

Sean took a packed-tent and lashed it to the bottom of his backpack.

Dermott secured three hunting knives to each side of each backpack, all handles angled to the front for quick access if they were needed. They worked in silence, in a calculative, practised fashion, moving together as one. Jerry watched them pack in unison, passing to each other and placing items in each bag.

"What did you-two used to do? Before prison?" he asked.

"What we used to do?" Dermott clarified. Jerry nodded. "Well, it was kind of... --secret. Military secrets... And, we... Like, worked for the military..."

Sean eyed Jerry, trying to read his curious expression for something more. "Why do you wanna know?" he asked cheerlessly.

"I'm... I was wondering..."

"More of this will be clearer soon... You'll understand."

A little later.
They walked towards the back-doors and into the stock-entrance bay, wearing their backpacks.

Dermott half-smiled, reaching the back-most door, he said, "So... Off to France then!..."

"France?" Jerry exclaimed.

Sean laughed. "Yeah. Why not?"

"What about my friends?"

"If we can't find them..." Dermott reassured. "If we can't find them," he repeated.

"We've got to make one stop first..." Sean said, meeting eyes with Dermott. He nodded back to his friend. "After we've checked out that barn your friends were staying in..."

One day later.
Dermott and Sean led Jerry into an unimpressive, featureless field of low grass. They crossed to a stunted oak tree and placed their backpacks in the shade of its branches. Jerry followed and took his own pack off and rested it with the others. Dermott took the spade that hung from the side of his pack and paced twenty steps from the oak, walking due East.

"Should be here, Sean."

"I'd say you're about right."

"What are you looking for?" Jerry enquired, stepping in behind them.

"You'll see."

The two men took turns digging with the spade, taking ten minute shifts. At a depth of three feet the spade-tip met something solid. Dermott crouched in the hole, widening it with his large, muddy paws. He scraped and dragged clods of mud from the hole and shoved them aside. Jerry helped to clear the piles around the hole, hoofing the hillock away with the side of his dirty blue Adidas Classics.

"Nearly there," Dermott told Sean, who gulped down a mouthful of bottled water.

"Good news."

"Nearly where?" Jerry enquired.

They cleared a flat shelf under the mud, where Dermott found a handle. He gripped the slippery metal and pulled.

The hatch lifted and balls of dirt rolled into the opening. Sean switched on his Maglite torch and shone it into the hole. Dermott started down, into the dimness. "What's down there?" Jerry asked, edging closer.

"You can come down, or stay here on look-out, Jerry, it's up to you..." Sean stated.

"I think I'll come down."

Dermott lowered himself fully and disappeared from sight. Sean shone the beam around and Dermott found a light-switch. He pressed the button and strip-beam fluorescents blinked on.

Dermott was standing in a small, square well made of wood and shoring; in front of him was a nondescript door and a thumbprint-reader. He pressed his thumb to the reader and the door *clicked* open and swung in an inch.

Sean found the ladder that ran up the well-wall and climbed down. Jerry followed behind them.

They entered a large space where two shipping containers, sixteen foot wide by eight foot high by forty foot long, had been welded together and buried under three feet of mud. Lights blinked on automatically, as the three men walked inside. Three thin aisles ran down the packed space, with six stainless steel racks built to the ceiling running between them. Each rack was loaded with machine guns, rifles, pistols, revolvers, shotguns, assault and sniper rifles, bullets and shells of all kind, body armour, gloves, boots, shin, arm and leg protectors, silencers, knives, helmets, shields, dehydrated food-packs, stun, flare and hand grenades, rocket launchers, medicine kits, saws, axes, batons, heavy-duty backpacks, binoculars, sights, and night-vision goggles. At the back of the container there were three spaces where machines, lathes, drills and other engineering equipment was arranged.

"Is this an armoury?" Jerry asked slowly.

"It's our armoury, bud," Dermott replied, a grin creasing his face.

"Why do you have this?"

"In case we needed it," Sean answered.

"In case what happened, happened?"

Dermott and Sean both shot Jerry a look, then went back to admiring and scanning their armoury, sharing his awe.

"Is that right?" Jerry pushed.

"Something like that."

"Is that a rocket-launcher?!" Jerry squealed.

"Err... Yeah."

"It's like some survivalist, end-of-days bomb-shelter-bunker like some crazy American redneck might have..."

"Huh, yeah," Sean muttered.

"Here's something that might interest you..." Dermott said, crossing to where Jerry was standing. He squeezed passed Jerry and unlocked a large cabinet, then slid back the panel on the front. "There's about twenty pounds of marijuana, freeze-dried; a few kilos of magic mushrooms, coke, heroin, speed... A few hundred ecstasy tablets... A few litres of liquid acid... Anything you could possibly want..."

Jerry's mouth fell open. After a moment aghast, he asked, "Why do you have all of this?"

Three days later. In Weymouth, on the B3155.

Dermott, Sean and Jerry rushed down the main road, passing a commercial estate, a MacDonald's and a KFC. They were running from a dozen slow moving infected that were pursuing them, gradually lurching up the street. They did not have their large backpacks on them anymore, and accelerated along the tarmac without hindrance.

They dashed down the main-road and ducked out of sight behind a white 2007 Daihatsu Materia.

"We're a bit fucked, huh, Sean?"

"We're not dead yet."

"How's your side?" Jerry asked Sean.

Sean touched his abdomen above his left hip. He pulled his shirt up and showed Dermott a large purple, black and green bruise. "It's healing. I'll be fine."

Seven infected rushed out into the road, drawn to the movement of the dozen-strong pack.

Dermott and Sean leapt from behind the Daihatsu and stood in the centre of the main-road. The infected instantly charged toward them, with the slow-movers following behind.

"What're you doing?" Jerry screamed, still huddled behind the Daihatsu.

"Having a break."

"Gettin' rid of this lot, bud!"

Jerry leapt to follow and stood with the others.

Dermott used the hammer effectively, diving into the group; Sean fought with his bare-fists, elbows, knees and boots; and Jerry swung a brick around, clutched in his hand, swatting the infected.

After a long, painful and reckless fight, Dermott, Jerry and Sean came away unscathed. A stack of the infected lay about the road around them, bleeding from vicious wounds all over their bodies and heads.

They turned around on the spot, then ventured further down the road. They could see the harbour with a thousand white masts pointing skyward.

"We're not far from the boats..."

"I'd suggest we go back and get our backpacks... I prefer having something to fight with."

"Me too," Jerry said. "I really-really miss the sword that Baz gave me..."

"You had a sword?"

"Yeah. It was a replica, a prop-one from a film," Jerry replied and laughed. "But my mate had the blade swapped-out and sharpened it..."

"If he hadn't, it wouldn't've been any fuckin' use..."

"Yeah, I know."

"A sword, huh? That's crazy... Maybe we should raid a museum or something..."

"I had the one from *Serenity*, then we swapped and I had the one from *Kill Bill*."

"That's quite cool, Jerry."

Later. At Weymouth Marina.
Dermott darted down the wooden-plank docks and undid the moorings of an expensive, but small speedboat: a twenty-four foot eight inch Yamarin 76 Day Cruiser with a Yamaha outboard engine. Sean and Jerry waited at the start of the footpath, watching the way they had approached from. They could see no infected at all.

Dermott waved to the others and they scurried along the dock with crooked backs, hugging their backpacks under their bodies. They climbed aboard the boat, tossing their packs in the back.

Sean twisted a screwdriver in the ignition, then pulled a panel from the dashboard and started to hot-wire the speedboat. The engine *grumbled* and came alive, as Dermott climbed aboard then joined him at the helm.

Jerry secured the backpacks in the compact cabin at the bow of the boat.

They exited the harbour slowly, watching the surrounding road.

Hundreds of infected lurched and waddled and sauntered along Westwey Road, Commercial Road, Trinity Road, Cove Row and the Nothe Parade. The boat picked up speed as they passed The Old Harbour Dive Centre, the Ferry Terminal, then the Weymouth Pavilion.

Dermott increased the speed again, as they passed the end of the Old Harbour and Nothe Fort.

They entered Weymouth Bay, then started across the English Channel.

Later.
They were halfway across the English Channel; they had travelled forty miles, nearly thirty-five nautical miles. Sean looked through compartments and pockets in the speedboat's dashboard.

"No," he said, "no binoculars..."

Sean let out a long exhalation, sounding like he was deflating. "I can't believe not one of us picked any up at the container..."

Dermott gritted his teeth, he said, "So we have to go in blind. In daylight. That's fine... If the plague isn't there, they may shoot us, or blow this boat up before we even get a chance to get to land... But it should be okay..."

"That sounds like fun," Jerry stated. "Getting blown up!"

"If there's no TV anywhere, no radio too, then I don't think it's going to be a friendly welcome... Besides, the wind probably took the plague on the first day to most of Europe..."

Dermott shook his head and sighed.

"Why do you keep calling it 'the plague'?" Jerry asked.

Sean opened his backpack and took out three cans of beer. He gave one to Dermott, one to Jerry, then opened the other for himself. He sucked away the froth from the can, then sipped from it. "Because that's what it is..." He gulped down a mouthful of beer.

"So, we could all be fucked? Everyone on the planet?"

Dermott and Sean exchanged a look.

"Yeah... Yep."

"Yeah."

"What if there are zombies in France too?" Jerry asked.

Sean and Dermott exchanged a look. "Either we turn back and try our luck on our home turf, or keep going..."

"So, the mainland?... Or back home?"

"Yeah."

"Well... Either way..." Jerry started. "We're fucked!"

"Yeah."

"Mmm-hmm."

Later.

They continued across the Channel, until they slowed, half a mile away from the village of Gatteville-Le-Phare, on the Northern coast of France, near Cherbourg.

They floated for a while on the surf, letting the current take the boat in slowly. White waves crested and broke around them.

Dermott, Jerry and Sean watched the coast very-closely.

Dermott saw an infected stalking along the shoreline.

"The plague is here too! Fuck it!... And if it's here, it's most-probably everywhere else too, guys..." Dermott stated calmly.

Sean stared at the coast and at the figure of the infected shuffling along.

"At least it gives us free-reign of the world..."

Dermott, Sean and Jerry stared at the beach and the shops and buildings that lined the beachfront.

Someone on the shore had spotted them.

CHAPTER 13 - ABSOLUTE NECESSITY - Birmingham

Night.
JAMES 'RANDALL' FIELD, 19 year old English young man – strolled into a bedroom he had never been in before and looked around. He was tall and wiry, with long muscular arms and legs. His hair was a top-heavy mane of dark auburn. He had a young face, wrinkleless and smooth. He had curious, dark coffee-brown eyes under twitchy and expressive eyebrows. His mouth was thin and almost lipless, always ready to fall into a half-smile. He wore a loose-fitting grey jacket, a baggy red *Flash* t-shirt over a stretchy, tight, plain-black long sleeve t-shirt, flared Smog jeans and blue-and-yellow Adidas Gazelle trainers. He tossed his backpack onto the bed with a bounce. He grabbed a jewellery-box and emptied the contents onto a bedside-table. He carefully selected the best pieces and secured them in numerous inside-jacket, trouser and backpack pockets.

He continued to rummage through the bedroom, opening drawers and pushing clothes around to reveal hidden objects. He pulled down several boxes from the top of a tall, thin double-wardrobe. A sprinkling of dust fell with the boxes making him sneeze.

Randall opened the closet and rifled through the contents, when an infected burst into the room through the half-opened door, and charged at him.

Randall was pummelled across his ribs. Tripping backwards, they walloped the wardrobe, splintering wood and breaking one of the doors off its hinges. The infected puked blood on Randall's legs, staining the denim. He kicked the infected away, grabbing a large hammer that sat in a holster, Duct-taped to the side of his backpack. He tried to hit the infected, but missed, then he and it ploughed through the bedroom-window, smashing the glass.

Randall and the infected rolled over the porch roof and fell down onto the front-lawn a few metres from the front-door. The noise attracted several more infected, who shuffled into the street then towards Randall, who picked himself up quickly.

He seemed like he was enjoying himself, a slight smirk on his face.

As the infected on the grass moved and sat up, Randall struck it, again and again, beating its head to pulp, then he ran for it.

Randall dashed around the side of the house and scrambled and climbed over the side-gate. A second after he hit the ground, the fist of an infected broke through the wooden-plank gate behind him. The claw opened and closed, then withdrew through the hole, when another appeared beside it, snapping the thin wooden planks with ease. Growls and groans issued from the other side of the gate.

Randall raced back into the house and into the living-room, when one of the infected on the front-lawn saw him through the lit interior of the house, and charged at one of the front-windows, smashing it with the flat of its forehead.

Randall bounded up the stairs and back into the bedroom. He slammed the door shut and wedged it with a chair.

Downstairs.
Five infected climbed into the house through four broken front-windows. They dragged themselves into the room, falling in on the carpet, staining it with putrid dark-red ooze.

The first infected clambered to its knees, then unsteadily onto its ankles. It groaned and made a loud *gaaah* sound, craning its neck to the plaster swirls of the ceiling.

Several more infected in the street were attracted to the groan, and shambled across the front-lawn, moving toward the house and forming a much larger pack.

Upstairs.
Randall sat on the ground on the other side of the bedroom. He used his back and feet to push the heavy-wooden bed inch-by-inch in front of the bedroom-door. Just as the bed wedged a final inch in front of the door, pushing the chair aside, an infected forced its arm through the gap, but it could not get in. The arm raked the air in figures of eight.

Randall laughed, momentarily relieved, then picked up his bag. "Not today, you twats!"

Another infected charged the door from behind, and the bed inched back a little, opening the gap into the room.

Randall's smile disappeared instantly.

He grabbed his backpack, slotted the hammer back in place, and climbed out of the broken bedroom-window and hoisted himself up onto the roof. Two more bags sat on the roof-peak where he had left them. He clung onto the gutters and pulled his body up and over them. A tile came loose and he threw it to the ground, vaguely aiming for an idling infected. The tile dashed into the lawn and stuck in place. His fingernails scraped the tile, then he found his grip and pulled himself onto the shallow pitch of the roof. He scrambled to his feet and crept upward.

Randall threw the other two bags over his shoulders and started along the roof, looking down at thirty-three infected, who clamoured around, unable to get to him.

He reached the chimney and found another item waiting for him – a weapon: a Super-Soaker 1500, a pump-action water rifle with a one litre bottled screwed to the back. He picked up the water-rifle and pumped the plunger on the underside of the front. He gently slid down the roof slope and stopped at the gutters, his Adidas trainers bending the glossy black plastic. He leaned forward and saw that more infected had joined the others and he counted the pack. There were forty-two infected barging into each other, pushing and shoving, some with the arms raised aloft, others with the arms hanging at their sides. Most were gazing up at the roof, eyes affixed to Randall's gangly form.

"Hey, you bastards!" he shouted.

He waited for two minutes, watching nine more join the others. He started to spray the water-rifle, aimed down at their heads and bodies. Squirts and streams of liquid shot out of the barrel in steep and long arcs.

The infected did not seem to care about the shower, and continued snapping and groaning up at Randall.

He plunged his hand into the side-pocket of his backpack and pulled out three Zippo lighters – a brushed silver-plate, a brushed brass and one with a simple, light-grey skull painted on its matte-black cover. He selected the brushed silver-plate Zippo and lit it. A candle-like flame exploded into existence. He tossed the lighter off the roof without flair.

The lighter spiralled into the air, falling, and hit one of the infected in the face, instantly igniting the liquid that soaked its hair and collar. Flames blossomed into life over its head, as it shook wildly. The lighter was ricocheted across the pack, alighting many of the infected. Those that were not immediately caught by the flames were trapped in the fray. The infected that were aflame bashed and barged and pushed against the others, setting most of the rest on fire.

Randall watched from the roof. A smile sat on his lips. His eyes reflected the fire, licking at fifty-one of the infected.

Later.
Randall climbed along a different road of roofs.

He reached a two-metre gully with a path forty feet below that divided two houses. Randall tossed each of his bags across the gap; each one rolled a little way down the pitch, but stopped before they fell to the ground below.

Randall took a running-jump.

He threw himself into the open air and, as he landed on the roof, as his Gazelles clipped the surface, the tiles gave way instantly and he smashed through into the attic. He fell, crashing through the attic, knocking into and crushing boxes, then plunged through the ceiling of the room below. He yelped, landing on a bed in a nondescript bedroom, covered in a pile of boxes, roof-tiles, wood, laths, and plasterboard. Fibreglass-fluff and dust floated in a cloud around him.

He groaned. "Ouchy... Fuck that hurt!"

Later.
Randall awoke. He stirred, groaning again and touching his left arm. A noise came from within the house and Randall's eyes snapped open. He sat up immediately and looked for a weapon.

He stood and wobbled a little, when he heard banging, then a scream. He stared at the half-open bedroom-doorway, when something moved behind it.

Randall backed away until he could go no further and pressed himself against the far wall, when an infected appeared and pushed face-first into the room. Its bloodshot eyes unblinkingly scanned the room. It *snarled* as it spat blood. Randall jumped onto the bed, then threw himself at the infected, tackling it and falling backwards into the upstairs hall.

He scrapped with the infected on the floor, and managed to knock one of its arms away from grabbing at him, then he pounded down repeatedly with his forearm on its neck. The infected slowly expired, gasping and spitting and wheezing and huffing.

Randall breathed heavily, then heard another stifled scream emanate from the downstairs of the house.

He picked himself up and walked downstairs slowly, cautiously, straining to listen for any more noises. He stepped straight into the path of an oncoming infected.

Randall stopped half-way down the stairs, then ran back upstairs, slamming the bedroom door shut behind him.

"Fuck! Fuck! Fuck! What about the crying woman?! Fuck! Fuck! Help her! No! Yes! Fuck! Go! Stay! Fuck! No!"

He looked around and around, then leapt onto the bed and tried to climb up into the attic, through the hole he made falling through. As Randall started to climb, the second infected banged on the door, causing him to shudder, nearly making him fall.

The banging and beating quickly became more violent.

Suddenly the fist of the infected smashed through the door and Randall fell. He jumped up on the bed again and climbed up into the hole, when the door broke open. The infected snatched and grabbed Randall's dangling legs.

Randall found his hammer in the attic and snatched it. He dropped, turning, and beat the infected across the temple. It tumbled across the bed and fell head-first into the wall and was dead.

Randall hopped down the stairs and opened the living-room door. He found a woman being fully infected by the virus. She was slathered in blood. She turned in front of his eyes, the colour draining from her skin, her eyes sinking into a dark, bloody-red.

The infected woman puked blood on itself and launched at Randall like a sprinter on a starting-post.

Randall yanked the door shut and backed away slowly into the kitchen. He put his head in his hands and leaned on the kitchen-countertop. He gritted his teeth, tensing all of the muscles in his upper body, shuddering with stress and fear.

"Fuck!" he screamed, balling his fists.

The next day.
Randall lifted a bag out onto the roof-tiles. He ate a bag of Kellogg's Crunchy Nut cereal with his hand. He looked out over a sea of rooftops, and saw something twinkle. He dropped the bag of cereal and snatched a pair of binoculars from its straps around his neck. He saw the side of an army truck, then the side of a military-green APC pass between two squat buildings many roads away from him.

Randall's eyes fixed on the last moment where he had seen the army truck.

He rushed to grab his bags and slung them over his shoulder.

He dashed along the rooftops, looking in a direction to intercept the APC and the truck.

The cereal box slid off the room and its contents rained down on the grass below.

The next day. Northampton – 3:01pm.
Randall sped down Bridge Street, the A508 road, on a black 50cc Peugeot Kisbee scooter. He swung around a stationary turquoise 1998 Volkswagen Polo on the Cotton End bridge and pulled to a stop next to the stone balustrades.

He stared down the River Nene, looking West, but he could not see anything.

He continued on down the A508, passing a large red-brick building with the names Latimer and Crick painted above the second floor.

Randall turned right into Delapre Crescent, then into Delapre Crescent Road and slowed upon reaching a park. He gazed down Towcester Road, the A5123. The APC and the truck appeared to Randall in brief flickers travelling South.

Randall accelerated the scooter, dodging around a sluggish, ambling infected, then skidded around a crashed-car, and hop-skipped up onto the curb, and drove into the park.

He swung the scooter around to travel in an intersecting path to the truck and APC, but it was a dead-end: blocked by a long wrought-iron fence. Randall spun the scooter to a stop and scanned for another exit, breathing heavily. His head spun around on his neck, trying to pick up any infected that might be close.

Randall took-off again, passing a small children's play-park, and found another exit that continued his journey parallel to the APC and truck, behind Queen Eleanor Primary School. He bounced off the curb and darted down Fawsley Road, a narrow curving path lined with houses, dodging around another crashed-car. He hopped up onto the pavement, when a fast moving infected charged at him from the open front-door of a house.

It knocked him off the scooter, with one swipe of its arm.

Randall slammed into the tarmac and rolled over, hearing his arm *crunch* beneath him. His reflexes were quick and he scrambled onto his fingers and toes, then leapt to his feet in seconds, skidding to a stop.

He immediately grabbed the oncoming infected by the front of its clothes and threw it over a garden-wall. He righted his scooter, when a shuffling infected appeared further down the road. The slower infected was joined by several more, who shambled into the road, twitching and shuddering as they crept between a zigzag of cars.

The faster infected rolled over and clawed the ground, then jumped to its feet and bounded over the wall. It charged at Randall, as he twisted the accelerator and shot away on the scooter. The infected chased him, arms flapping behind it, neck outstretched.

He stopped quickly, swinging an axe in a half-circle and hit and embedded it in the head of the infected. It tripped clumsily and fell over. The axe-handle *clacked* on contact with the tarmac.

Randall pulled away again, leaving the axe behind, and sped toward the group of slow infected. He aimed for the one at the front of the pack, when its head exploded with the hit of a silenced-bullet, shot from some distance. The other infected in the street turned in the direction of the muffled shot, and were then gunned down, one by one.

Randall slammed the brakes on and skidded, stopping a few metres away, when the APC and truck pulled up in front of him, the hydraulic brakes *hissing*. He stared at them with the look of relief and breathed out a huge lungful of air.

Moments later.
Randall was helped to climb into the back of the truck by Hastings, who returned to the cab where Bright sat behind the wheel. There were several people huddled in the back of the truck: Tetsuo, Foost and Brodie, Frank and Erin, Wilson and a few others. Randall eyed each of them in turn. "Hi," he said cheerily.

Hastings put his seatbelt on, making himself marginally comfortable next Bright in the truck's cab.

"New guy, huh?" Bright said. "How's he?"

"Yeah... Seems nice. First impression-wise."

Nahar was driving the APC, with Newton and Kara, Nancy and James, Alan and a few other passengers in the back.

Randall beamed from the APC behind the truck, to the other survivors around him.

"I can't fucking believe the army are here!" Randall said in an excited tone.

"They aren't the army... Well, a few are, but mostly we're all just survivors... I got out of Birmingham... Those two – Frank and Erin – got out of Manchester... Brodie got off a plane from America... The rest are from here and there," Wilson stated blandly. He grimaced and sat back, looking away from Randall. Brodie's head sunk.

Randall looked at Brodie, he asked, "Is the virus there?... In America?"

Brodie shrugged, replying solemnly, "Probably, yeah."

Randall looked at Foost, dressed in the dried filth of the past week. He shrugged. Tetsuo, who held a silenced-machinegun, looked back at Randall sternly and said nothing. Randall looked at Frank and Erin; Erin tried to sleep on Frank's shoulder, Frank looked shell-shocked and hugged her back tightly.

Randall turned to Wilson, he said, "Things look pretty bleak, then...?"

"Hmm."

Eight days ago. University of Birmingham, outside the Medical School.

Randall exited the Medical School, slinging his backpack over his shoulder. He wore a black *Punisher* t-shirt over a white long sleeve, Smog jeans and black-and-white Adidas Classics. He pulled both of the backpack's straps over his arms and clipped them together across his chest with a dull *clunk*. He let the door fall shut and immediately dodged around a student that was running inside. He walked out of the enormous, boxy Art Deco-Modern building, away from the looming and imposing block-shape. He hopped down the staircase outside the entrance and moved to his bicycle, which was locked to a hoop of metal to his left with several other bicycles.

He crouched beside the bike and undid his heavy-duty cotton-covered chain-lock and looped it across his body and *clicked* it shut. He pulled the bike free and threw his leg over it.

Randall pedalled away from the huge Medical School that backed onto the Queen Elizabeth Hospital, and turned up Vincent Drive.

He sped along, swinging around a slow moving car, hopping onto the pavement to avoid another, then jumping back into the road. He kicked down hard. The wind whipped through his tangle of hair.

A little later. At the O Bar on Broad Street.

Randall sat at the corner table on a stripy L-shaped sofa. A Jack Daniels and Coke sat in front of him. He looked at his watch. It read 11:45am. He slapped his thighs, waiting, then took a sip of his drink.

Two of his friends stood at the bar. They were ARMIN BRACK, 18 year old English young man of Israeli descent; and HIROSHI TOSHIDA, 19 year old English young man of Japanese descent. Armin was short and stocky with a furry, squat body and chubby, hairy arms. Under a full head of curly black hair his face was pinched and he had a soft, calmness to his big, dark eyes. He had a pair thick eyebrows that met in the middle above a long, thick nose. He had a charming smile with full, straight teeth. He wore a blue Ralph Lauren polo-shirt, charcoal-grey Calvin Klein jeans and black-and-gold Adidas Superstar Vintage trainers. Hiroshi was tall and lean, with gangly arms and legs. He had a crazy, fluffy, spiky pile of shiny black hair on his head, vaguely parted in the centre. He had deep, sincere black eyes that glimmered from under his thin brow. A small moustache and chin-tip beard framed his full-lipped mouth and natural smile. He wore a baggy white t-shirt with the image of the Japanese islands in black, in front of a red sun beside some Kanji characters that read *jishin kyuen nihon shien* which meant 'Support Japan with relief from the earthquake', black jeans and pewter black Vans trainers, with a tangle of wristbands, knotted friendship-bracelets and rubber charity-bracelets.

The barmaid placed two drinks in front of Armin and he paid and passed one of them to Hiroshi. They moved to the table and sat down with their friend. Armin saw Randall taping his thighs and made a *tut* sound. "Fucking hell! What's your rush, Randall?" Armin demanded.

"I'm supposed to be meeting Dill... Near Summerfield Park."

"That goofy idiot! Why the fuck would you wanna do that?" Armin asked.

"I'm helping him move house," Randall said with a sigh.

"Well, drink up and we'll see how far you go."

"He really needs the help, though. So I honestly can't stay too long."

"I suppose, if you have to," Hiroshi said and sipped his bottle of Budweiser. "We shouldn't keep you from helping."

"How was the lecture?"

"Fine... Went on for a while," Randall said with a smile. "I just popped in to talk to Suderis about the next lecture in the series."

"How was he? His usual fucking miserable self?" Armin asked.

"Yeah."

"I don't like that guy," Hiroshi said quietly. "He lords his experience over you too much. He's a prick."

"Agreed. I just wish he would fucking leave!" Randall said with a smirk.

"Or just curl up and die," Armin offered around a grin.

A little later – 11:59am.
Randall pedalled along Dudley Road, the A457 main-road.

He slowed behind another cyclist, then peeled away and accelerated along the road.

Twenty metres ahead of him an azure-blue 2006 Ford Mondeo collided with a black 2004 Toyota Avensis. The impact sounded like an explosion, *booming* and rushing down the road.

Randall skidded to a stop, the rubber of his tyre *squealing* against the tarmac. He stamped one foot down to steady himself, pulling his iPod ear-buds out of his ears, then looked behind him. The car that had been following him, a green 2002 Mazda 626, had careened off the edge of the A457. It ploughed across the pavement, grated against low lying posts and burst through the window of a Lidl supermarket. Glass shattered and the car disappeared inside the shop.

"What the fuck–...?" he murmured to himself.

Randall glared across the road to the entrance to Summerfield Park. He kicked down on his pedals and shot into the park between a blue-painted wrought-iron post and a brick pier. He darted passed a children's play-ground, built on a giant brick circle and accelerated across the park.

Three children lay in the park on their backs. One lay at the bottom of the slide, another had fallen off a see-saw and another had dropped backwards off a swing. Blood seeped out of their mouths. Several parents had collapsed around the perimeter.

Randall kicked on, the wind whipping across his face and fringe.

Three infected lurched into the Park from the East Gate.

Randall saw them and slowed.

One of the infected caught sight of Randall, and started to lollop towards him. It groaned and hacked, a snake of blood *hissing* out of its throat.

Randall swallowed, feeling his Adam's-apple rise and fall. He gritted his teeth, clenching the bike's handlebars.

Ten days later. North Hertfordshire.
Randall watched the world pass by through a thin slit in the tarpaulin sheet that hung over the back of the truck, thinking about Armin and Hiroshi, when it slowed to a stop. The engine *rumbled*, vibrating through the back compartment and the brakes *squeaked*.

Randall folded back the tarpaulin sheet, pushing it aside and looked out.

It was clear. There were none of the infected anywhere.

He glanced at the others in the back of the truck. In the week and a half that had passed some of the men's beards had grown at varying rates. Those that had scissors and shaving kits and that were bothered had still found the time to clean their whiskers, but others had not. Foost had an overall covering of dark, slightly-curly beard; Frank had a patchy goatee with a scruff of fur under his neck; Wilson and Randall had short, very-patchy beards; Brodie liked to clean-shave every other day, constantly attending to his appearance.

Sergeant Newton appeared at the back of the truck, he said, "We've found a message.."

Foost climbed out of the truck, Tetsuo and Wilson folded the tarpaulin completely back and hung off the back to see, and Brodie and Randall looked through the ripped-hole in the side of the truck, then let Frank and Erin, and the others see.

They saw Don Clement's message spray-painted on a large white-wall.

It read: "Go to London - Pickering Police-Station. Be careful."

Randall smiled again with relief. He gripped his knees.

The first light drops of rain began to fall, as the clouds darkened above them.

An infected sprinted into the road and sped towards the truck, moving from the direction they had come from.

Tetsuo fired the silenced-machinegun at it, using two bullets carefully placed, and took it down.

One second after the infected had fallen face-first into the tarmac, a shift in their focus alerted them to twenty-five more charging down the road at them.

Newton stared, then fired on them, as did Foost and Tetsuo.

"There are too many of them coming! And too quickly! Everyone should take cover!" Newton shouted and ran back to the APC and snapped the door shut.

Foost leapt in the truck, sitting on the back ledge. Randall took hold of his collar, his fist balled between Foost's shoulder-blades, and the edge of the tarpaulin. "Cheers," Foost said, then he opened fire on the infected.

The truck accelerated away, driving around the APC and taking the lead, when the infected reached the APC.

Inside the APC.
Newton and Kara fired out of thin-slit windows, as Nahar drove them away. Palm-hits and punches thudded against the sides of the APC, receding to nothing as it accelerated.

Outside.
Forty infected sprinted to follow them, trailing behind the two vehicles.
The rain poured down in a million sheets.

Later.
The truck pulled to a stop beside a hulking barn on a muddy track-road to a farm. The APC followed a moment later. Foost and Tetsuo were first to climb out, followed by Bright and Hastings from the cab.

"Sit tight, we'll check it's safe," Hastings told the others in the back of the truck.

Rain fell heavily, pouring off the roof of the barn in wide, conjoining channels, as the soldiers, and Kara, Bright and Tetsuo, divided and searched the surrounding area.

Newton climbed out of the APC and crossed to Hastings, who stood by the slung-open barn-doors.

They stood in the rain, gripping their silenced-machineguns.

"The world's seriously changed, huh?"

"You bet," Hastings replied. "I don't think I've understood everything that's happened."

"Me, either," Newton said with a sigh.

Rain soaked through their clothes.

"Have you had a chance to think about Lianne?"

"I haven't."

"Maybe you should."

"It's been, what, ten days since all-of-this began... If I say what the likelihood is..."

Newton patted Hastings' shoulder.

A little later.
The APC reversed into the barn next to the truck. The doors to the barn were closed and the APC was driven up behind them to ensure they could not be opened.

A fire had been lit in the middle of the barn, and everyone huddled around it.

The rain clattered against the corrugated-steel roof-sheets like a billion tiny stones dropped from the clouds.

A few of the other survivors and Bright, Newton and Nahar cooked a large bowl of chicken curry and rice.

"What about things you won't miss, then?..." Brodie asked.

"Most of the people I ever met," Randall admitted. "Except... Maybe ten people in complete, absolute total."

"Queues... Waiting behind all those people... Wasting loads of fucking time queuing," Wilson said grumpily.

"Complaints... Right now, we have the world to ourselves – except for all of those things... Hopefully once they're gone... No-one will need to complain about anything ever again... Because we might've survived it," Randall murmured.

"I agree with you on that," Brodie said slowly.

"Football... Bein' in a stadium full of people. Packed out to the roof," Foost added with a melancholy smile. His smile faded quickly and he sipped from a flask of water.

Hastings said, "My wife..."

Randall looked at Hastings and saw that he was hiding a deep wound. And he hid it well.

"I'm sorry to hear that," Erin whispered.

"I'm happy I'll never have to watch an advert again... With no TV, there's no advertisements... In fact, just the silence is really pleasing," Nahar said.

"I won't miss most of my life at all... At least now I can walk into a library and sit and read, no interruptions, no complaints, no noise, no mobiles..." Kara said. "I know it's only a little thing, but..."

"I'll miss being able to travel to France easily... In such a short time, you'd be there! It might take weeks to get there now, like it's the fucking Middle-Ages!" Frank growled.

"At least we don't have to shit in buckets and throw it into the street!" Wilson acknowledged.

"Well, while the water's still running," Hastings added with a slow exhalation. "And electricity..."

Later.

People were settling down and climbing into their sleeping-bags; two short rows of survivors lying next to each other.

Newton paced near the door, as Foost climbed down from a ladder that led to the roof.

"There're none of those things for a long-way around us, that I can see with the thermal-cam.."

Newton looked relieved. "You can make them out by their thermal signature?" he asked curiously.

"Yeah. They're still warm, like us."

"Yeah," Newton drawled sarcastically. "They're quite strange."

"But, at least, there's no sign of any...!"

"Yeah," Newton conceded. "That will make the next twenty minutes easier on me."

"Hmm."

"At least some people are still together," Newton admitted.

"Like Frank and Erin?"

"Yeah. And the rest of us."

Foost put the thermal-camera, a small unit the size of a shoebox, into the back of the truck. "I'll check it again in thirty," he said.

Newton nodded, raised his eyebrows, dropped them, then sighed. "I think I should get some rest," he said with a real yawn. "We'll be leaving quite early in the morning, so make sure we swap shifts. I'll assign everyone in the watch-rota," Newton added and patted Foost's shoulder warmly. "I'll do that now before I settled down," he finished.

Randall listened to them speak from his sleeping-bag, then fell asleep soundly.

The next day.

The group had assembled and were getting back in their respective vehicles once again, having packed away their kits and individual bags. Randall hung at the back of the both groups, watching them chat between themselves. He slid his pack beside the others, then Brodie helped him into the back of the truck. He found the far right corner was unoccupied and placed himself there.

Foost climbed down the ladder from the roof and signalled for the barn-doors to be opened.

Outside.
The rain continued. Huge puddles had formed along the dirt track that ran from the farm, passed the barn, to the main-road. A torrent of water still washed off the gutters. Muffled drumbeats pattered on the roof.

    The barn-doors *creaked* and groaned, as they shuddered with movement.

In the barn.
Newton and Hastings opened the barn-doors together.

    "See you at the next stop, mate," Newton said jovially.

    "See you then," Hastings said and jogged to join Foost at the truck.

    Newton crossed to the APC and climbed inside. He noticed Kara was watching him from two seats behind the passenger-seat.

    He shut the door and the APC moved.

    "You okay?" he asked Kara, catching her eye easily.

    "Yeah. Fine. Just keeping-watch. Watching your back," she replied with a practiced smile.

    Newton nodded half-officiously at her and turned back to the wind-screen. Water slicked the pane of glass. Nahar turned the windscreen-wipers faster.

Outside.
The APC and truck pulled away from the farm, vanishing behind sheets of rain into the distance down the dirt track.

    The downpour of rain continued, falling over the open barn-doors splashing on the mud below. The remnants of the camp lay still in the cool, calm of the barn.

The next day. North London – 7:28am.
The APC and truck were parked side-by-side in the forecourt of a small, side-road garage. The sign outside read: *Parkinson's and Sons*. They were parked in such a way that provided a means of getaway from the garage to both of the vehicles: through the side-door of the APC and through the ripped canvas-side of the truck. A stack of tyres and wooden pallets had been piled next to the truck to create a loose staircase up to the canvas-hole.

    Nahar and Hastings stood on the large flat-roof of the garage using binoculars to sweep the nearby area.

    On several of the roads around them large packs of infected roamed aimlessly.

    "This is not looking good," Nahar stated. "Not at all."

    "You're tellin' me," Hastings responded, breathing out despondently.

    "What're you going to tell Sarge?"

    "The truth–... We're stuck here for a little while."

    "What will he tell the others?"

    "The same thing, I think. We can't lie to these people."

    "Good."

    Hastings' brow furrowed. He glanced at Nahar, whose eyes were glazed and staring out across the rooftops.

    "Keep watching those packs – we need to find our way South as soon as we can."

    Hastings started away.

    "Not great, is it?"

    Hastings stopped, "What?"

    "My wife and son are probably dead. I keep feeling hollow... I see that you do, too," Nahar said, his voice breaking several times. "How can we help these people when we haven't helped ourselves? How do you feel about that?"

    Hastings nodded. "Yeah. Not great."

    Nahar nodded back to him, then turned back to the roads, putting the binoculars up to his eyes. "Newton thinks we need to do our job..."

"We should," Hastings answered. "We should."

He walked away from Nahar, and positioned himself at the other side of the roof.

A little later.

Hastings stood with Newton and Bright in the office of the garage.

"If we're stuck here for a little while, then we should make the most of it," Newton suggested.

"I couldn' agree withya more, boss," Bright added.

Foost entered. "We're all-sealed up, Sarge."

"Excellent."

"So, boss, whatja have in mind?"

Later.

Newton had assigned Foost and Tetsuo the watch on the roof, and Hastings and Kara to stay with the APC.

He stood at the front of the garage, near the shutter-door, and addressed the remainder of the group:

"We saw that sign two days ago... Who-ever wrote it must have found their way there. Must have got some plan together. Must have created some kind of safe-haven. We have to try for this place. We have to move on. We have to stay together and watch each others' backs. This is the only way. This is the way we keep on going. This is the way we have to be to stay alive... There are other chances. This is not our only hope. This is not our last chance... But we have to be pragmatic... We have to see if there are any other survivors out-there. Otherwise we're all that there is... But... That cannot be... We have to be safe. Find safety. Build our numbers... Those things out-there will turn us into them, if we let them. We cannot let them... We must beat them. Use what we've learnt to keep ourselves safe, unhurt and alive... No matter what challenges we face. We must keep on going. We cannot give up."

Later.

For the rest of the day, Tetsuo machined several knives and blades and showed people how to use them. Hastings, Foost, Kara and Newton showed others how to defend themselves with hand-to-hand combat practices. Bright taught marksmanship, but without the use of any bullets. Brodie worked on his equations, huddling in one corner, away from the others. Frank and Erin occasionally kept-watch on the roof, but did not join in with the training. Wilson and Nancy cooked for the group: a large bowl of rice each, with an assortment of vegetables in a Thai curry sauce. Nahar monitored the frequencies in the APC, spending hours listening to radio-signals that rotated through all main channels. He heard nothing.

A little after six, Kara and Hastings climbed the ladders to the flat-roof. They had eaten first and took first watch of the night.

They excused Foost and Bright, who sat on deck-chairs that had been there when they arrived.

They sat in silence for a long time.

"What did you do?" Hastings blurted, breaking the calm, quiet.

"I worked for Interpol... For the last four years."

"Was that fun?" Hastings said around a smirk. He sipped water from a canteen.

Kara met his eyes, unblinking. "Great fun. Actually."

Randall sat on the other side of the large roof, leaning against a ventilation duct. He heard their conversation clearly; there was no wind, no other noises, no ambient sound. He had enjoyed the silence when Foost and Bright had been up-there, but now, was consolidated with the soap opera equivalent.

"When did you sign up for the Army?" she asked.

"Sixteen. Then again at seventeen... After I'd been to the gym for a bit."

"Why did you join?"

"Danny... --Newton... Um... He was a year older than me at school, but we were mates through it all. We kinda fell into it together, after school... And re-sits..."

"D'you regret anything? Joining?"

"No," he said solemnly. "Otherwise I wouldn't be here right now," he added candidly. "I might be dead, or one of those things, instead of alive. Which is fairly good comfort."

Randall lit a cigarette.

Hastings glanced across at him, and he nodded hello.

Randall nodded back.

Kara arched her back and saw him as well.

"What's up?" Randall exclaimed.

"Nothing."

"Cool, then... I'll just smoke my ciggie, then," he said and turned away from them. "Just ignore me."

Kara settled back into her deck-chair first.

Hastings scooped the pair of binoculars from around his neck and swung the view across the main-roads. One was clear, except for two slow infected that crept into sight from behind a front-garden conifer. The other road was still filled with more than a hundred infected: a packed avenue that seemed never-ending.

He settled.

"What's your first name?" Kara asked.

"Evan."

Kara looked up at the sky and let her mind drift.

Hastings glanced at Kara, then bumped the back of his head lightly on the top-bar of the deck-chair. "Oohff!" He rested a moment. "Hmm... Where did you study?"

Randall pulled on the cigarette, watching a thin column of white smoke rise up into the sky.

The next day. One mile from Pickering Police Station – 6:46pm.
The APC and the truck were stuck in the road. Cars blocked both ways ahead where the road split. Dozens of cars gridlocked the road and prevented any further advance. The truck's engine *ticked* and *hissed*.

Inside the APC.
Newton stared through a long-range viewfinder and saw the situation clearly. The way ahead was not viable. The sky was starting to darken and night was coming. The road was looking faintly darker than it had the last time he had looked, only twenty minutes ago.

Newton looked at Kara, who sat in the back two seats behind him. "We need to scout ahead, before it gets too dark to find our way."

Kara nodded. She crossed to the side-door and unbolted it.

Erin turned the interior lights off and Bright unlocked the top-hatch and opened it. He climbed a few steps up the ladder that was welded to the wall of the hatch-opening and poked his head out, Stetson still in place. He glanced in all directions before bobbing his head down into the cabin. "Coast's clear for now, hun'," Bright said with a smile, his whiskery moustache pointing at the edges.

"Okay. Thank you," she whispered.

Kara opened the side-door and climbed out into the road.

Frank pulled the door closed behind her and bolted it quietly. He took his seat next to Erin.

On the road.
Kara crept alongside the APC, gripping a short-handle axe in one hand, and a silenced Sig Sauer P239 in the other. There was a walkie-talkie clipped to her belt that hung over her bum. She twisted between two cars and was in view of the front of the truck.

Hastings saw her.

She moved to the hollow of a shop-front, huddling in the crevice.

She angled her upper-body from behind the shop-window and glanced down the road.

Kara moved with speed and stealth, zipping between cars, hurdling bonnets and ducking into safe fissures between shops.

An infected stumbled into the street, out of the broken front-window of a Next clothing shop. There was a car three-quarters of the way into the shop-front, bodies and mannequins crushed underneath, clothing-rails and displays smashed around it.

Kara ducked behind a crashed canary-yellow 2002 Fiat Punto.

The infected slurred, groaning from deep within its body. It fixed on Kara, before she had time to see it.

As the infected moved to intercept her, Hastings thrashed at it with a long-handle axe. The impact of the blade smashed the infected aside, flinging it to the tarmac. Hastings twisted the axe and then stamped it down on the back of its head.

Kara stared at Hastings, as he hoisted the axe into his hands with total ease, as if it weighed nothing. "I didn't think you should go alone," he said. Then he smiled at her.

Kara smiled gratefully and warmly back at him, then continued on down the road.

"I didn't either," Randall pipped. "By the way."

Kara stopped dead in her tracks and turned. Hastings stared at Randall with wide-eyes and an open mouth. "What are you–...?"

"I get around quick, easy and fast. You-two could learn a lot from me!" Randall interrupted. "I thought I'd come along to share the wealth."

"Fine," Kara spat. "Let's get moving."

Hasting regarded Randall with a bemused half-smile. He slapped Randall's back and led him on with them. "You've got some balls, Randall... I nearly cut your head off..."

"You might of... If you hadn't been flirting!" Randall quipped.

One of the infected lurched into the street ten metres ahead of them, emerging from an alleyway between two shops. It groaned and strained its neck to look around. Fresh dark stains on its chin, neck and chest glinted in the streetlight.

"D'you wanna go ahead?" Hastings asked gesturing for Randall to proceed.

"Alright," Randall replied with a tilt of his head. He whistled and the infected snapped its neck to face him. It groped in front of it and found the edge of the wall.

Randall waited for the infected to move first, it shifted its foot forward, dragging its shoes across the rough concrete surface. It moved forward, *snapping* its teeth together, then Randall dashed forward, a baseball bat gripped in his hands and hanging over his back. Randall swung the bat. The end three inches of the bat and the face of the infected met. It twirled on its ankles and fell with a *crunch* on the road.

Randall let out a little laugh. "That was like a computer game!"

"That's sick!"

"Hey! What?" Randall said aghast, then swung the bat three times onto the infected, crushing the crown, and breaking the side of the skull.

"Come on," Kara said urgently. "Let's get moving. One on one is always a lot easier than when their in gangs!"

"I don't mind them in gangs!" Randall joked.

"You've gotta keep some composure, Randall," Hastings offered.

"I've got perspective. I don't need composure."

A little later.
They climbed the emergency-exit steps of a small office-building to reach the roof.

Hastings was first to reach the locked door-access. He swiped and slashed and chopped with the axe and the door cracked and broke open. Randall and Kara pushed the door through and slid outside.

They could see Pickering Police Station, still several roads away.

They saw the walled-courtyard car-park at the back of the Police Station, the academy beside and behind the main building, the tower standing out of the middle of the building complex, and parts the parade-ground that were not obscured by other buildings or trees.

"I see it... But, I don't want to say 'I don't believe it'," Hastings said softly. "I hope it's a good bet."

"It's there, alright," Kara said. "Mmm... Me too."

"Well it's fucking fantastic you-two can both state the obvious. We've got to find a way to get the vehicles there! Wasn't that the idea of us coming out here...?"

Kara shot Randall a look.

"Fine," Hastings said.

"Well isn't it?" Randall demanded.

"Yes."

"Get the map out."

The next day. Pickering Police Academy – 11:02am.
The truck pulled up first in front of the academy building. The APC followed quickly after it.

A dozen infected sprinted down the road, *roaring* and *wailing* in their wake.

Two men stepped out of the academy reception onto a small platform at the top of a curved flight of eight steps. They wore black balaclavas and ski-goggles, riot gear and heavy, steel-toecap boots. The men were armed with silenced semi-automatic-machineguns, which they clutched in front of them. They charged alongside the truck without a word and stood in the road, before any of the occupants had even pulled up the tarpaulin at the back.

Seconds later the men opened-fire, taking down each of the infected with one bullet; taking precise shots to every head or face.

Tetsuo and Randall whipped the tarpaulin from the back of the truck and threw it over the roof. Foost and Bright leapt out and stood behind the men dressed in black, lifting their own weapons.

Tetsuo launched out of the back of the truck, landing a few feet behind the men.

"Guys, what the fuck?" Foost said slowly, holding his unfired weapon in his hands.

The men pulled their balaclavas and goggles off. They were Harry Chapman and Marc Sheridan. Two more men exited the academy reception and stood framing the doorway: Craig Charlton and Glenn Meakins.

"Welcome," Marc started, "to Pickering Police Academy."

"Now, let's get you inside quickly... The door takes a little while to re-secure," Harry said.

The remaining survivors climbed out of the truck.

The APC's side-door opened and Newton, Kara, Nahar and the others joined their group and filed inside silently.

Inside the academy.
The group were led inside and found a grandiose reception room, with a dated and faded, beige and brown colour scheme. Adam Hilton, Marisa Flenkman, Angela Garcia, Melanie Cannon and about twenty others stood in waiting in the room, ready to greet the newcomers.

Marc shook Newton's hand.

"Why are these people here?"

"We saw you coming..."

"How many of-you are there?" Newton asked, slightly awed by the welcome.

"What you see here now, and about thirty, thirty-five, more," Marc stated and found himself surprised to hear his own words. And Newton could see that too.

"I'm so glad you saw our guys last night."

"We've been keeping-watch from here since day one."

"Really?"

"Quite a few people helped."

"I can imagine..."

"You probably can't... There are some interesting things happening. Interesting people for you to meet..."

Newton walked with Marc through the room. The main reception contracted in to a wide corridor that led outside to the parade-grounds. On one side of the corridor was a long window-wall showing the huge mess hall beyond, and on the other side were trophy cabinets, doors into classrooms, lockers, and administrative offices. They stepped in unison down the small flight of stairs onto the tarmac surface that covered a third of the grounds, the rest was a vast, finely-trimmed rectangle of perfect green grass. Beyond the parade-ground, Newton saw the police station and the tower. The sunlight warmed both men and they squinted in the sun.

Don Clement marched down the side of the parade-ground, along the wide concrete path that ran along the front of the barracks where the cadets would sleep. The barracks had a long awning built down its entire length, above and under it were windows to the inside, and benches positioned between each window on the ground level.

"Are the barracks clear?" Newton asked, his eyes following Don passed them.

"We've got the whole of the police station cleared. Including the barracks and the academy."

"That's impressive."

"It took a while," Marc said.

"How long have you been here?"

"Since day two."

"'Day two!... Makes it sound... --official..."

"We have to make sure someone watches the calendar."

"Ha... You're not wrong."

In the shadows under the barracks' awning, Reg Heron stood watching Newton and Marc crossing to the back-access to the police station, sweeping slowly across the centre of the parade-ground lawn, leaving their footprints behind them in the grass.

They entered the main block.

On the roof of the tower, Duncan Berry watched them enter. Then his gaze turned to Reg, lurking four storeys below him. He clutched a 7.62mm L96 sniper's rifle, still attached to its tripod. He took aim at Reg. Watched him lurk. Then walked away to the far edge of the roof, overlooking the front of the police station.

CHAPTER 14 - ADRIFT - Brighton Marina

CLIVE MEADWAY, 61 year old Englishman; and his wife MELODIE MEADWAY, 59 year old Englishwoman – stood on their sailboat, *The SurfRider*, a 40 foot Challenger off-shore sailing sloop, with their grandchildren: ANNABEL MEADWAY, 19 year old English young woman; BARNEY MEADWAY, 16 year old English young man; and, EVANGELINE 'EVIE' MEADWAY, 12 year old English young girl.

Clive had short grey hair, receded into a sharp widow's-peak, long white-grey sideburns and eyebrows, white bristles on his forearms, and an icy-blonde goatee-beard. He had a gentle, kindly face, wrinkled with age across his forehead, around his eyes and in laughter-lines. He had intense, brilliant-blue eyes, under light hoods and a wide, engaging smile. He was tall and well-built; the absolute peak of fitness for a man of his age. He wore a plain black t-shirt, a Captain's cap, denim jeans and slate-grey plimsolls. Melodie had shoulder-length wavy honeycomb-gold and grey hair, framing a mature and beautiful face. She had had very little cosmetic work done; eye-lifts and Botox around her eyes and the corners of her mouth. She wore minimal makeup, but still looked somewhat glamorous. She had quick, wise cool-blue eyes, highlighted on her lids with midnight-blue makeup and long lashes. She had a deeply graceful manner; the way she carried herself, walked, sat, all the product of a finishing-school's perfectionism in her youth. She wore a plain white t-shirt, olive-green trousers and white plimsolls; her jewellery included a black, Japanese Akoya freshwater-pearl necklace with matching earrings and bracelet, two platinum rings, one her wedding ring, and a Cartier wristwatch.

Annabel had dyed black hair, long and lank, with a quarter of the left side of her head shaved down to grade one. She had a pretty face, although it was disguised under a layer of extremely pale makeup, with dark rings around her dark, sparkling blue eyes, purple-black lipstick, a nose piercing, two snake-bite lip piercings, and a dozen studs, rings, bolts and chains through both ears. She had a small black neck tattoo of an upside-down cross below her left ear. She looked unapproachable and oppositional, like a goth and a punk hybridised; always presenting an expression of a bad attitude and little-to-no care. She was long and lean, but still a few inches shorter than her younger brother Barney. She dressed in complete black, from sleeves to socks: she wore a tight-fitting, long-sleeve, black t-shirt, black jeans and Doc Marten's boots with their yellow stitching coloured-in black with a Sharpie. On her wrists and around her neck were spiked and studded bands, chains and necklaces wrapped thrice around, and a custom-made SEIKO Arctura Kinetic wristwatch in stainless steel with a black face and black stripe around the handle. Barney had a slim to skinny build with a slight frame and gangly arms and legs for a boy of below-average height. He had short dark hair, overgrown by a few months, with a slight fringe that hung over his dark, intelligent sapphire eyes. He had slim face with fair, clear skin, high cheekbones and a round jaw. He wore a black leather jacket-hoodie over two t-shirts, one white and one black, baggy jeans and red Adidas Classics; he wore a custom-made SEIKO Arctura Kinetic Chronograph wristwatch in stainless steel with a black face. Evie had long hazel-brown hair, tied back into two twisted plaits with silver ribbon. She was small for her age and wore the clothes of a child a few years her junior. She had an enthusiastic, keen look to her glittering blue eyes, normally pointed at the pages of a book. She looked like a cleaner, sweeter and more natural version of Annabel, flashed-back seven long years. She was rambunctious and unruly if her understanding of a situation did not read well, if adults treated her like a child, or when her long adjournments to read were interrupted. She wore a pinky-grey fleece-jumper over a pale blue t-shirt with flowers embroidered on it, denim jeans and black plimsolls. She had a vintage Ingersoll Mickey Mouse watch, and a platinum necklace and matching teardrop pendant with a depressed ruby at its centre.

The Meadways were joined by another two couples: ROY MABEY, 63 year old Scotsman; and his wife JOYCE MABEY, 62 year old Scotswoman; and WALTER WAITE, 60 year old Englishman; and his wife SUE WAITE, 60 year Englishwoman. Roy had thinning, worn-off hair, bald on top and silver on the sides. His face was jowly, flabby and wobbled with every word. He had fuzzy eyebrows that sat on the brim of a long, wrinkled brow, hanging over thick lids and round, sober brown eyes, a thick nose and full, plump lips. He had a large, oblong frame with sloped shoulders and a pot-belly. His arms were strong and heavy, like a gorilla's, and similarly his legs were stocky, short and stumpy. He wore a faded navy t-shirt, baggy over his big frame, thick denim jeans and black plimsolls. Joyce had lustrous, thick white hair that cascaded around her face, over her shoulders and down her back. She had the look of a classic movie star from 1950s, sharp face with severe makeup and harsh, burgundy lipstick. She was slim and athletic, gym-fit and personally trained. She wore a dark-grey cardigan, loosely buttoned over a white silk blouse, a pair of three-quarter-length white cotton trousers and white canvas boat-shoes; she had a delicate gold necklace, bracelet and several rings. Walter had a full head of dyed-brown, thinning hair, swept and gelled back over his dry scalp, with ear-long ginger sideburns. He was short and skinny, but had started to form a belly; a fact he hated. He had a reddish-orange tan, faked and sprayed repeatedly many times a year, but this did not disguise any of his wrinkles. He had a short, pointy nose in the dead-centre of his face, ginger-brown bushy eyebrows and sneering mouth. He had an adenoidal voice, pinched and squeaky, tremulous and shaky. He wore a baby-blue sweater over a white t-shirt, black jeans and dark-blue canvas boat-shoes. Sue had reddish-brown hair, short and shaped like a helmet, curled behind her ears and parted down the middle of her forehead. She had small, deep-set eyes, and looked even further-set back by dark eye-shadow and -liner. She wore heavy, caked makeup that gave her skin a greasy sheen; thick-spread cerise-pink lipstick smudged around her small, severe mouth. She was small and bony, underweight and a little gaunt. She wore a black cardigan over a red blouse, a long denim skirt and white canvas boat-shoes.

The sailboat had been moored in the Brighton Marina the past few weeks, since Clive and Melodie's last jaunt to France, and bobbed on the water. The conditions were good and the sea lapped gently against the hull.

Clive prepared to set sail, aided by Roy and Walter. "You ready, guys?" he asked.

"Yep!"

"I suppose," Water murmured.

Other families and sailors made their own ways to their sailboats, lined along the marina; maybe sixty in total. Tall, white masts swayed on the water, tipping in a unison-line.

Barney stood near the mast, one hand lightly gripping it, the other hand cupped over his forehead, shading his eyes from the brilliant sunlight. He watched his grandfather, then looked at his grandmother.

Clive chatted with his friends on the decking-cover of the mooring, about to climb back aboard; their wives chit-chatted and clucked in the entrance to the cabin on the sailboat. Melodie winked at her grandson.

Barney turned to see Annabel and Evie standing behind their grandfather, waiting politely, patiently and silently. Annabel looked away, sullen. Evie stared about, bug-eyed, absorbing every bit of input she could take in.

Later. On the English Channel. 2 miles out of sea.
Clive, Roy and Walter stood at the back of the sailboat by the tiller; Melodie, Joyce and Sue sat in the cabin drinking tea; Annabel, Barney and Evie sat at the front of the sailboat. The bow cut through water as clear as glass, a few inches below their bare feet.

"How was Friday, at school?" Barney asked Evie softly.

"Good. We learned a few things," she replied sweetly.

Barney half-smiled. "How about you, Anna?"

"It was fine."

"Did you do any of your other lessons?"

"An hour."

"Good. I did two hours."

Evie left Annabel and Barney and tip-toed down the sailboat, passed the men, and climbed down steadily and easily into the cabin. As Evie entered, Melodie made a fuss of her, hugging her and stroking her long, straight hair.

"Are you hungry?" she asked, sitting back down, easing her granddaughter to perch on the tops of her knees.

"A little," Evie said and looked across at the fridge.

Joyce and Sue both smiled cheerily at Evie.

"Ooooh!" Melodie sung and she checked her Cartier watch. She said, "It's nearly twelve, so a snack won't hurt... It's practically lunchtime anyway... I'll bring some sandwiches up to the three of you, Evie."

Melodie stood, moving Evie aside. She patted her granddaughter on the bum.

A little while later.

Evie sat at the front of the sailboat, dangling her feet either side of the front peak, with her brother and sister close behind her. They ate sandwiches, when a scream rent the air. It had come from inside the cabin; and then Walter, standing with Roy and Clive, started to cough violently.

Walter patted his chest with the flat of his hand as coughs erupted from his insides.

Annabel, Evie and Barney stood to get a better view down the boat, alert to the disturbance, when Walter coughed blood down himself.

"Oh my!" Evie shouted.

Barney put his hand on her shoulder. "It'll be okay," he said calmly and turned Evie to face away from the stern.

Clive and Roy immediately moved to help Walter, when he staggered and convulsed, falling then hanging onto the side of the sailboat. A blood fountain gushed out of Walter's mouth. He cried and yelped, gasping for air.

Annabel and Barney stared wide-eyed at the bent-over figure of Walter, unable to see all of the blood. Annabel hugged Evie close to her. Barney's eyes fixed firmly to Walter, tightening.

Inside the cabin.

Sue coughed-up blood violently, arms crossed over her chest holding her collarbone.

"Oh my God!" Joyce screamed, then turned, panicked, to Melodie.

Melodie started putting away the food and condiments she had used to make sandwiches. She pulled a First Aid kit from the top of the cupboards and snapped it open.

Joyce rushed to help Sue, crouching beside her and taking one of her hands in hers. "Oh my God! Are you okay? Sue? Sue? Are you okay?" she begged. "Please speak to me..."

Sue convulsed in Joyce's arms, wriggling and gyrating. The colour in Sue's skin faded quickly and her movement slowed. She coughed up a mouthful of blood; it splattered her skin and dripped onto her blouse.

"Is she okay?" Melodie asked anxiously, looking at Joyce impassionedly.

Joyce turned to look at her friend. She was rendered unable to speak. "Oh, no! No!" she finally muttered.

Sue was taken by the infection. Her eyes sank into a dark, bloodshot-red. She grabbed at Joyce, hooking her nail-like claws into the meat of her shoulder. The infected vomited blood over Joyce's face. Blood filled her mouth, pouring over the corners. She pulled away, coughing and spitting.

Melodie stared at Joyce, then at Sue, wide-eyed. What appeared to be a complex mask of fear dissolved into nothing, and the woman that was left behind was filled with anger, determination, power, action and direction. She beamed with an unseen-before authority and definition. Melodie snatched a pair of scissors from the First Aid kit, squeezing them in her palm.

Joyce, coated in blood, was taken by the infection too. She *hissed*, spitting wine-dark ooze.

Sue, fully infected, pulled herself to stand and teetered on her ankles. Her hips rocked and the body moved with them. The infected stepped into the space in front of Melodie.

Melodie's left eyebrow raised.

On deck.

Clive and Roy stood either side of Walter. Roy patted his back, when his friend's body slid back and he sank to his knees. Walter puked blood over the deck, soaking his thighs, knees and shins with a widening pool. Roy and Clive backed away from their friend.

Walter's arms raised and his hands searched for the deck-rail. Fully taken by the infection, pallid and bleached hands found grip and the infected hoisted itself to its feet. It turned and charged at Roy, tackling him against the ship's railings. The force made Roy topple over the edge and he fell into the sea with a frothy splash.

The infected Walter turned again and immediately locked onto Clive. It leapt at him, but Barney hit and beat it with an emergency-oar, as Annabel threw Roy a floatation-ring.

"What the Christ is going on?!" Roy screamed from the water, kicking and splashing.

Clive looked straight into Barney's eyes and they both said the same thing, at exactly the same time: "Grandma!"

Inside the cabin.
The infected Sue stepped closer to Melodie, puking blood down itself. Its teeth *snapped* and *clicked* as it chomped the air.

It barrelled into Melodie, who stabbed it violently in the torso with the scissors. Even with the stab-wound, the infected kept pushing forward, raging against her and forcing her back. It swung its arms like an aerial front-crawl, wheeling beats down onto Melodie. She released the scissors, but shoved the infected backwards. She grabbed a magnetic kitchen knife from a bar on the wall, as the infected rushed back at her.

Melodie stabbed it repeatedly, aiming for the neck, but scoring it, slashing it and jabbing it where-ever she could. The knife punctured the infected multiple times in the face, arms, sides and chest.

Joyce awoke infected, coughing and hacking, spitting blood on itself, flicking ribbons of blood out of the sides of its mouth. Melodie rushed to the cabin-door, but was shoulder-barged into the wall by the infected.

She yelped in pain, the air knocked out of her.

Clive dropped into the cabin and helped his wife. They fought off the infected Joyce, throwing her into the cabinet-wall, smashing the contents to pieces.

On deck.
The infected Walter climbed to its feet and advanced slowly on the retreating figures of Barney and Annabel. They had left Roy in the sea with the survival-float, that Annabel had lashed to the railings.

Evie stood at the very tip of the boat, guarded by brother and sister. Barney swiped the air in front of the infected with the oar as it advanced on them. The oar *swished* and *whooshed* through the space, as the infected closed the gap.

"Don't worry. It'll be okay," Barney assured both of his sisters.

Melodie's head suddenly smashed through one of the cabin-windows. Chunks of glass skittered over the deck, bouncing around the feet of the infected, as it pressed on towards Barney and his sisters.

Barney lifted the oar.

Inside the cabin.
Melodie had been shoved hard by the infected Joyce through one of the windows, and Clive had been knocked onto the floor. The infected turned on Clive, its eyes scanning the ground, then becoming still on registering him.

Clive snatched a champagne-bottle from the sink, filled with ice-cubes, and clubbed the infected across the face. The impact swatted it and it fell and knocked against the bolted-down table and slid to the floor. Clive smashed its head with the bottle, breaking the skull open and stopping it abruptly.

On deck.
The infected Walter stumbled toward Barney, who hit it with the emergency-oar, shearing off one of its ears. A tiny tether of skin kept the ear from falling to the deck. Black-brown blood bubbled and coagulated around the wound.

Barney beat the infected backwards, jabbing at it with the end of the oar. He then pushed forwards, forcing the infected to retreat, stunning it with blows of the shaft of the oar.

Suddenly Clive appeared with a flare-gun and fired it directly into the infected Walter's face.

The flare exploded in a nimbus of white and blue and pink flames. The infected roared, raising and flailing its arms skyward. It took a few paces back along the deck.

Barney punted the infected under the chin, sending it tipping backwards and splashing into the sea. The flare *sizzled* as its face dipped under the surface, sparking and smoking.

Annabel rushed back to help Roy, who tread-water in the sea, clutching the survival-float. Evie followed closely behind her. They grabbed the wet rope and yanked on it as hard as they could, dragging Roy's kicking body through the waves.

Clive helped Melodie out of the cabin, holding one of her arms for stability, as Roy was helped to climb back aboard the sailboat. His clothes were soaked through and dripped persistently on the deck.

The infected sank into the darkness of the Channel.

Barney watched it disappear.

Roy panicked when he could not see his wife. "Where's Joyce? Where's Joyce? Where's Joyce?" Tears streamed out of his eyes. "Tell me!... What's happened to her?!"

Later that day.
Everyone sat silently on deck, when Roy sniffed, then cried out again. He blubbed and sobbed, trying at points to suppress the force inside himself, without any success. He had changed his clothes, but had wet his sleeves as he rubbed the tears from his eyes. Clive patted his friend's shoulder, Melodie resting against him, with Evie lying across her lap. Annabel sat to one side. Barney sat on the roof of the cabin, lightly kicking his shoes against the doors.

"We should go back to the harbour," Roy said slowly.

"We don't know what's going on... We should stay here, and think for a while," Clive comforted, speaking clearly.

Melodie hugged Evie and Annabel tightly between her arms, she said, "I think we should try and see, Clive... Not too close... But we could see."

"I have some binoculars... --in my bag... --in the cabin," Roy offered, stuttering and stammering, his voice breaking. It was obvious that Roy did not want to go inside; he did not even look at the cabin. Clive had had to hook another of his bags from the doorway of the cabin, to give Roy a change of clothes. The broken window at the side glittered with broken glass and traces of Melodie's blood. It looked like the mouth of a monster, frozen in a permanent scream, glass shards protruding at various points around the edges like sharks'-teeth.

A little later.
Clive tip-toed through the cabin, passed the stab-wound-riddled body of Sue, and the bottle-beaten body of Joyce. He crossed to where Roy's second bag was placed, with the other bags piled around it, and unzipped it open. He retrieved Roy's binoculars, pulling them free, letting the loose cable-strap fall out behind them.

Roy watched him from the broken cabin-window.

Clive turned, saw Roy's shrink-wrapped eyes, and screwed his eyes shut. He did not want to look at the bodies. He gritted his teeth and stepped towards the doorway.

Melodie stood beyond the door, staring at Clive's face. She saw his aversion to the scene and wore a soothing, sympathetic half-smile. Clive opened his eyes slowly, upon reaching the doorway. He saw Melodie and his spirits were momentarily lifted. He strode the last few steps towards her, ducking through the doorway, and met her outstretched hand with his. He hugged his wife.

Barney saw Clive's face as he hugged his grandmother, turning away from Roy. His soft expression faded, and anger and resolution replaced it.

Hours later.
The sailboat drifted about three hundred metres from the shore away from the surf. They were slightly further along the coast than the Brighton Marina, between the village of Peacehaven and the

town of Newhaven. They faced a huge, white and grey cliff-face that looked like the ripples of a curtain, undulating up and down along the coastline. Vast layers of chalk, clay and flint faced back at them like some enormous wall stretching away in both directions.

Clive looked through Roy's binoculars at the road that ran along the cliff-top. He gritted his teeth and grimaced, a dozen wrinkle-lines folding into his face.

He passed the binoculars to Roy, he said, "I can't see any people... --live people... --only the infected... It looks like a plague... God forbid it isn't."

Roy agreed with a maudlin expression covering his face. He shifted on the balls of his feet, not swaying with the boat, but swaying through and through. "I can't believe it!" he whispered. "What on earth has happened?"

Melodie looked worriedly at them both, holding Evie close to her.

Clive walked across the sailboat to where Barney and Annabel were sitting.

"Can I have a word?" he asked.

They moved to the bow of the boat.

Melodie hugged Evie, perched on the roof of cabin. She followed Clive and their grandchildren with her eyes, down the length of the boat. Roy watched them too; curious, but removed.

"Annabel, can you bring Roy, Evie and your grandma up here... --to this end of the boat... While Barney and I throw the bodies overboard and clean up the cabin?... Barney, can you help me do that?" Clive asked solemnly.

Barney thought for a moment, his eyes rolling skyward for a second, then he said, "Yes."

"Thank you," Clive said. "It'll help a lot."

A while later.
Clive and Barney threw the body of Joyce over the side of the boat and into the sea, and re-entered the cabin. They wore marigolds that Melodie had packed in her kitchen-bag, taped around the forearm with duct-tape, waxy aprons tied around their backs and cat-emblazoned tea-towels tied around their faces like cowboy bandits.

They stood at either end of Sue's body, looking down on the dozens of stab-puncture wounds.

"It's not a pretty sight," Clive offered.

"I don't think many dead people are," Barney quipped.

"I'm not sure they were entirely dead."

"Me neither."

"Let's get inside and finish cleaning up..."

"Okay."

Two days later. 500 metres from the coast – 10:48pm.
Barney sat on deck, while the others slept inside the cabin.

He looked through a book of coastal maps with a torch pressed between his neck and shoulder. He stared out across the channel at the vast water *sloshing* around the sailboat, lapping the sides, darkness all around, stars twinkling above his head.

He leafed through a few pages and stopped. He studied the map.

The next morning.
Clive tried to catch fish with a pair of fishing-rods, sat on the port side of the sailboat.

"I found a book last night. You should look at it," Barney announced, sitting next to his grandfather.

"The book with all of the nautical maps in it?" Clive asked.

"Yes."

"Did you find anything?"

"There are a few places we could try... The Isle of Wight, perhaps... It is an island."

"I'll certainly consider it. I'll have to have a good-look at the book..." Clive countered noncommittally.

Barney glanced at the stern of the sailboat, where Roy squatted. He stared out to sea, looking deflated, ruined and isolated. His back was crooked and his hands gripped the railing of the sailboat.

Annabel watched Roy from the starboard side of the sailboat, as Evie and Melodie played 'I-spy' with little inspiration. Annabel turned away, watching her brother and grandfather for a moment, before staring at the criss-crossed glimmers of sunlight glinting on the surface of the Channel.

"I see a ship!" Roy screamed. "I see a ship!" he repeated with more volume.

Clive and Barney stood up instantly, looking to Roy, who pointed South.

An ocean-liner was moving in the distance, across the horizon, 3 miles away from them.

"Oh my God!" Melodie shrieked. "That's incredible!"

Everyone joined Roy, looking out to sea, shading their eyes from the sun, as the ocean-liner shifted incredibly slowly up the English Channel.

"Barney, Annabel, start the engine!" Clive yelled.

Barney and Annabel sprang into action, rushing to the tiller and ignition.

Melodie used the binoculars to view the ocean-liner. Her mouth dropped open. "I can see something else too!... It's a life-raft! No, two!" she shouted.

"What? Where?" Clive asked and took the binoculars from his wife.

He saw both bright, basketball-orange life-rafts drifting away from the ocean-liner, being swept away on the large waves of the wake.

Later.
The sail-boat edged towards the first of two life-rafts that had been jettisoned from the ocean-liner.

"Cut the engine, Anna," Clive said quietly.

The sailboat drifted on the waves, shortening the distance to the raft.

Suddenly a woman appeared from the second life-raft. "Do not go near that raft! Please!" she squawked, waving her arms, panicked.

Barney looked at her, when an infected crawled out of the first raft and puked blood across the side of the sailboat. The infected was wearing the uniform of a barman, black and whites, blood-stained and ripped. One of the sleeves had been torn from the shoulder, leaving frayed edges of thread. The infected flopped and lolloped and tossed and turned on the mostly-inflated raft.

Melodie sucked in a sharp intake of air and Roy gasped, straightening.

Clive and Barney beat the infected with oars, hitting it in the face and arms to keep it from reaching the railing of the sailboat as the raft edged closer.

Barney stabbed the oar down and punctured the raft. Air *fizzed* and *hissed* out of the tear.

They stopped, watching the raft deflate and begin to sink. The infected flailed, marching and flapping on the spot, and then vomited blood in the water. Dark red and sea-water mixed around its ankles as it stomped more air from the inflatable. It met their eyes, struggling to find enough stable ground to kneel and then stand. It wavered on its feet, dropping to its knees with a splash.

Barney clubbed it one more time on the top of the head and it fell back on the raft and drifted away.

The woman – HARMONY JOINER, 29 year old Englishwoman – watched them, impressed. She had wavy blonde hair, expensively styled and trimmed, that fell in curls around her face and over her shoulders. She had a pretty face hidden under an excess of makeup and fake-tan. She had long lashes, emerald-green eye-shadow and bright, ruby-red lipstick. Her eyes were a misty grey, but fiery and quick. Her face was slim and pointed, a sharp nose, defined cheekbones and an arrowhead chin. She was gym-fit and lithe, poised on long, slim arms and legs. She wore a tight-fitting, low-v-neck turquoise vest-top, a pair of cream cargo-shorts and white-and-pink Puma Jago trainers; all of her clothes had blood-stains and scuffs and splatters on them. She sat on all-fours in the other life-raft, perched in the opening, eyeing the sailboat and the other survivors. An expression of calm and relief played over her features. "Thank God!" she exclaimed. "Thank God you saw us! Thank you!"

Another person in the second raft revealed himself. A man sat next to Harmony. He was ROMAN COSANZA, 47 year old American of Spanish descent. He had a full head of short-cropped dark hair, parted on the left, and slicked with hair-gel. He was average height, average build with nothing remarkable about his appearance. Between pairs of long black eyelashes he had dark, malevolent eyes under thick dark eyebrows. He was tanned and this darkened his eyes further. He had a slim face, but a wide jaw and brow, and a thick nose in the centre. His teeth were uneven and his smile was crooked. He wore a black suit over a grey shirt, with no tie, and smart black shoes; a thick plastic-band of a watch sat around his left wrist. His clothes were slightly ripped and blood heavily stained one of his arms, and his knees, lower legs and shoes.

Barney's and Roman's eyes met for a millisecond.

"Hey, watch out! Here you go," Clive said and threw a rope-line to Harmony.

She caught it with both hands and the rope tightened between them. A small wave formed at the front of the life-raft, as Clive and Roy pulled them closer.

Roman watched Harmony hang on to the rope, her thighs taught with muscle as her knees dug under the inflated rubber-ring of the raft and held tight as they were pulled closer.

"Thank you! Thank you, so much!" Harmony shouted.

A little later.
Clive and Barney looked at the coastal map book at the helm behind the tiller.

"I think we should head on. Keep going. Keep moving," Barney stated.

"I'm not so sure, kid," Clive said. "There will be more of those... --infected people out-there."

"Then maybe the Isle of Wight... Less people."

Roman moved to their position and asserted himself improperly on the decision-making process, to the chagrin and irritation of the others. He said, "I'd like my two-cents, if that's–... I'd suggest we try moving down the coast."

"And why's that?"

"Because an island will have a smaller population. If this virus has spread. I think your grandson is right."

Roy watched Roman from the middle of the sailboat. He eyed him suspiciously.

Barney, stood in front of Roman, looked at him the same way.

"We can decide in a minute... Think about all of the pros and cons."

Inside the cabin.
Harmony sat with Melodie, Evie and Annabel.

"We left New York three days before everything happened," Harmony began. "Wow! A week ago... A week ago I was buying shoes on Fifth Avenue... Hmm..."

Clive, Roy, Roman and Barney entered the cabin and found places to sit or perch.

Harmony cleared her throat.

Melodie stood. "I'll make something to eat..."

Three days ago. In the 'Kuysine' restaurant, on the cruise-liner – 11:56am GMT.
Harmony sat on her own in the huge, opulent, neon-lit restaurant. She wore the same tight-fitting, low-v-neck turquoise vest-top, the pair of cream cargo-shorts and the white-and-pink Puma Jago trainers: they were all spotless. A plate of untouched food sat on the table in front of her. She looked around at the busy surroundings; people milled about, serving staff dashed in between a myriad of tables, businessmen and hundreds of holidaymakers and the ship's staff shuffled around the periphery.

A waiter crossed to Harmony's table and placed a bottle of chilled Pinot Grigio next to her wine-glass.

"Thank you," she said and poured herself a large glass.

The waiter nodded and wandered away.

Harmony gulped down a mouthful, then sat back.

The room grew quieter and quieter. Then several of the waiting staff collapsed, dropping fully-loaded trays of drinks and dinners to smash and shatter.

Harmony started to rise from her seat, when she stopped herself.

Everyone who had been standing dropped to their knees then fell, crumpled on their feet, or lost balance and pitched over. Almost all of the people sitting at the tables, all around Harmony, had bent over and their faces were slumped on the table-tops.

Blood gushed out of the open, slack mouth of a passenger to Harmony's right. It poured and cascaded, running over the steaming roast on the plate under its head, dripping and coursing over the table-cloth and soaking it.

All voices stopped. Only the vaguely South American music tweeted from dozens of hidden speakers around the vast space. The almost-silence was freakish to Harmony, isolating and frightening.

She noticed several more of the passengers were leaking blood heavily from their mouths. One of the bodies hacked and lurched, then went still.

Harmony's eyes bore into the passenger, watching for any more signs of movement.

"Shit! This isn't happening," she whispered to herself.

She rose from her chair and looked at the wider room.

Another person stood, about forty metres from Harmony. He looked at the room as well, wide-eyed with fear, circling and staring, occasionally touching some of the bodies. He caught sight of Harmony and held up his hand, a sort of wave-greeting. Harmony replied with a similar gesture.

"What the hell is going on?!" the man shouted.

Before Harmony had a chance to speak, an infected had arisen from a table between them, off to the right. It groaned and hacked, blood dripping from its nostrils. It growled then arched its back, staring at the ceiling. Its head dropped and a gush of blood sloshed out and splattered on the floor in front of it.

The man's eyes widened impossibly further.

The infected scanned the room, then locked on to the man. It charged at him.

Harmony could only watch.

The infected bolted between several tables, as the man beat a hasty retreat. The hunt lasted a very short time. The man tripped on a body he had not expected to be there and fell face-first to the red-and-gold patterned carpet. He twisted onto his back, as the infected reached him. It shuddered, balling its fists, then dashed out a mouthful of blood onto the man. He tired to scramble away backwards, but the infected maintained its pursuit, striding after him. It shook again, then dropped onto its knees, dragging itself forward with its clawed hands. It clambered onto the man, ignoring his frantic punches and kicks. The infected puked blood over the man's face.

Harmony could not see them anymore, they had dropped out of sight behind one of the tables, one of the slumped-over passengers blocked her view fully.

She watched for a long time, until the infected clambered to its feet. She ducked behind one of the tables and scampered between several more to a pair of exit-doors. She scuttled and crawled to the halfway point before glancing back at the infected, it was making a line for her, followed by two others, including the man she had seen fall.

She stood then sprinted for the exits, bashing them open, then pulled them closed behind her. She found a stainless-steel stanchion-post barrier with twisted gold velvet-braid. She unclipped the rope-braid and picked up the stanchion and drove it through the door-handles, locking them in place.

Harmony turned to see the wide, grand corridor she found herself in. Several infected shuffled along, about twenty metres from her, dozens of bodies piled the way, both ways. She darted for an exit-door that led into a stairwell and up to the deck. She sprinted up the staircase, bounding two steps at a time.

A little later.
Harmony reached the deck. Dozens of bodies littered the walkway in both directions. A light rain of blood dripped from the next, smaller deck, above her. She could not see anybody left alive, she could not see any of the infected either.

She moved to the railings at the edge of the ship: they were a typical white metal grid with a teak balustrade running along the top, with life-preservers attached every ten metres. She looked down at the boiling sea below, swirls of white and blue, white-caps breaking.

"I wouldn't want to jump," a man said, making her jump and grip the balustrade tightly.

She turned and saw Roman. He stood casually in the middle of the walkway. He was a little bloodied, but his suit was not ripped at all.

"Why not? Have you seen what's happening right-now?"

"Yes."

"Then, what would you suggest? Stand and fight?"

"There are three thousand passengers and one thousand crew on this ship! How do you think your odds stack up against that? Two versus four thousand?" Roman stated calmly. "We have to get off this ship, but not now... If we get in a life-raft, then our chances of surviving will be very low. We're halfway across the Bay of Biscay. We'd likely be swept away in the currents. And lost at sea..."

Harmony eyed Roman suspiciously.

"We need to wait until the ship reaches the English Channel, at the least."

"How long will that take?"

"Three days."

"Three days!" she shouted, parroting him.

"Yes... For the most part, the ship runs on autopilot. Human-beings only really take command during the docking process, otherwise, they practically run themselves."

"So, what? Hide?"

"Exactly."

Harmony's brow furrowed and she looked worriedly around Roman, at the blood-smeared bodies that lay like discarded life-sized dolls.

The present. On deck.
Barney stared at the map showing the South coast of England in detail. He glanced across at the others. Harmony hugged her own arms, deep in thought. Roy whimpered, covering his face behind large, wrinkled hands. Clive watched Melodie; Evie on one side, Annabel on the other: Evie drew in a colouring-in book, Annabel scanned her Kindle screen. Roman stared out to sea, lounging against the outside of the cabin.

"We should go to the Isle of Wight," Barney said decisively, looking at his grandfather.

"Yes. Yes," Roman agreed.

Clive looked worriedly at his grandson. "We haven't got the petrol... So we'll have to sail there..."

Roman's teeth clenched together.

Two days later. At night.
The sailboat had been anchored and floated in the sea. Dark waves broke against the bow.

Roman sat on deck smoking a cigarette.

Barney watched suspiciously him from the cabin-door.

Inside the cabin.
Everyone slept soundly. Places had been organised for a fairly comfortable nights' sleep, although they were closely packed together.

Barney returned to his bunk.

The next day – 1:18pm.
Clive stood at the helm with Roman. His hands idled on the steering-wheel, as he kept a close watch on the newcomer. Roman leafed through the coastal maps book, looking at the same page Barney had been reading.

"So, what did you do, before all-of-this?" Clive asked genially.

"I–... Ahem," he said then cleared his throat. "I worked in a pet shop. I was the manager. It was in Florida..."

"A pet shop?"

"Yes. A pet shop."

"Really?"

"Yes. I had a lovely, little shop in Fort Myers Beach..."

"I didn't take you for a pet shop manager, Roman."

"Why is that?" Roman asked cagily.

"I thought you'd be a--... A--... I--... I'm not sure I thought you were... A bail-bondsman, maybe."

"A loan-shark?"

"Or something in law enforcement... Maybe a Police Officer."

"Oh, yes. A police officer, huh? Really?"

Clive looked at Roman. His interest seemed to have been slightly peaked. "Forget about it," Clive stated.

"Okay, then," Roman said mysteriously, then he looked back down at the pages of the coastal maps book. "I'll just keep looking at this book, then..."

Clive gritted his teeth.

From the bow, Barney watched Roman intently, while Roy talked to him about his youth in Devon.

On the other side of the boat.
Melodie, Harmony, Evie and Annabel sat in silence, watching the surf and waves.

Melodie tried to break the silence, she cleared her throat and looked at her granddaughters. "Do either of you have a stereo? We could try and find some music to listen to...? That'd be good, wouldn't it?"

"I have one!" Evie exclaimed.

"I have some music on my MP3 player..."

"Good. Good. Let's go and find something good to listen to."

At the helm.
Roman stared at the coastal map book intensely. "We could stop at this... It's a small, man-made island off the coast of the Isle of Wight."

"Oh yeah?" Clive asked, looking back at Roman. "Why there?"

Roman evaded Clive's eyes, then sat back a little, shiftily. He opened the book and showed Clive the location. "It will probably be deserted..."

Later that day. At night.
Everyone had assembled on the side of the sailboat, not far from a large, cylindrical multi-floored man-made island. This was The Bastion of Spitbank Fort, in the Solent, one mile off the coast of Portsmouth, near the Isle of Wight: it was built in the 1860-70s as a defence for the harbour of Portsmouth. It was a giant barrel-shaped building with armour-plating on the Channel-side of it and a small jetty on the land-facing side.

Clive used a flashlight to signal-flash to see if anyone was inside, or even alive. "Right, let's see..."

"I wonder if anyone will be in there," Harmony pondered.

"It'd be a miracle!" Melodie offered.

"It could happen," Evie started, "it looks fairly safe..."

Clive shone the flashlight into the room again.

After an agonisingly-long amount of time, a light flashed from within.

Everyone on the sailboat were shocked and relieved, but curious. A small cheer broke out amongst them; exclamations of joy, relief, curiosity.

Roman smiled menacingly. Only Barney saw it.

Ten days ago. On Preston Park Avenue, the A23 main-road, Brighton.

Barney and Annabel strode down the street together. Each of them had backpacks slung over their backs. They slowed and entered a large Victorian town-house. They wore similar clothes to the day at Brighton Marina.

Clive walked out of the living-room, intercepting Barney and Annabel in the hallway. "Kids, hello!" he said, opening his arms for a double-hug.

"How are you, grandpa?" Barney asked politely.

"Great! And you? Both?"

"Fine," Annabel answered.

"Good, thank you," Barney added.

A little later. In the living-room.

Clive and Melodie sat on one of the three two-seater sofas in the room, Evie flopped on the next with Annabel and Barney perched on the third. Clive and Melodie held cups of coffee, their grandchildren held glasses of fresh fruit juice.

"Now, I know you'll all be upset that your mum and dad can't come on the sailboat with us on Wednesday," Clive began. "But, you know they'll be doing some important work..."

"Yes."

"Mmm-hmm."

Evie nodded.

"So, how's about we just try to make the most of the trip?"

"Okay."

"Great!" Evie exclaimed.

"Good," Clive stated.

"I'm sure we'll have lots of fun," Melodie added.

"I'm sure we will," Barney agreed.

"So, what do you fancy doing this weekend? Before we go," Clive asked. "Today and tomorrow we can do anything you want to do."

"The cinema?" Melodie offered.

"Yeah!" Evie screamed. "The cinema!"

Annabel fell silent.

"We could go shopping?" Melodie asked.

"Yeah," Barney said. "Okay."

CHAPTER 15 - THE PLEA - Edinburgh

DAMIEN FLYNN, 33 year old Englishman – landed at Edinburgh International Airport. His Hollywood body and California tan glowed under the fluorescent lights of the plane and the refracted sunlight that bounced off the interior walls of the fuselage and seats. His slight wrinkles and age-marks, that he did not care to cover up, gave him a wily charm, even from a distance. He knew he was a handsome man, but never thought himself ridiculous. He stroked his hand through the thick mane of perfect black hair, ruffled it and swept it back across the top of his head. His bright blue eyes shone from under carefully tweezed eyebrows and maintained lashes. He was clean shaven without the hint of stubble from the journey he had just undertaken. He wore a pristine white shirt under a crisp black Armani suit, with comfortable but smart black shoes. He stepped off the Boeing 787-10X and onto the passenger-boarding-stairs, as he put on a pair of vintage, black Ray Ban sunglasses. Cool wind hit him and he took a deep breath. The air tickled his hair and he ran his fingers through it again, letting the breeze cool his scalp.

One of the stewardesses eyed him from the galley as he passed by and whispered something to another stewardess. He had seen that whisper many times.

He smiled, and nodded; his bored eyes hidden behind dark lenses.

He walked across the tarmac and entered a corridor with a glass out-facing window-wall. He followed several of the other First Class passengers and walked through into the departure gate. He crossed the huge, marble-floored hall and passed an HMV kiosk-store. He stopped and walked closer.

On the front-most rack of the shop, Damien saw a copy of his last production, a four season box-set of a television show he had filmed in Los Angeles: it was called '*Paradise Law*'. He picked up one of the boxes and looked at the back-cover. There were three pictures, all including his face in some form, and another in the background of his whole body. The price-sticker read: £39.99. He half-smiled to himself and put the box-set back. Maybe the airline had made the shop place this on the front shelf, he thought. The studio had sent him a small cardboard box with twenty copies of the box-set in it, for friends and family. He still had fifteen box-sets left to give away. They were sitting in a large cardboard box in his LA apartment, gathering dust beside his 1970s black PVC retro diner-bench that sat in his living-room, facing his Sony Bravia 70" LCD flat-screen television that was stylishly sunk into the wall. He would miss seeing all of the framed photographs that covered the hall and dining-room walls: every photo a picture of him with his arm around various A-, B- and C-listers, a few sports stars, a couple of politicians and two or three directors.

On the shop-wall behind Damien there was small section of books. Amongst them were '*Jubilee Junction*', '*Dr O'Neill's leisure*', and '*Highness and Lowness*' authored by John Ramsay.

He wandered idly through the airport chewing a stick of Doublemint, tugging his passport from his inside jacket pocket to give to the attendant at the Passport Control desk.

A little later.
Damien walked through the airport terminal, an iPhone pressed to his ear.

"I understand... I understand..." he said, leisurely pacing to the First Class baggage collection desk.

He held up a finger to gesture for the attendant at the desk to wait. The attendant nodded, pursing her lips, tilting forward on her swivelling office-chair. She stared at him.

Damien, between words, chewed his gum. "Listen, Hampton... I'm gonna have to go," he said and hung up. The attendant half-smiled and blinked flirtatiously. "Baggage for Flynn," he said with a perfected smile. Damien nodded, sliding the iPhone into his pocket.

"Yes, Mr Flynn... Right-away," she said, and tapped on the keyboard behind the top of the desk.

He thought about thanking the attendant, then turned to scan a few of the other First Class passengers, making a line behind him.

Outside.

At the exit, Damien was met by fifty-seven fans, who clamoured for his autograph. Damien conceded and signed four, before he saw his driver, and waved him over. His driver was MIKE ELVIN, 40 year old Englishman. He had a hard, long face with deep wrinkles for a man of his age. His eyes were world-weary and quick, his mouth thin and taught over a toothy jaw. He was large and powerful, dressed in a dark suit, white shirt, black tie and black, shin-high army-boots, with the high-ankles tucked under his trouser-legs. He used his size to push himself through, barging between several of the fans, to get to Damien. Once he was amongst them Mike took hold of Damien's luggage trolley, piled with his bags. He wheeled it towards a sleek, black 2009 Lincoln stretched limousine, ploughing through the remaining fans that waited between them and the curb. Damien signed three more 10x8" photographs of himself, when Mike parked the trolley beside the boot and opened the rear door for Damien.

"Nice to meet you, Mr Flynn," Mike stated and shook Damien's hand. "Mike Elvin."

"You too," Damien replied. "Look, I'm feeling slightly mobbed... I hope you're armed..."

"Get in, I'll clear this-lot, sir."

Mike held the door open for Damien and closed it behind him. He heard Mike tell the crowd to leave and they slowly shuffled away and dispersed. Mike loaded the luggage into the boot and climbed into the front-seat. He turned to Damien, across the space of two and a half metres. "I'm not only your driver, but also your minder slash bodyguard," Mike announced. "While you're in Edinburgh making this film-thing..."

Damien smirked. "Good to know."

"I bet there's shit-loads of wackos in America, huh?" Mike offered.

"Yeah... A few."

Mike squinted, looking at Damien, still wearing his Ray Bans.

"Well, just to let your mind rest... --Everyone on 'celebrity-babysitting' is armed," he said and patted two inches to the side of his heart.

Damien felt a little relieved.

"Can I ask you something, Mr Flynn?"

"Yeah... Shoot."

"How do these people out-here," Mike said, and gestured to the receding fans, "get to know you'll be arriving at this airport, on this flight, right-now?"

"I don't know... The media?... Social media?... In fact, probably my agent and PR company..."

"That must get quite frustrating?"

"It serves its purpose, Mike...

A little later. On the M9 headed Northwest.

Mike drove along the fairly empty motorway, slowing behind a purple 2006 Volvo V70 estate-car. He tapped the steering-wheel, eyes always scanning the road ahead and the three-surrounding mirrors. He glanced in the rear-view at Damien.

"Say, what's it like working in the film industry? In Hollywood, in America, I mean?"

Damien had heard every question before. "Y'know what, pal?... If you don't mind, I think I'm gonna get some sleep... Wake me up when we arrive at the hotel... Thank you."

Damien adjusted the pair of Ray-Ban sunglasses on his nose, leant back against the seat, ever-so slightly tightening the seatbelt, and tried to fall asleep.

Mike was visibly annoyed, gripping the steering-wheel, gritting his teeth, but Damien did not care or notice.

Damien screwed his eyes shut and pressed one ear against the cool padded seat-back.

A little later.

Mike coughed, jerking his arm out to take hold of the steering-wheel and make it steady. He cupped his hand over his mouth and cleared his throat. He settled and took a deep breath through his hand. Then he coughed-up a few spots of blood into his palm. He felt his heart-beat grow faster, breathing heavily. Then he died with a groan and a rasped-choking sound.

Mike's fingers dropped from the steering-wheel.

The limousine started to veer off the road, guided by a slight camber.

On the first bump against the curb, Damien was knocked against the door-panel and awoke. He saw that Mike had collapsed and was pitched to one side, leant against the side-window.

Damien released his seatbelt and scurried down the limousine to reach out to Mike, then a *booming* noise filled the space.

The limousine launched over the curb. The tyres, hopping and flexing, rammed through the wooden crash barrier, pulling the limousine along. Then the nose pitched down and the limousine dropped down the steep slope on the other side. The limousine rolled over and over again, battering Damien backwards, then up and down in a nightmare free-fall, left and right into the walls, hitting the roof, and smashing into the insides of the windows, knocking him out.

The limousine came to an abrupt stop when it hit the immovable trunk of a large oak tree.

Damien's body slammed to a stop, coming to rest half-across the backseat.

Later.

Damien awoke. Two of his fingers were broken and bent back and he was bruised and in pain. He looked across the inside of the car: it was wedged at a 45^0 angle against the oak tree, pinning three of the four doors shut. The remaining door was a crumpled concertina of metal, only the cracked safety-glass held firm in the deformed frame.

A few metres from the bottom of the slope and limousine, a country dirt-road wound away in both directions. A few Scots pine-trees dotted the surrounding area.

Damien held his head, disoriented. He felt a large bruise on the left side of his skull, under his hairline. Just as he tried to push the door open, an infected slammed into it from the other side. It growled and scratched at the door, trying to gain access to Damien. The infected punched and gargled and spat blood on the car.

Damien pressed himself against the opposite side of the limousine, as the infected punched the window repeatedly. It beat until a crack spider-webbed the centre of the glass. The infected fixated on Damien, staring through the veined, blotchy glass. It punched hard, breaking its own knuckles, and smashed through. The arm punctured the window and the broken glass cut its arms to shreds; strips and veins peeled back and hung like bloody, red rags and wires and spaghetti. Damien could see it was not aware of the injuries it was inflicting on itself. The infected forced its arm further through the hole, ripping more flesh away. It snapped its jaws at him, as it hocked and hacked and blood started to rise inside it.

Damien snapped to and remembered Mike's gun. He scrambled and clambered into the front of the car. He avoided using his hand with the broken fingers, holding it under his chest. He scrambled to the glove-compartment and opened it. There was a can of pepper-spray and a box of bullets, but no gun. Damien turned to Mike; his neck was broken and twisted in a horrific way, from his thighs down a crushed pâté of meat and seeping blood. His mouth hung open like a permanent yawn. The body convulsed and a mouthful of blood escaped, oozing down the tongue, over teeth and dripped over the lips and down the chin.

Damien went still, his arm frozen in the space above Mike.

The body did not move again.

Damien searched him, uncomfortably, with one hand. He found the gun in a holster under Mike's sweaty armpit and pocketed it. He looked down the centre of the limousine. It looked like a submarine that had been crushed under immense pressure, then hauled to the surface for inspection with all of the water drained from it.

He winced as he climbed back over the ripped and buckled front-seat. He crawled to the door where both of the hands of the infected were thrust and had punctured the hole in the shattered but toughened safety-glass.

Damien pointed the pistol at the infected, questioning it with his eyes. It was not a joke, he felt inside.

The infected vomited blood on itself and threw up bloody projectile at Damien. It splashed on the glass and spread across its own arms, running and coursing through the broken hole. It gushed again, painting the window oily, dark crimson. The light in the limousine dimmed.

He fired the gun through the smallest of holes between its arms and hit the infected through its nose. Blood, skull and brain exploded out the back of its head and it slumped to its knees, arms still trapped in the window. As the body slumped, in a natural prayer position, both its arms *cracked* and shattered and bent backwards.

The bullet sailed on and embedded itself in a Scots pine-tree.

As the shot rang out in the air, at the top of the hill, at the road, two more infected were attracted to the sound and dove down the slope towards the limousine.

Damien heard them coming, and saw them through a crack in the opposite window.

He struggled to free himself, kicking the pane of toughened glass, with the infected still attached to it, free from the frame. He used his jacket to cover the shards of broken glass that were wedged in the frame and fell out onto the ground, trying to land without falling on his broken fingers. He landed with a *thump* on the dirt and the wind knocked from his lungs.

Damien quickly picked himself up, cleared his throat, whipped his coat across his body, and made a run for it.

He dashed down the country-road that ran along parallel to the main-road, then curved away from the slope towards the entrance to a farm.

He reached a large barn, closer to him than the farmhouse along the road. He hurtled towards the barn.

The two infected from the main-road hotly pursued him, kicking clods of dirt behind them in their ragged chase.

As Damien ran into the barn, he beamed everywhere, spinning on his heels. He put the gun in his belt and picked up a pitchfork with his good hand, as the first infected bolted inside. He stabbed the infected straight in the heart, tipped it off its feet then leapt on it, as the second infected appeared in the doorway. Damien kicked down on the pitchfork, yanking it back and forth through the prone figure's insides, raking the organs apart. The first infected expired, when the second knocked Damien to the ground. They struggled, both flailing and whirling their arms to attack and to prevent attack. The infected threw out its elbow and caught Damien's fingers. He screamed in agony, rolling away on the hay-strewn floor.

Damien punched the infected, then elbowed its face, breaking its nose. It scrambled to its legs, as he pulled himself to his feet, then it dashed headlong at him. He dodged, then swung the pitchfork around. He used his elbow as a rest with his poor arm and gripped the shaft tightly with his good. He braced for the impact, as the infected charged into the forks. It impaled itself, but continued to advance, sliding Damien back until his shoes met the wooden-plank edge of a stable, scraping a wave of hay behind his heels. He pressed back and the infected *snapped* its teeth then puked blood, lessening and lessening after every moment. It seemed to yawn, gasping, then stepped back from Damien. It tumbled onto its backside, then lay down, partly propped up by the pitchfork.

A long moment later, Damien stepped out of the barn, unhurt overall, but breathing heavily and his leg cramped, and it made him limp. He could feel several bruises and strains forming along his right leg and arms. His hand still throbbed. He picked up the gun; it had been knocked out of his belt. He put it back.

His eyes drifted across the landscape. A few trees could have hidden more enemies, but he could see none. There appeared to be nobody within sight. No cars on any of the roads showing any sign of movement. This pleased him and frightened him in equal measure. He took a deep breath, pulling in a lungful of air. He retrieved his jacket from the muddy ground at the front of the barn and gently eased it onto his arm, then threaded his good arm through quickly.

He stared at the farmhouse, seeking any movement, then started to creep towards it.

He limped down the road. Luckily for him he had no blood stains on his clothes, had a glorious tan and so he felt he could not ever be mistaken for one of the infected. He had a gun, that was one thing. But he might be able to retrieve his stuff from the limousine later and get a change of clothes.

A little later. At the farmhouse.
Damien knocked loudly, gripping the gun by the barrel, ready to hit anything with the butt-handle. There was no sound, but something caught his eye in the front garden and he stepped forward. An old woman lay, face-down in the recently-cut grass. A puddle of blood by her mouth had dyed the grass a dark reddish-black.

> Damien tried the door. It was unlocked. He entered.
> "Hello?" he called out. "Is there anyone there?"
> The farmhouse was silent.
> He entered the small living-room and breathed a sigh of relief.
> Damien felt his pocket and took out his iPhone. There was no signal. He moved back into the hall, dragging his body then into the quaint, heavily-decorated kitchen and found an old, faded ring-dial telephone screwed to the wall. He tried the phone. There was a tone, but the Emergency Services 999 number did not work. He hung up and then searched the farmhouse.
> He went upstairs first, moving into the first room, then the next, then the next. He returned to the living-room when he was completely satisfied the home was empty and all of the external doors and ground-floor windows were locked. He cleaned his hands and found a splint to place between the broken fingers. He bit down on the ivory handle of a dinner-knife and snapped both his fingers straight. He screamed around the knife, tears filling his eyes, snot rushing out of his nostrils. He wrapped his fingers in clean gauze and fabric, then taped them together with several pieces of fabric-tape. After a few minutes he released the knife from his teeth and it dropped to the floor. After several more minutes, he found some flat-packed cardboard boxes and covered every ground-floor window, then taped the edges.

Later.
Damien checked every news-channel on the television. He flicked the stations, thumbing the remote control's buttons up and down. There were no people in any of the newsrooms.

> He drank black coffee, as night drew in.
> He pulled the curtains closed and switched the lights off. He was illuminated only by the television.
> His eyes fixed on the television, but his interest waned. He stopped on Channel 42 News.

An hour and a half later.
Damien idled on the sofa, staring blank-eyed at the television. A bubble *popped* on the surface of a cold cup of coffee that sat beside him on a sofa-side table. He took a sip from the coffee then placed it back on the table.

> On Channel 42 News – Something in the television studio moved.
> Damien sat up and watched intently. His eye-lids stretched open as he hunched forward and stared at the screen.
> A woman appeared, then ducked out of the camera's view. Then something moved in the background in the office behind the studio, beyond a half-frosted pane of glass. It was one of the infected. It stalked through the back office, creeping between desks and computer monitors.
> The woman crawled on her hands and knees into the studio, then slowly climbed to her feet, peering over the frosted-glass edge into the office. The infected caught sight of her. It raced at the woman, dashing through an unseen, open doorway into the studio. The woman turned, stood her ground and fought it with a fire-extinguisher. She swung the canister out, clipping the infected. It knocked her to the ground with several short, hard punches. She managed to twist on the ground and hammered the infected across its shins with the flat-base of the extinguisher. She rose and the infected struggled to its feet. The infected hung onto her clothes as she struck it again and they both fell off-camera.
> Damien found himself crouching in front of the television two feet away, staring at the screen as his eyes glazed and dried. He blinked and blinked again, moisture licking over his eyeballs. He pressed the volume control on the set and listened keenly.

He could hear the woman and the infected fighting. The infected hacking, coughing and groaning, liquid spilling onto the ground, damp and shallow *splashes*, shoes *squeaking* on linoleum-flooring, and the woman's panicked breathing, hushed yelps and anguished screams. She managed to push and roll the infected from on top of her, then slammed the extinguisher-side down on its forehead.

The loud *cracking* noise filled the small living-room.

Damien could hear her whistling, wheezing breathing.

The woman finally got up, and stood in front of the camera. She was LYNN OAKLEY, 28 year old Englishwoman - the weather-girl at the news-station. She was average build, well put-together and carried herself with a small amount of confidence and assertion. She had shoulder-length streaky-blonde hair, faded tangerine-makeup and coral-pink lipstick. She was an attractive young lady, although her makeup made her look more like an air-stewardess than an on-screen reporter, somewhat reducing her appeal. She had sparkling blue-green eyes, a charming, warm smile and perfect-straight teeth. She wore a tight, black three-quarter-length-sleeve top, a grey pencil skirt and comfortable black flats. She curled her hair behind her ears and flattened her blood-splattered top over her taught, gym-worked midriff.

"My name is... Lynn... Oakley," she began, then cleared her throat before continuing. "I'm not sure if anyone is out-there. If there's anyone alive... We received dozens of reports from all over the country about people dropping dead and the infected attacking people... No cities were unscathed..."

Lynn looked away from the camera, her eyes filling with water. She wiped her eyes, then beamed into the lens.

"After the first wave of reports, we didn't hear anything... And... And, at the same time, whatever was happening everywhere else, was happening here, too," she wept. She gave the address of the television studio and pled for anyone "to please come and help me", when the television-signal cut out, then immediately turned to static.

"I'm coming," Damien said soberly, staring at the screen.

Two days later. Near Hawick, 55 miles South of Edinburgh.
Damien stomped along a public footpath, marching ceaselessly South. He was dirty and bloody. His clothes were muddy, stained and ripped. He had re-wrapped his fingers in cloth and bound them to two splints this time. The bandage was grimy and crusty. He carried a small-backpack slung over one shoulder, a small knife in his injured hand and a large meat-cleaver in his good hand.

He was on a mission.

He pushed on South.

Two days later. Ponteland, 12 miles Northwest of Newcastle.
Damien ventured along the A696, wandering down the side of the road, scanning the way ahead.

Cars criss-crossed the road, some had crashed, others had merely parked.

Damien ducked behind a silver 2008 Toyota Yaris and glanced down the road.

Someone was coming.

He saw a woman in her early twenties from behind. She was holding a bow. The bowstring was stretched incredibly taught. An arrow was notched and trembled against the bowstring. She loosed the arrow and it sailed into the sky. The shaft wobbled through the air, then dipped downward and found its target. The projectile hit above the collarbone of an infected, piercing through its neck and lodged between its neck-vertebrae.

The infected tottered on the spot, then dropped to the ground.

Damien smiled, impressed, then stepped into the road. The archer knew he was there.

It was Eva Lamberton. She wheeled where she stood and saw Damien instantly, pointing a fresh arrow at his eye. She had a few loose brown curls, cascading around the sides of her face and down her back over her shoulder-blades, with the rest tied back in a ponytail. Her eyes were an intense, serious hazel and shone from under her small brow. A light speckling of freckles dotted across her cheeks and the bridge of her sharp, small nose. She was slight of build: a tiny waist, small breasts and rear; slim arms and legs made of thin coils of muscle. She had small, delicate hands, undecorated and plain. She wore a brown hoodie over a grey vest-top, faded, blood-speckled and dirty jeans, and muddy hiking-boots.

Damien raised his hands in mock-surrender. "Nice shot," he offered.

"Thank you," she said and lowered the bow and arrow.

Damien eyed her closely. "Where were you headed?"

"North," she answered pulling a backpack, bag and jacket from the ground behind her.

Damien looked at her curiously.

Four days earlier. Durham University.

Eva sat at her desk in her bedroom on the third-floor in the University College, her halls of residence. She touch-typed on her computer, adding the finishing embellishments to a six thousand word paper. She had several piles of books stacked beside her computer and others filling the shelving unit above the desk. She rocked her neck on her shoulders and it *cracked* twice. She stood and stretched her arms above her head, feeling her backbone stretch, vertebrae pulling away from each other, and her bra rise up around her breasts. She tugged the bra down, rolling her shoulders, then pulled her t-shirt down as well.

Midday-light shone through the gaps in the blinds that were pulled-down and closed across Eva's windows.

She pulled the draw-string on the side of the blind and the slats started to come together, folding itself upward. She squinted in the light and looked down onto the River Wear, where three two-man rowboats sliced through the water, leaving tiny wakes behind them. She looked down and across at Leazes Road and the Framwelgate Waterside, where the road followed the side of the river.

Something caught Eva's eye.

She scooped a pair of binoculars from a hook underneath the bookshelf. She pressed the eye-pieces to her sockets and started to focus. Eva found clarity and stared.

People along the road and bridge had started to collapse, twenty in total, she counted. One man, standing nearby, fell to his knees and remained there for a few seconds, before a gush of blood leapt from his mouth. The man climbed to his feet and raced off down the street.

A purple 2005 Saab 9-3 skidded and crashed into the barrier along the river-front, then hit a grey 2003 Honda Civic, before rolling onto its roof.

A woman chased a teenager across the bridge, before an errant yellow 2007 Mazda 3 collided with both of them.

She swung her vision across to the Elvet Bridge. A green 2010 Mini Cooper had collided with the bridge-siding and was stuck in place. A blue 2002 Audi A4 swung around the corner, then demolished the Mini, bouncing off its wheels on one side then pitched over the bridge and fell into the Wear. Water rushed over the car, filling the interior quickly.

Eva's eyes widened and she let out a tiny breath.

On Station Approach, the road that led up to the train station, a rust-orange 1996 Volvo 850 rammed into the side of a blue 2002 Ford Focus, before a grey 2007 Hyundai Santa Fe hit it. The Volvo leaked petrol on the road. A spark from the Ford Focus's engine ignited the petrol and the three cars were quickly taken over by flames. The Volvo exploded, splitting the other two cars in shreds and scraps of metal. A red and black fireball rolled upwards into the sky.

Eva scanned the city.

Everywhere she looked there were infected roaming and the dead laid down.

She opened her wardrobe and snatched a medium-sized camping backpack. She unbuckled and folded the top open. She placed a pair of walking-boots in the bottom, then packed clothes. She took a canvas bag from beside the wardrobe and unzipped it. She removed her bow from the bag, two leather wrist-straps, and found two full quivers in the bottom. She placed the bow gently on her bed and used Duct tape to attach the quivers to either side of the backpack. She took a shoebox, taped-shut, from the wardrobe and packed that into the bag. She unlocked and opened a small trunk in the bottom of the wardrobe and took out the contents: five hunting knives of various sizes, a pair of black Para-Ordnance P14-45 14-round .45 calibre pistols in holsters, six boxes of ammunition, a medical pack and a small-handle axe. She attached the knives in sheaths to her body: two were strapped to her right leg, one to her left, one under her arm by her ribs and the other at the bottom of the backpack. She put on a double-shoulder holster and clipped each pistol in place under her armpits. She zipped a tight, black hoodie around her body then took a durable, rough and worn leather jacket off its hanger, letting it fall to the floor. She hooked the jacket with her fingers then pulled it around her shoulders, then put the backpack on over the top of it. She looped her arm through the bowstring and secured it around the pack.

Seconds later, Eva dashed into the hallway carrying her full backpack and bag, and found an infected stumbling towards her. She recognised the infected; it was her neighbour two doors down, a Chinese student named Cliff. The infected Cliff alerted to Eva immediately and picked up pace, charging towards her, its arms raised in front of it.

Eva took a step forward, twisted her body around, then swung a 300° arc and cut the top of its head off with the small-handle axe. Its momentum drove its legs, and the infected carried on and lolloped into the wall and fell, weeping blood from its sliced brain. It landed a few paces behind Eva.

Eva moved to the kitchen and found it empty. She removed any foods that were suitable for travelling: small tins of tuna in olive oil and corned beef, small cans of soup and condensed milk, and packs dried food and pasta. She opened her drawer and took out three bars of chocolate, a bag of lighters, a sewing kit and an assorted set of scissors of varying sizes. She placed the food and things in her bag then threw it over her shoulder, where it hooked on the backpack.

A commotion broke out in the corridor and Eva paused at the door. Her hand rested on the door-handle, slack, ready to grip it and throw the door open. She looked through the long, thin pane of glass in the door and could not see anything. She huddled beside the door when she heard footsteps approaching.

The door opened and a man stepped inside. He looked across the kitchen and did not see Eva.

"I can't find her, sir. She wasn't in her room, but her things are gone."

Eva held her breath.

"Don't worry. I'll find her."

The door swung closed and the man was gone.

Eva let out her lungs and glanced through the glass pane again. The man was not there. She pulled the door open and crept into the corridor. The man was not there either. Her bedroom door inched shut, but she did not notice.

She bolted down the corridor to a flight of stairs and bounded down them two at a time.

Moments later.

Eva slowed reaching the bottom of the stairs and paused at the fire-escape exit-door. She eased the door open and saw an infected chasing a student across the lawn. She notched an arrow in place on her bow and she aimed at the infected.

Before she could let the arrow fly she saw a dozen infected corralling a group of students and staff towards a corner, where they pounced. Blood sprayed across the people as the infected launched in to attack them.

Eva removed the arrow and ran towards the tree-line, where she could see no enemies.

She jumped between two trees and sank to the ground on a patch of wet leaves. The river was one hundred feet from where she sat, down a steep slope leading away from the university. She used her binoculars to scan through the trees along the side of the university to the cathedral.

She picked herself up and dashed through the woods. She passed the Old Fulling Mill, and ran until she reached the South Bailey: an arched bridge that crossed the Wear on the South-West side of the university and the cathedral. She dragged her body up the short slope to reach the road level. She glanced up and down the bridge and saw nobody either way.

She started along the bridge.

A little later.

Eva jogged up Quarryheads Lane and passed Durham School, a boys school for ages 3 to 13 year olds. A few cars had crashed into each other and another had rolled off the curb into the trees that lined one side of the road.

She paused at the end of the road with a T-junction joining another road. She stood on the corner of Margery Lane, staring down Grove Street opposite her. There was no sign of any movement.

Eva peered around the corner slowly and looked down the tree-shaded Margery Lane. The road stretched away then veered off to the right. She could see another car, a yellow 2006 Fiat Punto Grande. It had collided with a streetlight, the bonnet crumpled around the pole. The two front doors of the car hung open, as was one of the back doors. Something about the car made Eva consider it for a little longer. Something inside the car moved and Eva fitted an arrow to her bow.

Two hundred metres down the Lane behind her, three infected lurched into the roadway.

Eva did not see them.

She made the corner and stood proud in the road.

An infected unhooked its arm from the seatbelt in the front passenger seat. Its leg fell to the tarmac, the sole of the shoe scraping on the rough surface. It had not seen Eva.

A noise broke the silence.

A scream.

It came from inside the school.

Eva crept to a window and looked into the room. A man had been chased into the classroom and was cornered by five young students that were all infected. The man was overwhelmed.

Eva turned back to the car and saw that the infected was almost upon her. She dashed backwards, when a car engine *roared*. The car sped up Grove Street towards her, then skidded at high speed. Eva saw a flash of the driver's face, pudgy and terrified, as he struggled with the steering-wheel, trying with all his panicked might not to hit her. The car slipped on its own tyre, *squealing*, and rolled, pitching down the road. The car was full of people. Screams erupted from within the car as it rolled away, *crunching* and buckling.

Eva gasped, as the infected reached for her, lurching at her, fingers clawing the air between them.

She dropped her bow and snatched one of the knives from her leg. She struck the infected across the neck, severing many arteries. The infected gurgled, but continued forward, blood surging out of the wounds. Eva dashed the knife into its ear and twisted. Its eyes rolled and it winked at her then looked skyward.

The car rolled again and struck the back of the Fiat, *crunching* on impact and spitting chunks of broken glass across the road. The driver was dead and pressed against the car's horn. The horn *droned* loudly in a warbling siren.

A door broke open in the school grounds and dozens of the infected, students and teachers, poured out.

Eva shoved the infected away, keeping grip on the knife, and ran, sliding the knife back into its sheath.

She sprinted down the side of the substantial house that faced the end of Quarryheads Lane and into a thick line of trees at the end of the back-garden.

Eva's bow lay on the road where she dropped it.

A mass of infected filled the street, drawn to the car's horn that *droned* on. They began to crowd the car. Two of the surviving occupants awoke to their own demise. They were infected where they were trapped. The crowd roared and vomited blood into every broken, cracked and twisted opening.

Eva charged between trees and shrubs and found a fence. She vaulted the wire-mesh with ease and found herself in a large allotment.

She could hear the car's horn *drone* fading as she put distance between herself and it.

She glanced behind her at the way she had come, and saw that three infected had followed her, but were trapped behind the fence. They groaned and struggled against the wire-mesh, pressing and pushing against it.

Eva marched along an aisle of dirt and stamped-down grass, ducking behind plants, vegetable planters and small trees. She found a two metre square shed that was away from the sight of the infected. She used her knife to snap the lock and quickly climbed inside.

She found a hoop-lock on the back and drove one of the prongs of a small gardening-fork through the space, keeping the door closed. She could still faintly make out the sound of the car's horn.

Gradually more infected began to join the others at the fence, suddenly disinterested by the car.

Later – 6:12pm.
Eva sat in the shed on a folded towel draped over the engine of an old lawnmower. She ate a can of tuna with a Swiss Army Knife fork.

She peered out of the shed's only window. It was dirty, misty and scratched, but she found a spot and cleaned it with spit and her hoodie-sleeve. She looked across the allotment using the binoculars to the other part of Margery Lane and the houses and flats beyond. She scanned the length of the Lane and saw five roaming infected. She moved back to the fence, and could make out twenty-three infected clamouring around in a loose line.

Two days later – 6:16am.
Eva sat in the shed, huddled next to the lawnmower in a sleeping-bag. Glimmers of daylight shone through the misty glass of the window.

She watched traces of dust ripple and wave through the air in the beams.

The car's horn had started to diminish. The *drone* faded and faded.

Eva sat up and took a can of pineapple chunks from her bag. She used the Swiss Army Knife to open the can.

Later. 2 miles North of Durham.
Eva trekked along train tracks, heading away from Durham. She carried her bow, gripping it in her left hand. She carried one of the hunting-knives in her right.

She strode on, determined and serious.

Two days later. Ponteland, 12 miles Northwest of Newcastle.
Damien cocked his head to one side. "North?"

"West, North, South... It doesn't matter at this stage."

"At this stage?"

"Where were you headed?" she asked defiantly, turning the questions on Damien.

Damien stared into Eva's hazel eyes. They were beautiful. He was momentarily stunned into silence. He cleared his throat. "...I was headed South... To London."

"Why?" she said, shaking her head.

"London seemed like a good place to start. I thought I might be able to help some other people..."

"You hadn't gotten very far."

"I hurt my leg," Damien admitted. "And my hand." He held up his bandaged hand, showing his two broken fingers. "I broke them... I was in a car crash. A few days ago. I think they're healing, though."

Eva scanned Damien with her eyes. "You're welcome to join me, I suppose," she offered.

"But, are we going to London?"

"I can't see any good reason to go there."

Damien stared down the A696 road. He saw thirty or more infected shambling down the road, moving in their direction. Eva glanced in an instant and counted twenty-six, before her eyes flicked back to Damien.

"I think we should discuss which direction we're taking, somewhere safer."

Eva looked down the road. She glanced at the fallen infected and jogged to it. Damien scampered to follow her. She tugged the arrow free from the corpse and wiped the thick, bloody mess from the end on its shirt-sleeve. Damien stared down the road, fixated momentarily on the crowd that seemed to be getting larger.

"Let's go!" Eva insisted, pulling Damien by the arm off the road.

They ran between cars and reached the edge of the road. Eva sprinted in front of Damien and they made their way down a path and into a Somerfield supermarket.

Several of the infected saw them and dashed towards the shop.

"They're still coming!" Damien screamed, as Eva found the metal shutters that secured the shop-entrance. She grabbed the shutters' bottom lip and yanked them down fully. Damien helped and in seconds they were closed. Eva wedged a knife through a small gap in the bottom, forcing the shutters closed.

The infected thrashed and beat at the shutters, causing a lot of noise.

Damien turned to the shop and took a few tentative paces inside.

"We have to make sure it's safe," Eva ordered.

"I agree. I very agree."

Eva handed Damien one of her hunting-knives. He studied it for a moment, then Eva's petite shape.

"Erm... How is it you have this?... Um, and the bow?"

Several dozen infected started to group at the entrance-door.

Later.

Damien and Eva stood on the second floor of the shop, looking through thin slit-windows at the street around the supermarket. Sixty-eight infected surged around the building, idling but fixed on the shop. The second floor was split into two halves: one side was an open-plan seating area with a small kitchenette, and the other half was a divided into three small offices, a stairwell, a unisex toilet and a storeroom.

"I'm Damien Flynn, by the way..." he said, staring down at the infected.

"I knew who you were," Eva stated. "I used to watch a couple of your programmes... I'm Eva."

"Nice to meet you."

Eva wandered away from the window and sat down on one of the seats. She put her feet up on the small coffee table that the seats encircled.

Damien sat opposite her.

"So, were you a fan?"

She let out a tiny laugh. "No."

"Oh... So... What did you do, before all of this? And... How old are you?" he asked, poised for a response.

"I was a student. At Durham. Studying law," she said following his eyes with her own. "I'm twenty-one."

"Law?... That's quite heavy."

"I enjoyed it. I didn't mind the work. Or the reading."

Damien's eyes drifted across Eva's chest. She saw it. He looked across at the small kitchenette.

"At least we can make food here. We should be okay for a while."

"We have to move from here as quickly as we can."

Damien was momentarily taken aback. "How quickly will that be?"

"I don't know. Until that big group move on."

"How do you know they will?"

Eva shook her head slightly. "I don't."

"And... If they don't?"

"Then the party will probably get bigger."

"How do you know that?"

"I read a lot of history books. It's siege warfare," she said.

"I don't think they see it that way."

"Then they'll get bored of waiting."

"So, why do we have to get away from here 'as quickly as we can', then?"

"Do you want to stay here?"

"I... I mean... I don't... --not want to stay, for a bit... While we're actually safe, inside, warm, sheltered..."

"We shouldn't stay any longer than we need to."

Later – 9:14pm.

Damien sat by the window, leaning on the back of a chair he had moved. He watched the infected massing and spreading on the street below. The streetlights had blinked on an hour or so ago and lit the area in a sickly orange glow. Creepy, stretched shadows flickered on the tarmac.

"They don't seem to be moving on."

Eva stood in the kitchenette. She was cooking stir-fry noodles with chicken and vegetables in a Thai sauce. "Let's just hope they do... Dinner's ready."

Damien crossed to the kitchenette as Eva passed him a bowl, and they moved to the seating area and sat down. Damien forked some of the noodles into his mouth and wiped his chin with a serviette.

"How long do you think the power will last?" Damien asked.

"I don't know... If there's no-one around to man the power-stations, then... I don't know," she replied.

Eva pulled her legs onto the seat and crossed them. She placed the bowl on the cradle formed with her crossed ankles and rested the fork on the side. The bowl steamed, swirling into the air in front of Eva's face.

Damien ate, but stopped when another thought popped into his brain. "Do you think we should try to find other survivors in Newcastle? We're fairly close."

"I passed by, walking along the train-tracks," she began, "and there seemed to be more infected near there."

"But, we were lucky... Maybe others might've been?"

"We were lucky," she agreed.

"Shouldn't we try to help?"

"Yes. Maybe. I don't know. No?" she paused, stabbing a green bean and eating it. "Most people will have to fend for themselves, until they get so desperate they venture outside."

"We've been outside for the most-part of this last week."

"I know that, Damien. But... Did you go into any cities or towns that were heavily populated?"

"No."

"Then that's why you're alive. No other reason."

"So the people in the cities are most-likely dead or infected?"

"I don't know. Probably. It would seem that way..."

"So why have you agreed to go to London with me?"

Their eyes met.

"I have no idea."

Three days later. Ponteland – 2:03pm.

Damien stood in the unisex toilet. He used a bar of soap and a wet flannel to wash his body. He had taken his shirt off and had soaked it yesterday to clean it, but still had his trousers on and they were feeling a bit sticky. He could not help stopping and staring at himself in the mirror. He was safe for now. He was alive for now. But he saw something in his eyes that he could not explain, nor had he ever seen in himself before. He judged himself. He scrutinised his own face. He stared into the deep, black wells at the centres of his eyes. He blinked and splashed water on his face.

A knock came from the door.

"Come in," he offered.

Eva entered. She shyly looked at the ground when she saw Damien was shirtless, then it disappeared and she looked at his reflection in the mirror.

"What's up?"

"Those things outside... --those people... --they're going."

"Three fucking days! Thank god!... What now?"

"It means we're moving. In twenty minutes."

"What?!"

"We're going. You haven't got time to do your moisturising and beauty regimen, Damien..."

"Oh, come on, that's not fair..."

One day later. Near Hexham – 7:32pm.
Damien and Eva stopped near the small clubhouse of the Tynedale Golf Club. They had been pushed West out of Ponteland, and found a dirt-bike during their escape. Eva had ridden with Damien hanging onto her back, wearing her backpack and clinging onto his and her bags. Many dozens of the infected had marred all of their routes, except West.

They had crossed the River Tyne before reaching Hexham. They had found the Golf Club by travelling along the south-bank of the river.

"Here should be okay for the night."

"Agreed," Damien added.

"Keep your eyes open."

"Yep."

The next day. Inside the Golf Club – 8:01am.
Damien watched Eva move to one of the windows. Spots of rain had started to speckle the window-pane. They had settled in a corner room with two windows on each external wall. There was a small kitchen next door and bathrooms across the hall. The room had a six-person table in one corner, pushed against the wall with stacked chairs next to it. There was a selection of padded seats that they had moved into the room to make beds with.

Within minutes a torrent of rain had begun to fall.

Eva looked across the golf course, as thousands of sheets of rain dropped from the sky. The distance she could see diminished quickly, as mist and dark grey cloud blotted out most of the daylight.

"Shit day," Damien said. "Shit weather."

"Yeah."

Damien sat on three soft-cushioned seats that he had pushed together to create a makeshift bed. He sat up and ruffled his hair. He rubbed his chin, felt the stubble thickening. "Maybe I should shave."

Eva glanced at him. She said nothing.

"I think I'll shave," he said with a nod.

Eva returned to her seat at the table and ate Cornflakes with long-life milk.

Later – 6:15pm.
Damien and Eva had covered the windows to black-out any light that could be visible from the outside and moved four small table-lamps into the centre of the room.

Damien had made pasta and sauce.

They ate in silence.

Outside, the rain poured. It hammered at the glass and the roof above their heads.

Damien studied a one-metre square map they had found in the clubhouse's office. He had the map spread across the floor and used a blue marker-pen to plot the course he had taken so far. He used a green marker to plot Eva's journey as well. He stopped and looked at Eva; she sat at the table reading a copy of *Fight Club* by Chuck Palahniuk.

Damien remembered Lynn Oakley's face, contorted with fear.

"I saw a woman," he said. "On the news. Before I left Edinburgh. She was in a news-room."

Eva placed her finger in the book and closed it. She turned to look at Damien.

"That was why I was travelling South," he admitted.

Eva regarded Damien for a moment. "To rescue her?" she asked with a hint of mockery.

"I don't know... Yes."

"If she's lasted this long, I doubt she'll still be in a television studio."

"But I still wanna try."

Eva furrowed her brow. "Why?"

"She's the only other person I've seen alive, apart from you."

"There will be others."

"How can you be so sure?"

"There has to be."

One day later. On the intersection between the M6 and the A69, Carlisle.

Damien and Eva rode mountain-bikes along the grass verge that ran down the side of the A69. They pedalled up the incline that led to the motorway.

The sun shone in a cloudless sky.

Damien saw an electricity pylon further along the road. "Hey," he called out to Eva, who was about four metres ahead of him. He pedalled a little faster.

She looked back at Damien and they slowed to a stop.

"What? Why are we stopping?"

"Wait here... I'll be back in a sec."

"Why? We're out in the open!"

"Just wait here. Please."

Damien jogged along the road and Eva held his bike. She glanced down the road behind them. There was no movement anywhere along the road.

Damien clambered up the first struts of the pylon until he reached a ring of barbed-wire. He wrapped a blanket over the wire, climbed over it, then started to scale the lattice tower, his fingers gripping the steel tightly. He reached the first arms that grew from the sides of the pylon. He found good footing and hooked his arm through one of the lattices. With his free hand he used binoculars to scan the Southern length of the motorway. Three infected wandered aimlessly about four hundred metres away. He swung the sight around to the Northern length of the motorway. He instantly saw movement. He pinched the focus dial between his fingers and the six-lane highway came into perfect clarity.

He saw John Ramsay and Piotr Hoogestern, Donald Etheridge, Jason Macpherson and Ella Lanning, Grant Sands and Mitchell Yates, Katya Volovaski and Jane Stapleton. They walked in single-file down the centre of the motorway in the middle-distance.

Damien saw that John had a pair of binoculars and was looking straight at him.

John and Damien waved at each other.

A little later.
John and his group walked up the motorway's off-ramp. Damien and Eva stood at the top.

As the two groups met, John shook Damien's hand, then Piotr shook it. Eva was immediately smothered in a hug from Ella and Katya.

"Whoa, you're Damien Flynn!" Jason exulted.

"Hi, yeah," Damien beamed.

"I used to watch *Temple,* back in Canada!" Mitchell announced, shaking Damien's arm, gripping his hand, then giving him a short, tight hug.

"So, where've you come from?" John asked.

"I started out in Edinburgh. Eva started in Durham... We tried to get into Newcastle, but it was totally overrun. More of those people on the streets in the city, and leaving there too..."

"Populated areas aren't safe," Eva added.

"I agree. That's what we've found," John said. "But, there are more survivors in the cities..."

"Where're you heading?" Damien asked.
"South... To London."
Damien glanced at Eva, who was already looking at him.
"I know that sounds a little like a contradiction... But London is where we have to go!"
"That's where I wanna go!" Damien asserted.
"Good," John said. "Great."

A little later.
The group made camp in an old, disused factory-building. They had settled in a large concrete box-room. They put out blankets, air-beds and camping-mattresses, then got into sleeping-bags and readied for bed. In the centre of the room stacks of bowls and cutlery sat in a collection beside a battery-powered camping lantern.

"At least we can all try and get one good night's sleep. The place is locked-up for the night..." John announced to everyone. He looked around at each of their faces. Damien saw that John's comment had put all of their minds at ease.

John crossed to Eva and Damien, who pitched their beds a little way from the others.
"One good night's sleep is better'n nothing," John said.
"Agreed," Eva replied.
"We're going to have to make the most out of them, when we can... We've managed to be safe every night so far," Damien added. "How about you?"
John nodded. "Our experience has been similar... It depends a lot on the place. Proximity to main-roads, train-lines and the areas that are most heavily populated."
Eva studied John's face.
"What do you expect to find in London, John?" Damien asked.
John looked at them in turn, shook his head a little, then addressed them soberly, "I hope there is hope."
Eva smiled at John.
He walked back to his sleeping-bag and picked up one of his axes. He walked away and sat on a small stack of wooden-pallets.
Damien nodded in John's direction.
"Do you know who he is?"
"John Ramsay... He's an author."
"Yeah!" Damien beamed. "I thought he was a recluse. Never left his home. Hid himself away."
"That's what I'd read too."
"You know a lot, Eva, don't you?"
"I'm going to sleep."

Later.
Everyone slept soundly. Except John, who kept-watch. He sat on the stack of wooden-pallets. He stared intensely at the doorway at the other end of the factory-room. He drank whiskey, a tiny-sip at a time.

At the other side of the room, Piotr sat awake. He read a book balanced on his lap, using a small Maglite torch that hung on a string around his neck to see the text.

Damien stirred and awoke. He saw John was awake, and shuffled out of his sleeping-bag. He stood and crossed to him.

John heard Damien moving, but did not move to look in his direction. He took another tiny sip, as Damien sat down next to him. John offered Damien the bottle, but he gestured: no.

"So... What is the actual plan, John?" Damien asked sceptically.
"London – that's the plan..." John replied. "Actually."
"Good, good... That is good... That makes me feel happy," he said in a deadpan tone. He cleared his throat. "I saw a woman, Lynn something, on TV... In a television news studio in London. Eleven days ago..."

John took another sip and said nothing.

"I want to go there, John, and broadcast a message," Damien stated. "We can help people."

John nodded, "Okay."

"I want to make sure who-ever is left alive, stays that way, stays away from the infected... If there's a message... If we can try to help people... I think we can all make a difference. Help people."

"I didn't think you were known for helping people."

"I didn't think you ever left your house!... I want to get that message out-there, John!"

"Okay," John replied blankly. He stood slowly. "It's Mitchell's and Jason's turn to keep watch."

John left Damien on the pallets. He crossed to Mitchell and woke him with a few gentle shoves. Mitchell came awake slowly and looked up at John, sleepily.

"My turn, boss?" Mitchell murmured.

"Yeah. Wake up Jason and make sure you both stay awake." Damien returned to his sleeping-bag and climbed inside.

Later.
Mitchell and Jason sat beside the wooden-pallets, leaning against them.

"...I didn't think I'd see Damien Flynn alive and in person," Mitchell said, "in my whole life."

"Me neither," Jason beamed. "It's pretty cool."

"It's fucking cool," Mitchell laughed.

Jason laughed. "You don't sound like you swear a lot, Mitchell...?"

"I don't. I didn't. It's fun. I never used to cuss at all," he said, then laughed again. "But, what-the-fuck!"

"It's the right time to start," Jason laughed.

"You're not wrong."

"So... What was your favourite episode of *Temple*?" Jason asked eagerly.

Later – 6:23am.
Outside there was a beautiful sunrise, glowing reds and pinks and blues. Clouds coasted across the horizon, but above the factory-building the air was a calm pale blue.

Inside, the group gathered the sleeping-gear and packed it into bags.

Damien walked out of one of the back-rooms, zipping his fly and wiping his hands on his trousers. He walked to Eva, who sat near their things, packing them away in her backpack and Damien's.

"This group is going to London... We can stay with them... We should be okay..."

Eva nodded. "Okay."

"Well, for now... If you get any compulsion to wander off with me, that's cool too."

"Good to know, Damien."

Damien beamed a smile at her.

Fourteen days later. At the graveyard.
John stood at the head of the group, now thirty-eight people strong, including Damien and Eva, Piotr, Ella, Grant and Mitchell, Katya, Jane and Gillian, Gemma and many others. One of the other survivors, a man called Leo, hovered shadily at the back of the group. They stood a distance behind John, sheepishly looking at each other.

John's legs buckled under his weight, and he fell to his knees in front of the graves of his wife and son, and started to cry.

"I'm sorry," John whispered through gasps and cries.

The group watched John, and nervously waited for someone to say something. But nobody stopped John from crying. The group bunched twenty metres from their leader, watching, waiting. In silence.

Damien looked at Piotr. He shrugged. Damien shook his head.

Gillian looked around the group, trying to read everyone's reactions. She smiled inwardly.

Eva watched John sympathetically and bit her bottom lip.

John cried uncontrollably. Through his tears, he said: "What do I do?!.. What am I supposed to do?!" His hands knotted into balls, gripping tightly, fingernails digging into the soft meat. Tears fell from his eyes, as the clouds shifted overhead, pointing rays of sunlight across the graveyard.

As if shocked by lightning, John pulled himself together, wiped away his tears, snorted, and cleared his throat. He stood, suddenly looking stable and determined. He gritted his teeth.

"I'm okay now. I know what to do."

Three infected appeared ahead of them, and charged towards the group. John grabbed his axe, before anyone else had time to react.

Damien and Piotr were the first to stop watching John, and reacted immediately, rushing towards the first infected, when a car sped into the graveyard, driving down the road to the crematorium.

The car skidded, then ran the second infected over, sending the body rolling through the air like a ragdoll into a gravestone, shattering its backbone and killing it instantly.

Relief flooded over John for a millisecond. And the rest of the group.

Damien and Piotr momentarily hesitated at seeing the car, stunned, but quickly-turned, as the first infected tackled them both to the ground.

John sprang into action and ran at the third infected, looking wild and ferocious, when the driver of the car and the passenger jumped out: Sergeant Danny Newton and Private Evan Hastings.

Gillian and the rest of the group watched, frozen, in stunned-silence.

Newton, armed with a silenced-pistol, shot the infected, splattering its brains. It tripped on the edge of a grave-plaque and tumbled to a stop at John's feet.

Damien and Piotr beat the other infected to death, away from the sight of the group behind a double-gravestone. They stopped when they noticed the men were dressed in soldiers' uniforms. They both breathed a sigh of relief, in unison.

A little later.
Newton and Hastings were with the group. They huddled near the car amongst a large group of huge headstones. John sat at the back of the group, away from the others. Damien and Piotr sat near Newton, and Eva and Gillian sat on Hastings side.

"We saw you walking along the motorway yesterday," Newton said. "We did try to intercept you-all earlier, but we ran into a little trouble... We have made a temporary-base in a police-station which has a training academy and a hotel next door to it... It's in the east-end of London."

"So, are you the army?" Gillian asked, sitting with her back straightened.

"We are... Not officially speaking."

"What does that mean?" Grant asked.

"Well. There's nothing left..."

A rumble of fear and panic swam through the group.

"We were in the army... There are some of us left. And we've been trying to help and gather other survivors... With your help we could–..."

"With our help?!" Gillian interrupted. "What help can we offer the army?!"

"Well," Newton stuttered. "You've made it this far."

"So?!"

"So?... So, you-all worked together to get this far... We have to stick together! And help others... If we can... Everybody has a skill, or set of skills, that will be useful."

John said nothing throughout this exchange. He listened as questions and answers rattled back and forth. Nobody seemed convinced, nobody's fears were allayed, nobody felt safe. Gillian eyed John from the other side of the huddle.

"How? How did you find us? Do you have a helicopter, or something?" Ella asked.

"No. We don't. We have a few people in the tallest buildings around London with telescopes and binoculars," Newton said, furrowing his brow.

Private Foost and Tetsuo Katsushika emerged from the road to the crematorium. They approached and joined the group, circling around the side to stand next to Newton.

Hastings stood and crossed to them, taking them into an aside.

"How's the transport?" Hastings asked.

"We've found a bus with some petrol in the tank... Bright and Kara are with it, coming to the entrance of the graveyard," Foost replied, when static came through on his walkie-talkie. "Excuse me a sec."

Piotr and Damien watched Foost walk away, pressing the walkie-talkie to his ear.

Tetsuo sat down on a headstone behind Hastings and Newton.

"Are there any – or do you know of any other safe-havens?" Gillian asked sternly.

"No others... None yet... None that we know of..."

Other members of the group asked more questions, without getting any solid answers from Newton. Gillian noticed this and watched them closely. John sat, listening but not participating.

Damien glanced at Gillian and stepped to the side of the group with Piotr.

"That woman is going to cause a lot of trouble."

"I thought the same thing," Piotr replied with a nod.

"John's gonna need to keep a cap on her."

"If he cares anymore," Piotr said and nodded at John, who rubbed his whiskery-beard and then massaged his temples. "He seems to have run out of energy."

"Or will-power."

"What about any other place outside of London?!" Gillian shouted at Newton.

Damien left the group and followed Foost, who walked away along the road.

Piotr ambled after them.

Before Foost had started talking into the walkie-talkie, Damien asked, "Where exactly are you based?... I'm not staying with you-lot... I'm going to go to a television studio to broadcast a message... It's going to tell everyone to go to one place..."

Foost eyed Damien for a long moment.

"Really?"

"Yeah."

"You? The actor?" Foost said with a laugh.

"I survived this far."

"Seriously?" Foost mocked. "Seriously?"

"Yes," Damien said sharply. "I want to help."

"Then, if you're being serious, tell everyone to go to Pickering Police-Station... We will try to meet them on their way there. We've been scouting around London the last week or so... And the out-posts might see others... One of us will see them coming..."

Damien nodded and smiled. "Good, then. Thank you, I suppose..."

Foost turned and walked away leaving Damien behind. He tried the walkie-talkie.

"Don? Come in, over..."

A strange static noise sounded from the speaker.

Foost opened the walkie-talkie and looked at a small screen displaying the signal in reception-bars. The bars showed there was a full signal, but no reception, no ability to broadcast or receive.

A little later.

Damien and Piotr walked passed Eva and Gillian, away from the group.

Eva watched them pass.

"This feels like a tiny amount of relief after all of this..." Gillian said to Eva. "But not enough."

Eva nodded, placating Gillian.

Foost passed them, walking toward the group. He took Newton aside, he said: "Something is blocking our radio-reception... I can't get through to Don... Or Marc..."

At the far back of the group, Kara and Hastings spoke guardedly.

A little later.
Hastings stood with Kara away from the group, who were eating sandwiches, when Newton joined them.
    "What're you two talking about?" Newton asked.
    Hastings and Kara shared a look.
    "We've decided to stay around here for a little while and put up more signs... Try to help people find you..."
    Newton stared at them, deflated. "That's probably a good idea... But... We might have a problem with our radios."

A little later.
Piotr helped Damien to climb a brick-wall at the side of a residential road.
    "You think we'll get as far as the TV station, just as you and I?"
    Damien looked at him, shrugged, and said frankly, "We've gotta try."
    They trudged on down the road.

CHAPTER 16 - WEALTH - The Bastion of Spitbank Fort

VICTOR CONWAY, 60 year old Englishman – walked out of his kitchen; a vast room equipped with every modern appliance available to those with an extraordinary amount of money and inclination. It resembled a professional kitchen with several cookers, ovens, refrigerators, freezers, hot-plates and every hi-tech food appliance worth using.

He strode into his living-space: an enormous room with a curved-wall that formed the outer-defences and perimeter of the building; The Bastion of Spitbank Fort, in the Solent, 1 mile off the coast of Portsmouth, near the Isle of Wight – Victor's immaculate, technologically-advanced and finely-designed private home and dwelling. He had a formidable receding-hairline, silver and white hair ringing his skull, dusty-grey eyebrows and silvery stubble. He had a deeply interesting face with dark amethyst-purple eyes, lightly hooded with wrinkled lids, a long, ridged nose and broad cheekbones. His mouth, surrounded by white whiskers, was serious and down-turned. He was below average height, but a stocky and imposing figure, with big hands and feet. He spoke with a deep, bassy and melodious quality to his voice. He wore a crisp white shirt, black braces crossed over his back, grey suit-trousers and smart, oiled black shoes; he wore a custom-made SEIKO Arctura Kinetic Chronograph wristwatch in platinum with a white face, several platinum rings on each hand, and a gold chain around his neck. He had eaten alone; a bowl of porridge with maple syrup, and a bacon, lettuce and crispy-onion sandwich with traditional Swiss mayonnaise.

He walked to one of the many windows and stared out to sea, across the English Channel.

He squinted in the sunlight, shading his eyes with his arm, seeing a freighter pass by.

Victor sipped from a tumbler of whiskey and ice, as someone entered the room – GABRIEL KROEDEN, 49 year old Englishman of German descent. He had short sandy-blonde hair, swept forward across a widow's-peak then parted. He had analytical, deep olive-green eyes that never remained still. For his age he looked young and was attractive, quite statuesque and impressively athletic. He had a bright, honest face; a thin pointed nose, high cheekbones, a slim mouth and a wide, sharp jaw. He was tall and imposing, but managed this by standing farther away from the people he spoke to. He had a deep, gravelly voice that boomed, even at a whisper. He wore a black tie knotted over a black shirt, a tailored three-piece black suit and smart, shiny black shoes; he had a custom-made wristwatch that looked like a black, dead computer-screen.

"Hello, Mr Conway," Gabriel said. "My name is Kroeden. Gabriel Kroeden... We have already met before..."

"Oh?" Victor said, watching the sea.

"In Seville, three years ago..."

"Hmm..."

"I wanted to come here personally–..."

"To what end?" Victor interrupted.

"I wanted to know what your plans were... --in weeks to come..."

Victor said, "I will be staying here, in my own home..."

"There will be extreme dangers in the future, Mr Conway... Things will definitely change... And depending on what choices you make, or perhaps what side you choose, you may have to watch a lot of people suffer... And suffer yourself."

Gabriel stared intensely at the back of Victor's head.

Victor's eyes never left the sea. "If I looked at you, Gabriel, I would go along with you... But I don't want to do that," he growled. "I just want to stay here."

Before Gabriel exited, he placed a small leather satchel, the size of a VHS cassette, on an table set against one of the interior walls. "Be careful, then... It may be prudent to make sure all of your staff are on the mainland, in eleven days time," he whispered.

Victor nodded, and Gabriel exited.

Sunlight broke out between two clouds, beaming down on Spitbank Fort.

Victor finished his whiskey in two large gulps.

After a few minutes, Victor heard a helicopter taking off and flying away from the structure.

He leaned out of the window and saw a black dot disappearing into the sunlight.

Victor crossed to the table, to the satchel, and opened it: it was a syringe-kit. He took out a vial of solution, with a label reading: Immunisation 4.0.1. and attached it to a syringe-gun that was enclosed in the satchel. He rolled his shirt-sleeve above the elbow of his left arm and injected himself. The syringe-gun made a *pfffsht* sound as he squeezed the trigger and the dose fired into Victor's vein. He grimaced as the needle punctured the skin.

After a moment, Victor picked up the satchel. He moved back to the window and dropped the syringe-gun, vial and the satchel out of the window. They were carried by the light wind and drifted away from the building and *plopped* in the water, sinking and vanishing from sight.

Victor pressed a small, emerald-coloured plastic button that looked like an alarm on the wall near the window. Moments later, Victor's butler – CLAUDE CADÍ, 66 year old Englishman of French descent – appeared at the doorway to the room. He had glossy black hair, slicked back over his head, and a small, greying box-cut beard. He was tall and lean with sloped shoulders, long arms and large, ape-sized hands. His face was grave and serious, deeply defined by long wrinkles and creases at the sides and under his dark-grey eyes. He wore a classic butler's outfit with a sleek, black tailcoat, light-grey waistcoat, a white wing-collared shirt, a black tie, morning trousers and smart, shiny black shoes; he had a vintage Cartier wristwatch around his right wrist. He cleared his throat, alerting Victor of his presence.

Claude carried another glass of whiskey on a tray, perfectly balanced on one arm, which he presented to Victor.

"Thank you," Victor said and took the glass. He sipped it, idling back to the window.

"Have you decided on lunch, yet, sir?"

"Not yet. I ate a little while ago...."

"The chef said that we have a large selection today of seafood and shellfish..."

"Good," Victor said vaguely. He took another sip. "One thing... Ensure every one of the staff has left the island by the end of this week... --back to the mainland... Including you... It will be just a temporary-butler and I, for two or three weeks... Make sure all of the larders and fridges are fully-stocked before then..."

"Yes, sir," Claude said with a nod, and exited.

Ten days later. At night.
An infected, dressed in a modern butler-outfit, lumbered down the living-space, with blood dripping from its mouth and nose. The infected hacked and coughed, spitting and spraying blood across the carpet in disarrayed polka dots.

Victor retreated rapidly in front of the infected, pacing backwards, keeping his eyes locked on it.

The infected made a *gaaah* noise, stumbling forward, splashes of blood dripping from the corner of its mouth.

Victor sighed, grabbing a vintage golf-club from a holder, and circled the infected as it strained to follow him. He swung and smashed it across the temple, sending it face-first to the floor. Victor swung up wide, then hit it. Then again and again and again and again.

He stepped back, looking at his temporary-butler's body, an expression of coldness etched into his features. He looked around the room, trying to locate something. He took a huge gulp of air, then placed the golf-club on the floor next to the infected. He exhaled slowly, looking at the room, feeling his heart beating hard inside his body. He picked up a glass of whiskey and sipped it.

One week later.
Victor stood alone, washing his underwear in one of the kitchen sinks in his vast kitchen. He listened to classical music that played through a sound-system linked with a wrist-watch-device, strapped to his arm next to his watch, to digital-receivers in each room of the building. The wrist-watch and the digital-receivers were connected through the house-system and showed the link with synchronised blinking neon-green LED lights on each device.

Victor finished, hanging the boxer shorts on a Victorian, six-lath pulley-strung clothes-airer that had been erected over one long sink. He dried his hands on a towel that had been folded next the sink.

He entered his living-space and the music followed him, dimming to nothing in the kitchen, and rising where-ever he moved.

Victor lit a cigar, a Colorado Claro, and blew smoke through one of the many windows, then manoeuvred a Celestron NexStar SLT 102 telescope into place. He looked through it, adjusting the lenses. He could not magnify far enough to see the details of Portsmouth's sea-front, so he crossed to another window, to another telescope exactly the same as the other, and looked through the eye-piece. He stared out across the English Channel. He moved the telescope, making a sweep of the sea. He could not see anything from his place.

As Victor walked away from the second telescope, he just-missed seeing a sailboat coursing into view.

Victor crossed to and sat in a large, leather armchair smoking his cigar. Beside the armchair's arms were two small side-tables; one had a bottle of McCutcheon whiskey and a half-filled glass of ice, and on the other table there was an ash-tray with a part-smoked Claro in it, and a tablet-computer.

Victor's head rolled on his shoulders and he stopped and stared emotionlessly at the ceiling.

Later. At night.
All of the interior lights had been switched off, or had not been switched on. The security display on the tablet-computer showed no movement anywhere inside the building, and that the light-levels were set to Off.

Victor slept in the armchair, snoring lightly.

Suddenly a light-beam shone through one of the vacant-windows, where there was not a telescope in place in front of it, awakening Victor instantly.

He sat a moment, disoriented, but staring at the windows, until the light flashed in again from the darkness.

He leapt to his feet and rushed to the window.

He saw Clive Meadway's sailboat.

Victor dashed to a long table where he had arranged many pieces of equipment: torches, flares, three gas-masks, boxes of matches, several diving- and hunting-knives, three other Seiko Kinetic wrist-watches, two first-aid kits and two small-handle axes. He snatched a torch and rushed to the window. He pressed the button and a beam of light sprang out of the window-hole, pointing straight out.

Clive and Melodie gasped.

"Did you see that?!" Roy shouted.

"Wow!" Harmony said breathlessly.

Barney eyed the window.

"Was that somebody? Do you think there's someone inside?"

"I don't know."

"I hope so... I hope that was someone..."

"I really hope so!"

Victor scooped up the tablet-computer and frantically but efficiently tapped the screen. The lights inside the structure all started to brighten. He pressed several more commands: a closed-circuit camera with a spotlight on its side came on, illuminating the sailboat, and showing the other survivors on the display-screen. He could see each of them; eight of them in total. Victor's eyes skipped across each face, every one looking up at the camera, squinting in the glare of the spotlight: Three people similar to his age, two younger adults, and three children.

Light started to flood the side of the sailboat that faced the building. Other spotlights and floodlights began to glow. Light flared up from inside the structure.

Victor moved to the window.

Clive flashed the window with the torch-beam again, seeing Victor's shape in the frame. "Sorry," he gushed, and moved the beam away from Victor's eyes. "Hello..."

The light, attached to the wall above their heads, shone brightly, making Victor almost indistinguishable behind the glare. "Good evening," he said, his voice booming down on the small party on the sailboat.

A little later.
Victor stood on a covered platform above a squat concrete mooring. He watched as a motorised-dinghy brought the first group to the mooring; the first four, and Clive at the back steering.

"Hello, again," Clive said sheepishly.

"Hello."

"Be back with the rest in a minute," Clive added and moved forward to help Melodie, Evie, Harmony and Annabel out of the dinghy and onto the mooring-platform. Victor helped them from the platform above.

Clive manoeuvred the dinghy back to the sailboat.

"Thank God," Melodie exclaimed. "Thank God you're still alive, and... And, that you would help us!" she beamed and gave Victor the briefest of hugs.

"You seemed in-need," Victor stated firmly.

"Oh, we are!" Harmony shouted. "We are, we are!"

"I am glad I can be of some help."

"Thank you, so much!"

Clive returned quickly with Barney, Roy and Roman, as Melodie and Harmony took the mooring-ropes and lashed the dinghy to the platform. Victor stared at Roman for a moment when he thought nobody would notice. Barney took it in, and helped himself onto the mooring-platform.

"Please," Victor began, turning to the structure with a gesture. "Come inside."

A little while later.
The group settled in the kitchen. Victor made some food for them all: a seafood pasta dish in a large pot with mashed potatoes and sea-kale.

Clive pulled a map out of his pocket and placed it on the kitchen-countertop. "We could push on to the Isle of Wight in the next day or so, I reckon."

"That would be sensible," Roy agreed.

"Could we not all stay here?" Harmony asked.

Clive shot her a look, then shook his head.

"There is only a limited amount of food here... I am sorry..." Victor answered.

"We should not impose," Clive stated firmly.

Roy agreed with a nod.

Roman watched Victor from the edge of the group.

Barney spied them all from the other side of the room.

"I can assure you, it is not that you would be imposing... I would happily say you could all stay, but there really isn't much food... I was the butler here, my master died a week ago," he said with a cough on the word 'master'. He looked at them each in turn. "That was when we lost contact with the mainland..."

"Oh my!" Melodie said.

"So, you're alone here?" Roman asked.

"Yes. Just me."

"I'm very sorry to hear that," Clive said.

"Yeah, really sorry," Roy added softly.

Later.
Victor showed his guests to some bedrooms.

"Thank you, Victor... For your courtesy and hospitality... Especially in a time like this," Clive said, and shook Victor's hand. His brow furrowed and he looked tense.

"Yes."

Victor left the others and went to his armchair and sat.

Later.
A noise awoke Victor from his sleep. He rose and stalked through his home.

He saw Roman disappearing down one of the spiral staircases that led to the lower levels of the structure.

He followed Roman to a large telecoms-room.

Roman listened to the end of a pre-recorded message: it was Marc Sheridan's police message, recorded shortly after his conversation with Don Clement. "...Go to Pickering Police Station... Be safe and keep your eyes open..." Once the message ended, Roman smashed all of the equipment with the back of a fire-axe. He smashed everything in the room, destroying irreparably all of the computers, servers, routers and monitors.

As Roman exited, Victor stepped out of the shadows, and followed him back upstairs.

Roman smiled to himself, knowing he was being followed, and walked into Victor's living-space. He took out a small test-tube that was filled with blood. He thumbed off the test-tube's seal, when Victor appeared behind him holding a black Beretta 92 pistol outstretched in front of him.

"I've seen you once before, Roman..."

Roman turned, half smiling, half sneering. He said, "I know, Victor... At one of the meetings... I told them, but they sent me here anyway..."

"Is that so?"

"What? That I was sent?"

"Yes," Victor answered coldly.

"Then why did I still come? Why would I still come?... They sent me here because I would know your face... I'd be able to identify you," he spat. Then Roman poured the blood down his throat. He smiled madly at Victor, his eyes bugging. "None of that matters now!"

Barney stepped out of the shadows behind Roman, as Victor aimed the pistol at the invader to his home.

"You won't get far, Roman."

Roman convulsed as the virus took him. He coughed-up blood, as his skin reddened then went ghostly-pale. He stared at Victor, shaking. The smile had left his face. He dropped to his knees, shaking. His fingernails dug into the carpet, then the infected launched at Victor, who fired on him.

In Clive's bedroom.
The gunshots rang out and snapped both Clive and Melodie awake. Evie and Annabel, who slept on the other side of the room, on beds that had been moved from one of the other bedrooms, sprang awake next to their grandparents.

In the living-room.
Victor fired again, and the infected Roman fell down. The bullets had knocked the infected back, and the final one had taken the side of his skull off.

The body hit the carpet, gushing blood.

Victor looked to Barney, who looked back, emotionless.

"Sorry you had to see that," Victor whispered.

Barney shrugged.

In Clive's bedroom.
Clive quickly pulled clothes on and ran into the corridor outside his bedroom holding a dented and well-worn cricket-bat.

"Don't worry, I'll find out what's going on!" he shouted, darting along the corridor.

In the living-room.
Barney looked across at the body.

"You know exactly what's going on, don't you?"

Before Victor could answer, his lips parted to speak; Clive emerged from the corridor and stopped in the doorway. The cricket-bat was gripped tightly in his hands. He saw Roman's body at once. Clive looked at Victor, and then his gun, and then saw Barney.

"What's going on, Victor?!... Barney? What're you doing out of bed?"

"That man was insane, and he wanted to kill all of us," Barney blurted.

Clive stared at Barney, trying to read him, when Melodie and Harmony appeared and shrieked at the sight of the body. Blood pooled around it, soaking into the thick-woven Persian rug underneath it.

"What's going on?"

"Is that Roman?"

"Oh my God! Is he dead?!"

"Everyone should get back to bed, I'll clear this up and explain a few things in the morning... Tomorrow."

"Yes," Clive agreed. "Let's all get back to bed... Barney?"

Barney started to join the others, slowly moving to follow. Clive put his arm around his grandson's shoulder. "What exactly did you see, Barn'?"

"Nothing... I wanted a glass of water. So, I went through there. I saw Roman being infected... He'd done it to himself."

"What d'you mean? He killed himself?"

"By using the blood like a poison."

"Is that all? Is that everything?"

"Yeah..."

They reached their rooms and Clive watched Barney enter his, before joining his wife and granddaughters.

Victor stared at Roman's body. He gritted his teeth then crossed the room to the far wall. Victor opened a cupboard, then unlocked a large inner-cupboard. He took a biochemical-suit from a rail where several others hung in a row. He put the suit on and crossed to Roman's body.

The next day. In the kitchen. In the morning.
Victor stood in front of the others. All of their eyes were fixed on him.

"...And after he smashed the communications-room, he told me he wanted everyone dead, and infected himself, somehow... I suspect he wanted to infect everyone in here, as Barney said..."

"He destroyed your communications-room? You had a communications-room? Seriously?... Is there any link to the mainland? Is there another radio?" Roy demanded.

Before Victor could answer, Harmony asked, "Is there a phone?"

"There was a message on the police radio band-width that Roman did not want us to hear... But I had already listened to it," Victor said.

"What did it say?" Annabel asked flatly.

"It said to go to Pickering Police Station in London... I wasn't going to go, as I thought I was safe here," he replied.

"You should come with us," she said.

Victor looked at Annabel, who was staring at him intensely. He said nothing.

Melodie turned to Clive who glanced at Roy, then they all beamed at Victor.

"We can't impose any longer, but you are more-than welcome to come with us," Clive offered.

Victor walked to a bookcase and pushed it sideways with a groan, revealing a hidden stairwell. He turned to the group. "You can stay two more days. But, when you leave... You'll need my help... Once you are all safe, I will come back here on my own... I have all the weapons and supplies you will need to get to London."

Roy spoke up, before Victor had entered the stairwell, he asked, "What did your boss do for a living, Victor?"

Victor smiled, he said, "He was in defence."

Two days later. At night.
Victor steered the group in a ten-man dinghy, whipping the outboard-motor this way and that to keep the direction straight. The dinghy had looked to Barney like the type of small boat that the SAS used in covert operations. Clive stared into the darkness at the front of the boat, listening to the slicing and *sloshing* of the water.

Rain poured from the sky, as it had all day. Clouds merged and swirled above them, cutting out all starlight. The journey soaked them all, but was relatively calm travelling in Portsmouth Harbour.

Victor cut the engine a short distance from the shore, and let the low waves bring the dinghy in. It took several minutes to retrieve the oars from underneath the passengers' seats and drop the tips into the water.

Barney and Roy helped to guide the boat in using oars on either side.

A little later.
Clive helped Victor out of the boat and joined the rest of the group. They stood in a loose pack on a large industrial dock with a private mooring. Warehouses surrounded the dock, tall and domineering. They were isolated from the rest the of docks, cut off by twelve-foot tall chain-link fences. The scene looked gloomy and grim; sheets of rain hitting each of them, splashing the dock and hitting the surf.

"Where to now, Victor?" Roy asked in a whisper.

Rain soaked all of their clothes, dripping in puddles at their feet.

"Here."

Victor walked to a doorway into one of the many warehouses around them. He swiped his watch on a non-descript digital-receiver, and both of the neon-green LED lights blinked in synch, then the door unlocked with a *clunk* and popped open two inches.

Victor tugged at the door, then swung it wide, and he walked inside.

The group watched, slightly impressed.

Clive looked at Victor suspiciously, but entered, leading the others inside and out of the driving rain.

"Come this way," Victor called from the darkness of a long corridor that led away from them.

They followed, and the door hermetically-sealed behind them with a suppressed *hiss*.

"What do you think this place is?" Harmony asked, her voice a hushed whisper.

"I'm not sure," Roy said slowly.

"Maybe it's a warehouse full of guns!" Annabel quipped. "Or missiles..."

"Annabel!" Melodie said sternly. "I suppose for now, we have to give Victor the benefit of the doubt."

"Please," Victor said, standing at the end of the corridor, his hand resting on a door-handle. "Welcome."

Victor pushed the door open and led them into a large, modern gallery-room. It resembled an open-plan safe-house, or bunker that would be built a mile under the surface of a mountain somewhere. There was a large fireplace beside a seating area for twelve, with a 50 inch Sony Ultra-Thin flat-screen television mounted on the wall. There was a large kitchenette extended from the side of the room, with a larder, freezer-room and two bathrooms adjoining through three narrow sliding-doors. A large wardrobe covered one of the walls, lining the back-side of the entry corridor. Victor flicked a switch and the fireplace ignited to life. Other spot- and floor-lights began to glow.

The group stared around the room with awe and wonder, wide-eyed and surprised.

"Make yourself comfortable, I'll be back in one moment," Victor stated, then moved to the door, inset in the middle of a blank wall. Clive watched him leave the room, as Melodie, Harmony and Evie moved to the kitchenette. Roy slowly followed them, opening the fridge first and pulling a bottle of beer out. He gulped down half of the bottle.

Annabel sat in the seating area, warming her hands by the fire.

Barney moved across the room and slid the door of a cabinet open. He smiled.

Clive followed Victor through the door and found himself in a huge garage with a large, window-walled office built into the front side. He crept to the doorway to the office and saw Victor.

Victor sat at one of three computer terminals typing.

Clive never took his eyes off Victor.

After a moment, Victor arose and turned to Clive. "Hello... I thought I asked you to wait in the living-area...?"

"What were you doing? Who were you talking to?" Clive accused angrily.

"Talking to?... Nobody... I was checking the computer... The mainframe, security, access... Checking the site was entirely safe. And... --There are two Land Rovers in the garage next door," Victor said. "They're the two cars you can take..."

Clive glanced into the garage and saw two identical black 2011 Land Rover Discovery 4s parked in front of a large shuttered-exit. The Land Rovers were both equipped with light armour-plating, studded tyres, and bullet-proofed and black-tinted windows.

Barney and Roy entered the room silently and stood behind Clive, when he rushed at Victor and away from their reaching arms.

Clive grabbed Victor by his collars. "What were you doing?! You were talking to someone! Why are you really doing all of this for us?!" he screamed. "I want to know! I want to know!"

Barney and Roy pulled Clive away from Victor, and Melodie dashed into the office. She looked at her husband and tried to calm him down with a hug.

"Why are you doing all of this?" Roy asked sceptically.

"I'm trying to help you... This is the only way I know that you will all be safe... We need to get you to that Police Station... If there is already a gathering there, then you will be safe with those people," he said, then straightened his clothes, and walked back into the other room.

Barney followed Victor, as Melodie and Roy continued trying to calm Clive.

"I don't trust him!" Clive exclaimed.

"That's fine, mate, that's fine! I don't trust him either," Roy said.

The next day. In the morning.
Victor drove the first Land Rover down a road, with Barney and Harmony as passengers. They drove in silence.

Clive followed in the second Land Rover, with Melodie, Roy, Annabel and Evie as passengers. Evie listened to music on a 3rd generation magenta iPod Nano, drowning out the sounds of the others' talking.

They drove down a country-road, and slowed to push-passed a crashed car with a deceased driver inside it.

Four days later.
The light was fading rapidly. Both Land Rovers pulled slowly into the grounds of a ruined cathedral outside a small farming village. Victor slowed, turning through a tight cleave between two walls.

Clive followed closely behind the second Land Rover. "How can we honestly trust him, Mel?" he asked, his eyes twitching.

"He's seen us well this far."

"This far."

"Yes. Now. Keep your thoughts to yourself."

"Why don't you trust him?" Harmony asked.

Melodie rolled her eyes.

"I don't know his agenda, Harmony. And I want to," Clive replied.

Clive's eyes never left Victor's Land Rover, when it slowed and stopped in part of the ruins. Victor climbed out of the front Land Rover's driver-side and waved to Clive.

Clive pulled in next to it, watching Victor closely.

A little later.
The group assembled on a partially-broken stone mezzanine-floor at the back part of the cathedral ruins.

    Victor handed out small, black tents which snapped open with an arm twist; much like ones used by the military or explorers on mountain-climbs.

    "Here you go," Victor said, handing out the final tent to Barney.

    "Thank you," he said quietly. Barney glanced across the group. Roy and Clive huddled together near the entrance, Annabel sat with her lower-legs dangling off the mezzanine-edge and Victor circled back to his backpack. A small fire had been built and covered to prevent the light of the flames from being seen from a distance. Melodie, Evie and Harmony made some food, also supplied by Victor; a vegetable, sauce and pasta dish.

A little later.
Everyone ate in silence.

    Victor walked up a set of stairs at the back end of the mezzanine, the only access to the floor, holding a silenced-machinegun in front of him.

    "From what I can make out, there isn't anyone for a long, long-way around... No people, no infected," he reported. He sat and accepted his food kindly from Harmony. "Thank you."

    Barney spooned a carrot and a piece of farfalle drenched in tomato sauce to his mouth. He watched Annabel, still sat at the edge of the mezzanine. She looked back at him and they half-smiled at one another. She turned away and continued to eat.

    Roy, Clive and Melodie ate, while Victor put out the fire with several handfuls of sand. He had placed small, solar-powered torches around the floor, which glowed on the ground and shed very little light on the walls.

A little later.
Victor sat with Barney, Roy and Clive around a fairly detailed pencil-drawing of the cathedral.

    "There is only one way through into this section of the ruins, and only one way up the staircase behind us, to get up here... I've set up a few motion-detectors along that way and near the entrance... And they link to this..." – he held up a palm-top device, then continued, "This will sound-out a dull beep if any of the detectors are tripped."

    Then the device *beeped*.

    They all looked at each other.

    "Is it a mistake?"

    "Is it a cat or something?"

    "Is your equipment faulty?"

    "No. It's all working fine."

    Roy and Clive instantly followed Victor, who grabbed the silenced-machinegun that he had leant against the wall, near the doorway to the staircase. He walked toward the edge of the mezzanine-level, pointing the gun down, as Clive and Roy dulled the torches around the floor.

    Victor flipped a lens-cap off the torch mounted on the top of the barrel, which instantly illuminated a woman standing on the ground below them.

    The woman was a mess; wearing shabby, dirty and blood-stained clothes. She was panting for breath. She lifted her arms in the air, surrendering.

    It was very dark and she was difficult to make out. The torchlight washed her muddy face with cold, bright light, wiping away all of her features.

    Barney appeared below Victor on the ground-floor, holding a silenced Beretta 92FS pistol and a flash-light, pointed at the woman, as she trembled and shook. "Please," she murmured.

CHAPTER 17 - LOCK YOUR DOORS - London

In an upstairs flat – PHIL BAILEY, 27 year old Englishman – sat at a piano on a long stool, guiding his pupil in how to play correctly. He had eyebrow-length dark hair, shaggy and uncombed, fashionably messy and parted in dozens of places; a light growth of hair came out bristly and patchy along his top lip and on the point of his chin. He was quite unremarkable with regular features and a forgettable face. His eyes were a blue-grey, interesting and engaging, and the only thing about him that stood out. He was above-average in height, but his slim frame made him look lanky and gangly. He had the look of many travellers; the shaggy hair, the almost-beard, the fashion sense. He wore a baggy t-shirt with the Quiksilver logo on the centre, flared and loose Smog jeans and brown Rip Curl Royal trainers.

The doorbell *rang*.

"That was a good effort today. I am quite impressed. What you need to work on is your speed," Phil said, summing up the lesson to his pupil – SHARON DELY, 11 year old English girl – as he led her down four short flights of stairs to the front-door. She had a big mound of curly, reddish-ginger hair piled on top of her head and spreading out down her back. She had a sweet face, dotted with freckles, bright blue eyes, a tiny nose and small, upturned lips. She was small for her age and skinny; she had long bony arms and legs protruding from a tiny torso. She wore purple leggings and a tangerine t-shirt under a shale corduroy dress, and amethyst-purple shoes with crimson flowers on the toe.

Phil spun the lock and opened the front-door. He found Sharon's mother – TORI DELY, 37 year old Englishwoman – waiting on the doorstep. She had a thicket of reddish-ginger hair, brushed back and noosed in a thick black-satin bow. She was pretty with almost-no makeup, porcelain skin, with a sprinkling of freckles on each of her high, smooth cheeks, and shapely, small lips. She had piercing, arctic-ice-blue eyes that were arresting and sharp. She was quite short, much like her daughter, but had grown into it; she had an attractive slim, athletic figure. She wore a fitted black business-suit, with flared trousers and a single-breasted suit jacket with two buttons and curved hems, a white shirt and Yves Saint Laurent suede black pumps. Tori paid Phil with a twenty pound note, and took Sharon's hand. "Thanks, Phil... How was she?"

"Great. Great... Can't wait to see what she brings next time... Great energy..."

"Good. Good. Thanks. Thank you. See you soon."

"Great. See you next week."

"Yep. See you then," Tori said and they started down the path, holding hands.

"So, how was your lesson?" she asked her daughter.

Phil closed the door and turned and started up the stairs, when he heard violent coughing from the outside that stopped him in his tracks. He swung back to the front-door, when Tori vomited blood on the reverse, splattering the glazed-panels. Thick, dark ooze streamed down the glass.

Phil's eyes widened. "What the hell?" he said aloud, exhaling, staring at his front-door.

He took a step down. Then another. Then another. Then he reached the tiled floor of the hallway. He slowly returned to the front-door, letting his curiosity take over, reaching up for the lock tentatively.

He turned the lock and opened the door achingly slowly, peering through the gap.

He immediately saw Tori and Sharon dead on his doorstep, blood gushing out of their noses and mouths.

Phil was shocked through his body. He stopped himself from being sick, covering his mouth and nose with his hand. With his other hand, he checked their pulses, but did not register anything.

He looked around, panicked.

Suddenly a red 2002 Vauxhall Astra crashed into a parked grey 2005 Renault Megane on the road, the other side of the hedgerow, at the end of the front-garden. Chunks of metal hit then fell through the conifers at the end of front-garden, as both cars split and broke apart.

Phil slowly crept down the path to the gate to see into the road. He touched the latch, when an infected charged at the gate, knocking him over backwards.

The infected lurched back, as if taking in a huge lungful of air, then puked blood on Phil's legs through the struts in the wooden gate. The infected was dressed in a long overcoat, a suit and tie, and smart shoes. Blood gushed out of its mouth, pouring and spilling down its shirt. The infected was a tall, lean man; ravenous and filled with a terrifying frenzy. It barked and yelped and snapped its jaws, pushing against the gate.

Phil let out a tiny scream, then quickly and shamefully scrambled to his feet and got up. He rushed up the path to the front-door as the infected awkwardly fell over the gate and climbed to its feet the other side. It started lumbering towards the house, gaining in speed and chasing towards Phil.

As Phil slammed the door shut, the infected punched through one of the glass-panels, sending fragments of glass to the doormat below.

Phil retreated to the stairs. "What the hell? What the hell?" he said, then bolted up the stairs.

Another infected charged at the gate outside and broke it down. It joined the other infected at the front-door and pounded on it, cracking another of the glass-panels.

Phil climbed the last step to get to the door of his flat on the third floor and put the key in the lock, trembling, when he heard banging coming from his neighbour's door. He stared at the door for a second, almost mesmerised. The door flew open and a large infected man rushed through and grabbed onto Phil. They tumbled down the staircase, bouncing down each padded and coarse-carpeted stair. Phil groaned as his head clipped a banister-rail.

The infected rolled down the stairs to the small landing at the bottom, but Phil grabbed onto another of the banisters and hung on to it, stopping himself halfway up. The infected hit the floor at the same moment the front-door broke open and the two other infected charged inside, two floors below them.

Phil clambered to his feet and dashed to his door and shakily unlocked it. He raced inside then shoulder-barged the door shut behind him, as the infected raced up the staircase after him. He bolted the door at the top and bottom and clipped the chain in place. He was breathing heavily and his arms shook from the shoulders. He panted for air, pacing back and forth behind his locked-door, when the fist of an infected smashed through the middle of it.

Phil ran.

He shot into his living-room, slamming the door behind him.

The infected punched holes through the door faster and faster, and more aggressively with each angry thrust.

Phil seized hold of one of the chairs from a small dining-table and wedged it tightly behind the door. He panicked and flapped his arms, pacing in circles, looking for something, anything: a weapon, any weapon, anything he could defend himself with. He searched the room with his eyes, and froze; seeing an African tribal mask on the wall, and leaning against the wall next to it, an authentic African tribesman's spear.

Phil snatched the spear, then saw something else: a two-foot long South American machete in a very-makeshift sheath of ropes, plastic-tape and strips of leather. He scooped the machete up and tied the string-belt around his waist. He made sure the blade was easy to get to, if the spear failed on him. He clenched the spear in his grip, standing in a pose he had seen and read about a thousand times in epic Roman or Greek sagas; legs spread and planted, arms gripping the spear handle, the back point pressed against the ground.

A long moment later.
Phil stood in waiting, clutching the spear in front of him, staring intensely at the door.

He was sweating. He could feel beads forming on the top of his nose, below his ears, across his forehead, and drip down from his hairy armpit and run down his ribs. He felt burning in his lungs, his breathing still ragged. His heart pounded. His head pulsed with heat. His muscles tightened and bunched, then quivered and shuddered.

He heard the noise of the flat's door finally smashing and breaking; enough for the three infected to enter.

Phil took to his fighting stance, waiting for a long moment. Waiting, waiting, waiting. Then something inside him spoke; it repeated, 'You're not a fighter. You're a coward,' over and over again. And he realised the voice was right.

He heard the first infected climbing into the flat.

He looked all around the room and stopped on the loft-hatch.

He jabbed the hoop-handle on the hatch with the spear-tip. Instantly boxes and ornaments and newspapers and crud fell out of the loft in a large cloud of dust and cobwebs and grit and grime.

Phil grabbed another chair from the dining table and climbed onto it. He peered inside the loft. It was very dark, but he did not know of any alternative. He angled then threw the spear through the hatch and quickly followed it, as the doorframe shattered with the force of impact from behind it.

Two of the infected charged through the flat, as the other concentrated on the noise Phil was making in the living-room. All three started pounding on the door, groaning and hacking.

Phil reached down through the small hatch-square and pulled the hatch closed, when the door smashed in, knocking the wedging-chair aside, letting the infected inside.

Phil sat in the darkness of the loft, panting for breath as the room below him was ransacked.

A little later.

Phil pushed free four roof-tiles and illuminated the loft a little. They dropped from sight and smashed on the ground below. Dust clouded the space, circling and wafting around Phil's body, pulling into his lungs, and escaping through the new ventilation-hole in the beam of light. Phil pushed his face into the hole and pulled in several lungs of clean, fresh air. He straightened and looked around the loft. There were cardboard and plastic boxes, several bundles of newspapers, picture-frames with dust-clotted paintings set inside them, stacks of old and rusting plumbing pipes, and a dozen ripped bin-liners with neatly folded clothes inside them. An old boiler sat near him on flattened-cardboard boxes that covered three quarters of the roof-joists.

The infected in the room below him continued to tear through the furniture, tipping over the dining table and upturning the two two-seater sofas. The television was knocked off its mount and smashed on the floor, then was stomped on as the infected circled, unable to find their prey.

Phil scrambled away, stepping on the roof-joists, trying to be as quiet as possible. He tip-toed through the loft and crossed over to a brick wall that followed a dividing-wall below. It was a very large house that had been chopped into many smaller flats over the last few decades, but the loft remained a large space with three vast segmented sections, covering the top three flats.

As he climbed his foot slipped and broke through a brace of plastered-ceiling laths.

Phil yanked his foot up, but the plaster-cracked hole tugged his shoe off. It fell to the floor of the flat beneath him.

An infected vomited blood on itself, then raced through the hallway, seeing the shoe. It looked up at the hole in the ceiling, then spat a little blood on the shoe, spraying out dark glossy ooze.

In the loft above, Phil heard crying.

He rushed, carefully, to the source. He stopped above a section of ceiling and crouched over it.

"Be quiet! There's one of them in your flat...!" he said in a loud whisper.

A girl sobbed. "I know – it's my brother!"

Phil swallowed, steadying himself on a roof-joist. Dust motes floated around him, falling from the roof and tiles.

"Stand by the back-wall," he said, as calmly as he could perform at that moment.

He waited a few seconds.

"Okay," she said, her voice wobbling.

He kicked through the plastered-ceiling laths and made a person-sized hole between two joists. He grabbed a dirt-encrusted towel that lay on one stack of boxes and smoothed the rough edge of the hole with it.

Phil saw, standing in the bathroom of her brother's flat – HELENA VAN TULEN, 24 year old Dutch young woman. She had a short-cut pixie hairdo, layered around the back and sides with a flat-ironed fringe parted on the left. She was very cute with dazzling topaz blue eyes, highlighted with modest and limited makeup. She had a slim, heart-shaped face with sharp, high cheekbones, a small angular nose, thin, rounded eyebrows, and wide, full lips. She was petite and slender, with thin, muscular arms and legs and a taught, athletic torso with small, round breasts. She wore a fitted white shirt, buttoned over a white Push Up bra, with the sleeves rolled up, tight denim Levi jeans and black Nike Flash trainers with silver ticks on the sides.

Phil reached down and offered his hand to her. "Grab hold! I'll pull you up!"

Intense banging made the door to the bathroom rattle and quake in the frame.

Helena stared at the door for a second holding her breath, then took Phil's hand. He lifted her up into the loft-space with relative ease. He never thought of himself as a strong person, but adrenaline surged through his body and some distant, almost-lost instinct to save another person's life grew inside him. He did not dwell on that thought for long.

"Thank god you aren't heavy," he quipped.

Helena ignored him. "How do we get out of here? Stuck up in the roof? There's no food or water. We have no way out. We're trapped up here – how do we escape?"

"We don't!" he asserted. "At least... Not for quite a while yet..."

Later.
Phil and Helena sat in the light of a single light-bulb, on a wooden-plank floor in the middle-section of the loft. There were considerably less boxes in the section of the loft, but more of an old assortment of furniture: armoires, chaise-longues, arm-chairs, wardrobes, desks and various chests of drawers. All were coated in a thick fur of dust. Cobwebs grew in every corner, under every piece of furniture, and criss-crossed every joist.

Phil sat on a high-backed arm-chair, his legs crossed underneath him. Helena sat on chaise-longue, leaning back against the raised cushion. Tiny eddies of dust floated around their heads.

"I still think we should try to leave," Helena said arching her back to look at Phil.

"We're safe here, for now."

Helena cleared her throat. "Do you have any family in London?"

"No... My parents are in the South of France at the moment. My brother's in Saudi Arabia..."

"Do you have a big family?"

"Not really... Just spread out... How about you?"

"It was just me and my brother... Lakke... That was his name... I was visiting him... I was only supposed to be staying for a little while..."

"What happened?"

"What do you mean?"

"I was teaching... I'm a piano teacher... I have no idea what's going on..."

"We had just come back from walking to the local shops. We got back to the flat. Then he went ballistic at me. I don't understand what happened to him. He was fine, one minute... Then he wanted to attack me, and did try... Then I locked myself in the bathroom."

Phil did not know what to say.

They stopped talking for a long time, stunned into silence.

Phil stared at Helena. She put her head on her knees and shut her eyes. He gritted his teeth.

Later.
Helena shifted on her seat. Phil watched her for a moment, then looked away.

"My mouth's so dry," Helena croaked.

"Yeah," Phil agreed.

They moved back to the hole in the bathroom ceiling. Phil poked his head through the hole and listened. There was no sign of any movement behind the door.

Phil steadily climbed into the bathroom, edging down slowly. He filled two plastic bottles with cold water.

The next day. In the morning.
Helena stood at another hole in the roof, staring through a gap they had made by pushing several more tiles out of place. She turned to Phil, who slumbered on a chaise-longue.

"We need to eat something," she said.

Phil snorted and sucked in dusty, dry air. "Huh? Huh? What? What?"

"We need to get some food, Phil."
"Huh? Oh. Yeah... I guess..."

Later.
Helena stood above Phil's flat, standing on the joists above the corridor. Phil eased back the lock of a roof-hatch then let the access door swing and fall open into the room. He looked through the hatch into his kitchen. There were none of the infected. They had seemed to have deserted the flat at some point during the night. He clambered feet-first into the hole and slowly let himself down.

He landed softly on the linoleum faux-floor-boarded floor with a tiny *squeak*.

Helena released a rope and it swung down through the hole.

He bagged several items from the counter: bread, tins of fruit, a couple of knives and some cans of Heinz baked-beans. Phil passed the bag up to Helena and she tugged it upwards. He refilled their bottles with water and put them in another bag. He plucked cheese, carrots, a lettuce and a cellophane-bag of peppers from the fridge and placed them in his bag.

Later.
Helena looked out of another hole in the roof-tiles of the middle-section of the loft. They had made several holes in both the front and back sides of the roof; to look out into the streets at the front and back of the house. They were on a crossroads at the front, and had a small park with a road running along the far side of it at the back.

Helena stood at the front, Phil stood at the back. They had been standing at the holes for several hours and had seen nothing but the infected. Helena used a pair of binoculars, occasionally removing them to look with her eyes. She blinked, adjusting to the weak sunlight.

"I taught piano-lessons, guitar-lessons, French horn and saxophone... And saved loads of money, and worked shitty cash-in-hand jobs anywhere I could find them... Any little bit of extra cash."

"For what purpose?" Helena asked, her curiosity peaked.

"So I could go travelling for six months at a time..."

"Travel where?"

"All over the world..."

"Really?"

"Yeah. I used to work in call-centres, but really hated it... So I started teaching music."

"Where did you go? Travelling, I mean..."

"Thailand, Laos, South Korea, China, Russia... South America; Peru, Chile, Brazil, Argentina... All over the world, really... I was supposed to be going to India, then on to Australia this summer..."

As Helena scanned the street, shielding her eyes from the dim sunlight, Don Clement flashed by on his motorcycle speeding along the railway-tracks beyond the dead-end of the road opposite the house. She swung the binoculars to her eyes and pressed the eye-pieces to her sockets. She caught another glimpse of Don on his motorcycle, speeding down the railway-track, then disappearing out of sight.

"Oh my God!" she screamed.

"What? What?!"

"I saw a man! A man on a bike...!"

"What?"

"Another person who's alive!"

"Where?"

"On the railway tracks, at the end of the road. We have to follow him!"

Phil looked at her apprehensively.

"If we follow him, he might know somewhere that's safe, and he can lead us there," she stated firmly.

Phil's brow furrowed and he felt worried.

A little later.
Phil and Helena climbed through a person-sized hole in the roof-tiles. They scrambled to the highest point on the pitch to see if they could locate Don, but he could not be seen.

"What are we going to do about food, Phil?"

Phil shrugged, climbing onto the roof of the neighbouring house. He saw further down the railway-tracks, then used the binoculars to look. Phil fixed on Don, as he drove the motorcycle around a bend in the tracks and vanished.

"He looks like just-a-bloke!..." Phil exclaimed.

"Have you seen any other 'just-a-blokes' around here?" she argued. "It seems to me like it's just you and me, and that 'bloke'... And thousands of those things..."

Phil sighed, conceding.

A little later.
Phil clambered down a large, wrought-iron drainpipe. He glanced at the roof, where Helena stood peeking over the edge, watching his progress. He glanced across at the road and saw three infected wandering aimlessly left and right. Two of the infected had been joggers and the other one was dressed in a cleaner's outfit.

None of the infected saw or alerted to Phil, who clutched the drainpipe and clung to it closely for a moment holding his breath.

The infected wandered away from the house, shambling off down the street.

Phil reached a cross-bar, about ten feet from the ground.

He could not see any more infected.

A little later.
Phil helped Helena climb down from a chain-link fence.

They hopped and jumped down a small grassy hill to the train-tracks.

Helena set off, walking at a pace.

Phil scurried to follow her.

"He was on a motorbike," Phil said.

"So?"

"So, it's likely that he'll be miles and miles ahead of us by now."

"We agreed to follow him, didn't we?"

"Yeah."

"So, let's follow him."

Later.
They had slowed in pace considerably. Helena, still at the lead, glanced back at Phil. He seemed to be blissfully unaware of their situation, contented and smiling, craning his neck to admire graffiti and some architecture.

"Hey! Look at that!" Helena exclaimed.

"What?"

Ahead of them, sixty metres down the train-tracks, a train had collided with a van that had veered off the road. The van was a mangled ashtray of nonsense under the immense carnage of the train-wreck. Nine carriages and the engine were bent over: twisted and cracked and distorted and pounded into dented, crumpled shapes. Five of the train's cars were crushed under three of the others, mashed and pressed under the intense collision. Metal was frayed and splayed and splintered and torn apart up and down every carriage.

One of the carriages lay across the Southbound tracks, buckled in the middle.

Phil crept a little closer to the train-wreck and saw that all of the windows were smashed.

"Let's get out of here!" Phil whispered, his eyes widening.

"Why?" she asked, sensing a similar foreboding.

"There could be those-people just waiting in those carriages..." he whispered. "Waiting for a noise, or to hear us talking too loudly... Just not-yet got up."

Phil and Helena stared at the black 1000cc Yamaha YZF motorbike Don had abandoned, before moving on.

Helena saw a trail in the long grass climbing up to another chain-link fence. "This way. He had to have gone this way. Look at the grass."

"What are you basing that on? Flattened grass?"

"The trail."

"That could've been anything. A dog or a cat..."

Helena shook her head. "I don't think he would've bothered to climb over that crash."

"Because you know this-guy so well?"

"Because it looks like he ditched his bike, then went this way! He probably had the same thought as you, as to why he didn't climb over the train..."

Later.

Evening was settling in, the light was beginning to dull. A light breeze had picked up and swept through the streets, picking up dust, grit and loose rubbish. Newspapers and plastic-bags fluttered in the air, circling and being taken by small whirlwinds.

Phil led Helena into a corridor in a block of flats and up the ancient stairwell. He could see and easily follow the trails left by Don, and the pursuing infected. They reached the second floor and found the body of the first infected wedged in the doorway. "Look, down there," Helena whispered. Her outstretched finger led to a space where two bullet-ridden bodies lay in a heap.

"Whoa."

"Look," she said. She gestured at the door and saw that there were bullet-holes in the opposite flat-door to where the infected had been killed. "Look... Here... And here, and here..."

Phil knocked firmly on the door twice. "Hello? Hello? Is anyone there?"

They waited a moment, then Phil kicked the door in, under Helena's direction. Daggers of wood split and splintered away from the frame and lock.

They rushed into the flat and found another dead body – the flat's occupant – another that Don had slain.

They searched the flat until they discovered the smashed window where Don had made his escape.

They glared out of the window and saw the cable that Don had climbed across, and just-saw Don disappearing over the roof-top, beyond the road-divide, and once again out of their sight.

It was getting quite dark outside, dark-grey cloud rolled overhead, and the orange glow of streetlight painted everything in a soft, bile-yellow neon.

There was a large crowd of the infected in the street now. Helena counted forty-nine. They had been attracted to Don's crossing and remained in place, aimless.

"I'm not going across there!" Phil exclaimed.

"Seriously? He just did!"

"What can I say?... That guy is ridonculous!"

"He's going somewhere!"

"I get that! But have you seen what's down-there?"

"Yes... But still, why don't you want to follow?... If he's got a destination?!"

"I'm not... I'm not really a follower... It doesn't... It doesn't look safe."

"You've got to change," Helena suggested firmly.

"So... We're following him?... I guess?..."

"Do you want to go first or second?" she asked bluntly.

"I suppose I'll go first," he said. Phil climbed out of the window and onto the cable. "I don't like the look of this."

"It'll be fine... The cable supported that guy."

"I'm not so-worried about the cable. It's those bloody things down-there!"

More infected swelled into the road below them.

A little later.
A quarter of the way across the cable, Phil's pace slowed. His hands had begun to tremble. Sweat coursed down his forehead, through his sideburns and tickled its way down his back.

Dozens of infected circled below him, packing together to immediately infect him should he fall. Several bloody hands reached up at Phil, clawing at the air.

He darted a look back at Helena, who mustered a smile and a nod, then he continued on.

A little later.
Almost-halfway across, Phil glanced back again. He saw Helena struggling with someone inside the flat, then they both disappeared from view.

A scream rent the air.

"Oh, fuck!" he shouted, wavering on the cable.

Several of infected nearest the block of flats arched their necks and looked to the source, staring at the smashed-open window and the void where Helena had just been standing.

Phil immediately started to climb back along the cable, awkwardly, but as fast as he could.

Inside the flat.
Helena struggled and fought with a man – DARRYL GRIFFIN, 39 year old Englishman. He had a large shaved head, balding but with signs of fresh, sparse growth. He was a huge, domineering and hulking man; he was over six foot eight with wide shoulders and built bulkily. He looked like a prop in a rugby team; a great big block of muscle. He had deep-set, dark and intense eyes under a heavy, wide brow. He was toothy, with thick slab-lips, a large bulbous nose and a strong, heavy jaw. He wore a grey boiler-suit with a sweat-stained white t-shirt underneath, and black ankle-high boots.

Darryl tried, with difficulty, to knock Helena out. He punched Helena and threw her around the flat, tossing her slight body into walls and against furniture. She kicked Darryl, but he snatched her off the floor and slammed her bodily against a wall. She was heavily-stunned and dazed, moaning and smacking her lips, her eyes rolling in their sockets.

Darryl dragged her out of the flat, when she came-to and kicked out again and again and again at him. He dropped her clumsily, but scrambled to pick her up in his huge bear-like paws. As Helena struggled, she kicked one of the bodies in the hall, soaking her shoe-tip with blood. Darryl pounded her against the wall, disorienting her, then right-hooked her in the abdomen. She gasped, trying to scream, wincing in pain, momentarily unable to breathe.

As Darryl carried Helena down the corridor, to the open front-door of his flat, the blood on her shoes smeared, scuffed and streaked stains down the rough-painted cream walls.

He entered his own flat and threw Helena to the ground next to his bed, then crossed to the door and slammed it.

On the cable outside.
Phil dangled from the line.

He furiously tried to climb back to the flat's window, hand-over-hand, burns and tiny cuts forming along his palms and fingers.

He moved quickly, faster than he had moved on his first attempted crossing.

The infected below him massed and surged around the space under the cable, and Phil's back. He could hear a chorus of moans and groans and coughs and rasping sounds.

One of his feet came loose and he kicked up when he saw one of the infected struggling to climb up on the front of a van to get a better shot at him. His ankle snapped around the cable and he scrambled back toward the flat.

A little while later.
Phil followed the trail of blood left by Helena's shoes down the corridor to Darryl's front-door. He froze where the bloody-smears stopped and faced Darryl's flat-door.

He quickly stopped himself from kicking in the door, when he had a moment of clarity. He could hearing his own breathing, the beat of his heart, the creaking of floorboards under old carpet. He padded down the corridor and raced back into the other flat. He grabbed his machete.

Returning to Darryl's door, Phil immediately kicked it in and rushed inside.

He found Helena's semi-conscious body lying face-down on Darryl's bed. Her jeans and panties had been dragged down to her knees to show her bare cheeks. Darryl stood over her masturbating frenziedly. He was so rapt in the action, he had not even heard the flat's front-door smashing open, or Phil's advance on him.

Phil stabbed Darryl in the back and side several times, jamming the wide blade-end of the machete deeply into the meat of Darryl's body.

Turning, Darryl's sought his attacker, who stabbed and thrust at him again, leaving the machete lodged flat through his abdomen and under his ribcage.

Darryl looked stunned and shocked; his eyes were wide with surprise. He towered over Phil, but this smaller man had got the jump on him. And that was a shock. Phil kicked out at him, clutching the machete-handle.

Darryl fell to the ground, winced and convulsed, then died on the carpet, letting out a long, final exhalation.

Phil rushed to Helena's side, pulling a blanket to cover her lower half. He tried to wake her gently.

She blinked and sat up slowly. She immediately saw Darryl's body on the floor, then noticed the sheet covering her and blushed.

Helena turned to Phil, then back to Darryl, she uttered one word only: "Good."

Later.
Helena helped Phil up the building-front opposite the flat.

The cable vibrated as Phil's foot left it. Their hands clasped and Helena hoisted him to the wall, where his trainers found purchase.

Once on the roof, they looked out over a sea of rooftops. In the distance was the large tower of Pickering Police Station. Streetlight glowed from every road, illuminating the borough in a sickly orange.

A light wind blew across the roofs, ruffling Phil's and Helena's hair. He pulled a beanie over his head and swept the hair from his eyes. He offered Helena another and she pulled it on.

They continued on, scurrying along the rooftop.

"Hey," Phil said.

Helena stopped, then looked back at Phil. "What?"

"We have no idea where we're going... It's night... What do you expect to achieve right-now?"

As soon as Phil had finished speaking, something exploded near the tall building less than a mile from their location. It was Pickering Police Station; where Harry Chapman had just detonated a 'distraction' for Don Clement to get inside the compound.

They stared across dozens of rooftops at the skinny grey and flame-lightened tower of smoke rising up into the sky.

"We should go there..." Helena suggested.

"Are you joking?!"

"No."

"That explosion will have attracted more of those-things towards it!"

"What if that was the man?"

"What if that was him getting himself killed?!"

"We have to look."

"For god's sake, Helena..." he growled. "Fine. Let's go," Phil conceded.

A little later.
Phil and Helena climbed down a slanting-roof and onto a wooden arbour. They crossed over to the next roof and up onto the peak.

Phil spotted Harry Chapman on the roof of the tall building: a small speck patrolling across the large flat-roof of a tower. He could make out that he was carrying a weapon, but could not tell it was a sniper-rifle.

Helena saw Harry too. "We might be able to make it there tonight!" Helena said excitedly.

"We should camp out for the night and move on in the daylight... We stand a better chance in daylight, I think – when we can see as best as we can... We can break into one of these houses," he said with a gesture. "And sleep in an empty bedroom... Before it gets totally dark..."

Helena reluctantly agreed with a nod, and they scaled back down the roof-top.

"If we can get into a bedroom and lock the door, we should be safe all night long..."

A little while later. In a bedroom.
Phil pushed a three-drawer, wide chest-of-drawers in front of the bedroom-door. They had covered the window with tape and wedged a painting across the curtains, pinning them down around the edges. One of the two lamps on the two bedside-tables was switched on, giving the room a feint pink glow from the flower-embroidered lamp-shade.

Phil glanced at Helena, who fingered through a clothing-rail in one of the two wardrobes.

"I'm gonna miss my friends... Back in home in The Netherlands."

"What made you say that?"

"I don't know... Shopping for clothes..." she idled with some dresses, sliding the hangers along the pole.

"They may be okay. You never know."

"I hope so."

Helena looked at the bed. "We are sharing this, aren't we?" she asked coyly.

"I guess so..."

A little later.
Phil and Helena lay in the bed.

"I remember sleepovers at friend's houses when I was in primary school... I wonder if any of them are still alive... I wonder where my parents are. They were on their sailboat... Maybe if they were at-sea... Maybe that might mean they made it..."

"I hope my mother is alive..."

They stared at the ceiling, swirls of plaster like the scales of a fish.

Sleep slowly took hold of both of them, and they fell asleep, exhausted.

The next day. In the morning.
Phil awoke with a start, but found the room still secure. Helena sat at the end of the bed. She read a Jackie Collins novel that had been set on the left-side bedside-table, next to a porcelain pot with various pieces of jewellery inside. She turned the page, then noticed Phil was awake.

"Good morning," she said. She offered him a jam sandwich that she had made for him.

"Thank you," he said and took a big bite.

"We should think about moving on..."

"Yep. Yeah. Making a move... Great. Let me just eat this and wake up properly..."

Later.
They darted along the side-wall of a garden and came to a gated-exit. Phil pulled a screwdriver from his backpack and prised the rusted-padlock open with a *snap*. Helena moved through the gate, then crouched behind a parked silver 2003 Nissan Altima.

Phil swept through the exit and pulled the gate shut, grinding the lock against the brick and forcing it in place. He ducked next to Helena.

"Which way do you think?" she asked.

"There," he pointed.

Helena dashed between two parked cars and around one that blocked the street. She stopped behind a Suzuki R750 motorbike. Phil joined her, gripping the machete by his side. She felt his breath on her cheek.

Later. Half a mile from Pickering Police Station.
Phil and Helena crept along a street lined on both sides with shops. They found themselves on the High Street – the main road that ran through Pickering, which eventually split into two minor roads that went north and south-east from a roundabout outside the Police Station. One road led away towards the Underground station and Barking, while the other was a route that led out of London through Dagenham and Romford to Chelmsford.

The glowing red dot of a laser-pointer shone onto the wing-mirror of a blue 2009 Toyota Corolla to Phil's left. He glanced at it, watching it shiver on the spot, then followed the line back to its source. It stretched all the way to the tower of Pickering Police Station. Phil saw Harry, who looked down on him through the sight of his vintage Parker Hale M-85 sniper-rifle.

He waved at Harry.

Harry took the rifle's sight from his eye and waved back.

"I think they've spotted us," Phil whispered, touching Helena's arm. He pointed to Harry.

Helena looked at the roof.

Harry stood up, lifting the sniper-rifle onto his hip. He saluted them.

Helena lips curled into a smile.

Later.
Harry shook Phil's and Helena's hands, allowing them inside, then tugged the side fire-exit door to the Academy closed. They entered a large classroom plastered with Army and Police posters, flyers, instructional diagrams, and regalia.

Phil breathed out heavily, looking around the room.

"Really-pleased to meet you," Harry said, grinning.

Helena smiled.

"You too," Phil said, patting Harry's armour-padded shoulder.

"We followed someone here... Did he make it?" Helena asked still beaming a smile.

"Um... I don't know... What did he look like?"

At that moment, Don walked into the room. Helena's eyes fixed on him in an instant. "Him," she exclaimed.

"Him," Phil repeated.

"Him what?" Don asked, confronted by two sets of eyes burning into him.

"We saw you... --coming here!" Helena blurted. "We... We followed you."

Don said nothing. His eyes twitched. Something stirred behind a blank expression. A tiny ember of pride.

"I can tell you, it's good having some more people," Harry announced. "People keep coming."

"How many of you are there?" Phil asked.

"There are nearly twenty of us so far!"

Later.
Phil, Helena, Harry and Don marched along a corridor that led to the Academy's vast mess hall and kitchen. It looked like any large dining-room at a university, hospital, large school or food court. There were sixty tables and booths dotted around the room, plastic-coated tops and blue-painted chairs. Along the left side was a window-wall, overlooking the parade-ground, allowing a generous amount of daylight in. This room had been cleared and cleaned by four o'clock on the first day. "Me and two others – Officer Leanna Picardi and Sergeant Terry Sowbridge – were the first to group together and deal with our situation inside the Police Station... And in here, in the Academy... We've managed to clear out the lower-ground floors of the Academy and Police Station," Harry stated.

"There must've been loads of those-people in here...?" Helena asked.

Harry's lip curled. "Actually, we didn't have many cadets in after the weekend. It was graduation for the current year a few days ago, so we only had basic staff and small numbers. It took a while, though... It did."

"What about the other floors?" Phil asked.

"We're working on them," Don interjected. He rubbed his beard and coiled hair behind his ear. "As many survivors as we find, we have to clear this entire complex as quickly as possible. Including the rest of the Police Station. We need places for people to sleep and eat and work and to live. We need places to start stockpiling weapons and food."

"How can I help?" Phil said.

"We need as many able-bodied people as we can get. I'll let you know..."

Two days later. In the barracks.
Light streamed into the space, shining along every surface that was not sprayed with blood. Several bodies lay scattered along the floor, collapsed in the stairwells and draped over banister-rails and open window-frames.

They had cleared out the ground-floor of the barracks earlier that morning and had moved upstairs to the first-floor. There were three floors, and on every floor there were four dormitories that each slept twenty cadets. On the ground-floor were dormitories one to four, on the first-floor were five to eight, and the second-floor were nine to twelve.

Phil, Don and Glenn Meakins crept along the barracks first-floor corridor. It was a long room lined with windows on one side – these overlooked the parade-ground – and four doors into the four separate twenty-man dormitories. They wore grey-blue police fatigues and riot-helmets, carried riot-shields, police batons and silenced-pistols. The uniforms were all lightly speckled with dried blood.

As Phil passed the first window, he saw Duncan Berry sauntering along the edge of the parade-ground, walking in the direction of the Police Station. Phil stopped to watch him, as Duncan turned suspiciously to glare back, showing him that he knew he was being watched. Then he strode away nonchalantly.

"Keep on task," Don demanded.

Phil's attention turned back to the corridor. "Sorry!"

Marc Sheridan entered the corridor from the other end where a fire-exit door led out onto a wrought-iron fire-escape, followed closely by Harry and Craig Charlton. They were all dressed the same and carried silenced-pistols, held in front of them, guiding their way.

Don came to the first door and paused. He looked at Marc, who nodded and raised his eyebrows.

Don swung the door open and disappeared inside, quickly followed by Phil, gripping the riot-shield in front of him. The door *squeaked* and *clicked* shut behind them.

Glenn stood behind the door, raised his riot-shield and took a defensive stance. He planted his feet down and prepared for an attack.

Inside Dormitory 5.
Don lifted the visor on his helmet to get a clearer look at the room. Phil watched him from just-inside the door. There were beds for twenty men, ten lining each wall. Beside every bed there was a bedside table and a skinny metal file-cabinet-type of wardrobe; these divided the spaces between every bed by three feet. Underneath some of the file-cabinets there were pairs of polished boots and trainers set next to each other neatly.

Five bodies lay in different places around the room. Two were lying on their beds. One had collapsed near the window on the far wall, bloody spray and gore spread around its face and mouth. Two had collapsed between their beds in a torrent of blood.

"Eyes on me," Don said, as he approached the first body.

A commotion broke the silence.

Phil turned to the door and through the frosted-glass saw one of the infected charge at Glenn, only to be swatted to the wall under the power he put behind the riot-shield.

Don stared at the window too, but not for long. He turned back in time to see one of the bodies in the room quiver, then start to move. It pushed itself up on bandy arms, wobbling.

The hand of the infected twisted and tightened into a ball.

"Phil!" Don shouted. "In here!"

Phil turned, as Don stood his ground in the middle of the room.

The body by the window stirred, then rose. The infected *snapped* its jaw at Don, prowling forward.

"Is this some kind of delayed reaction?" Phil asked.

Don nodded. "I guess..."

The first infected to move quaked on its ankles, shuddering. It growled, spitting blood. Don shot it through the bridge of its nose. The second infected stumbled forward and Don shot at it: two bullets ripped through its neck and shattered its fifth cervical vertebrae. The infected fell back into the window, hitting the wire-mesh that masked the entire frame. It flexed off the mesh and came blundering towards Don. It raised its arms.

Phil pulled in a breath and held it.

Inside the first-floor corridor.
Glenn battered the infected back huddling behind the riot-shield, as Craig fought with another forty metres along the corridor from him.

Craig clubbed the infected with a police-baton, stunning it for the briefest of moments.

Glenn mashed the infected against the wall, rolling along the faded, yellowing plaster, cracking and bruising it. He pounded against the shield, pressing the infected awkwardly into the brick. The infected groaned as a thick gush of blood ejected from the side of its head; then the side of its forehead split with a deep fissure.

Inside Dormitory 8.
Marc and Harry fought off seven infected, all of whom had been trapped in the dormitory for the past five days. Two of the infected were emaciated, starved-looking and ravenous. They led the charge on Marc, while Harry dashed across the room, leaping on and over beds, knocking wardrobes behind him to delay the pursuit of the other infected.

Marc rammed his pistol under the chin of the first infected and fired. A fountain of mess gushed into the air.

Another infected managed a punch, hitting Marc in the side, half-winding him. He winced and his knees almost buckled. He leaned over and found a wardrobe. The infected thrashed to get to him, spitting and coughing-up mouthfuls of bloody ooze. The riot-shield was coated, a broth of gore dripping down its length.

An infected side-swiped Harry and he tumbled to the floor. He fired, not looking where his aim was.

Two infected were caught by bullets. One bullet shattered teeth then the roof of the mouth. Another bullet ripped into the neck, ripping a wide gulley from front to back. The infected launched at Harry.

Marc barged two infected out of the way, as another ripped the shield from his arm.

Harry kneed and punched and kicked and elbowed the infected away from him, then scrambled to his feet, pulling a bed underneath him for support. He turned on the infected and leapt into the air. He landed on the riot-shield top-centre and his weight crushed the face and head of the infected, splitting the bone of its skull just-left of the middle, as if cleaved by an axe. Brains and blood spilled out onto the floorboards.

Seconds later, Craig burst into the room and opened fire. He expertly targeted each of the remaining infected and executed them in turn.

Marc lay on the ground, his helmet dotted with blood. He lifted the visor and looked at Craig.

Harry stood at the end of the room. He was breathing deeply. He lifted his visor and smiled. "That was intense!"

Inside the first-floor corridor.

Don, Phil and Glenn stood in a small, blood-soaked spot of carnage. The door to Dormitory 5 had been wedged open. Inside the dormitory, the bodies of the five infected lay in a pile by the entrance.

"Well, that was fucking terrifying," Phil offered.

"At least it's over," Glenn said.

"There's no time to celebrate yet, we've got six more dorms to get cleared."

"And then the first- and second-floor of the Police Station... And the tower... And the main building's upstairs too... And anywhere else we think we need, too!" Phil groaned. "Oh, yeah, the Hotel too...!"

"It doesn't have to be done all today," Glenn said. "Does it?" he asked, turning to Don.

Don looked at Glenn. "No."

The door to Dormitory 8 opened. Craig, Harry and Marc wandered into the corridor.

After the tiniest of moments, where Don, Phil and Glenn pointed their pistols at the others, they lowered them.

"Two down, six to go," Harry announced.

In the Communications Room inside Pickering Police Station.

Helena sat behind the desk. She was eating a chicken salad sandwich that had been brought to her by Angela Garcia. She nibbled on the corner of the bread, then replaced the half-sandwich on the plate. She sat back in the chair and sighed. The room was a well-lit grey box with a large built-in desk on one side with monitors and displays and various different equipment inlaid into it, and behind that were three rows of skinny-desks with six flat-screen monitors to each row, each had a headset-with-microphone hung on the top-right corner, in multiple matching order.

Adam Hilton came to the door and saw Helena. Their eyes met. "Sorry, I was looking for Angela..."

Helena picked up the plate and sandwich. "You just missed her. She just brought me this."

"You're...? – Helena, right?"

"Hi. Yes."

"I'm Adam," he said, and offered his hand.

Helena put the plate down and they shook.

"Pleased to meet you," he said.

"You, too," she replied.

Their hands separated.

"I'm getting together information about all of the survivors... Can I speak to you sometime? Get your experience down on paper...?"

"Sure... But, why?"

"Um, well," he began, "there needs to be an account of what's going on..."

"Oh. Okay, then."

"Great... I'll pop by."

Later. In the mess hall inside the Academy.

Phil ate a bowl of soup, cutting off a chunk of a bready dumpling with the edge of the spoon. He chewed on it. Glenn sat on the other side of the table. They had chosen a table near to the window and were bathed in warming sunlight.

"Good soup," Glenn mumbled around a large ball of dumpling in his mouth.

"Yes."

Glenn chewed. "I'm glad the morning is done with."

"Me too."

"It's not all going to be so bad, though..."

"I hope not."

"I hope not, too."

"Clearing out the barracks was tough," Phil admitted, mopping his mouth with a paper serviette.

Phil glanced out of the window. He saw Reg Heron and three other people exiting the barracks. They were carrying buckets of bloodied water, brushes and a mop-bucket filled with cleaning solutions. They wore breathable-fabric face-masks, blood-encrusted yellow plastic aprons, traditional green Wellington boots and yellow marigolds.

He watched the cleaning crew cross into a small room at the end of the barracks – the laundry room. They entered and moments later they exited. They moved back to the barracks carrying fresh soapy water.

Helena strode down the side of the parade-ground and Phil saw her and raised his hand. She waved back. She entered the Academy and pushed through the double-entrance doors into the mess hall. She made a line for Phil and Glenn.

"You're girlfriend?" Glenn whispered.

"No... A neighbour," he replied offhandedly. "We lived in opposite flats. Well, her brother and I did... Don't mention..."

Helena sat down next to Glenn. "Hi," she said. "How has your day been?... I met a few more of the other survivors today. Most of them seem nice..."

"Me too. This is Glenn."

"We met yesterday. Hi. How's your lunch?"

"Better than I usually get."

"I heard they finished the barracks."

"We've done the ground-floor and first-floor. Still have upstairs to go," Phil corrected.

"What are you doing with the bodies?" she asked.

"A few others are digging a hole near the back-road, behind the sheds along the parade-ground."

"A hole? Won't that get into the water supply."

"I don't think anyone's worried about that right now. As soon as it rains, all of the dead bodies and blood outside will wash into the ground and then we're all screwed!" Glenn offered.

"They're going to burn them."

"Oh. Good."

The next day. On the second-floor of the barracks – 10:10am.
Phil, Marisa Flenkman, Reg and Glenn crouched on all-fours, cleaning the floor. The blood-stained beds had been stripped and the sheets, covers and pillows were being burnt with the bodies. They wore the same breathable-fabric face-masks, cleaned yellow plastic aprons, traditional green Wellington boots and yellow marigolds that Phil had seen Reg and a few of the others wearing the previous day. They scrubbed at bloody patches on carpets and floorboards, on bed-frames and wardrobes, on bedside-tables and walls. All of the Police, Army and safety posters and motivational cards had been removed from the walls and bagged in bin-liners.

"This is awful," Reg croaked.

"Just think about it when it's clean," Marisa said calmingly.

"I can't."

Reg sat back on his knees and unhooked the face-mask from around one ear then the next. He was sweating and gasping for air. He took a few deep breaths.

"I have to get some air. I need a cigarette."

Phil and Glenn watched as Reg stood and crossed to the door.

Seconds after the door closed, and Reg was on the other side, his breathing completely settled and he strode away down the corridor. He reached the staircase and hopped downward, popping a cigarette in his mouth. As he reached the landing on the first-floor, a man was stomping up in front of him – Sergeant TERRY SOWBRIDGE, 51 year old Englishman. He was balding on top with a tuft-island of hair above his forehead and curly greyish-brown receding on both sides. He had a sloped forehead, round, ruddy cheeks and a double-chin, but with defined cheek-bones, jaw and a strong nose. He was six foot four and large-built, but not shapely anymore, more the figure of a retired rugby player. He still wore his Police uniform, cleaned and pressed. "Where're you off to?" he barked at Reg.

"Outside. Fresh air."

Sowbridge eyed the cigarette in Reg's mouth. He snatched it in a giant paw and mashed it between his finger and thumb.

"Fuck off outside, then."

Reg drifted away down the stairs.

Sowbridge stomped on up.

In Dormitory 11.

Sowbridge opened the door and found Phil, Marisa and Glenn cleaning further into the room.

"It's going well."

"Slow work, though," Glenn added.

"It will be. I'm starting on the next dorm now with some of the others," Sowbridge reported.

Later. In Dormitory 2 – 9:08pm.

Phil lay on one of the beds near the back wall. He had used the bed next to his as his personal armoury. His clothes were laid out next to an assortment of weapons: a silenced-pistol, an axe, a police-baton, his machete and a riot-shield. The room was dark, all of the lights were out and the only ambient light came from the window near to him and the corridor light, which was always kept on. A little streetlight shone through the window and between the wire-mesh affixed to the inside.

Phil rolled onto his side and stared at the wall under the window. His eyelids fluttered and he felt heat radiating through them. He pressed his hand to his eyes and rubbed lightly. He pinched his temples, massaged his skull, then rubbed the bridge of his nose.

A noise across the room made Phil roll over and sit up.

Helena stood a few metres away, next to the bed opposite his. She threw a hooded-jumper over her shoulders and pulled it off. She threw the jumper on the floor and kicked off her shoes. She unbuttoned her jeans, then rolled up her t-shirt. She wore the same white Push Up bra under the t-shirt, cupping her ample breasts. Phil laid back and stared at the ceiling as Helena pulled on a fresh t-shirt, an xxl size, and pulled her jeans off. She undid her bra and slid her arms under the t-shirt to extract it. She tugged her socks off and dropped them on the floor next to her shoes.

Phil's eyes shut, eventually.

Shortly after Helena could hear Phil exhaling deeply, then his snores, she fell asleep.

CHAPTER 18 - FAMILY MAN - Royal Tunbridge Wells

ROB ALCOTT, 31 year old American – sped down the A26 motorway in a black 2011 BMW X5. He wore a smart black suit, slate-grey shirt and smart black shoes. The car darted between other cars, people carriers, vans, motorbikes and lorries. It was like a sleek black blur gleaming along the concrete between average-speed, multi-coloured metal boxes.

Rob dialled a number on the car's in-built phone, as he drove faster and faster, immensely aware of every other car on the motorway around his own. He looked at the car's digital-clock, built into the dashboard, that glowed under the thin sheet of Perspex that covered it. It read: 11.29am.

Suddenly the car-phone *clicked* on, and started to ring.

The ringing built in volume, getting quickly louder when a man picked up: it was Mr Burton's voice that snaked out of the speakers. "Rob! I've been trying to get a-hold of you for the last few hours, where've you been?!" he said, quick and direct. His words cut straight to the point. "I–..."

Rob interrupted, he said, "Sir, I don't have time to explain where I've been... The virus is being released... --today! I have to go!"

Rob's hand lurched for the red-disengage button on the centre of the dashboard-display. Burton's voice came back calm, soft, flourishing. "I know, at twelve midday... It's no surprise, really, Rob... We have a defec.." The line *crackled*, then scrambled-*crackles* disguised Burton's last word: "Knapp..." through the *crackles*, then the line went dead with a *beep*. Rob's finger still hovered over the button, then it fell onto the gear-stick.

Rob slammed the brakes on, nearly hitting a green 2008 Honda Accord in a tiny moment of lapse, then turned abruptly off the motorway onto an off-ramp. The back end of the car had swung out, then the front-end righted and pulled it away up the incline. He tried to redial but got nothing.

He momentarily panicked, thoughts racing through his head. He slowed down behind a short row of cars at the junction. He swung passed them onto the wrong side of the road and sped away.

A little later.
Rob's car skidded to a stop outside his home, kicking a spray of gravel into the garage-doors, *pinging* off a hundred times in a tiny hail. He threw open the car door and ran inside.

He entered the kitchen-diner off the hall, and found his wife – RACHEL ALCOTT, 30 year old Englishwoman – standing by the kitchen-table. Her hair was cut in a short bob, lustrous and shiny auburn, with her fringe set above her arched eyebrows. She had a soft face, calm and easy; a small nose, full, pouty lips and bright grassy-green eyes. She was tall and lithe with slim arms and legs and a long, shapely torso. She wore a long-sleeve white v-neck t-shirt, a black pencil skirt and comfortable black pumps. She was feeding their daughter ALICE, 3 year old English girl. She had long sleek light-auburn hair, tied back in a Dutch braid. She was tiny and slight, an almost-perfect miniature of her mother. She wore a baby-pink v-neck t-shirt under a red-denim dress with lilac leggings and shiny red flats.

Rachel could immediately see something was wrong, the panic in Rob's eyes; the fear, the sweat beads on his forehead, the slicking of his hair with sweat, his ruffled suit-jacket and creased shirt.

"We need to get out of here. Right now. Please," he said so calmly it frightened Rachel. "Can you get our emergency suitcases now. And then we're leaving."

He dashed through the door in the side of the kitchen wall and dove down the staircase beyond, bounding and leaping the stairs to his study in the cellar.

As he reached the doorway to his study, Rachel stopped him, "What's going on? What's happening? Why are we leaving? Where are we going? Rob? Rob? Rob, answer me, please..."

"Please. Do as I ask. And do it as quickly as you can. Get Alice in the car," he commanded.

Moments later. In Rob's study.
Rob typed a code into his computer, when Rachel appeared in the doorway to his study, holding a black 9mm Smith and Wesson model 59 pistol, pointed at Rob's head.

"Stop. Stop what you're doing, Rob," she said, her voice shaking.

Rob spoke slowly, "We will all die if you don't do what I told you to do... For now, Rachel. Please... Put the gun down... --and just get the suitcases."

"Why should I?"

"Bad people are about to release a worldwide, airborne super-virus... The virus will kill ninety percent of the world's population over a thirty minute period... That will happen..." he checked his watch "...--in twenty-three minutes."

Rachel's mouth fell open, the gun dropped out of her hand and *clattered* on the floor, her shoulders sank, her eyes widened.

Rob typed a few more commands into the computer, then made it shut-down.

"We have to go now... Put Alice in the car, I'll get the suitcases..."

Rachel stared at Rob with an expression of shock and fear. He would have to deal with this later. He took her hand and led her out of the study. He picked up the pistol and wedged it at the back of his belt. They started up the stairs, back to the ground-floor.

A little later.
Rob loaded the last suitcase of four in the boot of the BMW, while Rachel climbed inside. Alice sat in a child-seat in the back, playing with a stuffed-lion soft-toy.

Rob took the pistol from behind his belt and put it in the driver's door-pocket.

"What about Michael?"

Rob put the car in gear and started away, "That's where we're going now!..."

The car tore away from the house.

As the car turned out of the driveway, Rob's house exploded in an eruption of brick, plaster, appliances, wood and other debris. The house quickly collapsed in on itself. A large tower of black smoke rushed up into the sky.

A little later.
Rob sped down the road, glimpsing the car-clock again – it read: 11.46am.

He slammed his foot down on the accelerator.

Rachel gripped the armrest and door-grip.

A little later.
Rob's car leapt a tarmac speed-bump, as it passed through a huge, Victorian wrought-iron and brick entranceway. They passed a sign that read: 'Westernby Private Preparatory School For Boys.'

The BMW shot up the driveway.

Outside the school.
The brakes on Rob's car *screamed*, as the car came to a stop, kicking up a cloud of gravel and mud.

Rob jumped out of the car, but then hesitated and turned to Rachel. "Stay here. If I'm not back with Michael in four minutes – drive to this place," he said and handed her a business card with a tiny map on the back. "And don't stop for anyone... Anyone!"

Rob nodded at her, looking her in the eyes until she nodded back to show her agreement. "Okay," she whispered.

He shut the car-door and ran up the huge stone staircase that led to the reception hall of the grand, main school-building.

Rob entered and knocked twice on the Staff-room door.

BRUCE FORSTER, 51 year old Scotsman – the school's physical education teacher– approached casually from the Great Hall. He had thinning to no hair on a round, incredibly sun-tanned head. He had heavy but grim features; a thick nose, deep brow, full cheeks, a wide jaw and a big mouth. He was short and wide; his shoulders were huge and sloping; his chest a large barrel set on a thick pelvis and sturdy, muscular legs; his arms were great coils of muscle. He wore a striped rugby jersey and jogging-bottoms with loosely-stretched, long rugby socks that bunched around an old pair of trainers. He said, "Hello Rob, how can I help you?"

Rob tried to look patient, and relaxed his shoulders, swept hair across his forehead, he said, "I was just-wondering if you could tell me what class Michael is in right-now, we have had a family emergency and I'm going to have to take him out of school for the rest of the day... I know this isn't normal practice, but this is of extreme emergency..."

Bruce led Rob into the Staff-room, he said, "What sort-of emergency, Rob?"

"It's private," Rob snapped. "I'm... I'm sorry... It's private family business."

Bruce ignored Rob's abrupt tone and apology, and found a class attendance and timetable book and checked it, he said, "Michael is in classroom 3b, in the middle-school."

As soon as Bruce had spoken, Rob sprinted for the door and bolted through the opening and ran.

Rob dashed into the Great Hall, his feet skidding on polished wooden floors, his head spinning for a second, a light sweat forming on his brow. He sprinted passed the kitchen entrance into the long corridor leading away from the hall, that acted as the main backbone through the school. The ceiling was low and veined with pipes, further down a ramp sloped away and the pipes were roofed under white-painted asbestos-tiles. The walls were dotted with posters for school events, eating healthily, homework clubs and after-school activities. Schoolbags were piled in two large alcoves along the wall opposite two of the dozen doorways into classrooms. Rob's shoes slapped the floorboards, echoing down the entire length of the corridor.

Rob made a turn into an adjoining corridor and slammed through a double-set of doors. He leapt up two stairs and ran down a large annex-building and into another corridor. He found the correct classroom – 3b – and without even knocking, entered.

"Michael, we're leaving, now," he said, instantly sighting his son.

MICHAEL ALCOTT, 9 year old English boy – got to his feet immediately, then looked around at the class, whose eyes followed him, then at his teacher. He was tall for his age, skinny and slim. He had a tiny, straight nose, high cheek-bones, and a small mouth. His hair was the same warm, thick cocoa-colour, like his father's, cropped and gelled and parted on the side as well. He wore his school uniform; a grey v-neck jumper over a grey shirt, red and green tie, black trousers and shiny, black shoes.

All of the other pupils stared at Michael – open-mouthed with the spectacle of Rob's entry. The teacher – FREDDIE SALMON, 24 year old Englishman – was sat in his seat behind the desk at the front of the room. He had a crew cut of dark brown hair, very shortly trimmed around the back and sides. He was tall with square shoulders; the physique of a swimmer or rower. He had a serious but arrogant face with a permanent sneering-smile in front of uneven teeth. He wore a loose-fitting light-grey suit with a dark, French navy shirt and smart brown-leather shoes.

A projector that was bolted upside-down to the ceiling *buzzed* and *whirred*, shining on an interactive white-board at the front of the classroom. There was a PowerPoint presentation on-screen, which the pupils had been studiously copying into their exercise-books in silence. Salmon looked from the board, to Michael, then to Rob.

Rob pushed between a few desks, nudging pupils aside, to get across the room. He grabbed Michael by the arm and pulled him away to the door.

"Wait," Salmon protested. He stood and got in their way, blocking the doorway, but Rob shoved him aside with a heavy swing of his arm. Salmon fell into his own chair and struggled to stay upright.

Rob and Michael sprang through the doorway and rushed down the corridor passed a clock that read: 11.59am.

At the bottom of the steps at the end of the annex-building, Bruce stepped in front of them and obstructed their path.

"Rob! Rob... There is a procedure for taking your children out of school early – you know that!..."

Rob pulled out his pistol and pointed it nonchalantly in Bruce's face. "In one minute, Bruce, none of it will matter... Believe me... Let us pass, right now. Or I'll shoot you in the face," he said icily, calmly.

Bruce questioned Rob with his eyes, but moved aside for them. "Okay. Okay, then."

As Rob passed first, Bruce grabbed at him, trying to knock the gun free. It *clattered* on the floor and came to a stop near Michael's feet. Rob shoved Bruce against the wall and pinned him there. Michael picked it up and placed it neatly in Rob's open hand.

"You didn't have to stop us!" he shouted, then pistol-whipped Bruce across his cheek, cutting it.

Bruce fell to the ground hard, touching the wound a second later.

Michael smiled at seeing Bruce being hit. "Come on," Rob told his son. "Let's go! Let's move!"

They bolted down the main corridor. Rob practically pulled Michael along.

They skidded to a stop when one of the infected stumbled out of the kitchen – it was one of the kitchen staff. It vomited blood over itself. It lurched into the space ahead of Rob and Michael, stopping them before the ramp. It groaned and hacked.

The infected took off, taking its first few tentative steps forward, letting gravity and momentum pull its weight down the ramp. It blocked their way to the Great Hall.

Rob looked around.

"What's going on, dad?" Michael asked calmly.

The infected snarled, pacing towards them.

"I'll explain later..."

"Shoot it!"

"No... I can't."

"Why not?"

"The sound will... --wake up more of them," he said slowly. Rob checked one of the nearby classrooms and found it empty. He pulled Michael inside and then wedged the door with a chair.

The infected reached the door and beat on the back of it, as Rob dashed to the windows, with Michael following behind him. He opened the window and lifted Michael outside, dropping him to the grass a foot or so below, then climbed out after him.

They squatted on the small strip of lawn for a moment, as Rob scanned the front of the school.

"Run!"

They dashed across the front lawn and to the BMW. Rob pulled the driver's door open and looked inside at Rachel. "Have you seen anyone else?" he asked, climbing in.

"No..."

"Good! That's good, at least..."

He started the engine then sped away down the long driveway.

As they drove away, two people – a woman and a child – ran out of the junior-school building. Michael saw them from the back-seat, but it was not clear who they were, or whether they were infected. He turned back to the interior of the car and sighed.

Rob turned out of the entrance-gate and noticed a silver 2002 Honda Civic skewed in the road.

He stopped the BMW, then turned to his children and wife, he said, "Keep your eyes closed..."

He saw the driver awaken infected, then flailed and struggled. The infected was wearing its seatbelt and was trapped in the car. It fought with the restraint, ramming its body and shoulder against the belt, punching and kicking the foot-well and dashboard.

Rachel watched, wide-eyed, unable to take her eyes away. "What has happened to that man?"

Rob shot her a look, he said, "We have to get somewhere safe, then I'll explain everything to you... I promise."

The infected in the Honda vomited blood over the inside of the windows, still struggling in its seatbelt-restraint. It growled and snarled, but the noises were muffled and hidden by the BMW's engine.

Rob put the BMW in gear and steered around the Honda, passing slow enough to catch a good glimpse of the infected occupant. It saw them through un-bloodied patches in the windscreen. It pushed its body against the seatbelt.

The BMW sped away.

A little later.

Rob was forced stop again. The road was blocked by two crashed cars: head-on collisions, bending, mashing and breaking the engine-blocks of both cars; a purple 2008 Mazda 3 and a crimson 2002 Volkswagen Passat. It was a mess of twisted pieces of engine and chassis. They were on a road that passed through a dense conifer wood. There was no way of getting around the crash, as trees lined either side of the road, closely planted together in disordered shady rows.

Rob stopped fifteen metres away, and got out. He stood with his foot lying in the foot-well, half-out of the car, staring at the crash.

"What are you going to do?" Rachel asked.

Rob shrugged, distantly. "I'm not sure yet."

He set off at a pace and walked toward the first car.

He looked inside the Volkswagen, it was a taxi – the driver and backseat passenger were both dead – slumped forward after the crash. The driver's legs were mashed under the dashboard by the impact. The backseat passenger wore a seatbelt, braced across their body, pinning them to their seat. Rob glanced through the back window and saw the handbrake was on. The driver dribbled blood from his mouth. The meter continued to *click*, adding more money to the passenger's tab.

He moved away from it, and looked at the Mazda.

Rob cautiously moved towards the second car, and saw that an airbag had gone off and that the driver inside could potentially have survived. He continued to step nearer, but slowed his pace. His eyes widened, inspecting the three-quarter deflated airbag. The driver's head was completely obscured by the fabric of the airbag, a white puffy-cloud that shone out behind the buckled bonnet of the car in the midday sun.

Rob hesitated before opening the passenger-side door of the Mazda, and stared at the figure inside. He checked to see whether the seatbelt was on, but it was not. As soon as Rob saw the clip was not in, the occupant – an infected – turned and launched itself at Rob, who fell backwards onto his lower-back, landing hard on the road, knocking some of the air out of him.

The infected out-stretched its arms and pawed the air, striking out at Rob in the open void of the passenger-seat. It struggled forward, freeing itself from the behind the airbag and pulling its feet free from the half-crushed foot-well.

Lying on his back, he managed to kick its clawing, thrashing arms away, knocking the infected back into the car. Then Rob sat up and shot it through the forehead. The bullet travelled through its head and shattered the driver's-side window, spitting bloodied glass onto the tarmac and into the wood beyond.

Rob got to his feet and dusted himself off, then reached into the car and finally checked the hand-brake was off – it was. He felt a twitch of relief untie one of the many knots in his upper-back and he shrugged his shoulders.

He kicked the gear-stick out of gear with a tired heel.

He turned to walk back to his car.

Rachel climbed out of the BMW, staring at her husband. Her eyes showed the panic inside her, that she ineffectually tried to bury. "Tell me what is going on right-now Rob," she pleaded. "Why did you shoot that man? Please... Please..."

Rob looked back at her with sympathy, a furrowed brow and pursed lips. He stared at Rachel for a long moment, walking towards her. He said, "I can't explain now... But I will. I promise." Then Rob saw one of the infected sprinting down the road toward them. "Rachel, get in the car right-now!"

Rachel turned and saw the infected running at her, and leapt in the car, gripping the inlaid-handles tightly.

The infected panted for breath, thick wine-blood discharging from its mouth and nose.

"Hey!" Rob called out.

The infected eyed him, and swung a wide line around the BMW to charge full-throttle at Rob.

He took a step back and waited.

The infected reached the BMW's blind-spot and he fired.

The bullet hit its throat and blew large chunks of meat and two cervical vertebrae out the back of the neck. The infected gasped as blood gushed freely through the sizable holes in each side of its neck. It dropped to its knees, opening and closing its mouth like a dying fish on the end of a hook. Its bloodshot eyes swung through the air. It almost looked like it was mesmerized by the pattern of sunlight shimmering through the foliage above it, but it was not. Rob put another bullet in the middle of its breastplate, punching it backward.

Rob crossed back to the Volkswagen and reached inside, when the backseat passenger puked blood on his hand and forearm; it was an infected twelve year old boy.

Rob shot it.

He pulled the gearstick out of gear, when he saw another of the infected running through the woods, rushing straight at him, darting between trees and shrubs.

Rob pointed the gun and fired. He hit the oncoming-infected in the eye and it fell clumsily to the ground, its right shoulder planting in the ground and making it roll over and over again.

He dashed to his BMW and got in, slamming the door. Rob drove forward and rammed the Mazda out of the way, when another infected ran at the car and slammed into the side of it bloodily.

Rob reversed twenty metres back from the infected, then let it run at them once again. He ran the infected down, then accelerated forward, scraping between the two cars to get by. Sparks skittered along both sides of the car.

Later.

Rob drove down a grit and mud track through another wood, not saying a word. He slowed and then finally stopped, winding his window down.

"Where are we going?"

Rob turned to Rachel and said, sincerely, "I'm sorry. But you'll have to be patient for a little longer..."

A camouflaged, armed soldier appeared out of the undergrowth and stepped toward the car slowly. The soldier raised a perfectly camouflaged rifle, creeping to a stop two metres from Rob's open window.

Rob did not let the soldier speak, he said, "My number is 58-66-71-58-11-08. Call it in."

After a few seconds of silence the soldier spoke. "You've been confirmed. Proceed down the track two hundred metres," he said gruffly. He waved them on up the road.

Another four soldiers stood at various points around the BMW, all concealed in the undergrowth, unseen by the occupants of the car, except Rob.

Rob drove down the track a little way. They passed a small clearing on the left side of the road, recently cut trees had been unearthed and moved to empty the space. The ground had been dug over and flattened with a roller. Rob thought nothing of it.

He came to a very-small concrete out-building with two innocuous grey doors set into the block. Two soldiers flanked the doors. They were armed with camouflaged rifles, but also had two pistols visible on either sides of their belts in holsters.

Rob and Rachel got out of the car, then helped Alice and Michael out of the back.

"This way," Rob said, leading them away from the car towards the out-building.

Another soldier, one that had been invisible ten seconds earlier, emerged from the ground beside the car and climbed behind the wheel. He started the engine.

Rob glanced at his car as it disappeared down the road. It was then that he noticed at least six other sets of eyes watching them from strategic positions in the wall of foliage and trees opposite and surrounding the out-building.

"Rob?" Rachel asked nervously.

"It's okay. Honestly. It won't be long before I can explain..."

They walked toward the doors and one of the soldiers swiped a card in a rough-hewn slot, almost indistinguishable from several other small cracks in the wall, and the door *hissed* and opened, a seal of mist escaping.

They entered a small, dim ante-room that had only two features; two doors ahead of them through which a double-wide staircase leading a long way underground was visible through large glass panels, and what seemed to look like a light-bulb above their heads. The door closed with a hermetic seal behind them.

"Where're we going?" Rachel asked.

"The only safe place left," Rob answered. Their eyes met briefly.

The light-bulb above their heads started to glow red.

Rob knew what this was. "This might hurt a little, kids... Rachel... I'm sorry, but I'll tell you everything in about five minutes. I love you."

"I love–..." but Rachel's words were cut off.

The light-bulb blinked ferociously fast and glowed intensely. Rob, Rachel, Alice and Michael winced in pain as their skin momentarily burned, searing with heat. Their teeth *buzzed* and vibrated and suddenly all of their hearts pounded. Their fingers curled and their shoulders sank. Their necks tensed and their abdomen bucked.

Later. Near the out-building.
A black five-seat Eurocopter Colibri came into view above the cleared space. The pilot swung the helicopter over the track, then banked back to hover over the clearing.

Two soldiers stomped into the middle of the track from hidden vantage points, and waved at the pilot.

"Confirmation code accepted," one of the two soldiers said into a wrist-band microphone.

CHAPTER 19 - EMPTY BOTTLE - Royal Tunbridge Wells

Doctor ELLIOTT STANGER, 37 year old Englishman – awoke to a muffled-sound. He had a thick, full head of dark-brown hair, shaved down to grade three; it stretched down his face in fluffy sideburns and merged into a unruly, heavy beard. He was a handsome man, behind the bush of a beard, the deep, dark-circled sockets and his glassy, opiated blue-green eyes. He was tall and broad, but his muscles had withered and he was a weak, faint shadow of his former self. He wore a long, white lab-coat over a brown jumper, grey shirt, black tie and dark trousers, and scuffed black shoes; he had a stethoscope hung around his thin, veined neck and a cheap watch on his wrist. He turned a bedside-lamp on and heard more muffled-sounds from beyond the door to the small dormitory where he had been sleeping. He was in a compact two-bed dormitory for hospital-staff. The other bed was empty. It was a small box-room that he previously been used as a storeroom and then converted into sleeping quarters. It was less than adequate. He had been awakened several times in the last four hours and this had not agreed with him at all. He ruffled his three-month-old beard and pinched the bridge of his nose several times, inhaling and exhaling through his nostrils. He scratched at the fluff on his cheek for a minute or two, trying to pull himself into wakefulness. His fingernails were getting longer; it had been maybe three weeks since he last cut them. He caught a rough hair and his nail gauged a tiny hole in his cheek.

Elliott got up slowly and popped a painkiller from a bottle in his lab-coat pocket, before standing with difficulty. He had trouble reaching out for the door-handle, being unsteadily led by his open palm.

He swallowed a few times, snatching then gulping a paper-cup of water, then opened the door.

Elliott stepped out into a corridor and found it completely empty, one way. He slowly turned to look down the other way, the muscles in his neck twinging. He immediately saw one of the infected pinning a man down, as he struggled on floor. The infected puked blood on him, spilling thick, glossy ooze into the man's wailing mouth.

The man screamed, as his mouth filled with blood, bubbling and splattering from the edges.

Elliott just stared, watching the infected gulping back down the flow of blood. His glassy-eyes stretched wide. He was totally perplexed. He felt like a wreck and daylight made him squint; he rubbed the deep, dark bags under his eyes. He looked scruffy and dishevelled and disoriented, but mesmerized and intrigued by what he was seeing. His mind wandered as his eyes bore into the crouching figure of the infected.

He continued to stare, fascinated and stoned, when three more infected entered the other end of the corridor.

Elliott unfroze, snapping to and gawping wide-eyed at them, petrified. Then he baulked and turned and ran away, passed the crouching-infected.

Elliott reached his office door, further down the long corridor, and unlocked it shakily as the three infected charged at him. Two of the infected had been nurses and the third had been a visitor. They were all soaked in blood. The infected were ravenous, accelerating down the space.

Elliott entered his office and slammed and locked the door behind him. He panted heavily for breath. He took another four pain-killers from the bottle and pulled a desk drawer open. He retrieved a bottle of vodka and gulped the pills down in a mouthful of poison.

The infected behind his door pounded on it.

Elliott sank to the floor and crawled into the foot-well under his desk.

Fourteen minutes ago. At Westernby Private Preparatory School for Boys.
KARYN FAULK, 41 year old Englishwoman – taught her class of eight-year olds in the junior school-section of the main school. This was built in a squared C-shape with a corridor around and classrooms off it, which kept four to eight year olds in eight classrooms. She had streaky blonde hair, tied back in a braid with a cropped fringe that reached her eyebrows. Beneath the fringe she had a striking, angular face; tweezed, arched eyebrows, professional-looking makeup, dazzling cobalt blue eyes, a sharp, small nose and full, wide lips. She was slim and petite with the body of a long-distance runner; she had

long lithe arms and legs, curved with muscle, and a flat, tight abdomen. She wore a white loose-fitting silk blouse over a sports bra, a black pleated skirt and comfortable one-inch heels.

Karyn wrote on a large, interactive white-board at the front of the class. The classroom was a large fifty-foot square, ten foot high space plastered with drawings and diagrams and posters and health-and-safety warnings and fire-exit signs. Several windows on the side-walls let flares of daylight inside, shining off the back-field of the school where there were a three-hundred metre running track, a football pitch and a large wood.

A projector bolted upside-down on the ceiling shone at Karyn, making the white-board in front of her glow with light, except where her silhouette prevented it, coating her back with light. She copied a sentence onto the white-board.

From behind her, over the course of a few seconds, most of the class started coughing.

Karyn smiled and tried to brush it off as a prank, she said, "Come on, you lot, it's nearly lunch time, you just have to pay attention for a little longer... Cut it out... Only a few more minutes..."

"Miss? Miss? Miss Faulk – Please turn around..."

Karyn turned and her mouth fell open, and her smile vanished. "Oh my God!" she whispered.

She saw that all of the fourteen pupils in her class had collapsed and were dead – with blood flowing out of their mouths and noses, and running over the edges of their desks – except one – ROBBIE SPRING, 8 year old English boy. He had long, dyed-black hair with a fringe that was swept over and down and covered one of his cool-blue eyes. He was small and unassuming; he had a skinny frame and low, sloping shoulders, thin arms and legs. He wore his school uniform; a grey v-neck jumper over a grey shirt, red and green tie, black trousers and shiny, black shoes. Robbie looked horrified, sat at the back of the class. His eyes shook and his hands gripped his arms, crossing his chest.

Karyn's eyes widened extremely. "Robbie?... Oh no," she moaned. Tears started to well-up in her eyes, and she turned away from her class, covering her face. Her body shook. One second later, without looking at Robbie, Karyn turned back to her class, then immediately checked the pulse of the nearest pupil to her. She swallowed, unable to find any pulse. She looked at Robbie, she said, "Robbie? Come to me please...."

Robbie got to his feet slowly and passed his dead classmates, being careful not to touch any of them. His shoes dragged along the floor. Tears streamed out of Robbie's eyes, wetting his cheeks completely with a sheen.

Karyn hugged Robbie closely to her, she said, "We should check the... --the... --the... --other classes... --the other classrooms... --to see what's going on..."

Robbie felt her shaking, felt her arms and thighs tremble against him. She slowly released her grip around him and looked into his eyes. He wiped away his tears. She nodded slowly at him.

"Okay... Okay... Okay," she repeated.

Karyn moved into the corridor, making sure Robbie was close-by and hidden behind her. She checked the first classroom. Everybody was dead, including the teacher. It was a horrible scene. A couple of the children had vomited blood over the whiteboard, over the floor staining the carpet, and across the space near the door. The teacher was slumped over his desk, head resting on the folded-open laptop that sat in the centre. He had also puked blood before dying. Blood and ooze soaked the laptop, his right arm and a third of the desk-top. His head twitched, as Karyn let the door go and it closed with a *click*.

Karyn crossed the thin corridor to the next classroom, and opened the door carefully.

The teacher had been infected, and it charged at Karyn. Her reflexes were good and they snapped into action, pulling the door shut with a light *slam*.

The infected banged on the door violently, punching at it, cracking the wire-inlaid safety glass in a thin panel in the door. The infected rammed its face against the panel, cutting it face and stripping away a thread of its nose. This did not phase it at all. The infected shoulder-barged the door and it *rattled* in the frame.

Karyn pulled on the handle, when she noticed the infected was not attempting to use it. She was still slow to release her grip on the handle, letting her hand hover over the twist of plastic gleaming under the fluorescent strip-beams that illuminated the hallway.

Then the infected punched through the glass-panel, snapping through the wire-mesh and grabbing at Karyn. Its hand was shredded at the knuckles, but it continued to claw and snatch at her, ramming it arm through the hole.

Karyn and Robbie ran through the junior school to the small staffroom and entered slowly. It was empty.

Karyn wedged a chair behind the handle, keeping it closed.

"I'm going to try and call the police..." she murmured. She picked up the landline-phone from the wall near the door, when a second infected appeared the other side. It banged on the glass panel, staring at both of them and spitting-up blood on itself and the glass. Karyn held the phone to her ear shakily, as the infected punched and barged and slammed ferociously against the door. Once again, the infected punched through the glass-panel. It wrenched its arm back and pushed its face through the broken-hole and puked blood. Thick, glossy mouthfuls dripped and splashed and trickled and slobbered over its lower jaw.

Karyn could not take her eyes from it, the ravenous animal that was tearing strips of skin from its cheeks and jaw.

Robbie pulled on Karyn's arm and gave her a look of terror. They ran to one of the windows, leaving the phone dangling on its coil. The phone *beeped* with the engaged-tone – then a *click* sounded and the phone went silent.

Karyn had to force and kick the window so that it would open wide enough for both of them to escape. They climbed out into the under-fives' playground. It was littered with large plastic climbing-blocks, slides and other large outdoors toys.

They heard a car engine roar.

Karyn held Robbie's hand and they darted to the end of the playground and vaulted over a two-foot high gate and launched around the side of the junior school-building, just in time to see a black BMW X5 speeding away down the driveway of the school.

"Hey! Hey!... Hey!" she shouted after the car, but it was long-gone.

She saw a cloud of exhaust and grit trailing behind the car, then it disappeared from view.

She retreated to hide behind one of the ten tall elm-trees that the junior school's car-park had been built around.

Robbie stood by another tree a few metres away.

Karyn crouched and looked around.

Something caught Karyn's eye and she stared along the front of the grand eighteenth century school-building, to the staircase leading up to the entrance. A glimmer of light shone across the main entrance-doors and Bruce Forster came limping into view. Bruce was bloody and a little bruised. He pulled on a hip-length leather coat and stumbled down the staircase. He clutched his ribs and was still bleeding from the wound on his head caused by the pistol-beating. He gripped a cricket-bat at his side. A few rivulets of blood dripped from his bloodied-arm and down the entire length of the bat. Drips of dark red fell from the tip of the bat onto each of the stairs as he stepped down.

Karyn and Robbie dashed towards Bruce.

"Bruce!... What on earth is going on?!"

Three minutes ago. On the A21 motorway.
JESUS 'CHOCO' CHIRINO, 27 year old Spaniard – was pulling-off the motorway in a Scania 40-tonne lorry. He had a short mane of fluffy dark curls, blending into a full beard down his long, curly sideburns. His eyes were dark brown orbs, shaded under a wide brow and curly, thick eyebrows. He was a few inches shy of six foot, had a muscular build overlaid with a coating of fat, and a small paunch for a belly. He was strong and physical, but had definitely let himself go; years of driving lorries with limited access to gyms had made it quite difficult for him to maintain his bulk. He did try to attempt sit-ups and press-ups every night before bed, but this was not very frequent. He wore a fleece-hoodie that was grease-blotched at the stomach and wrists, faded and tattered flared jeans that were hardened and rough at the ankles, an old grey t-shirt with a fashionably-distressed cartoon image of the Hanna-Barbera *Roadrunner* character on the chest, and comfortable, worn and cracked leather boots.

The motorway was in a virtual gridlock and Choco just-managed to manoeuvre the lorry through temporary gaps and onto the off-ramp. He swung the wheel and advanced up the off-ramp when two cars, on the overpass-bridge, collided at speed and crashed through the side-barrier and dropped into the two lanes of the motorway below. One of the cars immediately caught on fire.

Choco slowed, reaching the top of the ramp, as a car skidded into the lorry's path then mashed and clung along the front plane of the hulking vehicle. It bumped off the lorry hard and *crunched* around a large road-sign and came to a stop. The lorry was only moving at fifteen miles an hour, but it was enough, with a full payload, to pummel small cars around and out of its way. Choco had found that out three times since he began driving long-distance.

He jammed the brakes on and the lorry groaned to a stop. He switched on his hazard-lights and leapt out of the cabin. He dashed to the car and skidded to a stop on his boots, when he saw the driver had been infected.

The infected thrashed inside the car, then it projectile blood-vomited at Choco, soaking his thighs and legs from the smashed driver's-side window. It struggled in the seat, growling and flapping and punching with its hands. It stretched to reach out of the car, straining against the frame and broken glass.

Choco stared intensely at the driver, an expression of shock taught across his face.

The infected snarled and bubbles of blood boiled at its nostrils. It hacked and coughed and chomped. Its teeth made *clacking* sounds as it snapped its jaw, biting at the air between them.

Choco studied it for a moment, unable to move his legs.

The infected whipped its hands around the car and its little-finger *cracked*, hitting against the seatbelt release-button. The buckle released. The belt sprang back across its body.

"Fuck!" Choco screamed, backing away.

The infected scrambled to pull itself upright, struggling against the dented door. It managed ably to hook its fingers over the frame-edge and it climbed out of the broken-window. It ripped its hands on the broken glass in the frame, but it continued forward. It slipped out of the opening and hit the tarmac with a hollow *thump*.

Choco retreated quickly and clambered back into the cabin of the lorry. The engine roared and he sped away, as the infected crawled to its feet and started to chase him.

Three days later.
Choco sprinted through a wood, branches whipping across his face and body, when he came across Karyn, Robbie and Bruce. They were sitting around a makeshift camp in a small clearing. No fire had been lit. Their packs were piled closely in the centre of a small collection of supplies: canned food, three sleeping-bags and an assortment of weapons; three cricket-bats, a large axe, three hammers, two kitchen-knives and a large, long metal bar. Karyn knelt next to her pack, Robbie sat cross-legged reading a book, and Bruce sat on one leg, sharpening a gardening-sickle; a short wooden handle with a long curving blade for cutting long grass, corn and wheat.

Choco froze on the spot, holding his hands in the air, seeing each of them clearly.

"They are... --chasing..." he stammered. "They... They... --follow!"

The group stood.

Karyn snatched a hammer from the pile. Robbie took out a small hunting-knife. Bruce dropped the sickle and picked up the large axe.

Karyn stepped forward, she said, "How many are there?... Err... Ah... Um... Quanto mas?"

Choco stammered, he said, "T-T-T-Th-Three."

Karyn handed him a cricket-bat. They turned to the trees and bushes, as the first infected of the three emerged from the undergrowth, snarling and growling.

Now armed, Choco was fuelled to fight, and quite eager. He rushed at the infected and beat it with the cricket-bat, cracking a deep dent into the top of its head with the sharp wood-edge.

Bruce pushed passed Choco and killed it with a death blow from the axe. He swung up, then hacked its head off with one chop.

The second and third infected tore through the foliage, motoring straight by Bruce.

Choco hit the second infected, knocking it accidentally into Karyn's path. She reacted quickly and flicked out with her hammer. It clipped the chin of the infected and it took a few steps backwards. She looked ferocious as she attacked it, screaming out. The infected advanced, marching forward, and Karyn hit it under the chin again. The force of the hit knocked the infected onto its back. The short stem of a broken tree had impaled it through the side. Blood seeped around the wound. The infected gargled and spat blood, flicking its head to each member of the group.

Karyn turned the hammer in her hand and used it like a banker's-stamp. She battered its face, crushing it's cheek-bones and pounding its nasal bone into its brain.

Bruce rushed at the third infected and bulldozered it to the ground before it reached Robbie. He landed heavily on it, scrambling and turning over, struggling to reach up, and then snapped its neck.

Choco stepped back, watching Karyn and Bruce. "Whoa!" he said, then swallowed. "Thank... you... Thank you." Choco clapped his hands together and nodded at each of them, a silent prayer, including Robbie who stood in front of the packs, gripping his knife, guarding them. Choco's eyes watered and he struggled to suppress his tears. "Thank you!"

Karyn passed Choco. She looked at Bruce and Robbie, she said, "Are you both okay?"

"Ay," Bruce said with a confident nod.

"Yes," Robbie said. He watched Choco, still gripping his knife, then turned to Karyn. He nodded and his grip loosened, and his arm went slack. Karyn rubbed his shoulder gently.

Choco looked at the others, wiping his tears away on the fabric of his t-shirt.

A little later.
Choco wandered through the woods, searching around, looking for something. He recovered a large grey-blue backpack where he had tossed it, picked it up and swung it onto his shoulder. He walked back to Karyn, Robbie and Bruce, who stood nearby on a skinny mud-path.

They walked back to the camp, and they sat.

They ate cans of Heinz spaghetti, then pineapple-chunks.

"Where were you?"

"I live in Spain."

"Where were you, when this happened?"

"Oh. Si... I was... --driving... A lorry."

"A lorry?"

"Four... Ah... Forty tonnes."

"Right," Bruce said. "Where to?"

"To London. And you?"

Karyn stroked her face and blinked. "A school... Escuela?"

"Ah, si, si," he replied with several nods. "I was in... --a village... For two days... My petrol... No mas."

"Oh..."

"What do you think is going on?" Karyn asked, cocking her head to one side.

Choco shrugged, opening his bag. He offered them more food. He took out an apple, polished it on his t-shirt chest, and took a bite. He finally replied, "Maybe... the government... --or the army... --or the scientists made a... --an accident... A big accident... I don't know." Choco took another bite from the apple. He was much calmer now and his English was beginning to improve slightly.

Karyn was alert to their surroundings, her eyes danced across the trees and bushes around them.

"Where were you going to go, Choco?" Bruce said slowly.

"I don't know... If England is like-this... Spain is like-this also... I won't go to my home... I might be killed." He shrugged and took another bite of the apple.

Bruce started to gather their things and packed their bags.

"Will you stay with us?" Karyn asked, putting her hand on Choco's arm. She felt the bicep muscle under his skin and t-shirt.

Choco half-nodded, he said, "Okay. I will."

Two weeks later. At a farm.
Choco sprinted from a pursuing infected. He darted around a wall-corner and hopped over a rope that cut across the path. Bruce tugged the rope taught, causing the infected to trip over it clumsily. Its face dug into the mud and it fell to the ground lame.

    Choco and Bruce beat it to death.

    Karyn walked out of a nearby wood-shed where she had been hiding. She half-smiled, brushing hair behind her ear. "Good work."

    Bruce looked to Karyn, he said, "That leaves us the farmhouse empty."

    "This-one was the last for miles around," Choco said.

    Karyn turned to them both, she said, "I'll go and get Robbie from the barn, then we can start moving in... Can you-two take that to the ditch and set it alight...?"

    Bruce nodded. "Come on then, kid."

    "Si."

A little later.
Bruce made everyone a cup of tea. They sat in the kitchen of the farmhouse.

    Choco returned from looking around the house, he said, "It's okay, for now. There are three bedrooms. So I will sleep on the couch..."

    Choco was about to continue when Karyn silenced him. She heard something coming from outside, someone faintly shouting, "Hello?"

    Bruce crept to the window, picking up his axe on the way. He had heard the voice as well.

Outside.
Elliott walked down the driveway to the farm, passed a dormant and rusting combine-harvester. He had a limp and stumbled slowly, pained, toward the farmhouse, shouting, "Hello?" again and again.

    Bruce stepped out of the farmhouse and moved to intercept Elliott's path. He stopped a short distance from the farmhouse's front-gate, gripping the axe with both hands.

    "Hello... Where've you come from?" he bellowed.

    Elliott stopped walking. He was about twenty metres from Bruce. He looked at the axe suspiciously, then looked Bruce in the eye sympathetically. He said, "I'm from... I was... I was in a hospital... Pembury Hospital!... I'm a doctor... I hid for a week until I escaped... Please... Help me... I'm so hungry."

    Bruce stared at Elliott distrustfully, squinting and trying to divine the truth from his words.

    Elliott continued, "How many of you are there?... I saw there was a couple of you, when I walked down the hill a little while ago.... A small boy and a woman...? Is it just the three of you?"

    Bruce looked at the kitchen window, at Karyn, who watched them from inside. He swung his head back to Elliott and eyed him. He noticed Elliott was looking at the window as well. Karyn stepped away from the glass and was hidden in shade.

    "Why do you want to know?"

    "Because if it's just you and me, then that'll make restarting civilisation a problem," Elliott joked.

    Karyn appeared in the doorway to the farmhouse. "You saw us from the hill?" she called.

    Bruce turned to look at her, then faced Elliott, who crept forward.

    "Yes. From the hill back a ways... So, how many of you are there?"

    Bruce looked back to Karyn.

    She nodded.

    He said, "There are four of us."

    Elliott seemed momentarily taken-aback, he said, "Four?... Four?... That's all... Even still... That is more real-people than I've seen in over a week... It's actually great to be able to talk to someone... Even a stranger."

    Elliott's eyes glazed and he tried to smile, but he could not.

    "We're all nearly strangers."

"Yes," Elliott agreed smarmily. "That's quite right."

Four days later. At night.
Karyn ran as fast as she could into a ruined cathedral. She was dirty and tired, wet with sweat and bloody, anxious and panicked. Her clothes were ripped and muddy at the elbows, knees and shoulder.

She dashed between two broken walls, then climbed over another knocking stones down, then saw two parked Land Rovers. She froze, staring at the spotless cars, and reached out to touch one. She exhaled slowly, then sprinted between the cars and stopped suddenly when she entered a larger space with a mezzanine-floor above her. Her feet dug into the mud and she straightened.

Victor Conway's rifle-torch immediately shone in her eyes. Karyn froze, immediately putting her arms in the air, breathing heavily. Victor and the group on the mezzanine-floor stared down at Karyn carefully.

Barney Meadway emerged from the shadows in front of her holding his silenced Beretta 92FS pistol aimed at her head. A flash-light was pressed to the side of the gun, pointing the beam directly in her eyes. "Please," she murmured.

Barney lowered the torch. It shone on her shoulder and neck, allowing him to see her a little more clearly. He could hear her ragged breathing and took a small pace backward.

Clive and Roy stepped closer to the edge, neither of them raising their pistols at Karyn.

Karyn trembled, when Clive asked her, "Why were you running?"

Karyn replied shakily, "I'm being chased."

"By the infected?" Victor shouted.

Karyn shook her head, she said, "No... --by people!"

Clive instantly stood up to see if he could see anyone coming, when a dull, leafy-green gas-canister was tossed from behind a rubble-wall. It landed at his feet, straightaway releasing thick, smoky white gas with a constant *hiss*. Second, third, fourth and fifth canisters landed on the mezzanine-floor and at Karyn's feet on the grass below.

Karyn was the first to pass-out, collapsing on soft grass, then Clive and Roy fell limp onto the edge of the mezzanine. The remainder of the group fell into unconsciousness on the mezzanine floor, as the gas billowed and expanded and filled the area, spilling over onto the grass where Karyn lay in a smoky waterfall. Silence fell over the scene, as the canisters expelled the last of the gas with final *sputters* and *hisses*.

In the huge cloud of gas, Victor sunk away into the shadows wearing a gas-mask. He still held his silenced-machinegun gripped in front of him.

He vanished.

Under the staircase.
Barney crouched then clambered into a small tunnel and scrambled into a cave-like recess under the ruined structure. He carried a silenced-machinegun with him, slung over his back, and the silenced-pistol outstretched in front of him. He crawled along a heavy floor of rubble in the dark, dislodging bricks and stones with his shoes, the barrel-vaulted roof only six inches above him.

A little later.
Barney watched from the shadows, as four large soldiers in black fatigues carried the unconscious bodies of each member of his group from the mezzanine. They were gentle and were careful not to injure any of the group as they manoeuvred down the skinny spiral staircase to the ground-floor. They loaded the bodies onto hospital-style gurneys, that two other soldiers had wheeled into the space.

The soldiers lifted the gurneys onto guides and pushed them into a large armoured-truck. The back of the truck looked like an open-plan mobile-morgue, with low bunk-beds mounted atop one-another to fill the entire back-space, except for one thin passageway that ran between the bunks down the centre. They loaded the gurneys carrying Karyn, Clive, Roy and Melodie, Annabel, Harmony and Evie onto the truck, into the bunk-bed-structure, then locked them in place.

One of the soldiers placed transparent plastic face-masks over the mouths and noses of all of their captives and secured them around the back of their heads with fabric-elastic cords. The face-masks were linked to tubes that veined along the structure, meeting a large, flat gas-tank on the roof of the truck under a large plate of armour.

Barney could not see, but Bruce, Choco, Elliott and Robbie had also been loaded onto the trunk. They already had face-masks over their faces, keeping them sedated.

Barney backed-away into the darkness, still staring at the soldiers. He had vengeance and anger in his eyes.

A little later.
The armoured-truck pulled away from the cathedral ruins, disappearing into the night, leaving only red brake-lights as a trail.

Barney stepped out from behind a ruined-wall near the entrance. He watched them go.

As soon as he could not see the truck, he turned and walked toward the pair of Land Rovers. He opened the first Land Rover's driver's-door and climbed in.

Barney put the pistol he had been holding all night on the dashboard, rubbing his hand and wrist. He twisted the key that was already in the ignition, and the engine came alive. He drove after the truck, without any lights, guiding it through a little section of the ruins in almost pitch darkness and out onto the road nearby.

Later. At daybreak.
Barney steadily drove down a country road, using only the front side-lights.

Ahead five hundred metres along the road, the armoured-truck crested a hill.

Later. In Bromley, South-east London.
Barney drove down a road parallel to the armoured-truck. He paused at the end of road to watch the truck drive on, one hundred metres away from him.

He drove carefully, glancing around the street he was in, when an infected charged at the Land Rover and hit face-first against the driver's-door-window. A long crack webbed from the point of impact. Barney looked shocked for a moment, then continued on, unaffected and emotionless.

The infected sprinted down the street after the Land Rover, when Barney broke. It slammed into the back of the Land Rover and *crunched* against it, breaking its leg and pelvis.

Barney accelerated away.

The crippled infected lay in the road, arms out-stretched after the car, teeth *snapping* at the air.

A little later. On Sydenham Hill.
The Land Rover idled to the peak of a hill, when the petrol finally ran dry. The hill overlooked a long, wide stretch of the city of London. Early morning light glimmered and beamed out of a sky veiled in light grey cloud.

The car coasted for a few metres then stopped with a lurch.

Barney put the handbrake on.

He reached into the back-seat and found a pair of binoculars in one of two large bags, then turned and put the binoculars to his eyes. The armoured-truck pulled off the road and went out of sight. Barney swept the binoculars around to locate the truck but to no avail, for several minutes.

He gritted his teeth.

He glanced around the Land Rover and saw a large red-brick block of flats. The sign on the wall near the entrance-doors read: Frobisher Court. Barney hopped out of the Land Rover and darted across the road and up to the doors, where he shot the lock with the silenced-pistol. He quickly moved along the main corridor and found the lift. He pressed the button and stood in the cold silence, listening to the motors *whir* and *chug*.

The lift arrived and Barney found it empty. A broad pool of blood soaked one corner, and finger-, arm- and leg-marks smeared two of the walls. He entered calmly and pressed the button for the eighth floor. The lift shuddered then carried Barney upwards.

He stepped into a short corridor with four flat doors extending from it, and two emergency-exits at either end.

One of the infected stood in the corridor by flat 36, where the doorway was half-wedged open; an old lady lay on the floor, preventing the door from closing. The infected was a middle-aged man, thin and balding. Blood soaked its chest, covering an area where a bib would shelter. Its mouth chomped open and closed. Its teeth *clicked* as its jaws connected.

Barney lifted the silenced-pistol and the infected edged toward him. He fired and the first bullet tore through one of its ears, shredding it. He fired again and the infected was hit in the eye. It skipped backwards and hit the window behind it. Barney fired another time and the window shattered, throwing glass and the infected into the open air. Its arms flailed in the wind as it was dragged downward.

The body hit the ground with a *thump* and a *crack*, pooling with blood, motionless.

Barney booted the emergency-exit open and dashed into a small stairwell. He charged up the smoothed-concrete steps and shoulder-barged the roof-access open. The door swung wide and battered against a brace.

Barney ran to the edge and pressed the binoculars to his eyes. He looked for a long moment, sweeping back and forth. Then he saw the truck again, travelling in the direction of an enormous complex of buildings with a huge wall and fence lining its vast perimeter. The buildings included the Royal Observatory, the National Maritime Museum and the Old Naval College, backing off against the River Thames.

Barney swung the binoculars across the city, and something else caught his eye. He stopped on the river. A tiny dot coasted along the river passing the O2 Arena. It was a Thames-skiff with a small outboard moving slowly upstream on the grey-brown river, with three men aboard it. He watched as one of the men waved and pointed in the direction of the Royal Observatory. These men were Don Clement, Craig Charlton and Marc Sheridan.

Barney watched them intently for a long time.

A little later.
Barney climbed into the back of the Land Rover quickly, and quietly closed the door behind him. He gathered together supplies from the back-section and two bags, and filled a backpack. He stretched across the front-seat and took several boxes of ammunition for the pistol from the glove-compartment, set under the dashboard. He pulled a silenced-machinegun and silenced-sniper-rifle from the back-section and looped both over his shoulder.

He pulled a black beanie-hat over his hair, sweeping it away from his eyes, then threw the door open.

Later. In Greenwich.
Barney darted along a rooftop, then paused at the edge.

He put the binoculars to his eyes and saw the skiff ditched on the side of the river. He swept the view and found Don, Marc and Craig fighting seven infected in a large square plaza with a wharf on the waterfront at the back.

Barney instantly snatched the silenced-sniper-rifle and put the A-stand out. He flicked the lens-cap from the sight and took aim. He inhaled a deep gulp of air and held it.

He fired.

CHAPTER 20 - HOUSE DOCTOR - London

The Queen's House, National Maritime Museum – 5:22pm.

Doctor DONOVAN CROETZER, 54 year old Englishman – stood outside the grand entrance of the vast former royal residence. He was a slight man, no more than five foot six, with little to no build. He had aged badly and wrinkles were engraved around his eyes and mouth. He had thin grey hair, parted on the left side. He wore small, wire-frame spectacles that sat neatly on his big, rubbery ears. He was always clean shaven, and had remained that way even beyond the moment when the virus was released. He wore a three-piece suit and resembled a man from the 60s, prim and refined. He had mendacious eyes, tucked and sunken behind the fine discs of glass of his spectacles. His shoes were always immaculate and had been shined that very morning. He tapped the hard leather sole of his shoe on the top step of the twin front entrance-staircases.

Soldiers in black fatigues had made a large camp in the substantial ground: dorm-tents, mess-tents, communications and map-tents with tables and equipment, four CCTV vans, three large Ops tents and several other erections including toilets and food-stores.

A few army vehicles were scattered across the lawns, some parked neatly in rows, other strategically placed behind the perimeter gates, in case of intruders. From Park Row to the King William Walk the gates and walls had been reinforced and heightened. Three-metre tall wooden-plank guard-towers had been constructed at twenty-metre intervals along the walls on both sides. Every second guard-tower was manned by two soldiers, armed with silenced-machineguns.

Two larger, six-metre tall wooden-plank and -post guard-towers had been constructed either side of an 'air-lock' set of gates on the corner of Park Row and Park Vista. There were two twin sets of massive oak gates that extended from the perimeter-wall and -gate inward, forming an 'air-lock' for entering- and exiting-vehicles, eight-metres deep. These were manned continually with guards posted at stations on platforms below the towers, and in the towers themselves. From the lower deck the guards controlled the opening and closing of the gates.

Romney Road, the A206, that cut through the complex had been blocked off at both ends with huge metal walls on the Northeast side. Another 'air-lock' had been constructed on the Southwest side, exactly the same as the other, guarded and manned by twenty more soldiers.

At the Southeast corner of Greenwich Park, where The Avenue, Nevada Street and King William Walk met, near the statue of King William IV, another barricade had been built with another huge metal wall. Several soldiers were permanently grouped behind the barricade next to a small armoury.

Ostentatious and masterpiece paintings, costumes, suits-of-armour and antique furniture had been taken from the buildings and moved into various wooden crates on the front lawn at the side of The Queen's House, and had been covered in huge tarpaulins that were pinned to the ground at the corners. A team of soldiers dressed in black fatigues, ignoring the clamour of their colleagues, removed the antiques and packaged them safely.

Two soldiers in black fatigues stood either side of Croetzer, armed with silenced-machineguns. Croetzer saw, across the huge lawn and various tents, that a black-painted APC was pulling into the Northeast 'air-lock' – tagged with the words 'Gate A' in large, spray-canned lettering on the inside-facing side of the gates.

The APC stopped and the outer-gates closed with a minor *thump* behind it.

Four soldiers on each of the platforms, either side of the 'air-lock', swept the enclosed area for any of the infected, then waved to an eighth soldier, who opened the inner-gates with the push of a button. The inner-gates *creaked* and yawned, swinging into the complex.

Croetzer smiled menacingly, as the APC pulled along the start of Romney Road and stopped. The engine switched off and *ticked* in the afternoon sun.

"Good. New guests," he said quietly.

The group inside climbed out the APC, with the help of the soldiers who had been occupying it. The APC had a seated-section in the back for transporting soldiers, two benches bolted to the walls on both sides. The group was: Fiona and Nicola, Eileen, Baz and Harlan, Layla, Vivienne and Kit, Meredith and Nigel, and Bernie and Suthep.

They huddled and massed, staring in awe at the soldiers marching to and fro around them.

Fiona's eyes tightened, trying to make eye-contact with one of the soldiers. None looked at anyone in the group.

Nicola took Eileen's hand and Eileen squeezed it. She did not know whether Eileen was excited or frightened. She did not know which she was either. "I don't know if I like this," she whispered to her friend.

"We'll just have to see," Eileen replied, feigning cheer.

"What is this place?"

"Where have all these people come from?"

"Are they the army?"

"This is where they filmed Thor 2, isn't it?"

"Yeah... Over there, and around there," Suthep nodded.

Croetzer marched down the opulent curved staircase and walked through a bustling group of soldiers, who parted around him, and he stopped a few metres ahead of the group. He addressed them, "Welcome... My name is Donovan Croetzer and, as you can see, I am well-resourced and have managed to find a lot of help in this grave, horrendous time... And... We have managed to make some kind of temporary refuge here, in this place... We intend to try and find out what in the world has happened, and to help any survivors we find... We want to find more survivors, and we want to help them, like we will help you... This complex is more than sufficient and we are protecting it well."

Kit, Baz and Nigel all noticed, as Fiona and Nicola shared a look of concern.

"Please, come inside..."

Croetzer motioned for the group to move into the House, when Nicola asked, "What have you learned about what is going on?"

Croetzer smiled, he said, "I'll tell you everything I know over some food and drink... We are well-stocked and I think you will be happy... Go inside, I'll join you in the dining-room..."

The group slowly filed up the staircase and through the grand entrance-way into The Queen's House. They wandered into a plastic-sheeting-sided, low-ceilinged, long corridor that had been built as a temporary indoor 'air-lock' into the main building. A string of lights hung from hooks along the central-peak of the corridor.

There were only two doors along the corridor, one at each end; where they had entered, and a nondescript panel at the far-end.

Nicola and Fiona both noticed the lack of exits and slowed to the back of the pack, looking back through the grand entrance-way at Croetzer and his army.

"Tell me," Croetzer whispered.

Fiona and Nicola stared back and saw Croetzer with one of the soldiers.

"They are unarmed," the soldier said with a nod.

"Good... Proceed."

Fiona tried to read Croetzer's lips, but it was too late. The doors mechanically closed by themselves with a *boom* and a hermetic *hiss*. Daylight disappeared instantly as black-out shades covered the windows. The gloom in the corridor was immediately replaced by the glow of the electric lights above their heads.

The group huddled together.

"What's going on?"

"What's happening?"

The corridor visibly tightened on all sides and the air became heavy.

Outside.

Croetzer nodded and a soldier spoke into a walkie-talkie.

Croetzer beamed at the doorway, seeing the tent inside the hallway tighten.

Inside the entrance-corridor.

Fiona and Nicola immediately tried to push against the walls, but they did not move. Everybody quickly became very anxious very quickly, when a thick white gas started to cloud the room, coming from hidden ceiling- and floor-pipes and -vents.

Bernie and Suthep punched at the walls. Baz rushed to Fiona's side. Eileen's hand gripped Nicola's, squeezing her fingers together. Nigel tried to shoulder-barge the corridor wall. Meredith started down the corridor to the door at the far-end.

The cloud rushed around them.

All members of the group fell unconscious in a loose huddle.

The smoke filled the corridor, billowing over their bodies.

Later.

The first to awaken was Fiona. Her eyes unscrewed themselves, the muscles in her cheeks and temples relaxing finally. Her head felt foggy, heavy and her senses were dulled. She regained her balance, planting each foot on the concrete floor. Light spots and shadows danced across her vision. She had not even noticed the room she was in. Everyone of the group had been laid-down on their own bunk. They were in a large and long underground room with no windows and one access door, and lit by the weakest of light fixtures, sparsely placed along the centre of the ceiling. The room was divided by two iron-bar walls a metre apart, forming a corridor that split the room into two equally divided cells. There were fifty bunk-beds in each cell, and they mirrored one-another. Damp patches dotted the subterranean chamber walls.

Fiona tried to wake Baz first. He lay on the bunk beside here. He slumbered and moaned, then she moved on to Nicola, Harlan, Nigel and the others.

The whole group had been implanted in one cell, while the other seemingly remained empty. But there was one occupant in the other cell. The man was hidden under a large pile of rags and cloth in the farthest corner away from the others; his body was hidden in shadow and cramped behind the sturdy iron frame of the farthest bunk-bed.

Once everyone was awake, they examined the room.

"What the hell is happening? Where are we?" Nigel demanded.

"Who was that man?"

"What is this place?" Eileen asked.

"A jail... A dormitory..." Baz offered weakly.

"A prison-cell," Suthep agreed, nodding to Baz genially.

"Who were those fucking soldiers?" Harlan groaned.

"Who was that man?... Croetzer?" Layla asked. "Was that what he said his name was?"

"Why were we drugged?"

"Why are we underground?"

"Why are we in a fucking prison-cell?!" Harlan yelled, gripping the bars of the cage-wall.

"Are those-guys what's left of the Army?" Baz asked.

"I don't think so," Nicola replied.

"Me, either," Fiona agreed.

"Hey!" a voice called out from the other cell.

Everyone fell silent.

"Did you hear that?" Baz whispered.

The voice said, "It's no use asking questions... It's no use... It's pointless... You're prisoners now... And there is no way of escaping!"

Four days later.

The group sat in silence in the prison-cell.

The door unlocked with a *clunk* and they watched four soldiers in black-fatigues wheel several gurneys into the middle corridor of the room. They unlocked the single gate into the opposite cell with a swipe of an electronic access-card. The gate popped open with a *click*.

They pushed the gurneys into the second cell and deposited several new people on the camp-style beds. They were: Karyn, Elliott, Robbie, Bruce and Choco, Clive, Roy, Melodie, Harmony, Evie and Annabel.

Fiona and Nicola both watched avidly, hanging onto the bars of the cell. One of the soldiers noticed Fiona and Nicola watching, but did nothing. He turned away and continued to move the new survivors into their cell, and wheel the gurneys out of the cell, indifferent to the looks on their faces.

Once the soldiers had wheeled all of the gurneys out, Nicola and Fiona – joined by Nigel and Kit – pushed themselves close to the bars to examine the new guests. The soldiers marched out of the room and closed the single door.

Nicola called out, "Pike?"

A man emerged from the shadows at the far end of the cell and moved to check on the new arrivals. He was the prisoner who had been hidden under the rags. His name was PIKE, 49 year old Englishman. Pike looked like he was homeless; long, rough beard and straggly hair, poor, ripped clothes and sandal-shoes. He faced Nicola, cleared his throat, then spoke. "They're all still out..."

Nigel sat down, dejected, he said, "Forget them... We have to get out of here, ourselves... We have to come up with a plan!"

"It's safer in-here than it is out-there... Besides, we're fed here and... And you never know – this might be the way society has to be rebuilt at first... After everything that has happened..." Fiona said and sat down, watching Pike, as he leered over the others.

Nicola watched Pike as well, when he noticed her. He shook his head in a little gesture and looked back at Elliott's body. He randomly checked the pulses of the new-comers.

"What if Croetzer started the plague?" Nicola finally said.

Fiona's eyebrows drooped.

Near the River Thames.
Don Clement, Craig Charlton and Marc Sheridan fought with a pack of seven of the infected in a large square plaza with a wharf on the waterfront at the back.

Don and Craig moved like seasoned-professionals, covering each other's backs and Marc's, and improvising cleverly during the fight. Marc noticed their boyish pleasure in the fight, and occasionally caught smiles on their faces and joy in their eyes.

They managed to kill the infected between them, then ran to find cover. They moved like the army; stalking along in single-file, running closely to the walls next to them, pausing and passing each other, and showing extreme vigilance; pointing their silenced-machineguns ahead of them as they sped on.

Don turned into a side-street and jogged down it, with Marc and Craig following closely, paces behind him.

An infected darted into the road behind them, when a sniper-bullet cut it down. The men did not see the fallen infected as it ploughed into the tarmac and came to a stop with a *crunch* when it hit a high stone curb.

Don stopped them halfway down the side-street, he said, "Do you both actually think that truck came this way?... In this direction? Otherwise, I think we may've lost it."

Marc eyed Don and shrugged, he said, "The truck must've come this way... All these smaller roads lead this way. The others are mostly blocked with traffic and crashes..."

Craig glanced up and down the street, keeping a lookout. "Maybe we should get to higher ground... --while we've still got way-plenty of daylight left."

Don nodded, "Okay, good."

A little later. On Vanbrugh Hill road.
The trio scaled the brick-wall-side of a railway bridge. Their hands and clothes quickly blackened with soot, exhaust and smoke from the dirty bricks.

They climbed down to an Underground railway track, overgrown along its sides.

Craig descended first, followed by Marc then Don.

A little later. On a nearby rooftop.
Don climbed onto a small concrete shed and pressed a pair of binoculars to his eyes. Craig and Marc looked through rifle-sights up and down the railway track and surrounding roads, searching to see any infected. There were none anywhere in sight.

All of a sudden Marc said, "Boys – quick – look this way!"

He pointed in the direction of a flare that someone had fired. It arced into the air, fizzing red smoke, then dropped out of view quickly behind a tall office-building.

Don swung the binoculars to see Barney Meadway. The teenager stood on top of a apartment-building three hundred and fifty metres away, waving his arms in the air. His hands dropped and then he looked at them through his binoculars.

Marc and Craig waved back.

"What the fuckin' hell is a kid doin' out-here with a machinegun, a rifle and a pistol?!... And... --where the fuck did he get all that stuff?" Craig blurted, lowering the sight of his gun.

Don glanced at him. "I have no idea."

A little later.
Barney darted down a street, his trainers *squeaking* on the tarmac. A dozen infected chased headlong after him. In an instant, several bullets *whizzed* past Barney, but the shot-noises were muffled and suppressed. He faced forward, keeping his focus, when the infected nearest to Barney lurched backwards and was thrown down to the ground, a large bullet-hole blasted through its neck. Dark ooze spread from the wound, leaking and spurting and pooling on the road.

The second-nearest infected took a bullet through the nose and ploughed out of the back of its skull, making it trip and stumble and fall into an open car-door.

The third-nearest infected was hit in the breastplate, flinging it back out of Barney's peripheral vision.

Barney's feet stamped down on the pavement, as he kicked his way forward, swinging his arms, pushing onward.

The fourth, fifth and sixth infected all took hits to the face and neck, stopping them in their pursuit.

On a road-bridge one hundred metres away and above the road.
Don and Craig fired silenced-rifles on the pursuing infected, as Marc lowered a cable to the road below, into the open void of the bridge-tunnel. He passed the cable through his hands, dangling it over the edge of the barrier, swinging it into the space below.

Don took out the seventh infected with a shot through the heart, and then another bullet to the forehead.

On the street.
Barney ducked, dodged and weaved, giving Don and Craig better shots at their targets. The eighth and ninth infected were dropped seconds before they would have caught up with Barney, throwing both bodies backwards along their paths.

Barney reached the cable and leapt at it. Instantly Marc started to pull him up.

He watched the ground drop away from him.

Craig stopped shooting, dropping his gun on the road, snatched the cable, and helped Marc pull Barney up.

The cable swung and twisted, turning Barney around and around. He felt the fleeting sensation of dizziness, but it passed quickly, as he reached the arched brick-roof of the tunnel.

The remaining three infected collected below Barney, stretching their arms up at his receding boots, clawing the air. Their teeth snapped and *clicked*. He slid his silenced-pistol from its holster and pointed at each of the infected, and executed them in turn.

Don glanced over the edge, helping to guide the cable up safely. "You okay?"

Barney beamed up a Don and half-smiled. "Good. Thank you. You?"

Don could not help but smile back at the wide-eyed teenager they were lifting up to the road. Don stretched out his arm and Barney caught it in his.

A little later.
They sat on the edge of the road and huddled by a low brick-wall. Craig, Don and Marc listened to Barney.

"And this guy, Victor, gave us these cars and all these weapons... We were on our way to East London when we were ambushed by these men... Soldiers... Dressed in black... They took my family..." Barney concluded, "I saw from a hill a few miles back where the truck was going..."

"It's the black armoured-truck we saw from the river," Don added.

Craig nodded.

Barney nodded. "Yeah... They went to the National Maritime Museum... They have some kind of camp built there."

"We saw the truck and started tracking it in the middle of the night... We thought it was a group of more survivors trying to get out of the city..." Craig said.

Barney gritted his teeth and shook his head. "No. That was them."

"How old are you, mate?"

"Seventeen," he stated. "Do you have a map of this area?"

Before Craig could reach for their map, Barney took out one of his own and laid it flat between them. Barney pointed out a particular location: a section of green in the city. He said, "It's here... This is where the place is. This complex."

Then it began to rain. It started as a few light spots, then built in strength.

Barney took out a Sharpie and quickly drew many of the tents and entry points into the complex. "We need to get a better look at the whole place," he said meeting the eyes of the three men that sat beside him.

Later.
Don and Craig huddled in the gangway of a 53-seater coach. They laid on their knees and elbows, dragging themselves along the central aisle. It appeared that at the moment when the plague was release the coach had been stationary. Those who died immediately remained in their seats; those missing were those that had fled or were infected.

Several of the passengers looked serene in their death, while others had pain etched into their faces.

Don and Craig hid from the view from the road, as a large horde of infected flooded around the coach.

It continued to rain. It pitter-pattered, sounding like a million tiny nails hitting the metal roof-hull of the coach. Lines of water streaked down the windows, snaking diagonally and dotting the glass.

"It's just like old times," Craig whispered.

Don's head bucked a little and he half-smiled. "These fucking things," he said shaking his head.

"What d'you think of the kid?"

"Barney?"

"Yeah... I wouldn't be referring to Marc as a kid, you dope."

"He's a kid too," Don whispered. "Barney, though... He seems incredibly resourceful... --and brave... Or stupid."

"He's definitely interesting... --but creepy."

"Yeah."

"How many did you count?"

"Um... Sixty-three..." Don whispered.

"I got sixty-six."

Elsewhere.
Marc and Barney hid from the same horde of infected in a gated, mock corner-garden at the base of an office-building and a church, huddled under brown nylon hooded-ponchos in the rain. They were damp and wet patches had formed in several uncovered places on their clothes.

"So, you were following the truck... To what end?" Marc asked in a hushed tone.

"To get my family back," Barney stated.

"On your own?"

"I was going to try..."

Marc breathed in quietly, whistling up his nostrils. "At least you know some of your family survived the plague, kid.. I have no idea."

"I know I may've survived the plague. What worries me – today – is what's going to happen after."

"Me too," Marc agreed with a nod. "It's enough to worry about those things, let alone these new people too..."

Marc peered down the side-wall of the church, peeking through the leaves of several plants.

The infected horde massed and moved steadily away from them. He thought it looked like a march or rally against something, but it drifted aimlessly in no particular direction.

Barney crept close to the gate and stared at the coach, when Don's face appeared in one of the windows near the front; he was looking for them.

Their eyes met and Don held up his hand signalling for them 'wait there'.

Inside the coach.
Don turned to Craig, he said, "We have to come up with something to get us out of this bind... Barney looks like he's getting ants in his pants."

Craig looked out of the window at the sky, he said, "At least the rain's letting-up..."

Don opened a backpack and pulled out several magazines for his silenced-pistol. He stuffed them in his pockets and pulled the zip halfway up.

Craig crawled down the gangway over a couple of bodies, to the driver's body. He looked from the ignition – where the key was still in place – back to Don.

"It might start," he whispered. "Key's in!"

"If it doesn't, it'll cause more trouble than it's worth."

Craig agreed with a nod and backed away from it. He stared through the blood-splattered windscreen and saw a few infected turning the street-corner, and out of his sight. Several more lolloped into the road to fill their places.

Later that day. At dusk.
The horde had finally moved on. The last infected turned the corner onto Maze Hill road and disappeared.

Barney and Marc dashed across the road and joined Don and Craig in the coach. They climbed aboard and pulled the door closed behind them.

The last drops of rain coursed down the windows.

"I've got any idea," Barney exclaimed before anyone else could speak.

Two minutes later.
Don, Craig, Barney and Marc leapt from the coach, as it gradually gained speed. Don had wedged a brick on the accelerator, tied the steering-wheel to lock in a straight direction, and set off the coach's alarm. It *wailed* and shrieked.

They ran in the opposite direction from the coach as it continued away up the road, moving Northeast. It scraped along the side of a black 2006 Toyota Yaris, *squeaking* and grinding. It attracted several slow-moving and running infected, who chased after it and tried to board it through the open side-door. Other infected crowded after it and began to fill the road, massing and collecting in the wake of the coach.

A dozen infected charged into the road from an adjoining side-street and rammed face- and chest-first into the side of the coach. The force of the impacts rocked the coach on its axles onto its farther set of wheels.

Don rushed ahead of the others, as they darted into an alleyway. But he had to stop immediately: Don dropped to one knee and opened suppressed-gunfire on several oncoming infected, who had been alerted and drawn to the sound of the coach's *wailing* alarm.

Three bullets zipped through the air and took down the front three infected, making them tumble and trip and fall in front of the row behind them.

Craig passed Don, his boots beating the pavement, and Don took several shots by him. The bullets *whistled* around Craig and met an infected in three places: the chest, the neck and the mouth. As Craig reached the infected, he shoulder-barged it into the wall of the alleyway. It struck the wall and splattered with blood, graffiti-ing the brickwork with a postmodernist display of gore.

Don shot another infected five paces ahead of Craig with a kill-shot to the forehead, then a fourth and fifth with life-ending precision.

Barney and Marc followed Craig, then Don raced after them. They roared with adrenaline, hearts pounding, lungs burning, faces and armpits sweating profusely, throats blazing.

They ran into the next street, when they encountered a black-painted armoured-truck – not the black APC they had been tracking, but another. The APC was stationary and filled the void at the end of the road, blocking their path to the Museum complex over half a mile away.

Two soldiers wearing black fatigues leapt out of the cabin of the truck and pointed silenced-machineguns at the four survivors. "Don't move!" one of the two soldiers shouted.

They froze in a stand-off.

Don eyed both of the men with a furrowed brow and gritted teeth.

As did Craig and Marc, either side of Don.

Barney's eyes shot from one man to the other.

Don let his machinegun dangle on the belt around his shoulders and was slow to raise his hands.

Barney shot one of the soldiers in the Adam's-apple, then both sides opened fire on each other.

The second soldier shot at them, hitting the ground between Don and Marc as they scattered.

Craig fired at the side of the black APC, sending sparks and ricochets around the soldier. He moved quickly for the side of the street and darted back into the alleyway.

Eight more soldiers jumped out of the back of the APC to join the skirmish. Two others remained in the back.

One soldier was killed instantly by Don. A second was killed by Barney, when the others took strategic positions around the rear of the APC and fired back at them.

Don was pushed to the side of the street, near the alleyway.

Another soldier aimed and shot Marc through the cheekbone. He fell down and exhaled a final time. His breath was a visible mist.

As the fire-fight swelled, several infected became aware of the flares and noises of the gunfire.

Barney was separated from Don and Craig, pushing away to the other side of the street, as the soldiers averted their attention from the men and began shooting the infected that were swelling and surrounding them.

Barney stared at Marc's blood-soaked body in the middle of the street. He looked away as his eyes glazed over.

Don and Craig smashed an office window-wall with several bullets and ducked inside, as five infected sprinted down the alleyway behind them and rushed at the soldiers.

"I'll cover the front," Craig shouted, leaping the bottom five steps and taking a defensive stance on the small landing behind a raised reception desk, as Don bolted further up the stairs to the first floor.

Outside.
Barney tugged a grenade free of his bag.

He pulled the pin and pea-rolled it hard at the black APC. The grenade bounced short and stopped at a soldier's foot. It detonated and the soldier exploded in a fireball of blood and guts. Intestines sprang into the air like an unloaded spring. Bone and meat splattered the side of the APC, where the explosion had caused minimal damaged. The soldier that had been sheltering the other side of the APC had been knocked against the wall behind him and had broken his spine and neck. Two of the soldiers at the back of the truck had been disabled on the moment of eruption: one man had been thrown against the interior walls of the APC, impaling himself on a sharp-edged shelf of metal, and the second had been exiting the APC and was tossed upwards during the explosion, he landed on his ankle and snapped it in three places: his pelvis was also fractured and broken at several points. The soldier groaned, reaching out to his colleagues.

The roaring, *booming* noise of the grenade reflected off all of the walls around them, creating a momentary echo-chamber, alerting two dozen more infected to group and rush toward the scene, from all adjacent streets and locales. Interest was highly peaked.

The soldier with the broken pelvis groaned, when one of the infected charged towards him, snatched at his clothing and vomited blood over his screaming face. Blood filled his mouth and sockets as he whipped his head back and forth, spitting droplets.

Barney took another grenade out of his bag and gripped it tightly. His eyes stung and his ears rang with a painful, loud *chime*. His head pounded and his heart rushed. He glanced down the street. He saw the soldiers, occupied by the massing infected, firing on them, huddling to form a barrier of resistance. He noticed the APC had not been that badly damaged in the explosion and his teeth clenched together.

Inside the office-building.
Don heard the sound of the grenade-explosion and winced to himself.

"Fuck!" he yelled. He ran to a front-facing window. He was about to fire on the remaining soldiers, when he saw fifty-two infected grouping around the scene. "Double fuck!" he barked.

Don smashed the window with one bullet, then started firing on the soldiers, and the infected.

Downstairs.
Craig took the cue from Don, hearing the sound of gunfire from the floor above him. He sprang from behind the reception desk and down the stairs and shot out another of the downstairs-window.

He took aim and opened-fire on the soldiers, when the infected swelled and several darted in his direction. Craig took careful aim and executed each, in order, piling the infected in the open window-frame. "And a-five and a-six and a-seven and an-eight!"

Across the street.
Barney stepped out from evening shade covering the recess at the side of the alleyway and started firing on the soldiers and the infected. The second grenade was wedged in his pocket.

Guns flared as soldiers and the infected were hit from three sides.

Moments later.
Craig killed the last few infected with perfectly aimed single-shots.

All of the soldiers were dead or very-nearly dead.

Craig approached the front of the APC, with the machinegun raised in front of him. He passed Marc's body, looking at it with emotionless, indifferent eyes. He stopped at the side of the APC, where Barney joined him.

The residual burning embers of the explosion were dying out; tiny burnt traces of paint on the APC's side, pieces of stray rubbish that lay in the gutter, and the remains of the second man Barney Meadway murdered.

"Nice shooting, kid," Craig conceded.

"Thanks. Sorry. I didn't know what to do."

Don ducked out of the broken window Craig had been stood behind, pushing the pile of infected that had collected aside with the heel of his boot, and jogged to the other side of the APC to join the others.

"Hi," Barney said slowly.

"Hello."

"We'd better check those guys..." Craig said. "Hopefully one've 'em might be hanging on..."

"We might get some answers," Don agreed. He nodded to Craig and they moved down either side of the truck with an automatic unity of foot-paces and speed. They scanned the scene with the silenced-machineguns placed in guard-position in front of them. Barney scuttled behind Craig, pointing his own silenced-machinegun.

They reached the back of the truck.

There were ten soldiers. Eight were dead. One was paralysed, and the other near to death.

Don marched to the wounded soldier; two bullet holes were visible in his abdomen, a third was hidden from view. Don hauled the moaning and gasping body off the ground. The crippled soldier groaned and gasped. Barney took out his map and pointed at the complex that was marked.

"Is this the place?!" Don screamed. "Is this the place you've taken those people?"

The soldier's eyelids fluttered and his eyes rolled around in every direction, unable to focus. Don shook him.

"Is this the place?!" he repeated, shaking the soldier again.

He dropped the soldier on the tarmac, then pushed a silenced-pistol into the soldier's eye-socket.

"Tell me the exact location of where you have came from," he growled.

Barney glared at Craig. And saw Craig's complete accord with the situation.

The soldier sucked on his bottom-lip, rasping and struggling to breathe.

"Tell him," Barney shouted.

The soldier blinked several times, then he finally spoke, "That is the place you," he stammered. "...--The place you want... But..."

Don pulled him close, the veins popping at his temples, the creases between his eyebrows growing creases.

"...--But... You'll all die."

Don killed him with a shot to the forehead.

The next morning. Outside Croetzer's complex.

A black APC rolled down Park Vista, speeding toward Gate A. Then it smashed through the outer twin-set of gates. Wood cracked and splintered and fell apart as the vehicle thundered through.

Twenty-eight soldiers wearing black fatigues reacted instantly and opened fire on the truck, riddling it with bullets. Metal was shredded under the torrent and hail. The APC came to a stop as the back wheels wedged on the fallen outer-set of gates. The truck was ripped apart with gunfire, and smoke rose from many places. It groaned and *hissed* then slumped on its deflating tyres.

The soldiers stopped firing simultaneously.

A disquieting silence fell over the scene.

Another two soldiers climbed up the guard-towers on either side of the 'air-lock' and took aim down the street, standing side by side with the four guards.

One of the soldiers opened a concealed door and entered the 'air-lock'. He crept toward the cab-door, and threw it open, pointing his silenced-pistol into the cab. He saw that it was empty, there had been no-one driving the truck; the accelerator had been weighed-down with a brick. He pulled the brick free and turned to address his Major, when he noticed a long strand of thread. "Sir!–..."

A bundle grenades exploded, blowing the APC apart. The aurora-sunburst of fire tore through the frame and panels and seats and dashboard and rear-section and wheels and engine. Seven soldiers were killed instantly. Six more were shredded with shrapnel and would later die in triage. Four more were crippled. Six others were disfigured, dismembered and disabled. Five were safe. Shrapnel and debris blasted into the air, as a ballooning cloud of smoke filled the sky.

The near-side guard-tower was torn through by discs and shards of shrapnel. The soldier on the near-side had been hit across his face by a spiralling chunk of metal engine-tubing and coughed blood as he expired and fell to the ground forty feet below. The guard-tower quivered and tilted, *snapping* and breaking. The remaining soldier on the tower threw his hands in the air and flapped them, as the tower beneath him crumbled and toppled. The soldier hit the ground and impaled his shoulder on the metal spike-peg of a nearby tent. He screamed.

One of the soldiers, who was huddled behind one of the large, square corner-posts of the outer-skein of the 'air-lock', looked at his Major – GREGORY STANFORD, 46 year old Englishman. He was a tall, broad man with a large upper body and long legs. He wore a short blonde crew cut and no facial hair. He had a stern, war-hardened face, speckled on one side with scars. He had deep, bright eyes, a long thick nose, a heavy jaw, large, square teeth and a downturned mouth. He wore black fatigues, black boots and a black backpack with a tiny silver crown on the top, to signify he was a Major.

The soldier had the expression of pure shock on his face.

Stanford saw it. "Keep yourself calm," he whispered. He gritted his teeth and wiped mud and grime from his forehead. He stared around at the surviving members of the contingent he had ordered to be on guard-duty for Gate A. He saw the grotesque and ripped-apart bodies of comrades and recruits and people and friends and strangers and soldiers and men. He climbed up onto a lower-deck built around the bottom of the fallen guard-tower. He gripped the broken beam that had supported the perch of the tower. The top of the support glowed with a lava-like quality, exhaling tiny puffs of black smoke.

He stared down the road ahead of the complex.

Two more soldiers dashed to the remaining guard-tower, standing tall on the front side of the outer gates.

Stanford saw the men and averted his eyes from the road.

"You men, keep your eyes peeled. This is an attack!"

He looked at the demolished outer-gates and the large, broken opening to the inner-gates.

"Gleeson! Start rebuilding the gates. Bare it. Pack it up with shoring and wood," he barked. He watched as six soldiers dashed off and started erecting a new platform a few metres away from the fallen guard-tower, pressed against the perimeter-wall.

The man Stanford had spoken to nodded to his Major after the instructions, then ran between several tents and was gone from sight. His name was Captain NIALL GLEESON, 35 year old Englishman. He was long and lean, slimmer than Stanford, but more of an athlete: he had the body of a long-distance runner, lithe and muscular. His hair was shaved to grade one, a light, dusty brown. He had a long, angular head with a flat, sloped forehead, stubby nose and square jaw. His eyes were pale grey and squinted under a thin, low brow. He wore black fatigues, black boots and a black backpack with three tiny silver stars on the top, to signify he was a Captain.

Gleeson bolted between several more tents and darted towards a stock-pile of thick wooden fence-posts. He was quickly met by six soldiers who stood awaiting his orders.

Near the gate.
Stanford glanced along the perimeter-wall, when something caught his attention and he stared down the road again. He saw the first infected of eighty, racing down the street, moving straight towards the broken-open gate, where the skeleton of the APC still spewed thick, black smoke.

Dozens more infected were entering the street and joining the horde.

Stanford climbed to the lower platform of one of the guard-towers and glared down Park Row. He saw thirty more infected surging up the road.

A soldier climbed the still-standing right-side guard-tower. He reached the top of the ladder when a bullet hit him in the chest and he was thrown to the ground forty feet below.

Stanford immediately shouted, "Take cover! Everyone take cover!... There are people firing on us!... Find out where they are! -- And shoot back!"

Several soldiers hid behind the perimeter-wall and the smoking crater and wreck left by the APC.

Stanford charged into The Queen's House and bolted through the huge, marble-floored entrance-hall, where the inner 'air-lock' had been removed. He raced down a short, winding corridor, threw open the door to the cellar and leapt down the stairs. He sprinted downstairs to the underground prison where he met two soldiers who had been guarding the cells. They immediately stood to attention.

"What was that noise, Major?"

"Let me in," Stanford demanded, ignoring the soldier's question.

The door unlocked with a loud *clunk* after the soldier swiped his access-card.

Stanford entered the room and looked from one group in one cell to the other group in the other cell.

Stanford addressed both groups curtly, "We have some people attacking us... That noise was an explosion... And it made me think... It made me think quickly... And it led me to you... They must be here to rescue someone that is in this room!" he said icily, calmly. "That means someone in-here knows something! I'm not leaving until I have answers!"

Nigel stood. He said, "How the hell are we supposed to know anything?!"

Stanford withdrew a pistol from a hip-holster and shot Nigel in the face.

The booming *bang* from the pistol echoed down the long room.

Nigel's body bounced off the side of one of the bunk-beds and rolled onto the floor.

Stanford beamed into each cell, marching down the iron-bar corridor, looking at every face: Karyn, Choco, Bruce, Robbie and Elliott, Clive, Roy, Melodie, Annabel, Evie and Harmony, and Pike. And in the other cell: Nicola, Eileen and Baz, Harlan, Fiona, Layla and Vivienne, Kit, Meredith, Suthep and Bernie.

"Somebody start talking," Stanford barked.

No-one said anything, or moved at all.

Stanford shot Harlan in the eye.

Harlan's body slumped backwards against the back wall with a wet *thump*.

Stanford looked around again at all of his prisoners. Their blank and frightened faces stared back at him. He pointed with his pistol at three of them, then looked at one of the guards, he said, "Bring her, her and him.."

A little later.
The inner-gates had been temporarily rebuilt and shored with the fence-posts, under precise instruction from Gleeson. Other soldiers used spades and shovels to pile dirt and mud behind the wall, packing it tightly against the wooden wall.

Infected pounded on the other side of the outer-gate, clambering over the molten wreckage of the APC. Several infected had caught fire, but continued to beat against the compound's wall.

More infected flooded into the road beyond, pouring down Park Vista and up Park Row to Gate A.

Sunshine lit the infected from in front and Gleeson could make out easy identifications, if he had known their names, or had cared to know them. He shrugged, letting his shoulders drop, turning away from a crack in the wall.

The right-side guard-tower stood empty, but soldiers had gathered behind the perimeter-wall on quickly-constructed wooden platforms. They crouched on the platforms, peaking over the wall to aim at and then kill several of the infected. Gleeson had ordered them to take random, unpredictable pot-shots at the infected, with the aim to thin their numbers as quickly as possible.

Bullets occasionally hit the perimeter-wall, sending powder and grit and chips and chunks of brick flying, spoiling the facade of the outer-wall with dozens of tiny craters.

None of the soldiers could make out the locations of the snipers.

Outside the wall.
Over one hundred and fifty infected had assembled, with more and more joining every minute. They swelled and massed and lurched and pushed and stumbled and shoved each other, clamouring to get inside the grounds of the complex.

Bullets *whistled* over the heads of the horde of infected.

In the complex.
A soldier was hit by one of the bullets, pushing him backwards and spiralling over another soldier, who was rushing up the ladder behind him. The soldier hit the ground, narrowly missing kicking his comrade in the face.

Across the lawn, Eileen, Harmony and Roy were forced out of the entrance to The Queen's House in handcuffs. They were lined-up outside the front-doors by Stanford, who stood behind them menacingly, shielding himself from any gunfire.

The attack from outside the perimeter-wall stopped instantly.

Only the sounds of the infected could be heard. They clawed and beat and scratched and ripped and punched and hammered against the outer-wall and throughout Gate A. They packed into the space around the APC wreck, fighting to get their way inside.

Further down Park Row, beyond the wall.
A second huge, massing crowd of the infected swelled into the street and joined the others at the gates. They spread along the wall, beating against it.

Several hundred infected pressed to the complex-side, building in presence each passing minute.

In the complex.
Stanford held up a megaphone and spoke through it, "Tell us what you want!"

Silence enveloped the scene, as thirty or more faster moving infected charged at the gate, barging between dozens of others, joining the wave.

Soldiers lined-up down the length of the wall. They looked determined and ready-to-fight, or disturbed and fearful. Sweat slicked foreheads and hands all along the line.

"If these people here are your friends, you won't want to see them harmed," Stanford shouted through the megaphone.

He pointed a pistol at the back of Harmony's head, jabbing the metal deep into her hair.

Harmony wept.

A grenade landed on the ground behind the makeshift-gates and exploded. Two of the five soldiers behind the gate died that moment, and one was badly wounded. The other two soldiers were knocked back and were immediately blood-puked on, as the infected horde breached the gates and charged into the grounds. The infected stampeded through the opening, flooding inside.

The remaining soldiers started firing on the infected, moving from their positions along the wall to surround the breach. Piles of bodies quickly built-up on the ground in the 'air-lock' and behind the exploded APC.

A dozen soldiers charged across the lawn in front of The Queen's House to join the others at Gate A.

Another dozen raced up from Queen Mary Court and the Old Naval College and took positions to suppress the invasion.

In the confusion and fire-fight Eileen, Harmony and Roy were moved back to stand inside the front of the entrance-hall. Harmony broke free and tried to run away, darting towards a walkway between two tents, running straight across the complex towards Gate B on the other side. One of the guard-soldiers aimed, then shot and killed her.

Harmony's body tumbled and skipped then fell into one of the tents, collapsing it.

Stanford grabbed Roy by his collar and pulled him close. "You see what your people have done to us?! Can you see?!"

Roy whimpered.

The other guard-soldier held Eileen's arm tightly, pinning her in the small alcove in the wall inside the entrance-hall. She shivered and cried, tears streaking her cheeks.

Stanford stalked outside. "Take them back to the cells," he ordered, then marched along the front of the building to the communications tent. The *rattle* and *thunder* of gunfire sounded across the lawn.

Another soldier hopped up the entrance-stairs and stepped into the house behind Roy and Eileen. The soldier was wearing a gasmask, and his face was obscured behind it. He shot both of the guards in the temples, then pulled the gasmask off. It was Don Clement. He said, "I'm here to rescue you... I'm with Barney..."

Roy's eyes lit up. He asked quickly, "Barney? Is he okay? Where is he? I'm his granddad's best friend!"

Don stopped Roy, he said, "He's outside with a friend of mine keeping those people busy... Show me where the others are... We've got to get out of here as quickly as we can!"

A nearby rooftop, on the corner of Park Row and Trafalgar Road, the A206.
Craig shot at the soldiers in the walled-in perimeter using a sniper-rifle. He also fired on the torrent of infected making their way into the grounds. Heads split and dozens of tiny fountains of blood further dyed the clothes of the other infected around them.

Craig swung his sight across the soldiers, pausing for a moment. He saw several drop to the ground.

He picked up a walkie-talkie and pressed the button on the side with a *fuzz* of static. "Nice shooting."

"Thanks," Barney's voice called back.

The Meridian Courtyard, at the Royal Observatory.
Barney stood near the wall to Flamsteed House, leaning on the spiked-metal balustrade. From this place he could look out over Greenwich Park at The Queen's House, the Maritime Museum and the Old Naval College down across the sweep of the Park. A sniper-rifle was pressed to his shoulder and aimed at Gate A.

He opened fire and shot both the soldiers and the infected, knocking them down like target practice with tin cans. He shot indiscriminately, thinning both sides of the fight with precise aim.

The bodies of two soldiers dressed in black fatigues lay near the entrance to the Meridian Courtyard.

The rooftop, on the corner of Park Row and Trafalgar Road, the A206.
Craig peered down at the road and saw sixty more infected racing towards Croetzer's compound, barging through the huge crowd of the slow-moving infected that trailed towards and into Gate A.

A static-call sounded through on the walkie-talkie at Craig's side. "We have a bit of a problem..." Don's voice called out of the device.

Craig scrambled behind a small chimney and air-conditioning unit. He said, "What? What is it?" He reloaded his rifle.

"There's twenty people in here!" Don blurted.

Craig's mouth fell open. He looked at the walkie-talkie and thought of Barney. Craig gripped the walkie-talkie, he said, "Have you looked around? There may be a back-exit or some underground fucking tunnel...!"

Don replied, "I am underground, looking into two huge DIY prison-cells... We need more options..."

Suddenly the noise of a helicopter erupted, filling the air with noise.

Craig peeked over the roof-edge at the compound and, once-again, his mouth dropped open. All of the soldiers had disappeared. The helicopter sound built in volume, getting louder and louder, when four black twin-rotor Boeing CH-47 Chinook helicopters lifted into the air from the lawns behind The Queen's House.

In the lead Boeing CH-47 Chinook cockpit.
Croetzer and Stanford sat together behind two pilots.

"We left four-section and six-section behind!" Stanford stated grimly.

"Four-section will be making their exit on the River."

"What about six-section?"

"Some sacrifices must be made," Croetzer replied casually.

He cleared his throat – Stanford thought quite theatrically – then wet his lips with a reptilian flick of his slick, juicy-pink tongue.

The rooftop.

The Boeing CH-47 Chinooks banked away in formation and whirled through the sky, then were gone from sight and lost in rolls and waves of greying cloud.

Craig watched the helicopters vanish.

He stared at the front of The Queen's House, using his binoculars to twitchily scan the facade.

The immense horde of infected had advanced into the grounds, spilling through the hole in the 'air-lock' and pouring into the complex. They were slow to spread out, spanning the front of The Queen's House and a quarter of the lawn.

"Get to the front-doors, Don!... Run right-fuckin'-now and lock them!" Craig screamed.

CHAPTER 21 - WIDE APART

Jaipur, India.
ARI PURKYA, 43 year old Indian man – awoke on the vast, soft mattress in the bedroom of his hotel suite, a silk sheet draped across his body. He had thinning black hair, swept back off his forehead and face, bushy dark eyebrows and a thick, long moustache, trimmed lightly in the middle below his thick nose. He had dark, inquisitive eyes, hooded on top with dark bags underneath. He had an average-build, with the start of a small potbelly. He stretched his arm out from within a white silk kurta pyjama sleeve. He rested on his elbow, looking to his left through the open double-doors to the bedroom into the huge square den. Three large two-seater settees had been arranged in front of a large flat-screen 3-D HD TV; between each seat was a small side-table with psychedelic explosions of colour from long-stem firewheel flowers and fans of leaves that had flashes of persimmon and burgundy.

Purkya flopped back on the mattress and looked at the fine array of netting and decoration that webbed the canopy within the four-poster bed. The posts at each corner were ornately carved and inscribed beautifully.

Later.
Purkya led a young Indian beauty into his bed-chamber. Their hands met at the fingertips, barely touching. She danced around him and moved to the mattress.

Mid-afternoon sun beat through the cracks in the blinds that covered the skinny-cathedral windows.

A little later.
The girl kissed Purkya's neck, at first little kisses separated by moments, then increasing in passion with each new kiss. He felt twenty years old again. She was straddling him and bent forward and kissed him on the lips.

Purkya reached to the bedside-table and wrapped his small, dark hands around the stems of two full champagne flutes, bubbles *fizzing* and rupturing on the surface.

The girl swallowed a cough, covering her mouth and leaning away from Purkya.

She smiled and took the flute from him and sipped, when another cough erupted from her mouth, almost a bark.

"Are you okay?" he asked in perfect Hindi.

The girl held her hand up, hiding her face from him, coughing again and motioning to him that she was fine.

Another cough escaped her mouth, speckles of blood landed on the white-silk sheets.

Purkya sat up and back.

The girl turned on him. The colour had quickly vanished from her skin and beads of sweat dotted her forehead. She had a gormless, slack, emotionless face; her bloodshot-red eyes bore into him. Blood cascaded out of her blood and splattered over her breasts and thighs and onto his abdomen. He grabbed her hips, shoved her backwards and slid off the bed, momentarily unable to use his legs. He stared across the sheet, as the woman hacked and coughed, spitting blood.

Purkya stood, pushing back away from the bed.

The girl scrambled onto all-fours and scanned for him, her deep dark eyes wheeling around.

Purkya took an ornamental sword from the wall and drove it through the girl's open mouth. The blade sliced through her head and parted her hair at the back. He withdrew the sword and the body slumped to the bed, gushing with thick, glossy blood from the mouth. It looked like a garden-fountain, draining out with body-shuddering discharges of blood, soaking the silk sheets, bed and floor.

"Oh my God," he said calmly, exhaling in frustration.

His eyes moved to the balcony and he casually strode outside, pushing through the slated-wooden doors, stepping into the heat and the sun.

He crossed to the adorned and etched white-marble balustrade that edged the balcony. His hands found the lustrous, even surface of the balustrade-top and smoothed over it with his palms. He lit a cigarette.

Purkya looked down across the hotel's estate, away down the five-hundred metre long, raked-gravel driveway, to the main road at the end. Several cars had crashed into one another.

He saw several infected chasing down a couple at the end of the drive. They disappeared behind a small mini-market.

He took a pull on the cigarette, then exhaled slowly. He watched threads of smoke vanish into the air. He sighed.

Outside the hotel's entrance.
Purkya peered down to ground-level and saw a dozen people: tourists and hotel bell-hops and catering staff and receptionists. All of them had been taken by the infection and were ravenously clamouring together, finding their feet, trying to find prey. Something alerted them. They dashed and darted and stumbled around the asphalt, chasing down four survivors, who rushed away in the opposite directions. The small pack split and took off after each of the four.

He heard groans and howls and moans.

One of the survivors sprinted to his car, where one of the infected ploughed him to the ground and three more vomited blood over the man's face. A second later, the infected dispersed and moved away from the man, leaving him coughing and gagging on the road next to his car.

Several screams rent the air. They sounded as if they came from inside the reception, or from somewhere within the hotel. Maybe some of the floors below his room, he thought.

Purkya saw a dozen infected starting up the driveway. The group prowled and crept forward. Two of the infected shuffled to the front of the pack and broke out into a light trot. They increased their speed, accelerating towards the reception.

Purkya looked away.

Sixteen days later. On a small airstrip – 8:06am.
Purkya stomped along a metal gangway that led over the roof of a small out-building. He ducked down behind several other squat buildings that were constructed using breeze-blocks and roofed with corrugated metal sheets. His boots met the gritty, sandy ground and he heard the gangway *ping* and shiver as his weight left it. He trod across the roasting sand, his dark grey shalwar kameez lifting in the slight breeze.

The sun shone brightly in the sky. There were no clouds. There were no birds.

A 4-seat Cessna 180 Skywagon, heating in the sun, sat at the end of the runway.

Purkya motioned to a man on the other side of the airplane to pull the chocks free from the wheels. The man nodded and moved to the plane. His name was LENNOX RAWES, 30 year old Englishman of Ugandan descent. He had a short, scrappy afro that merged into thick, woolly sideburns and a scruffy, light beard. He was tall and slim, with thin shoulders and a small chest, wiry arms and legs, and a skinny waist. He had a warm, smile-dimpled face with a strong jaw, full mouth and wide nose. He wore a fitted black shirt, a pair of rough, worn flared Levi jeans buckled around his waist with a thick leather belt, and comfortable brown-leather hiking-boots. He was armed with a Kalashnikov AK-47 assault rifle type-1, strapped across his back. He grabbed the coiled string of the first chock and tugged it away from the tyre.

Purkya walked to a low-roofed out-building and went inside the shady, dark shack. It was cooler inside, but not much. He pulled the chain of an overhanging light-bulb and the room was illuminated by a dull orange glow. He picked up a backpack and two small suitcases and walked outside.

Lennox spun the propeller of the Cessna 180 Skywagon and it *burbled* and sputtered and shuddered and shook and wobbled and came to life.

The engine *roared*.

A man appeared from the shadows of a second out-building, shading his eyes. His name was CHOMAN NAGRA, 20 year old Indian man. He was skinny and bony, with little muscle or meat on his skeleton. He was small and gaunt, with bony shoulders, elbows, wrists and knees. He had a bright, cheerful face with a toothy, gap-filled smile and high, sharp cheekbones. He wore a baggy, dirty white shalwar kameez; a knee-length white shirt with loose white trousers and sandals. Choman called out in Hindi, but Purkya could not hear him over the plane's whirring engine.

Purkya waved to the young man and he skipped in front of the plane to him.

"There are those-people coming," Choman said in Hindi.

"Get these packs on the plane," Purkya shouted. "Then you and Lennox get aboard. Wait for me."

Choman nodded and gathered the bags Purkya had dropped in the sand. He took another Kalashnikov AK-47 assault rifle type-1 from a strap over his shoulder and walked back to the metal gangway. He climbed to the highest point and rested the rifle-grip on the tube-metal balustrade, twisting the strap around his hand for extra stability. He put his eye to the sight and instantly saw the infected coming.

Two hundred infected, dotted across the sandy scrubland in front of him, shuffled towards the airfield. They could hear the plane's engine whirring and sputtering.

Purkya glanced across to the airplane as Choman and Lennox pushed the rear in a half-circle on the small tail-mounted wheel, so that the airplane faced the dusty, uneven runway. The rotor-blade blew dust and sand in a heaping, clouding mass toward the tiny terminal building, and toward Purkya standing on the gangway above it.

He looked through the sight and took aim at one of the nearest infected. He took a deep breath.

He fired.

The bullet lifted the infected off the ground, gliding through the side of its head.

He aimed again and fired.

The second bullet *zipped* passed a toothless infected. It continued on, completely unfazed, its jaw dropping open and tightly pulling closed as it walked. The bullet travelled on and embedded itself in the shoulder of another infected several rows behind it. It continued treading forward.

He fired a third time.

The bullet smashed through the toothless top-plate gums and exited the back of its head.

Three infected lurched into a canter, hobbling and jogging, their arms swinging behind them.

"Oh dear!" he moaned.

Purkya aimed and fired, aimed and fired, aimed and stopped. He had not seen twenty of the infected that had crept in from the East and West, swarming for the terminal building and the first step of the gangway.

He bolted along the gangway, pulling his body along, gripping the balustrades in one hand and the rifle in the other.

He jumped the last three steps and met the ground with a bounding leap, kicking up sand as he darted for the open airplane door. He jumped inside, pulling the door shut with a *snap*.

"We are ready to go," Choman shouted in Hindi.

"Good," Purkya shouted over the engine noise. "Go," he said, and patted Lennox on the shoulder.

"Here we go, then!"

Lennox set the plane in motion and it eased forward down the runway.

Ten hours later. On an airstrip thirty miles North of Islamabad in Pakistan.
The airplane bucked and tilted through the air as the tyres hit the dusty ground with a bounce. The wheels met the dirt again and found traction. The Cessna 180 airplane slowed and immediately pitched slightly off to the left, towards the edge of the runway where the ground slipped away at a 60° slope. The airplane bumped over a tiny hillock of dirt and swung back onto the runway.

A man walked out of the small plank-hut that squatted at the side of the runway and stepped into the late afternoon, early evening sunlight. He shaded his eyes with his arms, as the plane's rotor-blades slowed and slowed and slowed. And the dust started to settle.

The man's name was VIKRAM OSHII, 55 year old Pakistani man. He was tall and slim, taller with a turban on his head; gangly and lanky. He had a long frame with stringy, slim and lithe arms and legs, and a tiny, taught waist. He had a charming, warm face; wrinkles were etched around his eyes and mouth and across his forehead. He had a bushy streaky-grey and black beard, with a long fluffy moustache. He had deep, dark eyes, under long joined eyebrows and above high, bony cheeks. His nose was a long beak, protruding from his shallow face, pointing out over his moustache and thin, pursed lips. He wore a long black shalwar kameez with a brown scarf knotted around his neck, black sandals tied up his ankles, and a grubby khaki-brown parka jacket over the top. Oshii casually put a hand on his own Kalashnikov AK-47 assault rifle type-1 that hung around his neck on a tattered rope-chord.

He watched the airplane come to a full stop, and Purkya climb out, followed quickly by Choman, who carried the airplanes chocks. Choman scrambled to stuff the chocks around the tyres, as Purkya walked slowly but with purpose towards Oshii.

"Welcome to Pakistan, my friends," Oshii said with one arm still resting on the machinegun and the other outstretched in a half-embrace. He spoke in perfect English, without any sign of a Pakistani accent.

"Hello, how are you today?" Purkya offered in perfect, accent-less English.

"You have survived many days," Oshii stated warmly with a nod.

"Yes. We have," Purkya said, still advancing, before slowing to a stop a few metres in front of Oshii.

"My name is Vikram. I am the only surviving member of my village... --eleven miles from here, North... When the plague began, it devastated my country."

"Not only yours."

"Really? Am I to believe this was not an isolated incident?"

"Yes."

Choman helped Lennox climb out of the airplane and they joined Purkya and Oshii, standing a few metres away from them.

"Welcome, friends," Oshii said graciously to the others.

"Hello," Lennox greeted.

"This place... --it's quite isolated... Have you seen many of the infected?" Purkya asked.

"As long as I keep my distance, they stay away... Where were you going?"

"England. Lennox and I have family there. We need to know whether they live or not."

"You may not get very far in that airplane, my friends," Oshii said.

"Why not?"

"You can try heading North to Kyrgyzstan, North-west to Tajikistan, or West to Afghanistan... You may get as far as Uzbekistan or Turkmenistan if you are lucky... What if you were shot at by survivors – those jealous of your having a plane? What if they shot your plane down?... You may make it to Georgia, or Armenia, or Azerbaijan or the Caspian Sea, but you may die before you get there."

"How would you proceed, then?"

"In trucks, my friends," Oshii said, finally releasing his light touch from the rifle and gestured for them to follow.

They crossed the dusty runway and walked straight passed Oshii's small plank-hut and scuttled down an overgrown track between two large, parched scrubby-bushes. Oshii led them through another small thicket of bushes at the end of the track and round a large mound of dark red mud. They passed a huge crater that Oshii had used as a funeral-pyre, burned out, but filled with the gnarled, charred body-parts of over the hundred infected he had dumped into it, and then set alight. The skeletons resembled a huge system of termite mounds, but twisted and broken, black and ashy, collapsed and entwined.

Oshii continued passed and around the edge of the funeral-pyre and vanished.

Purkya put a hand on the pistol in the back of his belt, as did Lennox. Sweat beaded on their foreheads. Choman walked between them, unafraid. They turned the corner, and Oshii was stood in front of them. His hand was raised and gripped a tassel on the fringe of a large tarpaulin. He tugged the sheet and the wind caught it, pulling it completely free.

Underneath the sheet was a British Army Bedford MK 4x4 personnel-truck.

"It is filled with dried food, ammunition, weapons and clothing... We will have to find a little more petrol for it, further down the line, but it works well, my friends," Oshii said with a smile.

Purkya, Lennox and Choman grinned.

"Why–... Why haven't you taken it anywhere?" Purkya asked.

"I had nowhere to go, my friend... Besides, I cannot drive."

Rhodes Capital, Rhodes, The Mediterranean.
MARTINA CORTEZ, 29 year old Spanish-American – had been awake since five thirty. She had a light tan, scorching Spanish eyes that glowed green, lips that were lean but shapely, high cheekbones, a sharp, small nose and perfectly-plucked eyebrows. She was extraordinarily attractive, distinguished by a tiny scar that ran one inch down her forehead to her left eyebrow, and a beauty-spot mole. She wore a white vest with a shirt tied around her waist, grey cargo shorts and pink-and-blue half-flip-flops, half-sandals. She strolled along the wooden-planked pedestrian walkway that ran alongside the Akti Sachtoun road that curved around the huge, ancient castle walls of Rhodes Town, the Old City, and along the Mandraki harbour. The Mandraki was the smaller of two harbours.

Across the harbour a small, two-hundred passenger Blue Star Ferry was pulling around the back-side of an enormous, towering four-thousand passenger cruise-liner called the Costa Fortuna. Alongside the cruise-liner, where it was moored, there were three windmills of grey stone with rose-terracotta roofs.

Martina covered her eyes for shade as she passed a pair of pristine Vespa scooters, followed by a battered, old Kawasaki. Behind several kiosks filled with dried puffer-fish, sponges, star fish and seashell-jewellery, three huge arches bored through the Old City wall creating two pedestrian walkways either side of a roadway.

One of the men in the kiosk nearest Martina nodded at her, smiling a toothy yellow-grin, beckoning her to come closer. "Parakaló," he said, smiling again.

Martina smiled back at the man but shook her head, she said, "Se efcharistó... Um... Thank you, no..." She swept a cluster of salty-dry hair behind her ear. She looked away shyly and continued along the harbour-front.

The sun was getting stronger and her lower-arms pulsed with heat. She took the sunglasses that hung across the tops of her breasts attached by a neck-cord, and slipped them on, tidying hair again behind her ears.

She glanced at her watch as five tourists shuffled passed her. It was 12:05pm.

She took a deep breath and picked up her pace a little. She was meeting Andre for a drink in twenty minutes and wanted to arrive early. And she hated walking in her half-flip-flops, half-sandals.

A few minutes later.
Martina passed the statue of four blue-rust coloured copper dolphins on a rocky outcrop.

She had seen them every day for the last three weeks, since she arrived in Rhodes.

She slowed to cross the road and enter the Old City through a twenty-foot arched entranceway that sat beneath two enormous round stone turrets. She felt tiny walking into the City, filing passed a tourist couple.

A few minutes later.
Martina wandered into Argykastron square passed a huge, stone staircase and paused near the large stone spire fountain with an iron owl perched where the point should be, as two pigeons scuttled by her feet. Another staircase led to a viewing platform where dozens of tourists were taking photos.

The square was becoming busy and lots of tourists skittered around looking at restaurants' menus and in shop windows and taking photographs and eating in the sun and drinking in the bars.

She crossed to the Palazzo bar and restaurant, and took a seat in the shade of the awning, with her back to the corner pillar of a long arched cloister that ran to the corner of the next building. She glanced up and saw that she was sat underneath one of three large, Arabic wrought-iron lights. She un-knotted her shirt from about her waist and pulled it on, buttoning it three times across her navel.

ANDRE CALDWELL, 37 year old Englishman – entered the square from the Sokratous road. He was lean and athletic with square shoulders, strong arms and legs, and a muscular chest. He was fit, healthy and active. He had golden hair, swept back and sideways in a side-parting. He had a handsome face, with a strong brow, deep, sincere blue eyes and a sharp, angular jaw. He wore a faded powder-blue shirt with the collar unbuttoned down his tanned chest and the sleeves rolled up, chinos, dark blue boat-shoes and a cheap diving-wristwatch. His chest- and arm-hair glowed gold against his tanned skin. Andre spotted her and moved to the table and sat in front of her.

"Good morning," he said cheerily.

"Good morning."

Andre took a moment, watching Martina as he made himself comfortable in the chair.

He cleared his throat and shook his wristwatch along his arm.

"So... Down to business?" he started, when a waiter cut between two tables and appeared beside theirs. "Ah, yes... What will you have, Miss Cortez?" and he smiled a set of perfect white teeth.

Martina stared at Andre, then looked at the waiter and smiled. "White wine, please."

"Good, I'll have the same... Something nice."

The waiter nodded and walked into the restaurant.

"Would you like to begin... --by explaining to me how you got my phone-number?"

"I had a contact in Russia... In Volgograd," she answered.

"Oh, I see... Mr Oborín?" he enquired with the air of personal satisfaction. He licked his lips.

"I presume he's dead now?" she asked, an eyebrow raised.

"You presume correctly," Andre replied, his eye catching on the waiter as he emerged from the restaurant holding a tray with two glasses and a bottle perched on top. He pursed his lips.

They both fell silent as the waiter pulled the cork and poured first Martina's, then Andre's. Beads of condensation immediately dotted the glasses and bottle. Andre wiped the side of the glass with a napkin and took a sip. He nodded to the waiter and he retreated back to the restaurant.

"You worried us."

"Oh?"

"Yes, you did," he continued. "You dropped off the face of the planet. And turned up in beautiful Rhodes... It is a lovely island... But you couldn't stay gone for long?... So, Mr Oborín gave you my number... And?"

"I found out from another source," she said sombrely, "something incredible."

"Now it's my turn to say 'Oh?'..."

"The virus... They're actually going to release it!"

Andre sat back on the bubble-gum orange seat and crossed his legs. He took another sip of wine. "I know."

Martina took her sunglasses off and her eyes stretched open. She sat forward and found herself gripping the table with both hands. She stared at Andre. He coolly sipped his wine.

"It's inevitable," he said after savouring Martina's expression for a moment.

Her throat began to choke. She sipped the wine and rested her hand on her chest. Her heart pounded.

"You knew?" she accused.

"Your research..." he said looking directly at her. "Every piece has come together now."

She wanted to stand, but her feet felt magnetised to the ground.

She swallowed.

Andre ran his fingers through his hair. He licked his lips.

"I'll give you some time..."

They sat for maybe fifteen minutes in silence. Martina finished her glass of wine and placed it on the table. Andre picked up the bottle to fill her glass, but she covered it with the flat of her palm and shook her head.

"When is this going to happen?" she asked, her brow furrowed deeply.

On a nearby rooftop.

A man clambered into position behind a 7.62mm L96 sniper's rifle resting on an A-frame. He popped the sight-covers from both ends of the sight, and lay down, and pressed his socket to the eye-piece.

The sniper took aim.

Outside the Palazzo.

Andre half-smiled and placed his glass down next to the ashtray. He lit a cigarette. Ribbons and jellyfish of smoke coiled and elevated into the air from the cherry.

"It's going to happen tomorrow," he replied, a smile playing across his mouth.

A bell-tower *boomed* behind them.

Martina watched as snakes of smoke drifted from Andre's mouth, between his thin lips, from his nostrils. Her mind raced. "Tomorrow?" she uttered.

A man, three tables away from them, sprang to his feet, steadying himself on the back of another table's chair. He coughed fiercely, patting his chest with force.

Andre glanced across at the man casually, then turned back to Martina.

Two tourists standing by the Bureau de Change behind their table erupted with violent coughs and barks.

An elderly couple in the square, about ten metres from Andre's back, fell to the ground.

Three children playing near the fountain collapsed.

A man climbing the staircase to the get out of the sun pitched backwards and tumbled down the steps, breaking his neck.

A tall waiter hung over the first-floor balcony of the Zorbas Restaurant Bar and Grill, above a tourist-appeal novelty and travel t-shirt store. He coughed, shaking his entire body. A mouthful of blood escaped his lips before he fell face-first over the balcony-rail and hit the ground. The weight of his body crushed his head, twisting it away from the body as it tumbled in the other direction.

Several people at a restaurant-bar across the square collapsed where they stood and sat.

Martina stood.

Andre stood. "Oh my God," he blurted. "It's happening now!... It was supposed to be tomorrow!"

Martina stepped back to the pillar, feeling her back press against the concrete.

A young couple collapsed on the balcony-bar above them, blood spilling out of their mouths. A light shower speckled the table around Martina and Andre.

A gunshot rang out across the square. The bullet hit Andre in the chest. He collapsed to his knees. Martina instantly stepped beside the pillar, ducking into a crouch. A dopey smile crossed Andre's face and his eyelids fluttered. He licked his lips then looked at Martina, his mouth moving but without any sound. He whispered, "It's Knapp..."

She stared back at him, tears filling her eyes. She flicked her vision to the rooftops around the square. She could not see anyone. She scuttled backwards on her hands and knees, watching Andre.

Another bullet zinged through the air and hit Andre in the centre of the back of his head. Martina darted aside, as blood and brain and skull sprayed the air and splattered the ground. Andre's body hit the stone ground hard, headless.

She snatched a menu off the ground and poked the corner of it beyond the pillar.

A bullet ripped a conker-sized hole through the card.

Martina tugged a ten-shot Taurus Millennium Pro PT140 pistol, eleven bullets with an extra one in the chamber, from the back of her jeans' belt. She held it inches from her face, when one of the infected charged from Pythagora street and leapt on a tourist who was panicking, standing motionless with hands clasped to their face.

Martina ducked out from behind the pillar and scanned the rooftops. She sank back. She had seen the sniper. He was directly opposite hiding between the roof-joints of two buildings. She sprang out from behind the pillar and shoulder-rolled to the next pillar. She charged along the cloister-front and barged through to the next restaurant.

One of the infected stood in her way idling on the spot.

She shot the infected in the eye. The bullet threw it backwards, making it tumble into a table and chairs, knocking them aside as it fell to the ground.

A woman screamed, running by the front of the restaurant, knocking over another table and chair, as three infected hotly pursued her.

Martina glanced between a break in the awning and saw the sniper moving.

On the rooftop.
The sniper jogged with the rifle swinging across his arms. He stopped next to a chimney and rounded it quickly, then threw the rifle up and put his socket to the eye-piece. He scanned the square as survivors and infected ran this way and that, careening around and over the tops of sixty or more bodies that littered the square.

      He crawled along the roof-tiles and took a new position. He looked through the eye-piece, when something caught his eye. He looked into the shaded corner of the square, where Martina was climbing expertly, and incredibly quickly, onto the balcony of the Plaka Seafood and Steakhouse.

In the restaurant.
Martina clambered under the low, shady ceiling and hid amongst the tables and chairs. Twenty people were dead at their tables, some with waiting staff lying next to them: most were face-down in their food or had impaled themselves on beer-bottles, wine glasses and cutlery.

      She pulled the pistol free, then crawled on her hands and knees to the furthest end of the balcony.

      Martina took a deep breath then stood. She took aim immediately and fired.

On the rooftop.
Three bullets *zipped* between Martina and the sniper.

      The sniper gasped. He was slow to tilt his head down, to catch sight of his own body, and saw three holes pierced through his chest in a perfect triangle. Three tiny traces of smoke escaped the holes, then blood boiled to the surface. He hocked and spat, a two-Euro splat of blood hit the roof-tile between his boots. He sighed.

In the restaurant.
Martina stared at the sniper as he wavered on his ankles, took a tiny step forward then plunged to the ground thirty feet below.

      An infected charged toward the body and stood over it for a moment. The infected lurched back, then puked blood over the sniper's face.

      Martina was momentarily captivated, then broke free with a shake of her head. She turned and saw that another infected had climbed the staircase inside the restaurant and pushed through onto the balcony behind her. The infected was a man of Arabic descent, dressed in a now-bloody thobe. He lurched forward, when Martina shot him in the neck. The bullet passed through a centimetre in front of its larynx. It gasped and mouthed, dark blood dripping from the fissure.

      She kicked the infected and it spiralled into a table, knocking it into one of the corpses and crashing to the floor.

      Martina sprinted through the restaurant and tore at the dried wood-blinds that covered a thin window. She forced herself through the window and landed with a *crack* on the roof-tiles of a neighbouring building.

      She stomped and bounded across several rooftops as ten infected sprinted down the tight street below her.

      She reached a stone arch that crossed the street and started across it. The stone *crackled* and grinded under her weight, then one of the edging-stones gave way. She plummeted off the arch and landed on a small tiled-awning above a shop. She clawed the air, catching a large plastic light with one hand and a telephone-wire with the other. She slowed her landing, but twisted her ankle and ripped a fingernail completely out.

      She groaned and touched her face, climbing to stand up. She kicked the flip-flop-sandals off her feet and pulled the pistol free. She glared up and down the skinny, paved road.

      A tourist twitched from the ground in a shop doorway.

      Apart from a dozen or more bodies, Martina was alone in the street. It felt momentarily peaceful, then several screams rent the air from different directions. Groans and growls echoed down the passageway.

Martina took a deep breath.

Three days later.
Martina stood at the helm of The Sun Chaser: a 2003 twenty-four and a half foot Jeanneau sailing yacht cutter. It had a three metre boom, with the sail catching the wind. A stable breeze buffeted the sails as she tightened a knot. The word *Athena* was inscribed on the back of the sailboat.

She watched the Mediterranean drift by, and Rhodes disappear on the back-horizon. The yacht bobbed and pitched on the low, lapping waves.

A man climbed out of the cabin and walked to her, steadying himself on some of the rigging. He was DANIEL WENDIVER Jr, 32 year old Englishman of Danish descent. He had tousled, stringy frosty-blonde hair that merged with fluffy white sideburns, a light, blonde moustache and small chin-beard. He was tall and lanky with ape-like long arms and legs and a short, stocky abdomen. He had a long, angled face with big, arching brows and high, wide cheekbones, a long and pointed jaw, a slim, straight nose and a wide full mouth. He wore an open white shirt, showing tanned skin and sparse blonde chest-hair, grey cargo shorts cut below the knee and worn-out blue-grey Adidas trainers with no socks.

"Where do you think we should go?" he asked.

"I want to go home. To Spain. I need to find my brother."

"But, we can help people here?"

"I don't care about other people."

"Then why did you help me? You saved my life."

"That's because I couldn't stand to see you infected."

"Really?" he said, smiling inwardly. He watched her for a moment. "We could help other people. On the way to Spain, I suppose...?" he suggested, rolling one of his sleeves up above his elbow. He smiled at Martina.

Martina half-smiled, focusing her attention back to steering the sailboat.

"I'll leave you to it... But, please have a think about it."

Martina nodded stiffly, then turned back to the sea. The island of Nisyros was becoming visible on the starboard side of the bow, beyond a wide expanse of Aegean blue waves.

Eight days later. South of the island of Kythira. South of the Greek mainland.
The *Athena* cut through the waves. Wind filled the sails and the sailboat glided onward at a brisk speed.

It was the lead ship in an armada of vessels. There were twenty-seven in total; a mixture of motorised formerly-charter yachts, sailboats, catamarans, Greek, Spanish and Turkish fishing boats, tourist seashell and dried fish-selling boats, and, several traditional Greek stripy white-and-blue wooden fishing-rowboats.

Daniel stood at the helm of the *Athena*.

Martina sat at the bow. Her legs hung over the breaking waves, and her arms rested on the metal rail of the forward pulpit. She was mesmerised and a tiny bit dizzy, watching the water flash by below and in front of her, sliced in two by the sharp edge of the boat.

On the deck of the *Escape*.
The *Escape* was a large sailboat schooner with three huge sails, taught in the wind, eighty metres behind the *Athena*.

A man stood on the deck. He replaced a pair of binoculars on the leather cord around his neck. He had been watching Martina for some time. His name was ANDREW ACKER, 48 year old Englishman of Swedish descent. He had curls of greying dusty-brown hair, piled on his head and growing long over his collar, and a short-cropped grey full-beard. He was tall and imposing, over six foot six, with wide shoulders and a strong build. He had an interested, engaging face with inquisitive, arched brows, deep, piercing blue eyes, a long crooked nose and strong jaw. He wore a brown wool jumper over a black shirt and black tie, grey trousers and black boat-shoes.

He studied Martina from his sailboat, a ship that dwarfed the *Athena*, but it had been Martina and her companion Daniel that had gathered the flotilla together, and that was why they led. Acker gritted his teeth.

The Raven Coffeeshop, Amsterdam, The Netherlands – 11:21am.
JULIETTE HALSTEDT, 21 year old half-English, half-Dutch young woman – stood behind the bar opening a bottle of Looza apple juice with a bottle-opener that hung from a string attached to her belt. She was radiant with a light tan and sleek dark hair; long and straight, hanging over her shoulders, with the left side shaved to grade two. She had an intimidating beauty, fine features, a sharp nose, slim lips and small, high cheekbones. Her body was slender and tightly muscled, with lithe arms, legs and a long, delicate neck. She had dazzling Capri-blue eyes that were quick and alert. She wore a short-sleeve black t-shirt, fitted three-quarter-length black jeans and black Vans; a silver necklace lay around her neck, resting on her chest, and several silver bracelets wrapped at her wrists. She dropped a straw in the juice and passed it to the customer that sat opposite her on a stool, the other side of the bar.

His hand reached out, and Jerry Hardbold took the drink and lifted the straw to his lips. He took a sip. "Thank you, very-much..." he proclaimed, beaming a smile. "I really needed that."

"No problem," Juliette said.

Their eyes met.

Eight hours later. In The Pancake Corner on Kleine-Gartman Plantsoen.
Jerry sat opposite Juliette at a table by the window. They stared into each other's eyes, elbows planted on the table-edges, hands knotted across the salt-and-pepper shakers. Their fingers played together.

A waitress crossed to them and their hands unravelled. The waitress placed enormous pancakes in front of each of them, then a condiment container between their plates.

"Thank you."

"Thank you," Juliette repeated. "Dank je wel..."

The waitress smiled, then retreated to the bar.

"This looks great!" Jerry beamed.

"Yeah. Mmm..."

Jerry picked up his knife and fork and started to cut the side of his buttery, sweet pancake. Maple syrup pooled at the incision and Jerry scraped a hillock of fresh whipped cream onto the fork and pancake piece. He put the fork down and looked at Juliette. She had just cut her fist bite. He sighed. "Y'know, I have to leave really early in the morning..." he murmured softly.

"I wish you could stay longer," she said and their eyes met again.

"Me too."

Two and a half hours later. On Rustenburgerstraat.
Juliette hugged Jerry tightly and they kissed. He swept hair behind her ear and leant close to her. They pressed against the wall of Juliette's apartment building. The street was a long line of tall red-brick tenements. At the middle there was a large overgrown lot with a wooden shack at the centre. Juliette's apartment overlooked the lot.

They kissed.

"I'm so glad I met you," he whispered.

Juliette squeezed him. "Me too."

Three hours later. In Juliette's apartment.
Juliette closed the door to her bedroom and flicked the light switch on with a *click*. She took her dressing-down off and hung it on a hook next to the door. She slid across the room and under the duvet, where Jerry lay waiting.

"You are so hot," he said, beaming a smile, his eyes squinting. "So hot!"

Juliette tucked herself next to Jerry. "You're alright."

They both smiled in unison. Juliette arched her back and they kissed.

One hour later.
Juliette's head lay across Jerry's chest, one of her arms hugging his front. He pulled the sheet up the bed, wrapping them both in it, tucking it around their bodies, and closed his eyes. Sleep quickly took him.

At Amsterdam Centraal Station – 6:01am.
Jerry wandered along the pavement, skipping passed the front of a coach full of tourists. He tugged his backpack over his shoulder as he dashed for the entrance.

Tourists and locals bustled passed him, entering and exiting the train station, as he went to the entrance. He took one last, longing look back at the city, then entered.

In Juliette's apartment – 12:22pm.
Juliette turned and rolled herself awake. She smiled and took a deep breath in. She opened her eyes and saw that Jerry was gone. A note sat on her bedside table. It read: Won't be gone for long... I will see you very-soon... Jerry x.

Juliette beamed a smile. She got up, wandered to her bathroom and turned her shower on, letting it heat up.

Later. The corner of Ruysdaelkade and Ceintuurbaan.
Juliette bounced down the side of the Ruysdaelkade canal, slowing before crossing onto the bridge at Ceintuurbaan.

She swung her arms, pulling her jacket across her back, her hands down the sleeves. She looked across the bridge and saw a man gripping the balustrade. She slowed.

The man pitched forward and collapsed at the same moment, vomiting a thick stream of blood into the canal. He gasped and stepped back, embarrassedly covering his face. He looked panicked and stared across the pavement at several locals who passed him by. Then another man collapsed. Then everyone in the immediate vicinity to Juliette fell to their knees, dropped flat, rolled over, crumpled or lay down. Only three other people remained standing.

Juliette stared from each person to the other, and they did the same.

"Is this a joke?" one of the people asked, crossing to one of the bodies. Then a tram flattened him, careening uncontrolled along its rails, the driver dead in his cabin.

Juliette screamed.

Sunset Park, Brooklyn, New York City, USA – 6:48am.
KRAYDER HELLIG, 45 year old American of Norwegian descent – strode out of the Yafa Newsstand and Deli on the corner of 4th Avenue and 45th Street. He was a huge bear of a man, over six foot four, heavyset, enormous and muscular, but coated with a thick layer of fat all over. He was darkly tanned which gave his weathered, cracked skin the quality of leather. He had long brown-black hair, matted and slightly dreadlocked, pulled back and tied up in a ponytail with a metal clip. His face was dominated by a great, thick, bushy beard spreading from sideburns to completely cover his thick, muscular neck. He had sensitive, brilliant blue eyes that glowed from beneath thick, wide eyebrows. He wore a pit-stained red t-shirt with a cartoon drawing of the Buddha on the chest, grubby and grease-stained Levi jeans and black ankle-high hiking-boots; a small bone skull, the size of a golf-ball, hung around his neck on a bootlace, and he had three large, plain silver rings on his right hand. Hellig started eating a chicken and pastrami cheese-melt sandwich with lettuce, 'slaw and cucumber, peeling back the paper-wrapper. He stuffed the sandwich into his mouth through his moustache, as he gazed up and down the street, before crossing. He saw the red-brown brick spire of St Michael's Catholic Church. A piece of chicken squeezed out between the slices of buttery bread and splat on the sidewalk with a ring of mustard-mayonnaise.

A Boeing 747-400 airplane soared through the air, ascending sharply, leaving a trail of white behind it.

Hellig pushed open the Pharmacy doors and walked inside. They had only been open for fifteen minutes and the clerk behind the counter eyed Hellig cautiously, as he restocked one row of popular anti-depressants.

Hellig wiped some mustard from his beard and smoothed it away on the thigh of his jeans.

"How can I help you, son?" the Pharmacist asked politely, looking with old eyes through deep, magnifying spectacles. He moved from behind the medicine-cabinets and stood behind the counter.

"I, uh, have a prescription for some pain-killers."

"Oh?"

"I do," Hellig confirmed, tugging the page of a prescription-pad from his pocket.

The Pharmacist read the page over the top of his spectacles, then nodded and disappeared behind a large shelving-unit filled with medicine.

A little later.
Hellig was moving down 45th towards the Gowanus Expressway. He clutched the paper-bag of drugs.

A man exiting his home slipped down the front-steps outside his front-door, dropping and bouncing down the last two, then managed to land on one foot and tumbled to the sidewalk between his open, spiked gate. The man fell flat on his back and lay there. Hellig hesitated before moving to the man, when he saw him stir and shift. The man's arms twitched and his foot kicked out.

"Hey," Hellig barked. "You okay, buddy?"

The man's head turned, swinging up and down the street, but not looking at Hellig at all. He stepped closer towards the man, arms raised in front of his body, ready to shove this man away. The man lost all of the colour in his face and his eyes turned bloodshot red.

A shrill scream filled the air.

Hellig's head swung around and he saw something in his peripheral vision, then he leapt for the sidewalk, as a black 2005 Daewoo Leganza back-ended a silver 2005 Mazda 5. Glass filled the air as the *crunch* and power of the impact rang out along the street.

Hellig rolled onto his back, as the man down the street got to his feet unsteadily. Blood dripped from the edges of his mouth as he struggled to stand up straight. The infected grasped onto one of the spikes on the front-gate of the house to stabilise itself, its ankles shuddering under its weight. Hellig saw the infected but could not help a groan escaping his lips.

The infected caught on to Hellig and started for him, shuffling at first but gaining in speed.

Steam rose from the smashed front-end of the Daewoo.

Hellig clambered to a stand and braced for the infected to reach him.

It picked up speed and charged towards him. He barrelled into the infected, caught it by its belt-buckle and lifted it off the ground. He threw the infected and it part-impaled itself on the front-gate spikes. One spike had been driven through its lung, while the two spikes either side had only-just jabbed into the flesh.

The infected roared and its arms flailed, pinned in place.

Hellig started down the street when the infected ripped itself free of the gate, blood gushing from the wound.

Another infected stumbled into the street from an open front-door ahead of him. A third wrenched the door of the Daewoo back on itself and it clambered out of the car. Fourth and fifth infected emerged from the street-corner. Fourteen more infected appeared in the street ahead of Hellig, others even further away.

Hellig bolted up the street to 4th, where ten cars had crashed into one another blocking the intersection. He saw fifty or sixty people lying on the sidewalk and road and blocking doorways and under cars and across the painted median-line and on the pedestrian cross-walks.

Five infected stumbled in a group in the direction of St Michael's.

He turned and ran.

Later.
Hellig slammed the door to his apartment. He pushed the bolt through, slid the lock in, twisted the dead-bolt, then attached the chain. He peered through the spy-hole for a long moment before deciding the corridor beyond was clear.

He pushed through the hallway and moved to his bedroom.

He slapped the wardrobe door open and grabbed a pre-packed backpack from the floor.

He slipped into the living-room and moved his old box-television set easily off a dusty trunk. He opened the trunk and took another full bag out. He slung the bag over his shoulder and pulled the backpack on over it. He pulled a large belt with four holsters on it: two with black Beretta 92 pistols in them, two with 20-inch machetes in them. He strapped the belt around his waist, where the guns sat; the machete-sheaths hung along his thighs.

Something caught his eye out the window in his living-room. He moved to it and saw a woman sprinting down the road. Then she side-stepped and ducked and hid between a greying-indigo 2008 Ford Galaxy Zetec people mini-van and a dull-crimson 2002 Honda Civic, on the other side of the street. She looked panicked and restless.

On the street.
The woman hushed her whimpers, one hand resting on the car's bonnet, the other resting on her knee. Her name was NATALIE FORTUNE, 23 year old American young woman. She had streaky blonde hair pulled back in a long ponytail. She was pretty, tanned and impeccably made-up. She had a small, round face with pouting lips, a button-nose and rounded chin. She had a small, petite frame, athletic and lithe. She wore a tight-fitting pink vest, black Lycra leggings and pink Reebok Classics. Natalie panted for breath, huddling between the cars.

She snuck a look and saw one of the infected determinedly stomping down the centre of the street. It gurgled and a mouthful of blood slopped out of its mouth, spreading down its chest. It had once been a hair-salon worker, and still wore the logo-emblazoned apron from its last shift: the words *Paula's Salon* were blood splattered across the chest.

Natalie took in a breath and crawled away behind the Ford Galaxy.

In the glass-fronted coffee-house behind her, two infected stirred: one moved back into the room, edging along the bar; the other crept closer and closer to the window-pane that stood between it and Natalie. Over a dozen bodies were scattered about the coffee-house, many were slumped over their tables, others were strewn across the floor as if a giant had gotten bored with his toys and tossed them away.

Natalie saw the infected in the coffee-house in the reflection on the shiny wall of the Ford Galaxy. She did not turn to look, but pulled her legs in underneath her body. She crouched for a long moment when a noise made her jump.

Hellig pulled a machete free of the skull of the hair-salon worker. Blood flecked the blade and asphalt.

Natalie peered through the Ford Galaxy's window and saw Hellig.

The infected in the coffee-house banged on the glass making it ripple. The other infected slouched towards it and patted the window with its hands, smearing it with bloody handprints. The second infected growled.

"Lady?" Hellig whispered.

"Hello?" Natalie said, appearing at the front of the car.

"Come with me," he said, motioning for her to join him, when six cracks split in six directions across the window. The hands of both of the infected beat the window again and a tiny kite of glass pinged outward.

Natalie dashed towards Hellig, when another three infected stumbled along the street ahead of them, temporarily blocking their path.

They froze in the centre of the street, watching the infected.

The glass window of the coffee-house shook again and cracks formed delicate spiders'-webs.

The infected passed by without noticing them.

The glass window shattered and the first infected tumbled out onto the sidewalk. The second infected was instantaneously gripping the broken edge of the frame and hauling itself out of the coffee-house.

Natalie grabbed Hellig's thick, muscular arm.

"Don't worry," he reassured her, "it's going to be fine."

"You say that now," she argued.

"Don't worry," he repeated.

Hellig stepped away from her and took out one of the Beretta pistols, screwing a silencer to the end with five quick twists. He stood between Natalie and the infected as they rose and circled the car.

Hellig shot the first infected as it tried to climb the steep bonnet and was punched backwards into the ankles of the second, knocking it to the ground. He took a few paces forward and shot the other twice in the face.

The three infected that had passed them returned, followed by several others.

Six more infected moved from the back of the coffee-house to the broken window.

Eleven infected exited a restaurant across the street; the entrance-door was propped open with a fire extinguisher. They grouped, pushing each other, jostling forward.

They had all been attracted to the noise of breaking glass.

"Excuse me," Natalie whispered, but Hellig had already seen the other infected.

"Come," he shouted, catching her hand and dragging her away down the street.

Three of the infected instantly burst with energy and took off after them at a sprinter's-pace.

Hellig hurried towards the open side of a 1976 Dodge Street van with paintings of Cowboys, Native Americans and Buffalo spray-canned across the side. He chucked Natalie in the back of the van and wrenched the door closed, as the first of the three infected reached them.

Hellig punted the infected in the groin, then shot the top of its head. A gush of blood escaped.

The second infected appeared and Hellig tossed a machete skilfully. It stabbed into the meat of its neck, wedging in place. The infected slowed and leant against a car, seemingly unable to notice the huge blade impaled below its chin. It wheeled around.

Natalie climbed into the front-seat and found the keys were already in the ignition. She squealed with delight. She twisted the keys and the engine came alive. She glanced at Hellig through a handprint- and splatter-smeared window, as he advanced on the third infected and punched it across the cheek. It was knocked to the ground, just like a knock-out punch in a boxing match, then the bear of a man stomped on the back of its neck with a violent *crack*.

The second infected staggered towards Hellig and he shot it through the nose, pulling the machete free before the body fell away from his reach.

Natalie shoved the passenger-side door open and Hellig climbed in.

The van took off down the street with a gathering slow-moving mass of the infected following it.

Natalie turned onto 2nd Avenue and swung around a head-on collision, bumping and bouncing over two bodies.

"My... My name is Natalie... Natalie Fortune," she said exasperatedly.

"Krayder Hellig."

Natalie beamed across at Hellig.

"It's Norwegian," he added. "I... I don't have an accent, because I've lived in the States for a long while."

Natalie nodded. "So... Where are we going?"

"To a port... We need to find a boat."

"Why?"

"To go across the sea."

"But, my... my family?"

"Are dead," he interrupted, "or one of those things..." He glanced at her – all of her concentration was on driving – her brow was furrowed and sweat had started to bead her forehead. "You will last a heck of a lot longer with me, Natalie..."

"That may be so," she started, "but I can't just go... Run... I've got to see..."

"You'll die. We need to get a boat. Find a way to cross the sea."

"So you can see your family?"

"No."

"Then what? Go where?"

"To England... Across the Atlantic... I need my revenge," he boiled.

"From who?"

"From a man called Knapp."

"Who?!" she exclaimed.

"I will explain it all to you later."

"How do you know this stuff? And why are you dressed like you were ready for this to all go down?"

"Later. I promise," he asserted.

"Then do that, but I've got to go to my dad... I live real close-by here. It's not far. Honest... I have to know if he's okay, or..."

She slowed the van and guided it smoothly around a pickup truck that was wrapped around a streetlight. They could both see the driver slumped over the steering-column. They passed the large Lutheran Healthcare Hospital and Dunkin' Donuts and continued down 2nd Avenue.

Hellig looked out of the window at the sidewalk. There were many bodies along the pathways, a few in the street and others in doorways and entrances. "Okay. We can go to your house," he conceded.

Natalie moved down a gear and drove at eleven miles an hour as they passed a huge car-park filled with cars. Beyond the car-park was an enormous, 8-storey white building – OEM Source, an electronics wholesaler.

Several infected stalked through the car-park and Natalie pressed the brake.

They watched as a survivor sprinted away from a gang of the infected, all twisting and racing between the cars, knocking wing-mirrors off and closing in on their target. They man yelled, then darted between a 2010 Dodge Ram Truck and a 2003 Ford Winstar mini-van and out of their sight. The infected circled the man and surrounded him. One of the infected charged first and vomited blood on the man, when another crept in behind it. The man was drenched by twin torrents of thick, dark ooze.

"Drive. We need to be fast."

Natalie accelerated down the near-mile long building that towered over the car-park off the side of the street. It was a gargantuan block squatting on a huge site. Hellig thought about how many people would be inside that building.

They came to the end of the OEM Source car-park and saw a large turquoise sign that read: Brooklyn Army Terminal – Making Space for Business.

"This is where we need to come back to," Hellig stated.

"Okay."

They saw a huge tower-block standing tall behind the row of businesses along 2nd, and Hellig thought again of the dead and the infected. They passed under the Belt and Shore Parkways and over Shore Road, turned right onto Wakeman Place, then took the second left onto Sedgwick Place. It was a road of white-painted wooden and red-brick colonial townhouses. American flags swung in the wind above several front-doors.

"This is it–..." Natalie began. "Oh, no!"

Two infected stood in the centre of the road.

Hellig gripped one of the machetes' handles tightly.

"I'll deal with these two. You get into your house... Get to your father."

He climbed out of the van and started for the first infected, who had arched its back and caught sight of Hellig. It shambled down the road toward him, its arms swinging at its sides, its mouth snapping shut as the first gush of blood geysered up its throat. Hellig marched up the asphalt and took a wild swing with the machete. The infected blinked twice as the blade passed through its neck, then its head peeled back off its neck and the body crumpled to the ground. Thick, oily blood sprayed out of the neck-hole and base of the head.

Natalie swallowed, then opened the passenger's side-door. She hurried across the road and rushed to her front-door. She shook whilst finding her key and stabbed it into the lock. She threw the door open and entered the den.

Hellig was behind her in a moment, using a torn cloth-piece of t-shirt to wipe the blood from his machete. He dropped the bloodied rag with a splat on the doorstep and moved inside.

Natalie's face was frozen.

Her father sat in a worn leather arm-chair. He was dead. A torrent of blood had run in columns from his nostrils and lips, staining his chest, tie and cardigan.

Her eyes filled with tears.

"We have to go, Natalie."

She was slow to nod, but she did. She turned to Hellig and stared at his face. He was emotionless and cold, but he looked determined and serious. She nodded at him again and sniffed back her tears. Hellig took her by the arm and guided her back to the van calmly.

A little later.
Hellig and Natalie crossed the car-park at the back of the immense OEM Source building to an NYPD Police harbour where a patrol station was set up.

The docks appeared to be deserted as they walked towards an NYPD Police patrol boat and climbed aboard.

Twenty-six days later. On an Panamax cargo container ship in the Atlantic Ocean.
Hellig sat in the bridge with Natalie. They ate bowls of pasta with chicken and bacon in a tomato and chilli sauce. The computer-controlled steering-wheel had been locked in place. A radar signal *pinged* on the side-wall.

One of the crew entered the room and checked one of the computers. His name was WOODY BARNES, 29 year old American. He was short and stocky, a little round at the waist with stumpy arms and legs. He had a kind, caring face with dimples on both cheeks. He had dark brown curls, almost always hidden under a thick, black woollen-beanie; a fluffy beard covered most of his face. He wore several t-shirts under a fleece jumper, hoodie overalls and a thick, durable jacket over the top; thermal leggings, two pairs of jeans and the overalls over them as well. He had strong, heavy boots, with stretched-plastic sleeves pulled over them to prevent water from getting inside. Woody approached Hellig, he said, "Everything seems to be running fine. No problems."

Hellig pursed his lips together and half-smiled, "Good."

Natalie looked at Woody and he smiled at her.

"Where's Cotton?" Hellig asked.

"He's... Um... He's in the mess, I think... --cleaning the stuff from lunch," Woody said nervously.

Hellig nodded. His brows lowered and there was something menacing about the smile he wore.

Tallinn, Estonia.
DEIDRICH VOLLER, 47 year old German – marched down Tööstuse street by the Kalamaja kalmistupark. He was tall and lean, healthy and gym-fit. He had sleek black hair swept back over his head, shorter on the sides and longer on the top. He was a serious-looking man with chiselled features and a striking, long nose; his brow was high and arching, his cheeks bold and wide, his mouth a long, reptilian slit. His eyes were an almost-impossibly dark blue and glimmered in the light. He wore a black suit with a white shirt, grey tie and shiny black shoes. Opposite the lush green park was a huge office-building with a white snaking-pattern down the sheet-glass wall and the top two floors had carmine-coloured plating. Voller strode passed one of the entrances, as a few people collected by it.

A black 2006 Mercedes C-Class cruised down the side of the road and stopped alongside Voller.

He checked his wrist-watch. It was a black and stainless steel Omega Seamaster Professional, water resistant to 600 metres. The time was 12:03pm.

The black-tinted driver's-side window lowered and a stern face nodded a greeting at Voller.

Voller's eyes met those of CLAUS LANGKJAER, 46 year old Swedish man of Dutch descent. He had loose, short brown curls of hair, cropped on the sides. He had a long face with deep, squinted green eyes and a long Romanesque nose. He was tall and lean with a long torso, and arms and legs. He wore a charcoal-grey suit with a white shirt, grey tie and shiny black shoes. "Good morning," he said in fluent German.

"I prefer English," Voller responded.

"That's fine."

"I did not expect to see you this morning, my good friend."

"I have news... --from Knapp... --from England," Claus proclaimed.

Voller circled the car and climbed in the passenger seat, pulling the door closed. "What news?" he demanded.

"Let's start moving first," Claus said pulling away from the curb and starting off down the road.

"How did you find me?"

"I never stopped watching."

"Tell me, then, what is this news you have?" Voller added

"The LKG are making their move."

Their eyes met, and then they both pulled snub-nosed SIG-Sauer 2340 .40 calibre pistols and pointed them at their respective hearts. It was a seamless, practised motion. They froze for a moment, breathless, before Claus averted his gaze back to the road and steadied the steering-wheel.

The car slowed to a stop at the side of the road near the turning for Graniidi street in a lay-by beside an aging, worn-out pumpkin coloured wood-clad house.

"We cannot just shoot each other, Deidrich," Claus said.

Voller looked from Claus's pistol to his eyes. He was reading the road, watching a pedestrian pass by across the road, in front of a car bonnet that reflected grey clouds.

"Let us go somewhere and talk," Claus added.

A little later. In the pub The Bear.
Claus sat with his back to the door and Voller sat with his back to the far-wall. They had replaced their weapons in their armpit-holsters but they were at immediate, automatic reach in an instant.

The pub was an encased square, panelled with grainy, dark-wood; it gave the room a subterranean, oppressive feel to it. Posters, beer-mats, foreign currency, flags, postcards, tin-signs and other advertising- or travel-related paraphernalia completely covered the area by the bar. Foreign paper-money hung like bunting along the inside of the top-shelf behind the bar; it all looked grey, faded or dirt-coated. Two ash-dried plants were bent-double either side of the doorway. Four frosted, misty, grubby windows glowed with grey light, above the plants, feeding very little light into the room. Three curly, coiled metal light-fixtures glowed with the warm reddish-brown of their tobacco-orange and stained lamp-shades and sick-yellow bulbs.

A barman screwed a damp tea-towel into a wet glass and twisted it. He was smothered by wrinkles and could have been ninety or more years old, or a human-basset hound hybrid. He had shocks of white hair poking out from under a brown and beige-lined flat-cap and around his ears. His eyebrows were the same: jagged mountains of white fluffy hair. Dark, coal-block eyes glowed from under the brows, barely visible.

Two other ancient patrons sat at separate tables: one near the door, playing cards with himself; and the other two tables over from Claus's back, reading a newspaper *The Eesti Ekspress*; both smoked bitter, strong tobacco roll-ups in their wrinkled claws-for-hands. Voller had spotted and measured each of them, as Claus pushed open the entrance-door, when they had arrived. Voller had not been to this pub before and was immediately suspicious of Claus's choice.

"You should start talking," Voller said, still in English.

The barman's head tipped back, but only to register a foreign language that he could not translate.

"I have had news from several sources that the LKG are bringing their timetable forward."

"I thought this was all dealt with."

"No," Claus said with a casual shake of his head.

"When?"

"Today."

Voller did not even shiver at the thought. He remained perfectly still.

"You don't seem surprised, Deidrich," Claus stated calmly.

Voller resisted responding straight away. He tilted his head left to right, right to left, analysing Claus for any tells. They eyed each other for a long moment.

The barman shuffled to them and placed two half-pints of watery lemon-coloured beer between them.

"Thank you," Claus said in clear Estonian.

The barman grunted and shuffled back to the bar, his slippers dragging across the worn floorboards.

"Why are you telling me this?"

"The only chance we have left... --is to stick together."

"You and I?"

"Yes."

"I thought you were here to kill me," Voller admitted.

"No... We've been friends for too many years, Deidrich... I would never."

Voller's shoulders relaxed underneath his suit, but gave nothing away to Claus.

"What's the plan?"

Claus checked his watch. It was 12:24pm.

"We have thirty-six minutes."

Voller's eyes widened a fraction.

"I have a safe-house where there is food, some weapons and equipment."

"And beyond that, my friend?" Voller asked.

"We have to get to England. And find Knapp."

"What makes you think he'll be there?"

"It's his homeland. If he wishes to survive everything that is to come, then he'll know his surroundings... And... If he isn't... You designed those things... We search every one of them until we find him!"

Voller was slow to nod. He saw Claus relax in his chair, the leather groaned.

"Agreed," Voller said.

"We don't have much time."

Thirty days later. In the Overvecht area of North-western Utrecht, The Netherlands. Near the N230 motorway.

Voller and Claus dashed across the roof of the Kendle International building and stood at the edge looking down.

"Fuck! There are a lot more of those things now, Claus," Voller exclaimed.

Claus stared at the roads and roundabout below them. His eyes glazed for a moment but he blinked it away. "It's part of the virus. The warmth... The warm weather these past few days has accelerated some of the hibernation and maturation process. What we're seeing now is only the tip of the iceberg..."

Juliette Halstedt appeared on the roof behind them. She had heard every word.

"Do you know how this happened?" she asked.

"We were part of an organisation..." Claus started, but his words drifted off.

"We will explain," Voller added. "When the time is right."

They stared over the edge of the roof.

On the road below.

Five and a half thousand infected surged and swarmed, massing and mixing, moving this way and that, aimless and undirected; lost and oblivious to those watching them.

At the graveyard, London. Twenty-three days after The Event.
John Ramsay crouched on the ground, his hands balled into tight fists. He cried uncontrollably. Through his tears, he said: "What do I do?!.. What am I supposed to do?!" His hands knotted into balls, gripping tightly, fingernails digging into the soft meat. Tears fell from his eyes, as the clouds shifted overhead, pointing rays of sunlight across the graveyard.

He fell into the darkness inside himself. Thoughts burned through his mind, lightning strikes of pain and clarity.

Then the darkness swallowed him.

John's living-room, The Isle of Mull. Twenty days earlier.
Picture-frames and the windowsill became clear, emerging into reality from the darkness. The sofas, the coffee-table, the walls and fire-place manifested in front of John's eyes.

He found himself with Graham Harding. Graham coughed. "Go to London... Live... Live... Living... People will flock there... You have to go... People will get there... --to safety... Go to your family."

John could not believe his ears. He started to shake his head, tears filled his eyes.

Graham coughed, then he shook his head.

"No... No... Everything is gone..." Graham stammered. "London... There will be more people... And some... More... And some... --hope... Find your sister." He coughed up blood, then looked at John, he said, "Oh shit..." then Graham Harding died. For several seconds his heart did not beat.

John stared at his friend across the room, unblinkingly. He clenched his teeth.

John leant across the space and took Graham's wrist, holding it to check for a pulse, water streaming from his eyes.

There was no pulse. None at all.

At the graveyard.
As if shocked by lightning, John pulled himself together, wiped away his tears and cleared his throat. He stood, suddenly looking stable and determined. He gritted his teeth.

"I'm okay now. I know what to do."

TO BE CONTINUED